"Is it true, my lord? Are you bedeviled?"

Kenrick smoothed the swatch of linen across Haven's injured wrist, scarcely able to resist placing his lips against the fluttering pulse that beat there.

"Am I bedeviled?" he said, so low it might have been a growl. "Aye, my lady. Lately more and more."

He spread his fingers and wove them between hers, catching her more firmly.

"Whether you are in or out of my sight, Haven, you affect me deeply."

He drew her closer, nearly edging her off the chair.

"Kenrick." She looked down at their joined hands and gave a small shake of her head. "We should not. This would be . . ."

With only the barest guidance, he lifted her hand and pressed his mouth to the soft skin of her knuckles. Haven's lips parted on a thready wisp of a sigh.

"What would this be?"

"Oh, faith," she whispered. " 'Twould be a mistake—if we . . ."

It was a weak protest when her lip was now caught between her teeth, her green eyes gone as dark and dusky as a twilight meadow.

Kenrick pulled her easily into his arms and silenced her with a kiss.

Look for these enthralling romances by Tina St. John

LORD OF VENGEANCE
LADY OF VALOR
WHITE LION'S LADY
BLACK LION'S BRIDE
HEART OF THE HUNTER

HEART
OF THE
FLAME

A NOVEL

TINA
ST. JOHN

BALLANTINE BOOKS • NEW YORK

Heart of the Flame is a work of fiction. Names, characters, places, and incidents are the products of the author's imagination or are used fictitiously. Any resemblance to actual events, locales, or persons, living or dead, is entirely coincidental.

An Ivy Books Mass Market Original

Copyright © 2005 by Tina Haack
Excerpt from *Heart of the Dove* copyright © 2005 by Tina Haack

Published in the United States by Ivy Books, an imprint of The Random House Publishing Group, a division of Random House, Inc., New York.

Ivy Books and colophon are trademarks of Random House, Inc.

ISBN 0-345-45995-4

This book contains a teaser for the forthcoming paperback edition of *Heart of the Dove* by Tina St. John. This excerpt has been set for this edition only and may not reflect the final content of the forthcoming novel.

Printed in the United States of America

Ballantine Books website address: www.ballantinebooks.com

OPM 9 8 7 6 5 4 3 2 1

To John,
my darling husband and dearest friend.
Forever, HB

ACKNOWLEDGMENTS

Each book begins with a dream—a glimmer of magic, which,
spun and smoothed, becomes something more. Something real.
To be able to spend my days (and a good many nights)
immersed in the magic of dreams spun to life
is a gift I shall always cherish.
For that, I thank you, my readers.

Special gratitude also goes to my wonderful publishing team:
Charlotte Herscher, Arielle Zibrak, and Karen Solem.
It's a joy to be working with you all.

❧ 1 ❧

Cornwall, England
May 1275

HE ENTERED THE place slowly, his footsteps hesitant now that he had breached the threshold. After so long an absence from his Father's house, he was not at all sure he would be welcome. He doubted he would be heard. But embraced or nay, his heart was heavy, and he knew of nowhere else to lay his burdens. The blame here, however, was wholly his own; he reckoned he would carry that for the rest of his days.

Fine silver spurs rode at the heels of his boots, ticking softly on the smooth stone floor as he advanced, their tinny music the only disturbance of sound in the vacant chamber. Unwarmed, unlit save for the hazy overcast glare that washed in through a high arched window, the vaulted space held the cool stillness of a tomb. Fitting, he thought, his eyes yet burning from the sight that had greeted him upon his arrival.

For a moment, as he reached the end of his path, the knight could only stand there, his limbs leaden from his days of travel, his throat scorched and dry like the bitter chalk of ash.

Golden head bowed, he closed his eyes and sank to his knees on the floor.

"Pater noster, qui es in caelis . . ."

The prayer fell from his lips by rote, familiar as his own name. Kenrick of Clairmont had said this prayer a thousand times, nay, countless repetitions—a hundred times a day for seven days straight, as was required every time one of his Templar brethren had fallen. Although he was no longer of the Order, he wanted to believe that where his vow was broken, some scrap of his faith might still remain. The prayer he recited now was for a friend and that man's family, for Randwulf of Greycliff and the wife and young son who once lived in this place.

Each breath Kenrick drew to speak held the cloying tang of smoke and cinder. Soot blackened the floor of the chapel where he knelt, as it did the walls of the small tower keep beyond. The place was in ruin, all of it dead and cold some weeks before he had arrived.

Rand and his cherished family . . . gone.

Kenrick needed not question why, or whom. The annihilation bore the stamp of Silas de Mortaine, the man who had held him hostage in a Rouen dungeon for nigh on half a year, and surely would have killed him anon, had it not been for his daring rescue a few months ago. Kenrick found it hard to maintain his relief at that thought now. While he was recuperating from his torture, Rand and his loved ones were meeting a hellish end.

All because of him.

All because of a secret pact he had shared with his friend and brother-in-arms, a pledge sealed more than a year ago at this humble Cornish manor near Land's End.

God's blood.

If he had known what it would cost Rand, he never would have sought his help.

"*. . . sed libera nos a malo . . .*"

Too late, he thought, bitter with grief and remorse. De Mortaine's evil was inescapable. His grasp was far-reaching. He was a menacing force, a wealthy man who dealt in dark magic and commanded a small army of mercenary beasts to assist him in his malevolent goals. He wanted the Dragon Chalice, a legendary treasure of mystical origins. Kenrick had stumbled upon the Chalice tales in his work for the Order. In truth, he had thought it mere myth, until he had held part of the fabled treasure in his hands and witnessed the astonishing breadth of its powers.

The Dragon Chalice was real, and the carnage here was merely one more demonstration of Silas de Mortaine's intent to claim the Chalice for his own. For Kenrick of Clairmont, who still bore the scars of his incarceration, the travesty surrounding him at Rand's keep was further proof of why he could not allow de Mortaine to win.

Not at any cost.

"Amen," he growled, then brought himself to his feet in the charred nave of the chapel.

For a moment, he allowed his gaze to settle on the wreckage of the place, at the modest gold crucifix hanging above the altar, unscathed. He bit back the wry curse that rose to his tongue, but only barely.

Not even God could stop de Mortaine from visiting his wrath on these noble folk.

A mild blasphemy to think such a thing, particularly in a place of worship. All the worse that it should come from a man once sworn into God's service, first as a novitiate monk, then, later, as a Knight of the Temple of Solomon.

"Saint" was what Rand and his friends had often called Kenrick in their youth, a name given in jest for his rigid nobility and scholarly ways.

But those days were long past. He would waste no further time dwelling on old memories than he would now afford his grief. There would be time for both once his business here was concluded.

As eager as he had been to arrive earlier that day, now he longed to be away. His scalp itched beneath the cropped cut of his hair, a lingering reminder of his captivity, when his head and beard had crawled with lice. He had cut it all away at first chance, preferring to be clean-shaven daily, his dark blond hair kept shorter than was stylish, curling just above the collar of his brown tunic and gambeson. He scratched at his nape, cursing the bitter reminder.

On second thought, he reflected, pivoting sharply, perhaps the niggling crawl of his scalp had more to do with the sudden feeling he had that he was not alone in the abandoned keep. There seemed a mild disturbance in the stillness of the air, as though someone—or something—breathed amid the death that permeated the place. Outside in the yard, one of the townsfolk who had witnessed the carnage waited with Kenrick's mount. The graybeard's portly form had not moved from where he stood.

Still, Kenrick felt eyes on him, surreptitiously watching. Waiting. . . .

"Who is there?" he called, the low command echoing hollowly off the vaulted walls.

No one answered.

His sharp blue gaze flicked into every shadowed corner, quickly assessing his surroundings. Nothing stirred. Nothing met his eye but cold stone and vacant silence. The chapel, like the adjacent tower keep, was empty. He was alone here after all.

That there were few around to meet him when he arrived, nary a peasant or neighbor willing to come forth and speak with him about what they might have witnessed, would have seemed unsettling had this not been Cornwall. Folk were different in this far-flung end of the realm. They kept to their own affairs, and they were not in the habit of welcoming strangers.

It had required a sizable fee to convince the man outside to provide his account of what had happened at the keep a fortnight past. Kenrick's head still rang with the terrible details: a band of raiders attacking the small manor in the night, the screams of women and children, plumes of fire and smoke as the keep was set ablaze, its inhabitants locked inside. . . .

He swore aloud, cursing himself and the uncaring God who had allowed this to happen. Rage churned in his gut as he quit the chapel for the yard outside.

The old townsman looked at him as he approached, and somberly shook his head. "Like I told you, m'lord. 'Twere an awful thing. Hard to think of anyone who might wish to harm Sir Randwulf and his family, kind as they were. Naught anyone could do about it, though. Whoever attacked this place came and went like ghosts in the dead of night. I don't reckon the poor souls had a chance."

Kenrick said nothing as he strode farther into the court, struck anew by the decimation. He paused only a moment, unable to prevent his eyes from straying across the scorched spring grass and muddy yard to where a child's toy cart lay overturned and broken.

A memory flitted through his mind. Rand's son, laughing as he tugged the painted wooden wagon behind him, fast as his five-year-old legs could carry him. Elspeth was there, too, Rand's pretty wife, waving to the three men—Rand, Kenrick, and jubilant Tod—as they passed her in the sunlit gardens of the keep. It had been the last he had seen of Rand and his family. He had come there to enlist his friend's help; instead he had delivered their death warrant.

"Stay here," Kenrick ordered the old man, not wishing to hear any more of what Rand and his family suffered. "I wish to be alone for a while."

"As you will, m'lord."

The solitude would suit him well in his next task, Kenrick admitted as he drew his dagger from the sheath at his belt. Above him now, the sky had turned from dull overcast to a mass of dark, gathering clouds. It would not be long before the cool sprinkle of rain that misted his face and bare hands would worsen to a downpour. He needed no better excuse to be quick about his work and have done with this place. Walking briskly, Kenrick left the courtyard and headed around the side of the chapel.

A small cemetery plot huddled in the shade of the westerly wall. The graves of Rand's forebears—thieves, scoundrels, and whores, Greycliff would admit with a reckless grin—lay burrowed beneath the staggered row of a dozen granite markers. Three oblong patches of raised brown earth indicated the newest additions to the plot. If Rand's neighbors avoided the place now, at least someone had taken care to see the slain family was properly laid to rest. Thinking on that somber event, knowing who lay buried under the damp mounds, Kenrick swallowed back a fierce wave of regret.

He entered the cemetery with reverent care, treading softly, his gaze searching out a squat pillar of chiseled stone near the back of the place, where the oldest of the graves were located. He had taken only a few steps when his spur clinked on something metallic beneath his boot. A pendant necklace, he realized, stooping down to retrieve it from the mossy ground. It was Elspeth's; he had never seen her without it dangling from around her delicate neck. The chain was broken now, the pendant dirtied from its time in the elements.

She would despair of its loss, even in death, for it had been a gift from her husband. Kenrick palmed the simple piece, fisting his hand around the cool metal. It belonged with Rand's wife; it seemed the least he could do to repair the crushed golden chain and bring the necklace back.

As he loosened the drawstring of his baldric pouch, he heard a rustle of movement somewhere nearby. Or perhaps it had only been the rain, which was pattering down a little harder than before, slapping gently on the rounded tops of the gravestones. He slipped the pendant into the pouch and stood up, pivoting to make certain the old man hadn't followed him.

No one was there. Only stillness, as it had been in the chapel.

The dagger he held felt cool and heavy in his hand, the sword sheathed at his hip an added measure of security he was fully prepared to use. In his fury over what had befallen his friends, Kenrick almost wished he would encounter Silas de Mortaine on this scorched plot of land.

His palms itched to deliver unholy vengeance . . . but first, the task at hand.

Kenrick stalked to the lichen-spotted marker at the far end of the cemetery and crouched down before it. With the point of his dagger, he found the hidden cleft in the chiseled design. Off-shape, no bigger than a child's palm, the secret compartment was disguised by the scrollwork and lettering hammered into the granite ages ago. Rand and he were not the first ones to make use of it. One of the early Greycliff brides had employed the marker to receive communiqués and gifts from a royal lover.

Now the stone held a secret of a far more dangerous sort.

Kenrick dug the sharp tip of the blade into the seam of the compartment, working the slender edge of steel around until the piece began to loosen. The granite rasped as it gave way, inch by inch. The final corner pried loose, Kenrick eased the wedge of stone out into his palm and gazed at the small compartment it revealed.

"God's blood." He exhaled the oath, tossing down his dagger and narrowly resisting the urge to drive his fist into the slab of granite before him.

It wasn't there.

The shallow hiding place carved into the tombstone, which had contained a folded square of parchment when he had sealed it up a year ago, was empty.

He stared into that vacant space, a thousand questions—a thousand dire possibilities—roiling in his head. Who had found the seal? How did they know where to look? How long had it been gone? Would they know how to use it, what to do with it?

And perhaps more crucial, now that it appeared he had lost it, how could he go about finishing his quest without it?

As it stood, he wouldn't have much time. It had taken him several years to realize precisely what he had uncovered, to understand the importance of protecting it from those who would use it for their own gain. Countless days and nights he had spent, toiling with his journals and ledgers, sifting out every fact from the troves of fiction buried within decades of dusty records and reportings of the Order.

"Christ on the Cross, how can this be?"

The final key to his discovery, enveloped within a single sheaf of parchment, now likely resided in the hands of his enemies.

He had not come this far, survived all he had, only to fail here and now. Nor would he permit Rand and his family to have died in vain. Placing the dislodged wafer of chiseled granite back in place on the grave marker, Kenrick pushed to his feet.

From the corner of his eye, he caught an unmistakable flicker of movement. His head snapped up, his gaze cutting sharply over his shoulder.

Damn it, he *was* being watched.

A fleeting splash of color moved near the wall of the chapel, too late to fully escape his notice this time. Kenrick caught a momentary glimpse of pale white skin and wary, wide green eyes. A mere blink was all the time she paused—just long enough for Kenrick to register the delicacy of the woman's heart-shaped face, which was caught in an expression of startlement as she looked back at him in that frozen instant. A drooping mane of unbound auburn hair framed her striking countenance, the rich russet-red tangles glowing like fire against the persistent gray of the morning. She was plainly garbed, a commoner by her modest attire of cloak and kirtle, but hardly plain of face or form.

As tense as he was, his blood seething over the loss of his friends and the prized item he sought, Kenrick was not immune to the beauty of this unexpected intruder. Indeed, he was tempted to stare, having found such incongruous beauty amid the smoldering ruins. His observer seemed in no mind to afford him the chance. Her eyes lit on the dagger still clutched in his fist, then she lunged, quick as a sprite, dashing behind the front wall of the chapel.

"Stop," he ordered, knowing he would be ignored and already vaulting to his feet in pursuit.

He ran around to the corner of the small church, his spurs chewing up the soft earth, his weaponry jangling with each heavy bootfall. His quarry was far lighter of foot, simply there one moment and gone the next. Into the chapel, he had to presume, for there were few places to hide, and there was no sign of her in the yard or on the gently rolling field beyond the keep.

"Where did she go?"

"Eh?" The old townsman looked up with a start as Kenrick thundered into the bailey, peering at him from over his grazing horse's head. "She, m'lord?"

"The woman—where is she?"

The graybeard looked to and fro, then shrugged his rounded shoulders. "I've seen no one a'tall, m'lord."

"You must have seen something. She was spying on

me in the graveyard and ran this way not a moment ago. You must have heard her footsteps at the very least?"

"Nay, sir. 'Twasn't no one come through here in a fortnight, save the both of us. I saw nothing, I assure you."

Kenrick swore under his breath. He was not imagining things, surely. A woman *had* been there. Watching him. With stealthy strides, he approached the open doorway to the chapel, the only place she could have gone. "Show yourself. You have nothing to fear," he said, stepping into the vaulted chamber. "Come out now. I wish only to talk to you."

The barest shift of sound came from a toppled cabinet to his right. The door to the piece hung askew on its hinges. Too small to hide but a child, yet it afforded the sole spot of concealment in all of the chapel. From the darkened wedge of space at the top, Kenrick saw the glint of a wary stare watching him as he approached.

"Who are you?" he asked, coming to stand there. He wished not to frighten the chit, but he wanted answers. Needed them. "What do you know of this place?"

When no reply came, he reached out with his booted foot and began to move aside the broken door of the cabinet to reveal its cowering occupant. There was a whine, then a fearful, animal growl as he bent down to peer inside.

"Jesu Criste."

It was not his stealthy observer after all.

A small red fox glared at him with hackles raised and teeth bared, trapped between the unyielding back of the cabinet enclosure and the dagger-wielding man who blocked its easy escape. The instant Kenrick withdrew, the little beast dashed out and fled the chapel for the safety of the outlying moors. Kenrick turned and watched it go, letting out his anxiety in a long, heavy sigh.

Where had she gone?

Whoever the woman was, she had managed to vanish.

Into thin air, he was tempted to think, as he scanned his surroundings and saw no trace of the lovely intruder.

"I wager it don't take long for the animals to come nosing about when there's no one here to shoo them off," said the graybeard from the village. He clucked his tongue as he ambled forward to where Kenrick stood. "Nothing of worth in this place for anyone now, man or beast. They burnt it all, save the stone of the keep and chapel. Sorrow is all that dwells here."

Maybe so, Kenrick thought, unable to argue that the destruction of the place had been as thorough as it had been brutal. But there was something else lurking here, too. Something beyond the death and cinder, and far more elusive than an errant forest scavenger hoping to root out its next meal from among the ruins. That particular *something* had a riot of long, rich, red hair, and the most beautiful face Kenrick had ever beheld.

And as sure as he had seen her, wherever she'd run to, he was certain she hadn't gone far.

❧ 2 ❧

BY NIGHTFALL, THE worst of the rain had passed. The air outside was damp and briny, bringing a chill into the vacant stone tower as Kenrick ascended to the private chambers abovestairs. He was alone now. The old villager had departed hours before, perfectly willing to leave Kenrick to continue his perusal of the manor without him.

Kenrick's torch flame wobbled in the draft that followed him up the spiraling stairwell, throwing long, eerie shadows against the curving walls. Were he inclined toward a belief in such things, he might have been tempted to think the place haunted, so vivid were his memories of the lives that had once inhabited this modest keep. He reached the top of the stairs and paused, assailed anew with recollected sights and sounds of Rand and his young family as they had been when they lived there.

Laughter echoed in his ears. Bright smiles and loving looks shared between mother and child, husband and wife, filled his vision as he strode into the empty family chambers on the second story.

A small table had been overturned near the entryway to the solar; Kenrick righted it with reverent care, striving to make no sound lest he disturb the sacred stillness

13

of the place. Elspeth's favorite chair stood near the shut-tered window, next to it a frame and stand that held her needlework, neatly set aside as though its maker were shortly to return. The torchlight spilled over the design as Kenrick neared, illuminating the pastoral scene in charred half-completion. The piece would never be fin-ished now.

He turned away, and his eye was then drawn to the large bed that dominated the other side of the chamber. Empty, unmade, standing as it likely was in those black moments of panic when the keep was overtaken by the raiders. Rand must have vaulted from his sleep in an in-stant to meet the intruders. The sooty remains of his boots stood near the fireplace, but his sword and dagger were both gone from their sheaths, which lay atop the charred bed as though tossed there in haste and forgot-ten. Elspeth likely had only a few moments to dress her-self and fetch little Tod before the place was overcome with smoke and blood and death.

How terrified they all must have been.

God willing, they hadn't suffered long.

Kenrick suddenly felt much an intruder himself, standing in the room where his friends would have been—indeed, should have been this very moment—sleeping peacefully in each other's arms.

The scent of old smoke was cloying, heavy in the room. He turned back toward the shuttered window and pulled the latch to permit a cleansing draft. The night breeze sailed in, crisp and cool.

Kenrick leaned into the wind, clearing his head as he breathed of the brisk, sea-tossed air. The urge to hurl his rage into the quiet darkness was too strong, even for his own rigid sense of control. Grief and anger tore from his throat like a lash.

He roared a violent curse, the bitter sound ringing in his ears as he sent his cry of fury careening into the night.

Down near the edge of the woods, a pair of green eyes, dimmed by fatigue and heavy with an unwilling sleep, snapped open. The pained roar that lanced the darkness jolted her awake where she had collapsed some time before.

How long had she been asleep?

Easily hours, for it was blackest evening now, and deathly still, save for the anguished howl that yet reverberated in the canopy of trees above her head.

Twigs and conifer needles jabbed her cheek where it rested on the ground. The tang of loamy earth mingled with the heavy odor of pungent herbs clinging to her skin and clothing. The rank smell offended her nostrils, but it was all she could do to lift her head a fraction off the cold, damp ground and peer around blearily at her surroundings.

She had collapsed just within the cover of the copse—yes, she remembered that now.

She had been running. Her feet had been too heavy to move any farther, all of her strength, feeble as it was, spent. The details were scattered in her mind, imprecise, elusive.

She had been fleeing from someone. The knight's face was but a flash of recollection: golden-haired, his features were bold, his blue eyes haunted, suspicious. Those piercing eyes had taken hold of her like a physical grasp.

Her hiding place had been found out, she nearly captured at the keep that stood abandoned across the way.

Not abandoned . . . decimated, whispered a memory that was struggling to surface. With the thought came more images of violence.

Smoke and blood.

Screams.

A child wailing in his mother's arms.

With a groan, she squeezed her eyes closed and pushed the visions away. There was little sense in them anyway, naught but a jumble of confusion lurking in a far corner of her mind. Consciousness itself had become a slippery thing. Days slid into night, and night into day; she could scarcely discern either anymore. It was getting harder and harder for her to hold onto wakefulness, nearly impossible to maintain focus even when her eyes were open.

Pain.

That was all she knew for certain. She was in constant pain now, a spreading fire that ate at her body as it slowly sapped her of her will and her senses.

There was a chill in the air where she lay, yet her body burned as though afire. Heat seared her from within, but no sweat rose to cool her brow. And she was so very thirsty. Her mouth felt as parched as sand, her tongue thick with need of water.

Blinking away the lulling pull of another slide into darkness, she forced her arms to lift her from the ground. Her limbs quaked, shuddering weakly as she hoisted her slight weight and dragged herself to a sitting position on the ground. The effort left her breathless, her temples pounding with the sluggish beat of her pulse.

Above her head, the tender spring leaves of oak and

ash trees glistened in the starlight. Barely unfurled from their winter slumber, they quivered in the evening breeze. Raindrops from a recent shower clung to their cupped folds. Summoning what she felt might be the last of her strength, she slowly got to her feet and reached for the precious droplets. She sipped from the leaves like a crude forest beast, feeding hungrily, but it was not enough.

Not nearly enough to quench the thirst that raged in her.

She had to find more water. She had to douse the fire that was consuming her. Rasping a breath through parched lips, she swiveled her head and looked out across the expanse of night-dark terrain that surrounded her. Something snagged her attention, making her grow quite still where she stood, watching, listening.

The wind howled, but above the raw scrape of branches and the soughing shift of tall meadow grasses was another sound.

Water.

Great rushing waves of it, rolling not far from where she was.

Feebly, she took a few steps, cocking her head toward the welcoming roar of the tide. The night breeze was cool outside the cover of the woods. It snatched the hem of her mantle and sent it rippling out behind her like a sail.

Above her, thin tendrils of clouds scuttled across the darkened sky, coal gray on black. Like fingers of smoke, reaching for her . . . closing around her throat. Choking her.

Materializing from out of the murky edge of recall, a punishing hand seized her in a death grip. She struggled

to breathe, her fingers grasping at the unrelenting vise
clamped onto her neck.

Dying . . . she was dying. . . .

"No," she whispered, clutching at her temples and
fighting the madness that seemed to pull at her from all
directions.

She remembered struggling, desperately striving to
free herself from strong, punishing hands. She had
managed—somehow—but only for a moment. Only
until a flash of metal danced before her eyes, a blink of
light amid the smoke. Then fired erupted in her breast.
Searing hot, bright as a thunderbolt. She could not see,
could not think. Darkness had descended quickly,
thicker than any roiling cloud of ash and soot.

He meant to kill her, but she had gotten away. Barely.

She stumbled into the meadow now, her hands flung
out and dragging through the spring rushes that stood
nearly waist-high. The air was crisp as it buffeted her,
but in her mind she gasped as though engulfed in a sea
of ash. Smoke was thick in her eyes as the memories
crowded in. She was there again, in the keep on the hill.

Death was with her now as it had been that night. It
pursued her with every hitching, awkward step she
took, chasing her with the same force of the night wind.
Before long, she knew, it would catch her. She did not
fear her eventual end, but neither would she yield to it
easily. Determined to fight to the last, she urged her legs
to carry her swiftly, her ear tuned to the soothing song
of the sea.

Water, she thought, the word like a balm on her
tongue. Water would cool the fire that was consuming
her body and slowly eating away at her wits. She needed
only to reach the nearby shore and she would be safe.

Hearing the roar of the surf, she ran faster. She was getting closer. The tall reeds of the meadow gradually gave way to scrubby, rock-strewn grass and moss. Soon it would be sand beneath her feet, then the gentle lap of the waves. She must be almost there.

Impaired by her haste and the delirium that seized her senses, she tripped on one of the jagged stones underfoot. She went down hard on the ground. Her breath was gone from her lungs in a whoosh as she struck hard earth, and a stab of intense pain wracked her left shoulder. Something warm and sticky oozed down her sleeve and onto her bodice.

Blood, she realized in a dulled state of wonderment.

Her end was nearer now than ever. The knowledge stunned her as she lay there, listening to her heart labor in her breast. So this was death? She mused over the idea, resigning herself to the coming darkness that robbed her of all further thought.

❧ 3 ❧

A SCUTTLE OF movement in the starlit distance caught Kenrick's eye. He lifted his head and peered into the night beyond the tower keep's window, studying the erratic path of someone walking quite near the ledge of the cliffs.

Nay, he corrected; not walking, but running. Recklessly traipsing along the treacherous drop that gave Greycliff Castle its name. The figure wore a light-colored cloak that obscured its owner's shape. The wide hem snagged in the violent wind that blew up from the sea, its edges flying out like wings of pale, tattered wool. Kenrick had seen that ragged garment not a few hours before, wrapped about the slight frame of the woman from the cemetery grounds.

"What the devil is she doing out there?" he murmured, confusion twining with an overriding sense of foreboding.

She was running dangerously close to the cliff's edge—almost as though she meant to run toward the water that crashed far below.

Was she mad?

Evidently, for she was going to dash herself over the ledge as he watched. Insane or despondent, he could not be sure, but he could not stand by and do nothing.

20

Honor compelled him to intervene and disallow death to visit this place so soon after it had taken his friends.

Kenrick backed away from the window, uncertain what he meant to do even though his feet were already moving him toward the door. He would never reach her in time. She was running as though in a blind delirium; one faulty step near the edge of the cliff would spell a swift, terrible demise.

No sooner had he considered the grim possibility than the woman suddenly lurched and crumpled in a heap on the ground. She lost her footing and down she went, prone and lifeless but a few precarious paces from the ledge.

"God's blood!" he swore, pivoting on his boot heel and heading for the tower stairs in a dead run.

His spurs bit into the smooth stone of the spiraling steps as he descended three at a time, urgency pounding in his temples. He crossed the sooty, scarred wood planks of the floor at ground level, torch flames undulating in their cressets as he passed. The keep's iron-banded door creaked sharply as he threw it open and leaped the short set of stairs to the yard outside. Damp sea air spat a fine mist on the night breeze. Kenrick swiped at the irritating sheen that salted his eyes, his gaze trained on the shapeless bulk lying lifeless across the field. She had not moved at all since he had seen her from the tower window.

Kenrick broke into a run. Bolting the distance of the grassy expanse of land, he reached the woman in mere moments. She lay facedown on the rock-strewn ground near the cliff's edge, still as the tomb. Far below, the sea roared, spewing great plumes of white as the waves crashed into the jagged rocks at the base of the cliff. The woman had been but a hairbreadth from disaster when she collapsed.

Not that she was spared death in escaping a certain tumble into the tide.

Expecting to find her cold, Kenrick touched the young woman's arm and was surprised to feel warmth against his fingertips. She was burning up. Heat radiated through the multiple layers of her homespun clothing. Her damp hair hung limply over her face, long russet strands littered with twigs and dirt. He lifted a sodden tendril to expose the pale, hollowed slope of her cheek. The scent of strong herbs clung to her as it had when he first spied her earlier that day.

Pungent, almost putrid, the smell of her wafted up on a gust of salt spray. Kenrick took his hand away from her flaming brow and turned his head into a draft of crisp fresh air.

Whoever she was, the woman was filthy and ragged— and unless he missed his guess, she was clutched in the lethal grip of an intense, raging fever.

Gingerly, he grasped her shoulder and rolled her onto her back. The oath he hissed was black and grim with understanding.

The chit bore a collar of bruises around her neck and a deep, bleeding wound at her shoulder. It reeked of infection and the useless herbal poultice that bulged under the bodice of her gown. She had lost a great deal of blood, more in recent hours, for the injury was wet and spreading even as Kenrick stared down at her. For certes she was dying, but when he leaned in close he caught the shallow but steady rasp of her breath.

There seemed little to do for her, save to make her comfortable in her final hours. He eyed her pale, begrimed face and shabby clothes. She looked as though she had been living in the wild for weeks. For what was not the first time, he wondered what this woman was about that she would be skulking around Greycliff Castle like a wraith.

Perhaps she had known Rand and Elspeth. Perhaps, mindless with fever, she had wandered there by chance, as she had been staggering about near the cliff tonight.

He would have no answers at all should the woman perish of her wound. He was hardly a trained healer to mend her, but even his crude battlefield skills would be better than none at all. Very carefully, Kenrick gathered her into his arms. Limp and lifeless, sodden to her bones, she was a fragile thing that he held as gingerly as he would a bird with a broken wing. To his dismay, the feather-light chit in his arms smelled more a sow's sickly castoff. Settling her against his chest despite her soil and stench, he carried her away from the promontory ledge of the sea cliffs and across the wide field to the castle.

He brought her into the hall, where he had earlier lit a fire in the brazier. The warm glow illuminated the long chamber, which Kenrick had commandeered as a stable for his horse since the outbuildings were charred beyond use. Now it would serve as infirmary as well. Retrieving a rolled blanket from his saddle tack, Kenrick tossed the thick swatch of wool to the floor near the fire and spread it out with his foot. He eased the woman down, arranging her on her back and cushioning her head with his leather gauntlets.

The wound that had looked so grim in the dark outside was not improved with the benefit of firelight. Blood soaked the front of her bodice and much of the mantle that covered it. The wound was not new, but torn afresh, likely in the fall she had taken in the moments before Kenrick had reached her.

He untied the ribbon that held her mantle together at her neck, then swept aside the ruined cloak. More blood marred the bodice of her simple gown. With a growl of distaste, Kenrick drew a dagger from his baldric and slipped the blade under the rough fabric. He rent it with one swift flick of his wrist, laying her bare so he could better see what he was dealing with.

What he saw was not good.

Old herbs and an oozing poultice spilled out from beneath a linen binding at her shoulder, the source of much of the woman's malodor. The cause of her fever was equally apparent, for what had been smooth, unmarred skin bore the thready purple marks of advancing infection.

The festering had spread from under the bandage as far as the middle of her chest and down her upper arm. Kenrick swore an oath as he rocked back on his heels and looked at her slackened face.

There was no movement in her, not even the vaguest flutter of her closed eyelids, their crescent fringe of dark brown lashes resting lightly against the rounded angle of her cheek.

He should take her to the village, see if she had kin there, seek the care she needed among the people who might better know her and care for her. But there likely wasn't time for that. It was near midnight, the village some miles inland; he could not hope to find help for her at so late an hour. God help her, he was all she had right now.

He would need stronger light with which to work. He got up and retrieved a tallow candle from the table on the dais at the head of the hall, then brought it back and lit it from the brazier. Kenrick positioned himself at the woman's side and leaned over her to remove the putrid bandage. He cleaned her as best he could, clearing away the blood and dried herbs that clung to her injury. Carefully, he probed the inflamed seam of the cut, assessing the damage, testing the skin around it while she was too senseless to feel any pain.

It was a knife wound, from the look of it. The puncture had not been terribly deep, but often it took only a scratch of tainted steel to kill a man on the battlefield. This woman, petite and lithe, stood no chance of weathering the infection if it worsened. As he continued to inspect the wound, something sharp scraped at his fingertip. Something metallic and jagged.

He scowled, running the pad of his thumb over the spot again to make certain of what he felt. She stirred slightly, moaning an incoherent word as he probed the area where the hard bit of steel was embedded in her tender skin.

He would need to work quickly, while the delirium of her fever held her deeply in its thrall. Kenrick's wineskin lay within arm's reach of him near the fire. He snagged its thin leather strap, pulled the vessel into his lap, and uncorked it. The wine cleansed his dagger, spilling in a small pool on the floor as he poured an ample amount over the blade.

"Forgive me," he told his unconscious charge as he prepared to extract the errant shard of metal from her wound.

Using his dagger, he gingerly worked out what appeared to be the tip of a blade, broken off where it had presumably connected with the bone of her shoulder.

He caught the triangular chip of metal in his palm—and in that same instant heard the woman draw a sudden, gasping intake of breath. Her eyes flew open, startlingly green, almost ablaze with intensity. Her hand flew out to him, latching onto the sleeve of his tunic.

"It's not too late!" she hissed, her voice urgent, her gaze trained on his but unseeing and wild with fever. Her slender arm trembled with fatigue, yet her grip on him was surprisingly strong. Unrelenting. "You must . . . you must . . ."

Kenrick stared down at her, perplexed. A cold knot of dread formed in his gut as her words trailed off. "You are safe now," he told her. Those fiery green eyes held him in thrall, sparkling like gemstones from within the wan, sullied face of a mudlark. "There is no danger here. Be still."

"It's not too late," she cried, though less vehemently now. Her lids drooping heavily, her eyes began to roll back in her head. "You can . . ." Her grasp on his sleeve loosened, little by little, until her arm dropped back down to her side. She spoke again, slurring just above a whisper. "You can . . . save them. . . ."

"What are you saying?" he demanded of her. "Not too late to save whom?"

She heard nothing, he realized. As quickly as she had revived, she was gone again, swept into the undertow of her continued feverish slumber. He waited, watching her closely as her features relaxed and her breathing returned to a shallow, steady pace.

"Jesu Criste," Kenrick swore, his blood yet racing as he recovered from the strange outburst. His palm was pricked by the small wedge of steel he held in his tight fist. He uncurled his fingers and turned the dagger point over in his palm. It was bloodied and warm from the heat of her body, a triangle of dark metal that seemed to pulse in his hand.

And there was something else peculiar about the errant bit of steel. Hastily, Kenrick held the queer object closer to the candle flame. The light glinted off the piece of blade in his palm. He peered at it, his gaze following a broken series of swirls and symbols etched into the small shard of metal.

He had seen its like only once before, in France some months ago, not long after he had been held prisoner in Silas de Mortaine's lair.

Behind him on the floor, the woman gave a soft, troubled moan. Had she been attacked by one of de Mortaine's hellborn minions?

It's not too late.

You can save them.

God's blood, but did she speak of Rand and his family? Could she have been present at the keep the night of the raid—the sole witness to what transpired? Did her incoherent ramblings mean there might be hope amid the carnage that was visited on Greycliff Castle?

Kenrick had to know. Her wound fever would likely not release her for some long hours, perhaps days. He could not tarry any longer in Cornwall now that de Mortaine might have another key to finding the Dragon Chalice. He had to make haste for Clairmont and attempt to begin reconstructing the information he had lost.

Which brought him back to the woman. . . .

If she knew anything about the attack on Rand's

home, or the secret that was missing from the cemetery marker, Kenrick needed to know. Whoever she was, if she had seen or heard anything that might prove useful at all, then despite his misgivings, he could ill afford to leave her behind.

❧ 4 ❧

SHE CAME AWAKE fighting.

The instant consciousness returned, her eyes flew wide open, darting wildly. Every muscle in her body went taut with strain. Under the blanket that covered her body, her limbs bucked with a sudden burst of rage. She twisted violently, her back arching off the cushion of soft bedding that lay beneath her.

"Easy now. 'Tis all right," a woman's soft voice cautioned her, the gentling words coming from directly beside the curtained bed. "Lie still. You are safe."

Safe?

Nay—hardly that, her senses warned. She could not possibly be safe when every muscle in her body ached, when her head was swimming with a sudden confusion of light and sound and scent. Abed in a chamber she did not recognize, feeling drained of all strength and wit, she could do little but attempt to shake off the disorientation and try to make sense of where she was.

The room was small but lavish. Tapestries depicting serene forest scenes and pleasant meadows lent color to the dark gray stone of the chamber's walls. Thick furs draped the foot of the bed. Sunlight streamed in through the narrow opening of an adjacent window, its gold-bright brilliance searing her eyes.

29

Near the edge of the large bed, the woman who tended her was wringing out a cloth over a bowl of water spiced with lavender oil and clove. The herbal liquid trickled softly into the basin, its perfume carrying on the afternoon breeze that sifted through the high tower room.

"I am glad to see you awake at last." Fair-haired, with caring blue eyes, the young woman leaned over the mattress and reached toward her. "This may be a bit cool at first," she said, then carefully swabbed the compress over her patient's brow and cheeks. Her touch was gentle, the soft woven cloth moist and soothing against her skin. "There . . . doesn't that feel good?"

It felt wonderful, but she forced her thoughts away from the physical comfort, unable to dispel the very troubling notion that despite the attention being given her, she was in danger here. The urge to flee the place was strong, as though a snare were set and about to spring around her.

Perhaps it already had.

"Where am I?" Her voice was naught but a bare croak of sound, rusty with disuse.

"You are in Devonshire, at Clairmont Castle."

A dim flicker of recognition sparked, then dimmed just as quickly, registering nowhere in her groggy mind. "Where . . . ?"

"Don't try to move," her gentle caretaker advised when she shifted, meaning to rise up to confront this strange place in which she found herself. "You are yet too weak from your fever and the wound—"

"Weak, mayhap, but she is awake. That's good enough for me."

The curt interruption issued from a deep male voice

on the other side of the chamber. A man had paused there, out of her line of vision at the threshold to the room. He stood at the door only for a moment, then entered on a long-legged stride, the solid thud of boot heels echoing in the sudden stillness of the place. He slowly came into view near the bed, wide-shouldered, golden-haired, his smoky blue eyes narrowed with the wary glint of suspicion. He looked vaguely familiar, the intensity of that sharp gaze a memory dancing just beyond reach.

"Kenrick," said the lady as she replaced the cloth in the basin of water. "Have a care my brother, and pray lower your voice. This is a sickroom, not a gaol."

He grunted, sober, thoughtful. Skeptical. "You were to call me when she roused, Ana."

"Aye, and I would have," she replied, evidently unmoved by the formidable presence of her lordly kin. "It has been but a moment since she woke. She should not be taxed. What she needs now is peace."

The piercing gaze never wavered. "And I need answers."

He strode to the foot of the curtained bed and stood between the two soaring posts at its base. Arms crossed over his chest, his broad frame all but filled the space, just as his arrogance—and his coolly restrained anger— seemed to fill the whole of the room itself.

He stared, studying her, breeding in her a bone-deep awareness that the danger she sensed in her fevered dreams was all the more real now that she was awake and facing it.

Facing *him.*

The urge to escape was as strong as it was spontaneous,

worsening the longer she was subjected to the piercing, blue-eyed scrutiny of this man.

Unnerved and apprehensive she turned her focus inward. It seemed so natural a response, an instinctual honing of her senses, summoning a well of strength she felt certain she possessed. She called to it in silence, searching with her mind for some clue as to who she was, where she was . . . anything that might shed light on this queer awakening.

To her dismay, she found precious little to grasp.

Everything seemed to dance just beyond her reach— even memory, which gaped dark and murky at the edges of her reasoning. All she felt sure of was that despite her caretaker's assurances, she was nowhere near safe, her present vulnerability tasting like a bitter potion at the back of her parched throat.

She fought the sluggishness of her body, trying in vain to command her limbs. It was no use. The coverlet weighed her down as though fashioned of lead rather than the fur-trimmed warm wool that cocooned her in the bed.

Neck constricted, a biting strain seeped into every tendon as she struggled to lift her head. Her shoulder ached with the effort, a piercing throb that she heeded with sudden caution. And surprise.

"I am injured."

"Yes," agreed the young woman at her side, "but your color is much improved today. Your fever has broken, Haven, and now you are well on the mend."

"Haven?"

"That is your name, is it not?" It might have been an innocent question, but the man at the foot of the bed made it seem an accusation. "Are you the woman called Haven?"

"Haven," she repeated, slowly testing the name on her tongue and finding it more familiar than anything else she knew in that moment. She stared, trying to absorb all that she was hearing. She was uncertain what to make of him or her present circumstances. She nodded once, wary with this queer disorientation. It felt as though she were adrift in a thready fog, random patches of her world obscured by mist, others providing slim and fleeting clarity. "Yes," she said, certain of this one thing at least. "Yes, that is my name. I am Haven."

He gave a curt nod, evidently satisfied with her answer. "I inquired after you in the village the day we left Cornwall. The folk there told me who you were, that you had some skill with herbs. They said you often visited Lady Greycliff with your potions."

In her mind's eye, Haven caught the sudden flash of a brief image: a woman's face, pretty but pained, and pale against the chestnut brown of her hair. She was seated on the edge of a large bed, clutching her temples in her hands, scarcely able to speak for the pounding of her head. Haven remembered giving her a pouch of herbs, telling her how to brew them to treat her frequent bouts with the ailment. At once, the anguished lady's name came to her. "Elspeth," she whispered.

"That's right." Her interrogator's gaze searched hers, probing for more facts. "You were acquainted with her, then."

Haven nodded, a burdensome effort for her head felt heavy on the bolster. "I knew her, yes. She was . . . kind to me."

"Do you know what happened to Elspeth and her

family? Did you know her husband, Rand? Were you there that night—"

"Kenrick," said his sister, cutting him off when he seemed intent to press further. "Hold your questions a while, I beg you. Can't you see Haven is exhausted? This is the first she's been lucid in the four days since she arrived here."

"Four days I have been waiting for answers."

"I shouldn't think another will make so much difference."

"You know what is at stake here, Ariana."

"Yes. Of course, I do. You know I do. But badgering this poor girl will not bring your friends back. Nor will it get you any closer to—" She broke off suddenly, as if catching herself before she said too much. She glanced at Haven. "Please do not let my brother upset you. I trust the pain in your shoulder has lessened?"

"Yes," she murmured, her thoughts yet churning on the notion that she had been senseless—and completely at these strangers' mercy—for so long a duration. *Four days*. The lengthy span of time was so unexpected. It had passed by her in such a blur and she could account for none of it. She frowned, confused by all she was hearing and seeing, yet unable to fully comprehend. "And you . . . have you been tending me all the while?"

"I've done what I could, but I fear I have much to learn about the healing arts."

"You saved me."

The lady Ariana gave her a warm smile as she squeezed her hand. "Not I. That credit must go to Kenrick. If anyone spared your life, 'twas him."

Impossible, Haven thought, looking in wary disbelief to his impassive face. His frost blue eyes watched her intensely, measuring her in some way, she was certain. From his strong brow, creased slightly from what must be years of practiced scrutiny, to the perfectly aligned nose and the firm mouth that seemed so wont to pass judgment on all he saw, Kenrick of Clairmont was a vision of rigid control.

Stoic, silent as he gazed at her, it seemed difficult to imagine he might have saved her from death. Haven saw no mercy in that handsome, untrusting face; only cool logic.

"You'd been stabbed," he told her grimly. "By the look of it, more than a sennight past when I found you wandering Greycliff in a state of delirium. The tip of your attacker's dagger had broken off inside your wound. It was poisoning your blood. If the blow itself didn't kill you, the infection from that bit of severed steel surely would have."

She heard his words, and knew that what he said must have been true. The aches of her body told her as much. The memory of searing pain flickered in the darkness of her mind, as did the vague notion of losing her footing on a night black cliff, of waves roaring very close to where she lay before unconsciousness swallowed her up. She could almost feel strong arms catching her, lifting her up, holding her when she had not the strength to hold herself. "I remember so little . . . most of it is dim . . . out of my reach."

"You were in a very bad way," Lady Ariana said. "Perhaps it is God's mercy at work that you do not recall much of what you endured."

"Perhaps," Kenrick muttered. He held something in his hand, Haven realized, watching as he uncurled his fist to reveal a small triangle of tooled metal. "Tell me, do you recognize this?"

"What is it?" Ariana asked, clearly surprised by this revelation. A note of wariness crept into her voice. "Kenrick, what do you have?"

"Anon, Ana. I would have Haven's answer first," he replied, his voice as cool as his gaze.

He came around the other side of the bed and held out his open hand. The broken bit of weaponry sat in the cradle of his large palm, a wedge of dark steel no bigger than his thumbnail. But scant as it was, the piece shone with peculiar allure. Light played off the intricate scroll-work that adorned it, dancing like a flame with every subtle movement of his hand.

Haven peered at it for a long moment, uncertain and yet . . .

Other images assailed her in that moment, unbidden images of darkness and violence. Of fire and smoke and brutal, slashing steel. Shattering screams and the metallic scent of spilling blood. She drew in her breath, quickly glancing away from the bewitching sparkle of the dagger's tip in Kenrick's hand.

"You were there when Greycliff was attacked," he said, not a question at all but statement of fact. "Tell me what you saw, Haven. You are the only living witness to the attack on Elspeth and her family. I must know what happened that night, everything. Who was there, what they did—anything you can recall, you must tell me."

In silence, she stared out the window across from the bed. She heard the impatient hiss of breath Kenrick exhaled, but she could not heed it.

"Who stabbed you with this blade, Haven?"

The images continued to fly at her, disjointed, unclear. "I don't . . ." She shook her head, closing her eyes against the onslaught of memory. "I am not sure what I saw. Nothing is clear."

"By the blood of Christ—you must think!"

"Kenrick," said his sister, rising to cut him off when he seemed intent on pressing further. "Enough, please. Let her rest a while."

"My friends are dead, Ariana. I do not take that lightly. As it stands, this woman is the only person who can tell me what might have transpired the night of the raid on their home. I need those answers." He fixed Haven with a piercing stare. "I *will* have them."

"But I have told you all I know," she protested, frustration rising in her breast. "I cannot remember what occurred. You know all that I do, I swear it."

"Indeed." He cursed under his breath then strode around the bed and toward the chamber door. "I trust your memory will improve along with your shoulder," he said, pausing with his hand on the latch. "Until then, you'll be staying under my watch while you recuperate."

Lady Ariana turned a sympathetic look on her. Instead of comfort, it brought a pang of alarm. Haven's memory might be sketchy, but she knew a threat when she heard one.

"Under your watch?" she challenged, anger flaring now.

"Aye," he replied easily. "Here at Clairmont."

He said it as though the matter required no further explanation. As though he would invite no questioning, nor permit her any other choice but to abide his own will.

Such domineering nerve—such arrogance!

Haven moved to push herself up on the mattress, but was felled by a jolt of debilitating pain. It robbed her of breath, stilling her instantly, even if it did not cool the outrage that was blooming hot in her belly. Lady Ariana eased her back down, concern soft in her eyes.

Where he stood across the room, Kenrick said nothing. He merely watched her with that judicious, unsettling gaze that seemed wont to turn her inside out. Pride rankled inside her, inflamed by the understanding that she was well and truly at his mercy—at least for now. Had she an ounce of strength, she swore she would have flown at him like a tempest. That maddening look of his said he sensed as much, and it worried him not in the least.

To her dismay, her voice, when she finally found it again, was weak with the slow ebbing of her pain. "Well, then. Do you mean to hold me here as your guest, sirrah, or your prisoner?"

"That, my lady, shall be up to you."

He turned away without another word, quitting the chamber and leaving Haven to simmer, made helpless by her lingering fatigue.

Pray, not for long, she thought, more certain than ever that her survival hinged on her escape from this place.

❧ 5 ❧

"**D**ID THE WOMAN confirm your suspicions about the attack at Greycliff?"

Kenrick glanced up from a journal that lay open on his desk. His brother-by-marriage, Braedon le Chasseur, reclined in a chair situated near the solar's cavernous fireplace, his sea gray eyes shadowed by dark brows and a fall of overlong raven hair.

Scowling, half-absorbed in his thoughts and the work spread out before him, Kenrick gave a shake of his head. "No. She claims to remember little of that night."

"Fever can rob a person of memory. I have seen it happen more than once."

Kenrick grunted, knowing there was sense in the statement yet unwilling to accept it. "She holds something back. I can see it in her eyes. She vows she is being truthful with me . . . but I don't know."

"Mayhap it is fear that keeps her from talking." Braedon turned a sage look on him. "Fear of you, my brother."

"Me?" Kenrick scoffed. "I have given the chit no reason to fear me. She is alive, is she not? She is safe and comfortable. Any fear she might harbor toward me is misplaced—nay, unfounded and foolish."

"Hmm."

39

The thoughtful response bespoke disagreement but Ariana's husband made no more of it. Kenrick watched him turn his attention to a small object in the cradle of his palm. He inspected the metallic shard, tilting it this way and that to allow the firelight to skitter across its polished surface.

"That she was present during the raid on Greycliff is obvious," Kenrick continued. "I reckon the chip of tooled steel you hold in your hand is evidence enough of that."

"Yes," the dark-haired warrior concurred, grim as he continued to peruse the item. "This dagger tip could have come from one place only."

"Aye," Kenrick said. "Anavrin."

Although thoughts of the place had consumed him for years, he had not spoken the word aloud in months.

Anavrin.

It was the realm of the Dragon Chalice itself, a mythical world that was said to exist alongside their own, ruled by benevolent immortals and guarded by soulless magi warriors who could shift their physical forms at will. Legend had it that some of those shapeshifters had been dispatched to the mortal world to aid in retrieving the Chalice treasure, after it had been stolen from Anavrin some hundreds of years ago by an unscrupulous knight who had connived his way past Anavrin's protective gates.

Most would call it fanciful fiction, mere fairy tale. But not Kenrick. Not Braedon and Ariana. They had seen too much of it—felt too much of the power and the pain—to maintain a blissful ignorance of the treasure and those who sought it.

Rand and his family had seen too much as well. And

Haven, whose tender body had endured the nearly lethal blow of a shifter's blade.

"She was there," Kenrick asserted. "She was nearly killed by one of them—strangled, stabbed, left to die—and yet she can recall none of it."

Braedon set the chip of tooled steel on a table beside him. "Naturally, you do not believe her."

The statement carried an irony that made Kenrick pause. "Would you? Knowing all that you know—Criste, having lived through it, closer than most—could you trust anyone who might have knowledge of Silas de Mortaine and that accursed cup he seeks?"

A measured silence was all the answer he would get from Braedon le Chasseur, the man once known by his dangerous reputation as The Hunter. Eyes gone stormy with contemplation, he looked away from Kenrick, toward the orange glow of the fire on the grate. As he turned, light played over the long, silvery scar that rode a jagged trail down the left side of his face. It was an old wound, given to him in the time before Kenrick or Ariana knew the man they would one day call kin.

Braedon bore other scars as well, the most savage of them earned but a few short months ago, in the bowels of an ancient abbey in France. The night that he, Kenrick, and Ariana experienced the true and terrible power of the mythical Dragon Chalice. None of them had emerged unscathed from that journey. Nor would they be eager to face such a test again.

Kenrick knew he need not remind his sister's husband of the danger they courted should Silas de Mortaine and his league of sorcerer's underlings learn of their escape and then turn their sights on Clairmont.

De Mortaine was a wealthy man with vast personal

connections, particularly among the Templars, where Kenrick had first encountered the evil nobleman. Powerful in his own right, de Mortaine was next to unstoppable now that he held one of the four sacred Chalice pieces. Only two remained. Kenrick's work had given him clues to their locations, but never had the treasure felt farther from his grasp.

"What of the seal?" Braedon asked, referring to the item Kenrick had sought, but not found in Greycliff's cemetery hiding place. "Will you be able to proceed without it?"

"I don't know. I had not yet puzzled out how to use the seal, did not know where it belonged, or what it would do. But I know it is a key to finding one of the Chalice pieces, and now I've lost it." He fisted his hand and let it fall hard against the surface of the table. "It has taken me years to put my findings together. Already de Mortaine holds a large portion of my work, but if they possess the seal as well . . ."

Kenrick broke off with a low muttered curse.

"Mayhap Randwulf of Greycliff destroyed it before it could be taken."

"Optimism from you, le Chasseur?" Kenrick chuckled at that, a humorless sound in the weighty pall of the solar. "Neither of us can claim to subscribe to that brand of faith. No, Rand would not have destroyed the seal any more than he would have surrendered it to the villains who raided his keep. Nothing would have torn its location from his lips."

"Not even the torture of his wife and child?" There was a soberness to Braedon's words that set a coil of ice in Kenrick's gut. "Don't think they wouldn't stoop to it. Nothing is sacred to these bastards. You know it."

A niggle of sick possibility rose like bile in Kenrick's throat. Randwulf of Greycliff was a strong man, a stalwart knight with an unbreakable sense of honor. He understood the gravity of what Kenrick had entrusted him with, and that trust would not have been breached. But at what personal cost?

"Damnation. What did I bring down on them?"

Kenrick's remorse was broken by the snick of the latch on the solar door. There was no rap, no delay for permission before the panel swung open on its hinges. Ariana entered the room with hands on hips, a look of censure snapping in her eyes.

"Do I interrupt?" She phrased it as a question, but it was clear from the stubborn tilt of her chin that she dared either of them to tell her she was unwelcome. "Pray, continue with your conversation, my lords."

Braedon cleared his throat.

"We had just concluded," Kenrick told her as she walked farther into the solar, narrowly regarding the both of them. He closed his journal before her gaze could fully light on the scrawled notes he had been writing. The subtle concealment of his work did not escape her shrewd notice, but she seemed to have other pressing matters to address.

"Do you mind telling me what just happened back there?"

"I merely asked the lady some questions."

"Interrogated her, I should say. You left her in quite a state, Kenrick. 'Tis not like you to be so rough and uncaring."

"Quite a lot has transpired these past weeks, as you well know. There are answers that must be found and little time to find them. I did not question the woman to be cruel." He reached for a tankard of wine on the desk and took a slow drink. "In any event, I think it prudent that we keep a close watch on this 'Haven' woman. She knows more than she is telling me, I'm certain. There is something amiss with her, something I don't quite trust."

"Did you consider for a moment that Haven might not trust *you*? That she might well be afraid of you?"

Kenrick frowned, glancing sardonically in Braedon's direction. "Clearly the two of you are well suited." At Braedon's answering smirk, he looked back to his sister, holding the snapping blue gaze she fixed on him. "Have I done anything to send the woman into a cower?"

Ariana gave an exasperated sigh. "Who knows the extent of what she might have suffered. Then to wake up in a strange place, injured and weak, finding herself among people she does not know—one of them scowling and grumbling at her as though she were a base criminal deserving of the stocks. For pity's sake, Kenrick, she is being kept here as your prisoner; you said as much when you confronted her a short while ago."

He felt the crease in his brow deepen at his sister's charge. An accurate one, he admitted with some reluctance. "I cannot afford any risks, Ariana. *We* cannot afford it."

"Kenrick is right, my love." Braedon rose from the chair he all but dwarfed, and strode to his wife's side. He put his arms around her, gently gathering her into a protective embrace. "Until we have more facts, we must be cautious with our trust."

"What are you saying?" She glanced from Braedon's face to Kenrick, worry etching the corners of her mouth. "What is going on here? For days, ever since you brought Haven here, the both of you have been discussing things in hushed voices and behind closed doors. Nearly every time I enter a room where you are, conversation ceases or makes an abrupt switch to mundane topics I know to be of no interest to either of you."

"We have not wanted to worry you, Ana—"

"Well, I'd say it is too late for that."

"You have already been through much, my love," Braedon began, but he was cut short by Ariana's dismissive little scoff.

She shook her head, creating a small tempest of movement in her long blond hair. "Husband, do you credit me to be some delicate thing that will break with the slightest whiff of distress?"

Braedon arched a dark brow. "Not at all."

."Then tell me what's happening. If there is trouble here, I want to know. All of it." She pinned a stern look on each of them, a softly censuring gaze that set both men to staring at their boots. "Dear Lord. It has to do with Silas de Mortaine, doesn't it? Your friends' deaths, the raid on their keep—de Mortaine is responsible, isn't he?"

"Yes." Kenrick nodded, remorse lying cold as frost in his gut. "Although if I blame him, I must blame myself as well. I should never have involved Rand in my findings of the Chalice treasure."

"Oh, Kenrick. What did you tell him about it?"

"It was not so much what I told him about the treasure, but what I gave him. Before I left for France last year, I entrusted Rand with the safekeeping of a key of sorts. On surface, it did not appear to be much—a bit of tooled metal wrapped in parchment—but it might be all that prevents de Mortaine from recovering another of the Chalice stones."

"Or the very thing that leads him to it," Braedon added gravely.

"And you believe that's why Greycliff was attacked?"

"We are certain of it, love."

"Mother Mary," she whispered. "Poor Rand and his family. Poor Haven, to have been made to bear witness to the horror of such a thing. My heart breaks for all of them."

Braedon smoothed his hand over her silken pate in a comforting manner, but the gaze he shared with Kenrick betrayed his unrest. His concern that the dark magic he had battled once before—that which had scarred him and nearly robbed him of the woman he loved—was clear in his stormy eyes. The danger might well come to roost once more, visited this time at very gates of Clairmont.

Kenrick knew the same dread. He had worn it like a robe since the day Braedon and Ariana had rescued him from imprisonment and torture at Silas de Mortaine's hands.

"The seal was missing from its hiding place at Rand's keep. That woman recuperating abovestairs is likely the only person who might know what happened to it. She is our sole witness to the attack that night. Any answers we might have will come only from her."

"And so you will keep her here on suspicion until she submits," Ariana replied. "Even against her will?"

"We must."

"Ah, yes. I understand." Her expression was schooled, but the challenge in her eyes had dimmed little. "I wonder though . . . how does this differ from the shackles that de Mortaine placed on you, my beloved brother? Is one prison any more justified than another?"

The question hung in the air of the solar, unanswered, for it was no simple matter to be viewed as either black or white. Was it?

Kenrick felt a muscle draw tight in his jaw. He need not justify his actions in this. Ariana was softhearted, ever compassionate. This was war. Undeclared, but bloody and serious all the same. And now his sister saw him as no better than the most heinous of villains, Silas de Mortaine.

When the silence stretched out, taut and unyielding, Braedon was the first to break it. "Come, wife. To our own chamber, if you will. I am late to training with the men and I would enjoy your company while I don my mail."

"Aye," she replied quietly. "Of course."

With one last glance in her brother's direction, a glance that went broodingly unacknowledged, Ariana accepted her husband's arm and accompanied him to the corridor outside. It was not until they had left and the door had closed firmly behind them that Kenrick let loose the black oath that rode at the tip of his tongue.

✖ 6 ✖

A TUB OF lukewarm bathwater sat vacant near the fireplace of Haven's chamber. Recently withdrawn from the fragrant, lavender-scented water, now dressed and seated on a cushion in the embrasure of the chamber window, she sighed as she ran a comb through her damp hair. She luxuriated in the feeling of cleanliness, in the soft slide of the fine bone teeth as she brushed out her long tresses, gathering the thick skein over her good shoulder to let it dry in the fresh morning air of the open window. The comb was a gift from Lady Ariana, as was the simple berry-colored gown that caressed her skin in silken luxury.

It had been two days since she had awakened in this place, confused and infirm, but already her strength was coming back. She was alert and out of the worst of the pain. She had her appetite again, and could move about without assistance—carefully, for her limbs were still unsteady, the strength in her left arm yet impaired by the healing wound. Each day, indeed each hour, brought more recovery, more physical strength and focus.

The same could not be said for her memory of the night she was attacked, however, a fact that troubled her much. As long as full recollection stayed out of her reach, it was clear that so, too, would freedom.

Her cage was the four tapestried walls of this chamber, her benevolent warden the kind Lady Ariana. This very moment, Ariana was searching out a pair of hose and slippers for her, for she worried that walking barefoot on the drafty floor might cause Haven a chill. In truth, her kindness thawed something cold in Haven's breast. Still apprehensive and wary, she had not wanted to like any of them, and a cautious voice inside warned that whether they were kind to her or nay, she would be wise to keep her distance.

Thankfully, Haven had seen little of the lady's disagreeable brother since that first day. Even now the thought of him and his arrogant ways rankled. It was primarily anger that fueled her determination to heal as quickly as possible. No man, no matter his reasons, would hold her against her will. She would regain her strength and then she would put Clairmont Castle far behind her.

She looked out longingly over the landscape that unfurled at the base of Clairmont's ancient motte. At the base of the hill, an open field, flowering in shades of pale yellow and violet, spread like a blanket toward a small orchard of blossoming apple trees. Farther still, a dense thicket of woods thrust up, dark and bristling with new spring leaves. Haven peered closer and spied a deer grazing on the dew-drenched grass of the meadow.

She settled back against the embrasure and for long moments contented herself with watching the doe, until a disruption somewhere out of earshot drew the deer to attention. It raised its head, scented some alarm, then bolted out of sight.

If only I could do likewise, Haven thought wistfully.

Soon, she would. As soon as she was able, she would

make her own escape. She would flee across that flowering field and into the cover of the woods, the same as the doe had done. She drew a breath of the crisp morning air and could almost taste freedom.

A rap on the chamber door behind her brought her thoughts back within the walls of her comfortable prison. "Enter," she said, listening for the now familiar snick of a key turning in the iron lock. She did not bother to turn around as the panel opened, unwilling to drag her gaze away from the endless beauty that lay so close, yet just beyond her grasp. "How far do Clairmont's borders stretch?"

She had expected to hear Lady Ariana's pleasant voice from across the room where she had entered, presumably returning with hose and slippers. Instead, a man answered Haven's query, the dark and familiar sound of him much too close for her peace of mind. "Farther than the eye can see from this chamber."

It was him—Kenrick, the golden lord of this place.

Her savior turned gaoler.

Haven's spine went rigid at once and she nearly dropped the comb in her haste to scramble out of the window. Pivoting, she put her bare feet on the floor and scooted off the deep-set embrasure to stand with her back pressed against the stone of the wall.

"I didn't mean to startle you."

"You did not," she replied, straightening as fully as she could and telling herself it was surprise, not fear, that sent her blood racing as she looked upon him. He had caught her unawares, entering unannounced, and intruded further by striding to the very window where she stood. He gazed out for a brief moment, then looked pointedly at her.

"You are trembling, Haven."

Was she? The knowledge jolted her to her core.

" 'Tis a chilly morn," she said by way of excuse as she inched away from his unwanted presence.

In truth, there was no bite in the air at all. If her body quivered when she stood beside Kenrick of Clairmont, she doubted she could blame the weather. Nor would she deign to credit it toward awareness of him as a man, despite that she could not tear her gaze away from the broad line of his shoulders, and the schooled expression of his striking face. There was a restrained power in his every move, a keen intelligence in his cultured voice.

"You know, before bringing you here, I had inquired after you in the village in Cornwall."

"So you told me when I awoke to find myself in your keeping, my lord."

"The folk there said you lived alone. That you have no husband or family. They said you had arrived in Cornwall not more than a year before, and that you plied your skill with herbs to make your living." He paused, as though testing her with his silence. "One or two folk might have called you a witch."

"A witch, am I?" She scoffed at that, finding more amusement than insult in the crude assumption. "The folk of that town are simple men with simple minds. Are you as well, my lord?"

Nay, he was not. She knew the instant the words left her mouth that this knight with the smooth, cultured voice was not an addlepated slab of brawn and handsome looks. His blue gaze was too shrewd, even as it casually perused her form. He was clever, and he was wise. A dangerous combination when paired with the sheer strength of his warrior's body, which she imagined could easily hold her in more complete restraint than any tightly tethered bonds.

"Do you think I cursed your friends in some manner? Is that why you have taken me prisoner here—to wring a confession from my forked witch's tongue?"

A wry smile played at the corner of his mouth. "I intend no such thing, Haven. Nor do I mean to hold you a prisoner in my keep. But I do want—nay. I *need* you to tell me all that you know about the attack on Greycliff."

She turned away from his probing gaze. "We have been through this already. I cannot tell you things I do not recall."

His voice was gentle, even while she braced herself for harsh male anger and intimidation. "Rand and Elspeth were my friends, Haven. What happened to them, what happened to you as well, was a cowardly act of brutality. I want to make sure the man who did this, and all those in league with him, never get the chance to hurt anyone again. He is evil, Haven. It's important that he be stopped, in any way possible."

"I do not see how I can help in that. It is as I told you, the attack is a blur in my mind. The details are . . ." She shrugged, but inside she was assailed with violent flashes of memory.

Sounds clashed with images, all of it hurtling dreamlike through her mind. She felt hands close around her throat. She shook her head, dispelling the vision before it could take root.

"I'm sorry, but the details of that night are lost to me."

She could not tell if he believed her. He watched her intently, saying nothing, then, finally, "I will not demand your cooperation in this, Haven. I know what it is to be a prisoner in truth, for I spent half a year in a madman's dungeon. He devised many creative ways of coercing information out of me—at times, I thought he might eventually be successful. When the torture was at its worst, I might have told him any lie to make it cease. I'm not going to do that to you. I don't want falsehoods from you, Haven. I cannot afford them."

There was an earnestness in his voice that took her aback. Had he come in raging and bellowing or with fists at the ready, she would have been more prepared. She would have been further convinced that the voice inside that warned of danger was correct. She found she did not know quite what to make of him.

"You were at Greycliff the night my friends were killed. The stab wound in your shoulder, the bruises that still linger at your neck from where your attacker strangled you—do you realize how close you came to dying yourself?"

"Yes," she murmured. "And I am grateful to you for helping me like you did."

"Then help me stop these beasts. There is an evil at work here that you would not wish to understand. Help me thwart it. Will you do that, Haven?"

"I have already told you as much as I know."

"You have yet to tell me what you were doing there that night. What brought you to the keep?"

"Lady Greycliff had sent for me."

A slice of memory opened in her mind. Haven saw the day clearly at first, she at work in her cottage preparing herbs, mixing dried sage and pennyroyal and sewing the blend into a small brewing packet. "I had been to see her often in the days before. She was . . . not well, and had requested an herbal of me."

He gave an understanding nod. "Elspeth often suffered headaches. There was little to help her when they were at their worst."

"Yes," Haven agreed. She saw no point in mentioning that it was melancholy more than headache that ailed the fragile lady in what would be her final hours. "I delivered what she wanted, and found her in quite a state. Her husband was away, gone for a sennight on estate matters to one of their holdings near Penzance. The lady herself was to have joined him but she was too ill to make the journey. I arrived at the keep and gave her my herbal, then sat with her awhile—easily hours, until I saw she was improved."

"So then the raid on the keep occurred while you were there with her?"

She shrugged, not certain of the details. "No. That is, I don't think so. I remember it was dark. Perhaps I went back to check on her? I do not recall the precise timing. Things become . . . hazy."

"What about Greycliff himself? Rand must have been there, too. Had he returned from his trip while you were there?"

"I don't know."

It was the truth; Haven could not recall specific facts from that fated night. Once darkness fell, once the flames and ash had begun to close in around her, she could make sense of little. She knew only the violence of the night's events, and the understanding that an entire family had been lost amid the carnage.

Just thinking on it, she could nearly feel the punishing vise of fingers at her throat, choking her whilst the smoke burned her eyes and seared her lungs.

In her mind's eye, she saw the white slash of a

grimace—the stark baring of teeth in a vicious snarl as her attacker squeezed the very breath from her.

"I need your help, Haven. I need you to tell me whatever you can about the man—or the beast—who attacked you at Greycliff Castle. Anything you can recall: what he looked like, what he might have said, if he took anything with him from the place . . . it is important that I have those answers."

"I'm sorry," she whispered, forcing herself to meet Kenrick's frank blue gaze. "There is nothing more I can say. I have told you all I remember right now."

For a long while, he said nothing. He merely studied her at too close a range, his intensity scorching her. Then he quirked a tawny brow in impasse.

"Very well, then."

He granted her leave from his questioning, but it was hard to mistake the lingering glint of suspicion in his eyes. He did not believe her, but true to his word, he would not force her into submission. She did not credit that he would afford her overmuch reprieve before he returned with more questions. For now, she would take what she could get.

"Give me your hand, lady."

Haven frowned up at him in question. "Why?"

"Your hand," he repeated, impatience flaring in his otherwise calm voice.

When she made no move to comply, he reached out and took her by the wrist. His fingers were warm and firm against her skin, his touch at once restrained yet commanding. With a subtle turn, her palm was open to him. He placed something in the center of it, then closed her fingers around a thin length of cold iron.

It was a key.

The very key to her chamber prison, she realized.

"What do you mean by this?"

"I give you choice," he said, his hand still cradling hers. He seemed to realize it at the same moment she did, for he withdrew his touch and took a step away from her. "I'm allowing you the freedom to decide where you go from here, Haven. You have nothing to fear from me or my kin. I'll not keep you prisoner; feel free to make Clairmont your home while your body continues to mend."

"But this isn't my home," she pointed out, determined not to warm to the man or his gesture of apparent consideration.

"You are welcome here as long as needed. You'll be fed and tended, and you will help my sister where she needs you about the keep. When you are fully mended, I will see that you are provided with a mounted escort back to Cornwall. In exchange, you have my protection, and the protection of Clairmont's guards."

"Do you think I require protection?"

He glanced to the bruises that ringed her throat, and down, to the bandage that wrapped her shoulder. "Someone tried to kill you, my lady. Don't think for a moment you are safe outside these walls."

"And within them?" she braved in a bare whisper, sensing a different brand of danger the longer she was held in Kenrick of Clairmont's penetrating gaze.

"You have my vow, Haven. No harm will come to you here. But I need your help as well. Trust me when I tell you that the lives of many—very likely all life itself— is at stake. What you know about the attack on Grey-cliff, what you may have seen, could prove immensely useful to me. Perhaps you will come to me with answers when you are ready."

She said nothing, watching as he slowly, deliberately, withdrew from the chamber. He closed the door behind him, but no key turned in the lock.

She wanted freedom, and now it seemed she had it.

Haven uncurled her fist and stared at the black metal key resting in her palm. Although she did not fully trust the gift, Kenrick of Clairmont had just given her wings to fly from this unwilling captivity. So help her, she would waste no time in using it.

❧ 7 ❧

FOR THE NEXT couple of days, Haven focused on her recovery. The fever had left her weak, sapping her breath and draining her limbs of much of their strength. To combat the effects of her injury, she rested often and used her waking hours to regain her stability. The freedom she had been granted by Kenrick was an added boon, for it afforded her the opportunity to walk about the castle and build needed strength in her legs.

Ariana accompanied her most of the time, an easy companionship that Haven was genuinely enjoying. On this morning, with the sun a brilliant orb shining down from a clear blue sky, Ariana had decided a bit of fresh air was in order.

She led Haven out of the tower keep by way of a side entrance used primarily by the kitchen servants. A guard stood his post at the door, armed with a deadly looking sword at his hip. He stepped aside as Ariana and Haven exited into the yard, lowering his head in deferential acknowledgment of the regal blond lady who greeted him warmly by name.

"Good morrow, Thomas. How fares your daughter today?"

"My lady," he replied, coming out of his bow. "She is

mending well. The spill rattled her pride more than aught else."

"Glad I am to hear it." Ariana's smile was sympathetic and fond as she turned to offer Haven explanation. "Some of the castle pages had been taking turns riding a pony about the courtyard yesterday morn when little Gwen, Sir Thomas's eight-year-old daughter, decided she wanted to join in. Evidently she took exception to the boys' taunting that she was too small and feeble to ride even a goat, much less the pony. She had them eating their words in no time at all. Unfortunately, the old bearded goat she rode out of the barn a moment later did not take kindly to helping prove her point."

"Oh, dear," Haven remarked, imagining what had likely ensued.

"Despite the brevity of her triumph, I don't expect Gwen will be mocked by the boys anytime soon. You know, Thomas, I suspect she deliberately chose the meanest of the goats on principle alone."

"She is a hard-headed one, that girl," he agreed with fatherly woe. "Has been since she was a mere babe."

"Yes, she has," Ariana said, laughing with him as he permitted a prideful chuckle. "Tell Gwen I'll come down to visit with her later this afternoon. I'll bring her a sweet from the kitchen."

Sir Thomas gave a warm nod, smiling. "She will be well pleased to see you, my lady. Thank you."

Ariana guided Haven away from the keep and on, along the path leading toward the kitchen outbuilding at the back of the castle.

"Poor Thomas has his hands full," she remarked to Haven as they strolled leisurely past the squat cooking house.

"How so?" Haven asked.

"Little Gwen's mother passed away in childbed nigh on two years ago, leaving her husband to raise the girl on his own. He is a good man, and he tries his best, but Gwen needs a mother." Ariana glanced to Haven with a sage look in her eye. "And just as badly, Sir Thomas needs a wife."

"Why does he not take one, then?"

"He is endeavoring to do so, I think, but the silly girl doesn't know what he's about," Ariana divulged in a hushed voice. "She works in the kitchens, a quiet maid named Enid. Sir Thomas bargained hard for his post at the postern door, and though he would never admit as much, I knew 'twas all so he could be standing nearby as shy young Enid makes her thrice daily rounds from kitchen to keep."

Just then, ahead of them on the path, a slender woman came around the corner of the keep and began a mincing walk toward the kitchens. She kept her head low, the elongated sides of her linen mop cap all but hiding her face. Ariana put her hand out to still Haven on the path, her gaze meaningful as the girl approached.

"Why, Enid. Good day," she called brightly.

The maid glanced up at once, seeming startled to be noticed, let alone directly addressed. She froze and bobbed a quick curtsy. "Oh! Good morrow, m'lady. And . . . miss."

"This is Haven," Ariana said, making introductions as the maid meekly drew close. "She is staying with us for a while as our guest, mending from a wound she took some days ago."

Enid nodded and politely offered her greetings. "My lady."

"I am glad I found you, Enid," Ariana interjected, her tone light and casually well-meaning. "We just passed the loyal knight on watch at the postern door, and I couldn't help but notice that the poor man has not been relieved from his post for some hours."

The maid's cheeks went pink with a sudden shy blush. "Sir Thomas, milady?"

"Yes," Ariana said, smiling now. "That's right, Sir Thomas. With the sun so hot today, he must be parched for refreshment. Would you mind fetching him a cup of ale?"

"Aye, of course." She looked mortified at the prospect, but immediately began smoothing her plain-spun skirts and patting at her floppy head covering. "Aye. I'll fetch it at once, m'lady."

When the girl had hastened away, Haven arched her brows at Ariana's crafty intervention. "You are wicked."

"I am," she readily agreed, laughing as she hooked her arm through Haven's and began strolling with her once more along the path. "But I have a notion about the two of them, and I wouldn't presume to meddle where I wasn't sure it would be helpful. Besides, I only want everyone to be as happily matched as I am with my husband."

It was not the first mention of her marriage that Lady Ariana had made in the time she and Haven had been getting to know one another. The mere thought of her husband seemed to light Ariana's features with an inner, luminescent glow. Her devotion was plain for anyone to see.

"Have you been long wed?" Haven asked, curious to know more about the man who had so captivated the heart of her new friend.

"Only a scant couple of months, though it seems we've been together always. Braedon and I were married at Clairmont soon after we brought Kenrick back from France this past February. He had run into some . . . trouble there."

Haven thought back to what Kenrick had told her the last time she had seen him, when he had come to her and informed her that he would not keep her against her will. He had admitted, much to her surprise, that he knew what it was like to be imprisoned.

"The trouble he encountered in France," Haven said. "Was that where he was held hostage?"

Ariana pivoted, nearly gaping. "You know about that?"

"Your brother told me he had once been a prisoner to a madman's torture. He said he spent half a year there."

"Yes," Ariana replied. The remembrance put a note of regret in her otherwise happy gaze. "He endured so much at the hand of Silas de Mortaine. Although he was beaten and tortured, my brother's scars are born on the inside. I doubt we will ever know the whole of it, for Kenrick keeps his feelings close. He is not one to open himself to others, or to admit his emotions. It has ever been the way with him, from the time he was a boy."

In some inexplicable way, Haven felt she understood what it was to conceal one's feelings. It seemed dangerous to her somehow, forbidden, in a manner she had not the words—or the memory—to explain.

She was less eager to admit that she might have anything in common with Kenrick of Clairmont. Nor did she expect he required a bit of sympathy or tender regard, least of all from her. If he shielded any part of himself from others, Haven guessed it was likely by his own design, for it seemed to her that the careful, remote knight did little without a calculated purpose behind it.

"Braedon helped me deliver my brother from his captors," Ariana was saying as they approached a bend in the path that led around the side of the large fortress, toward the front of the inner courtyard. "It turned out I was in quite over my head, thinking that I could negotiate alone for Kenrick's release. I had no idea what I'd gotten involved in, only that my beloved brother—my one true hero in all the world—was in harm's way and I had to save him."

" 'Twas brave of you to try."

Ariana dismissed the praise with a vague wave of her hand. "I can claim no such thing, merely that I was desperate to see Kenrick released. Braedon's courage is what truly saved him . . . and me as well. In order to rescue my brother, Braedon had to face Silas de Mortaine, and Draec le Nantres, a man who had been Braedon's friend until greed and his allegiance to de Mortaine persuaded him to betray that bond."

"What happened?"

"Before I knew him, Braedon made his living as a tracker for hire. He was called The Hunter, for that was what he did: retrieve outlaws or missing loved ones for a price. He was paid well, but it was not always the noblest of professions," Ariana confided. "Through his work, he ran across more than a few dangerous men, on both sides of the arrangement. One of those treacherous few turned out to be Silas de Mortaine."

They paused on the path, and Ariana lowered her voice as though reluctant to speak of the villain in anything more than a whisper.

"De Mortaine hired Braedon to locate and apprehend

a thief who had stolen something of great value from him. Braedon completed the task, unaware that it was a trap. Silas de Mortaine intended to kill him from the start, a fact that was well known by one of Braedon's own men, Draec le Nantres. It ended in a ruthless slaughter. Braedon survived, barely, but he lost many of his friends that day. He never went back to the life he once knew." Ariana's expression was grave as she held Haven's unblinking gaze. "These same men later took Kenrick prisoner. And they are also responsible for the raid you alone survived at Greycliff."

"Faith," Haven breathed, a shiver of black dread worming its way up her spine as her own murky recollection mingled with the horror Ariana had just described.

"I'm sorry, Haven. I hope I haven't upset you in telling you all of this."

"Nay. You haven't upset me," she replied. "These are things I need to know if I am to remember what I have lost to my fever."

"We are here to help you in any way we can." Ariana laid her hand atop Haven's in a gentle show of friendship. "But we need your help as well."

Haven nodded, accepting the kind gesture with a smile. She wanted to ask more questions, despite her fear of the answers, but a sound from the bailey drew Ariana's attention. There was the grating sound of clashing steel, then the mingled hoot of men's voices going up from an apparent gathered crowd.

"What is this about?" Ariana mused, frowning in curious speculation. Another metallic crash sounded, followed by a collective gasp of interest and awe. "Come, Haven. It sounds like Braedon is training the guards this morn. Let's go and have a look. I'll introduce you to my lord husband."

She led Haven around the side of the tower keep, to the inner bailey where a large group of knights had assembled. It quickly became apparent that the training involved only two men, the pair of them sparring in the center of the gathering. Above the heads and shoulders of the more than two-score spectating guards, Haven caught the occasional flash of sun-kissed steel and the good-natured goading of the pair of opponents as their blades struck and grated in mock battle in the yard.

"This is an unusual event," Ariana remarked with a look of surprise. "That's my brother's voice I hear."

Haven had already concluded the same, her ear immediately discerning Kenrick's deep, rolling timbre from the rest of the shouts and murmurs of the other men. She walked with Ariana toward the center of the yard, weaving her way through the circle of men in armor who parted slightly to permit the ladies a better look.

Haven's gaze rooted at once on the sight of Clairmont's golden lord, sparring before the crowd of gathered knights and castle folk. Like his opponent, he wore only breeches and boots, his tunic having evidently been stripped off earlier and now held for him by one of the attending squires. Bare-chested, his bronzed skin gleaming under the brilliant rays of the noonday sun, Kenrick was a fascinating vision of flawless masculine form and disciplined athletic strength.

Haven stared in silent awe at the concert of well-honed muscles that bulged and stretched as he raised his sword above his head, then swung it in a practiced arc toward his opponent. The strike was met with like agility from the man who sparred with Kenrick, a tall, dark-haired warrior who himself seemed built of steel and unerring, deadly skill.

The blades clashed together and held, grating force against force, neither man eager to give quarter, even in mock combat. The dark knight grinned through the spiky hanks of his raven hair that drooped into his face as he pressed against Kenrick's blow.

"I thought you said you were out of practice, brother."

Kenrick's answering chuckle held not so much as a trace of fatigue.

"I am," he replied, but then he flicked his wrist and lunged forward with his blade, putting the other man immediately on the defense of another well-placed thrust.

The raven-haired knight parried the blow and came around again, relentless. This time Kenrick deflected the oncoming blade, drawing a startled gasp from a trio of young maids who had since joined the crowd of spectators. The girls tittered behind their hands to one another, three pairs of eyes fixed on the skirmish in unabashed interest.

Haven suddenly felt no better than the fawning girls, for when Kenrick glanced over and saw her standing there with Ariana, she warmed with the onslaught of an instant, feverish blush. She quickly looked down, feigning interest in the patch of sparse grass at her feet.

"Shall we call a draw?" she heard him say to his opponent.

"Very well. If you wish a draw, brother, then call it."

"Nay, my stubborn lords. I will call the draw," Ariana interjected from where she stood at Haven's side.

Her arch command was softened by the jesting look

in her eyes, and in the wry tilt of her mouth. Haven glanced up in time to see the two men lower their blades, both grinning like boys and sweating like field hands. One of the squires rushed forth with a towel for each man, obediently waiting as they swabbed off, then took their tunics from another of the attending youths.

"Haven," Ariana said as the dark knight strode forward, shrugging into his simple shirt, "I would like you to meet my husband, Braedon."

As he drew near and the tunic settled over his head and shoulders, Haven caught an unhindered glimpse of his face. She took an instinctive step backward, struck by the presence of a terrible scar that slashed a jagged line down the full length of his left cheek.

"Lady Haven," he murmured in greeting, his deep voice rumbling like banked thunder.

"M-my lord."

Haven covered her rude reaction with a quick bow of her head, hoping neither he or Ariana had noticed her surprise.

But there was something more than merely the scar that set her pulse into a lurch, she realized the longer she stood before him. There was something lethal in him. Something that raised her instincts on alert, warning of a danger she could not fully comprehend.

Ariana seemed to know no such wariness around the man who was her husband. She embraced him lovingly, petting his glossy black hair and raising herself onto her toes to place a kiss on his stern mouth.

Haven brushed aside her unsettled feeling and smiled as Ariana recounted her morning to her husband. She was telling him of her plans to visit Sir Thomas's little daughter when Kenrick strode up, still mopping his short golden hair with the length of toweling.

"Good morrow, Lady Haven," he greeted her with a nod.

"My lord."

"I am pleased to see you up and about. How fares your shoulder?"

She glanced down, affected, just to be near him. " 'Tis healing well enough."

"We are trying to restore Haven's strength," Ariana offered, clinging to her husband's arm as her gaze volleyed thoughtfully between Haven and her stoic kin. One fine tawny brow began to arch in a manner Haven had observed but a short while ago, when Ariana had run into Enid on the garden path and lit upon a wicked plan. "Actually, Kenrick, I wonder if you might step in for me and finish the walk with Haven. My head is beginning to pound in this heat, and I have promised to look in on one of the knights' children who's taken ill."

"Oh," Haven began, not the least bit eager to put herself in such close company with the brooding lord. "I'm sure that will not be necessary. . . ."

"Nonsense," Ariana said, smiling. "Kenrick, you wouldn't mind terribly, would you?"

He shot her a look that said he could name a hundred things he would sooner do, but his voice betrayed none of his reluctance. "It would be my pleasure to walk with Lady Haven for a while."

"Excellent," Ariana replied. "Perhaps you might show Haven the gardens. They have begun to bloom quite nicely just this past week alone."

"The gardens?" Kenrick echoed.

"Aye. A lovely idea, don't you think?" A teasing

sparkle lit Ariana's gaze. "I trust you know where they are—just around the other side of the keep?"

"I will manage," he said, studying his sister's bright expression with a scowl beginning to knit his brow. To Haven he said, "I wonder if my sister thinks I might take you to the dungeon instead?"

Ariana shook her head at him in exasperation. With a sigh, she put her hand on his broad shoulder and rose up to kiss his cheek.

"Be nice," she whispered next to his ear, and then she was off.

Haven could only watch in bemused wonder as Ariana and her husband made their good-byes and strode away hand-in-hand, leaving her to the dubious company of Kenrick of Clairmont.

❧ 8 ❧

KENRICK HAD NOT at all been of a mind to take a leisure stroll about the grounds, with or without his pretty guest at his side. His work awaited in his solar, along with countless other more critical tasks than this unwanted play of accommodating host that had suddenly been foisted upon him by his well-meaning sister.

It was uncustomary enough for him to leave his studying behind to train in the yard, but he had awoken that morning with an itch to use his muscles. When Braedon had suggested a quick spar, Kenrick eagerly agreed.

Rare or not, he had not expected his appearance in Clairmont's bailey to draw such an avid audience, least of all Haven. Her presence among the ring of spectators had jolted him in a most peculiar way, the beauty of her face and the nearly physical weight of her clear emerald gaze watching him through the crowd catching him unawares.

Seeing her had put an unexpected tightness in his chest, and in points decidedly lower.

Kenrick cleared his throat.

"This way," he said to her, gesturing for her to walk at his side.

Although his tone conveyed only the barest edge of impatience, Haven hesitated to move. "Really, you

70

needn't trouble yourself to walk with me now. I'm sure you must have any number of things awaiting your attention—"

"Nothing that will not remain when I return," he said, uncertain why he did not take her offered leave when it had been all the excuse he sought not a moment before. He lingered, perhaps because she seemed uninterested in his company. Averse to it. "Have you no wish to walk with me, demoiselle?"

She considered his query for longer than he might have guessed, her small white teeth sinking into her lower lip as she stared up at him. She smiled then, slowly, and more polite than welcoming. "I would not presume to wish you here or away, Lord Kenrick. I meant only that the choice was yours."

"Very well. Then let us walk, Lady Haven."

She gave him a small nod, then began their stroll in thoughtful silence.

It was difficult to imagine that the malodorous, half-expired waif he rescued on Greycliff's rocky promontory was the same maiden who strode so gracefully beside him, her spine erect and proud, her regal gait showing only the slightest hint of effort. Garbed in a silk cotte that accentuated her every curve, her fiery locks swept back in a loose braid and carrying the scent of floral soap and lush spices, Haven looked as fine as any noble lady. The sallow, helpless wildling was good and gone, as if it had never existed. In her place was a woman of exceeding appeal, and no small amount of mystery.

Try as he might to hold her at a cautious distance as he would any stranger, Kenrick found there was a stronger part of him that wanted to know her better, to examine her as he would any puzzle.

Haven affected him simply by being, just as she did now, walking silently at his side as he led her past the bustle of the courtyard.

"I trust you are being provided with everything you need," he said, his inquiry sounding stiff and formal, almost stern.

"Yes," she answered. "I am."

"Your wound is being looked after?"

Haven nodded, sliding him a wary look that seemed to say she was less comfortable with his attempt at politeness than she might be with his gruff mistrust of the days before.

"And you are being well fed?"

At his further questioning, she paused, tilting her head to look at him. A small frown creased her brow. "Yes. I am regularly given more food and drink than I can consume."

"Very good. Your health is important to me, Haven. I want you to see that I am taking good care of you."

"Because you need something from me," she surmised, a note of challenge sparking in her eyes.

He did not confirm or deny his reasons, for he saw little point in it. Not that Haven awaited his response. She crossed her arms before her and faced him squarely where they stood in the center of the sun-filled bailey. As she spoke, her voice rose with the spark of her ire.

"Well then, my lord, let me assure you that I want for nothing. I am regularly bathed and fed. My chamber is never without a fire on the grate and fresh rushes on the floor. Lady Ariana has provided me with this fine gown and slippers. . . . Why, every prisoner should know such fine treatment."

Kenrick scowled, noting the furtive, curious glances tossed their way by some of the folk yet milling about the yard. None of Clairmont's subjects would dare such boldness, for since his return from captivity, Kenrick was regarded with a measure of caution—and not a little fear.

It was a situation that suited him fine when his days and nights were spent in solitude and secret study of the treasure that consumed his every waking hour.

Most everyone in the keep thought him bedeviled and best avoided, a fact that had not been entirely without design.

It would have been easy to exploit his mad reputation in that moment, when he stood as good as publicly confronted by the fiery brazenness of his injured female charge. He could feel the eyes on him, the ears trained to hear their broody lord unleash an unholy wrath on the hapless fool who dared to pique him.

For one tempting instant, he considered doing just that. But anger was never his way, and to his surprise he found that Haven's challenge intrigued him more than anything else.

Let the servants think it just another unpredictable facet of his nature that he allowed this woman to take him to task over an imagined slight. She had no cause to be angry with him, and he saw no need to goad her unnecessarily.

Kenrick lowered his voice to a private level, holding her impertinent glare.

"You are not a prisoner, Haven. I told you that not a

couple of days ago, when I disposed of the bar on your door. I have not confined you to your chamber, have I?"

"No," she replied archly. "My cage is a bit larger than that. Though not much, I expect."

He stepped closer to her, until his tall shadow blotted the sun from her sparkling green eyes. "Is that truly what you think?"

She gave him no immediate answer, holding her ground in stubborn silence.

"I realize I might have treated you somewhat harshly at first, Haven. But you may trust me when I tell you that it was not my intention."

Her pretty lips pursed in a moment of haughty consideration. "I find it a wiser thing to trust deeds over words, my lord."

Kenrick smiled, taken aback. "As do I, my lady," he replied, in full agreement and amused in spite of his own defense.

He flicked a glance over her burnished auburn head, his gaze searching the bailey for one of the young squires who served him.

He found one of the boys toting a bucket of slops out of the stables. Kenrick caught the lad's eye with a commanding look and gestured him forth. Dropping his pail at once, the squire dashed over to receive his orders.

"Aye, m'lord?"

"Take word to the stable master: I will need a mount and escort available at all times, provisioned to ride as far as Cornwall on my instruction. Once this lady is healed and fit to travel, I will see her returned to wherever she wishes to go. Understood?"

The squire bobbed his shaggy head. "Aye, m'lord. I'll go tell 'im what ye said."

"I trust that puts to rest some of your doubts," Kenrick said, looking back to Haven once the boy was gone. "You are as free as anyone here. I don't know what more I can do to convince you I am in earnest, lady."

She stared at him in mute contemplation, then quietly said, "Thank you."

"The gardens are this way. Unless you'd rather tour my dungeons?"

She smiled at his jest, a plainly unwilling warming of her otherwise cool regard for him. He held out his arm like a courtly gallant, and she stepped forward to join him. They crossed the rest of the inner bailey at an easy pace, a wary sort of truce stretching tenuously between them.

Kenrick watched the busy scuttle of the pages and squires as they went about their duties, the knights resuming their training, and the servants attending their day's business back and forth from the keep. Kenrick surveyed all of this mundanity with a keenly observant eye, but the whole of his interest—indeed, his every sense—was tuned toward the unusual beauty at his side.

There was something elemental, yet ethereal, about her very being. He had been told by the villagers in Cornwall that she was a common maiden, a simple healer, but Kenrick could see nothing common in her at all.

Fire leaped in her russet hair and in her sharp, gem-bright eyes. Delicate yet strong, she held herself with the bearing of a queen—a warrior queen, he mused, noting her rigid spine and the fine tendons that flexed beneath the fair skin of her hands as she toyed with a loose thread on her borrowed gown. Her gaze was distant, her expression a bit forlorn, as though she were lost somewhere deep inside herself.

Kenrick felt a pang of sympathy for her, understanding how distressing it must be to awake a stranger in one's own skin, uncertain where she was, or where she might belong.

But it was not his place to console her. Nor was it a burden he desired.

Still, he found himself hoping she might find some peace at Clairmont. More the better, should that peace bring along the full recovery of her memory of the night of the attack on Greycliff.

He was mulling over that eventuality when they rounded the far corner of the tower keep and came upon Ariana's splendorous gardens. Haven drew in her breath with a soft exclamation of awe.

" 'Tis lovely," she whispered, leaving Kenrick to venture into the heart of the glorious patch of Eden.

The garden spread out along one full side of the keep, its colors resplendent, mingled fragrances beckoning even Kenrick to draw a deeper breath in order to savor the sweetness of the many blooms and budding herbs. He had to admit it was a pleasing sight, although he had never given this area of the grounds much thought. In truth, he could not recall the last time he had been outside to enjoy his sister's hard work on the hundreds of flowers, trees, and herbs that flourished under her nurturing hand.

Haven stood in the center of the verdant sanctuary and held out her arms, tipping her head back to let the sun beat down full upon her. She seemed to forget he was there, indulging in a little twirl of pure, uninhibited joy. She came out of it almost as quickly as the urge had overcome her, shooting him a shy glance across the distance that separated them.

Kenrick's blood was pounding hard just to look upon her in the midst of so much fertile beauty. He took a step into the garden, his gaze rooted on her, his mind returning eagerly to an image of Haven's nude form, a form he had innocently glimpsed when he tended her wound at Greycliff.

There was nothing innocent about his imaginings now, however.

Realizing this, he forced himself to heel just inside, leaving no less than a dozen paces between himself and any further tempting thoughts where Haven was concerned.

Evidently, it was too late to mask his interest.

Haven had gone still where she stood in the center of the garden. She looked at him with the sudden awareness of a rabbit catching sight of wolfish eyes in the thicket. Her breasts rose with the shallow breaths she took. He could almost see her pulse beating at her throat while she waited for him to make his move.

He should have made his excuses, turned away, and left her there. God's love, he meant to, but there was something more powerful at work here. Something that drew him toward her when every bit of logic—every scrap of honor—warned him to keep his head.

Kenrick took a measured step toward her, stalking deeper into the sanctuary of the garden.

"I believe I've had enough sun for one day," Haven murmured. "Please, excuse me."

She nearly lunged to dash past him.

Kenrick reached out his hand, and stilled her with the barest touch of his fingers at her wrist. She froze, half a pace beyond him and less than a hand's width separating their bodies on the narrow garden path. He was still holding her wrist in his hand, the heat of her skin coursing through him like a living thing.

"Faith," she whispered, closing her eyes as he brought his other hand up between them. "Do not . . ."

But Kenrick was already touching her cheek, stroking the backs of his fingers along the silken line of her jaw.

He wanted to kiss her.

He knew little more than her name, knew not whether she belonged to another man or nay, but the urge to take her into his arms nearly rent those concerns to pieces.

He wanted her.

God's blood, how he wanted . . .

Mincing footsteps approached then drew to an abrupt halt somewhere behind him, followed by the wordless gasp of a female servant. Haven pulled her hand out of his grasp at once.

"Oh—mercy! Beggin' pardon, m'lord . . . and miss. Excuse me, but I didn't see ye there—"

Kenrick turned to find a mousy serving girl gaping at his back, her floppy white cap wilting over her head, an empty vegetable basket hooked over her thin arm. She stared as though encountering the devil himself and fearing for her very life. Kenrick realized he was likely glowering at the girl, though it was more from his own inwardly directed anger than for any fault of hers in coming upon them unawares.

"I've no wish to disturb ye." The maid backed away, nearly stumbling, dread looming in her wide-eyed gaze. "Beg pardon, m'lord. I'll be goin' now."

She did not wait for his leave. Flustered and quaking, she turned and bolted back whence she came.

"God's blood," Kenrick growled, disgusted with himself for the uncharacteristic breach of his control. "My apologies, Lady Haven. I had no right—nor was it my intent—to be so bold here."

Through a fierce blush that rode bright pink on her cheeks, she waved her hand in a mildly dismissive gesture.

" 'Tis all right," she murmured, but Kenrick could not help noticing that she took a couple of steps away from him, retreating well out of arm's reach. "I think I had better . . . I wish to return to the castle now."

"Of course. I'll take you—"

"No. Please, just . . . no. Excuse me."

Her denial was swift. Understandably so. She stepped past him in a rush of movement, hastening away without another word.

❧ 9 ❧

THE NEXT DAY, Haven was still rattled from her encounter with Kenrick. She could not believe he dared such liberties with her. Worse, she could not credit her own reaction to him.

His touch had left her shaken, though not from outrage as would be her right. Kenrick's unexpected caress had unsettled her in a way she dared not consider too closely. Not when her skin yet burned from the memory, her thoughts yet spinning from the tenderness he had shown her. There was danger in that silken touch. Just as there was an unspoken danger in the man himself.

She did not want to think on him at all, and glad she was that she had not seen him since their stroll the day before. She dearly hoped he would remain out of her sight this morn as well, for she had no wish to be reminded of their brazen exchange by the mere appearance of him in the hall or about the keep as she took her morning walk.

As it was, she would be taking that walk alone. According to the maid who arrived to dress Haven's shoulder wound, Lady Ariana was indisposed within her chambers and could not join her. Haven accepted the maid's news with a pang of disappointment and a note of true concern for her new friend.

"Is anything amiss, Mary? Did she say why she could not come?"

The maid, a young woman with a freckled face and shy demeanor, gave a shake of her head. "Nay, lady. She turned away her breakfast this morn and asked to be left alone to sleep a while."

" 'Tis nearly midday," Haven said. "I hope she is not unwell. Perhaps I'll go look in on her after a while."

The servant nodded agreeably as she removed the old bandages from Haven's wound and set them aside. With a warm, wetted cloth, she cleaned the area, then sat back to allow it to dry. "You are healing quite well, Miss Haven," she remarked. "Another sennight and I wager you'll be good as new."

Haven glanced down at her shoulder, where the ugly gash had indeed begun to mend. It was progressing quickly, already losing much of its inflammation. She could not look at the deep wound without thinking how close it had come to killing her. She might have had just days—perhaps only a few scant hours—before Kenrick of Clairmont happened upon her that night in Cornwall.

He had saved her life, and she should be grateful.

In truth, she was, but she could not help wondering if her golden rescuer didn't present another, equally lethal, brand of trouble. That he was involved in something suspicious was clear enough to any person with eyes and ears in their head.

Even his servants and the folk about the castle whispered of their lord's peculiar habits and secretive ways. He skulked about the keep and grounds like a wraith, always deep in thought, watching. It had not taken more than a few overheard whisperings to know that it was rumored he never ate or slept, that he studied the dark arts, and damnation awaited any who dared breach his sacred domain.

Haven doubted Kenrick wanted anyone's soul, but she did wonder what made the enigmatic lord so brooding and aloof. From what she could see in her short time observing the keep's goings-on, only Ariana and Braedon held any bit of his confidence, and even they seemed to be kept at a safe arm's distance.

Did anyone truly know the man?

It did not seem likely to her when he appeared to take great strides to ensure his own solitude. Kenrick of Clairmont was unreachable, certainly unreadable, and Haven did not doubt that there were many secrets lurking behind his cool blue gaze.

It was those secrets that made him all the more dangerous in her mind.

Although she could recall little of the life she lived before coming to Clairmont, she knew that to remain here now was to put herself at risk of further peril. Beyond the unsettling presence of the man himself, there was something deadly in this place. Haven could feel it pulling at her with as much force as that which warned her to flee at first chance.

But escape would take physical strength she presently did not have.

"There you are now," the maid said as she fixed the last binding of Haven's new bandage. Mary helped her to her feet, then assisted with her gown. With a whisper of silken luxury, the borrowed blue cotte settled over Haven's body like a cloud, the long skirts floating down to her slippered feet.

"Shall I show you to the great hall? 'Tis nearly time for the noontide meal."

"No. Thank you, Mary," Haven replied. "I think I will take a small stroll first and stretch my legs."

"As you wish."

The maid smiled, then gathered up the soiled supplies and quit the chamber.

Eager to continue her recuperation, Haven was not long behind the girl, venturing out of the chamber and into the corridor outside.

The folk had grown accustomed to her frequent walks about the keep, and, no doubt informed by their lord that she had his permission to do so, no one bothered her as she casually made her rounds.

As was becoming her habit, Haven first walked the length of the second floor of the keep. Most of the living quarters were situated on this level of the tower, a stroll of several hundred paces, which Haven took at a slow rate lest she push herself too hard, too soon. She felt less weakness every day, encouragement she needed as she planned for the time she would be strong enough to leave Clairmont as Kenrick had promised her.

And leave she would, Haven thought as she made one final pass down the corridor. As soon as she was able, she would accept Kenrick's offer of a mount and escort, and she would return to where she belonged.

Wherever that might be, she admitted, weathering a pang of dismay over the loss of her past.

Indeed, the loss of herself.

She felt only half alive as she walked the halls of this strange castle, awakened to a strange world and an existence that seemed somehow foreign, incomplete.

As black and disturbing as the memories of Greycliff's

attack seemed to be, Haven knew she would need to face them one day. Not for the sake of Kenrick of Clairmont and his secret cause. Not even for the sake of the family who had died that night in Cornwall, people whom Haven murkily recalled with a sense of mingled fondness and regret.

She had to remember the details of that night primarily for herself, because she felt certain the key to her own preservation lay somewhere in the shadowed depths of her slumbering mind.

The thought of what continued to elude her put a heaviness in her easy gait. She longed for the freedom of the outdoors, but knew she would not be permitted to leave the castle to stroll the grounds by herself. Kenrick's granted liberties were not entirely without limit.

Perhaps there was another solution.

With most of the folk preparing to assemble for the midday meal, Haven sought the tower stairwell that circled high into the keep. Wondering if it might open onto the roof of the tall structure, she began the spiraling climb up the the steep, narrow steps.

As she circled her way toward the top of the keep, passing another floor of living space, her legs began to tire. She paused to allow herself a moment of rest before trudging up the rest of the climb.

While she leaned against the curved wall to catch her breath, she felt a queer heaviness lingering in the air around her. She could not blame it on dankness or the close confines of the stairs, for just beside her was an arrow slit window that allowed the breeze to filter in and freshen the cool humidity of the stairwell.

But the feeling persisted, like a stillness that came before a storm.

It seemed to reach out to her where she stood, the prickle of tiny fingers skittering up her arms and neck, and into her scalp. The sensation drew her gaze up, into the shadows that lingered farther along the climb.

Curious now, she gathered her strength and continued up the steps.

She reached the uppermost floor of chambers and was dismayed to see no obvious means to the outside. Her path came to an abrupt end before a dark, iron-banded door that was barred with no less than two heavy locks. The unwelcome space was all shadows and gloom save the slim light that sliced in through another thin arrow slit window.

And now that she had finished her climb, she realized that the peculiar feeling she experienced before was still with her. If anything, it seemed to intensify the longer she stood there, contemplating the forbidding door at the top of the stairs.

This was *his* domain.

Haven knew it at once, her gaze straying to the solid locks that proclaimed the high tower chamber as none other than the private quarters of an elusive man with more than one secret to hide. Secrets so substantial he felt they needed to be stored within granite walls as thick as she was tall, bolted, and housed ninety feet off the ground.

The lure of discovery was a strong one, if hopeless, given the barrier that stood before her. Nevertheless, Haven could not help herself. Her skin yet tingling with the odd sensation, she reached out, moving her hand toward the door.

Her fingers had not even brushed the surface of the dark, oiled wood before she felt the rising flush of gooseflesh travel the length of her arm. The closer she reached, the more intense the feeling . . . until suddenly the bite of an unseen fire leaped out to meet her fingertips.

"What are you doing up here?"

Haven jolted at the sound of the deep voice and spun around. Dread coiled in her stomach. She knew who she would find waiting at the mouth of the stairwell, for there was little that escaped the notice of Clairmont's keen-eyed lord.

"I was merely taking a walk. I thought these steps might lead to the tower roof."

"They do not."

"No," she said, rubbing at the queer tingle of heat that still gripped her hand. "I can see that they do not lead there after all."

Kenrick glanced from her face to the undisturbed locks on the door. Then he strode toward her with a measured coolness that seemed at odds with the suspicion that sparked in his gaze. "This part of the tower is mine alone. You are trespassing here, lady."

"I am sorry. It was not my intention."

He grunted as though unconvinced and advanced another couple of steps, regarding her as he might a stranger . . . or an enemy. His gaze narrowed to dangerous intensity. There was no trace of the tenderness he had shown her in the garden the day before, only unblinking scrutiny and plain mistrust.

As he approached, Haven edged away from the door, gradually circling around him as he placed himself between her and the chamber.

"W-what do you keep in there?" she stammered, wondering what it was he guarded with such deadly caution.

"None of your concern."

He put out his hand and caught one of the big locks in his palm. When he gripped the knot of iron without so much as flinching, Haven's gaze flew wide. She was still staring, now scowling in confusion, as he tugged the lock to test its hold.

The peculiar heat that had leaped to sear her fingers not a moment ago seemed not to affect him in the least. The lock dropped back against the door with a metallic thud.

Faith, she thought, watching his every move. Perhaps he did possess a power such as the servants seemed to believe.

Haven tore her gaze away from him to glance down at her own hands. Although there was no indication of the heat that licked at her when she thought to touch the door, she could still feel the lingering warmth. Gooseflesh still stood beneath her long sleeves, where her skin felt alive and crawling.

"Tell me again, Haven, how it is that I find you in the one area that all in this keep know to avoid. More to the point, tell me why your expression is one of guilt that says you knew where you were heading."

"That's not true."

"Which, lady? That you were not warned away from this part of the tower, or that the pink staining your cheeks right now is not the stamp of a guilty conscience?"

"Both," she protested. "Neither!"

He scoffed, one tawny brow arching skeptically.

"I knew you permitted no one within your private chambers, but I knew not where they were."

"And the blush that still rides high on your cheeks?

What is it, if not the outward acknowledgment of wrongdoing?"

Faith preserve her, but she would never admit to him that any heat that resided in her face was caused from the unsettling nearness of his body. He could not know that she found it hard to breathe when she was gazing into the changing pools of his blue eyes, which turned so easily from placidity to turbulence.

He would be the very last to hear that she thought him heartbreakingly beautiful—beyond handsome, for that seemed a feeble word to describe a man like Kenrick of Clairmont.

Instead she held herself as rigid as a lance, forcing herself not to quirk so much as an eyelash when he moved ever closer, awaiting her reply.

"If not guilt, my lady, pray tell, what might it be?"

He reached out then, and for one breathless instant, she thought he might intend to repeat his brazen behavior from the day before. His fingers hovered very near her face, calling a deeper heat to fill her cheeks as she anticipated the uninvited seduction of his touch.

He held her gaze for too long, then his long fingers slowly curled into his palm as though denied their will. With an exhaled oath, he lowered his hand to his side.

"Do not let me find you up here again, Haven. Am I clear?"

She made no effort to curb her biting tone. "Perfectly, my lord."

"There is something more," he said when she turned to take her leave of him. Haven hesitated, pivoting warily. "What occurred between us in the garden yesterday—"

" 'Twas nothing," she said, glancing down, unable to hold his gaze.

"Nothing," he echoed, the low tone of his voice sounding skeptical, almost offended. "You should know that I am not in the habit of fondling my guests, Lady Haven. I had no right to be so bold, let alone do so before one of the keep's gossipy maids."

"Enid," Haven whispered, recalling the befuddled look on the kitchen servant's face as she had unwittingly interrupted them among the herbs and flower beds. "The maid's name is Enid."

Kenrick frowned, clearly unfamiliar.

"Sir Thomas—your guard on the postern door— wishes to court her, but he is too anxious to ask and she is too meek to realize his interest in her."

"Is that so?"

Haven nodded. "The child Ariana went to visit yesterday is Sir Thomas's daughter, Gwen. She had a mishap in the bailey yesterday and your sister wanted to look in on her and bring her a treat from the kitchens."

He clasped his hands behind his back and rocked on his heels, considering her with a look of intrigue and surprise. "You put me to shame, Haven. Here but a handful of days and already you know more of my keep than I do."

"I know that the folk of Clairmont seem uneasy in their lord's company. They fear you, I think."

"Do they now?" Kenrick studied her, neither confirming nor denying her observation. "What about you, lady? Do you fear me as well?"

"No," she answered, fighting to ignore the niggle of unease—of heated awareness—that coursed through her as he advanced the few paces that lay between them.

He wanted to intimidate her, she realized. From his crowding masculinity to his snapping blue gaze, he worked to make her tremble like the rest of the folk in the keep did in his presence.

But she saw through him in that instant. Holding his piercing stare, Haven glimpsed the solitude within him; a man who strove so hard to push everyone away.

In truth, she knew the same emptiness within herself.

"I think you have made your point here, my lord," she told him, refusing to let him cow her. "Now, by your leave, the midday meal is being served and I have asked one of the maids to save me a trencher in the kitchens."

"That's ridiculous," he said, as though scenting her small lie. "Granted, I may not be the most hospitable host, but I'll not leave a guest of mine to eat in the kitchens with the hounds. You will dine at the dais as any guest should expect to do—at the side of Clairmont's lord."

Kenrick held out his arm in a gallant sweep of motion, gesturing for Haven to walk ahead of him to the stairwell. She complied in careful silence, although he could see that the thought of enduring a meal at his side in the great hall was about the least thing she cared to do.

In truth he did not exactly relish the idea himself.

After his pawing of her in the gardens, and his near repeat of the error there in the corridor, he wondered if he could trust himself at all when it came to the bewitching beauty in his charge. He had been more gruff with her than he intended, desire and suspicion clashing like twin blades when he found her alone, sneaking about at the top of the tower stairwell.

He did not fully trust her—God knew, there were not many he permitted into his confidence—but that did not keep him from wanting her.

To endure an entire meal with her tempting presence beside him on the dais would be a hellish test of his will. It was too late to rescind his challenge, as she began a haughty march ahead of him to the stairwell.

Kenrick hesitated but a pace behind her, wondering again at Haven's presence in the far tower, her supposed accidental arrival at the very door that sealed from prying eyes and grasping fingers the tangible proof of the Dragon Chalice's existence.

Could she possibly know what he kept within that chamber?

Impossible, he thought, scowling as he considered the many ramifications of such knowledge. Besides himself, only Ariana and Braedon knew the truth. So it must remain, for all their sakes.

But it was hard to dismiss Haven's anxious expression when he had found her there, as if she sensed the power of what she had nearly stumbled upon.

Suspicion flared as Kenrick considered the flame-haired beauty who had come so unexpectedly into his charge. He told himself it was dark curiosity, and no small amount of mistrust, that had him watching her with such keen interest as he followed her down the spiral steps to the bustling great hall.

❧ 10 ❧

ALTHOUGH HER PAST remained a muddled pool in her mind, Haven felt sure that she had never experienced so conspicuous a moment as her entrance to Clairmont's great hall on the arm of the keep's enigmatic lord. The large banquet room was set for the midday meal, with cloth-covered tables and wooden benches situated in rows to fill the floor of the hall.

Many of Clairmont's residents—servants, knights, and common folk—had already been seated. All but a few turned looks of surprise and intrigue on the unlikely pair as they strode uneasily into the hall.

Murmured questions passed from ear to ear in their wake: Where did she come from? Who is she? What does he mean to do with her?

All things Haven herself wondered as Kenrick guided her in brooding silence up the long midway that passed between the assembly. At the head of the aisle was the elevated platform of the dais and high table.

Ariana occupied one of four large chairs at the dais table. To her left sat her husband. The hulking warrior spied them at once, his pale gray gaze under his raven's-wing brows observing her with a careful intensity similar to that which Kenrick possessed.

Haven's step faltered only slightly, for the same

tremor of wariness she had felt upon first seeing Braedon le Chasseur in Clairmont's bailey the other day assailed her anew. The closer Kenrick brought her to the dais, the less she was able to dismiss that there was something about Braedon's face—his very presence—that triggered a subtle warning in the back of her mind. Not quite a memory, but a niggling familiarity nonetheless.

Ariana seemed recovered of the ailment that kept her abed late that morn. She smiled as she held the dark warrior's hand atop the table, her slender white fingers laced between his large tanned ones in a decidedly affectionate manner. The pair rose as one when Kenrick and Haven reached the dais.

Ariana embraced her brother with a warm kiss on the cheek. "This is a pleasant surprise. I cannot recall the last time you dined with us here in the hall."

When the stoic lord merely grunted in acknowledgment, Ariana turned to Haven and caught her hand in a quick, friendly clasp. "You are looking better and more healthy every day. 'Tis good to see your recovery progressing so well."

"Thank you," Haven murmured. "I am eager to be hale again."

Very eager, she silently amended, thoughts of her promised release never closer from her mind than when her senses still thrummed from her encounter with Kenrick in the tower.

"I was told you were under the weather today," she said to Ariana with friendly concern. "Is aught the matter?"

Beside his lady wife, Braedon tensed. "You didn't tell me you were ill, love. What is it?"

"Oh, 'tis nothing," the lady replied with an easy wave of her hand. "I told Mary not to make a fuss. A little bedrest was all I needed. I am fine, truly."

The dark knight brought her fingers to his lips, placing a tender kiss on the back of her delicate hand. "You are certain that's all it was?"

"Aye, husband. I am well, I promise you. Never better."

Haven watched the loving exchange of glances that passed between the couple, feeling a bit awkward to be sharing the moment in Kenrick's brooding presence. She knew not how she would survive the duration of the meal when just standing beside him put a flutter of anxiety in her pulse.

"Two more place settings, please," Ariana requested of an attending servant who had come to pour wine at the dais. "This way, Haven. You may sit next to me."

Haven smiled, and allowed Ariana to lead her to one of the unoccupied chairs on the dais. To her dismay, Kenrick assumed the last, which meant he would have to lean across her to speak to either Ariana or her husband. Perhaps he would keep to his aloof ways and say nothing for the whole of the meal, Haven thought with fleeting hope.

Already he was too close to her, his large athletic frame engulfing the stiff-backed chair, his muscular arms crowding into her place at the table. His thigh rested so near her own she could feel the heat of his body emanating through the many layers of fabric that clothed her. She had a right to be offended, at the least incensed, having been made to endure his unseemly command that she dine beside him as his guest.

His guest, indeed.

Regardless of what he claimed or pretended, Kenrick would keep her there as long as he pleased, in whatever capacity he pleased. He would keep her under his careful watch for as long as it took him to decide whether or not he needed the information she had lost with the scorching of her memory.

Haven stewed on that notion while Kenrick and Ariana's husband discussed a theft that had occurred in a nearby village. Some artifacts from a chapel had been stolen—details Haven all but tuned out, her mind suddenly slipping back toward the night of the raid on Greycliff. She did not permit herself to venture too far into the darkness of those events, for there was a veil of pain and terror that hung between her conscious mind and the memories that lay charred and forgotten by the searing trauma that she had endured.

The edge of that veil was lifting, moment by moment, each hour since she had awakened from her fevered slumber. She did not want to know what lurked behind it. She was not sure she could bear the terror of the truth.

"Haven . . . ?"

Ariana's voice broke her out of the dark fog. "I'm sorry, were you speaking to me?"

"Yes," she said, smiling despite the note of concern in her blue gaze. "I asked if you wanted to try some of Cook's fish soup. It is one of his best dishes."

Haven nodded, and belatedly accepted the bowl of aromatic soup. "Thank you. I was just . . . thinking."

"You're distressed," Ariana observed, gently regarding her as she lowered her voice to a private tone. "You were thinking about the attack, were you not?"

"Yes."

"Have you been able to recall anything more? Anything at all?"

"Nay. Only what I have already told you." She let out a little sigh, and shook her head. "I don't think I want to recall much of it. I don't think I will be able to forget again, once the memories return completely."

Ariana's mouth flattened grimly, and she covered Haven's hand with her own. When she spoke there was no surprise in her voice, only a grave understanding. "There are dark forces at work, Haven. Very dark. You cannot know how fortunate you are that you survived to be here at all."

"Why would they attack Greycliff? What did they want?"

"That is what I had hoped you might answer for me," Kenrick interjected. "They were looking for something in Rand's possession. I need to know if they found it."

She shook her head. "I don't know what the attackers wanted. Why is it so important to you?"

He leaned back, a forbidding look in the taut lines of his face. His untrusting silence only made Haven more impatient.

"You won't tell me anything, but you expect—nay, you demand—my cooperation?"

An air of quiet tension stretched across the dais, a deliberate stillness that sparked Haven's anger. She looked from Kenrick's stoic expression, to Braedon's dark visage at the other end of the table, then to Ariana's gentle but witholding gaze beside her. Even she, who had been Haven's only friend since she had awakened in this strange place, would say nothing more.

"You ask for my trust when none of you will give me yours."

Ariana was the first to glance down in culpability under Haven's charge.

"Kenrick," she said quietly, "Haven is right. She has lived a part of this, as we have. She is involved, whether you wish it or nay, brother. And if you do not tell her, I will. There was a time not long ago that I was the one kept in the dark over this quest of yours."

"And the knowledge almost got you killed," he replied, not quite masking the devotion he felt for his only kin.

"The knowledge of the Dragon Chalice wasn't what nearly claimed my life. It was those who seek it—the same dangerous men who slew your friends and might have done like to Haven if you hadn't found her to bring her here. She has a right to know."

Like a silken thread catching on a thorn, Haven's mind snagged on two words Ariana spoke. "Dragon Chalice?"

"A myth," Kenrick said, slanting a pointed look on his sister.

"What of it?" Haven asked.

For a long moment, no one said a word. Then Kenrick drew his gaze away from Ariana and her grim husband to settle instead on Haven. "There is an ancient legend that tells of an enchanted land of great and powerful magic. This mystical realm, Anavrin, owed its existence to a special cup known as the Dragon Chalice, which granted its bearer many gifts: limitless wealth, complete happiness, and life without end. These gifts and more belonged to Anavrin and its people, until a mortal man stole the Chalice away from them."

Haven listened raptly, feeling doors creak open in the far corners of her mind. "I think I have heard of this treasure. It is . . . familiar somehow."

"Perhaps Rand might have said something about it to you," Ariana suggested, looking from Haven to Kenrick in question.

"Perhaps," he said, but there was little acceptance in his flat tone. "Only Haven can answer that for certain."

"I don't know," she said in total truthfulness. "I would have no cause to keep it from you if I knew."

Kenrick grunted as he began to eat his soup.

"How is it you know so much about this legend?"

"I have been studying it for nigh on ten years."

"For what purpose?"

"To see if there was any truth to the tale."

"And is there?"

He stared at her for a prolonged while, then shook his head. "No. There is no truth to it at all. The Dragon Chalice does not exist."

At Haven's side, Ariana had grown quiet. She turned her full attention on her meal, which she finished in haste. Too soon, she and her husband were making their excuses to retire, a departure that left Haven alone with her unhospitable host.

Even the servants seemed to pity her for her place beside their mysterious lord. They came and went from the dais with great efficiency, casting furtive glances at the woman who had come into their domain with no past— with barely a name—and who was being held in the keep as an unwilling witness to some horrible misdeed.

Their curious looks said they, too, thought her less a guest than prisoner here, although none would dare to sympathize, much less stoop to aid her. Not if it meant stirring the wrath of the man they claimed was either half mad or half lost to the dark arts.

And now there was this fairy story that spoke of enchanted treasures and kingdoms made of mist and magic.

"If you believe what you say about this Dragon Chalice, that there is no truth in the fable, then what has it to do with what happened to your friends at Greycliff? What has it to do with you and your sister, and the knowledge that you say nearly got her killed?"

"Some men will do anything in pursuit of a dream."

"Is that what the treasure is—a dream?"

He shook his head. "It is a nightmare. A very deadly one that I hope to put to rest."

"And so you study this legend every hour of every day, and keep it locked behind the double bolts of the chamber at the top of the tower stairs."

She had meant it only as an observation, a casual remark on his habits and the goal that clearly drove him, but the look in Kenrick's eye was grave with warning. "There is a reason the folk here know to stay away from that chamber. You would be well advised to do likewise."

"Do you mean to threaten me now, my lord?"

"Call it what you will. I am in earnest, Haven. Do not cross me on this."

"Oh, I wouldn't dream of it." She rose abruptly, and stepped away from her chair. "If you will excuse me."

Kenrick motioned for one of the servants to come

forth to the dais. "Lady Haven is finished with her sup. Please show her to her chamber."

"That will not be necessary," she replied, her ire directed at the cool blue gaze of Clairmont's arrogant lord. "I can find my way on my own. And you needn't worry—I won't venture out of my bounds."

❧ 11 ❧

"ARE YOU NOT hungry, Haven? You hardly ate at all yesterday and now you've barely had enough to break your fast this morning."

With mild disinterest, Haven eyed the lump of yellow cheese and broken loaf of bread that sat on the table near the bed.

"You should eat some of it," Ariana insisted, concern etching her fine brow. "You need to build your strength."

"Pray tell, what for? Your brother has informed me that he will keep me here so long as he wishes, whether I am fit or failing. My chamber door may be unbarred, but I cannot take a step within or without and not feel him watching me, forever judging me in that maddening way of his."

Ariana settled in beside her, seating herself on the edge of the bed. "What has happened, Haven? 'Twas clear that you and Kenrick had words before the sup yesterday. What is it? What went between you?"

At first, she thought to deny that Kenrick had upset her. Why admit such a weakness? Why acknowledge that he held any sway over her at all? But she was still angered from their conversation in the hall, and there was no denying that her encounter with him in the

101

tower had left her confused and angry throughout the duration of last eve's meal.

She tried not to consider what else had passed between them, nor to credit her unwilling response to his touch . . . to his very presence.

She would be mortified to confess that he affected her in that manner, even to Ariana. Worse and worse, should Kenrick somehow hear of the admission and mock Haven for her reaction to him.

"It was nothing," she said at last, hoping to dismiss the subject. "I had been walking about the tower corridors, merely stretching my limbs. I was doing naught more than wandering when I discovered myself on the uppermost floor."

Lady Ariana let out a small sigh. "Kenrick allows no one up there. The chamber is his alone."

"So he was quick to inform me. He made it very clear that I was trespassing there, and that I would be well warned to leave at once."

"Ah, I see. I am sorry, Haven. I fear Kenrick can be a bit . . ."

"Brutish?" she offered. "Surly? Overbearing?"

"Intense," Ariana said with a sympathetic smile. "You must understand, he is a very private man, very much involved in his work. I'm afraid he is not terribly skilled when it comes to being around other people— more and more, as of late. If he has said anything, or done anything, to cause you discomfort or upset, I am sure he did not mean it."

Haven wanted to maintain her outrage, but found it difficult to hold when it meant turning her anger on Ariana. Instead she gave a little shrug, begrudgingly accepting the offered excuses. "You will pardon me for saying so, but your brother is a boorish, infuriatingly broody man."

"At times." A smile teased at the corners of the lady's lips. "I wager the same can be said of all men from time to time, can it not?"

"Quite," Haven agreed, sharing the jest in spite of herself.

"Kenrick wasn't always like this—the way he is now. Years ago, when we were growing up, he was very thoughtful and kind. There was a sensitivity to him, a compassion fueled by his desire for learning and under-standing. When my mother was ailing and near the end of her life, she made my father promise to allow Kenrick to pursue his scholarly interests."

"Your father did not wish for him to do so?"

Ariana shook her head. "Kenrick was heir to Clair-mont, you see, and his duties to the demesne could not be shirked. My father honored my mother's wishes once she was gone, but he made a separate agreement with Kenrick. He could go to the church and learn, but he had to come back to Clairmont when the time came for him to be lord. Kenrick had hoped to one day be a priest."

"A priest?" Haven nearly choked to hear such an un-likely notion. "That is a calling that requires humility, is it not? And a kind disposition? From what I have seen, he has neither of those qualities."

"He had, once. A long time ago. It might surprise you to know that he was often called 'Saint' by those who knew him. Randwulf of Greycliff coined the name when the two of them were boys. Rand fostered here at Clair-mont. He is—*was*—Kenrick's closest friend."

At the mention of Greycliff, Haven grew quiet. She

could hardly think of the place or its folk without also returning to the carnage of the night the holding was destroyed. Visions that had been confined to the dark hours between dusk and dawn had since begun to haunt her in the daytime as well. They came unannounced, and with increasing clarity, although the visions lasted only moments and were gone as quickly as they had come.

This time, she felt the heat of fire too close to her skin. She was choking, struggling for every breath, hurting everywhere at once . . . desperate to escape. She was running, she realized, seeing the inferno blazing at her back. The night was dark as pitch save the blinding orange of flames leaping into the sky from Greycliff's tower and its surrounding buildings.

She was stumbling, lightheaded. Unable to maintain her balance. She threw a glance over her shoulder, her vision bleary, panting with exhaustion. Three shadowed figures were suddenly at her heels. One of the men went down with a howl, felled by a length of polished steel protruding from the center of him. A beastly, murderous roar shook the night. She would be next to fall. She knew it with stunned certainty.

Faith, but she did not want to die!

"Haven?"

The soft summons broke through the onslaught of memories, carrying her swiftly back to the present. When she glanced up, she met Ariana's concerned frown.

"What is it, Haven? You have grown so pale."

" 'Tis nothing. I am . . . I am fine."

Ariana took her hand and pressed it between her palms. It was a caring gesture, but Haven felt unaccustomed to such displays.

The contact unsettled her, and she pulled away. "I am fine."

"No, you are not. What happened to you at Greycliff? I know you are beginning to remember. I can see the horror of it in your eyes."

Could that be true? Was she so easily read? Haven got up from her chair and strode to the window across the room. "I do not recall everything. What I do remember makes little sense."

"But it is coming back," Ariana replied.

Her intuitive observation gave Haven pause. Although her memory was yet elusive, presenting only quick, confusing snatches of the truth, it was slowly returning.

Part of her wanted to push it back to the darkened corners of her mind, for what she saw was increasingly troubling and violent. But there was another part of her—the part that sought its own self-preservation—that urged her to embrace the full truth. To welcome it back with all haste, for with it would come a certain understanding.

And a certain power that currently eluded her.

"I realize my brother has done little to win your esteem since you've been here, but you should know that if anyone can understand what you have been through—what you might have witnessed in the attack on Greycliff—it is him. Kenrick will protect you if you let him, Haven."

"I don't need protection."

"Do you not? Are you so confident that whoever assaulted you will not be ready for the chance again? Have you any idea what these people are capable of?" When Haven said nothing, Ariana exhaled a small sigh. "Well,

Kenrick knows firsthand. So do I. And so does my husband, Braedon. We lived through it, though only barely."

"What happened?"

"We survived. That's all anyone can hope for when it comes to the villain I speak of. His evil seems to know no bounds."

"And now you think I am at risk from this same danger?"

"I fear you may be, yes." Lady Ariana smoothed her palm over her trim abdomen and something shadowed her otherwise bright gaze. "I fear the evil we encountered all those months ago in France may revisit us here, at Clairmont. Unless we take steps to thwart it. You can help, Haven. Anything you might have seen or heard that night—anything at all—you must make Kenrick aware."

Haven turned her gaze back to the open window and the hill that rolled beyond. She knew not what to make of Lady Ariana or her fervent plea. It seemed a reasonable enough request and yet she felt a reluctance to comply.

She knew not what to make of Kenrick of Clairmont either, all the more so now that she had spoken with his sister, a kind, intelligent woman who clearly loved him. Haven did not appreciate the feeling of beholdenness she experienced when she thought of how Kenrick had spared her life by tending her wound and bringing her into his home.

She owed him nothing.

Surely she owed nothing to any of these people. They had shown her kindness in her need, and for that she was appreciative. Still, it hardly meant she needed to get involved in their troubles.

Haven startled when a gentle hand came to rest on her shoulder.

"I will leave you in peace," Ariana said. "Perhaps tomorrow, if you like, you can accompany me outside in the garden. Cook is making capons in cream sauce, and I offered to gather him some fresh herbs."

Haven gave her a small nod. "I would enjoy being out of doors."

"Good." Ariana's smile was brilliant. "Tomorrow it is, then."

❧ 12 ❧

SLEEP PROVED MORE than elusive to Haven that evening. Each time her eyes closed, she was assailed by troubling images—memories surging stronger, brushing ever closer to the surface of her conscious mind. Unfolding like a dark dream, the night of the attack replayed behind her heavy eyelids. She thrashed on the bed, trying to shut out the vision, but it seemed her struggles only brought it into clearer focus.

She saw the smoke and flames, the shadowed rush of raiders pouring into the keep from all sides. She heard a scream, and a bellowed oath rife with fury. She smelled unsheathed steel, and, not long afterward, the coppery stench of spilled blood.

It's not too late!

The words echoed in her ears, rough and commanding. Familiar to her somehow.

Tell us where to find it!

In her fitful sleep, Haven tossed to and fro, the soft weave of the coverlet wrapping about her legs like ropes. She fought her bonds the same as she fought the onslaught of the dream that was no dream, but memory. Burning brighter now—as bright as the flames that rose to devour Greycliff Castle and those who had dwelled there.

Tell us!

Faith, but she did not want to be there, did not want to see any more . . .

"It's not too late to save them!"

It was the sound of her own voice that finally woke her. Confused, Haven jolted upright in her bed. She sat there panting, shaky, her brow sheened with perspiration. By all that was holy, was she going mad?

What did it mean, this gripping nightmare—these shrill, shouted words that still rang in her ears like thunderclaps?

There was more, she knew. More that would come from behind the veiled but parting corners of her recall. She did not think she could bear any further dreams this night.

No more memories.

The air in the chamber was stifling. The four walls were too confining. Haven threw aside the tangled bedsheets and slid her feet to the floor. One of Ariana's borrowed mantles hung on a hook fixed to the far wall. Haven slipped it around her shoulders and fastened its ribbon closure with a hastily tied knot.

The door to her chamber was closed, but no lock barred her from opening it. She pulled the latch and stepped out into the quiet corridor. All in the keep were abed at this late hour. Haven walked quickly but carefully and without sound, navigating her way down the curving hallway toward the rear stairwell of the tower fortress. She needed space. She needed to breathe, and to cleanse her head of the terrible thoughts that plagued her dreams.

Barefoot, she climbed the narrow stairs to the top of the tower roof. The wooden panel that held back the wind pushed against her with a great deal of force as she exited the stone portal and crept outside. She closed it as gently as she could, loath to reveal herself to any of the dozen guards who patrolled the battlements at any given hour.

Her heart was still racing from her disrupted sleep, her breath still rolling fast between her lips. She rested her back against the portal door and willed herself to calm. It was easier now that the night wind surrounded her. The bracing cold of a late spring evening breeze whipped at her hair and tugged at the loose hem of her chemise and cloak. She let the air buffet her, relishing the crisp chill that nipped her cheeks as she put her face full in the wind.

The memories no longer clattered in her head. They slowed, muted, faded to darkness with every deep breath she took into her lungs. But as the nightmarish visions slid back to the recesses of her recall, something new began to take shape inside of her.

It started slowly, a seductive whisper that compelled her feet to move. She stepped away from the sheltering wall of the tower portal behind her. The breeze grew stronger the closer she got to the roof's perimeter. Three more steps and she was there, her bare toes halted at the base of the waist-high wall.

Beyond the steep ledge was naught but air and empty space.

Freedom, said the whisper in her head.

Haven glanced around, observing the knots of watchmen stationed on the parapet and along Clairmont's curtain wall. None of them noticed her there.

Escape, came the hissed command of her subconscious. *Leave this place tonight . . . this very moment. It would be so easy.*

Easy? she thought, disbelieving her own madness to permit such a queer idea. Why, she would need sprout wings and fly from here like a bird to escape this rooftop intact.

Impossible! What insanity was this?

And yet, she could picture it so effortlessly—climbing onto the narrow ledge of the wall, standing there with only air to hold her, gripping her toes over the cold stone.

Leaping into the wind . . . and soaring as though her arms were spread wide as an eagle's strong wings.

With the notion came a peculiar tingling in Haven's fingertips. She felt warmth bloom, felt an uncanny strength begin to surge from somewhere deep inside her. She blinked and her vision was suddenly and astonishingly acute, unhindered by the opaque darkness of the midnight landscape surrounding her.

Movements caught her eye from all directions: sentries shifting and shuffling at their posts; tall grasses soughing in the dark, distant meadow; small night creatures foraging in the garden below, while an owl perched in the peripheral woods, silently observing its prey.

Near the barbican of the curtain wall, the guards were talking, voices low and muffled but becoming clearer. One complained of a nagging ache in his shoulder; another was busy boasting to his bored companions of his conquests on and off the battlefield.

Even from this fair distance, she could smell the nectar of Ariana's flowers blooming in the garden below the tower, the sweet perfumes laced with the loamy richness of fertile brown soil. She could scent the oiled metal of the sentries' swords and chain mail, the breath of a few men carrying the tang of overmuch ale.

In that moment, Haven's every sense seemed sharper, keener.

And the urge to leap—to reach for freedom—began to fill every fiber of her being.

"Oh, faith," she gasped. "What is happening to me?"

She shook herself out of the dangerous impulse and backed away from the wall.

"What is wrong with me?"

The tower door pressed against her spine. With grasping fingers, she searched the cold iron latch and pulled the door open. The wind swirled as though to bar her exit, but desperation gave her strength. She yanked the rooftop panel ajar and slipped inside, heedless of the fact that it banged shut behind her.

She had no idea what nearly overtook her out there. She knew only that something dark was closing in, and she was not at all sure she would be prepared to face it when it did.

If allying herself with Kenrick of Clairmont might help, perhaps it was time she stop fighting him.

A fire waned on the large hearth of Kenrick's solar in the tower. The warmth was all but gone, naught but embers keeping the small flames alive. He paid the cold no mind. Bent over his desk, goose-quill pen bobbing madly, he jotted his thoughts down into one of his many journals. The records he had made on behalf of the Templars had led him to visit several locations, two of which eventually yielded pieces of the Dragon Chalice. A third site, a chapel located in the wilds of Scotland, had been on his mind for a long while, although he had yet to venture so far north to investigate. But it was the question of the possible fourth that vexed him now. He felt he was so close to seeing the pattern, yet it eluded him.

He flipped through more of his written reports, then went back to his writing. Halfway down the page, an idea struck him. His hand paused, then the quill dropped to the book with a soft thud.

"Yes, of course," he murmured, abandoning the journal for a text that had been folded into the pages of another heavy tome. He withdrew the sheet of parchment and held it to the light of a candle at the center of the large working space. The writing on it was better than a year old, and faded. Kenrick read the coded Latin with a shrewd eye, unhindered by its complexity, for the language employed was one of his own creations. "How did I not see it before? The location was all wrong."

He went back to his writing, utterly immersed in his work. He had no notion of the hour, nor did he care when his mind was racing with thoughts. Very often, more nights than not, he forfeited sleep for the benefit of further time devoted to his study of the Dragon Chalice. Time he dearly needed, now that he was all but certain Silas de Mortaine and his cohorts were sniffing around England.

He had beaten the bastard at his game once; he was determined to do so again. Permanently, if he had aught to say about it.

With a low-voiced oath, Kenrick scratched his quill along the page, intent on his work. He was scarcely aware of his surroundings, until the careless bang of the tower's roof door reverberated down the stairwell to the lord's chambers. Then he was attuned entirely. Frowning, suspicious of who might be awake and prowling at this late hour, he stealthily crossed the room and pulled open the solar door to the corridor outside.

Haven had just paused there, her hand raised as if she meant to knock.

"Oh."

It was a gasp of startlement, but she recovered herself at once, giving him a cool glance. He could smell the fresh night air on her skin and in her hair. She wore one of Ariana's cloaks over her chemise, the dark blue wool contrasting richly against the fiery waves of her hair.

"I saw light beneath the door and I—well, I did not mean to disrupt you."

"You haven't." Behind him in his chamber, a night candle guttered with a fatty spit of sound. "It is late for you to be yet awake and walking the corridors."

"Yes, I know. I . . ." She shrugged. "I could not sleep."

"Nor I, although that is hardly unusual." His brow creased as he took in the sight of her windblown hair and night-kissed cheeks. "You've been on the battlements."

Her chin went up a notch, evidently assuming his curiosity was censure instead. "Was that another area of your keep that's forbidden to me? I didn't know. Please excuse me."

"Haven, wait. I did not mean—" He broke off and ran a hand through his hair in frustration. "Do you think we might ever manage a simple conversation without locking horns?"

She glanced down at his teasing remark, but the smile on her lips was weak, haunted somehow.

"Is anything wrong? You seem upset."

"No, it is nothing. I should not have bothered you—"

He reached out and caught her by the arm. "What is it? You obviously came to my door for a reason. Tell me what this is about."

She shrugged, but distress stormed in her eyes. "I may have . . . I remembered something about that night. I have no idea if it is important or nay."

"Why don't you let me decide that. Come in, Haven."

He held the door open with his forearm and gestured her inside. She entered warily, her eyes sweeping the chamber. They settled on his disheveled desk and the collection of texts that lay in various stages of perusal atop the wide surface of the working space. Kenrick strode around her to discreetly close the journals he had been studying in the moments before her arrival.

"Tell me what it is you remember," he said as he stacked the thick volumes and set them aside.

She was clearly disturbed by what she recalled, for her usual fiery demeanor was quelled a bit as she regarded him from across the room. She swallowed, then began to recount the events of that fated night. Most of it was familiar to Kenrick, details he had gleaned from his observation of Greycliff Castle and his talks with the village folk.

Haven told him how she had gone to the keep that day with herbs for Elspeth. The raid came in the dead of night, and while she could not say why she had been delayed there for so long that she was present for the attack, Haven did recall new details of the hell that was unleashed on Rand and his family.

"Everything happened very fast. The fires came first, the stables and outbuildings, then, amid the chaos, the raiders moved into the keep itself. There was screaming and bloodshed . . . many deaths dealt in the blink of an eye."

"Did you see any of them?" Kenrick asked, loath to press her, but he needed to know. "Was one of them—their leader, mayhap—a tall man with fair hair? He might have sent his lieutenant to do the deed instead. A mercenary with dark features and a crest bearing dragon insignia?"

Haven shook her head. "I could not say. It was difficult to see anything . . . the smoke, it was everywhere. 'Twas so hard to breathe."

She closed her eyes and he could tell that she was reliving the moment again, right there, before him. The horror of it drew a deep tension into her face, creasing her brow and lining the corners of her mouth in taut whiteness. She exhaled a sharp breath and met his gaze once more.

"Something was said by one of them. Something . . . confusing."

"Go on."

"They were looking for something. They wanted to know where to find it."

Kenrick's every muscle stilled, tensed. "Do you know what it was they wanted?"

"No."

"Do you know if they found what they sought?"

"No," she said, a measure of agitation lacing her voice. "All I know is that they were looking for something, and they shouted for him to tell them where to find it. They said it wasn't too late—that he could still save them if he gave it up."

"Save who?" Kenrick asked, his stomach knotting in dread.

Haven turned a somber look on him, her mouth quivering. "His family."

Kenrick's answering oath was low and bit from between clenched teeth. "The soulless bastards. Did he tell them? Did Rand give them what they wanted?"

She shook her head. Her voice was very quiet. "I don't know."

Kenrick absorbed the news with a mixture of regret and hope. He knew Greycliff was a strong man, with strong ideals. His word was his bond, and he had given his pledge to keep the seal a secret, to keep it safe. But the thought that he might have done so at his own family's peril put a sick and gnawing remorse in the pit of Kenrick's gut.

He had asked so much of his friend. Too much.

"Is there anything else you remember of that night?" he asked Haven, putting aside emotion to better deal with the facts as he was presented them. "Have you told me everything now?"

"Yes, that is all that I know," she answered.

She walked toward where he stood, pausing within arm's reach. Her gaze strayed over his desk, past the neat stack of journals to an item that lay near the edge, half-hidden beneath some parchments. The fine gold chain of the pendant glinted dully in the meager light of the solar.

"That necklace," Haven said, frowning as she moved to retrieve it from the desk. "I remember it . . . This was Elspeth's."

"Yes."

"I never saw her without it."

"Nor did I," he answered soberly, watching as Haven carefully handled the broken chain and the simple gold filigreed heart that slid along its length. "I found it lying in the cemetery at Greycliff, the same day I found you there."

She glanced at him only briefly, then returned her attention to the fragile gift Rand had given his wife as a token of his love. "One of the links is broken."

"Yes. It must have come apart in a struggle, or after . . ." Kenrick let his grim speculation trail off, not wishing to think about what his friends had endured. "I have cleaned it, and I've tried to repair the chain, but it's very delicate. My hands are clumsy, better suited for the sword or the pen."

"May I try?" She turned a hopeful, determined look on him. "I would like to, if you don't object."

"Of course. Do what you can. There is a small hammer right there, if you need it."

Haven bent over his desk, her face screwed in concentration. As she examined the broken link, Kenrick fetched her a new candle and lit it from the fire. "It may help if you warm the metal, to make it more pliable."

She accepted his advice and his assistance with an easy agreeability, her focus trained wholly on her work. Kenrick caught himself smiling as he watched her, for he could appreciate that sort of focus.

He could appreciate far more about her as well, watching her elegant fingers manipulate the tiny chain. Her eyes held fixed on her work, unblinking and sharp. Her lips pursed slightly as she looped the severed end of the chain back onto the broken link, then brought the candle close. She heated the section of chain in the wobbly flame, then drew it away.

As she reached for the little mallet, a lock of hair slipped from behind her ear. She swept it back, but the fiery tress was stubborn. It fell back down along the side of her face.

Before he could stop himself, Kenrick was reaching out. He caught the springy tendril of molten silk in his fingers and gently lifted it away. He heard her indrawn breath, saw her nimble hands falter with the pendant.

"So you can see better," he said, hooking the lock back where it belonged and holding it there with probably too much pleasure.

"Thank you," she whispered, resuming her restoration of the chain, and working in haste, he thought. "What will you do with this once it is repaired?"

"I'll return it to Greycliff, where I found it. That is where it belongs, with Elspeth."

"She must have meant a great deal to you, to take such care."

Kenrick considered the casual comment with a small twist of irony coiling in his heart. "She did. She was the wife of my closest friend."

And there had been a time, long ago . . .

He shut out the thought before it could take hold, refusing to dwell on regrets or things never meant to be.

Elspeth's heart belonged to Rand, and always had. He begrudged them nothing—now or then—for the love they shared.

His infatuation with the fragile Elspeth had been his own dark secret, one full summer of agony as he watched Rand charm the pretty maiden into becoming his bride.

Kenrick had been a sober youth of fourteen, already engrossed in his pursuit of learning and study. He had been a mere boy, reserved and awkward, particularly when compared to his friend, the rakish jester Randwulf of Greycliff.

He had never breathed a word of his feelings for Elspeth, not to a soul. That same year, he left for his studies at the church, and, not much later, the Templars. As it turned out, neither calling had suited him. The more he learned, the more he became aware of greed and corruption. His faith had crumbled along with his vows.

And while he was not immune to the allure of a pretty face and form, or the pleasures to be had in the company of a soft, willing female, he had permitted none to captivate him beyond a temporary passion.

He was careful and distant, and always in control.

Until recently.

Kenrick watched her in studying silence, still holding the lock of her hair between his fingers and not trusting himself to speak, let alone move.

Haven said nothing, either. With a few taps of the small mallet, the broken pendant link was restored. She slowly straightened and met his gaze. The tendril swung back down along her cheek as Kenrick reluctantly released it.

"There you are," she said, holding out her hand, the chain dangling from her fingertips. "I've fixed it."

He took the pendant from her and set it down on the desk. "Thank you."

A fetching blush crept into her cheeks as he considered how badly he wanted to touch her. He wanted to kiss her, though he had no right to desire such a thing.

As she blinked up at him, a chill swept her from out of nowhere, making her shudder as though gripped by cold that he did not feel. She vigorously rubbed her arms, frowning in evident distress.

"Kenrick," she whispered abruptly, "can I tell you something? Tonight when I was on the battlements, I . . . I'm not sure how to describe it, save that I feel as if something is happening to me. I think . . . faith, but I fear I may be going mad."

For a long moment, Kenrick said nothing. She had never addressed him so informally, as a confidante. An intimate. That she did so now, when she confessed her fears and looked to him for reassurance, stirred something deeply protective in him.

Something far too possessive.

Despite the impulse to act on his feelings—to touch the satiny opalescence of her cheek, even if only to comfort her—he managed to hold himself in check.

"You have been through a great deal, Haven. To be confused is only natural. But I have seen madness, and I can assure you that you suffer no such thing. Would that you didn't have to remember what happened at Greycliff—no one should be exposed to such a thing. But you survived. You are healing, and soon you will be well."

She nodded mutely, then asked, "Are we in terrible danger if these men you seek turn their sights on Clairmont?"

He would not lie to her. Not when she had already borne witness herself to de Mortaine's wrath. "It will be bad, yes. But if we are clever, and if we do not waste precious time, we may be able to stop them."

"How? What do they want?"

For a moment, one fleeting instant, he considered telling Haven the whole of it. But the knowledge could put her further in jeopardy, and there was also a cynical part of him that warned him not to divulge the stunning secrets of what he had found in his work for the Templars. Few knew about the Dragon Chalice and its power. Those who did were either dead, or set upon a course to claim it—whatever the price.

Bad enough his work had involved Ariana and Braedon, and, tragically, Rand and his family.

He would not put anyone else in jeopardy over the accursed cup and the lure of its dark, wondrous magic.

"What they want is something they will never get so long as I am alive to stop them," he told Haven, holding her bewitching emerald gaze. "So long as you are under my roof, you need not fear them or their evil ways. You are protected with me, Haven. I give you my promise."

She said nothing, merely looked at him as though she waited for his touch to comfort her. To his utter astonishment, she was the first to move, reaching out to place her palm lightly against his cheek.

"Thank you," she told him quietly.

Kenrick stared, incapable of speech so long as her touch lingered. He held himself very still, rigidly so, not daring to breathe as every muscle in his body tensed with the sweet warmth of her fingertips resting so tentatively on his skin.

"I should leave you to your work."

Relief warred with regret as she slowly drew her hand away.

"Goodnight," she whispered, but Kenrick remained silent.

He watched her step aside of him and cross the threshold to the corridor outside.

His work did await—urgent work—but yet he remained transfixed in the doorway of his chamber, his gaze following Haven's lithe form as she padded softly away and into the darkened shadows of the keep's long hallway.

When he looked down to the clenched fist of his hand, he found he had snapped his writing quill in two.

✌ 13 ✌

ALTHOUGH HER REST that night had been fitful, Haven rose to a morning filled with sunshine and gentle May breezes. Ariana greeted her shortly before noontide, making good on her promise to take her to the castle's garden for a day of ladies' duties about the grounds.

To Haven's delight, she had brought a basket of food and watered wine from the kitchens so they could break their fast outdoors. Munching on smoked fish and warm bread, the two women partook of their meal amid the flower beds and plots of herbs, both content to be away from the confines of the castle.

Haven relished the open space of the garden. Among the rosemary and sweet woodruff there was a sense of peace. Her disturbing memories, and the queer feeling that had overcome her on the roof last evening, were banished by the fragrant air wafting off the spring flowers and the explosion of color that surrounded her on all sides.

Seated on a turf bench across a small path from Ariana, Haven reached into the basket they shared and withdrew a sprig of mint from among the bundles of savory spices gathered for the evening's supper. She chewed a bit of the refreshing leaves and watched as Ariana trimmed a clump of bay laurel from a nearby shrub.

With her memory returning in only scattered bits and pieces, Haven knew not where she truly belonged. Not in Cornwall, she felt nearly certain of that. And likely not here, either. But it was tempting to picture herself living out her days in a place such as Clairmont. The place did not quite fit her—much like her borrowed gowns and too-snug slippers—but there was a calm here she was beginning to enjoy.

Clairmont held its own brand of enchantment, a thought clearly shared by Ariana, who glowed with serenity and life amid the flowers that surrounded her in the small garden. She was a woman at peace with her place in the world, and Haven envied her that feeling.

"You seem quiet today," Ariana remarked after a time. "Does anything trouble you?"

"Nay." Haven gave a vague shake of her head. "I am just thinking."

"I hope you know that you can talk to me, Haven. We're friends, are we not?"

Her welcoming smile set a twinge of emotion in Haven's heart. She recalled little of her past, but she had the keen feeling that there were few she counted among her friends. It seemed almost a foreign notion to her, something she had purposely denied herself. She saw no reason to do so now. In fact, she was glad for the company. Glad to think she had at least one ally in this strange, if pleasant, landscape.

"I was merely thinking how good it feels to be out of doors. I like these gardens very much."

Ariana beamed. "They are my pride, if you want to know. I've planted all of these beds myself."

"They are lovely."

"You may clip some flowers for your chamber if it pleases you."

"You wouldn't mind?"

"Of course not," she replied, leaning over to give her hand a warm squeeze. "There are violets in the corner, and lily of the valley over there, shaded beneath the arbor—"

Ariana paused mid-sentence, her expression brightening as the sound of horses' hooves pounded onto the cobbled bailey. "It must be Braedon and Kenrick. They've returned!"

The two men had been out since before dawn, away on matters not divulged to Haven. Now Ariana got to her feet and brushed at the flecks of dirt and scattered greenery that had gathered in her lap. A pretty flush filled her cheeks, her smile wide and dazzling, evident joy reaching all the way into her sparkling blue eyes. She brought her thick, honey blond braid over her shoulder, then hooked her basket of neatly gathered herbs onto her arm.

"Will I suit?"

Haven nodded approvingly. Ariana looked as fresh and promising as daybreak itself. Not that her lord husband would demand such perfection. From all Haven had seen of the lady and her beloved raven-haired warrior, she could greet him dressed in rags and ashes and he would beam at her with nothing short of husbandly pride.

Ariana took a jubilant couple of steps, then abruptly turned back to look at Haven. "Well, are you coming?"

It hardly seemed she could refuse, even though she dearly wanted to. The thought of seeing Kenrick again after her visit to his chamber last night brought a peculiar flutter to her stomach.

As she strode alongside Ariana, Haven found herself smoothing the folds of her own skirt, which, she noted with some dismay, bore smudges of dirt and the trace stains of the berries she had collected. Her fingers had fared none the better, spotted purple in more places than not. Her hair shunned the obedience of the prim braid into which Ariana had attempted to train it that morn. Loose coppery strands blew on the breeze like streamers despite Haven's efforts to tame them back behind her ears.

With some degree of resignation, Haven left off fussing with herself. Thrusting her chin up, letting her hair stray as it willed, she gripped the handle of her basket and attempted not to fret over her appearance, which would never match Ariana's golden grace and warmth. There was no point in trying.

After all, she reasoned with herself, she had no one to impress.

Haven clung to that thought as they rounded the soaring east wall of the tower keep and came into the courtyard of the inner bailey. Try as she might to be unaffected, it was difficult not to stare at Kenrick of Clairmont when he stood beside his white charger outfitted in gleaming chain mail and a surcoat of deep blue silk.

The splendor of him as he drew off his helm and coif fair stole her breath. If she thought him endearingly handsome when he was bent over his desk, pensive and frowning as he scribbled his secret writings, this new side of him—this golden warrior—was utterly devastating.

He was magnificent. So much so, Haven nearly groaned with desire just to look upon him.

Thankfully she was spared the indignity when in that very moment, Ariana gave a little cry of excitement and launched herself into her husband's waiting arms. Braedon lifted her off the ground as though she weighed naught but air and spun her around in a quick circle in the bailey. They murmured private words to each other, then pressed their lips together in a loving kiss that seemed like to never end.

Haven looked away from the affectionate display, and her gaze was snared at once by Kenrick's level stare.

"Good morrow, my lady."

"My lord," she replied with a courteous nod of greeting.

He took her in from head to toe, a slow, measuring glance that set butterflies of awareness batting around in her breast. "I see you've been in the garden today."

She willed herself not to look down at her berry-stained skirts, waiting to catch that dissecting gaze as it picked her apart, flaw by glaring flaw. Instead, when their eyes met again, his held only a note of curiosity. Perhaps something more, although she was never sure how to read his stoic expression.

"Apparently there will be capons in cream sauce at this eve's sup," she told him. "Lady Ariana and I were collecting rosemary and fennel for the recipe."

He strode forward and reached out for her basket. Pressing one strong, elegant finger to the edge of the container, he tipped it slightly to inspect its contents. "And elder berries?"

"For a pudding."

As he reached in to pluck one of the glossy fruits from the basket, Haven's mind returned to their encounter in his chamber the night before, when that same hand had caressed her cheek, and idly toyed with a lock of her unbound hair. She had longed for more then, and, faith preserve her, she did so now as well.

"How went the trip?" Ariana asked, drawing out of her husband's embrace to question both men.

Haven thought she spied a note of reservation passing between Kenrick and his dark brother-by-marriage, but it was gone quickly, replaced by an air of masculine command.

"It went much as expected," Braedon said.

"You are back earlier than planned."

"Aye," Kenrick agreed. "But only for the night. We'll be off again on the morrow."

"So soon?" Ariana wrapped her arms a bit tighter around Braedon's trim waist. "Did you find anything while you were away, any news that might prove helpful?"

"There have been some developments," Braedon said, tenderly tracing his fingers along Ariana's cheek. "Naught to worry about."

She shot him an arch look. "You know how I feel about secrets, my lord."

"I do, and I will tell you all, my lady." He glanced subtly in Haven's direction before meeting his wife's expectant gaze. "We can talk in the keep, after I tend my mount. Mayhap you will be kind enough to fetch me a bath. Lord knows, I could use one after riding all morn."

"Very well," she sighed. With some apparent reluctance, Ariana released her hold on her husband. "I shall meet you in our chambers as soon as Haven and I collect a basket of eggs for the kitchens. Do not keep me waiting overlong, my lord."

The scar on Braedon's left cheek drew tight with his answering grin. "I wouldn't dream of it, my lady."

As the ladies departed, Braedon crossed his arms over his chest and blew out a slow, appraising sigh. "It is a rare thing, to be sure."

"What's that?" Kenrick asked, unable to tear his gaze away from the unpracticed sway of Haven's hips as she walked.

"To find such beauty, fire, and wit in one woman." Braedon angled a knowing look on him. "That brand of fortune is usually reserved for men more deserving than either of us."

"Aye." He shrugged. "I wager so, now that you say it."

For all his casualness, Kenrick paused to consider the truth in Braedon's observation. Haven was indeed an unusual woman. Beautiful, of course, as any man would readily admit, but her appeal went much farther than that.

Much to his dismay.

Spirited, intelligent, she was as intriguing as any puzzle Kenrick had ever known. He wanted to uncover each of her mysteries, solve the many riddles that made the lady into the elusive, alluring creature she was.

Haven was fire and beauty and wit—everything Braedon had said and then some. She defied description to Kenrick's way of thinking, and that alone made him want to know more.

"The lady is a fair, many faceted jewel," he admitted at last, voicing his thoughts aloud. "She surpasses mere beauty, do you ask me."

Braedon grunted in reply as he went back to his work.

Kenrick's attention, however, had turned eagerly elsewhere, toward the vixen who lit up the drab bailey courtyard like a burst of pure amber light.

"Have you ever seen such a face or form so lovely as that? Or hair so lustrous? 'Tis like skeins of silken flame. And her eyes—by God, those unusual emerald-hued eyes are alive with a thousand flecks of gold and silver and colors I vow I've never seen the like of before . . ."

Braedon's sudden outburst of laughter shattered the vision Kenrick had been lost to in that moment. He scowled at his sister's husband, who now sat back on his haunches to regard him from under his dark forelock. The man was clearly quite amused.

"By the Rood," Braedon chortled. "Have a care, my stricken brother. Else you'll have me believing you've traded your formulae for the mooning lyrics of the troubadours."

"Believe what you like. And I'll thank you to piss off," Kenrick gibed back, chagrined to think he had made a fool of himself, even with the man he considered a close friend and kin. "Besides, you were the one to start the subject. I was merely elaborating on things you yourself had said."

"Fair enough," Braedon said, clapping him good-naturedly on the shoulder. "But I was talking about my lady wife. Pray tell, which lady might you have been talking about?"

The smug bastard did not wait for Kenrick's reply, which likely would have been accompanied by the wooden brush he held in his hand. Still chuckling, Braedon tossed down his packs and sauntered back into the stables with his mount.

* * *

With her basket tucked under her arm, Haven followed Ariana past the stables to the area of the bailey where the pens for the livestock were located. A brown milk cow mooed as they passed her square patch of grazing turf. Piglets snuffled and rooted about in their pen, chasing their mother as the large sow roused from a nap and shuffled to the far corner of the containment, her afternoon doze evidently disturbed by the two women strolling by.

Ariana covered her face with the edge of her long sleeve, discreetly shielding her nose although the earthy smells of the animals and their pens was hardly offensive. Haven noted Ariana's hastened pace, the faintly queasy look that spread over her countenance.

"Does he know?" Haven asked.

Ariana looked over at her quizzically.

"About the babe. You may not like secrets, but you are keeping one of your own. Your husband does not know he is to be a father, does he?"

"Wha—" She ceased walking and blinked at her in disbelief. "But I am just a fortnight past my time. How could *you* possibly know?"

Haven glanced at the lady's trim stomach, knowing it was too early to see signs there. Her nervous stomach could have been nothing more than a passing ailment, or the delicate senses of a woman born of noble blood, but the truth of it was in Ariana's eyes. And in the tender look that came over her when she thought no one was watching. It was in the loving way her hand liked to drift down and caress the growing child in her womb.

"I have treated more than one expectant woman with my herbs. The signs are there, if you know where to look. Why do you keep the news from him? 'Tis plain enough for all to see that he holds affection for you."

"Affection?" Ariana laughed, a musical sound of amusement. "Yes, I dearly hope so!"

She resumed walking, her gait easy now that they were gone from the larger animals and crossing an open grassy area.

"Why do you not tell him, then?" Haven pressed, curious all the more. "Do you fear he will not feel the same affection for his child?"

"No," Ariana answered at once. "No, never that. Braedon is a very loving man. Family is important to him. 'Tis just . . . well, there is much about him that I cannot explain. He is hard on himself, believing he has many flaws. He is concerned that some of them will be passed along to his children."

"And what do you think?"

"I think his children will be very special, and I am honored to be the woman to carry them and raise them. To love them, as I so adore their father."

She smiled at Haven, and might have said more if not for the sudden complaint of a rooster who had been pecking at some grit as they drew near. The strutting cock flapped his wings, then suddenly darted beneath a cart at their approach.

And, farther along the path, came the commotion rising from a number of fowl. The cacophony grew more frenzied as the women approached the squat little building that housed the hens.

Nervous fluttering and the clucking of dozens of birds continued as Ariana unhooked the latch and opened the door. Haven stood just behind her.

"Something certainly has them upset," Ariana

remarked over her shoulder as she ducked beneath the
low eave of the henhouse door. "Have a care when you
enter, Haven. There is a dip just on the inside of the
door. I should hate for you to lose your footing and hurt
yourself."

To Haven's mind, the hens seemed due more caution
than the worn earth of their coop's floor. Clearly agitated, most of the score-and-a-half birds had already
scuttled off their nests as Ariana then Haven stepped inside. Feathers and dust stirred as the flock ran hither and
yon inside the cramped coop, complaining loudly.
Wings flapped, beady eyes darted in alarm, and the din
of clucking and crowing amplified toward a state of wild
panic.

"Whatever is the matter in here?" Ariana mused
aloud. "They hardly get so agitated if one of the cats
manages to sneak into the coop."

She shooed a large speckled hen out of her way, then
turned back to motion Haven farther inside. The coop
was low-ceilinged and dim. What scant light filtered in
through the roof's wooden slats was swimming with
dust motes from the continued beating of the earth floor
as taloned feet scratched and scuttled in a dance of anxious upset. The chaos within worsened by the moment,
the noise building to almost deafening heights.

"Good lord, what a queer mood they're in!" Ariana
exclaimed. "Hand me your basket, Haven. I'll collect
what we need."

Haven reached out to give her the small container,
and as she did so, one of the few birds remaining on its
nest suddenly launched into the air, screeching. Heavy,
graceless wings beat in a panic as it flew at the women.

Haven saw the bird coming and quickly drew Ariana

aside. The hen's sharp claws caught in Haven's hair and raked her cheek. She brought her arm up to shield her face and eyes, for the bird was in a blind fury, pecking and attacking wherever it could.

"Watch out!" Ariana cried from behind her. "Haven, come. Let's get out of here now!"

Ariana's advice was sound, but a fraction too late. Before Haven realized what she was doing, she drew the slim dagger from Ariana's girdle sheath. Snatching the feral bird by the leg as it came at her face again, Haven flipped the dagger in her hand and slew the hen in an instant, sticking the dagger into the plump breast of the creature. She tossed down the unmoving carcass and backed toward the door where Ariana waited. The remaining hens continued their chatter and fluttering, but a wariness had settled over the coop with the slaughter of the one.

The door to the henhouse flew open behind the women, spilling light from the bailey into the cramped confines of the outbuilding.

"What the devil is going on in here?"

Kenrick of Clairmont's voice boomed over the din of the nervous birds and sent them scattering to the corners of the coop. His sharp blue gaze lit on his sister's stricken face, then settled on Haven.

"Jesu! Your face is scratched bloody—and your arm. What just happened?"

"Th-the hens," Ariana stammered. "Something upset them, and they tried to attack us. Poor Haven took the brunt of it. Had she not pushed me out of the way, no doubt we would both be standing here thrashed and bleeding."

"Are you all right?"

At Kenrick's low query, Haven glanced up and met his eyes. She nodded, uncomfortable with his gentle regard. "I didn't mean to kill the animal. I reacted . . . on instinct, I suppose. Before I had the chance to know what I was doing."

He exhaled an oath. "The bird means nothing. Thank the saints you have such instincts, my lady. I know a few Templars who would envy the accuracy and speed of your battle wits."

Was he teasing her? Haven felt certain he was, but she knew not what to make of him. Although he made light with his jest, his expression was one of total seriousness and concern. Scowling, he looked to the angry welts on her arm.

"You need care for those. And for your face." He touched her cheek with the pad of his thumb, an unexpected gesture of tenderness that took her aback. His finger came away from her face stained with a bright smudge of red from cuts of the bird's sharp talons. "You're certain you are all right?"

"Yes," she replied, unable to speak in anything more than a whisper when the warmth of his touch still lingered on her skin.

Faith preserve her, but the man's very presence rendered her nearly incapable of thought, much less speech. It was a decidedly uncomfortable feeling, to be so aware, so physically affected. She inched slightly away from him, averting her gaze from the potent intensity of his blue eyes.

"I'm so sorry, Haven," Ariana said, taking her hand. "I truly don't know what might have caused this, but I feel simply terrible that you were hurt."

"As do I," Kenrick added. "I shall have to think of a way to make it up to you."

"That won't be necessary," Haven said. " 'Tis just a few scratches. I am fine."

Ariana arched a quizzical brow at her brother, but spoke instead to Haven. "Come along now, and let's look after your cuts."

With a nod of agreement, Haven allowed herself to be led away from the livestock area and back toward the tower keep. She could still feel Kenrick's gaze on her as she departed, the power of his stare warming her every step across the wide courtyard. She should have ignored the sensation, but she could not prevent her head from turning slightly, just enough to cast a surreptitious look over her shoulder to where he stood.

"He has been watching you for days, you know."

Haven quickly turned away and shot an uncomfortable glance at Ariana. "Aye, he watches me like a hawk trained on its prey."

"Nay," the lady countered, a warm smile playing upon her lips. "He watches you like a man watches a woman. His interest is obvious, though I somehow doubt he would admit it."

"I am sure I wouldn't know."

"Well, I would. I have seen the look often enough to recognize it."

Some of the warmth Haven knew began to cool when she considered how many other ladies Ariana's handsome brother might have charmed with his strong, golden appeal and swaggering confidence. To her chagrin, she could not help asking. "Just how often have you seen it in him?"

"In Kenrick?" Ariana gave an amused laugh. "Oh, never."

Haven turned a frown on her, confused.

"I have never seen such a look in my brother, but I have seen it aplenty in my lord husband." She patted her stomach and gave a sidelong wink as she guided Haven into the cool shade of the castle. "After all," she said, her voice lowered to a private whisper, "how do you imagine I find myself in this happy state?"

❧ 14 ❧

ALTHOUGH THE DAY'S trip had given him a new direction to explore with regard to the Chalice treasure, Kenrick found his thoughts occupied with other things. He had finished up in the stables alone, for once Braedon learned of the incident in the henhouse, there was little to keep the warrior from heading to the castle chambers to make sure firsthand that Ariana had not been injured.

As for Kenrick, once divested of armor and riding gear, his own path inside the keep ended at Haven's door. He knocked lightly, and was greeted by the round, wimple-framed face of a servant girl as the panel opened.

"I've come to see about the lady Haven. Is she within?"

"Aye, m'lord. She's here."

The maid dipped her chin and stepped aside for him to enter. Behind her several paces, seated in a chair beside the fireplace, was Haven. A basin of herbed water steamed atop a pedestal table next to her, carrying the scent of lavender and sage across the chamber.

"Do I interrupt?" he asked.

She gave a nearly imperceptible shake of her head. "Mary was just assisting me in cleaning up my scratches. We were nearly finished."

Kenrick stepped farther into the room and turned to the maid. "Allow me, if you will."

"M'lord?" Mary blurted, gaping at him as if he had just announced he meant to take up embroidery.

"I wish to make amends for the bad manners of my livestock," he said as he took the damp cloth from the girl's slack fingers. He saw Haven's slight smile and offered a further apology. "Perhaps I wish to make up for some of my own bad manners as well."

"Thank you, Mary," Haven said as the girl made a hasty and thoroughly befuddled exit.

"I trust you are not too shaken from what happened outside today."

She shrugged in dismissal. "I'm fine. Just a few scrapes, nothing more."

"Good." He strode to the basin and dipped the swatch of linen into the warm water. "You may have your revenge tonight at supper. I've told the cook to add one surly hen to his famed dressed capons."

Haven laughed, a rare sound that warmed Kenrick as fire itself. It drew him nearer as he wrung out the cloth. To his regret, her humor faded a bit as he hunkered down beside her, one knee on the floor. She gave him a look somewhere between humiliation and disdain. "This is not necessary, truly."

"On the contrary," he told her with mock sternness. " 'Tis entirely necessary."

Brooking no argument, he carefully reached out and took her hand in his.

Her skin was warm and soft as feather down against the sun-browned roughness of his fingers. He turned her palm over and rested it in the cradle of his hand as he gingerly swabbed at the angry red scratches crisscrossing the inside of her forearm.

"Your servants will think you mad when Mary tells them their noble lord is in here mopping up my scant abrasions."

Kenrick wiped away a thin smudge of dried blood and grinned up at her. "The servants already think me mad. Have you not heard them whispering about my strange habits? The odd hours I keep? About how I am known to disappear into my chambers for days—even a sennight at a time—to scribble in my journals and ledgers?" He shrugged, looking back down at the ivory elegance of the hand ensconced in his. "This—ah, lady, this is easily the least mad thing they've ever seen me do."

"So, is it true, my lord?" she asked after a long moment. "Are you bedeviled?"

Kenrick smoothed the swatch of linen across her delicate wrist, scarcely able to resist placing his lips against the fluttering pulse that beat there. Her abrasions were cleansed, but yet he held her hand, unwilling to release her. He glanced up and met her uncertain emerald gaze.

"Am I bedeviled?" he said, so low it might have been a growl. "Aye, my lady. Lately more and more."

He spread his fingers and wove them between hers, catching her more firmly. She did not try to pull away. Nay, she held him as he did her, their hands joined and locked, her thumb idly stroking his.

"Whether you are in or out of my sight, Haven, you affect me deeply."

He drew her closer, nearly edging her off the chair.

"Kenrick." She looked down at their joined hands

and gave a small shake of her head. "We should not. This would be . . ."

He rose up on his knees before her. The slightest flex of his arm brought her to the very edge of the chair. With only the barest guidance, he lifted her hand and pressed his mouth to the soft skin of her knuckles. Haven's lips parted on a thready wisp of a sigh.

"What would this be?" he murmured against her velvety fingers. Heaven, he thought, permitting his tongue to taste the sensual cleavage between her thumb and forefinger.

"Oh, faith," she whispered. " 'Twould be a mistake . . . if we . . . if we—"

It was a weak protest when her lip was now caught between her teeth, her eyes gone as dark and dusky as a twilight meadow.

He pulled her easily into his arms and silenced her with a kiss.

Where he had expected a virginal tentativeness, a reluctant hesitance, he instead found melting, heated fire. He filled his hands with the delicacy of her face and neck, splaying his fingers through the heavy mass of her hair. The light perfume of the herbal water mingled with the warm, womanly scent of her skin.

Kenrick breathed her in, feasting on the headiness of her allure like a drunkard gone too long without wine. For too long had he denied himself such an indulgence. Too long, if a mere kiss could render him so lost.

But it was not as simple as that. He could not blame this feeling on deprivation or basic physical need.

Haven was his intoxication.

He needed only see her to be intrigued. Her strange beauty, her sharp wit and fiery manner—all of it conspired to bewitch him. She challenged him on many levels, her uncommon frankness as engaging as her secrets and the murkiness of her past. She was mystery and contradiction, and she was seducing him with her very presence under his roof.

Even now, she stirred him to his core.

This simple kiss, naught more than a beardless youth might steal from a dairy maid, had caused a swift conflagration in his veins. His blood pounded with want of her, beating an almost audible tattoo in his temples and reverberating further down his body. Like a jolt of lightning, fever shot through to his very bones, searing him as sure as fire itself.

She slipped her hand around his neck, granting him further access as he dragged her closer, widening his thighs to settled her deeper into his embrace. His arousal surged tightly in his breeches, straining for her.

He broke their kiss to trace his mouth along the slender line of her jaw, and down, to the warm hollow of her throat. Haven dropped her head back, moaning softly as he nipped the tender skin. She trembled in his arms.

"Something is happening to me," she gasped, her breathless whisper sounding ragged beside his ear. "Something is . . . happening."

God's blood, but he felt it, too.

Pleasure, like a living physical thing, flowed between them. The heat of her body poured out from everywhere they touched—fingertips, mouths, skin that ached to be rid of the barrier of clothing. Her hands skated over his back in trails of pulsing fire. Her skin where he tasted her seared his tongue like a fever. The hairs on his arms rose as though drawn by gooseflesh.

This was not mere desire, but something deeper.

Something unfathomable. The sensation licked at him from within and without, building until he could hardly bear it.

And with the sensation came need. Pure, unbridled need. Kenrick shook with the fierceness of it. He felt an animal need rise in him, a stunning need to have her—right there on the floor of her chamber if she would permit him.

For one mindless instant, he thought she might.

She moaned and writhed in his arms, but then he realized she was pushing him away.

"N-no, please." She broke out of his embrace, a troubled look on her face. "No."

"What is it?"

She glanced down, averting her eyes when he tried to reach for her. She crossed her arms protectively over her breasts and flinched more than shrugged. "My shoulder," she said quietly, as though the excuse sounded feeble, even to her own ears. "It pains me."

He sat back on his heels, some of his fever cooled by the knowledge that he might have been hurting her.

"I'm sorry," he said, searching for some measure of logic when his blood was yet thrumming with desire. "Is there anything that you—can I get you anything for the pain?"

"No." She would not look at him. "I think . . . I think you should leave now."

Her cheeks were flushed pink, her lips tinged dark as berries from the passionate kiss they had shared. There was a tortured look in her eyes, apparent to him even though she seemed determined to avoid looking at him now. And he could not help noticing the way she rubbed her palms over her forearms as though to wipe his touch from her skin.

Did she find him so distasteful, then? Could he have so grossly misinterpreted her reaction to his embrace, his kiss?

Kenrick rose without saying a word.

Perhaps it was good that this incident had occurred. Better that he learn her feelings now than later. He had not planned a seduction when he arrived at her door—God knew he did not need the distraction from his work—but he was not fool enough to believe he would not have taken the opportunity. He still wanted her, a fact that angered him as much as it bemused him.

He strode across the room, willing himself toward a state of reason and calm.

Yes, better that he put Haven out of his mind now, before she had the chance to sap any more of his questionable self-control.

"My apologies," he said as he lifted the latch on the door and stepped into the hall. "This will not happen again."

He pulled the door closed behind him, and swore to himself that his words were nothing less than cool, rigid truth.

Haven sat on the floor near the fireplace for long moments after Kenrick had shut the door and departed. She could not move, did not trust her legs to hold her.

"Oh, faith," she whispered into the empty chamber. "What does this mean?"

She held herself in a loose grip, her palms moving quickly up and down her arms, trying to dispel the queer feeling that had overcome her. Her limbs felt as if they were being faintly pricked by scores of pins and needles. Her head was spinning, her ears humming with the oddest tickle of sound, as though a thousand bees swarmed inside her mind.

Indeed, her entire body seemed alive and quickening with the odd shimmer of sensation.

It had startled her, how quickly the feeling had come upon her. Once it started, she had been unable to think, been scarcely able to breathe. Even now, alone in the chamber, she could not comprehend how deeply her kiss with Kenrick had stirred her.

She had wanted to feel his mouth on hers, despite her hesitation. She had wanted his arms around her, had wanted his gentle touch.

Truth to tell, she wanted him still.

But this overriding feeling that held her in its grasp went beyond anything she knew, surpassing any notions of simple human desire.

This feeling was a dangerous one.

It was powerful, and it carried an unfathomable allure.

She looked down at her arms, to where the scant dusting of fine golden hairs had risen as her body had begun to stir at Kenrick's touch. Those scattered, gossamer fibers were still standing on end. Her skin seemed luminous and pale beneath the scratches left from the hen's sharp talons, the delicate webbing of her veins more sharply defined across her opalescent wrists.

And there was more, she realized.

Something that she had found curious before and now made all the more unsettling.

She untied the laces of her gown and slid the garment over her shoulder. The bandage that covered her wound became visible as the bodice dipped low on her chest. Haven looked down at the pristine white linen, contemplating what she might find.

She had to know.

She reached over and lifted one edge of the bandage.

It came away easily, not even the slightest tug on the healing skin beneath the binding that Haven herself had applied that morning. Mary had wanted to help, but Haven had turned the maid away, preferring to do it on her own now that she was feeling stronger.

In truth she had not wanted the girl to see what lay beneath the bandage. She would not have understood. Haven herself was not quite sure what to make of it. Now she had to know.

With trembling fingers, she pulled back the square of undyed linen.

It came off the wound as clean as it had gone on that morning, not so much as the faintest stain to mar it.

There was no stain . . . because the wound that had been raging and nearly lethal just a few short days ago, was all but healed.

❧ 15 ❧

MORNING WAS SLOW to arrive that next day, and Kenrick greeted the dawn in a rare foul mood. He had gotten little rest the night before. That fact alone would have been unremarkable, save that his inability to sleep was due less to his obsession with the puzzle of the Dragon Chalice and more with a mystery of another kind.

That of the spell a certain flame-haired witch was weaving over him.

She had occupied his thoughts from the first he had seen her, but after yesterday's kiss—after the embrace that had seared him as certainly as a live flame—Haven lingered in all of his senses. She drew him like no other, in spite of his intention to maintain his distance. A man would need to be dead to resist her.

Either dead, or a saint.

Saint indeed, he thought wryly, scoffing at his old nickname. Never had it seemed more a jest.

His feelings toward Haven were anything but saintly, and the vow he had given her the day before may have sounded noble at the time, but it felt as flimsy as vapor to him now, when it would take little convincing to turn down the corridor that led to her closed chamber door. With an oath, he took the stairs instead, his stride long and purposeful as he quit the keep and headed for the bailey courtyard.

He was glad for the day's business that would take him away from Clairmont for several hours, despite that the task would be an unpleasant one. When Braedon and he had been out the day before, they had heard word of a band of riders spotted in a village in Devon. The group of outlaws had harassed a church and ransacked a nearby abbey.

Senseless destruction, unless one knew what these brigands sought.

And Kenrick knew all too well.

From the descriptions he and Braedon had received, the mercenaries could be no other than the ruthless minions of Silas de Mortaine.

A retinue of twenty Clairmont knights stood assembled in the wide yard of the inner bailey. A precaution, should things turn ugly on the sortie to Devon. The men's mounts were saddled and waiting, as was Kenrick's white destrier and Braedon's black. The knights greeted their lord's arrival with serious faces and a ready gleam in their eyes, for they knew they stood a good chance of riding into battle today.

God willing, they would have that battle.

Kenrick prayed they would be met and challenged, for until all four pieces of the Dragon Chalice were in his grasp, a feat that he might never accomplish, the only way to be assured of the security of Clairmont and his loved ones was through his sword.

He mounted up just as Braedon strode out of the keep. Ariana was with him, and Kenrick could see from the shadows lingering beneath her eyes, the trace lines edging her mouth that she, too, was aware of the day's

goal. She paused just outside the door and embraced her
husband for a long moment, then nodded silently as he
pressed his forehead to hers and whispered private
words. They kissed, and parted. As Braedon descended
the short steps into the bailey, Ariana lifted her hand to
wave somberly to her brother.

"Godspeed," she mouthed.

Kenrick tilted his chin in reply, then donned his helm
and took the reins from an attending squire. With a look
to Braedon as the dark warrior mounted his charger,
Kenrick gave the signal for the retinue to head out. The
score of soldiers fell in line behind the two men who
rode side by side under the portcullis gate of the barbican.

As the clop of horses' hooves sounded in the shaded
arch, Braedon drew alongside Kenrick and said in a con-
versational tone, "The incident in the chicken yard yesterday must have given your guest quite a scare."

"Haven?" Kenrick said with a shrug. "She did not
seem overly shaken. A few scratches was all she suffered, nothing more."

"Hmm," Braedon grunted. "I wondered, as she seems
intent on hiding in her chamber today. Perhaps something else has upset her."

"Who could know what the woman is about?" Kenrick scoffed, unwilling to look at the smirking knight at
his side. Sunlight beat down upon them as they cleared
the gate and put their mounts onto the road leading
away from Clairmont Castle. "There is no logic in her at
all, from what I've seen."

"Mayhap you have not looked close enough. Women
have their own logic, I'll grant you. And what a sweet

reasoning for the man who endeavors to understand his lady."

"I have no time to understand Haven. There are more pressing matters at stake here. She is but one piece of a puzzle I aim to solve, that of the attack on Greycliff, and nothing more."

" 'Tis a smart tack to take. Logical, certainly." Braedon gave a sage nod of his head. "But try telling that to your heart. Tell it to hers, for that matter."

Kenrick let out a bark of laughter. "I'd no idea my sister had wed such a romantic. I assure you, Lady Haven's heart concerns me no more than I wager mine concerns her."

"Truly?" There was an edge of amusement in Braedon's voice. "Is that why she watches our departure from the tower window?"

Kenrick turned a swift, questioning glance on him, searching for signs of jest. There was no mockery, but there was a glint of smugness in the dark knight's eyes, and in the smile that tightened his facial scar into a silvery line against the swarthiness of his left cheek.

"Look for yourself, do you not credit me. I'd venture she has been haunting her chamber window since the moment you strode into the bailey this morn."

Scowling, Kenrick pivoted to gaze behind him, to the steep tower that rose up behind Clairmont's protective walls. There, high in the keep, Haven's chamber window stood open onto the bailey below. There was a rush of movement from within the darkened room, a hasty blur of pale silk as a slender arm quickly closed one of the shutters.

Kenrick turned back toward the ribbon of dusty road that lay before him. "She despises me."

"More illogic to your mind, I take it?"

"Nay. It is rightly due. I wager I earned her scorn and then some after last evening."

"Oh? What did you do, intimidate the poor girl with more interrogation?"

"Worse. I kissed her."

Braedon let out a chortle of laughter that drew the stares of several accompanying knights. "You kissed her."

"I did more than that, if you must know."

"God's blood," Braedon said, leaning in close for none to overhear. "You didn't force her—"

"Christ!" Kenrick replied, aghast. "I am not so long deprived—or depraved—that I would resort to that. Or so I like to think. When it comes to this lady, too often I know not what I am capable of. She does things to my head, that one."

"She is exasperating," Braedon supplied.

"Yes."

"Frustrating."

"That, too."

Braedon seemed to be enjoying a somewhat private smile now, his gaze following the horizon as though lost in his own thoughts. "Easily the most bothersome female you have had the misfortune of knowing, is she?"

Kenrick felt himself nodding his head in total agreement. "Yes and yes. You understand me, at least."

Again the enigmatic grin, only this time it was turned on Kenrick. Braedon reached over and clapped him on the shoulder. "Oh, I understand you, brother. No doubt more than you can know."

"She is becoming a . . . problem for me."

"Women are a complication, to be sure."

"Aye, well, this one affords no easy solution."

"I thought you enjoyed a challenge?"

"I find I have plenty of that without the added distraction of Haven." He navigated his mount around a deep rut in the track of the road. "If you found yourself in my situation, what would you do?"

"You mean forced into close quarters with a woman who tempted me toward outright madness when I wasn't looking for ways to entice her into my bed?"

"Precisely."

Braedon looked askance at him, his mouth tugging into a wolfish grin. "Why, I married her."

It was difficult to share in his friend's humor when the solution to Kenrick's own trouble was so far out of reach.

Marry her, indeed. Wedded bliss was for people like Braedon and Ariana.

For Rand and Elspeth.

Not for him.

He was not the sort to dream of simple days around the hearth and home. He had no skill with people and the making of pleasant conversation. Nor had he the patience to immerse himself in the trivialities of everyday life. His mind yearned for greater challenges, bigger quests.

Regardless of how happy he saw his sister and her husband, or even the joy he had witnessed between Rand and Elspeth, Kenrick could not imagine that same light shining one day on him.

And as for love . . . ?

Well, save that notion for the bards and poets. To him, love was simply the grandest myth of all: intangible, immeasurable, insubstantial. An illusion he had no intention of grasping for on faith alone.

He was a man driven by proof and evidence—principles that had not served him well in his aspirations toward the church and his service as a Knight of the Temple.

Faith was a concept he found difficult to embrace . . . like love.

If something could not be held or weighed or measured, how could it exist?

The Dragon Chalice was real enough; his quest for the treasure was all he could truly embrace now. He had devoted years to finding it, and so he would continue that quest until the cup was safely in his hands, or until he breathed his last. He could ill afford to let thoughts of lust—or love—distract him from his course.

"I should let her go."

He had not been aware he'd spoken the words aloud until he glanced up and saw Braedon looking at him.

"She has not fully regained her memory about the attack on Greycliff. Do you not need the information she may have trapped in the corners of her recall?"

"I will manage without it."

"When you brought her to Clairmont, you were adamant that you needed whatever secrets she might hold."

"And now I say I will fare better without her underfoot. She has become an unwanted distraction."

"Not so unwanted, I wager."

"All the more reason for her to be gone at once."

"Ah, naturally." Braedon's tone suggested wry amusement. "And I suppose this makes logical sense to you?"

Kenrick glared over his shoulder, well aware that he

was hemming himself into a corner with all this talk of women and feelings. "I am glad to keep you entertained, brother, but the ride to Devon will pass much faster if we cease our prattle and instead look to the road."

Braedon's grin widened. "I see no problem here. I can ride and talk at the same time. Can you not?"

But Kenrick was already giving his mount a nudge of his spurs, leaving the party of knights to ride ahead on his own.

The last thing he needed on today's sortie was to be distracted with thoughts of Haven and what he should or should not do about her. Bed her, wed her . . . neither was a solution he was willing to entertain, despite that there was a degree of temptation in both ideas. Kenrick shut it out, however, training his mind on the task at hand.

That task became all the more consuming as the hours of travel passed and the riding party came upon the quiet village of Devon.

A small farming burgh plunked down in the middle of a shallow valley, the town had no fortress to guard it. The smattering of huts and cottages lined the road on either side, squat buildings made of dark timber and wattle-and-daub. Humble villeins came out of their homes and in from the fields to greet the retinue, their expressions of worry battling with flickering hope as the party of armed knights advanced into their midst.

Kenrick nodded to them as he rode past, a sober greeting that let them know there was naught to fear from this band of strangers garbed for war. He and his retinue cantered on, to the head of the settlement where stood the chapel and abbey.

Little seemed out of place until Kenrick and his company neared the small stone church and monks' quarters. The thick oak door of the chapel was closed tight, but it bore the deep, punishing grooves of a battle ax's blade. Its iron latch had been smashed from its fixtures, the meager security breached by the invaders who had trampled so carelessly on this hallowed ground.

They were met by a priest of middling age, whose kindly face and pale hands bore evidence of the struggle recently endured. Other village men had similar defensive scrapes and cuts, and all looked ready to fight again should they need to.

"Good morrow," Kenrick said as the holy man and two of the townsfolk approached. He made summary introductions, then cut straight to the business at hand. "What can you tell me about the men who did this?"

The priest gave a somber shake of his head. "There were several of them—five, if I counted aright. It was too dark to get a good look and they did not linger long."

"Was anyone hurt?"

"Nay, m'lord. They did not seem bent on murder, thank Providence."

"They was demons, do you ask me," cut in one of the village men. "Who else would ride in at dead of night and sack a place of worship?"

"What did they take?"

"We are a poor parish, m'lord," said the priest. "There is little of value to be had in our small chapel, save a golden cross that stood on our altar. 'Tis gone now, regrettably."

Kenrick studied the holy man and the lamentable state of his domain. "I would like to look around."

"As you wish, m'lord." The priest gestured toward the church grounds and began leading the way. "If you like, I will show you where the cross had been in the chapel."

Kenrick drew off his gauntlets and dismounted. He paused there, pivoting to address a handful of his men with low-voiced orders. "Ride out and search the outlying area. Bring word to me here if you find anything telling."

Half a dozen knights formed a group and fanned out to fulfill his command.

Braedon leaped down from his horse, his expression grim with understanding as he came to stand beside Kenrick. "This had to be le Nantres's work."

"I would credit no one else, save de Mortaine himself."

Braedon's lip curved into an almost animal sneer. "Silas prefers not to get his hands dirty with petty raids and thievery. Draec, however, has no such qualms. Nothing is below his grasp."

He would know better than most, Kenrick thought, seeing the animosity gleam in his brother-by-marriage's eyes. Braedon had once been associated with Draec le Nantres, although it was years ago. Draec had been a trusted friend of the warrior once known as The Hunter— until greed for the Dragon Chalice bred a betrayal that in the end had spilled much blood and delivered many deaths. Braedon had barely escaped the slaughter; most of his accompanying knights were not so fortunate.

It was le Nantres again, scarcely three months ago in France, whose relentless pursuit of the Chalice treasure ended with Ariana lying wounded and dying in Braedon's arms. They had needed a miracle to save her, and so, by what could only be explained by the magic of the Chalice itself, they had received one. Kenrick was far too practical to think they might be so fortunate again.

"This way, sirs," the priest called from the blade-scarred door of his church.

Kenrick and Braedon followed, leaving the rest of the men to stand guard outside.

The chapel was quiet and dark, lit only by the flames of a dozen candles that burned in a modest iron candelabra in the nave. The altar cloth was scorched on one end, but it had been carefully smoothed out and replaced where it belonged. The priest genuflected, then strode serenely to the front of the chapel.

"It was here, you see?" He pointed to the vacant center of the altar, his tonsured head shaking in slow remorse. "I am not a man to be swayed by material things, but this cross had been a special gift to our humble parish, which makes its loss all the more troubling. The cross was presented to us by the abbot of Saint Michael's Mount some years ago."

A knot of coldness began to ball in Kenrick's gut at the mention of the island abbey off England's southern coast.

" 'Twas that alone which the brigands stole. Can you fathom such a thing?"

Yes, he could.

Saint Michael's Mount had been the very place where Silas de Mortaine obtained the first part of the Dragon Chalice—Avosaar, the Stone of Prosperity.

It hardly seemed coincidence that his minions would have now stolen an artifact related to that holy site. For what was not the first time, Kenrick cursed himself for the prolonged imprisonment that cost him so much of his work on the Chalice lore. And to have lost his findings to de Mortaine and his soulless henchman, Draec le Nantres—the thought seethed inside him like poison.

Scowling with the folly of his past mistakes, Kenrick slanted a look in Braedon's direction. He spoke in low tones, paused some distance from the altar and well out of the cleric's range of hearing. "These raids had a purpose, and this theft was not random at all."

"No," Braedon agreed. "How long do you think it will take them to find the path that will lead them to more of the treasure?"

"When they search like this—sacking every abbey and chapel in the realm—they can count on luck alone to guide them."

"Sooner or later, even a fool will strike true. These are no fools."

"But they are desperate, and desperation makes a man careless. Their carelessness will buy us time to head them off before they find another of the stones."

"How much time?"

"A week or two." Kenrick hissed an oath between gritted teeth. "Likely not enough."

"That is a slim tether on which to tie one's hope."

"Slim indeed, but it's all we've got right now, my friend."

"And if, as you suspect, they have the key you hid at Greycliff? How long then?"

His mood growing more grave by the moment, Kenrick had no answer for this inevitable question. As it was, he had no chance to contemplate it, for outside the open door of the chapel came the steady pound of a horse's hooves. One of his dispatched knights jogged into the dim confines of the church, urgency written in the taut line of his mouth.

"What have you found?"

"A campsite, my lord. It appears to have been recently used."

Kenrick stalked the length of the chapel aisle, his every muscle primed for confrontation. "Where is it?"

"Not far from the village, in a forest to the west."

"Show me."

With Braedon close behind him, Kenrick followed his man to the horses waiting outside. The group mounted up and set off at a gallop, heading for a strand of pine and oak a short ride from the village square.

As the young knight had said, the campsite appeared to have been only lately abandoned. And in some haste, Kenrick thought as he jumped down to inspect it. Although it seemed unlikely, perhaps its makers had fled in the midst of a struggle. The trod earth bore the scars of horses' hooves, the indentations bearing the deep scoring of rearing beasts and the chaotic scuffle of spurred boots.

Braedon was already dismounted as well and crouched on his haunches near the still-smoldering remains of the small campfire. He picked up a stick and jabbed it into the smoking embers. "They're not long gone. An hour at most."

Kenrick raked a hand through his hair, scarcely able to bite back his oath of anger.

So close.

To have missed them by so slim an amount of time

grated against the logic that assured him they could not have gotten far.

"There is blood here," he remarked idly, his gaze drawn to a trail of dark droplet stains soaking into the hard-packed sand of the campsite perimeter. "At least one of them is wounded. And from the tracks they left, it appears the party has divided to ride in separate directions."

Kenrick pivoted his head to scan the outlying areas beyond the small forest clearing, searching for further signs of the brigands' departure. They might have taken any one of the paths through the towering woods, although none would have been an easy escape.

"We could split up, and try to catch up to them." Braedon stood up and met Kenrick's stare. "Injuries will slow them down and we've still several good hours of light. Even without the aid of my old skills, I can pick up a trail this fresh."

Kenrick did not doubt it. Braedon le Chasseur—once known as The Hunter for his uncanny ability to track and retrieve anything, or anyone, that had gone missing—did not make idle boasts when it came to his gift. Despite that he had forfeited his skills some months past, he was yet a formidable warrior.

But as much as Kenrick relished the idea of apprehending any one of de Mortaine's minions, he felt their efforts would be better spent elsewhere. The discovery at the village church had given him another thought. One that just might put him a few steps closer to claiming one of the two remaining Chalice stones.

"Shall I tell the men to prepare to ride?" Braedon asked, breaking into Kenrick's already deep concentration.

"Yes. We ride, but for Clairmont, not into a chase our enemies might well be expecting."

Braedon gave him a quizzical look, his dark brows knit in a frown. He was a man of action; no doubt his hands itched for the confrontation they might find after a day of searching for de Mortaine's men. Kenrick's did too, but he was patient, calculating the value of a satisfying skirmish versus the benefit of time he could use in gaining firmer hold on the Dragon Chalice.

Very likely Braedon recognized the direction of his thoughts. Though quick to strike, the warrior was reasonable when he needed to be, and he trusted Kenrick's judgment. That much was clear in his answering nod of agreement.

"We return to Clairmont," he said, then turned and shouted the order to the rest of the knights who stood by awaiting command.

With Kenrick on his white charger leading the way, the retinue prepared to depart the glade.

As the party assembled and turned back onto the road, a pair of keen eyes watched in stealthy silence from deep within the cover of the woods. The large figure blended in well with the darkness surrounding him, aided by drab attire and a face grizzled by a shadowy growth of beard.

Quiet as the tomb, as still as stone, he waited.

He watched, one hand curled around the cold hilt of his sword. The weapon had been drawn without a sound, held low but ready to strike with swift, lethal purpose.

Every breath he took was measured and unhurried.

Everything about him bespoke of calm reason and the assured patience of death itself.

Everything, save his eyes, which burned like the embers of a banked fire . . . quietly smoldering, waiting for the opportunity to ignite and consume all in his path.

❧ 16 ❧

KENRICK IGNORED THE first few quiet raps on his
solar door. He had sequestered himself in his tower
quarters upon arriving back at Clairmont, knowing
with a renewed sense of clarity how much work he
had to do, and what little time in which to do it.
De Mortaine's men were getting closer. They were getting desperate, if the ruination he saw that day were any
indication.

All their searching would eventually bring them to
Clairmont.

Part of what they sought was here in Kenrick's
keeping—a crucial part—and it would not take Draec le
Nantres long to figure that out once he learned that Kenrick, Ariana, and Braedon had escaped France whole
and hale a few months ago.

Tuning out a further knock that sounded on his door,
Kenrick continued transcribing his current set of figures
and diagrams.

Usually his silence was indication enough to the servants that he wished not to be disturbed. Tonight, which-
ever page or scullery maid it was who waited in the
corridor beyond was disinclined to take the hint.

Overbold and persistent, another rap sounded on the
thick oak panel.

"I do not wish to be disturbed," he growled at last, impatience biting in every clipped syllable.

To his vexation and surprise, the latch on the unlocked door began to open. Irritated, Kenrick looked up from his work on the desk as the panel pushed inward, groaning on its hinges.

"You did not come down to the hall tonight. I thought you might be hungry."

Any impatience he felt at the intrusion was lost the moment he saw that it was Haven standing in the doorway of his solar. She held a tray of food and slim decanter of wine. The aromas of roasted meat and creamed vegetables drifted into the room.

"What's this?"

"Supper, if you want it."

"Supper," he mused, setting down his quill. "This is an unexpected gift. After the way we left things between us yesterday, I shouldn't think you'd mind if I starved up here."

"If you don't want it—" She started to edge back into the corridor.

"Nay, don't go." Kenrick got up from his desk and walked around to the front of it. "I appreciate your consideration, Haven. And find I do have an appetite after all."

Gesturing to where she could set down the tray, he waited as she complied, then leaned against the large table and casually inspected what she had brought him.

The trencher contained a tempting array of the evening's fine fare: a large chunk of gravy-drenched beef, green beans and onions thick with a rich cream sauce, a wedge of cheese, a half loaf of bread, and a flagon of spiced warmed wine. Kenrick stirred through the lot of it with the accompanying poniard Haven had supplied. He poked the slender knife into a piece of the meat and lifted it to his nose. It smelled as it should, rich with herbs and slow-simmered juices. Nothing of note beyond Cook's usual flair with a sauce.

Everything on the trencher looked acceptable. Nothing seemed amiss.

Kenrick took the vessel of wine and poured a bit into an empty cup sitting on the edge of his desk. It swirled in the bottom of the tankard, deep red, fragrant with mulling spices and nothing more.

"I trust everything meets with your approval." Belatedly, he realized Haven was watching him with a quizzical, somewhat insulted gaze. "I bring a peace offering, but you examine it as though you expect I might poison you."

Kenrick gave a vague shrug of his shoulder as he set the cup of wine back down on the desk. "An unfortunate force of habit."

"Oh?" she asked, one dark amber brow arching on her forehead. "And who is it you trust less with your stomach, my lord—your cook, or me?"

He met her teasing smile and gave her a wry smirk of his own. "Let's just say a man learns to be cautious when he spends half a year in an enemy's dungeon. The only thing less enjoyable than the daily beatings was the rancid food I was forced to ingest. I might have gladly taken a dose of poison over the maggoty bowls of gruel that de Mortaine provided."

His tone was light, but in truth, he really did not want to think about his months of captivity abroad. He certainly did not want to discuss with Haven the seemingly endless torture and solitary confinement he endured.

"I'm sorry," she said softly, offering sympathy he did not want or need.

Kenrick shrugged. "I survived."

He turned his attention eagerly back to the tray of food. The meal she brought was a sore temptation to his empty stomach, and so he began to eat.

"My thanks for the supper," he said as he wolfed down a succulent chunk of the beef. "I'll take the tray back down to the kitchens when I am through."

It was an abrupt dismissal, one he was somewhat reluctant to give when Haven was standing before him in the firelight glowing from the solar's hearth. Her pretty face and glossy auburn hair were gilded in warm hues, her green eyes bright as gemstones. The simple gown she wore seemed to skate over her figure, hinting at the soft curves of her shoulders and bosom, and caressing the gentle flare of her hips.

She made an exceedingly enticing picture.

Too much so, when thoughts of her were never far from his mind's reach. To see her now, alone with him in his private quarters after a long day on the road, set in motion a swift and particularly distracting calculation.

From where she stood, no more than an arm's length separated them. Less, were he to take the slender hand that was presently tracing a whorled knot at the edge of his desk, and haul her to him. Beyond her to the right, some five long strides, was an upholstered bench situated near the fireplace. Past that, it was precisely nine paces to the threshold of the adjoining chamber, where his large bed stood.

Fewer than twenty steps lay between Haven standing anxiously near the door and Haven lying beneath him on a cloud of sable furs and soft down coverlets.

In spare moments, he could have her unlaced and undressed, gloriously bared.

Damn and damn!

Curse this importunate proclivity to see patterns and solutions with every glance. With a growl of frustration, Kenrick reached for the cup of wine and downed it in a single gulp.

"It must be difficult for you."

Haven was peering at him in question, and for a moment he wondered if the wicked musings of his mind had been evident on his face.

"I can see that it still troubles you—your imprisonment. To think you were there half a year. It must have been unbearable."

"That was not what I, ah . . . ." He cleared his throat. "Aye, well. It was worse in the beginning. After a while, one day blended into another."

"But to endure that time, never certain what day might be your last . . ."

"Is that not what being born and living is—enduring our existence without knowing when the end might come?" He permitted a teasing, cynical smile when she glanced up at him, her brow creased. "Anyway, I realized early on that my captor did not want me dead so much as he wanted to loosen my tongue. And weaken my mind."

"Why would he do that?"

"Because I had information he needed."

Her gaze slid to the assortment of papers, maps, and writings that littered his desk. "Did you give it to him?"

"He managed to obtain some of what he sought—too much, regrettably—but not all."

"And whatever it is you fear was lost to him at Greycliff," Haven said, "will now help lead him to the Dragon Chalice."

Kenrick met the too-shrewd gaze she turned on him, careful to maintain an air of casual disregard. "I told you, the Dragon Chalice is a myth."

"Yes, that is what you told me." Unblinking, she stepped closer to him. "Much of my memory was scorched away that night, but do you reckon the fever robbed me of all good sense as well?"

In the wake of his answering silence, she blew out a sharp sigh and shook her head.

"The men who killed your friends went there for a reason. You've asked me what it is they were looking for, but I think you know. Why were Rand and Elspeth and their child killed, Kenrick? Tell me what it was that cost them their lives that night."

"I did," he replied, voicing his regret aloud for the first time. The burden of it had never seemed so heavy. "They're dead because of me."

"What happened?"

Kenrick felt his mouth twist with wry reflection. "Before I was captured by Silas de Mortaine, I served as a Knight of the Temple of Solomon. My duties for the Order involved reporting on various holy sites, chronicling purported miracles and other unexplained occurrences in England and abroad. These reports, I would later learn, had been commissioned by one of the Order's most influential, and dangerous, patrons."

"Silas de Mortaine?" Haven guessed.

Kenrick nodded. "He was paying handsomely for my work, and once I heard the first mention of the Dragon Chalice—an enchanted cup thought to be rent in four pieces and scattered across the realm—I realized that my findings were less harmless reports than detailed maps that might aid de Mortaine in claiming the treasure."

"What did you do?"

"Without divulging too much of my work, I took my concerns about de Mortaine to my superiors. They knew he was a ruthless man, with unchecked power, but they were enjoying his substantial contributions too much to turn him away. They commanded me to submit my findings to him or be banished from the Order. It wasn't the first time my eyes had been opened to the greed and duplicity of my fellow man. But I swore it would be the last."

"So you left the Templars."

"Yes. I left that very night, with the whole of my work as well. I came home to Clairmont—it was little better than a year ago—and I made the Chalice my own quest."

"What about Rand?"

"Soon after I returned to England, not long before I would be captured and imprisoned by de Mortaine, I entrusted Rand with a crucial piece of my findings. It was a metal seal: two rings intersecting, with a small cross at its center. Although I know not how it might be used, I am certain it is a key I will need to find another of the Chalice pieces."

"Another?" Haven was frowning slightly, looking up at him in expectant silence.

"Aye," he said. "Silas has already recovered one of the four."

It was an unfortunate truth, and one he hoped would help mask his careless slip.

There were just two parts of the Dragon Chalice yet to be found. Another resided in this very keep since Kenrick's rescue two months past. The golden cup bearing the Stone of Light, or Calasaar by its Anavrin name, was presently kept under Kenrick's close watch.

Too late to make it seem a subconscious effort, Kenrick reached over and began organizing his work, shuffling his diagrams and unencrypted notes into a neat stack. He turned them over, facedown on the desk.

Haven's expression was soft, understanding. "I won't betray your trust, Kenrick. You needn't hide your work from me."

"I merely remove the temptation. You've heard too much already. Trust me when I say you are better off not knowing any more of what's contained here. Too many lives have been forfeited. No doubt more will be spent before it is ended."

She absorbed that news with a sober look. "I had no idea drawings and words could be so dangerous."

"Dangerous enough to take down kings," Kenrick replied. "Perhaps entire realms."

"Is that what Silas de Mortaine seeks—to claim a king's throne?"

"He wants power. Wealth. Immortality. Everything the Dragon Chalice promises. And he is being aided by forces nearly beyond comprehension," Kenrick divulged with more than a little gravity.

"What are you saying?"

"The men who serve him, beasts whose origin can only be the darkest brand of magic, have no regard for human life. Nor does he."

Haven's gaze had taken on a haunted quality as he spoke. She seemed to fade somehow, the candlelight flickering in unseeing pupils that were growing large against the pale emerald hue of her eyes. She looked a bit unsteady.

Kenrick reached out to her, holding her arm in a gentle but firm grasp. "What is it?"

She blinked as if to clear away a thought that had taken her unawares. "I don't know. Something you said seemed familiar . . ."

"You are remembering things, aren't you?"

An uncomfortable expression skittered across her features. "I . . . I am not sure. Some things seem so close to the surface—fleeting details, words, faces—yet other things dance just out of my reach. You cannot know how frustrating it is to know little more than your name and a few scant details of a past that seems so incomplete, so unfamiliar."

"Give it time, Haven. All will come back to you, I am certain."

She nodded slowly, glancing down at her hands, which had begun to fidget with the long tail of the braided girdle circling her hips. "In truth, that is partly why I am here tonight. I wanted to speak with you."

"Oh?"

"You said once I was stronger, you would let me leave." At his grunt of acknowledgment, she rushed on. "My shoulder is healing well and my memory, as you say, will surely restore itself given time. You told me that when I was better, you would provide me a horse and escort so that I could go back—"

"Out of the question."

"—back to where I belong," she finished, dropping the end of the belt and scowling at him now. "How can it be out of the question? Did you or did you not make such a promise to me?"

"I did."

"And now you will break it?"

"There have been developments of late. Greycliff's at-tackers are on the move. They've been leaving a trail of death and destruction behind them, and now they are getting closer to Clairmont."

She started pacing, concern etching her brow. "All the more reason for me to leave. If I am in danger anywhere, surely it is here. I don't wish to wait around for them to find me. I may not survive them a second time."

"Nothing will harm you here."

"How can you be certain of that? You've said yourself these men are dangerous, that they will stop at nothing to get what they are looking for."

"Aye."

"Then how can you know that I am safe here?"

Kenrick reached out to her, halting her in the midst of another agitated step. He caught her stubborn chin and gently turned her face up toward his. "You are safe be-cause I will protect you. With my sword arm and my life, Haven. No one will do you harm without first com-ing through me. And I will not permit that to happen. Do you understand?"

She closed her eyes, dark brown lashes shadowing her flushed cheeks. "You are the one who does not under-stand. Your protection is another sort of threat to me."

"I offer it willingly, without a price to be paid, now or later."

"I know." When she lifted her lids, slowly daring to meet his gaze, her green eyes smoldered with verdant fire. "And that is precisely why you are a threat to me, Kenrick. I fear you are a threat to my heart."

Kenrick's exhaled oath was as bemused as it was

blasphemous. With great effort, despite that he wanted to bring her close, he held Haven away from him to search her eyes for answers.

"What have you done to me, lady? I see you and I stand enchanted. I touch you and I want to possess you. God's blood, but when I kiss you I feel . . . for the first time a long time, I feel—"

"Alive," she whispered, as though knowing his very thoughts.

He held her face in his palms, stunned by the intensity of emotion shining back at him through her eyes. "Yes. Alive." With a tender touch, he smoothed his fingers over the silken softness of her cheek and forehead, tracing the elegant arch of her brows. "So," he murmured, emotions churning inside him. "What are we to do, my lady?"

She pressed her cheek to his chest. "I don't know. Please understand that I cannot stay here. Not any longer."

"Where, then? To Cornwall? What awaits you there?"

"I don't know—I don't know!" She heaved against him as though to thrust him from her heart as she was pushing him from her arms. "But I don't belong here. This much I do know. I feel it."

"Nay. What you feel is fear. There is naught here that will harm you."

She shook her head and tried to move away from him, toward the door. "I'm sorry. I must go."

He let her get only as far as to lift the latch before he took three long strides and was standing directly behind her. He pressed his palm to the rough wood of the panel, closing it and meeting very little resistance.

She would not face him. She froze where she stood,

her spine held rigid before him, her breath coming fast and shallow. Kenrick brought his free hand up between them to trace the spiraling wave of a lock of her hair. He petted her gently, wanting only to soothe her.

Nay, in truth he wanted to do more than soothe. So much more.

He inhaled the scent of her, his voice low and rough as he spoke very near her ear. "You wish to leave and I have promised you that you could. Now I find I have no wish to let you go."

"Kenrick," she whispered, little better than a sigh. "Please . . ."

He smoothed his palm along the delicate line of her shoulder, and down the slender length of her arm. Her hand was still on the latch. He wrapped his fingers around hers and coaxed her grasp to loosen. "I would keep you here to know that you are safe, that I might protect you, but that is only a partial truth. I would keep you here because it is what I desire. I desire you, Haven."

"No," she barely whispered.

He spoke over her feeble objection, intent to rid himself of the burden of feeling that had been weighing him down for days. Ever since Haven had so unexpectedly entered his life. "You intrigue me more than any woman before, more than anything I've ever known. You have bewitched me with a foul brand of magic, my lady." A self-mocking laugh hissed between his teeth. "I like to think I am a man of some reason, but all my logic scatters when it comes to you. I hate this weakness you've put in me, but it is there, and I'll be damned if I can deny it."

She dropped her chin down, pressing her forehead to

the slab of thick oak that barred her exit. The sigh that sifted past her lips might have sounded of defeat had she not then slowly turned to face him. Her emerald gaze was heavy-lidded, but lit with a fire that stirred him at his core.

"I cannot let you go, Haven." He bent his head toward hers, eyes fixed on the verdant spark that beckoned him nearer even as her mouth trembled around a soundless protest. Kenrick stroked his fingers along her cheeks, his slow, praising caress coming to rest at the silky softness of her parted lips. "I want you to stay, lady. God, how I just . . . want you."

"Kenrick."

His name was naught but a thready whisper breathed against his lips as he dipped his head and pressed his mouth to hers. Only the merest brush of contact, he kissed her tenderly, calling up every measure of control he possessed to keep from claiming her with the urgency his body demanded.

Haven's lips were nectar sweet, pliant beneath his.

Heat coiled deep in his loins.

Blood pounded through his veins, primal and unfettered.

He, the saint, the scholar, the stoic one, was all but lost—to the tentative sampling of a simple kiss.

"Do you know how much I want you?" he murmured, breath panting, arousal licking at him like live flames. "Do you know what you do to me? God's blood, my lady, you must *feel* it."

Her answering gasp, the sudden quake of her limbs, told him all. Teasing, testing, he kissed her again, playing the tip of his tongue along the seam of her mouth. With his coaxing, she parted for him, permitting him past her lips with a moan that nearly undid him where he stood.

The soft fabric of her cotte rasped under his palms as he slid his hands down the length of her graceful spine. She shivered in his arms, a deep tremble that echoed the passionate tempest building within his own body. His fingertips brushed the crisscrossing laces that bound her bodice together.

He toyed with one of the little knots, easily loosening it, and all the while lavishing her with kisses that trailed from her lips, to her ear, to the warm column of her delicate neck. Haven's scent filled his nostrils, the twining perfumes of lavender soap and sensual woman proving an intoxicating blend. He breathed her in as he tasted the satiny softness of her skin, delighting in the low mewls of pleasure that fanned so warmly against his ear with her every gasp and sigh.

The second knotted lacing slipped free a moment later. Two remained, but already the snug bodice gave a bit in his hands. Haven's arms wrapped about his neck. She arched into him, and Kenrick pulled the network of binding laces until they slackened even more.

She was so incredibly soft, so passionately alive, this enigmatic lady who burned like fire in his embrace. Kenrick stroked her hair, marveling in the burnished tendrils that felt softer than silk against his hands. Possessively, he coiled his fingers around one glossy auburn wave, and pulled Haven deeper into his embrace. She opened her eyes to peer up at him in the firelight, her gaze dusky with desire, shadowed by the heavy fringe of her lashes.

The bouyant pressure of her breasts, nestled against his chest, rising with every shallow breath she took, proved a temptation too sweet to resist. Kenrick brought his hand around the front of her lithe body and filled his palm with the pert fullness of her bosom, molding his hand around the swell of one perfect breast, then the other. Her nipples beaded hard as pearls beneath the fabric of her bodice, exquisite little buds he longed to taste.

With trembling fingers, Kenrick felt his way down the fragile cage of her ribs and along the bewitching flare of her hips. He gathered the gentle folds of her skirts in his hands, subtly drawing them up, kissing her all the while. At last he found the hem of the generous fall of silk, and then the smooth warmth of the bare limbs beneath.

Haven sucked in her breath as he slowly drew his fingers up the length of her thigh.

"What are—oh, faith," she gasped brokenly, a twitch of muscle jumping as he teased the soft skin of her bare hip. "Kenrick . . . what are you doing?"

"Touching you," he murmured against the fluttering pulse at her throat. "Touching you, my beautiful lady, as I have wanted to for far too long."

She gave neither consent nor protest. Her head dropped back against the chamber door, a ragged sigh rushing past her lips as he let his senses marvel at the fiery vixen who responded so enticingly, so passionately, to his every stroke and caress.

Her skin felt like living, molten silk under his fingertips. He trailed a sensual path along the line of her body, astonished at how touching her so intimately could feel so indescribably good. He smoothed his hands over her warmth and felt as though somehow she were the one stroking him, coaxing pleasure from every fiber of his being.

"Sweet witch," he whispered, bending his head to

suck at the soft curve of her neck, "what is this spell you weave over me?"

"You are the one weaving spells," she said, her voice husky, catching in her throat as he plumbed the hollow of her throat with his tongue.

Kenrick moved his hand to grasp the arc of her pelvis, pulling her to him. Their bodies pressed sensually together, her softness melding into his rigidity. He explored the exquisiteness of her bare skin, his fingers dancing ever closer to the thatch of heaven nestled between her thighs.

Haven writhed, arching her back ever so slightly as though to guide his questing fingers to the place that he so fervently wanted to be. The flossy curls brushed against his fingertips as she moved, her sweet, moist scent registering in some primal part of him that knew only lust and want and greed to be sated.

The call was fierce.

Potent.

He struggled against it, knowing that to submit to the hunger that urged him to obey her unschooled cue would surely do him in. She moaned as he drew his fingers away from the lure of her femininity, retreating to safer ground.

God's wounds, but she could not know how close he was to taking her already. His arousal strained hard between them, thick and pulsing and needy. It only worsened as Haven twined her arms tighter around his shoulders, meeting his kiss with a rising hunger of her own.

Weakly, he indulged in her unpracticed embrace, one hand holding the tender small of her back, the other fisted in her rucked up skirts, deliberately bound there as though leashed and unable to be trusted. In truth, he did not trust himself at all in that moment. His need was too strong, his will too close to snapping.

When Haven's warm, wet tongue pressed against his lips, sliding along their seam as his own had done to her a moment ago, he should have refused her. He should have set her away from him.

Should have indeed, but instead he let her in.

Worse and worse, he caught her firmly in his arms and pressed her spine to the solid barrier of the chamber door, pinning her there with the length of his body. He grabbed her hands, which were now flat against his chest, and hauled them up above her head, holding her fast.

He kissed her hard, hiding none of his need for it was too wild to be contained. Although he could never tire of her sweet mouth, he dragged his lips down her neck, and lower still, to the sensual rise of her breasts. With his free hand, he scooped one glorious mound out of its confining bodice and feasted on the rosy nipple and pale swell that surrounded it.

"I think I will die if I do not have you, Haven." The admission rasped between his teeth as he grazed the succulent bud. "God, how I need you now."

She gave a soft cry, her body taut and heated against him.

"Do you know what I want of you? Tell me you understand." He blew out a sharp breath. "God's love, lady—tell me you are not a maiden still, or worse, the wife of another man."

The answering whimper carried an unmistakable note of distress.

"Tell me," Kenrick said, pausing only momentarily,

working to hear her reply over the heavy rhythm of his feverish pulse. "Haven . . ."

"I—"

She broke off, shaking her head, and a new sort of tension began to seep into the luscious curves that pressed so heavenly against him.

She could not tell him any such thing, he realized.

She could not say if she was virgin or bride because she could not remember.

"Ah, Criste." He brought his hands away from her at once, running his fingers through his hair as he pivoted away. He slammed his hands down on the edge of his desk. "Jesu Criste. What am I doing?"

As badly as he wanted her, he could not allow himself to go any further. She was not his to take—not by any means. And he did not have so little honor that he could willingly seduce a woman without the certainty that she had not already given her heart to another man. If she loved another, someone she did not yet recall, Kenrick did not wish to open himself to that brand of torment.

Better that he rein in now, before he became any more lost to the sweetness of Haven's body.

"Kenrick," she said softly behind him. "Please. 'Tis all right . . . I didn't . . . I don't want you to stop."

"No." His bark of laughter was self-mocking, edged with the harshness of his still frenzied lust. "I won't do this. Not to either of us."

He heard her tentative footsteps draw near. Her hand came to rest on his shoulder. "Kenrick?"

He shrugged away from her touch, yet too enflamed to endure her tenderness.

"You need to go now, my lady." He permitted himself only the briefest glance at her over his shoulder, fleeting,

yet long enough to see the confusion—the unbanked
fire—in her eyes. "Please, Haven. Just . . . leave me.
Now."

He swiveled his gaze away from her, his grip so tight
on the desk he thought the oak would crush in his fists.
Not two paces behind him, Haven let out a broken sigh.
He thought she might have said something more, but
then, mercifully, he heard the soft swish of skirts, followed by the click of the latch on his door. The panel
creaked open, then closed softly at her heels.

A chill breeze drifted in through the open window of
Haven's bedchamber. Like a wisp of cold breath, the
night air skated across the disheveled surface of her bed
and up the length of her bare leg. The ribbon of coolness
streaked along her skin, but did little to assuage the heat
that yet lingered from her impassioned encounter with
Kenrick.

Although long past midnight, hours since she had
been abed, sleep eluded her. She was anything but rest-
ful, having spent the time alternately tossing, turning,
and pacing, since she had fled Kenrick's quarters for the
sanctuary of her own. Now she lay atop rumpled furs
and coverlets, nude despite the chill in the air, trying to
will her body to calm.

Her head hummed, her limbs tingled, and her heart
beat with the intensity of a brewing storm.

But that was not the worst of it.

At her very core, deep inside the part of her that was
raw emotion and pure feminine feeling, she burned.

Kissing Kenrick, touching him—faith preserve her,
wanting him so desperately—had left her awash in a
pleasure so clear and bright it was wont to consume her.

Like glittering, beckoning fire, her passion for him had nearly overwhelmed her. She had not wanted to stop the madness he stirred within her, not this time. Despite that she knew, somehow clearly knew, that what would pass between them was wrong—*forbidden*—she wanted him. Even now.

Kenrick had awakened in her something wild and elemental.

He had given her but a taste of passion, and then denied her. He had all but thrust her away from him physically, a thought that stung when she knew with full certainty she would have permitted him anything in those heady moments of bliss. She would have stayed with him there in his chamber, breathing him in, drowning in his touch . . . a willing thrall.

She would have lain with him, but he did not want her.

Wise to take that as a blessing, she thought sullenly.

Fighting the continued quickening of her body, the unabating drone of her senses, Haven threw aside one of the fluffy feather bolsters and sat up in the midst of her tangled coverlets and blankets.

The breeze outside had grown stronger. It riffled the edge of the curtains that had been drawn back from the bed. Haven welcomed the chill, filling her lungs with deep, cleansing drafts of fresh night air. More, she thought, glad to feel some of the tumult within her begin to subside.

Her chemise lay draped at the edge of the bed, glowing stark white in the lightless space of her chamber. She retrieved the undergarment and slipped it over her head, then pivoted to put her feet on the floor. Rushes crackled softly underfoot as she took the handful of steps to the deep-set window of the adjacent wall.

The barest sliver of moon peeked out from behind black clouds. Calmer already, Haven turned her thoughts to the cool skate of the wind, and to the endless quiet just beyond the stone embrasure. She closed her eyes, tilting her face to catch the rush of crisp air as it swept over her.

Tranquillity descended like a veil, pushing away her earlier turmoil.

Yet something rippled beneath the surface of her intuition.

Something troubling and sharp.

Dangerous.

Haven snapped her eyes open on an indrawn breath.

Although she could see nothing to justify the sudden jangle of her senses, neither could she dismiss the feeling that took firm hold of her with so little warning. She stretched her thoughts outward, searching for the source of her alarm. She heard naught, saw naught, but then . . . something.

Like an icy hand coming to rest on the back of her neck, a streak of wariness shot through her. Whatever it was, it scented her. It hunted her, she was certain of it.

Haven instinctively recoiled.

Nay! she thought, inwardly admonishing herself for the cowardice that made her shrink away. If there was reason to be wary, if there was aught to fear within or without the castle stronghold, she had to know.

Mustering her resolve, Haven crept back toward the gaping blackness of the high tower window. She stood firm and ready, peering out at the night landscape and into the fringe of deep woods that ran the perimeter of Clairmont's western wall.

Nothing was there.

Her feeling of foreboding was passing, all but gone now.

Yet she was certain that somewhere in the dark below, nearer than she cared to think, malevolence loomed.

HEART OF THE FLAME

❧ 17 ❧

KENRICK RAISED HIS sword and brought it down hard on his target.

The blade connected in a punishing clap of sound that echoed in the stillness of a predawn mist that cloaked the castle's back bailey. It was a killing blow, striking deep into the thick torso of his unmoving opponent. The training dummy spewed a shower of wood splinters from yet another savage impact; its helmeted head wobbled on the pike that held it in place.

Kenrick eyed the weakness with grim satisfaction, offering no quarter. With a growl of pent-up fury, he delivered the final strike, the force of contact sending the battered helmet in a rolling tumble into the dirt of the tilting yard.

The knight on watch at the postern door was the only nearby witness at this early hour. He nodded in greeting to Kenrick, then briefly left his post to assist. As the knight jogged over to retrieve the errant helmet from the ground, Kenrick drew back his mail coif and wiped a sheen of sweat from his brow.

He wore light armor for this morning's impromptu exercise, the drape of chain links giving his arms a degree of added resistance as he worked. The burn of his straining muscles was a comfort to him. In fact it felt good, for the ache was a welcome distraction from an ache of another kind that he had been nursing since his aborted seduction of Haven in his chamber last night.

"I wager this fellow's seen better days," said the postern guard as he replaced the training dummy's head back onto the pike. "You've an admirable skill with the blade, my lord."

"Thank you," Kenrick replied, reluctant to accept the praise when he knew each of the men in his service was sworn to give their lives in protection of his. "You are Sir Thomas, are you not?"

The knight paused, offering him a nod of deference. "Aye, my lord. I am he."

"You have a young daughter—Gwen, is it?" Kenrick asked, recalling what Haven had told him a few days ago.

"Aye, my lord. She is my firstborn." Sir Thomas's expression muted into one of concern and not a little worry. As though the hammer of a mad lord's rage were about to drop on him and his family. "If the girl has been a bother to you in some way . . ."

"No. Not at all," Kenrick said, dismissing the notion with a shake of his head. "Nothing like that. I understand there had been an incident recently, that she'd been hurt. I merely wanted to inquire after her health."

"Oh." Relief poured into Sir Thomas's tired eyes. "Aye, that. My thanks for your concern, my lord. Little Gwennie is just fine now."

"Good," Kenrick replied. "I am glad to hear it. Let me know if there is anything you or your family requires, Thomas. You've long been a loyal knight—to my father, to my sister, and to me—and I am grateful for your service."

The knight beamed as if he had just been dubbed anew, and by a royal hand at that. "Aye, my lord," he said proudly, then took his leave to resume his post.

Kenrick continued his practice for a while longer, until the pink hues of dawn became the clear light of a risen day.

Servants hurried past him to assemble the great hall for breakfast, bringing baskets of fresh bread and cold meats into the keep from the kitchen outbuilding nearby. Kenrick watched with a sense of satisfied curiosity as Sir Thomas attempted pleasant conversation with the blushing maid, Enid, on her multiple trips in and out of the postern door.

On one of those trips out, a brawny arm held the door open for her from inside, the palm of the large hand identifiable at once by the silvered tracery of scars that covered the warrior's calloused skin.

Braedon exited on Enid's heels, hailing Kenrick with a wry grin.

"I've been dispatched on high orders this morning. My lady wife wishes to know if Clairmont's lord means take his breakfast in battle gear at the table or in the tilt yard."

"Neither. I lost track of the hour. Do not delay the meal on my account."

"Ariana will be disappointed. So will a certain other lady, I wager."

Kenrick glanced sardonically at Braedon and sheathed his weapon. "Haven waits for me in the hall as well?"

"As lovely as I've ever seen her, even if her eyes seem a bit troubled. It doesn't appear she slept well last night . . . nor do you, now that I am looking at you."

"Sleep is rare enough for me. Last night was no exception."

His inability to relax was no secret about the keep, but he saw no need to divulge the details of the indiscretion he shared with Haven in his chambers. Not even to Braedon, who was the closest thing he had to a friend.

Haven was the primary cause of his current state of restlessness, but his new thoughts on the Dragon Chalice were a very close second.

"I believe I may have found a further clue," he told Braedon in a confidential tone of voice. "There is an entry in one of my oldest journals about a holy site where unexplained healings have occurred. This place, Glastonbury Tor, lies along the same set of lines that connects both Saint Michael's Mount and Mont St. Michel. My calculations had been off only slightly, but I'm confident I'm on the right path now. I'm certain I'll find a key to another of the Chalice stones at Glastonbury. I mean to leave soon."

Braedon was listening in thoughtful silence. "This place—Glastonbury Tor? I have heard of it. 'Tis located not far from Cornwall, is it not?"

"It is."

The dark knight needed not to speak the words for Kenrick to know what he was thinking. Cornwall, the place where Haven had spent the last year—where her past might yet wait for her return—might hold answers for Kenrick of another sort.

"She is affecting me deeply," he admitted. "Her memory of the attack on Greycliff is only partially restored; the rest of her past remains elusive. I will find no true peace with her until I know her heart can be mine in full.

If I will lose her to her past at any time, I prefer to do it now."

Before she comes to mean even more to me, he thought, refusing to voice the weakness aloud.

Braedon nodded slowly. "If there are answers to be had in Cornwall, or at Glastonbury Tor, then I pray you find them."

He placed a brotherly hand on Kenrick's shoulder, the look in his gray eyes grim with understanding.

Beyond them, at the postern door of the keep, a commotion was rising from within the castle. The clipped thud of sentry boots reverberated off the stone walls of the keep's entry corridor a moment before the door swung open.

"Where will I find Lord Clairmont?" inquired a guard's voice of Sir Thomas on his watch.

Concern edged the inquiry, immediately setting Kenrick's instincts on alert.

"I am here," he answered, already walking over to meet the knight who he now saw was accompanied by one of the villagers.

"My lord."

The knight inclined his head in greeting, as did the cottar, who swiped the cap off his graying pate in a deferential, if unnecessary, show of respect.

"What is it?" Kenrick asked, impatient with formalities of rank when it was clear that something was amiss this morning. He did not like the feel of it one bit.

"There has been an incident in the village, my lord. The villeins have apprehended a man—"

" 'Tis a poacher, m'lord," interrupted the cottar as though excitement prevented him from holding his tongue a moment longer. Puffing out his chest as he spoke, his ruddy face and narrow-set eyes beamed with pride. "My boy Ralph got 'em with a pitchfork when the bastard tried to escape with one of the new lambs."

"He is dead?"

"Nay, m'lord. He lives, but he's hurtin'. My boy stuck 'em good in the belly, he did."

"Where is this poacher now?"

"Down in the barn at the village, m'lord. Ralph and some of the other lads are holding 'em there for ye. He's a mean one—spittin' angry to be caught."

"Poacher, my arse," Braedon snorted under his breath at Kenrick's side. "There is treachery here. It smacks of de Mortaine's influence."

Kenrick nodded. "My thoughts exactly. Shall we go question this trespasser and see if our suspicions are confirmed?"

"Lead the way," Braedon said, his hand resting on the pommel of his sword.

The dining hall was nearly filled with Clairmont's folk as Haven and Ariana made their way toward the dais. Ariana greeted those they passed, her kind smiles and cheerful demeanor not unlike a candle reaching light and warmth into a dank, dreary room.

Ariana's left hand rested lightly on her abdomen, a loving cradle for the babe that slumbered there. On her finger, her golden wedding band sparkled in the flicker of torches and the pale illumination of the morning sun that slanted down from the high windows of the hall.

"Have you been feeling unwell anymore when you wake?" Haven asked as they continued on through the shuttling throng of castle folk.

"Nay," she replied, smiling. "I am feeling better every

day. The babe is strong, and I think 'tis time that Braedon knows he is to be a father. In fact, I intend to tell him this evening."

"He will be naught but pleased, I'm sure," Haven assured her.

Ariana beamed. "I hope so."

Haven walked along at the lady's side, truly excited for her joy. But she was not quite able to ignore the shadow of anxiety that dogged her steps at the prospect of seeing Kenrick that morning.

Where Ariana and Braedon were immersed in the bliss of their union, with happy news of the babe to come, Kenrick and Haven could claim only confusion and obstacles between them.

And desire, she thought with a pained twist of her heart.

She yearned for him with a fierceness she could hardly comprehend.

And there was more to the feeling.

Something that went deeper than the physical ache he conjured in her with a mere glance . . . with a simple touch of his sensual hands. As much as she wanted to deny it, she could not dismiss the awakening Kenrick stirred in her very soul.

A forbidden stirring that she feared to acknowledge, let alone embrace.

It was dangerous, this feeling she had for him, of that she was certain.

". . . his leman, do ye say?"

Up ahead of her a few paces, Haven caught the murmured hush of gossiping voices. Two servant girls whispered back and forth, giggling as they shuffled along with the crowd gathering for breakfast.

"I swear it," hissed the second maid behind her hand. It was Mary, Haven realized once she heard her shrill voice and saw the freckles that spattered her cheeks. "I've seen them alone more than once. Why, just last night she came creeping out of the lord's chamber—"

Ariana cleared her throat in a pointed warning behind the tittering girls.

"To your table, Mary. That is quite enough."

"Aye, m'lady," the maid gasped, red-faced as she turned around and saw them standing there. Her companion and she slunk away to find their seats without another word.

"I am sorry," Ariana said to Haven. "I will speak with her later."

Before Haven could confess that nothing Mary said was untrue, a disruption caught her attention at the back of the feasting hall. A knight had come in from his watch with news that had the other guards talking among themselves in cautious voices.

"What is it?" Ariana asked of a passing servant who had just returned from their table. "What is going on?"

"A poacher, my lady. He's been caught down in the village. The men say word arrived not a moment ago."

Ariana blew out a troubled sigh. "And my husband? Where is Lord Braedon?"

"I understand he and my lord Kenrick have both gone down to see about the matter, my lady."

As the news of the intruder was dispensed, Haven weathered a gnawing pang of dread. "Oh, no. Something is wrong here. Ariana, last night . . . I was in my chamber when I felt the queerest sensation. It was evil, and I felt it staring up at me from outside the castle."

Ariana's blue gaze took on a worried sheen. "What are you saying?"

"I'm not sure. But Kenrick and Braedon—they're in danger, I know it. I have to warn them!"

The lambing barn stood an unassuming structure amid the timber outbuildings of Clairmont's village. Beyond its battered wooden door, huddled beneath low-ceilinged rafters lit with only the barest shafts of morning light from outside, easily a dozen cottars had crowded together to observe the morning's unusual arrival. The motley group of men talked among themselves, low murmurs and speculative wagers on how long the poacher might live with the gut wound that was slowly bleeding him dead in one of the stalls.

Kenrick strode through the assembled knot of villeins, followed close by Braedon and the old cottar whose son was responsible for apprehending the would-be thief.

"There be my boy," he crowed, pointing a gnarled finger toward a towheaded young man who stood guard outside the berth, pitchfork still in hand. His ruddy face took on higher color as Kenrick approached, his fingers going a little whiter where they gripped the long handle of the pitchfork. "The bastard ain't died yet, has 'e, Ralphie?"

A rather sickened look came over the young cottar's face as he shook his head in answer to his father. The expression of remorse and shock deepened at the sound of pained moaning and thrashing that rolled out from within the stall.

It was obvious the boy had never drawn another man's blood before, let alone inflicted a mortal wound. A visible shudder worked its way along his lanky limbs.

If he were made to endure his post a moment longer, the poor lad would probably either piss himself or lose his stomach on the spot.

Kenrick nodded at him in grave understanding as he came to stand beside him. Inside the stall, slumped against the timber wall and clutching a bleeding midsection, was a swarthy man with shaggy black hair and a thick growth of beard. He was panting like an animal, his teeth bared in a grimace of agony. A slivered eye rolled in Kenrick's direction, glinting with pain and, did he not mistake it, something darker.

Something malevolent, if the prickling of Kenrick's nape and Braedon's low growl of warning were any indication.

The cottar's son nervously rushed to explain what had happened. "He sneaked in here 'fore dawn, m'lord. At first I thought a wolf broke in to take one of the lambs, for all the snarling and bleating I heard in here. I grabbed this fork thinkin' to drive it off. Didn't see 'til after I stuck him that 'tweren't no wolf, but a man. God forgive me—he's dyin', I think."

"You did right," he told the anxious youth. "You did only what you had to, Ralph."

"Aye, m'lord." The young man stood there, staring as though unable to move.

"Set down the pitchfork and take the rest of these gawkers outside," Kenrick calmly commanded him. A glance to the knight who had accompanied them down to the village brought the soldier to his side. "Stand guard at the door. No one enters. Understand?"

The knight nodded, then helped corral the curious villeins and escorted them out of the barn.

Kenrick stood at the head of the open stall, listening

to the small crowd disperse, his gaze trained on the bleeding man who crouched low in the shadows. Braedon flanked Kenrick's left arm, his expression rigid, hand twitching in readiness where it hovered above his sheathed weapon. When the folk were gone, the barn door having creaked to a close, Kenrick spoke.

"I suppose it was only a matter of time before de Mortaine sent his hounds to sniff around my keep. What were your orders?"

The man said nothing. He kept his head down, his barrel chest heaving, wheezing belaboredly with the effort to breathe.

"Who commands you—de Mortaine, or Draec le Nantres?"

No response, save the rasping pull of his lungs.

"I admit, I am surprised they would send just one of you—a dullard at that, if a stripling cottar could fell you with a field tool."

A curse rolled between tightly clenched teeth, but the mercenary said no more.

"Not of a mind to talk, are you?"

Braedon's sword came out of its sheath with a slow, lethal-sounding hiss. "I imagine I could loosen this cur's tongue."

The man slanted a narrow glare on the blade now poised a hairbreadth from his nose. "Go ahead and cut me. I don't fear death, and I am already dying."

Kenrick spared him only the briefest lift of his brow. "Yes, you are."

"Aye," the swarthy mercenary agreed, "and sooner than later. So why should I tell you anything? Unless you mean to staunch this river of blood, I've nothing to gain from helping you."

"I cannot stop the bleeding, no."

The man snorted smugly.

"I can slow it, however," Kenrick added. "I could have you bandaged up and held under my watch for the next few days—more than that, perhaps a couple of weeks. Long enough to get the word out to de Mortaine that you have betrayed him to ally with us in the quest for the Chalice."

"I have no idea what you're talking about."

"No? You expect we believe you are merely a vagrant, poaching lambs from my village and deer from my woods?"

"I care not what you think."

"Mayhap you'd like to see what you really came here looking for," Kenrick drawled, a menacing edge in his voice.

Braedon snapped an askance look at him, unspoken caution for Kenrick to take care in what he divulged. Dying or nay, this "poacher" bore the stamp of de Mortaine's control. Worse, the oxlike bulk and sinister mien bespoke an even greater threat.

An otherworldly one, born of the same dark magic that wrought the Dragon Chalice itself.

But Kenrick knew precisely what he offered, and to whom.

"The death that awaits you here in this barn is an easy one, that is true. But unless you tell me what de Mortaine is up to, I've a mind to show you another end. One that will be aught but easy, I promise you." Kenrick narrowed his gaze on the dulling eyes of the Anavrin warrior. "Talk," he said, "or I will see that you meet your death amid fire and pain unlike anything you've ever known."

The big head pivoted at the coolly issued threat. Understanding dawned in the slitted look the mercenary fixed on Kenrick.

"*Calasaar,*" he whispered, his pale tongue curling around the word in obvious, reverent wonder. The thick black beard split to reveal a grin of sharp yellowed teeth. "So, it is here after all. Le Nantres's guess was right."

"Where is Draec now?" Kenrick demanded.

"Closer than you could know." The man's ensuing chortle dissipated into a deep, wheezing cough. He spat blood onto the already red-stained straw.

"Tell us," Braedon snarled, pressing his blade to within a hairbreadth of the miscreant's throat. "What is the bastard up to?"

The man cursed them low under his breath, his string of black oaths swallowed up by a sudden commotion brewing up outside the lambing barn.

The guard posted there issued a stern order, but a female voice rose above it.

"I will not be turned away. You must let me in there!"

Dear God.

Haven.

"Keep her out," Kenrick called, hoping the sentry would obey him. "Do not permit her in here."

The sounds of struggle, of stubborn female determination, rang on the other side of the rickety barn door.

"You do not understand! Please, I must warn him. He could be in danger—"

In a confusion of creaking hinges and hasty scrambling, the panel burst open and Haven dashed into the gloom of the small outbuilding. She was breathless, her face flushed. She must have run on foot from the castle to the village. Her eyes were wild as she searched the dimness of the cramped space and found Kenrick.

Braedon's choice oath was echoed by Kenrick's own.

"God's blood," he shouted to his flummoxed guard. "Get her out of here!"

But it was too late. Haven was already running to his side.

And out of the corner of his eye, Kenrick saw the injured man begin to lunge to his feet in the stall. He leaped forth, snarling like the beast he truly was—a blur of seething darkness and biting talons that sunk into the bulk of Kenrick's shoulder.

❧ 18 ❧

HAVEN'S SCREAM TORE from her throat. The cry of shock, of bone-deep horror, rent the musty stillness of the barn as she saw Kenrick come under surprise attack from behind. The man who leaped on him—for she had been certain he was a man in the moment it took for her eyes to adjust to the gloom of the small barn—now bore the shape and manner of a beast.

Shifter.

The word was a hiss of memory that skated across her mind like a razor-sharp lance.

Night-black, bristly with a coat as thick as any wolf's, the creature seemed to possess an immense, other-worldly strength. It clung to Kenrick with sharp claws, its sudden writhing weight on his back driving him down on one knee. Savage jaws flashed bright and frenzied as the wolf sought to rip through the chain mail to the flesh of Kenrick's shoulder and neck.

The beast meant to kill him.

Shifter.

Haven shook away the pull of recall that seized her, all her focus—her very heart—rooted on Kenrick. She jolted forward, running the three steps that separated her from the spot where he struggled, but Braedon's stern voice halted her before she could reach him.

200

"Stay back!"

Braedon's sword was already swinging down in a punishing arc. The long blade of steel sunk into the side of the wolfish creature. It howled and thrashed, recoiling in pain.

Kenrick twisted out from under the bulky black body and threw it to the ground. His own blade sang a metallic shriek as he drew the weapon and drove it home.

Everything had happened so fast.

Haven looked to Kenrick, relief spilling over her to see that he was alive. He stood before her, torn and bloodied from the fight, his face hard, as unforgiving as his sword, which was gripped in his hand and dripping with the lifeblood of the creature who would have killed him in those frenzied moments. At his feet lay the beast.

Save that it was no longer beast, but man.

Dark, dying eyes stared back at her from a face gone slack with the coming of the end. One large hand lay stretched out in her direction, hard fingers reaching toward her as though to entreat her while those dulling eyes held her in unspoken contempt.

In that moment, her gaze compelled by all she had seen—by what was rippling into her mind like a returning tide—Haven could not move.

She knew him.

Faith . . . she had seen this man before.

His breath rattled out of him in a slow, broken wheeze. And in the moment before life dimmed from his glittering gaze, the thick black beard split into a leering, bloody grin.

This man, this vile creature, had recognized her, too.

He had been at Greycliff that night, she was certain of it.

He had stood near her in the smoke-filled darkness of the keep as it went up in flames. Heaven above, but she could hear his growling voice grating in her ear—a shout gone up to spare no one, not even the smallest child.

Horrific words.

A hellish command.

"Haven." Kenrick's voice sifted past the jolting awareness that had so suddenly overcome her. He took a step toward where she stood. "Haven, it is all right now. 'Tis over."

She shook her head, an unconscious denial that she felt to her very marrow.

"No," she murmured, knowing for certain whatever had transpired there was not over.

The danger she had sensed the night before was only intensifying. It was brushing up against her, twisting around her legs like a cat. She saw it in the sightless gaze of the man who stared at her even now, his dead but leering grin chilling her like ice at her nape.

"I have to get out of here," she gasped.

"Haven."

"No." Kenrick held out his hand to her, but she flinched away from him, taking a few careless steps in retreat. "I have to . . . get out of this place. I cannot . . . Oh, faith, I cannot breathe."

Pivoting on her heel, she stumbled forward, back toward the open door of the barn. She pushed away the sentry's hand as he tried to catch her, to hold her at his lord's command. With a wordless cry, Haven righted herself and bolted into the blinding sunlight outside.

Kenrick called out to her, but she could not bring herself to halt or turn back. She flew out of the barn and began running.

Running from the disturbing truth of what she had witnessed in the barn—and from the sudden flood of memories that rose to choke her when she thought of the horror that had transpired at Greycliff Castle some weeks ago.

Kenrick saw the look of distress in Haven's eyes in the instant before she fled the barn. While few sane people would credit what had occurred—the incredible transformation that had played out as the Anavrin shifter vaulted into his attack—Kenrick felt certain that in some way, Haven did understand. There had been a flicker of recognition behind her astonishment, a reflexive jolt of awareness that said this had not been the first time she had witnessed the dark doings of Silas de Mortaine's henchmen.

Haven might have recognized the evil at work, but she could not be expected to cope with the stunning horror of it, certainly not alone.

And if any of de Mortaine's minions yet lurked about Clairmont's grounds, the very last thing Kenrick wanted was to think of Haven unwittingly meeting up with them in her current state of panic.

"Go after her," Braedon said, confirming Kenrick's look with a grave nod of his head. His mouth twisted as he glanced in the direction of the fallen shifter. "I'll manage this offal without you."

Without further word or delay, Kenrick lunged for the open door of the barn.

A field hand stood outside near the fenced yard. He glanced at Kenrick's fierce expression, then gestured toward the path leading to the steep castle motte. "She headed up that way, m'lord."

But Kenrick had already spied her fleeing form on the road. He ran to his mount and vaulted astride it. A jab of his heels sent the white charger into a full gallop on the dusty path. He would catch up to her quickly, save that Haven suddenly veered off the path and into the forest ridge that ran along one side of Clairmont's property.

"Haven, wait!" he shouted to her, but she paid him no heed.

With an oath, Kenick urged his horse into a faster pace, hauling on the reins when he reached the place where Haven had disappeared. His feet hit the soft earth with a thud as he jumped down to follow her on foot. A section of ancient stone fence had been toppled in this spot. Kenrick leaped over the lichen-covered rubble and stretched his legs into a sprint as he chased after Haven.

The forest thicket was dense with new spring growth. Heavy ivy twisted on the ground, crisp green leaves crushing underfoot. The tightly woven ground cover proved a boon, aiding Kenrick in quickly spying Haven's path through the bramble and farther into the woods. She had run with aimless haste; Kenrick tracked her with careful expedience.

And he found her soon enough.

He spotted a bright patch of blue among the verdant expanse of the forest. Resting her back against a moss-patched slab of boulder, Haven's shoulders fair shook, her chest rising and falling with the swift breaths she took into her lungs. She heard his approach and immediately jumped to alertness. Her head pivoted toward him, the loose strands of her hair flying about her like auburn fire.

"It's all right," he told her. "You don't need to run from me. It's all right."

She moved away from the rock, a cautious look flashing in the wildness of her eyes. She took a hesitant step, and for a moment Kenrick expected her to begin her flight anew. But she did not.

"Kenrick," she cried, and launched herself toward him.

He caught her in his arms and held her close, his heart racing, clenching tight as a fist to feel her clinging to him with such need. Such undeniable trust.

Kenrick lifted her face and pressed his mouth to hers. It was a chaste kiss, one of comfort and understanding. Of reassurance that she was safe with him.

"Are you all right?"

She did not seem capable of speaking. A strangled sound caught in her throat, but she gave him a small nod.

"Jesu Criste," he swore against her heated brow. "Don't ever run from me like that again."

She burrowed deeper into his embrace. Never had he felt this vulnerability in her, this total trust that he would protect her, and that she would accept that protection. He realized suddenly that she was trembling. His fiery lady, who seemed to fear nothing short of death itself, was shaking with a tremor that seemed rooted in her very core.

"Why did you come down here?" he asked, his own voice unsteady as he held her. "Why would you risk such a thing?"

"I had to warn you."

"Warn me of what?"

She clung to him a bit tighter, her arms wrapped about his waist as though to never let go. "Last night, after I returned to my room . . . I thought I saw something outside the keep. I . . . *felt* something. Something cold and dangerous that seemed to be reaching out for me through the dark. It was him, Kenrick. I didn't know it last night, but when I saw him back there, after he attacked you—"

"You've remembered something."

Kenrick did not ask it of her, for there was no need. He had read her expression in the barn, just as he could now read the source of her distress in every quiver of her limbs.

"Something has come back to you, hasn't it?"

"Yes." The whisper was but a trace of sound that he felt more than heard.

"There is no need to fear the memories, Haven. They cannot harm you."

She twisted her face away from him, squeezing her eyes closed as if the memory of that fiery night seared her just to think on it. "You don't know . . . you cannot know . . ."

"Tell me. You must tell me what you remember."

When she finally spoke again, her voice was quiet but steady with certainty. "He was there, Kenrick. That man, he was one of the raiders who attacked Greycliff."

"Is he the one who attacked you?"

She slowly shook her head, then gave a weak shrug of confusion. "I don't know. I don't think so . . . but that face—I'd seen him before. Back there, in the barn, as he was dying, he looked at me as though he had seen me before as well. He reached for me. Faith, but I swear he looked right through me."

Kenrick gathered her close, resting his cheek against the delicate shell of her ear. "Think on him no more. He cannot hurt you now."

"He was at Greycliff, I'm certain of it. He was one of the men who killed your friends."

Although it had not taken Haven's confirmation to convince him of that fact, Kenrick's blood seethed anew when he thought of Rand and his family being butchered by beasts like the one lying dead in the lambing barn. "I will see every last one of his kind dead at the end of my blade," he vowed.

"His kind," she murmured, a note of distress catching in her throat. "Kenrick, there is a name for his kind."

"Shapeshifter," he said. "I know what he is—what he *was*. That cur back there is one of several such men under the command of Silas de Mortaine. I have seen them change from man to beast, even mirroring the form of another man."

Haven's grasp on him loosened, then slowly broke away. She pulled out of his arms to take a handful of steps back, holding herself as though to ward off a deep chill. "Faith, Kenrick, but you speak of this with such calm acceptance. Have you no idea the power de Mortaine holds if he commands this brand of magic? How do you expect to fight enemies like these?"

"With steel and will. The same as any other battle."

"This is not a simple battle. You know that." She pivoted to look at him, her pretty face marred with scratches gained in her flight, her sensual mouth lined thinly white with anxiety. "Kenrick. I do not think this is a battle you can win."

Her doubt made him bristle. "I will, or I'll die trying."

A look of sadness passed over her features. "My dear, foolish lord. Don't you see?" She caught her lip between her teeth but seemed unable to bite back the little hitch in her voice. "That is verily what I fear the most."

Kenrick stared at her through the small space of coolly shaded forest that separated them. He had never seen her look more vulnerable, nor more openly caring of him. Her body trembled, but despite the small quiver of uncertainty that gripped her, Haven held herself with the regal poise of a woodland queen.

He had told himself—and her—that he would not touch her again, but that pledge fell away like an autumn leaf drifting on the wind.

Three paces brought him to the place where she stood.

With reverent fingers, he tilted her chin up and gazed softly into her eyes. There was no need for words. Kenrick dipped his head down and brushed his lips over hers, kissing her with tender care and an affection that ran deeper than he thought possible. Slowly, they parted, only to join again, mouths meeting with sweet abandon and an honest need that neither was able, or willing, to deny.

"I don't want to let you go," Haven murmured against his lips.

"Nor I you," he admitted, his voice thick and husky, little better than a growl. "But we cannot stay out here. You will be safer behind Clairmont's walls. Besides that, I am unfit to hold you so long as I wear the taint of that creature's blood on me."

With great reluctance he pulled away. Their hands remained joined, fingers laced together, clinging tight.

"Come with me, Haven. It is not safe out here. Let me take you back to the keep now."

The invitation smoldered with meaning, but he could not hide his desire for her. Feeling the danger that had been so close to them that morning only made him yearn more deeply for the comfort of his lady's embrace.

For the warmth of her sweet curves nestled against him, skin on skin.

She knew what he asked of her; those quick green eyes were dusky with understanding. She gazed at him in silence, then moved toward him with a welcoming acceptance that nearly undid him where he stood.

❧ 19 ❧

THEY RODE WITHIN the weight of a knowing silence from the village back to Clairmont Castle. Perched sidesaddle behind him, Haven clung to Kenrick's firm waist, her cheek pressed against the solid warmth of his back. There was comfort in his nearness, an indescribable sense of belonging.

Of trust.

Despite all she had seen that morning, she felt safe with him.

Despite the shadowy pull of memory that lapped at the edges of her mind like a dark, rising tide, she felt certain that no ill would befall her. Nothing evil could touch her when she had Kenrick holding fast to her, his strong fingers caressing the sensitive skin of her wrist while he guided the horse up the motte and into the shelter of Clairmont's inner bailey.

He reined in, then dismounted and helped her down. A squire took the horse's lead and walked it to the stable, while two others rushed over to assist Kenrick in removing his tunic of chain mail.

"Tell the servants to send a bath to my chamber," he instructed one of the attending youths.

"Is everything all right, my lord?" asked the boy. He was staring at the bloodstains on Kenrick's tunic and mail, blood that told the tale of a death served but a short while ago. Then his glance slid to Haven and the scratches that marred her cheek and brow from her abandoned flight. "What happened, my lord? I pray your injuries are not grave."

"The blood belongs to another man," Kenrick assured him, wrapping his arm protectively around Haven's shoulders. "Send for the bath, and a flagon of wine as well. Go on, lad, and be quick with it."

With an obedient nod, the squire loped off to carry out the order.

Haven knew it was unseemly to cling to Kenrick like she was, but after what she had seen, she needed his support. His strength was reassuring in ways she could not explain, and the mere presence of him—his touch alone—banished all dark thoughts the way no balm ever could.

She cocooned herself in his embrace as they crossed from the stable yard to the keep. Despite the intimacy of the picture they must have displayed to the folk, no one murmured a single untoward word. A few pairs of eyes glanced up in curiosity, peering in quizzical speculation at their lord and the unlikely woman under his arm, but not so much as a whisper followed their ascent up the short steps to the tower.

To the sanctuary of Kenrick's private solar.

Although he had not said as much, Haven knew where he would lead her once they were behind the closed door of his chamber.

She knew it the instant before he kissed her in the forest glen. She knew it when he asked her to return with him to the castle. And she knew it now, as they strolled through the entryway of Clairmont's majestic fortress.

Almost unconsciously, Haven paused, drawing herself out of Kenrick's warmth. Doubt niggled at the edges of her mind, warning bells that tolled a dim alarm. There would be no turning back once she took the first step that led to his bedchamber.

"Kenrick . . ."

She meant to deny him, but the words would not come. Only dark thoughts seeped into her mind, clawing at her with renewed force now that she was separated from him and standing apart in the cool shade of the corridor.

"I will keep you safe," he said quietly. "My sword arm and my life. That was my vow, Haven."

"Yes."

She closed her eyes, hearing the sincerity of his promise. Believing it. Savoring the sweetness of what she had found in the arms of this warrior with a poet's soul.

When she lifted her lids, it was to see Kenrick waiting patiently before her. He extended his hand out to her, his strong fingers cutting through a nimbus of sunlight that poured down from a high arched window at the end of the corridor.

Kenrick of Clairmont, the unreadable, unreachable lord, wanted her.

He needed her, perhaps as much as she needed him, if the intensity of his gaze told her true. His blue eyes captivated her in a stare that was both strong and vulnerable at once. He said nothing, merely reached out to her in wordless entreaty.

Haven slipped her fingers through his and climbed with him up the circling stairwell.

The solar at the top of the towering keep was locked as always, Kenrick's private quarters and the secrets he protected within barred from all. He paused there and withdrew a key from his baldric to free the iron latch, which fell open in his palm. He pushed open the thick oak door and led Haven within, his easy grasp on her hand a steady reassurance as he brought her into the large chamber.

The pale radiance of morning lit the broody solar from between the slats of half-opened shutters. A thready spring breeze drifted in, riffling the pages of the journals and ledgers that lay on the large desk nearby. Haven watched as a loose sheet of parchment lifted on the slender breeze and skated to the edge, a hairbreadth from slipping to the floor. Knowing that Kenrick was ever protective of his work, sensitive that no one observe what he studied, Haven waited for Kenrick to release her and attend the desk and its neat array of documents.

But he paid little mind to the errant parchment . . . or anything else. His focus seemed unerringly fixed on her as he guided her into the center of the sanctuary that so few were permitted to breach.

And so long as he was touching her, holding her in the simmering intensity of his gaze, Haven paid heed to little else as well.

With the edge of his thumb, he tenderly dabbed at the scratch on her cheek. His hand lingered at her face, idly stroking the sensitive skin near her ear. Slowly, his fingers drifted toward her mouth. It took no coaxing for her to meet his touch with with a slight brush of her lips; no persuasion at all for her to tip her head back and accept his gentle kiss.

Kenrick's lips met hers with warm restraint, the soft caress of his mouth wringing a sigh of pleasure from somewhere deep inside of her.

He broke away too soon, a look of anguish in his eyes. "My lady, this will change everything between us. I need to know you understand."

"Yes," she whispered, fully willing to give him whatever he wanted of her. "I know what I am giving you, Kenrick."

"Do you?" He searched her gaze with an intensity that stole her breath, his big, warm hands framing her face. "I would have you, Haven, and allow no one else to come between us. Now or later. The thought that there might be someone in your past, anyone who might rightfully claim you once your memory is restored—"

"No." She shook her head, refusing to accept even the possibility. "There is no one else. I know it with every particle of my being. There is no one . . . save you, Kenrick."

He stroked her brow as she whispered her assurances, his eyes darkened to stormy indigo, smoldering with such desire it left her legs weak beneath her.

Tenderly, he bent his head and kissed her once more.

Where their earlier encounters had been wild with a passion barely containable, now, when acceptance of what was to pass between them smoldered so surely in their gazes, they proceeded with measured care, with a slow and welcoming tenderness that burned all the hotter for its patience.

For long moments, they held each other thus, their kisses playing out, deepening in unhurried sweetness as the breeze danced across the floor and the sun stretched fingers of embracing warmth around them.

Haven lost herself to the pleasure of Kenrick's kiss, to the power of the man who held her as though she would shatter in his strong arms if he did not have a care. In spite of the heat in his gaze, and the need that fairly thrummed through him and into her, Kenrick was tender and patient.

He wanted her; there could be no doubting that. But their pace would be hers, and Haven could think of no stronger spell than the one he seduced her with in that moment.

Her head was reeling, her body fairly humming with the potent sensations he stirred in her with just one endless kiss. His fingers were firm against her nape, curving strong and warm on her skin as he pulled her closer to him. Dizzy with desire, Haven hardly heard the knock on the chamber door.

"That will be the bath," Kenrick murmured across her lips, reluctance edging every word as he broke their kiss and put a small space between them. His gaze was hooded, lazily confident and deepest blue as he stepped back from her, then called for the servants to enter.

In no time at all, the round wooden tub was set and steaming water poured to fill it. A decanter of warm mulled wine and two cups were placed on a hearthside pedestal. The group of servants completed their task in mindful silence, with quick efficiency, but even those spare moments out of Kenrick's embrace seemed to last forever.

Already the cold of his absence was seeping into the core of her, the darkness of memories struggling to surface loomed like a chasm splitting wide before her, unsettling the ground beneath her feet. She turned away, battling the sudden rush of unpleasant thoughts, of disturbing recollections, that rose to assail her in the moments she was out of Kenrick's arms.

Behind her she heard the soft scuff of retreating feet,

then the quiet thud and snick of metal as the servants made their exit and the chamber door closed on their heels.

Kenrick's hand brushed the back of her neck as he swept her unbound hair aside, baring her skin to his touch . . . to his kiss.

"You are trembling, Haven."

"Am I?"

"Aye, lady. Like a leaf before a storm. Do you not wish to be here with me? God's love, how I want you— I need you—but I could never cause you any fear or distress."

"No." She gave a weak shake of her head. "Never. 'Tis just . . ."

"Tell me." His mouth seared the delicate hollow behind her ear, his low rolling voice driving the darkness of her thoughts back into the shadows.

"The memories," she whispered, scarcely able to speak for the dizzying sparks of pleasure that ignited with Kenrick's every stroke of his fingers, every seductive press of his lips as he kissed a trail of heat along her neck and into the curve of her shoulder. "My memories are dark. They grasp at me sometimes. I can feel their claws sinking into me, dragging me down . . ."

"You are safe," Kenrick murmured. "There is naught to harm you here."

"There is no safety where the memories would lead me. I can feel that much. And today, that man in the barn—I just . . . I don't want to relive that night anymore. It hurts to think on it."

"I know, sweeting. I know." With gentle hands at her shoulders, Kenrick slowly turned her around to face him. "No one should be made to witness the hell you knew in Greycliff's raid. I would make it better for you if I could."

Haven burrowed into the warmth of his arms, pressing her cheek against his chest. "You do make it better. Just feeling your arms around me banishes the horror of it . . . and the pain."

"Then let me hold you, my lady." Taking her hand in his, he guided her toward the waiting bathtub near the fireplace. "There is only us now. Let's wash away all traces of that night and this morning. Let me hold you."

She walked the few scant paces with him, her fingers caught loosely in his. He brought her near the steaming pool of the bath, stripped off his soiled tunic and tossed it aside. Bare chested and glorious, he began to slowly disrobe her. Haven stood there, his willing thrall, as he untied the laces of her gown. The silk cording whispered out of its neat row of eyelets, then softly fell in a small coil at her feet.

Kenrick bent his head and kissed her as his deft fingers sought the loosened bodice that now sagged in a revealing crush between her breasts. His hand slid within, seeking out and finding the aching buds of her nipples. The little peaks surged tighter at his touch, yearning for more of his caress. She wanted more . . . so much more.

There was no curbing her small moan of dismay as he left off, moving his hands away from the needy ache of her breasts to slide her loosened bodice over her shoulders.

The gown made a slow descent down the length of her body, leaving her standing before him in naught but the thin covering of her shift.

"Still you tremble," he murmured, his heavy-lidded gaze dragging up to meet her own.

"From pleasure," she said. "And from anticipation."

His smile was a wicked twist of his lips that fair stole her breath. So handsome was he, her golden lord. As handsome and as darkly skilled as the most learned sorcerer.

"What is it you crave of me?" he asked, deviltry gleaming in the muted indigo of his eyes. "My touch, perhaps?"

She could not speak, for in that moment he cupped her breast in his palm, smoothing the pad of his thumb over the taut crown of her nipple, which rose like a pebble beneath her chemise.

"Mayhap you crave my kiss."

The sweet torment of his touch was compounded at once with the heat of his mouth on hers. He teased her lips with a sensual joining that sent quivers of sensation to the very core of her being. Too soon, he broke their kiss to trace his mouth along her jaw, then down the column of her throat. He sampled her skin with what seemed a barely restrained hunger, his teeth nicking here and there as he made a moist, burning path to the shallow dip at the base of her neck.

She dropped her head back and let him plunder at will, only vaguely aware of the scuttling chill of air that hit her bared flesh as Kenrick untied the ribbon of her chemise and eased the fine undergarment off her body.

A note of tenderness dimmed his gaze as he caught sight of the bandage wrapped about her shoulder.

"Will it hurt you at all . . ."

"No," she replied, moved by his gentle care, which was unnecessary. The wound did not pain her any longer. It was all but healed in the short time since she had been at Clairmont, the new skin concealed by the pristine bandage that covered it.

Kenrick gave her no time to think on the queer healing of her injury. He stooped down before her, tasting his way into the heart of her bosom.

With caressing hands and a questing mouth, he laved her breasts both in turn. Jolts of desire arced through her as he suckled her nipples, teasing the tender buds until she could scarce endure the pleasure. He kissed the narrow space between them, pausing to sample the bouyant swell and the sensitive skin beneath it.

Then his kiss drifted lower still.

Haven sucked in a breath of shock to feel his mouth skim along her belly. His tongue darted into the cleft of her navel, the sensation so purely sensual—so unexpected— she jerked in reaction. He steadied her with gentle hands splayed at her hips.

"Trust me, sweetness. I want you very much, but I vow I will take things slow between us now."

Haven's answer was a deep, throaty sigh. "Oh my dear, noble lord," she gasped, body quivering at his every touch. "Your skilled restraint is like to be my undoing."

But he seemed disinclined to give her quarter. Every seductive stroke of his mouth and lips and tongue made her yearn for more. As though he sensed this about her, he proceeded with maddening patience, as if he meant to sample every inch of her in his own time.

Such exquisite torment.

He paused in his slow unraveling of her senses, and drew back from her slightly. Where his mouth had ceased its exploration, now his gaze began to drink her in. Haven felt the heat of that gaze like a thousand fingers of flame. Tickling, teasing, his eyes traced a path of hungry indigo fire from her own yearning gaze, to her parted lips which still tingled from his kisses, to the rosy crowns of her breasts, and on . . . to the smoothness of her belly, and the thatch of dark amber curls nestled between her thighs.

His gaze was so nakedly lustful it scorched her, but if she burned, it was with wanton bliss. And a keening need for more of all he would give her.

"You are beautiful, Haven. So incredibly soft. Every bit of you so tempting."

Kenrick was on his knees before her.

Faith preserve her, but he was poised so close to the core of her femininity that his rough, fast-soughing breath stirred the flossy patch of down. He bent forward, and shocked her with the sudden press of his lips against her.

Haven arched taut at the contact, torn between moving away and toward the unexpected contact. But Kenrick's hands were firm at her hips, holding her in place as his tongue slid along the crevice of her womanhood. She cried out, unable to bear the sweet torture of his intimate kiss. His tongue was slick and hot, parting her like a flower. Her body wept for him, drawing taut as a bowstring with every flick of his sorcerer's tongue. He found the bud of her desire and sampled it with dizzying strokes, working a spell of dark seduction on the part of her that knew no shame.

But he took just a taste, enough to wring an anguished moan from her lips, and then he was gone.

"You are sweeter than any honey," he whispered, his voice thick as he glided his hands down the length of her thigh. "Softer than the finest silk."

He pressed a kiss to the tender skin, and gently lifted her slippered foot onto his lap. Her shoe came off as his lips teased the slight bend of her knee. As though she were made of glass, he carefully placed her bare foot down on the woven mat of rushes. Then he did likewise to her other leg, masterfully removing the last of her clothing and leaving her standing before him utterly nude and trembling with sensation.

"Your bath awaits, my lady."

His stare narrowed slightly as she shook her head.

"Our bath," Haven corrected him.

Her fingers toyed at the rolled waistband of his trousers. The drawstring ties hung down from the knot that held his remaining clothing. She could not keep her gaze from drifting to the pronounced rise of his loose-fitting garb. His arousal strained high and proud, the blunt tip outlined by the linen draping him like a tent.

Haven swallowed, her throat parched with desire. Kenrick stood before her like some lord of legend, a towering golden idol of sinew and strength, and seductive splendor. He looked more warrior than poet now, an unholy vision of pure masculinity that called to something deep and primal within her.

Her wanton gaze would not leave that part of him that was steel and silk combined. She caught the tail of one drawstring cord and tugged it loose. Her fingers brushed against him—only the slightest whisper of contact—but his arousal leaped within its fabric confines. Haven smiled up at him, knowing the impatience he wore so visibly in his taut expression. It had been hers but a moment ago, the resonant pulse of desire still thrumming through her like the beat of tiny drums. She knew the exquisite anguish of longing, and she wanted to deal it as surely as had been dealt to her.

She leaned in and placed an open kiss on Kenrick's bare chest, suckling the flat disk of his nipple between her teeth. Her tongue circled the male bud, drawing it tight. Then she withdrew, denying him when he grew still under her mouth, his breath rasping out of him on a curse.

She went back to the tied points of his hose and braies, allowing her fingers to drift across the hard plane of his abdomen before she sought another of the knotted strings. Kenrick jerked under her barest touch, his golden skin sheening and hot beneath her fingertips. He made a strangled sound in the back of his throat, an impatient sound that gave Haven a measure of supreme satisfaction. When he reached down to assist her in undressing him, Haven placed her hand over his, halting his impatient fingers.

"We are to take this slowly," she said, reminding him of his own pledge that nearly drove her to madness. "No rushing, was that not what we agreed?"

His answering chuckle was deep with amusement. "You are too clever by half, sweet witch."

Haven only smiled, then returned to the enticing completion of her task. A second tied knot came free with measured deliberation. The others fell in likewise fashion, slowly, one after another, until just one slender strand remained. Kenrick watched her with smoldering interest, a purely male smile curving the corner of his mouth.

Holding the indigo fire of his gaze, she tugged the final lacing that concealed him from her full view.

Kenrick's low oath held far more reverence than curse

as Haven slipped her palms between the slack linen and the velvety firmness of his hips. She eased his trousers down, sinking to her knees before him as she smoothed her hands along his legs from muscular thigh to tendoned ankle. His feet were bare; he had no doubt removed his boots surreptitiously while she was busy losing herself to the seductive wonder of his touch.

Haven carefully stripped him of his hose and braies, then she leaned back to look upon the naked splendor of her golden warrior.

He was magnificent.

Faith, but it had been easy enough before to see why the castle maids whispered of him with girlish shades of pink in their cheeks, all of them flirting with the aloof overlord as much as they stood wary of his stoic, secretive manner.

Now, gazing upon him here, Haven knew the weight of that feminine desire some hundredfold. Kenrick was a vision of masculine perfection, from his golden crown of close-cropped hair, to his broad shoulders, bronzed chest, and trim, muscular waist.

And there was more perfection the farther she dared to glance.

Although she had anticipated nothing less, seeing that part of Kenrick that was unabashedly, impressively male, stole her breath. She could not keep from staring at the rigid beauty of him . . . nor could she resist the sudden overwhelming urge to touch.

His flesh leaped at the first brush of her fingertips. Haven stroked him softly, utterly intrigued with the incredible satin smoothness that sheathed so much steely strength. His sex was thick and large in her palm, its heavy girth filling her hand from the tips of her fingers to past her wrist. A drop of moisture beaded at its blunt crown, a silky warmth that dampened her fingers as she dared to stroke him.

At Kenrick's low growl, Haven dragged her gaze up the golden length of his body. He was watching her with an intensity that made her stomach quiver. His sensual mouth was held taut, his fine nostrils flaring with every breath that rasped into his lungs. And his eyes—mercy, but the look in his eyes was so feral, so heated and raw, Haven knew not whether her boldness pleased him or enraged him.

"If you wish me to stop . . ." she said, her voice trailing off as she glided her fingertips along the underside of his shaft, from the thick base of his sex to the glistening head. "I don't know quite how . . . to touch you."

"Aye, you do, my lady. You are but a breath away from unmanning me where I stand."

His hands played over her bare shoulders, and along the curve and swell of her breasts. Haven reveled in his touch, in the hungered way he stroked her skin. His fingers were warm and strong as he caressed her nape, then plunged them into the mass of hair that cascaded down her bare back. He lifted the heavy tresses, crushing and sifting them through his fingers and letting her hair fall in waves around her.

"Come up here now," he commanded her in a rough whisper.

Haven obeyed the gentle pressure of his hands beneath her arms, allowing him to assist her back onto her feet. He stroked her face, frowning slightly as his finger traced around the inflamed scratch that slashed down the slope of her cheek. With a tender look, he leaned to retrieve a small folded cloth from the edge of the bathtub. He bent to soak it in the steaming water, wrung it out, then carefully blotted at her small injury.

She was in no pain at all, but his tender ministrations soothed her. Each stroke of his touch, each caring glance, delivered her farther and farther away from the disturbing events of that morning. With Kenrick there was only light and warmth and peace. There was trust as well, something that did not come easily to her . . . or to him.

Haven accepted his care now, and the sensual promise of what was to come. She brought her hands up to caress his back as he cleansed her, her fingers tracing along the sinewy ropes that twisted and flexed as he moved. Their bodies brushed together, her breasts against his chest, their thighs smoothing together in pleasing friction with every touch.

She did not realize he had set down the cloth until he was tipping her chin up to meet him as he bent to claim her mouth in a passionate kiss.

Haven's senses swirled wildly under the heat of his lips on hers. His hand drifted down her body, down and down, until she felt his fingers wade through the curls between her legs. One blunt finger slid into the moist cleft, parting her to his brazen touch. She groaned as he teased her dewy folds, spreading sensual fire through every fiber of her being. She felt her limbs begin to quake beneath her, like butter melting in the sun.

"Sweet witch," he murmured along the edge of her mouth. "My beautiful, mysterious lady . . . I think the bath must needs wait."

Haven opened her eyes to meet his gaze. Her heart was racing. Inside, she felt molten and shimmering with a need she could not define. Kenrick kissed her again, this time with a fierceness that nigh overwhelmed her. His tongue slid past her lips, past her teeth, thrusting with an animal need she felt echoed within herself.

"Yes," she gasped when her breath was once again her own. "Oh, Kenrick . . . yes."

He hesitated not for an instant.

Sweeping her up into his strong arms, he turned away from the wreathing steam of the bathtub and carried her across the solar to the adjoining bedchamber. Haven nestled into his firm chest, drowning herself in the delicious scent of his bare skin. Part spice and warm man, part musk and rich claret wine, he was an intoxicating balm to the fever raging in her blood.

In the short time it took to reach the large bed in his private antechamber, Haven was all but lost to him. He set her down on the thick mattress, plush fur tickling her backside as she sank deeply into the coverlets spread over the bed.

Now that she was there, now that she was looking at his bold, naked form as he looked down at her from beside the bed, Haven knew a shiver of doubt.

Forbidden, her conscience warned.

Forbidden to touch his kind.

Forbidden to care for him.

His expression muted as he gazed at her, from needful hunger to intuitive concern. "What is it, love?"

"I don't . . ." She gave a weak shake of her head on the bolster. "I don't know . . ."

He bent down to smooth the hair from her brow. "If you do not wish to lie with me," he said, the coarse sound of his voice betraying the deepness of his need, "I will not force you. You must know this."

"Yes, I know. There is nowhere else I want to be than here . . . with you."

His answering smile dazzled her. His mouth curved with affection and not a little satisfaction as he reached out to take her hand in his. He placed her palm flat against the center of his chest, where his heartbeat thudded with rapid strength. She felt his life vibrantly pulse there, saw his honesty, his soul-deep honor, gleaming in the dark gemstone blue of his gaze.

"Your spell is thorough, sweet witch. I am yours to command." He lifted her hand to his mouth then, kissing each fingertip with reverent care. "If you wish me to stop . . . at any time . . . you need only say it."

Haven closed her eyes at the sweetness of his declaration. She knew he spoke true; no matter his own need, he would cease if she willed it.

But turning him away was the last thing she wanted when she searched her heart for a reason for her trepidation. Kenrick was all that was solid and good in her life now. Indeed, already his touch was chasing away the darkness of doubt that had been grasping for her.

Forbidden. . . .

The warning was just a whisper now and fading. Haven knew not where it came from, nor why she should mistrust her feelings for Kenrick.

She opened her eyes to find him standing beside the bed unmoving, stoically awaiting her decision. He still held her hand. Haven slowly retracted it, clasping her fingers around his and guiding him toward her. He sat down beside her on the mattress, glorious in his nudity, his sex thrust high and eager between his thighs.

"You are certain?" he asked.

Haven nodded once, met his probing gaze, then nodded again.

His exhaled sigh held a weight of feeling that said much of his desire for her. He kissed the heart of her palm, a slow, sensual kiss that sent spiraling flames into her very core. With his gaze locked on hers, Kenrick guided her hand down to the blunt spear of his manhood and wrapped her fingers around him.

Haven delighted in her further exploration of this fascinating part of him that responded so deliciously to her touch. As she stroked and teased him, Kenrick began a likewise exploration of her. Bracing himself over her, with one hand fisted beside her to prop up his weight, the other hand made a tactile study of every exposed inch of her skin.

"You feel like velvet under my hand," he told her, worshipping her breasts and arms, then her belly and the tender skin of her hips. "You feel like velvet flames, warm and soft and bewitching enough to consume a man's mind." He gave her a wicked smile. "And a man's body."

Haven could not respond, even if she'd had her wits enough to offer a clever reply. Her mind was caught in a heavenly conflagration, her body as well, for Kenrick's touch was venturing to places far more sensitive.

Places far more sacred.

She bit her lip but could not contain her soft mewl of pleasure as Kenrick's fingers cupped her mound. He teased her there, making her writhe and yearn for more.

"So wet," he murmured, playing at the petals of her womanhood with wicked mastery. "So sweet."

He pivoted, and slowly descended on her with a deep, carnal kiss.

Haven's spine arched at the stunning heat of his mouth closing over her sex. He nuzzled her close, breathing her in. Faith preserve her, but he was lapping at her, suckling her with the devilish tip of his tongue.

Something queer began to happen to her as Kenrick feasted on her so passionately. She felt weighted down, coiled and captured by unseen bonds. She could not move, could hardly breathe for the sudden stiffness of her body. All thought, all feeling, centered on the shocking pressure—the sensual heat of Kenrick's kiss.

Pleasure shot through her like a bolt: pure light, piercing, rooting her beneath him on the bed. His kiss deepened, and she heard herself cry out in helpless wonder. Heat shimmered along her limbs, her madness climbing when she felt the blunt penetration of Kenrick's finger sliding inside her.

"Kenrick," she whispered. "Oh, faith . . ."

She could say no more, for he began a rhythm of thrusting and withdrawing that left her incapable of anything but the rapt indulgence of this spell he wove over her. She climbed a crest of astonishing pleasure, so intense it made her want to weep. She soared higher, and higher still, until she felt certain she could bear no more. But Kenrick's masterful seduction gave no quarter. She cried out, breaking into pieces under his touch, spiraling in a tempest of utter, wordless joy. She fell as on a cloud, aware of naught but the shattering wonder of the moment.

"Criste, you are sweet," Kenrick growled, positioning himself atop her as she continued her heavenly descent. "I need you, Haven . . . now."

She felt his hardness pressing at the mouth of her womb. She was still reeling with pleasure, her body slick with passion, her legs slack and welcoming. The blunt head of his sex nestled easily at her threshold, a demanding presence that she craved like nothing she had ever known before. He nudged slightly, making clear what he meant to do.

"Yes," she sighed, tilting her pelvis to better greet him.

Haven moaned as he lowered himself to kiss her. Their mouths met in a hungry joining, and with a firm thrust of his hips, he buried himself fully inside her sheath. An exquisite fullness warmed her as their bodies adjusted to their mating, Kenrick moving only slightly, and she lying beneath him in a state of dazed bliss, tremors of pleasure still arrowing through her.

"We are a perfect fit," he said, dipping his head down to kiss the tip of her nose as he rocked within her in a controlled rhythm. "Do I please you, my lady?"

She gave him a lazy smile. "Aye, my lord. I am well pleased."

"Good."

He grinned, a broad and satisfied look of male pride. He flexed his hips again, his gaze on hers, watching as he claimed her. Each stroke deepened, each thrust held more power, until the heat between them surged into something primal and wild. Kenrick rose up, bending her knees to take her more fully. He was animal, and Haven delighted in his loss of control—in the power she seemed to wield over him as he rode her to the crest of his own release. He gave a coarse shout as his body constricted, the muscles in his chest taut, tendons in his neck engorged as he threw his head back and roared his pleasure.

He put his hands beneath her and lifted her up off the

mattress, withdrawing just as the heat of his spilling seed rained onto her thighs. The musky essence of their passion was a heady perfume, his sweat-sheened golden skin glittering like starlight. Haven could not resist tasting him. She bent her head and kissed the hollow of his shoulder, tracing her tongue along the salty-sweet warmth of him.

"God's love, woman," he panted as the shudders slowly subsided. "You will ruin me, I swear it. I'll never want to leave this room."

Haven nestled against him, fervently wishing they could stay there without end. But from a shadowed corner of her mind, an insidious voice warned that like the pleasure she had just been shown, this idyll she was living at Clairmont could not possibly last.

❧ 20 ❧

FOR SEVERAL GLORIOUS days the idyll did continue, and Haven found herself becoming more enmeshed in life at Clairmont, more a part of the keep and its folk. And every hour proved her more charmed and bedazzled by its enigmatic, golden lord.

Where Kenrick's work during the day kept him occupied and lamentably out of her company, by night he had shown her a sensual openness that knew no bounds. The passion he stirred in her was deep and lasting, a gift that almost compensated for the long hours that kept them apart while he sequestered himself behind the locked door of his private chambers in the tower.

On this particular day, a sunny morning that dawned bright and cloudless, Kenrick had invited Haven with him for a stroll in Ariana's gardens. She went gladly, unable to marshal her broad smile as he escorted her out into the courtyard. They walked with hands linked into the gated patch of flowers and greenery situated just below the towering keep.

"I have a surprise for you," Kenrick said as they strode into the center of the garden. "Close your eyes."

She shot him a questioning, curious look.

"Close them."

She obeyed, biting her lip as he guided her by the

232

hand to a point somewhere deep within the heart of the natural sanctuary. Her nose filled with the perfume of blooming flowers and fresh, fertile soil. There was something more as well, the faint aroma of baked bread and warm honey.

"Very well," Kenrick whispered beside her ear. "You may look now."

Haven opened her eyes and breathed a sigh of wonderment. "Oh, Kenrick! It is beautiful."

A small blanket, dusted with rose petals, had been spread on the ground, nestled among the flower beds and traveling ivy. At the center of it was a tempting collection of bread and cheese and sweets, all neatly arranged in a shallow basket. It was an enchanting sight, one that tempted her stomach and her eyes.

"Do you like it?"

She turned to look at him, beaming her joy. "Yes. I like it very much."

"Come."

He brought her forward with him onto the blanket, then seated himself near the basket. Haven joined him, folding her legs beneath her as she absorbed the glory that surrounded her. Nothing pleased her more than seeing Kenrick so close beside her, a smile curving his sensual mouth.

She could not resist his lips; she leaned over and gave him a tender kiss. "Thank you. This is lovely."

"I am pleased you approve, my lady." He reached into the basket for one of the honeyed tarts. "Try this."

He fed the sugary confection to her from his fingers, watching her eat it and smiling when she could not contain her moan of enjoyment. They shared much of the breakfast in companionable silence, reclining in each other's arms, content to be together in the tranquillity of the garden.

Her stomach happy, her heart squeezed with joy, Haven reached up to stroke Kenrick's face. "This is bliss," she said, curling into his arms on the blanket and watching as a hawk sailed high above. "I don't think I've ever known this much happiness."

Kenrick caught her fingers in his and brought her palm to his lips for a chaste kiss. "Nor I, lady. In truth, I did not think it possible."

Haven smiled up at him. "Mayhap we're dreaming. This could all be a fanciful imagining—our picnic among the flowers, the beauty of the sky above us . . . the warmth of your arms around me. All of it seems too rich to be reality."

"You have been like a dream in my bed, sweet witch." He gave her a lazy grin, but the spark of masculine interest in his eyes was anything but indolent. "Whatever spell you've cast, lady, you have cast it well."

He bent forward to kiss her parted lips, but the sound of approaching footsteps cut short the tender meeting of their mouths.

"Ahem," murmured one of the keep's young squires. He dropped his head in an apologetic bow, his downy cheeks sweeping red over his untimely intrusion. "Begging pardon, my lord. Lady Haven."

Kenrick cleared his throat as Haven hastily extricated herself from her sprawl across his lap. "What is it, Alfred?"

"Your mount is saddled and awaiting you in the stables, my lord."

He was leaving again? Haven's joy dissipated a fraction at this news.

"Thank you, Alfred," Kenrick replied, his gaze slanting toward Haven as she drew back on the blanket in a bit of a sulk. "I'll be along in a short while."

The youth nodded agreeably, his cheeks yet filled with color. His downcast eyes went furtively to his lord and the woman whom most of the keep regarded as Kenrick's leman. Not far from the truth, she admitted with chagrin.

When Alfred was gone, Kenrick moved closer to Haven on the blanket.

"Even my servants are under your spell, beauty. Poor Alfred could hardly keep his eyes from straying to you despite my presence."

He teased her nose with a curling end of her unbound hair, but she refused to let him win a smile that easily.

"They are sheepish around me because they know."

Kenrick lazily arched a brow. "What do they know?"

"That their lord has taken a common girl to his bed."

"I have done no such thing."

Haven frowned at him in question.

"You are the most *uncommon* girl I've ever known. And who I choose to take to my bed is hardly the business of the folk of Clairmont."

"You are too clever to believe that, I think." Haven huffed out her breath, only halfway mocking exasperation. "I am but another of their lord's odd interests. It is all they speak of lately, although they are careful to do so in hushed voices and behind shielding hands."

"Ah." Kenrick seemed to consider the matter at length. "And this makes you uncomfortable."

"A little, yes," she admitted.

"Then I shall assemble the keep in the hall tomorrow and speak with them about it."

"Nay!" she said, then laughed when she spied the teasing gleam in his eyes. "Do you seek to mortify me even more by calling attention to our . . . indiscretion?"

"Not at all," he answered, and suddenly his expression was all soberness with something tender underlying the serious tilt of his mouth. "The very last thing I wish is to make you uncomfortable, my lady."

"And I thank you for that, my lord."

He stroked his thumb along the line of her brow, then down the slope of her cheek. "I should think the gossip would end, were I to cease making you my mistress."

Haven went still, thinking at once how empty she would feel without Kenrick's touch, without the sheltering warmth of his embrace or the stirring sensuality of his body next to hers. She could suffer a thousand whispering gossips, but now that Kenrick had shown her the fire of passion, she wondered how she would endure a single night without him.

But she had presented him with a problem, and true to form, Kenrick meant to solve it.

"In truth," he said at last, his fingers pausing in their gentle play about her face and throat, "in truth, I have been giving the matter some thought. I had hoped I might discuss it with you upon my return later today, but now is likely as good a time as any."

"As you wish," Haven murmured, fearful of what was to come.

"It has been becoming apparent that I cannot let things go on between us like they have been. As pleasant as they may be."

Pleasant.

The word grated on her like a shard of glass. Could it be that what she had thought to be nothing short of paradise was, to him, merely a pleasant diversion? Could she have been so foolish to think she meant something to him—that she might have reached through to the heart and soul of him?

Kenrick's deep, thoughtful voice carried a note of finality. "Decisions need to be made, Haven. I wager the sooner, the better."

"Of course," Haven replied, or mayhap she merely thought the words. She was finding it hard to swallow past the knot that was rising in her throat, so she could not trust that she might have command of her voice.

She blinked up at him, awaiting his judgment.

Dreading it.

"I have important issues to attend here, life and death issues. I cannot afford to be distracted by the petty whisperings of my folk. Nor the whims of a mistress. Do you understand?"

Haven nodded, but only barely. She wanted to pull herself out of his loose embrace and run until her legs would carry her no farther. But she had no will to leave him, not even when he was sitting there, telling her he no longer wanted her.

"I have business in town, but in a few days I plan to travel to Cornwall and the village where you lived before the attack on Greycliff. I mean to look for answers about your past, and where you truly belong. I cannot continue on like this, waiting for your memory to return."

"I see." She closed her eyes to absorb the weight of his words, and felt his fingers beneath her chin. He lifted her face up, compelling her to look at him.

"I need to know that you understand, Haven. I cannot keep you as my lover any longer . . . I want you as my wife."

Haven was holding her breath, unaware of that fact until it rushed out of her in that next instant. "Your wife?"

"If it pleases you."

It did please her, immensely. But she could not help but notice that Kenrick spoke only of practicalities and logical solutions—nothing of his feelings for her. Nothing of love.

"I do not know what to say."

"Customarily, a woman either says yea or nay."

"Of course," she said, half laughing at her own fluster.

"Of course you will, or of course you won't?"

She met his intense stare and stifled a further giggle of emotion. "Yes, Kenrick. I will happily be your wife."

His smile warmed her thoroughly, though not more than his kiss. For long moments, they held each other in the peaceful Eden of the garden. Haven's heart was still soaring when Kenrick finally led her back into the castle so he could prepare for the trip that would take him away from Clairmont for several hours.

Ariana and Braedon were coming out of the solar together at the same time Kenrick and Haven strode into the keep hand in hand.

"Good morrow," Kenrick's sister said, her bright gaze lighting on the pair with keen interest. "You two are up and about early this morn."

"We just broke our fast in the garden," Haven replied, no doubt beaming her joy. "Kenrick surprised me with a picnic . . . and something else."

Ariana turned a wide-eyed look on her brother, but

before she could question him, Kenrick announced their plans.

"I have asked Haven to remain here at Clairmont . . . as my bride."

"Oh, Haven!" Ariana threw her arms around her in a tight hug. "That's wonderful!"

Braedon extended his hand to Kenrick, then offered his congratulations to Haven as well. "This calls for celebration."

"Yes, it does," Ariana agreed. "It happens that we have two things to celebrate: your happy news, and ours. Braedon and I will be welcoming the arrival of a babe later this year."

"Congratulations," Haven replied, thrilled for her friend and the dark knight who glowed his pride as he beheld his pretty wife.

"My best as well," Kenrick added with marked approval.

"Nothing pleases me more than to see the both of you happy," Ariana said. "We shall have a grand feast this evening to mark the occasion. Come with me, Haven. There is much we'll need to do."

Haven found herself easily swept up into Ariana's excitement. Before she was led away in hand by her sister-to-be, Kenrick caught her in a quick embrace. "I will see you upon my return later today."

"Aye, my lord," she whispered, melting with pure ecstatic wonder as he kissed her. "I will see you soon."

❧ 21 ❧

THE MORNING PASSED quickly enough in Kenrick's absence, for Ariana presented Haven with a list of things that must be done in preparation for the feast that evening, including a jaunt to a nearby village market.

With Braedon and a Clairmont guard overseeing their excursion, Haven and Ariana walked from one vendor's stall to another, perusing the wares and discussing the splendid meal Ariana was planning for that evening. By her rapt descriptions, it was to be a feast as grand as any Clairmont had ever seen.

"We have much to celebrate, after all," she said, hooking her arm through Haven's as she led her toward a table heaped with fine fabrics and lace.

The market was a churning hive of patrons and gawkers, the entire area abuzz with chattering, haggling, and general good cheer.

"Stay close," Braedon advised in his brooding way. "There are too many people here this morn. Too much opportunity for trouble."

"My husband worries overmuch," Ariana said, slanting him a teasing look. "Especially now that he knows I carry our child. Suddenly I am made of glass, isn't that right, husband?"

"I've not known glass to be so stubborn," he groused,

240

but could not hide his gentle regard. He playfully drummed his finger on her pate. "Nay, this pretty head is not glass at all, but hard, impervious steel."

Ariana gasped in mock affront. "For that remark, sirrah, you will come with me and help me choose a goose for tonight's sup. Or perhaps we should truss a disagreeable gander instead. Will you pardon us, Haven?"

Haven nodded, warmed by the affection so clearly shared between Ariana and her husband. She could only hope she and Kenrick might share the same bond in their marriage.

Marriage.

The word had meant little to her until Kenrick had said it that morning. He wanted her to be his bride! For all the murkiness and uncertainty of her past, her future at least seemed bright with promise.

Hope bloomed within her, as colorful as the silks that spread out before her on the vendor's table. Giddy with thoughts of her life to come, Haven picked up a length of wispy red sendal and held it out before her to watch it catch the light. The sun was blazing high in the noontide sky; through the swatch of rich cloth, it glowed like gemstone fire, dazzling her vision.

" 'Tis a beautiful bit of fluff," said a low voice that was tinged with a queer sense of familiarity.

Haven lowered her arms, feeling a knot of cold dread form in her stomach.

A man stood next to her at the vendor's stall, his longish black hair gleaming like polished jet, his smile deadly cool in his profanely handsome face. He wore a dark cloak that could not quite hide the dragon that snarled in rampant pose on the breast of his tunic. He was a menacing figure, clearly graced with the devil's own arrogance.

Although she did not know him—prayed she did not—Haven sensed at once that he was dangerous. He hung back with obvious deliberateness, standing in the shade of the canopy with no wish to call attention to himself. In reflex, Haven threw an anxious glance over her shoulder to see who might spy them together.

"Lady Ariana has her husband's full attention in another stall," the cunning stranger informed her. "Your guard is out of earshot. He will take no notice unless you give him cause to come over here, Haven."

Faith.

He knew her name.

"I had heard you might have found your way inside Clairmont's own keep, but I scarce could credit it until I saw you with my own eyes."

"Who are you?" she whispered, needing to know what he was about even while she waited in dread of the answer. "How do you know me?"

The hawkish brow furrowed, his dragon green eyes narrowing. "Do you jest?"

"Tell me," she said. "Should I know you?"

He tipped his head back and let out a low, disbelieving chuckle. "That is rich, indeed, when we have taken orders from the same man for nigh on a year. What is your game here, vixen?"

"I'd say you are the one playing games, sirrah."

Haven let the ruby cloth fall back on the table and made to pivot away.

When she would have alerted the Clairmont guard to her distress, the dark-haired warrior hissed a warning. "Not so fast, lady. You and I needs have ourselves a talk.

Unless you'd like word to reach our mutual employer, Silas de Mortaine, that you are not dead in the Greycliff raid as he presumes."

At the mention of the villain's name, Haven froze.

Their employer? The very man who inspired such contempt and wariness at Clairmont was somehow tied to her?

Nay. She refused to accept what she was hearing. She needed answers that made sense to her, and felt with growing dread that this man could give them to her.

"What do you know of that night?"

He stared at her long and hard, then breathed a wry oath. "What do I know of it? Evidently more than you recall. Is it all lost to you?"

She gave him a small nod. "Please. You must tell me everything."

Someone—or something—followed him.

Kenrick had felt the weight of watching eyes on his back nearly since leaving Clairmont's gates. His observer was stealthy, keeping out of sight and just far enough behind as to not betray his position. But he was there nonetheless.

Kenrick had taken a forest path that day instead of the road, intending to shortcut his travel distance at the expense of a slower ride. He had also tired of the cat-and-mouse dance playing out between him and the cur who stalked him too doggedly to be careful.

When the opportunity arose, Kenrick veered off the woodland trail and plunged his mount into the thick spring growth of the forest. He rode with haste, using the cover of the greenery and his knowledge of these woods to aid him as he made a circle in his course and came up a short distance behind his pursuer.

The rider was a large man, doubtless a knight by the way he sat the saddle and no mean commoner despite his humble clothing. His mount was a well-bred palfrey that balked a bit when its reins were pulled back and the beast was made to halt on the path.

Kenrick hung back, the observed now the observer, and waited as the rogue with the earth brown hair and hulking shoulders swung his leg over the cantle and dismounted without a sound.

Kenrick, too, left his saddle on silent feet that crushed not even the smallest pine needle as he then crept a stealthy path toward the stranger. He drew a small blade from his baldric sheath and moved quickly, carefully through the ferns and bracken.

In no time at all he was standing behind him but an arm's length away.

"Turn around knave, and show yourself."

The man's spine stiffened, then straightened, his shaggy head swiveling but a fraction to mark the threat at his back.

"Slowly," Kenrick advised, pressing the dagger none too gently through the tousled, dullish brown hair until it rested against the base of the miscreant's skull. "Your game is up; I have let you dog my steps long enough. Face me as a man, or I will run you through where you stand."

The broad shoulders gave no sign of resistance or intent to fight. On the contrary, they slumped a mild degree, then lifted in a resigned shrug. "I should have found a better way to approach you, Saint. But too much is at stake. I had to be sure."

Hearing his old nickname—hearing the voice that spoke it, a resonating baritone that he knew too well—Kenrick scowled.

"Turn around," he demanded, not trusting his ears.

The man did as instructed, carefully pivoting under the pressing threat of the dagger until he was facing Kenrick straight on.

"God's blood—*Rand*."

"I saw you outside the village in Devon," his friend said. "You and some men had come upon a fresh campsite in the woods."

"You were there?" Kenrick asked, stunned to think it.

"From under the cover of the thicket, I watched you and your group leave."

"You said nothing. Why? Did you not trust me?"

"I had to be sure. You see, I'd been tracking the shifters, too. It was I who spilled some of their blood that day. Though not enough."

Dark-bearded, begrimed, unkempt from what had surely been weeks on the run, Randwulf of Greycliff stared back at Kenrick with hardened hazel eyes. Lines of tension bracketed a mouth that had so often been upturned in laughter or the telling of a bawdy jest. His face was lean and grim now, lifeless, the horror of what he must have endured these many days stamped in the bleakness of his expression.

"Good Christ," Kenrick swore, sheathing his dagger in a state of astonishment. "I thought you dead. After what I saw at Greycliff a fortnight ago . . ."

Rand winced nearly imperceptibly. When he next spoke, his voice had a sharp edge, black with a simmering fury. "They killed my family, Saint. Elspeth, my beloved, is gone. Jesu, even little Tod. Bloody devil's minions—they slaughtered my wife and son before my very eyes."

"I know." Kenrick's gut twisted sickly. "I am sorry, Rand, more than you know. I brought this on you. I am wholly to blame for involving you in my quest. If I had known what it would cost you—"

Rand dismissively shook his head. "It was my choice to aid you, Saint. I would do it no differently now. The blame for what occurred at Greycliff rests on one man: Silas de Mortaine. It was his band of changeling beasts who sacked my home and slew my family. I live, only to see every last one of them dead at the end of my blade, and to send de Mortaine to the depths of the hell that spawned him."

It was a sentiment Kenrick well understood, and shared. "De Mortaine grows bolder every day. His shifters have even found their way to Clairmont. Just the other morn, one of them was killed in a barn in our village while poaching livestock."

"Shifters," Rand spat. "They and all their devil's kin are good for naught but the grave. Soulless wraiths, all of them, for that is how they descended on Greycliff the night of the attack, aided by one of their own who wormed into my keep through lies and trickery. We never saw them coming, Saint. They never gave us the chance—six of them at least, pouring in amid the dead of night, armed with steel and fire and demons' magic. They descended as wolves on my few guards, tearing out their throats, moving through the keep as a pestilence to consume all in their path. I killed a few, but not all. They were after the seal you entrusted to me," Rand said grimly.

"I know. I feared as much when I saw the empty hiding place and the three fresh graves in Greycliff's yard."

"I tried to keep it from them, but to save Elspeth and Tod—"

"Say no more, Rand. You did only what you had to do."

"It mattered naught. They killed them anyway." Rand swore an oath. "After the raid had ended, when the shifters left and I awoke in the smoking ruins of my home, I buried my family. My wife and son in two of the graves, a dead guard in a third to pretend my own death, and then I left Greycliff. I cannot go back there, Saint. Not until this is done. Mayhap not even then."

"There will always be a place for you at Clairmont. My home is yours, Rand."

Emotion stormed through Rand's hazel gaze as he gave a grim tilt of his chin. "I want vengeance for what has been done. I have come because I am the one in need of your help now. Will you give it, Kenrick?"

"Anything."

His old friend's mouth curved in the ghost of a smile, but it was with a bleak look that he accepted Kenrick's offered hand. The two men briefly embraced, Rand as rigid and cool as the sword that rode in a sheath at his hip.

"These are treacherous times," Kenrick said as they parted. "Few can be trusted when it comes to the Dragon Chalice."

"Aye," Rand agreed. "Would that the lesson did not come at so great a price for my loved ones. I knew the wench who came to Elspeth with her witchy herbs was peculiar, but I never thought—Jesu, not even in my darkest dreams did I think she would prove so deadly."

Fingers of icy cold suddenly traveled down Kenrick's neck. "A healer, did you say?"

"Healer," Rand scoffed. "Nay. A shifter bitch who pretended frienship and betrayed us to the others of her kind, may she rot. I never knew a greater satisfaction than when I turned her dagger on her own heartless breast and ran her through."

Haven was still standing at the silk vendor's stall, numb with shock, when Ariana approached. Braedon was with her, a fresh wrapped goose tucked under his strong arm.

"Have you decided on any of them?" Ariana asked with bright cheer as she came to stand beside her at the table of pretty fabrics. She picked up the crimson swatch with an admiring eye. "This one would make a lovely garland for the dais. Don't you think so, Haven?"

She could not answer, merely acknowledging with a vague nod of her head.

The dragon knight was gone some time before, having delivered his troubling revelations—and an impossible, all but unthinkable proposition. Haven's mind was reeling from the encounter, her memory now mercilessly clear and unbroken. The darkness of her recall had been thrown into starkest light by everything she had heard.

She remembered it all, everything Draec le Nantres had told her.

Ariana's hand came to rest over hers in concern, the gentle contact jolting her out of her dark musings.

"Haven? What is it—are you all right?"

"Oh. Yes, I'm fine. The sun is a bit warm, is all. I think I would like to return to the castle, if we might."

"Of course," Ariana agreed.

"I'll tell the guards to ready our mounts," Braedon said, scowling, his eyes cutting from Haven's pale face to his wife. "We have stayed too long as it is. I don't like the feel of this place much."

When he turned to summon one of the knights who accompanied them to the market, Ariana moved in closer to Haven and wrapped her arm around her shoulders. "You're sure 'tis just the sun that has you so peaked?"

Haven looked into the honest and caring blue gaze of Kenrick's sister—a woman who would recoil in terror if she knew who she truly was—and perpetrated a further deception.

"Nothing is wrong at all. You have no cause to worry."

❧ 22 ❧

NOTHING WAS THE same to Haven when she returned from the market with Ariana and Braedon. She looked upon Clairmont, and her kind, unwitting hosts, with new eyes.

Shifter's eyes.

How she wanted to deny what Draec le Nantres had told her, about her role in Greycliff's attack, her forsworn fealty to the villainous Silas de Mortaine, her duty to her clan and her kingdom to see that the Dragon Chalice was returned . . . no matter the cost in the mortal lives of these Outsiders.

Her enemies.

She wanted to deny it all, most especially the knowledge of the queer and powerful gift that set her apart from these folk. She had felt it moving within her for days now, the twisting, shimmering prickle of change that ran beneath the surface of her skin.

Her glamour.

It had been slumbering until now, weakened by her fever and the scorching of her memory, but no more. She felt its strength coursing within her now, alive and awaiting her summons.

There had been a time not long ago, she recalled, that her glamour had given her great pride. To walk among the Outsiders, simple people who possessed no such magic—indeed, not even the ability to understand it, much less recognize its superiority—had made her feel unstoppable. It had made her feel immortal in many ways, although that was a gift denied her race.

Where shifters enjoyed the unregulated power of their magic on the Outside, in Anavrin the shapeshifting glamour of the Magics was arrested, kept on short leash by the ruling class of the Immortals, who possessed no conjuring skills. It was an age-old war, one that would come to a head again if the Dragon Chalice remained lost to the mystical realm that required it for survival.

This was Haven's legacy, and now, her curse.

As she paced the floor of her chamber, she contemplated the terrible turn her life had taken in so short a time. That morning she had been filled with a joy she had never known. Now she felt the fragile pieces of her world crumbling around her feet.

A selfish part of her wanted to pretend she had never seen Draec le Nantres that day. She wanted to deny everything she had heard—including the brazen offer he had made her, to ally herself with him instead of Silas de Mortaine.

Le Nantres was a man with his own secret ambitions. He had the seal that the raiding shifters had stolen from Greycliff; he needed Haven to help him determine how, and where, to use it.

She had been a spy once for Silas de Mortaine, when she'd been sent to befriend Rand and his family. Now Draec wanted her to report to him instead, delivering what she could of Kenrick's further findings about the locations of the remaining Chalice stones.

Draec's offer was clear: Help him, and he would see

that Haven returned to Anavrin safely. Cross him, and she knowingly put in jeopardy all she held dear.

For in permitting herself to care for these Outsiders at Clairmont—indeed, by allowing herself to warm to Greycliff's family when she had been covertly sent to the keep to spy on Kenrick's friends—Haven had committed the highest sort of crime against her clan. Her heart was opened to the enemy and she therefore branded a traitor to her kind.

She was Shadow now, a state of existence that was rare among the shifter warriors dispatched from Anavrin to seek the Dragon Chalice. To turn Shadow was to turn traitor.

Her life was forfeit if they found her, her fealty to her clan's mission now compromised by her love for Kenrick. The other shifters would sense her change on sight. They would hunt her with the same ferocity with which they hunted the errant pieces of the Dragon Chalice.

Haven had heard of others in her clan who'd been weakened by mortal emotion. A scant few were rumored to be in hiding somewhere on the Continent; the rest had been mercilessly hunted and executed.

With the shifters getting closer to Clairmont all the time, Haven knew she could not last long before they came for her. They would kill her. And then they would kill those she loved.

Faith, but she could not bear to so much as think of it.

She could not permit another horror like the one unleashed on Greycliff Castle.

Siding with le Nantres was no more noble—no less treacherous—than an alliance with Silas de Mortaine himself, but her other alternatives held too many risks, too much pain. Not the least of which being her thoughts toward Kenrick.

As difficult as it would be, her heart urged her to go to him at once and tell him everything. She owed it to him, even if he would hate her for it.

According to the servants, Kenrick had returned to Clairmont with a guest a short while ago, but retired to his solar immediately upon arrival. With the feast yet a few hours away, Haven knew not how she would endure the time alone with her thoughts. For certain, she would not be able to bear the entire meal with so great a weight hanging between them.

If only she could see him, if only she could have one moment to determine what his reaction might be to her terrible truth that burned like acid in her belly. She had to do something, for pacing the confines of her chamber was like to drive her mad.

With a sense of resolve, and a dread that threatened to consume her, Haven quit her tower room and headed for the lord's solar on the main level of the keep.

She was surprised to find the door left ajar, no one within the meeting chamber at all. Kenrick had been there but a moment ago, for a healthy fire burned in the large grate and on a table situated between a pair of cushioned chairs, two empty tankards sat alongside a drained wine decanter.

Something else lay there as well. The glint of flat, hammered steel reflecting the firelight drew her attention as she cautiously entered the chamber.

It was a blade, she realized when she had taken but the first step toward it. The tooled dagger compelled her with its stunning familiarity, with its bewitching dance of light on the dragon hilt and engraved blade of exquisitely rare Anavrin steel.

It was a shifter's blade, this one intact and perfect, where the one that had felled her at Greycliff—her very own weapon, turned on her by a man who had every right to wish her dead—had broken off where it had struck her in her shoulder. She wondered how Kenrick had come by the piece.

More worrisome to her now, she wondered how the dagger had been discussed between Kenrick and whomever had been seated with him in the solar.

Haven picked up the weapon and held it in her palm. The instant the cool blade touched her skin, she experienced a sudden, traveling sense of power. Her fingers were alive with the kiss of a thousand needles. The sensation spread, running up the whole of her arm and into her shoulder, then down her spine.

Like fire itself, the strength of her magic engulfed her, warming her. The air about her became charged with a quavering, thrumming intensity. This accoutrement of her past, of her true home, called to something deep inside of her, showing her what she was and would always be.

Her glamour rippled just below the surface of her consciousness, an alluring whisper that urged her to let it free.

"No. I will not."

Haven dropped the shifter blade back onto the table with a clatter. She spun around—only to find Kenrick standing behind her in the open doorway of the solar.

"Have a care, lady. 'Tis a shifter's dagger, and their witchery knows no bounds."

She put her arms behind her, quelling the pulsations

of her rising glamour and praying the queer pricking of her skin would abate. Unsettled by the stirring of her true nature, her discomfiture only worsened as she stared at Kenrick's stoic countenance.

"A dagger just like that one was used on you the night of the attack at Greycliff," he said, striding into the solar and closing the door behind him. "The night you were attacked by raiding shifters on orders of Silas de Mortaine."

Haven swallowed on a suddenly parched throat. "How is it you have this blade?"

He stood near the table now, and reached out to retrieve the weapon from where Haven had dropped it. Shrugging, he turned his mouth down in casual regard. "I cannot be sure precisely where this one came from. Braedon and I slew a fair number of the beasts in France some months ago. It might have belonged to any one of them."

His disdain for the breed—for her breed—was evident in the darkness of his tone. The loathing she saw in him put a knot of fear in her heart.

"Did your travel today go well?" she asked, making anxious conversation while the weight of what she had come there to say to him pressed down on her like iron rods. "Mary tells me you brought a guest back with you."

"I met an old friend." His chin lifted, but his gaze was narrow, measuring. The dagger was still gripped idly in his hand. "We had much to catch up on, it turns out."

She attempted a cheery smile. "Will your friend be joining us at tonight's feast?"

"He will."

"Well, Ariana has put together quite an affair,"

Haven said with a breeziness she did not feel. "She has prepared an impressive menu and plans to deck the great hall with silks and spring garlands. She does too much for me, I think."

Kenrick's grunt of acknowledgment held a strangely predatory tone. "My sister has a giving heart. She trusts easily, and looks for the good in people—at times, to her own detriment."

"She is a good friend to me," Haven said, wary of the coolness in his steady blue eyes as he looked up from the light dancing on the blade to meet her gaze. "I would never do aught to hurt her."

"I am glad to hear it, Haven. For there is nothing I would not do to protect my sister, indeed all of the folk who live within my keep and trust me as their lord."

He seemed lost in thought for a long moment, and Haven struggled to find words to fill the quiet.

"Kenrick . . . there is something—"

"Trust is a very fragile thing," he murmured, the low growl of his voice silencing her in midstream. She could only watch in wary silence as he lifted the dragon blade and traced it, untouching, up the length of her long-sleeved arm. "It is hard-won, sometimes never fully given."

He did not look at her, merely watched the tooled dagger as it crested her shoulder and began a slow, skating path toward the neckline of her gown.

Faith, did he already suspect her secret? she wondered, feeling a new layer of fear worm its way into her heart.

"Trust is the most binding gift a man has to give . . ."

The blade's razor edge slid beneath one of the ribbons that laced her bodice.

". . . and it can be lost with the slightest, careless slip of one's hand."

Haven let out a pent-up breath, glancing down at the silken lacing as it severed and fell away.

Kenrick's gaze was flinty hard, but heated when he finally looked at her again. She could not read him, but she could sense the rawness of his emotions. A battle stormed in his expression, somewhere between fury and hunger. Whatever he felt in that moment, it was animal and immediate, and it sent a frisson of nervous anticipation down Haven's spine.

"Do you trust me, lady?"

She nodded, hardly capable of speech as the dagger subtly sliced through the rest of her ribbon lacings.

Some cautious thread of sanity warned that he was dangerous in that moment. She could not dismiss the idea that he was threatening her with this sensual game as much as he teased her. His gaze was too wild to be harmless. He was a man as skilled in combat as he was in study or seduction, and it was with no small degree of wariness that she reminded herself of that fact.

She had her glamour now—in truth, she knew she would be a fair match for any man if she called upon her magic—but she would not use it against Kenrick, no matter what his intent with her might be. His power over her was strangely thrilling, even through her fear.

"Do you trust me?" he asked again, framing her face in his hand, stroking her cheek with the pad of his thumb.

"Y-yes," she whispered. "I trust you."

"Do you want me, lovely witch?"

"Oh, yes," she gasped, her hands coming up around his back when he leaned in to kiss the tender skin below her ear. "Yes. I want you. Kenrick, you must know that I will always want you."

"Nay, lady," he murmured against her jaw line. "I can be sure of no such thing. Show me that I can believe anything that you would tell me."

His command emboldened her and she kissed him with all of the passion she felt for him. Their mouths melded together in a fevered joining that neither seemed able to control. There was fury in Kenrick's kiss, and a need for domination like she had never known in him before. He sought her complete submission, and Haven felt herself bending to his will with eager surrender.

He guided her hand down the hard length of his body, placing her where he wanted her. "Show me how you want me."

With questing fingers, she slipped her hands beneath his tunic. His skin was so warm to the touch, like velvet over solid steel, his heartbeat thudding fiercely in her palm. She caressed the silken sinew of his chest and down along the ridged firmness of his abdomen.

He sucked in his breath when her fingers found the rolled waistband of his breeches. That same breath rasped out of him on an oath as the laces were untied and his sex sprang free and heavy into her hands. Haven stroked him with wordless reverence, marveling as ever at the wondrous feel of his body and the power of what his pleasure did to her.

He moaned, and she was the one to melt. He trembled, and she felt her own legs weaken beneath her.

There was so much that needed to be said between them, so much that would need mending, but Haven was fast losing herself to the sensual spell of Kenrick's body. Touching him was not enough. Recalling how wild he had made her with his own brazen kiss, Haven slowly knelt before him on the floor, and took him into her mouth.

His groan of pleasure was a sweet reward that only made her more adventurous. She suckled the smooth crown of his manhood, teasing it with her tongue. The taste of him made her mad with desire and eager to explore every silken inch of his sex with her mouth. She feasted on him without inhibition, letting his hands guide her, his sharp moans of passion and deep, fevered sighs showing her just how to please him most.

She reveled in his body's reactions, wanting more of him. Needing all that he would give her. But just when it seemed he would lose himself to her, instead he seized her under the arms and hauled her up onto her feet. He was panting hard, his jaw rigid, eyes so deep a blue they seemed nearly black.

"God's blood, you are a ruthless witch."

She reached for him, but he pushed away her hands, denying her with a feral look of hunger. He spun her around in front of him, then bent her over the back of the chair. Her skirts went up around her hips in a whoosh of fabric, exposing her to him in the most intimate way. It made her anxious, but she did not fight him. He was too needy with desire, and she was too willing to submit to him in any way he wanted her.

His probing fingers met with the slick moisture between her legs. He parted the damp petals, teasing her with the thought of penetration, his stiff member sliding along her cleft. Haven cried out, unable to bite back her longing.

"Tell me what you want," he said, wickedly tormenting

her with the sensual caress of his heated, heavy flesh at
the gate of her womb.

"You," she gasped. "I want you, Kenrick. Please . . ."

"I shouldn't want you like I do," he muttered, his
voice sounding rough with throttled emotion. "God's
love, but I should not need you like I do."

With a raw curse, he thrust inside her, as deeply as she
could take him. Haven arched up as his sex seated fully
within her sheath, filling her in one endless stroke. At
once she was panting, breathless with the onslaught of
climax. Every flex of Kenrick's hips drove her farther to
the edge, the intensity of his need—his fevered quest for
release—making her dizzy with sensation. She cried out
his name as pleasure buffeted her, radiating over her in
waves of pure light and boneless awe.

He soon followed her over the edge of a shuddering
climax, thrusting hard, his hands gripping her pelvis in a
bruising frenzy. At the last moment, when she would
have done anything to hold him there, he withdrew
from her on a coarse shout, denying her the heated spill
of his seed.

When the cool air of the chamber fanned her naked
backside, she realized he had turned away from her entirely. She pivoted from her prone position over the
chair to find him hitching up his breeches. He glanced at
her only briefly, coolly, she thought, then focused his attention on finishing getting dressed.

Haven eased her rucked skirts down in a state of
uncertainty. A sudden emptiness pressed down on her,
worsened by the impersonal look in Kenrick's eyes as he
poured himself the last of the wine and downed it in a
single gulp.

"Kenrick," she began, more worried now than when she had first come there. "This had not been my intention—"

"Nor mine, I assure you," he agreed, his voice devoid of all feeling.

Her nerves jangled with alarm to see him go from furious passion to chilling remoteness. He set the empty cup down on the table, then casually walked to his desk across the solar and seated himself behind it. The large piece of heavy, carved wood stood between them like a portcullis dropped on the castle courtyard.

"I had hoped we might talk . . ."

At her trailing voice, he lifted his head, frowning. "I have much that requires my attention, Haven. We'll talk after the sup tonight."

She stood there for a moment, stunned that he was shutting her out so coldly. Aloof as ever, stoically detached, he was once more the unreachable lord. The same forbidding man she had first encountered upon awaking in this unfamiliar place.

"Kenrick—"

"Tonight, Haven," he said again, then picked up a goose quill and began writing on a square of parchment as if she had already left the room.

❧ 23 ❧

"OH, MY. I knew the gown would suit you." Ariana beamed at Haven, stepping back to allow her room to swish the flowing skirts of the iridescent green kirtle. With a smile dancing in her eyes and a gentle hand at Haven's elbow, she turned her to face the tall looking glass stand. " 'Tis a perfect fit. Lovely beyond words."

Haven gazed into the unfamiliar reflection and saw an image of dazzling unreality standing before her.

"I take it you approve?" Ariana asked, coming up to stand at Haven's shoulder and meeting her gaze in the smooth pane of glass.

"Yes, of course I approve. It is beautiful."

"Then it's yours."

"Mine?" Haven turned to look at her, astonished at the generosity Ariana continued to show her. "I . . . I don't know what to say. This is . . . an extraordinary gift. You have given me so much already. I don't think I should accept—"

"Nonsense." Kenrick's sister gave her a stern look that held more humor than fire. Her delicate hands came to rest on the small rise of her belly. " 'Twill be close to a year before I am able to wear the gown, so there is no point in letting the moths get it in the meanwhile."

"Ariana," Haven said, shaking her head. "You are very generous to offer, so thoughtful, but I—"

"No more protests, I insist. The gown is my gift to you, Haven." She reached out and squeezed her hand. "Accept it as my friend . . . and my sister-to-be."

Unable to keep from admiring the stunning kirtle with its gold-shot embroidery and liquid, elegant skirts, she spun once more to the looking glass. Not even Anavrin magic could conjure the feeling of euphoria she felt wearing such an exquisite garment.

As she pivoted and posed, permitting herself a moment of childlike giddiness, Ariana brought a brush and began combing through the unbound tangle of Haven's hair. "Shall we put it up tonight?" she asked, lifting the mass of auburn waves into an improvised crown atop Haven's head.

It might have been a good idea, were it not for the necklace of bruises that still ringed her throat. They had faded in the time she'd been at Clairmont, but even in the dim light of the ladies' chamber, the marks were unmistakable. Some of Haven's joy evaporated at the sight of them. It was almost easy to forget they were there, to deny where they had come from . . . and why.

Very gently, Ariana let the glossy tresses fall back down around Haven's shoulders. She arranged one long strand so that it curled around the front of her neck, artfully masking one of the darkest of the remaining bruises. " 'Twill be pretty no matter how you wear it. And I have a pendant that will look stunning against your creamy skin."

Smiling over the kindness Ariana had bestowed on her, now and for the whole of her stay at Clairmont

Castle, Haven reached up and clutched the lady's slender fingers with heartfelt affection.

Although she had come into this keep innocently enough, everything now was drastically changed. The knowledge of what she was seemed a burden Haven could hardly bear. The thought that she might lose her dear friend and Kenrick as well, put a bleak hurt in her very soul. She had never known such warm acceptance. How she regretted that her past was rising up to steal it all away.

"Thank you, Ariana. For everything."

"You're welcome." She set the brush down on a side table. "I'll go fetch the necklace."

"Ariana," Haven asked as she turned to cross the room to the door. Uncertain suddenly, she smoothed the long silk skirts, her palms oddly moist and trembling. "Do you . . . do you think he will like it?"

"Like it?" Ariana laughed. "You outshine the sun and stars together in that gown, Haven. Trust me, once he sees you, my brother will have trouble looking at aught else tonight."

"I want to look nice for him," she admitted, shy despite the warmth, the bone-deep excitement, she felt just to think of Kenrick, despite the unsettling encounter they shared in his chamber that afternoon. "I hope he favors the color."

"He will adore it," Ariana assured her. "As much as he adores the woman in it."

Was it true? Haven wondered as Kenrick's sister departed the chamber to retrieve her promised bauble. *Did he adore her?*

Could Kenrick possibly feel any measure of the affection she held for him?

Not a couple short days ago, she might have hoped so, but now she couldn't be certain how he might truly regard her. She dared not presume such a miracle could in fact be real. Particularly after his strange behavior that afternoon. His coolness after such a heated encounter made Haven fear that she had misread his affection for her.

But hearing Ariana state it with such surety caused a flutter of hope in Haven's heart. It no longer frightened her, the queer trembling of her soul, the heady rush of feeling that bloomed within her each time she thought of her handsome lover.

Kenrick.

Her beloved, she admitted, if only to herself—and to Ariana, who had come to hold many of her secrets in trusted confidence.

Save the most damning one.

The weight of what Draec le Nantres had told her was unbearable. Her unwitting duplicity pressed more heavily on her with each passing hour, making her mad with the torment of carrying so black a secret. If Kenrick had seemed the least bit accepting when they'd met in his chamber today, she might have told him then. She should have, but faith preserve her, she'd been too afraid of his rejection.

If only she could go back to the day she first met Kenrick. To the moment he found her near Greycliff manor and rescued her from the fever that had robbed her memory, and the death that would have claimed her. If only she had never met him, never known what awaited her at Clairmont.

The kindness.

The kinship.

The love.

There was still time to end her masquerade. She was in over her head, to be sure, but she could right this before disaster swallowed her whole. And so she would, she vowed to the wide-eyed, frightened-looking reflection staring back at her in the glass. She owed it to Kenrick. To Ariana, and even Braedon, who had been willing to embrace his wife's newfound friend despite any of his own misgivings. She owed the truth to everyone at Clairmont, for there was not a soul in the demesne who had not touched her in some way, however small.

And because of her, they were all at terrible risk.

All the more, now that she—shifter born—had forbiddenly permitted these Outsiders into her heart.

"Here it is," Ariana brightly announced as she returned to the chamber, pendant in hand.

The necklace sparkled with the rich jeweled hues of verdant emerald, honeyed topaz, and dazzling crystal. Each stone was cut into a teardrop shape of graduating sizes, the smallest one nearly the length and width of her thumbnail.

"This belonged to my mother, and several previous ladies of our line. According to family lore, it was once worn to London court and nearly lost the same evening, when Queen Eleanor herself enviously remarked upon its beauty."

Haven could not offer praise enough for the precious heirloom that was draped about her neck by Ariana's nimble fingers and suddenly bobbed suspended between Haven's breasts.

"Perfect," Ariana pronounced, standing back to admire the crowning touch. In the mirror, her pleased expression suddenly changed to one of concern. "Haven? What is it?"

"Nothing," she replied, finding it difficult to form words when her tongue was suddenly so thick. Moisture seemed to spring from out of nowhere to mist her eyes, blurring everything in the room.

Ariana's spontaneous embrace did little to help the matter. Haven's vision swam. She swiped at the wet tracks that coursed down her cheeks. "I don't . . . I don't know what's happening to me," she murmured, unable to stanch the flow.

"Hush now," Ariana whispered, her voice sounding oddly constricted too. "You mustn't cry. If you keep this up, you will have me crying, too!"

She gave a strangled little laugh, and suddenly both women were sniffling and wiping at their tears.

"Enough of this foolishness. Enough!" Ariana ordered, although she seemed equally hard-pressed to recover herself. "We'll be gathering for supper in a short while and it simply will not do for you to make your stunning arrival with puffy, red-rimmed eyes."

She reached out and took Haven by the hand, steering her toward the wardrobe. "Come and help me decide what I should wear. I am plotting a seduction of my husband for this evening, and I need to find something suitably irresistible."

Haven returned her friend's impish smile, more than content to put her troubling thoughts aside for a while and play along.

"Damnation!"

Kenrick fumed at his carelessness, watching a stain of black ink begin to spread across the page of his open journal. His tunic sleeve had tipped the small well of ink before he could stop the error.

He blotted at the seeping pool as it ran across the page, but it was useless. His last two hours of work were wasted. The calculations and drawings he had been attempting to transcribe into his journal were now rendered illegible by the widening edges of the black mark that soaked into the parchment like so much spilled blood.

With a roar that went deeper than any irritation at a ruined set of figures, Kenrick picked up the journal and heaved it against the adjacent wall of the chamber. The leather-bound book cracked apart on impact, pages fluttering as it dropped like a dead weight to the floor.

"Focus," he chastised himself, vaulting out of his chair and raking his fingers over his scalp in abject frustration.

He had been thinking about her.

Haven had left his solar chamber several hours ago, shut out by his deliberately cool demeanor and the thick oak door that sealed him off from the rest of the keep, yet her presence lingered.

After what he had learned about her from Rand, Kenrick did not want to think about Haven any more. He did not want to see her. God knew, he did not want to crave her as he had when he'd found her in this very room earlier that day.

He had ravished her like a beast, slaking his passion and his anger on her body, but still he burned for her.

In his mind, she was his enemy. She was a shifter spy and a cold liar. If what Rand had told him were true, then Haven's heart was as black and evil as death itself.

He could scarcely believe she might be in league with

Silas de Mortaine. Knowing her as he did, it seemed impossible to reconcile so heinous a truth.

Haven had seemed so genuine and kind. She had become so much a part of Clairmont in the short time she was there recuperating from her injury and the loss of memory that kept her from knowing who—and what—she truly was. Kenrick could hardly deny that she had become a part of his life as well.

Had it all been a cruel mistake of fate, or merely part of a shifter game contrived to aid her in a bigger plan?

His mind worked hard to reject the idea . . . or perhaps it was his heart that struggled to accept he could have been so blind.

If all he heard were true, Haven would be the worst sort of betrayer, a fact he meant to prove out that night at the feast.

Kenrick had not let Ariana or Braedon know about Rand's arrival at Clairmont, or the damning information his friend had delivered. The servants knew only that there would be a guest at the supper that evening; Rand had been given a private chamber in the keep where he was bathing and resting after the weeks spent living on the run. If Greycliff saw Haven before Kenrick was prepared, he knew his old friend would stop at nothing to finish her on the spot.

While Kenrick understood, indeed, shared some of that killing rage, he needed to handle the matter in his own way, on his own terms.

He slid a glance across the solar, to a corner where a long tapestry hung, suspended on polished wooden rings. Ten strides brought him before the colorful length of embroidered silk. He reached out, and clutched a handful of fabric in his fist. A quick jerk of his wrist brought the piece down in a crumpled heap at his feet.

A narrow stretch of darkness lurked behind the tapestry, the stairwell it had concealed climbing steeply up to the top of the tower keep . . . to the locked and forbidden chamber that contained a secret of otherworldly, deadly power.

"On my own terms," Kenrick growled low under his breath.

Stepping into the wedge of inky blackness, he took the long flight of hidden steps three at a time.

⁊ 24 ⁊

HAVEN COULD SCARCELY contain her anxiety as the summons went out to announce the evening's supper. She had rather hoped that Kenrick would come to fetch her personally, for despite his coolness that afternoon and the worry that continued to assail her over what she would confess to him that night, she longed to see him. But she understood from Ariana, who had obtained it from one of the servants, that he was occupied with pressing matters in his solar and had asked to not be disturbed until the meal was called.

"It is better this way, actually," Ariana told her on the side as they quit Haven's chamber and descended the spiral stairwell from the family quarters above. "Now when my brother sees you it will be before a room filled with scores of people. It will drive him mad to sit near you at table and not be able to touch you for some long hours. I expect this meal will pass as the most trying one he's ever had."

Haven permitted a nervous laugh as they neared the bottom of the stairs. "I don't know how you come by your wisdom," she said, smiling conspiratorially at her accomplice in this endeavor to bewitch their unsuspecting lords. "But I do hope you're right."

Ariana winked. "Fear not, dear friend. You will make my brother the envy of every man in the hall this eve."

"Not every one," Haven replied, taking in the beauteous sight of Ariana garbed in exquisite indigo sendal.

The wispy silk gown traced her curves as though sewn to her form. Long skirts, nearly sheer, so fine was their weave, fell in fluid motion to the floor around her dainty leather slippers and in a train behind her. Edging the hem of the elegant skirt and the long bell sleeves of its sky blue overtunic was an embroidered braid of cream satin, sewn with gemstone beads and pearls. With Ariana's every graceful step along the corridor toward the great hall, the gown's luxurious adornments twinkled gaily, catching in the torchlight of the keep.

Everything about the dress was a study of perfection on Ariana, including the daring neckline of the bodice, cut to expose just the right amount of decolletage flushed pink with the same glow that radiated from Ariana's serene face.

"Lord Braedon will be enchanted, to be sure," Haven said, eager to see Ariana's effect on her brooding warrior of a husband.

"I warrant there are times when a woman must call upon every bit of magic she possesses, wouldn't you agree?"

Haven returned her friend's smile, though inwardly the jest was lost on her. Her mind was racing forward to the end of the evening, when she must face the inevitable.

She had to tell Kenrick tonight. There could be no more delaying, no more wishing for the opportune time when it might never come.

She loved him.

He commanded her heart, and she needed him to know that. He needed to know everything. She would tell him all tonight, after the meal was ended and they were assured time alone.

She would lay bare all her secrets, and pray he would find a bit of acceptance—a bit of mercy—in his heart.

"Here we are," Ariana said as they arrived at the entryway of the banquet chamber. "Are you ready to make your entrance, Lady Haven?"

In truth, she wasn't at all sure, but Ariana's eyes were bright with confidence, instilling a measure of the same in Haven. With anticipation sparking through her like tiny currents, she mustered her courage and came to stand in the open archway of the tall double doors.

Before her in the hall, people milled about like bees at the hive, flitting hither and yon as they assembled to take their seats at the long trestle tables spread out across the floor. Haven's gaze pierced the crowd, straining to find the dais through the churning throng.

At last there was a break in the press of bodies. A pathway cleared in her line of vision, and she followed it with eager eyes, holding her breath as her gaze traveled across the room and up, onto the raised platform of the head table.

Kenrick was standing there. He was flanked by a small group of other men, Braedon and some of the Clairmont knights among them. But Haven only had eyes for the handsome, golden lord who ruled her heart. He saw her in the same moment she saw him. His intense blue stare reached to her from the distance that separated them.

Haven's heart gave a little leap as their gazes locked.

Something unreadable flickered in his silent regard—

a momentary glint of surprise, mayhap desire, she wanted to believe—as his astute eyes took an obvious assessment of her attire. She stood there, anxiously waiting for his smile. For a welcoming lift of his hand, or some subtle warming of his features . . . anything but the stoic countenance that met her across that crowded hall.

It did not come.

He only stared at her, motionless and silent, his eyes cold, steady, piercing. . . .

Bleak with a certain measured expectation.

Haven frowned, confused.

But then he shifted slightly, and cold understanding began to dawn. That one small step he took, a deliberate movement, subtle though it was, drew her attention to a tall, broad-shouldered man who stood behind Kenrick on the dais. She saw a mass of thick chestnut hair crowning a harsh, hawk-like face that was only partway revealed through the distance. The face was a shadowed specter of another she had known—leaner, less jovial than it was meant to be.

Still, there could be no mistaking it.

She blinked, recognition instant despite the logic that told her it could only be a trick of the light. Her lips parted on a silent oath of wonder.

And all the while Kenrick watched her, those crystalline eyes cutting through her like twin shards of razor-sharp glass.

"Oh, no."

Haven gasped the words, understanding now what this was about. Stricken with dread, she quickly backed away from the entryway. She took a handful of steps into the corridor, stumbling in her haste.

Doubled over, her back pressed to the cold stone of

the wall, she clutched her stomach, which was twisting into itself with a stabbing jolt of alarm.

"No, no, no . . ."

Ariana was at her side at once. "Haven? What's wrong?"

"It cannot be." Like a stone tossed in a fathomless lake, her heart plummeted, sinking into a black, frigid void that knew no end. "No . . . not like this. Not now."

She pushed away from the corridor wall, every instinct urging her to run. Had her feet not felt so leaden, her heart not so constricted in her breast, she might have done just that. As it was, she only managed another two paces before Ariana caught her by the wrist.

"Haven, are you ill? For heaven's sake, tell me what's wrong."

"Let me go. Please."

Kenrick's sister held fast, worry knitting her forehead. "Not until you tell me what this is about. Let me help y—"

"Please!" Haven hissed, urgent as she wrenched her hand from Ariana's well-meaning grasp. "Please, just let me be. I don't . . . I don't feel well," she improvised, lamely grasping for the first excuse she could find. "I need to be alone for a while."

She didn't wait for Ariana's reply. Choking on panic, on bitter fear and stunned disbelief, she fled for the tower stairs.

❧ 25 ❧

IT WAS SETTLED now.

He had wanted his answer, and so, by God, he had it. Haven's guilt-stricken look the moment she spied Rand at the dais had said it all.

She had betrayed him. Perhaps all this time, playing him for a fool. Pretending to be of feeble memory, lying to him about what had happened at Rand's keep those weeks ago. Using him to obtain information about his findings on the Dragon Chalice.

A cursed shifter, deceiving him each time she kissed him, mocking him with every silken sigh and pleasured moan she had breathed beside his ear as they made love.

And he, fool to the end, had been praying she would prove his suspicions wrong.

When he saw her in that emerald-hued gown, a confection befitting a goddess, it had taken every ounce of his control not to gape in dumbstruck, mortal admiration. Never had she looked more stunning.

Never had she been more treacherous, for as he had glimpsed her across the distance of the great hall, bedecked in silken finery, her eyes more dazzling than the jewels that winked at the heavenly valley between her breasts, Kenrick had felt a deep and growing hope burn from some protected corner of his soul.

Hope that what he felt for this woman, this temptress witch who could seduce him with a look, was forged of something stronger than mist and moonlight.

In that flashing instant of time, he had entertained a wishful scenario where Haven was pleased to see Greycliff alive. Kenrick had imagined the warm smile she directed at him softly melting into astonishment when she spied the man whose family had taken her into their home as a healer and friend to Elspeth. Sheltered her and fed her, trusted her as one of their own.

Much the way she had been accepted here at Clairmont.

Kenrick had expected disbelief perhaps, shock certainly, when she laid eyes on Rand, whole and hale after her account of his horrific death at enemy hands.

Disbelief he got, and shock as well. Whether a trick of his mind or something else, he could have sworn he saw a note of relief—uncomprehending, yet heartfelt and true—bloom in her eyes as she saw that Rand was alive. Whatever emotion played there, it had been quickly overridden by a look of unmistakable dread once she glanced back to Kenrick and met his studious, knowing gaze.

Standing there on the dais after her sudden retreat, Kenrick exhaled a black oath. Time to have done with this business entirely. With murmured excuses, he quit the high table and stalked through the settling crowd of assembled castlefolk. Ariana met him halfway across the floor.

"Kenrick, I am worried about Haven. Something is terribly wrong with her."

"Aye, there is," he growled, his jaw clamped so

tightly, it was a wonder the bones didn't shatter under the pressure of his rage.

"I have never seen her in such a state. Someone should look after her at once."

"Where has she gone?" he asked, hardly pausing for the answer.

"To the tower." When he lengthened his stride, Ariana hurried after him. "Wait, Kenrick. I want to go with you."

He threw a look over his shoulder, his commanding glare halting her in her tracks. "Stay, Ana. Go to your husband. Tell him no one is to come upstairs until I am through. Do you understand?"

Worry bled to sudden wariness in his little sister's blue eyes. "You're upset with her. Why? What is happening?" She glanced toward the dais and drew in a sharp breath. "My Lord. Is that—? Rand . . . *he is alive?*"

"Do as I ask, Ana. Tell Braedon to say nothing to Greycliff or to anyone else about what goes here. This matter is mine to handle."

"Kenrick, I don't understand. How can Rand be standing here when Haven said—"

"Nothing she has said—*to any of us*—means a thing."

Ariana looked to him, her lips parting in an expression of doubt. "What do you mean to do to her?"

"What I should have done the moment I first began to suspect her lies."

Haven fumbled with the last of the delicate laces of the gown, her fingers trembling, nearly useless in her state of utter distress. Breath hitching, she loosed the final fastening and shed the beautiful clothes like a snake coming out of its skin. It was all she could do, unable to bear the weight of the silk and velvet and beads when the press of her heart, her very soul, felt as onerous as a hundred stone weight.

In her white chemise, her feet bared of the soft kid slippers Ariana had given her, Haven hurried to the coffer at the end of the bed and threw open the lid. Her old dun kirtle and woolen mantle were folded inside, washed and mended sometime during her stay at Clairmont. She took them out, carefully setting aside the lavender sprigs that she had crafted one of the sunny mornings she had spent conversing with Ariana in the castle's garden. The flowers were so tender, nearly sapped of all life after just a fortnight gone from their vine.

How fragile this mortal world was.

How easily its precious gifts could be lost.

Tears threatened on that thought, but Haven held them at bay. She could blame no one but herself for what was happening now. She owned it all. What was lost to her tonight could not be measured, nor, she feared, could it be won back.

And as much as she mourned her own sad circumstance, she felt it tenfold for the pain that her part in this must have caused Randwulf of Greycliff. He had lost his wife and child—his dearest family. The part of her that was still shifter, the warrior who had been silenced all this time by the searing of her memory, whispered that Rand's losses were but casualties of the battle that waged around them for the Dragon Chalice.

What a feeble justification.

She could not fathom the person—nay, the unfeeling creature—who could parcel life and death into such neat compartments. For certain, she no longer knew the woman she once was. She would never be her again, now that Kenrick and his kin had shown her what it was to truly live.

To truly love, with all one's heart.

She closed the lid of the bedside chest and rose to her feet. Dressing hastily, she threw her old garb over her head and smoothed down the rough-spun skirts, just in time to hear booted feet pause outside the closed chamber door. She hadn't bothered to bolt it. Whatever wrath she faced now, she would face with courage . . . and total honesty, no matter its cost.

The iron latch snicked free of its cradle and the heavy panel swung inward.

Kenrick walked in without a word.

She heard his purposeful strides come to pause in the space behind her.

Haven, who had feared so little in her life, now shook with dread. Not for the thought of facing his fury, which would be fierce, understandably, but for the emptiness she knew would be hers in a few precious moments.

"I can explain," she murmured, summoning all her strength to turn and face the man she loved. The man she had unwittingly deceived with her very presence in his keep. "Until this afternoon, I did not know what I had done. But my memory is back now—all of it."

"A miracle, to be sure," he scoffed.

"Kenrick, I would have told you everything . . . I had planned to, this very evening—"

He cut her off with a sharp command. "That pendant belongs to my family. Take it off."

She obeyed at once, unclasping the golden chain and feeling the cool weight of the gems slide down between her breasts, where her heart thudded so desperately. "Ariana let me wear it," she said feebly, holding the necklace out to him in her palm.

Without acknowledging, indeed, without so much as looking at her, Kenrick took the pendant. He tossed it onto the bed behind her with a curt flick of his wrist.

"I can hardly believe Randwulf of Greycliff is standing down there, alive, in your hall—"

"No doubt. It came as a shock to me as well, when he approached me today to tell me of the hell he lived through."

"I hadn't thought—faith, but I hadn't dared hope— that anyone survived. I am so relieved that he is well."

"Relieved," Kenrick replied, his tone bitingly flat. "The look on your face seemed not to speak of relief. Guilt, I thought. And fear that you had been found out."

Haven's gaze welled with the rise of hot, stinging tears. "I feared that you would think the worst of me. That is the very reason I delayed telling you today about all that occurred at Greycliff the night they were attacked. I feared you would not accept me once you knew the full truth. I fear it all the more, now that I am standing here before you."

"Better to deceive, is that your way of thinking?"

"No. I had no wish to deceive you, or anyone else. You were the one who brought me here. I only wanted to be left alone."

"You would have died of your injuries."

"I might have preferred that," she whispered, a stabbing bite of pain twisting in her heart. "What of Rand? Does he know I am here?"

"Nay," Kenrick answered. "He knows none of it yet.

I wanted to see for myself if my suspicions were correct, before I told him I was housing his family's betrayer."

"I did not betray them, Kenrick. Not intentionally."

He gave a humorless bark of laughter. "Intention hardly matters when a gentle lady and her young son are lying dead in cold graves."

"Would that I could trade places with them. I would have, even then. Elspeth became my friend at Greycliff. I cared for her and her family. I did not want to see them harmed. You may find that hard to credit now, but it is true. As dear as they were to me, it is nothing compared to what I feel for you. I love you, Kenrick."

His expression wavered no more than his stance: rigid, unyielding. Despite her clothes, which rasped against her skin as she trembled, Haven felt all but naked, utterly vulnerable, standing there before him. Her chance to explain herself was spent; nothing more she said now would convince him she spoke true.

Looking at him, knowing how he valued fact and truth—how he loathed deceit—she understood his anger. Not even her magic could shield her from the ice of Kenrick's mistrust.

"Say something. Please."

An interminable silence stretched between them.

Her heart aching, Haven waited for something from him, some indication of what he was feeling. But she could not read him. He would not permit her that. His steely logic sealed him off like a gate slammed tight against her.

Impenetrable.

"Kenrick . . . do not do this. Please," she said, reaching out to grasp his arm. "Don't shut me out with your silence."

"What would you have me do, lady?"

She made a noise of frustration, somewhere between a sob and a curse. "Bellow your rage at me! Demand recompense for my actions." She took his hand, and brought it up toward her face. It hovered there, unmoving. "Strike me if you will—that I can bear!"

His strong fingers, rigid and radiating heat where they held near her cheek, slowly curled into his palm. He refused to touch her now, even in anger. "No. I am not going to shout, nor raise my hand to you, Haven. That would require passion. Something I don't have for you. Not anymore."

A cry broke from her throat, ragged against the stillness of the chamber. "Can you put me out of your heart so easily?"

"I already have." He glanced up, meeting her gaze for the first time since he had entered the room. "Would that I had banished you sooner, before you worked your shifter's witchery on anyone else in this keep. For that is what you are, is it not? You are a shifter."

Shame made her chin heavy, but she forced herself to hold her head high, to not waver under Kenrick's accusing gaze. "I am Anavrin-born, yes. I was sent to the Outside with others of my clan to seek the Dragon Chalice and see it returned to our kingdom."

"Shifter," he accused, his tone cold as any steel. "One of de Mortaine's minions. You made a clever spy—indeed, you had me fooled. How long would you have waited before you summoned your kin to attack Clairmont as they did Greycliff? Or do they come as we speak?"

"I have summoned no one, nor did I when the raid occurred on Rand and Elspeth's home."

"You would have me believe it was coincidence that you were there?"

"Nay, it was not coincidence. I was sent to their keep to gather information about the Dragon Chalice. Silas de Mortaine knew of your visits to Greycliff, and he suspected you had given Rand a portion of your work. I was supposed to search for answers and report back to him, but I found nothing. Rand kept your secret well, never speaking of your agreement nor betraying your trust in any way."

"Yes," Kenrick said. "He is a true friend."

Haven winced at the implication, then continued. "I knew the longer I delayed at Greycliff, the more likely that reinforcements would be sent to investigate. Before I could warn Elspeth and Rand of the danger they were in, de Mortaine ordered the attack on the keep. I had no idea it was coming." She took a fortifying breath, recalling the horror of that night. "The raiding shifters swooped in like a tempest. No one stood a chance against them."

"And what of you, Haven?" Kenrick's voice was wooden, flat. "What did you do during all of this bloodshed— join in with your clan?"

"No!" she gasped. "No, I tried to help Elspeth and Rand escape the raid, I swear it!"

His gaze was hard with suspicion.

"You don't believe me."

"No more than Rand himself, I expect." He gestured to her neck, where the faint marks of punishing fingers still lingered. "Those bruises you said you suffered in the attack. Rand told me how he had been betrayed to de Mortaine. He explained how he turned the betrayer's own blade on her breast, how he would have choked the life out of you, had he not lost hold of you amid the smoke and fire of the raid."

Haven nodded slowly. "His rage was uncontrolled; he would have killed me, I am certain. I would not have fought him. But one of my clan would have slain him not long afterward, and then he would have stood no chance at all of saving his family."

"What are you saying?"

"The smoke was thick, so thick all around us that it concealed me like a cloak. I shifted out of his grasp and fled into the night."

"Jesu Criste," Kenrick swore, raking his fingers through the golden waves of his hair.

"I would have told you all of this tonight, I swear it, with or without the surprise of Rand's presence."

He stared at her, his jaw held taut. "Show me."

"What?"

"I want to see you as you truly are, in your shifter form. Show me. Now."

"No," she said, recoiling at the idea. "I won't—I cannot! I do not want to be what I was."

" 'Tis too late for that, don't you think?"

She shook her head in mute denial. "I am no longer that person. That part of me is dead now. It has been, whether I remembered my origins or nay, nearly since the day I met you. Since the moment I fell in lo—"

"Do not say it again, Haven. Spare me any more of your lies."

"It is the truth, whether or not you choose to believe it. I love you."

"Nay." He reeled on her and seized her by the wrist before she knew what he was about. "You speak of love? There is but one thing a shifter truly loves."

He pivoted, and stalked across the width of her chamber, her arm caught in an unrelenting grasp. His long strides carried them into the corridor and to the stairwell that led to his private chambers in the tower. He did not free her until they were standing in the middle of the room.

She took in the space with a wary eye. His desk was in uncustomary disarray, one journal swept off the surface entirely and lying broken apart on the floor. At the opposite end of the room, a large tapestry had been rent from its hooks and left where it had fallen, exposing a flight of narrow, darkened stairs.

"Kenrick," she gasped, feeling real terror as her body raced with the sudden quicksilver tremors of her glamour rising in alarm. Tiny needles of sensation pricked the tips of her fingers and raced along the length of her limbs. "What is this about?"

"The truth, Haven. Finally."

He turned toward his desk, his hands reaching for a small wooden chest that sat there, its size and shape no bigger than a lady's mending box.

"If 'tis love that drives you," Kenrick said as he lifted the coffer from its place, "then let us see it now."

"What is the meaning of this? What is in that chest?"

"I expect you know what it contains." He turned around to face her once more, his eyes hard with judgment. "The very thing you've wanted all along for your employer, de Mortaine."

Haven dared not move, her gaze rooted to his despite the pain it caused to see such loathing reflected back at her.

Especially from him.

"Kenrick, please . . . what is in there?"

He was standing very close to her, no more than the width of the little box between them. This close, Haven felt the current of a thousand bolts of lightning thrumming from within the confines of the chest. Whatever it contained was alive with power, as strong as any magic she had ever known. It pulsed through her limbs and up along her spine, raising the fine hairs at the nape of her neck.

By all she was, every drop of Anavrin blood that coursed within her veins, she knew now what the coffer contained.

There could be no mistaking it.

Calasaar.

The Stone of Light—one of the four cups of the Dragon Chalice.

Holding the small casket before him like a prize, his knowing blue gaze impaling her, Kenrick reached to the front and lifted the hammered brass clasp.

"This is what you wanted, Haven," he told her grimly. "Open it."

She would not lift the lid, Kenrick knew. She could not allow herself so close to the treasure that was wrought from her kingdom's enchanted forge. He knew this, and so he did the deed himself. His fingers grasping the lip of the casket's hinged cover, he slowly opened the box.

Haven instantly took several steps back, but was barred from flight by the solid weight of the desk behind her. She stared at the gaping mouth of the coffer as though transfixed. Unmoving now, she stood frozen, save the visible tremor that traveled the length of her slender arms to the tips of her elegant fingers. Kenrick could hardly tell if she so much as breathed.

"*Calasaar,*" she finally whispered. "It was here all along."

Light emanated from the heart of the golden cup, one fourth of the most incredible treasure in all of Christendom. Each of the four pieces of the Dragon Chalice bore a winged serpent, coiled about the stem and clutching in its talons a priceless stone of immense power. For this cup, the stone was illumination itself—purest white, shining clear with a life-giving heat that just a few months ago had brought Kenrick's own sister back from the abyss of darkest death.

But as it healed some, it could also harm others.

Especially Haven.

Where Anavrin's shifters were charged with assisting in the return of the Dragon Chalice, for them to touch any part of it was to court a hellish death. Kenrick had heard a horrific tale of how Silas de Mortaine once punished a shifter by forcing her to hold one of the four sacred cups. She perished in a ball of flames, paying a steep price for daring to defy her evil employer.

"What now, Kenrick?" Haven asked quietly. There was fear in her eyes when she at last looked up at him. In their jewel-green depths, he saw a keen sorrow he tried hard not to acknowledge. "Will you command me to touch this cup as I stand here before you?"

"You think I want you dead?"

"Don't you?"

He couldn't answer. Emotions warred within him. Clashing feelings of rage and regret, pain and passion, competed for dominance in his heart. He knew not what to feel, or what he wanted from Haven in that moment.

"Here," she said suddenly, and lunged toward the box he held. "I will make it easy for you. Easy for both of us—"

"No!"

As her hand shot out, Kenrick seized her by the wrist. A mere heartbeat away from placing her fingers against the Calasaar cup—a fractional instant before she would have sought her own death by its deadly magic—he stopped her. The fine bones in her wrist went taut with strain.

She struggled against his hold, surprisingly strong, and flexible as a willow switch. Pinioned, she nearly twisted free. One hand loosed, she made another grab for the cup.

With a curse, Kenrick dropped his spellbound parcel to take Haven in both hands. She startled, flinching as the wooden box and the cup it contained fell from his grasp and thudded softly to the floor, its freefall tumble cushioned by the thick rug beneath their feet. He kicked the priceless vessel out of range, hearing it roll onto the wood planks some distance away.

"Why?" she cried. "Why did you stop me?"

"Because as much as I loathe what you are—" He broke off, his voice a harsh whisper very near to her face. "God's blood, but as much as I wish to deny you ever existed, I do not crave your death. But I do want you gone."

"Kenrick—"

"Go. Go now, before I have the chance to think on what I am doing in letting you leave."

"Kenrick, please. Let me explain—"

He thrust her away from him. "Go!"

A raw sob tore from her throat. She held her arms out to him, beseeching, weeping mutely. Her hair was a halo of auburn fire, her skin luminescent—almost shimmering—infused with light from the torches in the corridor outside the tower chamber.

But there was something more than mere rushlight surrounding her, he realized. In that moment, her face stricken with anguish, her fingers reaching for him, she was enveloped in a glittering, twisting sheath of glowing power.

"Jesu," he whispered, awestruck by the change coming over her.

He said her name, but he did not think she could hear him. Her features were transforming, veiled by the brilliance of the magic that had been unleashed. Her mane of long hair spread over her, golden-red, shortening to a glossy pelt. Her eyes tilted up at the corners, stretching, pupils elongating as her face took on a wilder form. She arched her neck and gave a sharp-pitched howl as the change swept over her, faster now, becoming something feral, something fierce and untamed.

The light grew brighter, nearly blinding him.

Kenrick shielded his face with his arm, transfixed by this impossible reality. He peered through slitted eyes, searching for the woman who had been standing before him, engulfed in the shimmering wonder of her glamour.

She was gone.

Haven was there no longer, but in her place stood a beautiful, terrified looking little fox.

Just like the one that had eluded him at Greycliff the first time he had laid eyes on Haven.

"God's love. It *was* you that day at Greycliff. And when the hens attacked you and Ariana here at Clairmont, provoked by an unseen alarm . . . it was because of you."

The vixen gave a short, high-pitched whine, hesitating only a heartbeat before it darted out of the tower chamber.

❧ 26 ❧

K ENRICK BOLTED INTO the corridor, disbelieving yet unable to deny what he had just seen. Dashing ahead of him, the fox was naught but a streak of pale russet fur and fast-flying feet.

It made an abrupt turn for the stairwell, its speed too much for Kenrick to keep up. He heard the startled cry of a servant on the stairs, then the crash of pottery. Taking the steps several at a time, he passed the maid who was now stooping to pick up the shards of a broken water jug.

"Have a care, m'lord! There be a nasty beast loose in the keep!"

Kenrick lunged on without acknowledging the warning.

As he cleared the last step, he nearly crashed into Ariana, who had just come out of the great hall. Her eyes were wide, her hand held at her breast in recovering composure.

"Good lord," she gasped. "A little fox just ran through here in a wild panic! However do you suppose it got in here?"

Kenrick could not answer immediately. His emotions were clashing like a thunderstorm inside him, but he held them on a tight tether, meeting his sister's worried look with one of cool resolve.

"What happened with you and Haven?" she asked him, her gaze searching his. "I saw her face as she fled the hall tonight. What has happened, Kenrick?"

"She is gone," he answered tersely. "She's gone, and she will not be back."

"Kenrick—" Ariana frowned. "What did you do to her?"

He scoffed at the protective tone in his sister's voice. "She betrayed us, Ana. All of us. By her own admission to me, she was in league with Silas de Mortaine."

"No!" Ariana shook her head as if to physically deny the possibility. "No, that's impossible. How could that be true—"

"How?" Kenrick cut her off with a bark of humorless laughter. "I saw it with my own eyes not a few moments ago, when the woman before me changed into a cunning little beast."

"What are you saying?"

"The fox you saw just now as it fled the keep was no mere animal. Haven," he said, the name falling uneasily from his tongue. "She is a shifter, Ana."

"Sweet Mary," Ariana gasped. "Kenrick, I'm so sorry. I never saw it in her, never would I have guessed . . ."

"No one was more deceived by her treachery than I."

"It seems too cold, hard to believe she could do such a thing. I don't want to believe it, as I know you must feel as well . . ."

Ariana reached for him in comfort, but Kenrick shrugged her away. He did not want sympathy at that moment. God knew, he despised pity.

"Where is Rand?" he demanded sternly.

"He waits in the hall with Braedon. Everyone is wondering where you went. They will want to know . . ."

"No," Kenrick snapped. "This is my mistake to rectify. I will do it on my own terms."

With a curt summons to one of the keep's sentries posted nearby, Kenrick called for two horses to be readied for several days' journey.

"Will you go after her, then?"

"Go after her?" He cursed low under his breath. "Nay, Ana. To me, she no longer exists. I mean to go after the one thing that does matter—the Dragon Chalice. Rand and I will set out for Glastonbury within the hour."

Her breaking heart seemed wont to burst from her breast as she ran. The meadow grasses were damp and cool against her belly, slapping hard in her face as she cleaved through them, not daring to rest until the lights of Clairmont castle were mere pinpricks on the distant hill.

Only then did she pause.

Only then did she allow her glamour to fade and recede.

She came up from her crouched position and stood amid a blanket of moonlit heather, fully changed, a woman once more. Panting from exertion and a bone-deep regret that weighed on her heart like iron bonds, Haven appeared no different than she had the moment before her betrayal was discovered, garbed in her simple kirtle and leather slippers.

But in her heart she knew she could never be the same as she had been before.

Too much had occurred.

She had allowed a breach she could not reclaim.

Haven pivoted, looking one last time on all that she was leaving behind. Clairmont stood in silhouette, dark gray stone and golden glow spilling from its windows and from the torches lining the perimeter walls.

Kenrick was on the other side of those walls, full of hatred for her. Ariana and Braedon would be as well, once they were told of her deception. There was no hope in thinking she could make a home there, among the Outsiders. She was too different from them, too tainted by the stain of her past and the magic that yet flowed through her shifter veins.

Tears filled her gaze, blurring the lights. She looked away from the short happiness she had known in Kenrick's home, in Kenrick's bed, and focused on what lay ahead of her now.

Bleak as it was, her future rested on the decisions she made from this point on.

She was compromised, but she would not be so easily defeated.

Draec le Nantres had given her a shred of hope in his proposition that day outside Clairmont. He had given her what was, perhaps, her only choice.

With a heavy heart and a fiery resolve, Haven set off on the path that would take her to the market town, where le Nantres had said he would be waiting for word from her.

❧ 27 ❧

THE WEATHER HAD been kind the nearly two days it had taken Kenrick and Rand to make the ride from Clairmont to the pastoral meadowlands of Somerset, home of Glastonbury Tor. Now that they had arrived, stopping to rest their mounts just within sight of the queer hill with its little church perched atop it like a crown, the afternoon skies threatened with rain.

"Storm's coming," Kenrick said as he eyed the bunching clouds with weary scorn. The trek up the steep tor would be arduous without the added trouble of slick mud and wet clothing. "Looks as though we'll be staying the night in town. No sense pushing the horses or ourselves now that we're here."

"I'd rather we pressed on, Saint."

Rand fixed him with a determined look. Around his neck he wore Elspeth's pendant, repaired and returned to him by Kenrick upon Rand's arrival at Clairmont. Absently, the warrior's calloused fingers toyed with the delicate filigreed heart that rested at the base of his throat. Rand stroked it like a touchstone, and his gaze was dark with purpose.

"The sooner we finish here, the sooner we can begin searching for the next piece of the treasure . . . and the sooner I can have my vengeance on Silas de Mortaine."

Kenrick had known his friend was bitter with rage for the deaths of Elspeth and his son, but the days on the road with him had shown a darker side of Rand. His heart was cold, black with grief and deadly determination. He was a man consumed by hatred, all of it centered on de Mortaine and those who would aid him in his search for the Dragon Chalice.

Rand spoke of little else but his plans for revenge. He was single-minded in his purpose, even more so than Kenrick himself had been on his own years-long quest for the Chalice treasure. Rand had eagerly absorbed all that Kenrick told him of his findings and his theories on the locations of the remaining pieces. He had sworn to ride beside Kenrick every step of the way—wherever it led them—if it meant he would one day have the pleasure of slaying Silas de Mortaine.

"We've come this far," Rand pointed out, his hazel eyes flinty in the overcast light. "I'll get no sleep in town when I know the treasure could lie just at the top of that hill."

Kenrick glanced to the tall mound of earth in the distance. Even from here, he could see the maze of rings that circled the base of the tor, seven levels of an earthen labyrinth carved by men long centuries dead.

It was said that an ancient king and his army slumbered within the great mound, awaiting their revival. It was also said that Joseph of Arimathea had carried the Cup of Christ to this very spot in ages past, and buried it somewhere on the tor. If Kenrick's suspicions were correct, it was not the Holy Grail that waited on Glastonbury Tor, but another sacred cup—one that would be a match for the bejeweled, golden goblet he carried in one of his saddlebags.

He had not told Rand about Calasaar, for despite the friendship they shared, Kenrick felt this new Rand—this wounded man who was only a small part of the reckless adventurer he once knew—might let his want for vengeance shade his judgment.

Kenrick knew well how easy it was to let emotion rule one's better sense. His time with Haven had been proof enough of that. His weakness with her had put his quest, and perhaps his beloved kin and keep, in great peril.

Even now, Haven might be working to realign herself with de Mortaine. She knew about the seal that was missing from Greycliff, and after their painful confrontation at Clairmont, she now knew about Calasaar as well. Kenrick was not about to risk a further mistake, nor would he watch as Rand submitted his sense to the anger that festered within him.

And so he kept the Calasaar cup secreted away on his saddle, held close until the time he might need it.

"What say you, Saint? You'd be the last man to let a little water keep you from proving a point. You know that damned cup is up there, just waiting for you to take it."

Kenrick absorbed Rand's words with as much resignation as he did pride. It was true; nothing could dissuade him once he'd seized upon a problem and meant to solve it. His gut told him that one of the Chalice stones was, in fact, waiting somewhere on the tor, so close he could almost feel the vibration of its power passing through Calasaar and into him.

He was so close—he was certain of it.

Rand gave a knowing chuckle and cuffed him on the shoulder. "I'll meet you at the top, my friend."

With a nudge of his heels, Greycliff sent his mount into a canter across the flat meadowland that lay shrouded with the mist of the oncoming rains.

Kenrick let him go but a furlong's distance before he, too, was spurring his horse onward, toward the final hour's ride that stood between him and the crest of that mysterious jut of earth.

The inn was crowded with seamen and traders and other unsavory types. He paused to scan the many haggard faces, looking for a glint of recognition, of expectance, in any pair of the scores of eyes that turned on him as he entered the coastal gathering place. None seemed inclined to stare overlong at the warrior who strode in alone, an air of contempt in his every move.

He was dressed as fine as any wealthy lord, his dark cloak swirling in his wake, brushing the tops of his gleaming leather boots, and dancing around the length of polished steel that rode in a gem-encrusted sheath on his hip. The knight crossed the small public room in stormy silence. His gaze was hard, flinty as he approached the innkeeper for word, as he had been instructed.

"Le Nantres," he announced himself in a growl, impatience edging his clipped tone as he put down a handful of coin in payment.

The man behind the bar gave a discreet nod. "Right, sir. This way, if you will."

Draec followed his portly guide away from the teeming public room and up a short flight of stairs toward the back of the establishment. He shared none of the innkeeper's serviceable haste, taking his time as he talked along the narrow hallway an indolent distance behind the man. He did not appreciate being made to bend to another's demands, even when those demands had come from a chit as appealing as the one who'd summoned him that night.

"This be the one," said the innkeeper, halting as he gestured to the door of a private room.

As Draec approached, the man meekly edged away, leaving him alone at the threshold. Once the innkeeper was gone from sight, Draec turned his attention back to the door. It was slightly ajar. The wench was bold; clearly, she had expected him not to refuse her requested meeting. She'd even made him pay for the lodgings. He had to admire her for her cheek, if nothing else.

Light spilled out from the open space near the latch, the welcoming crackle and glow of a hearthfire emanating from within. Draec splayed his hand against the cool panel, and pushed it wide.

The shifter beauty stood not a half dozen paces away from him, her fiery mane and slender figure cloaked in a long mantle of shimmering gold velvet. The fabric caught the light of the twisting flames on the hearth, making Haven sparkle like living fire herself.

A table had been set with a warm meal and an uncorked flagon of wine. Two glasses bore samples of the decanted claret, their bowls glowing ruby red. At the other side of the chamber stood a large bed, its four posters draped with gauzy curtains that had been parted and tied back on the side facing the door. Although half in shadow, he could see that the coverlet was turned down as if to invite a decadent tryst.

Draec felt his blood quicken at the thought.

He hadn't imagined the unattainable lady, this deadly shifter spy, could be such a willing temptress. But he had noted something peculiar about her when he'd seen her that day near Clairmont, and although he had not been able to put his finger on just what that peculiarity was, it had not been far from his mind in the time since.

It had been something in her eyes, he had decided, thinking how her bewitching green gaze had seemed softer than before. Softer than any shifter's detached and emotionless stare.

But that softness was gone now, Draec determined, studying her face.

"Something has happened to you," he mused aloud. "Clairmont found you out, did he?"

"I didn't come here to talk about him," she replied, her voice as cool and steady as a blade. "You and I have better things to discuss, wouldn't you agree?"

She untied the ribbon at her throat, and let the mantle fall. The lush fabric slid down her curves like a lover's hand, slow and appreciative, until it pooled on the floor at her feet. All she wore was a simple silk gown of feathery weight, which floated about her shape like a veil. The garment was an effective tease, an artist's shroud— or sorcerer's conjuring—that hinted tantalizingly at the feminine perfection it concealed.

She was the very picture of seduction, and well she knew it.

Draec felt no shame as he drank in the unearthly beauty before him. He was never one to deny himself a gift freely given, particularly when it came wrapped in a package as delectable, and as personally advantageous, as this. He smiled the devil's own smile, anticipating the pleasure—and the imminent fruition of his quest—that was to come.

"Dare I hope, lovely vixen, that this meeting means you've given my proposal some thought?"

Her jewel-bright gaze did not waver so much as a fraction.

"Yes," she said, unflinching as he approached. "I have decided to accept your offer."

❧ 28 ❧

A SMALL, TOWERLESS chapel stood at the crest of Glastonbury Tor. Dedicated to Saint Michael for having slain a dragon on this very spot, the modest church was comprised of a square nave and narrow chancel. For the small group of monks who resided in the grand abbey at the base of the high hill, visiting pilgrims were no unusual occurrence. In fact, over the years, a few profit-minded brethren had encouraged the curious with reports of unearthed tombs belonging to King Arthur and a well that was said to flow with water originating from the Holy Grail itself.

Although strange lights and unexplained events were rumored to occur atop the tor, it was the abbey grounds below that elicited the most interest from travelers seeking miraculous cures and treasure hunters seeking other, material boons. With the spring rain wetting the countryside, few observers had been present to take notice of the two men who had made a cautious ride up the long sloping back of the oblong-shaped hill.

Nor was anyone hovering around to question them on their purpose during the couple of hours they spent carefully examining every nook and hidden alcove for signs that would lead them to one of the Chalice stones.

The church was a small structure, its central chamber, the nave, no more than two score paces in any direction. Beyond it, through an arched threshold, was the priest's chancel. It was in this narrower space that Kenrick first saw a familiar symbol. The light was fading fast outside, with the rain shower and the approach of twilight throwing the chapel into dusky gloom. While Rand went to find torches to light, Kenrick stooped to retrieve a flint from one of his satchels.

As he crouched on the glazed tile floor, his eye caught a subtle design beneath the dust underfoot. He smoothed it away with his palm and swore a quiet oath. He cleared more of the fine grit, revealing the tile directly below the arch that separated the nave from the chancel.

"The torches, Rand!" he called out. "Bring them quick!"

Rand's heavy bootfalls echoed from the other section of the church. He held two small pitch lights and an iron candelabrum from the altar. "What did you find?"

"Here," Kenrick said, pointing to the glazed tiles. "You won't see them from that angle. You'll have to crouch down."

Rand came down to where Kenrick was, and followed his tracery of the design. On the floor between the two rooms was a series of scrollwork symbols: circles interconnecting, crosses stretched between the intersections. Scarcely discernable, the symbols had been etched under the glaze, gray enamel on gray stone tile, all but invisible unless one knelt before the archway.

"What does it mean? How will it lead us to the stone?"

"I'm not sure . . . but the answer is here." He took one

of the torches and struck his flint to light it. "Take this," he told Rand. "Search the floor of the nave for more of these designs. I'll keep looking in here."

He lit the second torch as Rand pivoted to check the other chamber. It was not a few moments before an exhaled oath echoed from the adjacent nave.

"Saint. You'll want to have a look at this."

Kenrick pushed to his feet and hurried to where his friend's voice had issued.

Rand stood in the center of the nave, his torch held out before him. He was not looking at the floor, but at the walls, now cast into relief by the flickering flame of the pitch torch. What had seemed smooth stone was something other altogether. Kenrick drew up beside his friend and looked to the wall that housed the arch leading to the chancel antechamber. He could not help but gape in wonder at what he saw.

"Holy Mother of God."

Rand held one of Kenrick's diagrams out to him. The symbols were nearly identical. "I'd say we found something, my friend."

"Aye, we have," he agreed, not certain he even breathed now that he was staring at the tactile evidence of his imminent success.

Or his most spectacular failure.

He knew the symbol of the cross and spheres was a key that would lead him to a piece of the Dragon Chalice, and now here it was, the pattern repeated in dizzying array on the thick stone wall not an arm's length away.

The problem was, he had expected the symbols to mark the location of the treasure. All he could see here was the empty space of the nave and the darkened chancel on the other side of the archway.

They had reached a dead end.

Perched on the edge of the bed, Haven held her full glass of wine and watched as Draec le Nantres sampled the tray of food she had served him. Reclining near the hearth like a negligent prince, he was on his second glass of claret and having the devil of a time keeping his smoky, sensual gaze from fixing on her body as he listened to her plans for their covert alliance.

All lies, of course.

Her brazeness was purely illusion. Not much different than the diaphanous gown and velvet cloak, both crafted of Anavrin magic, and meant to conceal the drab attire she wore since her flight from Clairmont. She had given Draec le Nantres a picture of invitation, of willing alliance, and so far, he was taking the bait. But there was still a chance her plan could fail.

She needed to stall him for time, give the herbs a chance to be absorbed and work their own magic on his muscular limbs and dangerous mind.

To her good fortune, le Nantres was a man of great appetite. To her chagrin, that appetite did not restrict itself to just food and wine. He wanted her, and had been making that point quite clear as the hours wore on in the private chamber of the inn.

"You are making me feel like a glutton, lady. Won't you come down by the fire and join me in this meal? It is quite delicious."

Haven gave him a coy, if calculated, smile. "I'm content to watch you enjoy it. Besides, as I've told you already, I took my supper before you arrived."

The noise he made in the back of his throat was something of a growl, sulky, yet full of masculine confidence that made her wonder if any woman had ever denied the rogue what he wanted. "A taste, at least. Then we can discuss the more pleasant aspects of our alliance."

She lifted a brow, but did not move from her seat across the chamber.

"Nay?" he asked with idle amusement. "Very well, stubborn minx. I will bring the decadence to you."

With strong, elegant fingers, he plucked a glazed berry from its sauce of rich, baked honey, then got up from his position on the floor to approach her. His gaze was dark with a powerful sensuality that seemed accustomed to the chase, and to conquest. But there was the slightest falter in his otherwise flawless stride.

He did not seem to notice, she thought; more the better.

He reached the bed and seated himself beside her, one hand braced behind her, the other holding the sweet dark berry at her lips. He gave her a wickedly handsome smile that dazzled when he was but a breath away from her on the mattress.

"Open your mouth, beauty, and taste the sinful treat you would deny yourself."

Her eyes on his, Haven obeyed the deliberately sensual command. The pungency of pennyroyal was evident to her trained palette, its subtle flavor filtering through the thick honey sauce. She betrayed nothing of her thoughts as she chewed the berry under his close scrutiny.

"Hmm?" he grunted, evidently pleased at her compliance. His voice was as dark and warm as silk. "You know, I could be content watching your enjoyment tonight as well."

He stroked his fingers along the length of her arm and Haven sidled away. "There are still a few things we must make clear," she said. "Things I must know before I am comfortable to . . . proceed with our arrangement."

He leaned back, his blunt chin going up in consideration. "What more do you need to know? We have agreed to help each other—you will assist me in finding the other Chalice stones, and I will see you returned to Anavrin, whole and hale, once I claim the Dragon Chalice for my own."

"Yes," Haven said, "that is our agreement. But you are asking me to place a great deal of trust in you. How can I be assured that you will uphold your promises to me?"

His mouth pursed thoughtfully. "You wound me, lady. I realize some would question my methods, call me a scoundrel, but I do have some honor. I am a fair man—so long as I am getting what I require in the bargain."

"And what, precisely, do you require in our bargain?"

"You help me find the remaining Chalice stones, and assist me in obtaining the one held by Silas de Mortaine, and I will see you back to your homeland." He chuckled, and when he spoke there was a faint slur in his words. "Until that time, there iss naught to bar us from enjoying each other's company . . . iss there?"

He scowled suddenly, no doubt alerted to the vague thickening of his devil's tongue. She would need to distract him lest he discover her intent too soon.

"There is something I would know," she said, turning to face him on the edge of the bed. "Why would you risk going against Silas de Mortaine to get the Chalice? He is a formidable man with a great deal of power, both here and in Anavrin. He already has one of the sacred Chalice stones, and he has a good number of my clan at his command. To defy him is to court death. You must know that."

"What does it matter my reasons?"

"If I am to ally myself with you, I would have you tell me."

"You say that to defy de Mortaine is death?" Le Nantres's expression had become very grim, troubled by unspoken demons that writhed within the dark green depths of his gaze. "To allow the Dragon Chalice to slip through my fingers is death to me. What man would not be tempted by the lure of immense power—of eternal life?"

"There are some."

"Clairmont?" Draec scoffed. "Can you be so sure? He has gotten closer than anyone to deciphering the riddle of the Chalice. What drives him to it if not the promise of its many gifts?"

"I suppose he thinks he is doing what is right, what is just, by keeping de Mortaine—or anyone else—from using the Chalice for their own designs. Mayhap he also enjoys the challenge to be found in so intriguing a quest."

"Ah," Draec purred. "The thrill of the chase. Few men can resist that. I wonder, lovely Haven, how long did Clairmont have to chase you before he caught you?"

Haven shifted slightly where she sat, feeling Draec's gaze narrow on her in measured observance. He pinned her with his piercing green eyes, but already his pupils had begun to round under the lulling spell of her herbs.

Still, he was a big man, a seasoned warrior whose honed body might resist such an affront. She only hoped he would succumb before his masculine patience wore out.

"If I allowed myself to be chased and caught, it did serve to bring me closer to my enemy and his secrets. You here on the Outside often fail to consider that silk is sometimes stronger than steel." Haven offered le Nantres a considering smile that felt too tight on her lips. "Anyway, as you say, what matter his reasons for seeking the Dragon Chalice? Every man will have his own cause for wanting the power it wields. Kenrick of Clairmont is no different than the rest of your breed."

Le Nantres gave her a lazy look that belied his keen perception. "Did I not know better, shifter, I would think I detect a note of bitterness in your voice. I thought your kind was immune to such mortal emotions."

Haven thrust out her chin and spoke in a curtly superior tone. "Disdain is what I feel for the days I was held little better than a prisoner in his keep."

"A prisoner garbed in pretty gowns and sparkling jewels," Draec drawled, plainly remarking on the way she looked when they met so unexpectedly outside Clairmont's walls.

"They knew not who I was."

"And now they do?"

"Yes, they know."

"I am surprised Clairmont and my old friend Braedon did not kill you on the spot. They will, once they learn you have sided with me."

"All the more reason for us to put our alliance to work without delay," Haven replied. "I do not belong here on the Outside. I will not be safe until I'm back in Anavrin."

"And so you shall be, lady. Once the Dragon Chalice is mine." Draec raised his glass to his lips and drained it in one swallow. He set the empty glass on the floor beside the bed a bit clumsily, then leaned back on the mattress, propped by his bent elbow. "Tell me what else you know about Kenrick of Clairmont and his quest for this treasure."

"I can tell you that he believes he knows where another of the stones is hidden."

"Where?" Draec asked, not bothering to hide his impatient interest. "Did he give you the location?"

"No. But I saw his writings, and I was able to conclude what he'd been guessing at."

"Tell me. Damn it, name the place!"

"Land's End," she relented after a moment, praying he would swallow her lie as readily as he swallowed the herbed wine. If he did, and if she should fail in her plan tonight, at least she would be sending le Nantres leagues away from Kenrick's true destination. "There is a small church on the promontory of the cliffs. Clairmont means to search there for one of the Chalice stones."

"This is the truth?"

"I swear it on my life," Haven vowed, prepared to accept the consequences. "But even if he is correct in his deductions, he will fail to find the stone, for he is missing a crucial piece of the puzzle. Something you claim to have."

"That's right." Draec's chuckle was deep with appreciative humor. He inclined his head in a courtly show of respect. "I have the seal, and now I know where it belongs. You see, Haven? This is why we make an ideal team."

She shared his smile, but hers hid a wary sense of calculation. "Show me the key."

"What makes you think I brought it with me?"

Now it was Haven's turn to laugh. "You would never entrust it to someone else, nor would you risk leaving it out of your sight, where anyone could steal it back from you. Let me see it."

"Later, perhaps," he said, then stretched out on the bed. She started to get up, but his arm snaked out and he seized her by the wrist. His tug was playful, but firm. "Join me, Haven. You have been tempting me sorely all evening with that witchy gown of yours. Patience never was one of my virtues."

She had not intended for things to progress so quickly, but she let him pull her down beside him on the bed. As she stretched out to face him, her free hand worked to loosen her braided silk girdle. The long length of cording slid out from beneath her hips, and she tucked it at her back on the mattress, holding le Nantres's dragon green gaze all the while.

"Isn't that better?" he asked when she had settled in before him.

"Yes, this is . . . nice."

His chuckle was sly and not a little alarming. "I'm not a fool, you know. And you are not a skilled liar, lady."

Haven's face must have registered her jolt of anxiety, for Draec's grip suddenly tightened on her wrist. "What game do you play?"

"I do not—"

He thrust her arm up and over, holding fast to her and

pinning her to the bed with the hard length of his body. "You do, Haven. And I do not like—uhhh!"

A shudder wormed its way through his body and down the punishing muscles of his arm. He squeezed his eyes closed, and when they opened, he seemed unable to focus. "Damnation . . . what is this?"

He released her wrist as if he had no choice, rubbing his eyes and gripping his temples in both hands. He groaned, his face twisting into a grimace.

"You'd better lie down," Haven told him, quickly extricating herself from his reach.

He fell back on the bed, his brow sheened with perspiration. "My ears are ringing . . . mouth is . . . bone dry." He licked his parched lips. "Christ, I need a drink."

"Nay," Haven said, easing him back down when he tried to rise from the mattress. "You have had enough wine, I reckon. Lie down now, and relax."

No longer heeding the illusion of her seductive garb, Haven released it. She stood before him in the simple kirtle and slippers that she had taken from Clairmont Castle.

"What have you . . . done?" le Nantres croaked. He shook his head, scowling, then blinked at her in sudden, dawning understanding. "Witch," he snarled through bared teeth. "You . . . have drugged me."

Haven said nothing, merely worked in all haste to secure him while he fought the effects of the herbs. She slid off the bed with her girdle trailing in her fist, then ran to his right side. He gave little resistance as she took his hand and tied it to the tall post of the bed. With the long tail of the braided rope of silk, she fit his other wrist likewise to the opposite post.

Draec jerked against the makeshift shackles, jostling the heavy bed, but the tether held fast.

"Let me up . . . damnation! Let . . . me . . . up!"

Satisfied with her work, Haven paused to look down on his supine body, which dwarfed the big mattress. The snarling dragon emblem on his tunic seemed to glare up at her, eyes blazing with a fury matching that of the warrior who bore the beastly symbol on his chest. Le Nantres growled in outrage, but he could do little else when the intoxicating potion she fed him was speeding through his system.

"I think you would be better advised to rest a while, Sir Draec."

"No—damn you!" He struggled some more, futile rage that spent precious strength.

"The herbs I put in your food and wine will not kill you, but they will make you sleep, and your head will be terribly sore come the morning."

"Can't sleep . . . the beast . . . 'twill swallow me . . ." He thrashed his head on the bolster, fighting invisible demons with a fear that seemed very real. "Cannot see . . . cannot . . . breathe."

"The herbs have already taken hold of you," she said, hearing the nonsensical murmuring as he writhed on the bed. "Rest now. You only make the herbs work faster when you fight it."

He gave a half-hearted attempt to rise up off the mattress, but seemed not to have the strength. He fell back down with a frustrated expulsion of his breath. "Foolish chit! You're letting de Mortaine win," he said, anger flaring in his sharp green eyes as he struggled to speak through the hazing effect of the herbs. "You have no idea . . . he will destroy . . . I need . . . must have the Chalice . . ."

The herbs were dragging him under swiftly now; his eyes rolled in dazed slowness, shuttered longer and longer by the fall of his thick dark lashes. The tendons in his arms relaxed, slumping as the pull of sleep claimed him. One last epithet was lost midstream as his breathing deepened to a low snore.

Faith, she had done it. The dragon lord was subdued.

"Sleep well, le Nantres."

Now to find the seal.

Haven made a quick search of his person. She emptied the pouches on his sword belt, then ran her hand under his tunic, praying her instincts were correct, that he would keep the seal close to him at all times. Her fingers brushed over a cord of thin leather looped about his neck. She followed the line of it, to where it had slid in his struggles.

Haven smiled when her hand closed around cool metal. She gave a hard tug and the object came free of its tether.

She pulled the seal out into the candlelight, her gaze tracing the very pattern Kenrick had described to her all those nights ago. Twin circles overlapping, with a small cross floating at the heart of their intersection.

Feeling hope rise from the ashes of her past mistakes, Haven seized the metal seal in her palm and dashed out the door.

❧ 29 ❧

PUTTING HAVEN OUT of his mind had been difficult during his waking hours, but Kenrick found he could not bar her from his dreams. He dreamed of her smile, her thoughtful gaze, the beautiful face and siren's body that masked her witch's heart.

By day, he held fast to his rage at her betrayal, at his own stupidity.

She had proven him an utter fool.

He, the man of reason, the student of logic and patterns, had been bested by pretty lies and false embraces. He should despise her, and in truth, a part of him did. That she was likely teamed with his enemies at this very moment was enough to fuel his anger ten times over.

She *was* his enemy, he reminded himself harshly on those occasions when he felt his heart soften toward the woman who had seemed so lost when he found her, so vulnerable and in need of his protection.

By day he forced his heart to harden and shut her out, but at night, when he closed his eyes and saw her there with him—fiery, sensual Haven, as she had been before he knew the truth—it was all he could do to keep from reaching for her. All he could do to keep from pulling her close and tasting her deceitful kiss one more time.

He should have learned, for in the end it was always the same.

Even in dreams she proved him her fool, laughing soundlessly as she faded to mist and slipped away through his grasping fingers.

On this night, with Rand on watch in the tor chapel and Kenrick having made camp outside, Haven came to him in sorrow. He felt her touch brush softly against his cheek, drawing him into the dream. His slumbering mind saw her as clearly as ever, kneeling beside him on the soft grass, her mane of flowing auburn hair and graceful shoulders limned by silver moonlight.

He would have thought her an angel if not for her tears.

She said nothing as she gazed down at him, her eyes welled and glittering with moisture. One fat tear spilled over, rolling down the delicate slope of her face. He might have caught the errant droplet, but he willed himself not to reach out, not to touch, lest he lose her so soon after she had arrived.

Her sadness confused him. It moved him, registering somewhere deep inside him, but she gave him no chance to question her.

Slowly, silently, she bent down and brushed his mouth with a tender kiss.

It had been just days since they had parted at Clairmont, a few scant nights since the last one they spent together, but to Kenrick, feeling her lips so warm against his own, it seemed he had gone a lifetime away from Haven's kiss.

His hunger surged at once, desire arrowing through him like a spark igniting parched fields. But he did not let it rule him. He dared not rush the dream that felt so real, so right. He kept his hands at his sides, rigid in his control, as the midnight vision of Haven drew back to look at him in thoughtful silence.

His breath caught as he gazed upon her and realized she wore nothing but the dark velvet of the evening around them. The tips of her breasts peeked out from beneath the fiery veil of her hair, which tumbled about her in long coppery waves. Her skin was pale, ethereal, luminescent. Her fingers were just a bit unsteady as she reached out to pull away the cloak that blanketed him on his makeshift pallet on the ground.

She leaned into him then, slipping her flattened palms under his tunic and up his bare chest. Her touch was feather-light, but it inflamed him like a brand. She stroked every inch of his skin, as if memorizing him by feel, her nails grazing across the discs of his nipples, her palms curving around the bulk of his shoulders and down along his biceps.

Already he was growing hard, his manhood stiff and straining in his braies. When she bent down to kiss his mouth again, Kenrick could not contain his groan of animal need. But he did not pull her to him as his want for her would have him do. He let the sensual dream proceed at its own pace, fearing it would not last, and praying it would never stop.

Through the lustful daze of the kiss, he felt Haven's fingers stray down his belly, trailing over the muscles that ribbed his abdomen, and lower still. Her palm smoothed over the top of his breeches to the thrusting ridge of his arousal. She stroked him wickedly, knowing his body's rhythm, stirring his desire toward the breaking point.

Kenrick arched his hips to meet her sensual caress,

willing the dream to take him further. He needed Haven's touch. He wanted her, even now, despite her betrayal.

He felt the ties of his breeches, then his braies, tug loose in her fingers.

"Criste . . . yes . . ." he heard himself hiss as her warm hand curled around his unfettered shaft. "Don't stop."

She said nothing, but continued to stroke his fevered flesh. God help him, but she did not stop, not even when he was full to bursting, shuddering under her hand and not a hairbreadth from spilling his seed in her palm. He had never known such raw need. No woman had ever commanded him as Haven did—in his dreams or waking. And he cared not which this was before him now. He knew only that he needed her, that he had to have her.

"Please," he begged the moonlit witch who had since poised herself astride him in the dark. Her naked thighs straddled his hips, a few cruel inches separating him from the paradise of her warmth and the release that only her body could give him. "Haven," he whispered, "sweet witch . . . take me inside you. Let me feel your heat all around me."

Her smile was wistful, sweetly sad. With her teary gaze locked on him, she slowly seated herself, sheathing the full length of his sex inside of her. God's love, but for a dream, she was searing hot and wet as she contracted around him, coaxing him into a pleasurable tempo as she rode him in the quiet darkness of the glade.

Kenrick watched her move atop him, each grind of her hips, each subtle withdrawal, tightening the leash of his control. The tether she held him on was thin and growing thinner. She knew it, the crafty witch. She knew how close he was to losing his hold, and she delighted in the wicked torment.

He felt his climax building, rising, bunching at his core. Haven held his gaze and took him deeper. The tight glove of her body clenched hard around him, contracting, the quickening of her release demanding his own.

He could hold it back no longer.

With a throttled moan of pleasure, he spent himself, surrendering all control to the midnight vision of his lady of fire. Trembling with the force of his release, he needed to touch her, to hold her, to know the softness of her skin pressed flush against his own.

In defiance of the rules of the dream, Kenrick reached out to her.

His hands settled on hips that were warm and pliant under his fingers. He squeezed her tighter, waiting for her to dissipate to vapor as she had every other night she had come to him in his dreams. But she did not fade away. She did not mockingly leave him in silent laughter and mist.

"Haven," he said, disbelieving as he came up off the ground and caught her in his arms where she yet straddled him. "I thought I dreamed you here."

She made a desperate sound in the back of her throat and tried to move away, but he held her firmly. It should not please him so to be holding her again, but it did. Too much, he thought, when the sting of her deceit was still so raw, the ramifications of that deceit yet undetermined.

But she was truly there with him, not a dream, though she lay under the dark skies like heaven in his arms.

And the tears that glistened like starlight on her cheeks were not illusion, either. They, too, were real.

She swiped at them with impatient fingers, struggling beneath him. "I must go. I should not have come here, not like this."

Kenrick rolled aside to let her up, watching as she hastily dressed. She glanced back at him, her gaze meek, apologetic.

"This was a mistake—"

"If it is, 'tis but one among many we both have made," Kenrick replied, feeling no regret for what they had just shared.

"No, this is different. Each moment I delay here puts you in greater risk."

He laughed at that, finding it ironic that she would be concerned with his well-being after all he knew about her now.

"It is true," she said quietly. "I don't expect you to understand."

When she turned away as if she would leave him there without a further word, Kenrick got to his feet with a curse. He grabbed his breeches and tugged them up over his hips, then caught her by the arm before she could take another step. "What wouldn't I understand? That no matter what we have shared, you are sworn in deadly service to Silas de Mortaine? Or that you are playing me still, even now?"

Her downswept gaze was not swift enough to hide the note of regret in her eyes. "You have every right to hate me, I know that. But know this too: I am here not because I mean to deceive you in any way. That was never my intention. Nor did I come here to make love with you."

"Why, then?" he asked, cautious to see what seemed true emotion in her clever shifter gaze.

"Please—Kenrick, I am a danger to you. Now more than ever."

"Now I at least know what you are. That is a benefit denied me all the time you were deceiving me in my keep . . . and in my bed."

She wrenched out of his hold with a small cry. "Let me go."

"What is your hurry, sweet witch? Does your clan await word from their spy of where I am?"

" 'Tis nothing like that—"

He scoffed. "What makes you think I'll believe that you are not prepared to lead de Mortaine and his minions to this very spot so they can finish me once and for all? Mayhap they are already here, laying their trap while you seduced your fool one more time."

"Can you really think so little of me?" She looked up at him with earnest, tear-filled eyes. "I would give anything to take back what has come between us—all of it. I would never betray you to anyone, not for any reason . . . because I love you, Kenrick. I love you with all my heart."

How cold would that heart have to be to tell so deep a lie with such evident conviction? Kenrick let her claim sink in for a long moment, saying nothing to accept or refute it. The very last thing he needed was to involve himself with Haven again, not when he was this close to finding another of the Chalice stones.

And yet . . .

How hard it was to look at her now, when his body was still warm from loving her, her scent yet clinging to his skin like the most exquisite perfume. How hard it was to see the distress in her soft features, the sorrow in her eyes, when time stretched out and he remained rigidly silent, unable to decide how he felt in that moment.

"I cannot go back to my clan now," she said quietly. "I am changed because of you, Shadowed by the love I feel for you. There is no turning back. I have betrayed a convenant of my kind, and that betrayal is what puts you in danger when you are with me. I came here tonight to say good-bye in the only way I knew how. But more importantly, I came here to return something that belonged to you."

He frowned, uncertain at her meaning until his eye strayed over his things and caught the faint glint of moonlight on metal. He bent down and reached for the satchel he had been using as a bolster while he slept. Sticking out from beneath the flap was an object he thought never to see again. He picked up the item and held it under the pale glow of the moon.

"The seal," he said, astonished to feel it as real in his hand as Haven herself had been not a short while ago, pressed against his bare skin.

"Le Nantres had it."

"Jesu . . . how did you manage to get this back from him?"

"Aye, wench. How did you manage?"

Kenrick glanced over his shoulder to find Rand standing but a few feet away from them, his sword gripped menacingly in his hand, a murderous look simmering in his eyes.

❧ 30 ❧

THE LAST TIME Haven had seen so lethal a look in Randwulf of Greycliff's eyes, she had been stuck at the killing end of a dagger, her throat all but closed off by the punishing grip of his hands as he sought to squeeze the life from her.

That she was standing before him again, facing his thunderous rage, made her stomach coil with fear and a pained acceptance that she deserved all the black hatred he would deal her now.

"You," he snarled. "I thought you dead. By the blood of Christ, I had hoped you as dead and gone as my beloved wife and son, murdered because of you."

"What I did to you and your family is unforgivable," she admitted. "You have every right to wish me dead."

"Wish it?" His bark of laughter was short and rife with loathing. He took a menacing step forward, raising his sword. "Nay, shifter. I'll do more than wish it now."

Haven forced herself to remain where she stood, prepared for Greycliff's wrath. But to her surprise and Rand's obvious confusion, Kenrick stepped in front of her. He guarded her with his body, placing her behind him in a protective, sheltering stance.

"Step aside, Saint. You cannot know who—or rather, what—it is you mean to defend. This black-souled beast brought my family's deaths. She crept into my home like a vermination, befriending Elspeth with her witch's potions and binding spells. She is a shifter, as vile and treacherous as they come."

"I know who she is," Kenrick answered soberly. "And I know what she has done."

"You . . . know this? If that be true, then how can you put yourself near her? God's blood, Saint. How is it you can move to protect her?"

Kenrick's voice was stern, unyielding. "Put down your weapon, Rand."

"I will have retribution for my family's lives—not even you can stand in the way of that. This shifter wench will pay."

"Stand down—" Kenrick began, reaching for his own weapon.

Haven halted him with a softly voiced command. "Kenrick, no. You needn't defend me in this, my lord. Nothing can. Your friend is right; I am responsible for his loss."

Rand stared at her as if waiting for her to wield her shifter's magic. Haven took a few steps toward him, dismissing with a shake of her head Kenrick's advice to keep her distance while Rand was still holding his weapon at the ready, his chest heaving with rage.

"I'm sorry for what happened to Elspeth and Tod. I cared for them, too."

"Lies!" he scoffed.

"I know you won't believe me, but it is true. I cared for them, and that is what brought my clan to Greycliff that night. You see, they were hunting me—with as much determination as they hunted for the Chalice secrets you were keeping for Kenrick. I was sent in to spy and to recover the seal, but I did not report back as I was instructed. De Mortaine became suspicious, and he sent a number of shifters in to find me. My ties to my clan are severed completely. I cannot ever go back to them."

Rand snorted in rejection. "Why should you be trusted? Because you can put a tear in your eye and declare to feel affection for something other than your accursed Dragon Chalice? It would take no magic to do that—only a lying tongue and a lack of mortal conscience."

"What I've told you is the truth. Would that I could bring them back to you, I would do it. I would trade my life for theirs, were it possible."

"Spare me your empty sentiment," he scoffed. "Tell me, can you feel loss, shifter? Can you feel remorse?"

Haven's gaze slid toward Kenrick for an instant before returning to meet Rand's hard stare. "Yes. I know loss. And I know remorse like a pit of darkness I may never climb out of." She nodded her head, reflective in her silence. "I know regret . . . as deeply as I have come to know love these past precious days."

"What about you, Saint?" Rand looked at him now. "You seem to know her better than I could say. Do you believe her?"

Kenrick's stoic expression was unreadable, but he inclined his chin in agreement. "She has brought the seal from le Nantres. No matter what else she has said—to either of us here tonight—she has delivered the boon we needed. She had no need to bring it, and she did so at great personal risk."

Rand's voice was hard with skepticism. "How can you be sure this is not a trap?"

"It is no trap," Haven interjected. "I am here to help you. My word is my honor. I stake my life on it."

"Aye, you do," Rand agreed, refusing to be swayed so easily when his heart clearly ached for all he would never again have. "Your life is at stake, lady. For if this be a shifter trick, and we find ourselves circled by de Mortaine and the rest of your hellborn ilk, you can be sure of one thing. You will be the first to die—by my hand."

"I am here in earnest," she vowed, her gaze turned to Kenrick. "I give you my oath."

He seemed to accept her word, his expression solemn, but lacking some of its previous cool edge. There was a note of forgiveness in his eyes, and, she hoped, a small measure of trust. She might never win back that particular precious gift, but this was a start.

Kenrick sheathed his sword. "Time is wasting. The Chalice treasure is what matters now. What say you, Rand?"

For a long while, Greycliff did not move. Then, slowly, his hazel eyes flaring with scarcely banked fury, he relaxed his stance before them. "We've come too far. Let's do this. But Saint—she comes with us. Whatever your feelings, I don't trust her out of my sight for a moment."

"No," Kenrick said, slanting a concerned look at Haven. "It might be dangerous for her in there. If one of the Chalice stones is in that chapel—"

"It's all right," she interrupted, knowing he sought to protect her from the deadly power of the Dragon Chalice, yet loath to come between the two friends any more than she had. "I'll go with you to the chapel. I want to be with you."

A muscle ticked in Kenrick's stern jaw as he held her gaze. A string of denials played in the dark blue of his eyes, but he voiced none of them aloud.

With a nod, he simply said, "Then let's go."

"Remember my promise, shifter," Rand warned in a toneless whisper as she made to walk past him. "Cross us, and you are dead."

The three of them entered the chapel on the tor, Kenrick keeping Haven near him despite Rand's grudging acceptance of her. He did not worry that his friend would lash out at her in cold blood, but he knew Greycliff well enough to believe that the threat he issued outside would be made good the instant he scented trouble.

Kenrick could not completely absolve Haven of her deception in the time she was at Clairmont, but he shouldered much of the blame himself, for it was he who brought her there, he who allowed her into his life. Even if he struggled to credit the depth of her feelings toward him, he did believe her when she said she cared for Rand's family. He had seen that in her as her memory had been returning at Clairmont, before she knew her true origins. She cared for Ariana, and despite her Anavrin roots, she had become a part of the fabric of Clairmont.

Kenrick could not fault Haven for the legacy of her shifter birth, but he saw no room for himself in the world she inhabited. Nor for her in his.

Her words came back to him as they lit torches and entered the empty chapel. In the afterglow of their lovemaking, she had professed to love him. She had then confessed to Rand that she knew the taste of loss and regret. That she had returned with the seal after the way Kenrick had left things with her at Clairmont—after the

. way he had driven her off in his own explosion of blind rage—seemed evidence enough that she was an ally and not an enemy to be kept under suspicion.

Still, his reason warned that she was yet a shifter. Perhaps controlled more by her Anavrin blood than any bond she claimed to feel for him or anything else.

He prayed he could trust her, for if she proved him wrong this time, he doubted any one of them would live to walk off this hill at the end of the night.

"This way," he said, leading them into the square space of the nave.

Their torches cast shadows in every direction, filling the small chamber with a bright orange glow. Kenrick strode to the wall that contained the arch between nave and chancel, raising his light out before him. The flame played over the intricate etchings, illuminating the tracery design that he and Rand had discovered upon their arrival.

"The design of the seal matches it perfectly," Haven said. "Two circles, intersecting over a cross."

"But where does the seal fit?" Rand asked. "There must be nearly a hundred like symbols. Which will show us to the Chalice stone?"

"We'll try them all," Kenrick said.

He handed his torch to Rand and approached the slab of carved stone. It looked to be a simple enough thing, until he placed the seal against one of the symbols and realized it was a close fit, but not quite. He tried another and met with like frustration. It almost seemed as though the designs shrank the barest fraction the instant he laid the seal against them, preventing him from finding the key symbol.

"We will be at this all night," Rand remarked when he had tried a dozen or more without success.

Kenrick was inclined to agree. He stepped back and raked a hand through his hair. "They all look to be a perfect fit, but none are."

"Let me try." Haven held out her hand. "Please. I want to try."

Kenrick placed the seal in her upturned palm and watched as she cautiously approached the dizzying network of designs.

"What are we looking for, Saint?"

Kenrick shook his head. "I'm not sure. Perhaps a hidden room, an alcove that might hold the Chalice stone . . . I cannot be sure, but I know it is here."

Haven studied the symbols in silence, her head pivoting from one end of the design to the other. She was thoughtful, deliberate, as if she trained her Anavrin senses to guide her to the correct place to set the seal. At last she had decided.

"I think I see the one place it will fit," she said, glancing back at Kenrick over her shoulder.

At his nod, she turned back and reached out to settle the seal where she indicated. There was the softest sigh of sound as the odd key locked into place. Then a low and rising rumble grew from somewhere deep within the tor itself.

"Haven, get back!"

Kenrick lunged for her, catching her below her arms and dragging her away from the wall not a moment too soon.

From out of the glazed tile floor—indeed, from below, above, and on all sides—shooting flames erupted inside the nave. The fire expanded like a wall in the center of the chamber, blocking their path. The wall of symbols, and the key Haven had retrieved from le Nantres, were never farther out of reach.

Haven struggled to get out of Kenrick's hold. "Faith," she gasped. " 'Tis incredible!"

"Aye," Rand snarled. "Why, it seems that hell itself has just opened its gates before our eyes. Thanks to you."

Haven shot him a look of confusion. "Look beyond the flames. Do you see it?"

Kenrick followed her direction but saw nothing save the blinding conflagration that roared from the very spot they had been standing a moment ago. It sealed them off more effectively than any amount of towering granite or steel. "There is naught to see, Haven. Naught but fire."

"Nay!" she insisted. "The cup is there—one part of the Chalice treasure—on the other side of the flames. It sits on a pedestal of gleaming marble. How can you miss the sparkle of the golden bowl and the deep red stone that glows brighter than a ruby in its core?"

"She's lying," Rand said. "I told you she would seek to deceive us with her witchery. Now do you believe me?"

Kenrick held his friend at bay with an upraised hand. "Let her speak."

"The cup is there. I see it as plain as I see both of you."

"And the flames?"

She nodded. "The cup is on the other side of the flames."

"Damnation," Rand cursed. "To have come this far—to be this close only to fail!"

"We've not failed yet." Kenrick contemplated the soaring barrier of fire that crackled and twisted a few paces away. "If the treasure is visible on the other side, out of the fire's reach, then we have not lost it."

"What do you propose to do?"

Kenrick unhitched the toggle flap on his shoulder satchel and slid his hand inside the leather bag. His fingers curled around warm metal; into his palm pressed a coiled dragon stem on a cup of pure gold. He withdrew the priceless treasure in measured silence.

"By the Rood, Saint. Is that what I think it is?"

Haven took a wary step away from him, putting healthy distance between herself and the Calasaar cup.

" 'Tis one part of the Dragon Chalice, the Stone of Light," Kenrick said.

The cup reflected the flames like sparks of pure illumination, refracting the beams into prisms of dancing light. Rand watched in transfixed awe. Haven looked to Kenrick in stark fear.

"Don't worry," he said. "I know the danger it poses to you. I'll not let it near you."

Rand stared in fascination. "You didn't tell me you had this. God's blood, my friend. If another cup exists like this one, 'tis no wonder de Mortaine pursues it like a demon. The piece is exquisite—easily worth a king's fortune."

"Four of these make up the Dragon Chalice. There is no wealth great enough to buy the power of the Chalice as a whole."

Rand's oath was quiet, reverent. "What will you do with this piece now?"

Kenrick considered Calasaar with a judicious eye. "This cup saved my sister's life some months ago. I don't pretend to know the full power of the Dragon Chalice, but I know it is immense. Perhaps it will be strong enough."

He glanced back at the wall of fire, not quickly enough to escape Haven's notice. Wide-eyed, her face stricken with realization, she took a half step toward him.

"Kenrick—no. You cannot do it. You cannot mean to cross."

He met her worried gaze with a look of determination. "The other cup is there? You see it plainly."

For a moment she did not answer. He could see warring emotions play in her eyes, in her expression that went from concern to doubt to pale fear. "Kenrick . . . the risk is too great. We cannot be sure of anything, least of all that you can do what you are contemplating."

"I have to try."

Rand looked between the both of them, his brow furrowed. "I know you are not thinking to traverse that hellish veil of flames, my friend. You will go up like a cinder."

"I don't think so."

Rand swore a vicious oath as he yanked one of his leather gauntlets from his baldric. He held it out before him, then tossed the glove toward the fire. It incinerated in an instant, dissolved to naught but smoke and ash.

"Have you lost your mind? There must be another way past this obstacle."

"There is no other way. And even if there was, we don't have the time to find it," Kenrick said, every instinct telling him this was the answer despite his logical mind's protestations that he invited certain death.

He could not allow his doubt to overshadow his faith.

He trusted Haven's word. He trusted his own heart that this was the sole solution.

He looked to Haven, her beautiful face gone white as snow, her lips parted in silent denial. He memorized her in that moment, the sweet witch who had stolen his heart, then he gripped Calasaar a little tighter, and turned to take a vaulting leap into the flames.

❧ 31 ❧

IT WAS MADNESS that possessed her in that moment Kenrick took the Calasaar cup and prepared to make his leap across the flames. Madness, perhaps . . . and a love so strong, Haven needed less than a heartbeat's pause to know what she had to do. She could not let him make the uncertain journey alone.

As he took the first step, Haven grabbed his hand and held fast. Clinging to Kenrick as to life itself, she turned her face into his shoulder and followed him through the wall of soaring, twisting fire.

Behind her closed eyelids, a piercing orange glow filled her vision like a blinding brand. Heat engulfed her, enveloping her from head to toe as they sailed through the conflagration. Flames licked at her from all sides, stealing her breath, searing her thoughts.

Haven knew a sudden jolt of panic, uncertain which source of fire burned her more intensely—that of the chasm they were leaping, or the power of the Dragon Chalice clutched tightly in Kenrick's other hand.

Either one could easily destroy her—should destroy her—but it was too late to let go. Kenrick's fingers were strongly wrapped about her own, giving comfort where fear and fire might have swallowed her whole.

He did not release her, not even when their feet finally,

335

safely, touched ground on the other side of the soaring inferno.

While he refused to let go of her, Kenrick set down the Calasaar cup, placing the priceless treasure on the tiles at their feet. Then he whirled on Haven and seized her upper arms in strong, trembling hands. "Criste, woman! What the hell were you thinking?"

He gave her no chance to answer, pulling her against him in a fierce embrace. He held her tightly, his heart thudding heavily against her while the wall of fire crackled and twisted behind him. He swore an oath, then grabbed her face in his palms and kissed her with a desperation she had never before felt in him.

"I couldn't let you do it alone," she murmured against his mouth, her own hands clinging to him as though to life itself. "I couldn't bear the thought—"

He cut her off with a snarl that sounded more relieved than angry. "Do you realize the risk you just took? Silly little fool . . ."

He kissed her again, deeper this time, and Haven knew there was nothing she would not risk where this man was concerned. She loved him, and that made everything else pale to insignificance.

"Saint!" Rand's voice carried through the flames that yet separated them from where he stood on the other side of the chapel antechamber. "Saint, do you hear me? Speak to me, friend! I cannot see you."

"We are here," Kenrick answered, his gaze holding Haven's like a caress. "We crossed safely."

"And the Chalice stone—is it there as she claimed?"

"Aye," Kenrick called back. "It is here. Just as Haven said it would be."

He released her at last and walked past her to where

stood the pedestal she had described. Haven heard him exhale an uncertain breath as he lifted his hand to retrieve the second piece of the Dragon Chalice. His fingers flexed, then closed around the stem of wrought gold.

His reverent oath was both awestruck and triumphant as he pivoted on his heel with the ancient treasure clutched in his fist.

"We did it, love. We did it."

Haven dared not get too close to the cup, for the heat of its forbidden power could sear her just to look upon it. But look she did. Her curiosity drew her toward the treasure that was both beautiful and deadly to those of her kind.

Her eye was caught by the intricate carving that formed the small dragon base and pedestal of the cup, and to the sparkling bloodred stone clutched within the beast's sharp talons. Blood and fire twined together in the molten core of the rare treasure. Life and death, beating as one.

"Vorimasaar," she heard herself whisper.

Kenrick nodded. "Stone of Faith," he said, smiling as he offered the translation of the Anavrin word. His gaze grew reflective as he admired the golden cup in his hand. "It was in the darkest hour of their darkest day that Braedon and Ariana found its mate, Calasaar, all those months ago in France."

Haven lifted a brow at the irony. "The Stone of Light, recovered amid bleakest darkness."

"And now Vorimasaar is ours, won through trial by fire," Kenrick remarked. "Perhaps the flames that stood between us and the location of this cup were merely illusion—the final test for the one who sought the Stone of Faith."

"Perhaps," Haven agreed.

Perhaps it was that same faith that protected her from the killing power of the Dragon Chalice when she and Kenrick leaped those flames together. Even though he had been holding Calasaar away from her in his other hand, it had been beyond dangerous for her to put herself so near it, to connect herself to the forbidden artifact by touching Kenrick while the cup was in his grasp.

If the Anavrin lore were true, it should have killed her.

Instead she was standing there at Kenrick's side, whole and hale, save the ache of knowing that their time together was quickly coming to an end.

She was Shadow now, no longer the Seeker entrusted on a mission to help recover the Dragon Chalice. She had broken the laws of her blood, and there was a steep price to be paid. By her honor—by her dying breath, if need be—Kenrick and the other people she had come to love would share none of that cost.

Haven knew not where she would go, but one thing was certain.

She could not remain with Kenrick once he left Glastonbury Tor.

Haven had grown very quiet. She kept a safe distance from the Chalice stones, an understandable wariness when they both knew well the danger the treasure posed to anyone with shifter blood running in their veins.

Kenrick knew no such fear, and it was difficult to contain his pride when he was holding so great a prize in his hands. In his one hand, Vorimasaar burned with the dark fire of rubies. In his other, he held the white-hot strength of Calasaar and its icy jewel.

Kenrick could feel their pull as he held them apart. They hummed with an intensity that was increasing every moment, drawing inward like a vise, tightening. The space between them vibrated with waves of visible power.

"What is happening?"

"I'm not sure. They want to join. I can't . . . keep them . . . apart."

"Be careful," Haven called to him, worry lacing her voice. "Kenrick, please—"

"Stay back!"

No sooner had the warning left his lips did the two Chalice pieces collide together in his fists. Light exploded before his eyes, shooting out in all directions. The force of it hit him like a blow to the stomach, knocking him backward, almost off his feet.

Behind him some distance, Haven cried out in shock. "Kenrick!"

"By the Cross," he breathed, astonished at the dazzling show of light that played out before him. He stumbled a couple of paces, his gaze transfixed on the two cups that were now melded as one and spinning like a child's toy on the floor of the chapel antechamber.

Calasaar and Vorimasaar, two parts of a greater whole.

Kenrick would have bent to retrieve the treasure, but Haven's hand on his shoulder made him pause.

"Kenrick," she said, her own gaze fixed straight ahead of her, rooted on something other than the mated half of the Dragon Chalice.

He followed her look and what meager breath

remained in his lungs leaked out of him on a low-voiced oath.

For the fusion of the two cups into one of greater power was not the only miracle taking place at that moment.

At the far wall of the chapel antechamber, where only stone had been before, a window of clear glass had formed. Nay, not a window, Kenrick realized suddenly. It was an open door—a portal overlooking a place that should exist only in dreams.

"Oh, faith," Haven gasped, disbelief blooming in her eyes.

"Criste," Kenrick swore. "Is it possible? Can this be what it appears?"

"Yes," she replied softly. "Kenrick . . . you have found one of the two portals to the kingdom of Anavrin."

❧ 32 ❧

"**G**OD'S LOVE," KENRICK murmured, entranced by the vision of paradise that lay resplendent on the other side of the portal.

Trees verdant with leaves, and flowers of every color spread across a landscape rich with dark brown earth, rolling grasses, and crystal lakes. Far in the distance, the many peaked towers of a massive castle fortress rose pristine white, glittering in the sunlight as though mortared with stars plucked from the heavens themselves. Endless blue skies stretched above it all, as if to say that God himself had blessed this place above all others.

It was as though he gazed upon Eden reborn, and it nearly robbed him of his breath to know that such a place existed.

"What manner of punishment was it to be made to leave such a place as this?" he wondered aloud, then turned to find Haven with her back to the portal. "Will you not look at your birthplace, my lady?"

"Nay."

Hearing the note of pain in her voice, he went to her. He walked around to stand before her, stroking her slender shoulders in a light embrace. "Why won't you look,

341

Haven? What keeps you from facing the splendor of your homeland?"

"I just . . . cannot."

"What is it you fear? That you will not be able to look away once you steal your first glance?"

She said nothing, but she could not hide the distress from her eyes. He knew her too well now. He understood her heart—God's truth, at times he felt as if their hearts shared the same beat, the same joy and pain.

"Haven, turn and look at what awaits you."

With obvious reluctance, she glanced to the open archway behind them, to the pure white light pouring out like a beacon of welcome. As if she could not resist the power of that tranquil glow, Haven slowly lifted her hand, reaching toward it. The light reached back, twining about her arm like a delicate vine of shimmering iridescence.

Kenrick himself felt the pull of Anavrin's allure, the promise of a sanctuary so pure and everlasting, it could only be met in a place of mists and myth. Only an extraordinary woman like the one standing before him could have been born of such magic, such miraculous wonder.

Anavrin was where she belonged.

He could see that now, more than ever. Her freedom, her very life, waited on the other side of that archway. He would not selfishly wish her to remain with him, outside the peace and safety of her true home.

"Kenrick!" Rand's shout carried over the flames that still divided the chapel. "Bring the treasure, my friend. Time is wasting. I'll ready the horses, then we must be away at once."

"He is right," Kenrick said, scarcely resisting the urge to touch the delicate shell of her ear as she stood in the twisting light near Anavrin's threshold. "We cannot delay what must be done."

She did not look at him. Her voice was very small, far-away somehow. "You will pursue the last of the hidden Chalice stones with Rand?"

"Yes. Serasaar cannot be far from my reach, especially now that I have its two mates to help guide me to it."

"First you will have to leave the tor."

"Aye. And I won't do that until I know you are safe where you belong. We cannot be sure how long this portal will remain open. You must go, my lady. Now."

His command was stern, more stern than he would have thought himself capable of in that moment. But despite the firmness of his tone, Haven's hand began to fall back down to her side. She turned to face him, her eyes glittering with unshed tears. The light of Anavrin's portal danced like flames in her watery gaze, imbuing her with an incandescent, otherworldly beauty that stole his breath.

A slow blink snuffed the lingering glow, as though she meant to deny it a place within her.

"I cannot," she said, a simple denial that broke her voice. "Anavrin is no longer my home. Even if I could return to my old life there, I would not. I will not leave you. Not when I can feel danger closing in on this place like a vise."

"I am not asking you, Haven. I am telling you. Damnation—there is no choice!"

She seemed immune to reason at that moment, defiance edging her voice and the stubborn tilt of her chin. "The others of my clan are moving in on this place. I can feel them this very moment, getting closer—"

"Then I will deal with them as they come. This is my fight, lady. Leave me to it. I need to know that you are out of harm's way."

From the other side of the chapel, Rand's heavy steps echoed, followed by a ripe curse. "Riders on the approach, Saint. I count four of them, armed to the teeth from the look of it. Bring the damned cup and let's go while we still can!"

"It is too late," Haven said quietly. "They know we're here. We cannot run, for they will surely find us."

She was putting herself in the equation, a fact that did not sit well at all. "There is no we, Haven. There can't be. Not anymore. You are marked—you said it yourself. You will be killed if you remain here on the Outside."

Her small hand came up to frame his jaw. "And you and Rand will be killed if I go."

He was scowling at her, furious that she would defy him when her very life hung in the balance. But her gaze was so serious, so courageously accepting of what she was saying, that he could hardly hold his anger.

"The Dragon Chalice is more important than any of us, Kenrick. Anavrin's survival depends on its return. Perhaps the survival of your world—the Outside world—depends on it, too."

Kenrick's oath hissed through his teeth.

"Too many have paid the price for that accursed cup. There is no certainty that any of us will walk away from this hill today."

"No," she said, "there is not that certainty. But together we at least stand a chance."

For a moment, one insane moment, Kenrick considered possible strategies for the three of them to combat the four shifters riding in for the attack. One by one, he discarded each plan. All were too risky to work, putting the Chalice treasure—and Haven—in too great of peril.

He was not sure there would be a way out this time.

And over Haven's shoulder now, he watched as the light from the Anavrin portal was beginning to dim. It was closing, and she remained firmly rooted before him, her eyes flashing with fiery determination. Too soon, the light was extinguished entirely, sealing off the gate to her homeland.

As the portal closed, the wall of flames at their backs shrank down, snuffed by an unseen magic. Only thin puffs of smoke and ash-covered stone remained.

"Together," Haven said, barely a whisper. "Trust in me. It is our only chance."

Before he could argue any further, before he realized what she was about, Haven rose up on her toes and kissed him. It was a fleeting contact that he wanted to savor, but as quickly as the sweet pressure of her lips had come, it was gone.

And so was she.

Moving so fast he could scarcely credit it, Haven withdrew from his arms and whirled away, striding like a warrior queen across the smoldering embers of the chapel floor. She marched past Rand and on, heading for the entryway and the coming retinue of her Anavrin clansmen.

Clutched tightly in her hands—to Kenrick's infinite bewilderment and furious disbelief—she held his sword.

❧ 33 ❧

THE ANSWER HAD come to Haven in a flash of instinct, all her shifter senses training on a single, risky thought. In her compromised state—a queer suspension between the magic she had been born with, and what, through love of an Outsider, she had since become—she could not be sure her plan would work.

But it was their only hope.

She sensed the malevolent intent of the riders coming up the tor. Her ear picked up the ring of metal riding gear and chain mail armor. Her nostrils filled with the scent of the slaughter to come. There would be much blood spilled today. Not only hers, as the hunted betrayer of her clan, but Kenrick's and Rand's as well.

Anger seethed within her at the thought. Her fury stirred like a tempest, mingling with the waking power of her glamour. She called it forth, summoning all she had as she stalked the torchlit corridor of the chapel.

She was shifter born, descended from a long line of Anavrin kings and sorcerers.

More than that, she was a woman with a heart full of determination, and that made her dangerous.

Haven gripped Kenrick's sword in tight hands before her, while she honed her senses on transformation.

She gathered the images in her mind, cobbling them,

346

sculpting them as from clay, until she had a clear vision of the glamour she sought. Her skin tingled with the coming of the change. She felt her body shimmer toward illusion, the mirroring of another human form.

It was one of the most difficult things for a shifter to accomplish, perhaps impossible now that she was Shadow. Haven pushed aside her doubt and concentrated on the face and form that would become hers. The image began to slide over her, molding to her like a veil.

It took all her strength to hold the illusion in place as she neared the chapel door and heard it bang open as the shifters who hunted her forced their way into the small stone structure.

Behind her all of a sudden, she heard a vivid curse, and the hard clip of boots on the slate floor of the corridor.

Kenrick.

He had followed her out, with Rand directly behind him.

Before either man could utter a word of surprise at what greeted their eyes, Haven whirled on Kenrick with his own sword, stopping him with the deadly point of the blade at his throat.

"Don't move," she warned him in a low voice not at all like her own, and watched as his logical, mortal mind grappled with what he was seeing. "You'll want to do as I tell you. Trust me."

His keen gaze lit with recognition as he glanced at the length of steel poised beneath his chin. He knew it as his own sword, and when his friend took a nearly imperceptible move toward his defense, Kenrick held him off with a slantwise look of denial. Rand edged back into the gloom of the corridor, concealing himself from view.

"Excellent work, ladies," Haven drawled, swiveling her head to fix a caustic glare on the four shifter guards who lumbered toward her in the corridor. "Had you been any slower to arrive, Clairmont here would have made off with the Chalice treasure *and* your shifter quarry."

"Le Nantres," said the larger of the four, his dark eyes fixed on the illusion Haven struggled to maintain. "Did you come here alone?"

"I had two of your kind with me—for all the good they did me."

"What happened?"

The image of Draec le Nantres shrugged nonchalantly. "They got careless. Amazing what the mere touch of a Chalice stone can do to a shifter. You'll find their cinders inside."

One of the four approaching shifters lifted his nose to the still air of the chapel and breathed in deeply. The sensitive nostrils flared and twitched. "There is something else inside this place as well. Shadow," he said, advising the others. "I can smell her."

A frisson of fear snaked its way up Haven's scalp. How long could she hope to maintain this ruse? Her apprehension made it hard to hold on to her glamour. She felt her skin tingle with the first ebb of transformation, the slightest waver of retreating power. It was all she could do to train her senses back on her illusion.

And her silence put a note of doubt in the larger shifter's narrowing gaze.

"Aye, I can smell the traitorous little bitch as well, and she's still breathing. Where is she?"

Haven parted her lips to speak, but it was Kenrick's voice that met her ears first.

"Le Nantres stabbed her," he said, growling the words with a good deal of venom and glaring at Haven's illusion with a hatred she nearly believed herself. "The bastard cut her down without mercy and left her for dead back there."

The shifter leader still seemed skeptical, but the hand that now rested on his sword relaxed somewhat. "Show me. My men will guard your prisoner."

He turned his head to motion to the three others, and Haven knew it might be her only chance to strike.

She pivoted away from Kenrick and, with a cry of desperation and fury, swung the long steel blade into the shifter leader's side. He was dead before he hit the floor, blood and life draining onto the slate tiles at her feet.

Kenrick's sword was a leaded weight in her hands, the action of wielding it requiring too much of her precious strength. Haven felt her precarious grasp loosen on both the weapon and the illusion she had fought so hard to manufacture.

Like a pebble tossed into a tranquil pool, her glamour rippled away in waves, shedding Draec le Nantres' image and revealing her true form.

"Bloody hell!" bellowed one of the three remaining shifters, his eyes black and feral with the fever of the hunt. "It's her!"

A chaos of shouts and steel and deadly rage erupted all around her. In a blink, Kenrick had seized his weapon from Haven's trembling hands and moved her out of the path of the carnage he would wreak. Rand joined the fray, roaring a bloodcurdling curse as he brandished his own blade and leaped in to fight at Kenrick's side.

Haven dared not shelter her eyes, regardless of the hellish scene playing out before her. She feared for Kenrick and Rand, knowing how viciously the shifters would fight, armed with weapons and magic and the black hunting rage that had led them to the chapel on the tor. She sought shelter in a darkened corner of wall, out of striking distance, yet near enough that she might step back in if she could be useful.

The three shifters fought hard, but they stood little chance against the seasoned men who fought like two halves of a deadly whole.

The first went down with a howl of animal pain, cleaved apart by Kenrick's punishing sword.

A second had transformed to a snarling beast, its wolfish jaws snapping and slavering as it leaped at Rand's throat. The knight's blade was a flashing bolt of bloodied steel, plunging into the shifter's big body. It, too, was dead soon enough, stuck through like a pig on a spit, while Kenrick slew the third shifter and threw it to the floor like so much offal.

As quickly as the battle had begun, it ended.

Haven ran to Kenrick, unable to stanch her tears as he caught her in his arms. She wept with hardly a measure of control, relief and fear and joy buffeting her all at once. She felt drained of everything, unable to do aught but cling to him as he lifted her into his arms and gently carried her out of the chapel and into the sunlight outside.

"Hush, love," he whispered fiercely against her brow as she drew in a sobbing breath. "I'm here. It's all right now."

"Were you hurt?" she asked, managing at last to speak. "Did they hurt you?"

"Nay, my lady. Thanks in no small part to you. That was some trick you managed, mirroring Draec le Nantres. I won't question how you did it, but I'll thank you never to show me that blackguard's face again. Or any other man's, for that matter."

He was jesting, she realized dimly. Ever her protector, he was trying to cheer her when his heart was still beating like a drum against her, his muscles yet bunched and tense from the deadly battle he had just fought.

"I wasn't sure if I could do it. I feel so tired . . . I am so weak, Kenrick."

"You can rest now, Haven." He brought her to where their mounts waited, grazing in the shade of the small chapel on the tor. "Will you be all right for a moment out here?"

She lifted her head with a measure of alarm. "Where are you going?"

"To retrieve the treasure we came for," he said, gently stroking her cheek, "and to help Rand with the mess we made back there."

"Oh. Of course," she said, nodding.

Slowly her wits were returning, if not her strength. Her conscience issued a warning as she gazed into Kenrick's earnest blue gaze. Her trial was not over, despite their victory today. They may have vanquished the shifters who had come for her this time, but they would not be the last. There would be another and another, so long as there were shifters working with Silas de Mortaine. And so long as she was Shadowed by her love for this man.

Kenrick knelt down beside her in the soft grass of the

chapel hill. "Are you sure you are all right? You look as pale as frost."

Haven dismissed his concern with a smile and forced a firmness into her spine as she sat up. This too was a trick of her glamour, for inside she was as weak as pudding, scarcely able to remain upright on the ground. "I am fine, really. The illusion was difficult. It has tired me a bit, that's all."

He was frowning at her, not appearing overly convinced. "I will be but a moment. Wait for me here."

She nodded, then watched in mingled sorrow and relief as he strode away and disappeared into the chapel.

❧ 34 ❧

HE HAD EXPECTED to find Rand removing the dead shifters from where they had fallen, for it would be foolhardy to leave such evidence for anyone to happen upon once they were gone from the tor. But as Kenrick walked the darkened passage through the heart of the little chapel, the bodies remained where they had fallen, and his friend was nowhere to be seen.

He was about to call out to him when Rand suddenly came out of the chancel antechamber. In his hands, he cradled the golden bowl of the Chalice treasure. Abruptly he noticed Kenrick standing before him, and his head snapped up.

"You left it back there," he said, a note of accusation in his voice. "Calasaar was remarkable on its own, but together with this second cup—"

"Vorimasaar," Kenrick said, his eyes holding steady on his old friend. "The one we found today is called Vorimasaar—Stone of Faith."

"The two cups melded together into this one?"

Kenrick nodded. "They were drawn toward one another with a force no man could contain. The power of the Dragon Chalice will increase with the recovery of each stone."

353

"Amazing," Rand mused, "Goddamn bloody amazing."

He held the cup out before him, turning it to and fro and watching as the stones caught the scant light of the torches bracketed on the walls. Prisms of red and white reflected back in his face, illuminating an expression that was more bitter than bedazzled. When he spoke, his voice was grim with purpose.

"If we push the horses, ride all night, we should make the western coast by sunrise. It will be faster to sail than travel on land, so we'll hire a boat once we get there. We'll put in for Scotland before either le Nantres or de Mortaine catches wind that we've been here today." He paused in his careful admiration of the mated cup that was both Calasaar and Vorimasaar, and turned a gauging look on Kenrick. "What say you, Saint?"

"It's a good plan," Kenrick agreed. "Save for one thing."

"What's that?"

"Haven."

A scowl darkened Rand's brow. "What of her?"

"She's too weak from this ordeal today, from much of what she's been through of late. She is putting on a brave front, but that's all it is. She will never make the trip."

Rand grunted. "I wasn't aware that she was part of this." His gaze was hard, unforgiving. "She is a shifter, my friend. You have seen the treachery of her kind, just as I have. Nothing will change what she is. For Christ's sake, it is unnatural what she is—inhuman."

Kenrick balked internally at the assertion that Haven was less real, less human, than he himself. "She is flesh and blood, the same as you and I. She feels natural enough in my arms. Her heart beats the same as any other."

"She has bewitched you into thinking so. Cut her loose while you can, Saint. She has bound you to her with her shifter's magic."

"Yes," Kenrick admitted. "Perhaps she has."

Rand stared at him incredulously. "I do not believe what I am hearing now! Nor can I credit the looks I have seen pass between the both of you. God's wounds, Saint—tell me you don't love her."

The swift denial he grasped for could not be summoned to his tongue. His feelings for Haven went deep, far deeper than he wanted to acknowledge. To Rand or to himself.

But love?

There was no logic at all in the idea that he might be in love with Haven. They had passion together, but there could be no future for them. She was a shifter, forbidden to be with him and by her own account a fugitive from her clan. He had to think of Clairmont, and the recovery of the Dragon Chalice. The least sensible thing he could do was surrender his heart to Haven.

And yet . . .

"You and I are standing here now because of her," he told his old friend, neither confirming or refuting the stunning realization. "If not for Haven's help, we would be the ones lying bloodied out there, not those shifter guards. We owe Haven our lives today."

"Today, yes, I'll grant you she proved more than useful. But she is a hindrance to your quest for the Chalice and you know it," Rand countered. "She will slow you down, make you careless. You will never get close to the

Dragon Chalice so long as you are torn between protecting her and seeing this thing through."

He was right, of course. There was no arguing the logic in Rand's assertion. But to Kenrick the alternative hardly seemed fair, let alone palatable, particularly after all he and Haven had shared.

"What would you have me do, leave her here?"

The fact that Rand did not immediately reply was answer enough. "You have spent much of your life reaching for this prize. You must do what is right. One piece of the Dragon Chalice remains, perhaps no more than a fortnight's travel out of your grasp, by your own guess. You want the Chalice; I want de Mortaine's head. We can both win, Saint."

"Are you sure this is about doing what is right?" At Rand's rigid look, Kenrick let out a sharp exhalation. "The only way to ensure that Silas de Mortaine never gets the Dragon Chalice is to destroy it. That is all that will stop him—and the beasts who ride at his command. If we take that cup from this hill, then we should take it out to sea as far as we can and drop it to the very bottom. Where no one will ever find it."

Rand twisted the cup between his fingers. "I would sooner see de Mortaine choke on it as I shove it down his throat."

Hearing the fury in his old friend's voice, Kenrick understood the depth of Rand's ruthless drive. "Having your revenge means that much to you?"

"It's all I have left. It's all de Mortaine left me with." Rand lifted a bleak gaze on him, his broad jaw set with firm resolve. "I'm taking this cup, and I'm heading north to find the final piece. And when I do, I will use it to lead the blackguard to me, and I *will* have my revenge."

Kenrick nodded, unable to hide his resignation. "You have thought this over for some time."

"I have," he admitted soberly. "Every waking moment of every endless day, I have thought of nothing else. My decision is made, Saint. All that's left is yours."

Haven's arms felt leaden, her body drained and wrung out. It was all she could do to grip the reins of her stolen shifter's mount and hold herself in the saddle as the palfrey galloped through the marshy field that spread out at the base of the tor's labyrinth mound.

Her heart ached for the way she had left Kenrick. Not even a word of farewell, but she knew that had she lingered any longer, she would not have had the will to leave at all.

And she had to leave.

Her own safety meant little, but now that she was turned Shadow, there would be no sanctuary for her or those for whom she cared. Finding her—destroying her—would be the goal of every Chalice Seeker who prowled the cities and sleepy burghs in league with Silas de Mortaine.

Her love meant death now.

What happened at Greycliff was terrible; what would be visited on Clairmont as payment for her transgressions against the laws of her kind was sure to surpass the most horrific nightmare.

That unbearable thought urging her on, Haven put her heels to her mount and turned the horse onto the road leading away from Glastonbury Tor.

She knew not precisely where she would go, nor how long she could ride when every bit of strength seemed sapped from her. The illusion she had effected in the chapel had taken too much out of her. Never had she felt so weak and helpless, so devoid of power.

She could scarcely stay upright. She did not think she could make it much farther.

The steady gait of her mount was all she knew, the only sound she could hear. Her head lolled on her shoulders. She was fading quickly now, too drained to continue. Her shoulders began to slump, her spine slowly slackened, too weak to hold her.

"Kenrick," she whispered, her last conscious thought rooted on the man she loved more than life itself. "Faith, let him be safe."

And then she was slowly sliding into darkness, falling. Falling. . . .

Amid a steady pattering of rain that boded a coming storm, Randwulf of Greycliff put his heels to his mount and sped away from the chapel on Glastonbury Tor. He did not slow, nor did he look back even once. His course was set.

And so was Kenrick's.

The palfrey saddled beneath him snorted into the misting spring air as Kenrick turned in the opposite direction of his friend. He looked toward a fresh trail that cut a clumsy path down the other side of the hill.

Haven was gone, fled on one of the horses down that steep road not long before. She meant to leave him, and the loss hit him harder than any physical blow.

Kenrick knew what he had to do, even before Rand had pushed him to decide. He was just realizing it now, feeling it more deeply than anything he'd ever known in his life.

He loved her.

He loved Haven more than anything else in this world, and before another moment passed, he needed her to know that.

With a snarl of pure male determination, Kenrick sent his mount in a brisk gallop down the tor.

❧ 35 ❧

SHE CAME AWAKE fighting.

The instant consciousness roused, her eyes flew wide open. Every muscle in her body went taut with strain. Under the blanket that covered her body, her limbs bucked with a sudden burst of rage. She twisted violently, her back arching off the cushion of soft bedding that lay beneath her.

"Easy now, Haven. Be still, love. You are safe."

She turned her head and looked into an intense blue gaze she knew like her own heart.

"Kenrick."

His name was little better than a sigh on her parched lips. Never again did she think to see his handsome face, or to hear the soothing rumble of his voice. It was him, really and truly, gazing upon her with such affection.

"I have missed you, sweet witch. All of Clairmont has been awaiting your return to us."

Elation soared within her, then swiftly crashed as a bird on broken wings.

"Kenrick—" She raised herself up on the bed, her eyes wide with fear. "What have you done! You should not have brought me here. I tried to tell you, it is too dangerous—"

"Where did you think I should take you?" he said,

slowly shaking his head as he smoothed a damp tendril where it clung to her cheek. "When I caught up to you on the road below Glastonbury Tor, you could scarcely lift your eyelids. You needed care."

"You should have left me there," she said, pushing him away when all she wanted was more of his touch, more of the comfort just seeing him gave her. "You should have let me go. Don't you see? I am Shadow now. The others will hunt me wherever I go."

"Because of your affection for me?"

She closed her eyes for a moment. "Because of my love for you, yes."

"Then it only seems right that I stand beside you, whatever may come." When she turned her head away from him, fearful of that eventuality, Kenrick gently coaxed her back to him with his fingers at her chin. "My arm and my life, lady. Both are pledged in your service."

"But you don't understand . . ."

He did not let her finish, silencing her with a tender kiss. "My arm and my life. And now my heart, if you will have it."

Haven said nothing at first, afraid to speak for the foolishness that might leap from her tongue. She hardly dared think it. Hardly dared to hope.

Staring at him in wild anticipation, she could take the wondering no longer. "Your . . . heart?"

He gave a deliberate nod. "I love you, sweet witch. I have been waiting for you to wake so I could tell you just how much."

Haven's breath faltered, a small sob catching in her throat. "You love me?"

"With all my heart and soul. I was too fool-headed to credit it, until I thought I'd lost you at the tor."

At first she did not believe she heard him right. But he was looking upon her with such tenderness, such deep emotion, Haven knew her ears had not deceived her.

The weight of what he was saying—the realization of what it truly meant, in light of what had occurred at the Glastonbury chapel—settled on her like a blanket of warm, downy wool.

"Oh, Kenrick. It was you," she said, astonishment all but robbing her of her voice. She felt tears well in her eyes, hot, joyful tears that spilled over and ran down her cheeks in twin trails of moisture. "It was *you*. The wall of fire did not burn us—Calasaar did not consume me as it would any one of my kind—because of you."

A note of skepticism flickered in his schooled expression. "You give me overmuch credit, my ladylove. What did I do, after all, save put my faith in the power of that accursed Chalice?"

"You put your faith in me, my lord." She lifted his hand to her lips and pressed a kiss to the strong fingers that felt so right wrapped around her own. Now that she was touching him again, she never wanted to let him go. "Don't you see? At that very moment in the tor's chapel, you finally trusted me. You believed in me."

"Ah, love. I have not been fair to you. I did not want to believe . . . to hope that what we shared was real. I was afraid to trust my own feelings, and so I barred you from my heart for too long. Will you forgive me?"

"Forgive you?" She laughed softly through her tears. "Kenrick of Clairmont, my magnificent lord . . . my forever love. You have saved me. Again. Always."

"Sweet Haven." He caught her in his arms and held her in a loving embrace. "You have saved me as well. Never doubt it. Together we can face anything, including those of your clan who are fool enough to step onto my domain."

Warmed by his words, knowing he meant them in earnest, Haven drew back to look at him. "I do not think there will be a need. None will seek me here. Not now."

"But if you are Shadow, I thought—"

She slowly shook her head. "To love an Outsider is to become Shadowed. That is rare enough. I have never known the cycle to progress beyond that level. To my knowledge, it has never happened to any shifter in all these millennia."

"If not a Shadow, then what?"

She had thought the joy that swelled within her knew no bounds, but understanding how extraordinary a gift Kenrick had given her made all previous elation pale. Her happiness soared to new heights as she looked upon the man who had become everything to her. "If one of my kind falls in love with one of yours and is loved in return, with a full and unguarded heart, then the Shadow becomes Shielded."

"Shielded, as in protected in some way?"

Haven smiled. "Yes. There is no shifter magic can touch us now. We are truly safe, as is everyone we care for in this keep. You love me. That is the true magic that occurred at Glastonbury Tor. And love is, as any sorcerer can tell you, stronger than the most powerful spell . . . stronger, even, than the Dragon Chalice itself."

"I will let nothing come between us, Haven. Never again."

"My love," she whispered, kissing him and holding him close.

"I would give you something more, Haven, if you will

have it. Something already promised, as I recall, though done with a woeful lack of finesse."

Befuddled, yet quivering with an excitement she could barely contain, Haven watched as Kenrick slowly dropped down on one knee beside the bed. He took her hand between both of his and kissed each of her fingertips.

"My truest love. My only love . . . beautiful, bewitching Haven of Anavrin. You are my heart and my soul, the source of all my faith and happiness. Will you please—I beg you, sweet lady—honor me by becoming my bride?"

"Yes," she sighed, coming down off the bed to wrap her arms around him. "Oh, Kenrick. Yes. Yes!"

She was weeping as he kissed her, the salty taste of her tears mingling with the heady sweetness of his mouth. Her heart felt full to bursting, every particle of her being alive with the fiery magic of the passion they shared.

"Well, this is certainly a happy sight."

They broke their embrace only slightly to look toward the open door of the chamber, where Ariana and Braedon now stood. The other couple was smiling, Ariana's the delighted grin of a romantic, and Braedon's the wry smirk of a man pleased to see he was not the only one to be snared and besotted by a special woman.

"Perhaps now we will get the whole tale of what occurred at Glastonbury Tor," Ariana said, delight gleaming in her eyes as Braedon hugged her close.

"Aye," agreed the dark knight with a slanted look at Kenrick. "This one has said nary a word—indeed, he's not left your side for a moment—these past two days."

"Haven is all that mattered to me."

"More than your quest for the Dragon Chalice?"

Kenrick answered his brother-by-marriage without taking his eyes from Haven. "More than anything."

Braedon grunted but there was no venom in it. "You see what we have been made to deal with, Lady Haven? All he's seen fit to tell us are the barest facts: Vorimasaar was found, you all barely managed to escape alive, and at this moment, Randwulf of Greycliff is sailing for Scotland to pursue the last of the Chalice stones."

"God willing, he will find it quickly and destroy the accursed cup before Silas de Mortaine catches up to him," Kenrick remarked. "That was our agreed plan when we parted at the tor."

Haven could see the concern he had for his friend. And the doubt. Rand was so angry, his heart so full of hatred because of the beloved family he had lost. Haven's guilt for her part in that tragedy would likely never fade, despite that Kenrick at least had absolved her of the unwitting role she had played.

"God be with Rand," Ariana said quietly, a prayer that was echoed by all in the room.

When the moment passed, Ariana came forward and bent to catch Haven in a fond embrace. "We are glad you've returned, Haven, and that you are well. I trust we'll have time to talk again and catch up on what has passed."

"Yes," Haven said, feeling undeserving of the kindness she was enjoying. "I am . . . Ariana, I am so sorry for deceiving you. All of you. I'm sorry for everything."

Ariana dismissed her concern with a gentle look. "I have missed my friend and I am beyond pleased to know that I will soon have a sister." She kissed her cheek, then moved to join her husband across the chamber. "We'll talk when you are up to it. If my brother will spare you, that is."

"In a day or three . . . perhaps," he said, giving Haven a smile that warmed her from her forehead to her toes. "My bride-to-be and I have a future to begin and I don't plan to delay another moment."

True to his word, Kenrick hardly waited for Ariana and Braedon to say their good-byes before he gathered Haven into his arms and pressed his lips to hers.

It was magical, his effect on her, an enchantment she submitted to willingly, wantonly.

In his arms at last and forever, Haven's old life fell away like an empty shell she no longer needed. She knew only the love of this man, and the passion that leaped to life like fire between them.

And as he slipped in beside her on the large bed, she knew that their future—and the strong generations they would create together—had already begun.

HEART OF
THE DOVE

The Irish Sea, off the coast of England
June 1275

A HUGE WAVE gathered under coal black skies and
rolled with deadly menace toward the side of the boat. It
hit much as the dozens that had come before, a fist of
crushing force that exploded against the wooden hull,
rocking the vessel and spewing a sheet of drenching
water over the already sodden deck. The boat lurched
heavily under the pummel of the storm, the protesting
strain of its joints screeching over the steady clap and
roar of thunder.

Randwulf of Greycliff sat apart from the rest of the
ship's few passengers on deck, his back pressed against
the sheltering wall of the sterncastle, steadying himself
for the hurling pitch and swoon of the storm. It had
only worsened since their departure from Liverpool's
harbor.

Three travelers had joined them in the port town

when they docked for supplies that morning, two men and a young woman. The man and his wife moved off to share the cover of a moth-eaten blanket with five other passengers, but the other man who boarded with them seemed no more inclined to mingle with the others than Rand himself. One arm lashed around the railing, he sat not far from Rand on the same side of the deck. Rain pelted his uncovered head and beard, wetting shaggy dark hair to spiky bristles.

"You look as miserable as I feel," the man called to him, chuckling wryly. With his free hand, he held something out to Rand. A hammered metal flask glinted in the brief arc of light that broke as another bolt ripped jaggedly overhead. "Irish whiskey. Have some, friend. It will warm you."

Although he had done nothing to warrant mistrust, Rand decided he did not like the man's look. Ignoring the offer, soaked to the marrow of his aching bones, he pulled the dripping hood of his mantle down a bit lower on his forehead and steeled himself to ride out the churning squall.

The weather had been unseasonably harsh since he had set out on this journey more than a fortnight past. His destination, Scotland, was still several days north— easily more, if the conditions of the sea did not clear up. And judging from the furious roil of the thick, sooty clouds overhead, he doubted there would be any mercy forthcoming.

In truth it seemed the farther north he sailed, the more ferocious the ocean's turbulence became. As though God Himself knew of the unholy purpose that drove him and sought to dissuade him with the unrelenting lash of the elements.

Let Him rage, Rand thought with grim savagery as another gale shouldered the side of the vessel and sent it groaning in a listing starboard plunge. The women on board screamed as the boat dipped sharply and took on more water.

Rand did not so much as flinch where he sat. He refused to cow to the vicious tumble of the waves. Biting rain needled his face as the storm spat and hissed all around him. Let the ocean swell and the winds tear him apart. Not even godly fury would be enough to turn him away from his goal.

Revenge.

It was his sole intent now, all of his hatred focused on one man . . . if that's what the villain he sought truly was. Rand doubted it. Born of flesh and blood, perhaps, but there could be no shred of humanity left in the one called Silas de Mortaine. Not when he commanded a small army of changeling beasts from another world, sentries conjured by some manner of sorcery to aid him in his quest for wealth and power. De Mortaine would stop at nothing, and woe betide any who stood in his way.

Even innocents, for on his order but a month past had come the brutal deaths of a woman and child . . . Rand's wife and son.

They had been everything to him—life, love, more blessings than were deserved by him, he was certain of that. But they were gone now. With the slayings of fragile, sweet Elspeth and little Tod, Randwulf of Greycliff no longer had anything to live for.

Save to avenge them.

And he would, justice delivered with the slow and

agonizing death of the one who took them away from him in a hellish night of fire and screams, and the waking nightmare of their blood spilling before his very eyes.

Rand carried the tool of his vengeance with him on the boat. Its weight knocked against his hip with the roll of the deck, an artifact secured within a leather satchel and concealed beneath the wide fall of his cloak. There was nothing Silas de Mortaine wanted more than the treasure that Rand and his brother-in-arms, Kenrick of Clairmont, had claimed from an abbey church at the crest of Glastonbury Tor some two weeks ago.

That treasure, coupled with the final piece Rand was headed for Scotland to find, would be all the lure he would need. De Mortaine was certain to rise to the bait, and when he did, Rand's retribution would be dispatched by ruthless, savaging steel.

He did not expect he would survive to savor his victory. Nor did he delude himself with the notion that he might join his family in the hereafter when his heart was blackened with hatred, his hands soon to be willingly stained with the cold-blooded murder of his enemy. But it mattered naught. Elspeth and Tod's deaths would not go unmet, even at the price of his very soul.

"For them," he muttered under his breath.

The crash of another wave slammed the side of the boat, spraying briny water into his eyes. With the answering lurch of the deck, the young woman from Liverpool gave a sharp cry of distress. She flung her arm out to reach for a small purse that had come loose from her belongings. The tide washed across the deck, carrying the little pouch swiftly toward the edge. Too late to be retrieved, the errant purse rode the pull of the retreating wave right into the sea.

"My mother's brooch was in that bag!" the woman wailed to her husband as he gathered her close to comfort and protect her.

"Best keep a tighter hold on your treasures. Wouldn't you say, friend?"

Above the din of the storm, Rand heard the voice of the man seated down the deck from him. The query—and the oddly phrased advice—was directed at Rand, rather than the couple huddled across the deck. Rand lifted his head to peer at the stranger through the pelting rain. Dark eyes stared back at him from under the fall of a thick forelock, their narrowed, unflinching look too focused to be mistaken for anything less than cunning.

"I am not your friend," Rand growled in warning, "and I've a blade at my hip that's itching to convince you of that fact. I don't like your look, sirrah. I'd advise you to back off."

The man gave an abrupt shout of laughter. "You advise me, do you?"

"That's right." Beneath his mantle, Rand wrapped his fingers around the hilt of a dagger sheathed on his belt. "I won't tell you again."

There was something peculiar about the stranger's face. Indeed, something peculiar in his very being. The sheeting rain seemed to distort his features, sharpening the man's bearded jaw, bulking his dark brow. The eyes that stared at Rand with such boldness seemed lifeless and devoid of color now. In the scant light, they took on a feral glint.

The stranger grabbed the railing of the deck and

hauled himself to his feet. He chuckled, his mouth filled with sharp, bared teeth. "You arrogant, stupid . . . *human.*"

Silas de Mortaine's shapeshifter guard spat a savage threat, his features no longer those of a man, but swiftly changing into the huge black bulk of a snarling wolf.

Pillow Talk

"I should pack my things and find another place to stay."

"You don't have to do that. In fact, I wish you wouldn't."

"This thing, my being here—it clearly isn't a very good idea." Emma's gaze lingered on Beau's eyes, his lips, her body tingling with memories that refused to fade. "It's not just us. We're adults, and I'm sure we can figure out a way to make sure that what happened here this afternoon isn't repeated."

Rising from the cushions, he paced a few steps into the room, his muscles flexing as he crossed his arms. "I swear to you, it won't be."

"You're sure? Because those boys of yours—I can already see the wheels spinning in their little brains, and they're far too precious to hurt."

"You have my word." His words had the ring of an oath, serious and solemn. "I'll be your host, your protector, your friend if you need one. But as for any more than that—"

She frowned at him. "What if I need a partner instead?"

* * *

Dear Reader,

Do you love road trips or hate them?

As someone who lives in and travels by car through the great, *big* state of Texas, I spend many hours behind the wheel, often in rural areas beyond the reach of internet or even decent radio reception. I've come to enjoy those long days spent talking, snacking and simply watching the road spool out before us, allowing my imagination to play with story ideas as big and fluffy as the cumulus clouds that drift across the sky.

On several such trips, we've passed sprawling wind farms, their towering turbines dotting a landscape once better known for oil field pumpjacks, cattle and miles of empty space. The sight prompted me to daydream about changes to the landscape and the conflicts that can occur between the old ways of doing things and the new, as different people learn to occupy the same space—or to fight it out to see which ones will prevail.

In *Deadly Texas Summer*, not only is wildlife biologist Emma Copley working to make sure wind turbines can operate without harming protected birds of prey, she is also struggling to live in safety after leaving an abusive marriage. Yet her very presence in a tiny coastal South Texas town is seen as a threat by others, including Beau Kingston, the handsome and powerful owner of a sprawling ranch under siege from harsh modern realities. But some changes, he will soon learn, bring far more danger—especially his attraction to the one woman who could destroy his legacy.

I hope you'll enjoy Emma and Beau's story. And the next time you're stuck in a car for a few hours, enjoy a daydream or two on me!

Colleen Thompson

MEGAN HART

precious and
fragile
things

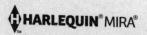
HARLEQUIN® MIRA®

ISBN-13: 978-0-7783-1417-2

PRECIOUS AND FRAGILE THINGS

Printed in U.S.A.

HARLEQUIN®
™ www.Harlequin.com

First, to my friends and family who read this book in its many stages—thank you. It's a better book because of you.

To my agent, Laura Bradford,
for not curling her lip when I first told her about the book,
and for believing in it all along.

To Superman—
I wouldn't be able to do this without you.
Thanks for catching the kids.

To my spawn—
I love you both,
even if I did throw you out the window as "research."

January

1

This was the life she'd made.

Cheese crackers crunching beneath her boots. A tickling and suspicious stink like milk that had been spilled in some unfound crack coming from the backseat. An unfinished To Do list, laundry piled and waiting for her at home, two overtired and cranky children whining at her. This was her life, and most of the time Gilly could ignore these small annoyances that were only tiny details in the much larger overall picture. Embrace them, even.

But not today.

Please, shut up. For five minutes. Just shut up!

"Give Mama a few minutes" is what Gillian Soloman said instead, her voice a feathery singsong that belied her growing irritation.

"I'm thirsty, Mama!" Arwen's high-edged, keening whine stabbed Gilly's eardrums. "I wanna drink now!"

Count to ten, Gilly. Count to twenty, if you have to. C'mon, keep it together. Don't lose it.

"We'll be home in fifteen minutes." This would mean nothing to Arwen, who didn't know how to tell time, but to Gilly it was important. Fifteen minutes. Surely she could survive anything for fifteen more minutes, couldn't she? Gilly's voice snagged, ragged with the effort of keeping it calm, and she drew in a breath. She put a smile on her face not because she felt like smiling, but because she didn't. Kept her voice calm and soothing, because an angry tone to the children was like chum to sharks. It made them frenzied. "I told you to bring your water bottle. Maybe next time you'll listen to me."

Gilly made sure she'd signed the check in the right place and filled out the deposit envelope appropriately. Looked over it again. It was only a check for ten bucks and change, but if she messed up the amount written on the envelope, the credit union could and would charge her a fee. It had happened before, unbalancing her checkbook and causing an argument with her and Seth. The numbers blurred, and she rubbed her eyes.

"Mama? Mama? Mama!"

Gilly didn't even bother to answer, knowing the moment she said "what?" that Arwen would fall into stunned silence, nothing to say.

Fifteen minutes. Twenty, tops. You'll be home and can put them in front of cartoons. Just hold it together until then, Gilly. Don't lose it.

From the other seat came Gandy's endless, wordless groan of complaint and then the steady *thump-kick* of his feet to the back of Gilly's seat. *Bang, bang, bang,* the metronome of irritation.

"Gandy. Stop kicking Mama's seat."

For half a second as her pen wavered, Gilly thought about abandoning this venture altogether. What had she been thinking, making "just one more" stop? But damn it, she needed to cash this check and withdraw some money from the ATM to last her through the week, and since she'd already had to stop to pick up her prescription at the pharmacy…

"I wanna drink now!"

What do you want me to do, spit in a cup?

The words hurtled to her lips and Gilly bit them back before they could vomit out of her, sick at the thought of how close she'd come to actually saying them aloud. Those weren't her words.

"Fifteen minutes, baby. We'll be home in fifteen minutes."

Thump, thump, thump.

Her fingers tightened on the pen. She breathed. She counted to ten. Then another five.

It wasn't helping.

Last night: she fumbles with her house key because Seth locked the door leading from the garage to the laundry room when he went to bed. She stumbles into a dark house in which nobody's left on any lights, carrying handfuls of plastic bags full of soap and socks and everything for other people, nothing for herself. She'd spent hours shopping, wandering the aisles of Walmart, comparing dish towels and bathroom mugs just so she had an excuse to be by herself for another hour. She took the long way home with the radio turned up high, singing along with songs with raunchy lyrics she can't listen to in front of the kids because they repeat everything. Scattered toys that had been in their bins when she left now stub her toes, and she mutters a curse. In the bedroom, lit only by the light from the hall so she doesn't wake her sleeping husband, the baskets of clean, waiting-to-be-put-away laundry have been torn apart by what, a tornado? Clothes all over the floor, dumped as though she hadn't spent an hour folding them all.

Even now as she remembered, Gilly's fingers twitched on the ATM envelope and rage, burning like bile, rose in her throat. Seth's excuse had been "I needed clean pajamas for the kids." She'd gone to bed beside him, stiff with fury, the taste of blood on her hard-bitten tongue.

She'd woken, still just as angry, to the sound of Seth slamming dresser drawers and his plea to help him find a pair of clean socks, though of course they were all in the very basket he'd trashed the night before. In the shower Gilly had bent her head beneath lukewarm water that too quickly ran to chill. She'd been glad when he didn't kiss her goodbye.

At breakfast the children each wanted something different than what she'd put on the plate in front of them. Shoes wouldn't fit on feet, coats had gone AWOL, and every pair of Arwen's tights had managed to get a hole. The cat got loose, and the children cried, no matter how much she tried to reassure them Sandy would be just fine.

They'd been late to Gilly's doctor appointment. On any other day being on time would've meant a fifteen-minute wait. Today, the sour, scowling nurse informed them they'd almost forfeited their appointment. Arwen pinched her finger in a drawer, and Gandy fell off the rolling stool and cracked his head. Both children left the office in tears, and Gilly thought she might just start to cry, too.

The day didn't get better. There was whining, there was fussing, there were tantrums and yelling and threats of time-outs. And of course, though she'd spent hours in Walmart the night before, she'd still forgotten to buy milk. That meant a trip to Foodland. That meant children begging for sugary cereals she refused to buy. More tears. Pitying looks from women in coordinated outfits without stains on the front and well-behaved children who didn't act like starving beggars. By the time they'd finished their grocery shopping, Gilly was ready to take them both home and toss them into bed. She'd made one last stop at the ATM.

One last stop.

"Mamaaaaaa!"

The whining rose in intensity and persistence. The kicking continued, ceaseless. Like all of this. Like her life.

Count to ten. Bite your tongue. Keep yourself together, Gilly. Don't lose it. Don't lose it.

Gilly made herself the Joker. She wouldn't have been surprised to feel scars rip open on her cheeks from the smile she forced again. "Ten more minutes, baby. Just ten. Let Mama do this, okay? Now listen. I'll be right back."

She turned in her seat to look at both of them, her angel-monsters. Arwen's eyes had gone squinty, mouth twisted into a frown. Gandy had snot dribbling from his nose and crusted goo at the corners of his lips. He'd spilled a juice box all over his pale blue shirt. They looked like the best of her and Seth combined. This was what she had made.

"I'll be right back," Gilly said, though frankly she wanted to start running down the highway and never look back. "You both stay here and keep your seat belts *on*. You hear me? Seat belts on. Do not get out of your seats."

Good mothers didn't leave their children in the car, but the ATM was only a few feet away. The weather was cold enough that the kids wouldn't broil inside a locked vehicle, and she locked them in so nobody could steal them in the five minutes it would take her to finish her task. Besides, she thought as she slid her ATM card into the machine and punched in her PIN, dragging them both out into the freezing, early evening air would surely be worse than leaving them warm and safe in the Suburban.

Frigid wind blew, whipping at her hair and sending stinging pellets of winter rain that would've been less insulting as snow against her face. She blinked against it, concentrating on punching in her PIN number with fingers suddenly numb. She messed up. Had to cancel, do it again.

Slow down. Do it right. One number at a time, Gilly. It'll be okay.

She deposited the check, withdrew some cash, shoved her receipt and her card into her wallet and got back in the car. The kids had been silent when she opened the door, but within thirty seconds the whining began again. The steady kicking. The constant muttering of "Mama?" Gilly swallowed anger and tried desperately to scribble the amount of her withdrawal from the ATM in her checkbook, because if she didn't do it now, this minute, she would forget and there'd be another overdraft for Seth to complain about, but her hands shook and the numbers were illegible. She took a deep breath. Then one more. Willing herself to stay calm. It wasn't worth losing her temper over any of this. Not worth screaming about.

Five minutes. Please just shut up for five minutes, or I swear I'll...

Not go crazy. Not that. She wouldn't even think about it.

Gilly put the truck in Drive and pulled slowly out of the parking spot. The strip mall bustled with activity, with Foodland getting its share of evening foragers and the office supply store just as busy. Gilly eased past some foron in a minivan who'd parked askew, brake lights on, and mentally threatened them with violence if they dared back out in front of her.

This part of the strip mall had been under construction forever—the promise of a popular chain restaurant and a couple upscale additions had made everyone in Lebanon salivate at the thought of getting some culture, but in the end poor planning and the economy's downturn had stalled the project. They'd only gotten as far as building a new access road, slashing like a razor on a wrist through what had previously been a tidy little field. Gilly stopped at the stop sign and looked automatically past the empty storefront to her left, though all that lay at the end of the road in that direction were dirt and Dumpsters.

The passenger door opened, and Gilly looked to her right. She blinked at the young man sliding across the bench seat toward her. He slammed the door and grunted as he kicked his duffel bag to the floor. For one infinite moment, she felt no terror, only confusion. "Where did you—?"

Then she saw the knife.

Huge, serrated, gripped in his fist. She didn't even look at his face. And she wasn't confused any longer.

Cold, implacable fury filled her and clenched her hands into numbness. All she'd wanted to do was go home, put the kids to bed and take a hot bath. Read a book. Be alone for a few precious minutes in peace and quiet before her husband came home and wanted to talk to her. And now…this.

The tip of his knife came within an eyelash of her cheek; his other hand gripped her ponytail and held it tight. "Go!"

There was no time for thought. Gilly went. She pounded her foot so hard on the accelerator the tires spun on ice-slick ground before catching. The Chevy Suburban bucked forward, heading for the traffic light and the road out of town.

He has a knife. The press of steel on flesh, parting it. Blood spurts. There is no smell like it, the smell of blood. That's what a knife can do. It can hurt and worse than that.

It can kill.

Gilly's hands moved on the steering wheel automatically. With little conscious thought, she flicked her turn signal and nosed into the line of traffic. Night had fallen. Nobody could see what was happening to her. Nobody would help her. She was on her own, but she wasn't alone.

"I'll do what you want. Just don't hurt my kids."

No smile this time, but it was the same voice she'd used just minutes ago with her children. It was her mother's voice, she thought. She'd never noticed. The realization sent a jolting twist of nausea through her.

"Mommy?" Arwen sounded tremulous, confused. "Who's that man?"

"It's okay, kids." This was not her mother's voice, thank God. It was the one Gilly used for things like shots and stitches. Things that would hurt no matter what she said or did. This voice broke like glass in her throat, hurting.

Gandy said with a two-year-old's wisdom, "Man, bad."

The man's gaze shot to the backseat as if he only now noticed the kids there. "Shit." He moved closer. He gripped the back of her seat this time, not her hair, but the knife stayed too close to her neck. "Turn left."

She did. The lights of the oncoming cars flashed in her eyes, and Gilly squinted. Slam on the brakes? Twist the wheel, hit another car? A checklist of choices ticked themselves off in her brain and she took none, her fury dissolved by the numbness of indecision and fear. She followed his barked orders to head out of town, away from the lights and the other cars. Away from safety. Away from help.

"Where do you want me to go?" The big SUV bounced with every rut in the road, and the knife wavered that much closer to her flesh. She'd bleed a lot if it cut her. She didn't want her children to see her bleed. She'd do anything to keep them from seeing that.

The man looked over his shoulder again. "I'll tell you when to turn."

The Suburban headed into farm country, past silos and barns, dark and silent. Gilly risked a look at him. She took a deep breath, spoke fast so he'd listen. "I have sixty dollars in my purse. You can have it. Just let—"

"Shut up and drive!"

No other traffic passed them, not even a car coming the opposite direction. Salt and grit spattered against the windshield, smearing it. She turned on the windshield wipers. She didn't oblige him by driving fast.

If he didn't want money, what did he want? Her mind raced. The truck? The vehicle wasn't the kicky, sexy sort of car she'd always assumed people wanted to steal. It was far from new but well-maintained, and had cost an arm and a leg, but she wasn't attached to it.

"Look, if you want the truck, you can have it."

"Shut up!" The knife again dipped close to her shoulder, close enough to brush the fleece of her jacket. The blade glittered in the green dashboard light.

He didn't want the truck. He didn't want the money. Did he want…her?

Both children wailed from the backseat, a sound that at any other time would have set her teeth on edge. Now it broke her heart. The road stretched out pitch-black and deserted before them. No streetlamps out here in Pennsylvania farm country. Nothing but the faint light of electric candles in the window of a farmhouse set off far down a long country lane.

"What do you want?" Her fingers had gone past numb to aching from holding on so tightly to the steering wheel.

He didn't answer her.

"Just let my kids go." She kept her voice low, not wanting Arwen and Gandy to hear her. "I'll pull over to the side and you can let them out. Then I'll do whatever you want."

Only fifteen minutes had passed. She'd have been home by now, if not for this. The man beside her let out a low, muttered string of curses. The knife hovered so close to her face she didn't dare even turn her head again to look at him. Ahead of them, nothing but dark, unwinding road.

"Just let my kids go," Gilly repeated, and he still didn't answer. Her temper snapped and broke. Shattered. "Damn it, you son of a bitch, let my kids go!"

"I told you to shut up." He grabbed the back of her neck, held the point of the knife against it.

She felt the thin, burning prick of it and shuddered, waiting for him to slice into her. He only poked. No worse than a needle prick, but all it would take was a simple shift of his fingers and she'd be dead. She'd wreck the car, and they'd all be dead.

Just ahead, lights coming from a large stone farmhouse settled on the very edge of the road illuminated the pavement. A high stone wall separated the driveway from the yard. Though the snow this winter had so far been sporadic, two dirty white piles had been shoveled up against the wall.

Yanking the wheel to the right, Gilly swerved into the driveway. Gravel spanged the sides of the car and one large rock hit the windshield hard enough to nick the glass. She slammed on the brakes using both feet and sent the truck sliding toward the thick stone wall and concrete stairs leading to the sidewalk.

Into the slide or away from it? She couldn't remember, and it didn't matter. The truck was sliding, skidding, and then the grumble of antilock brakes shuddered through it. The truck stopped just short of hitting the wall. Gilly's seat belt locked against her chest and neck, a line of fire against her skin. The carjacker flew forward in his seat. His head slammed into the windshield and starred the glass before he flew against the side window and back against his seat.

Gilly didn't waste time to see if the impact had knocked him out. She stabbed the button that automatically rolled her window completely down, and with a movement so fast and fierce it hurt her fingertips, unbuckled her seat belt and whirled over the center console to reach into the backseat. Arwen was crying and Gandy babbling, but Gilly didn't have time for speech. She reached first to the buckles on both booster seats and flung the freed seat belts with such force the metal hook on one of them smacked the window.

The inside lights had been on when they pulled into the driveway, but now the porch lights came on, too. It would be only moments before whoever lived in the house came to the door to see who was in their driveway. Gilly had driven past this house and barn a thousand times, but she'd never met its occupants. Now she was going to trust them with her children.

"No tears, baby." She pulled Gandy back with her over the center console.

The carjacker groaned. A purpling mark had appeared on his forehead, a starburst with beading blood at the center. More blood dripped from his nose to paint his mouth and chin. His eyes fluttered.

"I love you," she whispered in Gandy's sweet little boy ear as she lifted him out the driver's side window. She heard his cry as he fell to the frozen ground below, but hardened her heart against it. No time, no time for kissing boo-boos. Arwen balked and protested, but Gilly grabbed her daughter by the front of her pink ballerina sweatshirt and yanked her forward.

"I love you, honey." She heard the man starting to

swear. She'd run out of time. "You take Gandy and you run, do you hear me? Run as fast as you can inside the house!"

Gilly shoved her purse strap over Arwen's shoulder, grateful the bag had been on the floor in the backseat. Wallet. Phone. They'd be able to call Seth. The police. Incoherent thoughts whirled.

Then she shoved her firstborn out the window, noticing the girl wore no shoes. Irritation, irrational and useless, flooded her, because she'd told Arwen to keep her sneakers on, and now her feet would get wet and cold as she ran through the snow.

Gilly had her hand on the door handle when he grabbed her again.

"Bitch!" The man cried from behind her, and she waited for the hot slice of metal against the back of her neck. Time had gone, run away, disappeared. "You'd better drive this motherfucker and drive it fast or I'm gonna put this knife in your fucking guts!"

He reached over, yanked the gearshift into Reverse and slammed down on her knee. The engine revved. The truck jerked backward. Gravel sprayed. Gilly twisted in her seat, reached for the wheel, struggled for control, fought to keep the truck from hitting the kids. The headlights cast her children in flashes of white as they clutched each other in the snow. The back door opened and a Mennonite woman wearing a flowered dress and a prayer cap planted on her pinned-up hair appeared. Her mouth made a large round *O* of surprise when she saw the truck spinning its wheels and hopping backward onto the road like a rabbit on acid. When she saw the weeping, screaming children, she clutched her hands together and ran to them, her own feet bare. Gilly would never forget the sight of her children in the rearview mirror as she sped away. She couldn't see their faces, only their silhouettes, backlit from the porch light. Two small figures holding hands in the dirty, drifted snow.

"Drive!" commanded the man who'd taken over Gilly's life, and she drove.

It took her at least a mile to realize he hadn't stabbed her. His slamming hand had bruised her knee, which throbbed, and he still had her tight by the back of the neck, but she wasn't cut. The truck slid on a patch of black ice and she didn't fight it. Maybe they'd skid and wreck, end up in a ditch. She couldn't think beyond what had happened, what was still happening now.

Her babies, left behind.

"Not the way it was supposed to go down. Fuck. Fuck. Fuck!"

He repeated the word over and over, like some sort of litany, not a curse. Gilly followed the curves in the road by instinct more than attention. She shuddered at the frigid night air from the open window and kept both hands on the wheel, afraid to let go long enough to close it.

"Damn, my fucking head hurts."

Blood covered his shirt. He let go of her to reach toward the floor and grab a squashed roll of paper towels. He used a few to dab at the blood. Then he pointed the knife back at her. It shook this time.

"What do you want from me?" Her voice didn't sound like her own. It sounded faraway. She felt far away, not here. Someplace else. Was this really happening?

He snorted into the wad of paper towels. "Just drive. And roll up the fucking window."

She did as he ordered, then slapped her hand back to the wheel. They'd only gone a few more miles, a few more minutes. Ahead, a traffic light glowed green. She sped through it. Another mile or so, and she'd hit another light. If it was red, what would she do? Stop and throw herself out of the car as she'd thrown her children?

She risked a glance at her abductor. He wasn't even looking at her. She could do it. But when she got to the light, it didn't oblige by turning red, or even yellow. Green illuminated the contours of his face as he turned to her.

"Turn right."

Now they were on a state road, still deserted and rural despite its fancy number. Gilly concentrated on breathing. In. Out. She refused to faint.

The man's voice was muffled. "I think you broke my fucking nose. Christ, what the hell were you doing?"

Gilly found her voice. Small, this time. Hoarse, but all hers with nothing of anyone else in it at all. "You wouldn't let me stop to get my kids out."

"I could've cut you. I still could." He sounded puzzled.

Gilly kept her face toward the road. Her hands on the wheel. These were things that anchored her, the wheel, the road. These were solid things. Real. Not the rest of this, the man on the seat beside her, the children left behind.

"But you didn't. And I got my kids out."

He made another muffled snort. The wad of bloody paper towels fell out of his nose, and he made no move to retrieve it. He'd dropped the knife to his knee. Not close to her, but ready. Gilly had no doubt if she made any sudden moves he'd have it up at her face again.

"Well, shit," he said, and lapsed into silence.

Silence. Nothing but the hum of the road under the wheels, the occasional rush of a passing car. Gilly thought of nothing. Could think of nothing but driving.

Her mind had been blank for at least twenty minutes before she noticed, long enough to pass through the last small town and onto the night-darkened highway beyond. When was the last time she'd thought of nothing? Her mind was never silent, never quiet. She didn't have time to waste on daydreams. There were always too many things to do, to take care of. Her thoughts were always like a hamster on a wheel, running and running without ever getting anywhere.

Tomorrow the dog had a vet appointment. Arwen had kindergarten. Gandy needed new shoes. The floor in the kitchen badly needed a mopping, which she meant to do after paying the last round of bills for the month…and if she had time she wanted to finish reorganizing her closet. And through it all, the knowledge that no matter how many tasks she began, she'd complete none of them without being interrupted. Being demanded of. Being expected to take care of someone else's needs.

Tonight a man had held her at knifepoint and threatened to take away that tomorrow with its lists and chores and demands. If nothing else, no matter what else happened, how things turned out, Gilly would not have to heave her weary body out of bed and force herself to get through one more day. If she was really unfortunate, and a glance at the twitching young man beside her told her she might be, she might never have to get out of bed again.

The thought didn't scare her as much as it should have.
He shifted. "I need to get to Route 80."

"I'm not sure…"

"I'll tell you."

In a brief flash of light from the streetlamp, she saw
his forehead had furrowed with concentration. Gilly
looked to the road ahead, at the lights of oncoming cars
and the lit exit signs. The man ordered her to take the
exit for the interstate, and she did. Then he slumped in
his seat, head against the window, and the sound of his
tortured breathing filled her ears like the sound of the
ocean, constant and steady.

In the silence, uninterrupted by cries and demands,
Gilly let her mind fall blank again as she drove on.
Her rage and terror had passed, replaced by something
quiet and sly.

Relief.

2

Thud, thud. Thud, thud. Thud, thud. The truck's wheels passed over asphalt cracks with a sound like a beating heart. For an hour or so her abductor had told her which roads to take, what highways to follow. Some were small, obscure back-country lanes, some major four-lane roads, all of them dark and fairly clear of traffic. She didn't know if he meant to dodge pursuit, was lost, or had a plan. He'd listened to the radio for a while, switching stations, pausing at a commercial for the built-in navigation service that came with all the newer model cars.

He'd run his fingertips over the dash. "You got that?"

"No. It was only an option when we bought the truck, and we didn't take the option."

On the radio, the soft-voiced operator assured the sniveling woman that she was going to be just fine. The commercial narrator reminded everyone what a lifesaver the service was. The man had seemed pleased and switched the station, finally settling on the weather.

They were predicting snow. His eyes had closed several miles back. His breathing had slowed, joined with the heartbeat of their passage, to soothe and lull her further into blankness.

Into quiet.

When Gilly was growing up, her best friend's house had been full of constant noise. Danica had four brothers and a sister, plus a dog, a cat, a bird and several tanks full of fish. Her parents yelled a lot, mostly to be heard over the rest of the roar. Gilly loved spending time at Danica's house, but she'd often come home from a visit with her head whirling, slipping into her solitary bedroom and putting her head under the pillow to muffle even the silence that almost always greeted her.

It wasn't until she'd had kids of her own that Gilly realized noise was normal. Most families lived with it. Shouts, laughter, calling to each other from room to room. The burble of the radio, television. These were the sounds of normal families. She'd come to appreciate the noise of normality, but could never quite relish it the way she now savored the silence in the car. It had been a long, long time since she'd been in silence like this, been granted the choice to stay silent, herself.

Gilly drank the quiet like it was wine, and felt nearly as drunk from it. No whining, no complaining. Nobody asking to stop to pee or to change the radio station. Nobody ignoring directions. Nobody grumbling she was going too slow or too fast. Nothing but an occasional sigh from the man in the driver's seat beside her, or the clink of metal to remind her he still had the knife ready at his side.

The man beside her came awake with a snort and flailing arms. The knife hissed through the air scant inches from her hand and arm, then knocked against the center console, rattling it. Gilly swerved across the center line and back, heart pounding. The man sat up and scrubbed at his face with the hand not wielding the weapon.

"Fuck!"

Gilly shifted in her seat and repositioned her hands on the wheel. She didn't say anything. Her abductor muttered and tapped the hilt of the blade in his hands, then apparently decided to pretend he hadn't been sleeping at all. Maybe he thought she hadn't noticed.

"Where are we?" he blurted as if he didn't realize she ought to be the one with the questions.

Gilly told him by tilting her head toward the road sign they'd just passed. They'd been on the road for two hours. Her thoughts drifted briefly to Arwen and Gandy. Had Seth picked them up yet? Were they home, safe in bed? It was past their bedtime, and Arwen was impossible in the mornings if she didn't have enough sleep....

"I asked you a question!"

The rap of the knife's blade against her shoulder made the car jerk beneath her startled hands. Gilly yelped, though he'd only tapped her with the flat of it. She steadied the massive truck, visions of rolling the huge vehicle punching any other thoughts from her head.

"Pay attention!"

"Sorry," she said, but she didn't sound it. She tried again. "Sorry."

She told him out loud, though by now they'd passed another sign. She watched him scowl at the white letters on the green background, and wondered if he couldn't read. He pulled a crumpled piece of paper from his pocket and held it up, turning on the map light to look at it.

"We need Route 80." He shook the paper at her. "You didn't go the wrong way, did you?"

The unfairness of the accusation stung her into response. "You're the one telling me which way to go!"

She regretted her outburst when he bared his teeth, blood grimed in the cracks, and lifted the knife.

"I have a knife." His voice was hoarse.

"I know you do."

"Don't talk to me like I'm some kind of fucking idiot."

If he was going to cut her, he wouldn't do it while she was driving. He'd make her pull over first. Wouldn't he?

"Sorry."

"Okay." He seemed to think they'd reached some sort of mutual agreement. Gilly didn't know what it might be, but she wasn't going to argue.

"We haven't passed Route 80 yet."

He held up the soiled scrap of paper again. "That's where we need to go."

"We haven't even made it to State College," Gilly said, not pointing out they'd have been long past there if he hadn't made her take such a crazy, circuitous route.

Gilly waited to hear what he'd say next. He didn't speak. The tires thudded. She felt him staring.

"We're going to need gas," she said at last, since even though she loved the quiet, craved it, it frightened her. "Depending on how far we're going."

He leaned close to her to look at the gas gauge. She expected a whiff of sweat, of dirt. An angry or scary odor, something bad.

He smelled like soap and cold air. For the first time she noticed he didn't even wear a winter coat, only jeans and a worn hooded sweatshirt with a zipper. In the green dashboard illumination she couldn't tell the color, but everything on him was dark. Hair, eyes, the growing scruff of a beard she could just make out. A quick glance at his feet revealed huge and battered hiking boots.

"Fuck." He leaned back into his seat. The knife seemed forgotten at his side, but she wasn't sure she could trust that impression. One sudden move and she could find herself with four inches of steel inside her.

Later, when it was all over and she could be totally honest with herself, Gilly would think it was that clean scent of soap and fresh air that let him keep her. That and the silence. People assumed it was the knife, and she never disabused them of that notion, but Gilly knew the truth. He smelled good, and he didn't talk much. It was wrong…but right then, it was enough.

They drove a few more miles in the silence before he sighed heavily and rubbed his eyes. "How much longer before we have to stop?"

She looked at the gauge. "We have less than a quarter of a tank."

Her captor made a muffled sound of disgust. "Next gas station, stop."

They weren't on a particularly populous stretch of road, but it wouldn't be long before they found a station. He leaned forward again to punch the button on the radio and found only static. He punched the button to play the CD. The familiar words of a lullaby, albeit one unconventional and untraditional, blared from the speakers.

"What the hell is this?" He turned down the volume.

Her smile felt out of place but she couldn't stop it. *"Bat Boy: The Musical."*

He listened for a moment longer to the words, a mother's gentle promise to nurture the unloved and unwelcome bat-child found in a cave and brought to her home. The song was one Gilly liked to sing along with, but she didn't now. When it was over and the next song from the campy rock musical had taken over, he stabbed the button on the stereo to turn it off.

"That's weird," he said bluntly. "You listen to that with your kids in the car?"

She thought of Arwen, who hadn't seen the show but loved to sing along with the songs, too. "Yes."

He shook his head. "Damn. What's it about?"

His voice had a smoker's rasp. He talked slowly, as if choosing each word was a mental strain, but he didn't slur his words or use bad grammar. His voice matched the rest of him, unkempt and battered.

"It's about Bat Boy." Gilly's eyes scanned the road signs, looking for one that showed an exit or gas station ahead. "It's...it's just fun."

"Who the hell is Bat Boy?"

She hesitated, knowing already how the answer would sound. "He's half human, half bat. They found him in a cave down in Virginia."

"You're shitting me." Even his curses were clipped and precise, as though he was speaking written dialogue instead of his own thoughts.

"It's a story," she said. "From the *Weekly World News.* I don't think it's real."

He laughed. "No shit."

"There's a gas station ahead. Do you want me to pull over?"

She tensed, waiting for his answer. He shrugged, leaned forward to check the gas gauge again. "Yeah."

She signaled and slowed to exit. Her heartbeat accelerated and her palms grew moist. Anxiety gripped her, and a sense of loss she refused to acknowledge because she didn't want to think what it meant.

Apparently he remembered the knife, for now he pulled it up and waved it at her again. "Don't forget I have this."

As if she could. "No."

Ahead of them was the parking lot, busy even at this time of night. Bright lights made Gilly squint. She pulled the truck up to the pumps and turned off the engine. She waited for instructions, though normally being told what to do chafed at her. Now she felt as though she could do nothing else but wait to be told what to do. How to do it.

He leaned close enough to kiss her. His breath smelled like Big Red gum. "Give me the keys."

Gilly pulled them from the ignition and passed them into his palm. His fingers closed over hers, squeezing. She winced.

"If you so much as flick the headlights, I will gut you like a deer. You got that?"

She nodded.

"I'll pump." He waited, looking at her. She saw a flicker of apprehension flash across his face, so fast she wasn't sure she saw it at all. He held up the knife, but low so anyone looking at them wouldn't see it through the windows. "Don't get out of the car. Don't do anything. Remember what I said."

She expected him to ask for money. "I don't have my purse."

He made that sound of disgust again, and now he sounded contemptuous, too. "I don't need your money."

He folded the knife and put it into a leather sheath on his belt, slipped the keys into his pocket, then opened his door and went around to the pump, using the keyless remote to lock the door. He fumbled with the buttons and the handle, finally getting the gas to start. Then he went inside.

Gilly sat and watched him. After a moment, stunned, she realized this was the second time he'd let his attention slide from her. She sat a moment longer, seeing him choose items from the cooler, the racks of snacks and the magazine section.

From this distance she had her first good look at him. He was tall, at least six-two or -three, if she judged correctly. She'd seen his hair was dark, but in the fluorescent lights of the minimart it proved to be a deep chestnut that fell in shaggy sheaves to just below his shoulders. He didn't smile at the clerk and didn't appear to be making small talk, either, as he put his substantial pile of goods on the counter. He motioned to the clerk for several cartons of cigarettes, Marlboro Reds. He was spending a lot of money.

He didn't hurry. He didn't look nervous or wary. She could see the knife in its leather sheath from here, peeking from beneath the hem of his dark gray sweatshirt, but this *was* rural Pennsylvania. Deer-hunting country. Nobody would look at it twice, unless it was to admire it.

Outside, the gas pump clicked off. Gilly shifted in her seat. Inside the market, her abductor pulled an envelope from his sweatshirt pocket and rifled through the contents. He offered a few bills to the clerk, who took the money and started bagging the purchases.

This was it. She could run. He wouldn't chase her. If he did, he couldn't catch her.

She could scream. People would hear. Someone would come. Someone would help her.

She breathed again, not screaming. The white-faced and thin-lipped woman in the rearview mirror could not be her. The smile she forced looked more like the baring of teeth, a feral grin more frightening than friendly.

Time had slowed and stopped, frozen. She'd felt this once when she'd hit a deer springing out from the woods near her house. One moment the road had been clear, the next her window filled with tawny fur, a body crushing into the front end of the truck and sliding across the windshield to break the glass. She'd seen every stone on the street, every hair on the deer's body before it had all become a haze.

Today she'd felt that slow-syrup of time stopping twice. The first when the man slid across the seat and pointed a knife at her head. The second time was now.

She wasn't going back. Not to the vet appointments, the ballet practice, the laundry and the bills. She wasn't going back to the neediness, the whining, the constant, never-ending demands from spouse and spawn that left her feeling on some days her head might simply explode. She didn't know where she was going, just that it wasn't back.

When he opened the driver's side door, he looked as startled as she must have been when he made his first appearance into her life. "I…I didn't think you'd still be here."

Gilly opened her mouth but said nothing.

His eyes cut back and forth as his mouth thinned. "Move over."

She did, and he got in. He turned the key in the ignition and put the truck in Drive. Gilly didn't speak; she had nothing to say to him. With her feet on the duffel bag he'd squashed onto the passenger side floor, her knees felt like they rubbed her earlobes. He pushed something across the center console at her: the latest edition of some black-and-white knockoff of the *Weekly World News,* not the real thing. The real thing had gone out of publication years before.

"You care if I smoke?"

She did mind; the stench of cigarettes would make her gag and choke. "No."

He punched the lighter and held its glowing tip to the cigarette's end. The smoke stung her eyes and throat, or maybe it was her tears. Gilly turned her face to the window.

He pulled out of the lot and back onto the highway, letting the darkness fall around them with the softness and comfort of a quilt.

3

"*Roses don't like to get their feet wet.*" *Gilly's mother wears a broad-brimmed straw hat. She holds up her trowel, her hands unprotected by gloves, her finger-nails dark with dirt. Her knuckles, too, grimed deep with black earth.* "*Look, Gillian. Pay attention.*"

Gilly will never be good at growing roses. She loves the way they look and smell, but roses take too much time and attention. Roses have rules. Her mother has time to spend on pruning, fertilizing. Tending. Nurtur-ing. But Gilly doesn't. Gilly never has enough time.

She's dreaming. She knows it by the way her mother smiles and strokes the velvety petals of the red rose in her hand. Her mother hasn't smiled like that in a long time, and if she has maybe it was only ever in Gilly's dreams. The roses all around them are real enough, or at least the memory of them is. They'd grown in wild abundance against the side of her parents' house and along gravel paths laid out in the backyard. Red, yel-

low, blushing pink, tinged with peach. The only ones she sees now, though, are the red ones. Roses with names like After Midnight, Black Ice, even one called Cherry Cola. They're all in bloom.

"Pay attention," Gilly's mother repeats and holds out the rose. "Roses are precious and fragile things. They take a lot of work, but it's all worth it."

The only flowers that grow at Gilly's house are daffodils and dandelions, perennials the deer and squirrels leave alone. Her garden is empty. "I've tried, Mom. My roses die."

Gilly's mother closes her fist around the rose's stem. Bright blood appears. This rose has thorns.

"Because you neglected them, Gillian. Your roses died because you don't pay attention."

"Mom. Your hand."

Her mother's smile doesn't fade. Doesn't wilt. She moves forward to press the rose into Gilly's hand. Gilly doesn't want to take it. Her mother is passing the responsibility to her, and she doesn't want it. She tries to keep her fingers closed, refusing the flower. Her mother grips her wrist.

"Take it, Gillian."

This is the woman Gilly remembers better. Wild eyes, mouth thin and grim. Hair lank and in her face, the hat gone now in the way dreams have of changing. Her mother's fingers bite into Gilly's skin, sharp as thorns and bringing blood.

"You love them," Gilly's mother says. "Don't you love them?"

"I do love them!" Gilly cries.

"You have to take care of what you love," her mother says. "Even if it makes you bleed."

Gilly woke, startled and disoriented. She didn't know how long she'd slept, how far they'd gone. Didn't know where they were. She rolled her stiff neck on shoulders gone just as sore and stared out to dark roads and encroaching trees. Steep mountains hung with frozen miniwaterfalls rose on both sides. A train track ran parallel to the road, separated by a metal fence.

Had she seen these roads before? Gilly didn't think so. Nothing looked familiar. The man took an unmarked exit. They rode for another hour on forested roads rough enough to make her glad for four-wheel drive, then turned down another narrow, rutted road. Ice gleamed in the ruts, and the light layer of snow that had been worn away on the main road still remained here. A rusted metal gate with a medieval-looking padlock blocked the way.

He pulled a jangling ring of keys from the pocket of his sweatshirt and held them out to her. "Unlock it."

Gilly didn't take the keys at first. It made no sense for her to defy him. In the faint light from the dashboard his narrowed eyes should have been menacing enough to have her leaping to obey his command even if the threat of the knife wasn't. Yet she sat, staring at him dumbly, unable to move.

"Get out and unlock the gate," he repeated, shaking the key ring at her. "I'm going to drive through. You close it behind me and lock it again."

She didn't move for another long moment, frozen in place the way she'd been so often tonight.

"You deaf?"

She shook her head.

"Just fucking stupid, then. I told you to move. Now

move your ass," he said in a low, menacing voice, "or I will move it for you."

This morning she'd stood in her closet, picking out clothes without holes or too many stains, jeans with a button and zipper instead of soft lounge pants with an elastic waist. She'd dressed to go out in public, not like the stay-home mom she was. She'd wanted to look nice for once, not dumpy and covered in sticky fingerprints.

She should've worn warm boots, not the useless chunk-heeled ones that hurt her feet if she stood too long. No help for it now. She'd chosen fashion over function and now had to face the consequences. Gilly got out of the car. Immediately she slipped on some ice and almost went down, but managed to keep upright by flailing her arms. She wrenched her back, the pain enough to distract her from the tingling in her drive-numbed legs.

Frigid air burned her eyes, forcing her to slit them. Her nose went numb almost at once, her bare fingers, too. The padlock had rusted shut, and the key wouldn't turn. Her fingers fumbled, slipped, and blood oozed from a gash along her thumb. It looked like ketchup in the headlights. Gilly clasped her hands and tried to warm them, tried to bend her fingers back into place, but they crooked like talons.

At last the key turned with a squeal, and the hasp popped open. She slipped the lock off and pushed the gate forward. Ice clinked and jingled as it fell off the metal. The gate stuck halfway open, grinding, and she pushed hard, her feet slipping in the icy ruts. Her palms stung against the cold metal; she had a brief vision of the movie *A Christmas Story* and the boy who stuck his tongue to the pole, but fortunately her hands didn't stick. She grunted as she shoved once more. More pain in her back, her hands, her freezing face, her cramped toes. The gate groaned open the rest of the way, and the truck pulled through.

It didn't stop right away and for one panicked moment Gilly thought he was going to leave her behind. Then the red glare of the taillights came on, bathing everything in a horror-show haze. Once open, the gate wouldn't close. Gilly pulled the sleeves of her jacket down over her palms to get a better grip and protect her hands, but that only made them slip worse. She tugged, hard, and fell on her ass.

The truck revved. Gilly got to her feet, slipping and sliding. He hadn't stabbed her. He wasn't going to drive away and leave her here to freeze, either. She ran anyway as best she could on frozen toes. Her fingers slipped again on the door handle. Gilly climbed back into the truck and slammed the door.

He drove for another thirty minutes along a road so twisted and potholed Gilly had to grip the door handle just to keep herself upright every time the truck bounced. Trees pressed in on them. Some branches even snaked out to scrape along the truck's side. At one point, the battered driveway took a steep pitch upward. The tires spun on loose gravel. They were climbing.

At last, the man stopped the truck in front of a battered two-story house, bathing it in the twin beams of the bright headlights. *House* was too flattering a term. It was more like a shack. A sagging front porch with three rickety steps lined the front. Green rocking chairs, the sort with legs made from a single piece of bended metal, lined the porch. Gilly had seen chairs like that in 1950s pictures of her grandparents vacationing in the Catskills.

He turned off the ignition. Darkness clapped its hand over her eyes. Gilly blinked, momentarily blind.

"Get out," the man said without preamble.

He opened the door and stepped into the glacial night air, then shoved the keys into the pocket of his ratty sweatshirt, slammed the door shut and headed toward the house without hesitation. He quickly blended into the dark.

Without the light of the headlamps to guide her, the distance from the truck to the front porch became instantly unnavigable. She already knew the ground here was frozen and hard. At best she'd fall on her ass again. At worst, she'd end up with a broken leg.

Gilly put her hand on the door. Tremors tickled her, and her fingers twitched on the handle. Her feet jittered on the duffel bag. Only her eyes felt wide and staring, motionless while the rest of her body went into some strange sort of Saint Vitus' dance.

She was dreaming. Was she dreaming? Was this real? In the dark, the silent dark, Gilly had to press her twitching fingers to her eyelids to convince herself they were open. Like a blind woman she felt the contours of her face, trying to convince herself that it was her own and uncertain, in the end, if it was.

The slanting shack began to glow from the four windows along its front. The light was strange, yellow and dim, but it gave her the courage to open the door. The meager glow was just enough to allow Gilly to make her stumbling way to the front porch steps, and then through the door he'd left open.

She entered a small, square room with a sooty wood-

stove on a raised brick platform between the two windows along the back wall. Now she could see why the
light coming from the windows seemed so odd. Propane, not electric, lights illuminated the room. She
wrinkled her nose against the smell, which reminded
her of summer camp.

Despite the stains and dirt on the carpet she could
see it was indisputably green. Not emerald, not hunter,
but mossy and dull. The color of mold. The furniture
grouped around the woodstove was faded brown plaid
with rough-hewn wooden arms and feet. The two long
sofas facing each other across a battered coffee table
looked in decent enough condition, but the two chairs
beside them had seen better days. Time or rodents had
put holes in the plaid fabric, and stuffing peeked out
here and there. The scarred dining table had four matching chairs and a fifth and sixth that didn't match the set
or each other. Someone long ago had tried to make it
pretty with an arrangement of silk flowers, now dusty
and only sad. A larger camping lantern, newer than the
wall sconces but unlit, also sat upon the table.

To her right Gilly saw the kitchen, separated from the
living room by a countertop and row of hanging cabinets. Through the narrow gap between them she saw
another table and chairs. Off the kitchen she thought
there might be a mudroom or pantry. She glimpsed
the man standing at the refrigerator, mumbling curses.
Maybe at the emptiness, maybe at the stench of mildew
and age that she could smell even from here.

Gilly closed the door behind her with a solid, re-
morseless thud.

"Smells like a damn rat died in the fridge."

Gilly wasn't positive he spoke to her or just at her.

She swallowed her disgust at the thought and looked around the room again. Through the door immediately to her left she spied a linoleum floor and the glint of metal fixtures. A bathroom. The doorway farther back along the wall hinted at a set of steep, narrow stairs. That was it. Upstairs must be bedrooms.

"I need to take a piss," he told her matter-of-factly. Carrying a large battery-powered lantern, he brushed past her and into the bathroom. Next came the sound of water gushing, then a toilet flushing. At least the facilities worked.

Her own bladder cramped, muscles that had never been the same since her pregnancies protesting. When he came out, she went in. He'd left her the lantern. She peed for what felt like hours. At the sink, washing her hands, a stranger peered out at her from the cloudy mirror. A woman with lank hair, dark to match the circles under her eyes, and skin the color of moonlight. She looked like her mother.

She'd run away just like her mother.

She tried for dismay and felt only resignation. Her eyes itched and burned, and not even splashing cold water helped. She breathed in through her nose, out through her mouth, her stomach lurching. She didn't puke. Eyes closed, Gilly gripped the sink for one dizzy moment thinking she would open them and find herself at home in front of her own mirror, all of this some insane fantasy she'd concocted out of frustration. Wishful thinking. Maybe crazy would be better than this.

When Gilly came out of the bathroom, she found the man sitting at the dining room table. He'd lit the lamp there and spread out a bunch of wrinkled papers. He held his head in his hands like the act of reading them all had given him a headache.

Gilly cleared her throat, then realized she hadn't used her voice since they'd stopped for gas. Four, five hours ago? Less than that or longer, she had no idea. She waited for him to look up, but he didn't.

He ran his fingers again and again through the dark lengths of his hair, until it crackled with static in the cold air. Gilly waited, shifting from foot to foot. Awkward, uncertain. Even if she did speak, what could she possibly say?

He looked up. Under the thin scruff of black beard, his face had fine, clean lines. Thick black lashes fringed his deep brown eyes, narrowed now beneath equally dark brows. He wasn't ugly, and she couldn't force herself to find him so. With a shock, Gilly realized he wasn't much younger than she was, maybe three or four years.

"My uncle," he said suddenly, looking up at her.

Gilly waited for more, and when it didn't come she slipped into one of the battered chairs. She folded her hands on the cold wood. It felt rough beneath her fingers.

He touched the pile of papers, shoving a couple of them toward her. "This was my Uncle Bill's place."

Gilly made no move to take the papers. She found her voice, as rusty as the gate had been. "It's…quaint."

His brow furrowed. "You making fun of me?"

She expected anger. More knife waving. Perhaps even threats. Anger she could handle. Fight. She could be angry in response. Instead she felt hollow shame. He'd spoken in the resigned fashion of a man used to people mocking him, and she *had* been making fun.

"Was it a hunting cabin?"

"Yeah." He looked around. "But he lived here, too. Fixed it up a little at a time. I used to come here with him, sometimes. Uncle Bill died a couple months ago."

Condolences rose automatically to her lips and she pressed them closed. It would be ridiculous to express sorrow over a stranger's death, especially to this man. Her fingers curled against the table. Surreal, all of this.

You're not dreaming this, Gilly. You know that, right? This is real. It's happening.

She knew it better than anything and yet still couldn't manage to process it. She stared across the table. "He left you this cabin?"

"Yeah. It's all mine now." He nodded and gave her a grin shocking in its rough beauty, its normality. They might've been chatting over coffee. This was more terrifying than his anger had been.

She looked around the room, like maybe it might look better with another glance. It didn't. "It's cold in here."

He shrugged, pulling the sleeves of his sweatshirt down over his fingertips and hugging his arms around himself. "Yeah. I could light a fire. That'll help."

"It's late," Gilly pointed out. She'd been about to say she needed to go to bed, but she didn't want him to get the wrong idea. Fear flared again as she watched him run his tongue along the curve of his smile. He was bigger than she was and certainly stronger. She wouldn't be able to stop him from forcing her.

"Yeah" was all he said, though, and made no move to leap across the table to ravish her. He blinked, cocking his head in a puppyish fashion that might have been endearing under other circumstances. "Let's go to bed."

Stricken, Gilly didn't move even when he pushed away from the table and gestured to her. Her throat dried. *Lie back and enjoy it,* she thought irrationally, remembering what a friend of hers had said a blind date gone horribly wrong had told her to do. Gilly's friend had kicked the would-be rapist in the nuts and run away, but Gilly had given up the chance for running back at the gas station. Even if she ran, now, where would she go?

He went to the propane lamps and lowered the flames to a dim glow, then jerked his head toward the steep, narrow stairs. "Beds are upstairs. C'mon."

On wobbly legs she followed him. She'd been right about the stairs. Dark, steep, narrow and splintery. Festooned with cobwebs and lit only by the lantern he carried.

The stairs entered directly into one large room that made up the entire upstairs. More propane sconces, wreathed in spiderwebs furry with dust, lined the walls beneath the peaked roof. The windows on each end were grimy with dirt and more cobwebs. A waist-high partition with a space to walk through divided the room in half widthwise. A low, slatted wall protected unwary people from falling down the stairs.

"Beds." He pointed. "You can have the one back there."

He meant beyond the partition. Gilly realized he didn't intend to follow her when he handed her the lantern. She passed the double row of twin beds, three on each side of the room, then went through the open space in the middle of the partition. On the other side was a sagging full-size bed, a dresser, an armoire and an ancient rocking chair. A faded rag rug covered the wooden plank floor.

"Cozy," she muttered and set the lantern on the dresser.

The man had already crawled into one of the beds on the other side. Gilly, mouth pursed with hesitant distaste, pulled back the heavy, musty comforter. The sheets beneath were no longer white, but still fairly clean. Nothing rustled in them, at least nothing she could see.

She unlaced her useless boots and slipped them off with a sigh, wriggling her toes. She hadn't realized how much they hurt until she took off her boots. Without removing her coat, Gilly crawled into bed and pulled the knobby cover up to her chin. The thought of putting her head on the pillow made her cringe, and she pulled her hood up to cover her hair.

His voice came at her out of the dark. "What's your name, anyway?"

"Gillian. Gilly."

"I'm Todd."

She heard the squeak of springs as he settled further into the mattress. Then exhaustion claimed her, and she fell asleep.

4

What finally woke Gilly was not a warm body burrowing next to hers and the stench of an overripe diaper. Nor was it the sudden blaring of a television tuned permanently to the cartoon channel. What woke her this morning was the numbness of her face.

She hadn't slept without nightly interruption for more than five years but now her eyes drifted open slowly. Gradually. Bright morning sunshine dimmed by the dirt on the window glass filled the room. She'd rolled herself into the covers, cocooned against the bitter winter air. Her hood, pulled up around her hair, had kept her head warm enough. Her face, though, had lain exposed all night. She couldn't feel her cheeks or her nose or her lips.

The night rushed back at her. Her heart thumped, and her mouth behind the frozen lips went dry. Gilly sat up in the sagging double bed, fighting to untangle the covers that had protected her through the night.

She managed to push them off. On stiff legs she got

out of bed and hugged her coat around her. Her boots were gone.

Everything in the dusty attic room shone with an unreal clarity that defied the fuzziness of her thoughts. How long had she slept? The sudden, panicked thought she might have slept for more than just one night, that she'd been gone for days, forced her into action.

In the light of day she could no longer take solace in the dark to hide her actions, to excuse her decisions. She'd made a terrible mistake last night. She could only hope she had the chance to fix it.

Gilly pounded down the stairs, breath frosting out in front of her. She hurtled into the living room and stumbled over her own feet. She caught herself on the back of the hideous plaid sofa.

From the kitchen, Todd swung his shaggy brown head around to look at her from his place at the stove. "You all right?"

She didn't miss the irony of his concern. "Yeah. Thanks."

By the time she walked across the living room and entered the kitchen, her stomach had begun to grumble like thunder. The last thing she'd eaten was half a granola bar Arwen had begged for and then refused because it had raisins in it. Gilly swallowed against the rush of saliva.

"Hungry?" A cigarette hung from Todd's mouth and wreaths of smoke circled his head. He lifted a spatula. "I'm making breakfast. Take your coat off. Stay awhile."

Gilly wrinkled her nose at the stench of smoke and didn't laugh at what he'd obviously meant to be funny. With her stomach making so much noise she couldn't pretend she wasn't hungry, though she didn't want to admit it. "I'm cold. What time is it?"

Todd shrugged and held up a wrist bare of anything but a smattering of dark hair. "Dunno. I don't have a watch."

Her stomach told her she'd slept well past eleven. Maybe even past noon. It grumbled again, and she pressed her hands into her belly to stop the noise.

Gilly looked around the kitchen. The propane-powered appliances were old, like the chairs on the porch, straight out of the 1950s. Green flowered canisters labeled Flour, Coffee, Sugar and Tea, and a vintage table and chairs set stuck off in one corner prompted her to mutter, "You could make a fortune on eBay selling this stuff."

Todd swiveled his head to look at her again. "What?"

"Nothing."

From the stove in front of him came the sound of sizzling and the smell of something good. A wire camping toaster resting on the table held two slices of bread, a little browner than she preferred. Her stomach didn't seem to care.

"Toast," Todd said unnecessarily. He pointed with the spatula. "There's butter and jelly in the fridge."

All this as casual as coffee, she thought. All of this as though there was nothing wrong. She might've woken at a friend's house or a bed-and-breakfast. She shuddered, stomach twisting again. She fisted her hands at her sides, but there was nothing she could grab on to that would stop the world from turning.

"Christ, move your ass! Put it on the table," Todd said, voice prompting as if she was an idiot.

She jumped. The command got her feet moving, anyway. Not from fear—he didn't sound angry, just annoyed. More a point of pride, that she wasn't so scared of him she couldn't move, or so stupid she couldn't figure out how to eat breakfast.

Remembering his comments the night before, Gilly hesitated to open the refrigerator. She expected to recoil from the smell of dead rodents and had one hand already up to her nose in preparation. The interior of the appliance was not sparkling; age would prevent that from ever being true again. But it was clean. The caustic but somehow pleasant scent of cleanser drifted to her nostrils. Food filled every shelf, crammed into every corner. Jugs of milk and juice, loaves of bread, packages of bologna and turkey and deli bags of cheese. The freezer was the same, bulging with packages of ground beef and chicken breasts. No vegetables that she could see, but plenty of junk food in brightly colored boxes, full of chemicals and fat. The sort of food she bought but felt guilty for serving.

"You went shopping."

"Even bastards gotta eat," Todd said.

Gilly pulled out the jumbo-size containers of jelly and margarine, not real butter, and set them on the table. She shifted on her feet, uncertain what to do next. She wasn't used to not being the one at the stove. The bare table beckoned, and she opened cupboards in search of plates and cups, pulled out a drawer to look for silverware. The tiny kitchen meant they needed complicated choreography to get around each other, but she managed to set the table while Todd shifted back and forth at the stove to give her room to maneuver.

When at last she'd finished and stood uncertainly

at the table, Todd turned with a steaming skillet in one hand. "Sit down."

Gilly sat. Todd set the skillet on the table without putting a hot pad underneath it, but Gilly supposed it wouldn't matter. One more scorch mark on the silver-dappled white veneer would hardly make much of a difference.

Todd scooped a steaming pile of eggs, yellow interspersed with suspicious pink bits, onto her plate. Gilly just stared at it. She smelled bacon, which of course she wouldn't eat, and which of course he couldn't know.

Instead she spread her browned toast with a layer of margarine and jelly and bit into it. The flavor of it burst on her tongue, igniting her hunger. She gobbled the rest of the bread and left only crumbs.

A teakettle she hadn't noticed began to whistle. Todd left the table to switch off the burner and pull two chipped mugs from one of the cupboards. Into each he dropped a tea bag and filled the mugs with the boiling water, then pushed one across the table at her.

He took his chair again and settled into the act of eating as naturally as if he'd known her all their lives. He ate with gusto, great gulps and lip smacking. His fork went from the plate to his mouth and back again, with little pause. Watching him, Gilly was reminded of the way their dog crouched over his bowl to keep the cat from stealing the food. Her stomach shriveled in envy. One piece of toast wasn't going to be enough.

He paused in his consumption long enough to look up at her. "You not eating? There's plenty. I made extra."

The sudden loud gurgle of her stomach would make her a liar if she said no. "Maybe some more toast."

The smooth skin of his brow furrowed. "You don't like eggs?"

Gilly pointed to the skillet. "Ah...they've got bacon mixed in with them."

Todd licked his lips. The gesture was feral and wary, as though she was trying to trick him and he knew it, but wasn't sure how to stop her. "Yeah?"

"I don't eat bacon," Gilly explained. Her stomach gurgled louder. She'd no more eat the breakfast he'd cooked than she would kick a puppy, but the smell *was* making her mouth water.

"Why not?"

"I'm Jewish," she said simply. "I don't eat pork."

Todd swiped his sweatshirt sleeve across his lips. "What?"

Gilly was used to having to explain herself. "I don't eat bacon. I'm Jewish."

Todd looked down at his plate and shoved the last few bites of pig-tainted eggs around with his fork. When he looked up at her, she noticed his eyes were the same shade as milk chocolate. "You don't look Jewish."

The comment, so ripe with anti-Semitism, was one she'd heard often and which never ceased to rankle. "Well, you don't look crazy."

He cocked his head at her, again lining the rim of his lips with his tongue. From any other young man the gesture might have been sensual or even aggressively, overtly sexual. On Todd, it merely made him look warily contemplative. Like a dog that's been kicked too many times but keeps coming to the back door, anyway. Mistrustful, waiting for the blow, but unable to stop returning.

"Uncle Bill always made the eggs that way up here,"

he said finally. "He called them camp eggs. But I can make you some without bacon, if you want."

She wanted to deny him that kindness, to keep him as the villain. Her stomach gurgled some more, and she couldn't. "I'll make them."

She pushed away from the table, heat stinging in her cheeks. Why should she feel guilty? He was the bad guy. He'd held a knife on her, kidnapped her, stolen her vehicle. Put her kids in danger.

"Can you use this skillet, or…" His voice trailed off uncertainly from behind her. "Or do you need one that didn't have pig in it?"

Again she thought of a kicked dog, slinking around the back door hoping for a moment of kindness, and the heat burned harder in her face. That she doubted there was any utensil in this cabin that hadn't at some point touched something nonkosher didn't really matter. He was trying to be considerate. This, like his concern when she'd tripped, was scarier than if he'd shouted and threatened. This made him…normal.

And if he was normal, what did that make her?

"No, I can just wash it out. That one will be fine."

He scraped the remains of the skillet onto his plate and handed it to her. She washed it, then opened the fridge and pulled out the cardboard carton of eggs. She opened two cupboards before she found a bowl and rinsed it free of any dust that might have gathered. She cracked the first egg into it, checking automatically for blood spots that would make it inedible.

The skin on the back of her neck prickled. He was watching her, of course. What else would he look at but this woman in his kitchen, a stranger he'd stolen? Gilly broke another egg with crushing fingers, bits of shell falling into yellow yolk.

"How long have you been Jewish?"

It wasn't the question she'd expected. "My whole life."

Todd laughed. "I guess that's about how long I've been crazy."

Crazy.

She'd thrown out the term offhandedly, the way most people did, not meaning it. The way Todd had, himself. His tone had told her he didn't think he was crazy. Not really. Gilly didn't think he was crazy, either. Gilly knew crazy.

Crazy was having a chance to escape and ignoring it, not just once, but many times. Crazy was wanting to escape in the first place.

Her stomach lurched into her throat, bile bitter on the back of her tongue. She swallowed convulsively. She wasn't hungry anymore. She beat the eggs anyway and poured them into the skillet along with some margarine. The smooth yellow mess curdled and cooked. Gilly knew she wouldn't be able to eat it now no matter how hollow her stomach. She removed the eggs from the stove and turned off the flame.

She sipped in a breath, forming her words with care, keeping her tone light and easy. Casual as coffee. "Where are we, by the way?"

"My uncle's cabin. I told you last night."

Keeping her back to him, Gilly gripped the edge of the counter. "No. I mean…*where* are we? We drove a long time. I fell asleep. I don't know where we are."

A beat of silence. Then, "I'm not telling you. Jesus, you think I'm stupid enough to do that?"

Last night he'd held a knife to her and she'd been angry; this morning, faced with the kindness of breakfast and his sullen but nonaggressive tone, Gilly had to dig deeper than her fear to find even a thread of fury. She drew in a breath and then another. She gripped the counter so hard her knuckles turned white and one nail bent and cracked.

She turned to face him. "Todd. That's your name, right? Todd, you have to take me back. Or take me someplace. Let me go."

He wasn't looking at her. He shook his shaggy head and got up from the table to stalk to the living room with a handful of paper napkins he used to build up the fire in the sooty woodstove. He went to the table and picked up a bulging folder, then took it to the woodstove where he crouched in front of its warmth, sifting through the papers. Every so often he threw one of them into the blaze.

"Please," Gilly said from the kitchen.

Todd ignored her, bent to his task with a single-minded self-absorption. He muttered as he worked, but she couldn't make out the words. Gilly moved to the living room, wanting to draw closer to the fire's warmth but feeling as though it was up to her to keep a proper distance between them. There had to be something for her to say or do to make him listen.

If she ran away now, would he chase her? Gilly's head felt fuzzy, her thoughts mangled, but everything in the cabin seemed too sharp, too clear. Looking at things straight on hurt her eyes. She couldn't blame exhaustion since she'd had the longest night's sleep she'd had since before being pregnant with Arwen.

She'd felt this way before, when the pain of childbirth

had made time stretch on into an unfathomable and interminable length. When the drugs she'd been taking for a sinus infection had made her feel as though she were constantly floating. Now it was the same, every minute lasting an hour, her head a balloon tethered to her shoulders by a gossamer thread that could snap at any minute.

You did this to yourself, Gillian. You know you did. Now you pay the price.

It was her mother's voice again, stern and strong. Gilly thought of the dream she'd had while driving. Roses and thorns and blood and love.

The fire warmed the room and she shrugged out of her coat. She hung it on the back of a chair. "Todd."

Todd shuffled his pile of papers together and held them out to her. "Read this."

Her first instinct was to say no, but wouldn't it be better to do what he wanted than to antagonize him? Gilly sat on the plaid couch and took the offered papers. The first was a bank statement. The name at the top of the account was Todd Blauch. The previous balance was for a little more than five thousand dollars. One withdrawal had been made a couple weeks ago for the entire amount. That explained the envelope at the minimart.

She explained what that meant. He gave her that look again, the one that said he knew she mocked him, he just wasn't sure how cruelly. "I know that."

"You told me to read them."

"I know *that* one," he said. "I need help with the ones under that one."

She took a look. The legal-size sheets would have been incomprehensible to her even without the crumpling and staining. It was some sort of legal docu-

ment. A will. All she could really make out were the
names Bill Lutz and Todd Blauch. There was a bunch
of mumbo jumbo about property lines and taxes. Deeds.

"Is it the will saying you've inherited the cabin?"

Todd sighed. "Yeah. But there's too many words
on that paper. Lots of little words always mean there's
something they can catch you on."

"I'm pretty sure that's all it says," Gilly told him.
"But I'm not a lawyer."

"That would've been my luck," Todd muttered. "To
get stuck with a lawyer."

"You're not stuck with me."

Todd stuffed the papers back in his folder. "Shit,
Gilly."

"You took my boots." It wasn't a question.

He stared at her sideways, head cocked and his thick
dark hair hanging over one eye. "Yeah."

"So I couldn't run away."

He shrugged but didn't answer.

Gilly screwed up her courage with a deep breath.
She lifted her chin, determined her voice would not
tremble. "Do you want sex?"

He looked as stunned as if she'd slapped him across
the face. Her words propelled him from the couch. Todd
turned from her, facing the woodstove, his shoulders
hunched.

"Jesus. No!"

"If that's what you want," she continued, her voice a
calm floating cloud that did not seem to come from the
rest of her, "then I will let you do whatever you want…
if you let me go…."

He whirled around, and to her surprise, his tawny

cheeks had bloomed the color of aged brick. "I don't want to fuck you!"

Gilly shook her head, immensely relieved but inexplicably offended. "What do you want me for, then?"

"I didn't want you at all, I just wanted the fucking truck. Jesus fucking Christ. Shit!" He smacked his fist into the palm of his hand with each invective. "What the hell?"

She pressed her hands tightly together to prevent them from trembling, but nothing could stop the quaver in her voice. "I just thought…"

He tossed up his hands at her, forcing her to silence. He lit a cigarette, staring at her while the smoke leaked from his nose in twin streams like the breath of a dragon. The steady glare was disconcerting, but she forced herself to meet it.

"You think I stole you?" Todd said slowly. "I mean, you look at me and you think I'm a guy who takes women?"

"You *did* take me!"

"Yeah, well," he said, "I didn't mean to."

I didn't mean to.

It was one of the things Seth said when he wanted to sound like he was apologizing but really wasn't. Gilly hated that phrase so much it automatically curled her lip and made her want to spit. The noise forced from her throat sounded suspiciously like a growl.

"How could you not mean to? I was in the truck. You got in with a…with a knife!" Her words caught, her voice hoarse. "How was that an accident? What happened? Did some big wind come up and just blow you into my car?"

"I didn't say it was an accident. I just said I didn't take you on purpose!"

"There's no difference!" Gilly cried.

Todd stared at her long and hard. "There is a fucking difference."

Shouting would solve nothing and might, in fact, make things worse. Gilly made herself sound calm and poised. "I want you to let me go, Todd."

"Can't."

His simple answer infuriated her. "What do you plan to do with me, then?"

He shrugged, sucking on the cigarette until his cheeks hollowed. "Hell if I know."

"Someone will find me."

He stared at her, long and hard, through narrowed eyes. Todd didn't look away. Gilly did.

"I don't think anyone *will* find you," he said. "Not for a while, anyway, and by then…"

"By then, what?" She stood to face him, but he only shrugged. She softened her tone. Cajoled, tempting that boot-kicked dog closer with a piece of steak. "Look. Just give me my boots. I'll hike down to the main road and…hitch a ride. Or something. Find a gas station."

He snorted laughter. "No, you won't. You'd never make it. Christ, it's…" He stopped himself, wary again, as if telling her the distance would give her any sort of clue where they were. "It's too far."

"I'd make it," Gilly said in a low voice.

"No," Todd said. "You wouldn't."

Images of a mass grave, multiple rotting bodies, filled her brain. Gilly swallowed hard. Fear tasted a little like metal, but she had to ask the question. "Are you going to kill me?"

Todd started. "No! Jesus Christ, no."

There was no counting to ten this time, nothing to hold her back from rising hysteria. "Because if you are, you should do it now. Right away! Just do it and get it over with!"

Todd flinched at first in the face of her shouting, then frowned. "I didn't bring you here to kill you. The fuck you think I am, a psycho?"

Gilly quieted, chest heaving with breath that hurt her lungs. Her throat had gone dry, her mouth parched and arid. Todd stared, then shook his head and laughed.

"You do. You really do think I'm crazy. Fuck my life, you think I'm a fucking psycho."

Gilly shot her gaze toward the front door and expected him to step in front of her, but Todd just tossed up his hands.

"Go, then," he said derisively. "See how far you get. People die all the time in the woods, and that's ones smart enough to have the right gear with them. You don't have gear, you got nothing. See how long it takes your ass to freeze."

"The police," she offered halfheartedly. "They'll be looking for me."

"Where?"

He had a point, one she didn't want to acknowledge. "They can trace things. The truck, for one."

"The fuck you think this is, CSI?" Todd shrugged. "Maybe. Maybe not."

Gilly looked again to the door and then at the floor in defeat. "Please. I'll give you whatever you want."

"You can't give me what I want," Todd said.

Gilly went to the front windows and looked out at the yard. Her truck was there, but she had no keys. The forest ringing the patchy, rocky grass looked thick and unwelcoming, the road little more than a path. He was right. She wouldn't get far. Running out there would be stupid, especially without shoes.

She had to be smarter than that.

"I need to clean up," Gilly said finally. "Brush my teeth, wash my face…"

She trailed off when he walked past her. He picked up a plastic shopping bag from the dining room table, and for the first time she noticed there were many of those bags on the chairs and beneath the table. He tossed her the first one.

It landed at her feet, and she jumped. Gilly bent and touched the plastic, but didn't look inside. He'd bought more than groceries.

"Go ahead." Todd poked at the other bags on the table. "Look."

"What's all this for?" Gilly sifted through a stack of turtleneck shirts, one in nearly every color.

Todd pushed another handful of bulging plastic sacks toward her. "I had all my stuff with me. You didn't have anything."

Gilly pulled out a pair of sparkly tights. She said nothing, turning them over and over in her fingers. They were her size. She didn't even know they made sparkly tights in her size. She looked up at him.

Todd shrugged.

She let the tights drop onto the rest of the pile and wiped her now-sweating palms on her thighs. Her heart began to pound again.

"All of this… You bought enough to last for months," she said finally.

Todd stubbed out his cigarette in a saucer on the

table and lit another, flicking the lighter expertly with his left hand. He sucked deep and held it before letting the smoke seep from between his lips. "The fuck am I supposed to know what a woman needs? You needed shit. I bought it."

Gilly steadied herself with one hand on the back of a chair. "I won't be here for months."

Todd flipped the lid of his lighter open and shut a couple of times before sliding it back into his pocket. Without answering her, he stalked to the woodstove and piled a few logs on the fire it didn't need. His faded flannel shirt rode up as he knelt, exposing a line of flesh above the waist of his battered jeans.

If she could stab him there, he'd bleed like any other man. The thought swelled, unbidden, in her mind. She could run at him. Grab his knife. She could sink it deep into his back. For one frightening moment the urge to do it was so strong that Gilly saw Todd's blood on her hands. She blinked, and the crimson vanished.

Gilly sifted through the contents of the bags. He'd bought soap and shampoo, toothpaste. Shirts, sweatpants, socks, a few six-packs of plain cotton underpants in a style she hadn't worn in years. No shoes, no gloves or scarf, no hat.

She rubbed her middle finger between her eyes, where a pain was brewing. It seemed he'd thought of just about everything. Nothing fancy, all practical, and probably all of it would fit her. She thought she should be grateful he hadn't bought her something creepy like a kinky maid's outfit. She thought she should be happy he'd bought her clothes and wasn't going to skin her to make a dress for himself, that's what she should be grateful for.

Gilly gathered as many of the bags as she could. "Is there a shower?"

"Outside. There's a tub in the bathroom."

The plastic shifted and slipped in her fingers as she took the bags and went into the bathroom. She shut the door behind her. There was no lock. The room's one small window slid up easily halfway, but then stuck. She would never fit through it. And if she did, where would she go? How far would she get with no coat or gloves and nothing but socks on her feet, with no idea where she was or how to get anywhere else? Todd was right, people died all the time in the woods.

"You didn't bring any water?" This comes from Seth, looking surprised. "But you always bring everything."

Not this time, apparently. Gilly shifts baby Gandy on one hip and watches Arwen toddle along the boardwalk through the trees. There are miles of boardwalk and lots of stairs at Bushkill Falls, and who knew it would take so long to walk them, or that there'd be no convenient snack stands along the way? Gilly's thirsty, too, her back aches from carrying Gandy in the sling, her heart races as Arwen gets too close to the railing.

Gilly is the planner. The packer. The prepared one. Seth is accustomed to walking out the door with nothing but his wallet and keys, and if he slings the diaper bag over his shoulder it's without bothering to look inside. He trusts her to be prepared. To have everything they could possibly need and a lot of stuff they won't.

"I can't believe you didn't pack water," Seth says, and Gilly fumes, silent and stung, her own throat dry with thirst.

That had been an awful trip. Walking for miles to see the beauty of the waterfalls that she'd have enjoyed more

without the rumble of hunger and a parched mouth distracting her. And that had been along set paths, no place
to get lost, in temperate autumn. What would happen
to her if she set out without shoes into the frigid mid-
January air and tried to make her way down a mountain, through the forest, without having a clue about
where she was going?

No. She had to plan better than that. Be prepared.
Because once she started, there'd be no going back.

First, she'd get cleaned up. The tub, a deep claw-foot,
was filthy with a layer of dust and some dead bugs. The
toilet was the old-fashioned kind with a tank above and
a pull chain. It would've been quaint and charming in
a bed-and-breakfast.

Gilly set the bags on the chipped porcelain countertop and pulled out a package of flowery soap. Her skin
itched just looking at it. Further exploration brought
out a long, slim package. A purple, sparkly toothbrush.
The breath whooshed from her lungs as if she'd been
punched in the stomach. Gilly let out a low cry, holding on to the sink top to keep her buckling knees from
dropping her to the ground. Shudders racked her body,
so fierce her teeth clattered sharply.

He'd bought her a toothbrush.

The simple consideration, not the first from him,
undid her. Gilly pressed her forehead to the wall, her
palms flat on the rough paneling. Sobs surged up her
throat and she bit down hard, jailing them behind her
teeth. She cursed into her fists, silent, strangled cries
she didn't want him to overhear. She didn't want to
give him that.

Count to ten, Gilly. Count to twenty if you have to.
Keep it in, don't let it out. You'll lose it if you let it out.

You'll lose you.

Gilly clutched at her cheeks and bit the inside of her wrist until the pain there numbed the agony in her heart. He'd given her opportunity to escape, and she hadn't taken it. Had been unable to take it.

She was crazy, not him. She was the psycho. It was her.

Quickly, she ran water from the faucet. It was frigid and tinged with orange, barely warming even after a minute, though it did turn clear. She splashed her face to wash away tears that hadn't fallen. When she could breathe again she forced herself to look in the mirror. Her eyes narrowed as she assessed herself.

She'd dreamed of her mother speaking words she'd never said. Never would've said. Gilly didn't need a dream dictionary to parse out what the dream meant, her mother with the flowers that had sometimes seemed to mean more to her than her family. Blood. The responsibility of roses.

Looking at her face now she saw her mother's eyes, the shape of her mother's mouth. She'd heard her mother's voice, too.

"I am not my mother." She muttered this, each word tasting sour. She didn't believe herself.

Her ablutions were brief but effective. Staring at the clothes in the bags, Gilly felt herself wanting to slip into disconnectedness again. It was tempting to let the blankness take over. She forced it away.

She changed her panties but kept her bra on. Apparently he hadn't thought to buy her one. She put her own jeans back on, her own shirt. She didn't want to wear the clothes he'd bought her. She wanted her own things, even if the hems of her jeans were stiff with dirt and her shirt smelled faintly of the juice she hadn't realized was spilled on it. She folded the rest of the clothes and shoved them back in the bags.

Gilly combed her hair and tied it back with the po-nytail holder from her jeans pocket. It was Arwen's. Her fingers trembled as she twisted the elastic into her hair. They'd stopped by the time she finished using the sparkly toothbrush.

Todd had put more wood in the stove, and now the room was almost stifling. He sat on the couch, staring at nothing. Smoking, tapping the ashes into an old cof-fee can set on the table in front of him.

"Feel better?" he asked without looking at her.

"No."

Todd sighed. "I'm not an asshole, Gilly. Or a psy-cho. Really."

She didn't say anything.

He looked at her, anger smoldering in his dark eyes. The sight made her step back toward the insignificant safety of the bathroom. Todd got up from the couch and made as though to step toward her.

"You afraid of me?"

She shook her head, not quite able to voice the lie. She was suddenly terrified. In her hands the plastic crinkled and shifted, and she clutched the bags in front of her like a shield.

"Shit," Todd said. "This is all a bunch of shit."

Then he stormed to the front door and out, slamming it behind him. A few minutes later she heard the truck's engine roar into life. Gilly dropped the bags and ran to the window, but he'd already pulled away.

5

Gilly had always prided herself on keeping cool in an emergency, but now she flew to the door, flung it open, ran out onto the freezing front porch. The truck had disappeared. She ran after it anyway.

She couldn't even hear it by the time she crossed the snowy yard and reached the gravel that began the rutted road. Rocks dug into her sock-clad feet and she hopped, slapping at her arms to warm herself in her long-sleeved but thin shirt. She ventured a few steps down the road, which grew immediately shadowed by the trees.

A layer of snow, perhaps two inches deep, interspersed with rocks and ice, blanketed the ground. It hadn't been a good winter for snow. Bitter-cold temperatures had abounded since late October, and one large storm had closed schools across the state, but that was all. None of it had melted, and piles of it were still all over the place, but no more had fallen. Gilly looked at the moody gray sky, clouds obscuring the sun. This spot was up high. Close to the sky. The wind pushed at the trees and lifted the tips of her hair. Was she going to run?

She looked again down the empty road and knew she wasn't. Not like this, anyway. Not unprepared. Sparkly tights would not protect her feet. He hadn't bothered to tie her up when he left, but he hadn't needed to.

"Moss," she muttered aloud, turning back toward the cabin. "Something about moss."

Growing on a side of a tree. Something about finding and following a stream. She knew snippets of information about how to find her way out of the woods, but nothing useful.

The smartest thing to do would be to steal the truck and drive away, something she'd have to do when he got back. With that in mind, Gilly headed back into the cabin. She closed the door behind her and looked down at her muddy socks. She stripped them off and dug around in the plastic bags until she found another pair. They had kittens on them. Sparkly, glittery kittens.

Socks in hand, Gilly sank onto the floor and cradled her face in her hands. She didn't cry. Her feet and hands were cold, and she shuddered, wrapping her arms around herself. The floor was filthy, but she couldn't seem to care. How had she ended up here, in this place?

Quiet. Everything was quiet around her. Her knees ached, her thighs cramped, and a chill stole over her in the overheated room. Still, Gilly didn't move. She had nowhere to be, nothing to do, nobody tugging on her for attention. She was still. She was silent.

She sat that way for a long time.

Without a watch or a clock, Gilly had no way of knowing how long Todd had been gone. At last she could no longer stand even the luxury of idleness. She had to *do* something.

With nothing to keep them occupied, her hands opened and shut like hysterical puppets. Gilly paced the room, step by step, measuring her prison with her footsteps. There had to be a way, some way to take advantage of his absence. In the end, she could think of nothing, could make no decision.

She understood without hesitation she was breaking down, that she'd broken down the moment at the gas station when she'd stayed in the truck instead of escaping. Her split from reality was shameful but not surprising; that she'd wondered for years if she would one day step off the deep end did not, now, make her feel better about having taken the dive.

She was too strong for this, damn it. Had always forced herself to be too strong. No fashionable Zoloft or Prozac for her, no trips to the therapist to work out her "issues," nothing but sheer determination had kept her functioning. And yet now…now all she could think about was her mother.

Gilly had grown accustomed to hearing her mother's voice. Dispensing advice. Scolding. She knew it was really her own inner voice. She hadn't realized until a day ago that she'd used it out loud, too.

She thought of her mom now, not hearing her voice but remembering it, instead.

"We're normal," her mother says. "You think we're not, but we are. Other families are just like this, Gillian. Whether you believe it or not."

Gilly doesn't believe it. By now she's spent too much time at Danica's house. She understands that most other people's mothers don't spend days without showering or

*brushing their teeth, without getting out of their night-
gowns. Most mothers are able to get up off the floors
of their bedrooms. They don't cry softly, moaning, over
and over and over again while rocking. Most people's
mothers wear bracelets on their wrists, not scars.*

*A cliché has prompted her mother to say it. Spilled
milk, a puddle of it on the table and the floor. Gilly
knocked it over with her elbow and would've cleaned
it up before her mom even noticed, but it's one of the
days Marlena has made it out of the dim sanctuary of
her bedroom. She weeps over the spill, gnashing her
teeth and pulling at her hair as she gets on hands and
knees to mop up the spill with the hem of her skirt.*

*"This is normal, Gillian," her mother mutters over
and over. "You think this isn't, you think we aren't. But
we are!"*

Gilly had stood watching as blank faced as she felt
now.

This is different. You're not her. This isn't like that.

But it was worse, wasn't it? What Gilly had allowed
to happen, no, what she'd *chosen to do* was worse than
anything her mother had ever done. Because Gilly
couldn't blame any of this on being crazy. She'd worked
too hard against insanity.

A plastic bag tangled in her ankles as she paced, and
Gilly paused to kick it away. She looked at all the things
he'd bought her and kicked those, too. Scattering the
brightly colored turtlenecks made her feel better for a
moment, gave her some power.

She gathered up the clothes and stuffed them back
in the bags. Gilly looped the handles over her arms and
took all the stuff upstairs. She was moving on autopi-

lot, but having something to do made her feel calmer. Allowed her to think.

She pulled open the top drawer on the dresser and prepared to put away the clothes. Inside she found a sheaf of photographs, some in frames but most loose. She picked up the top one.

A dark-haired boy stared out at her. He stood beside a tall, bearded man wearing a blaze-orange vest and holding a gun. The boy was not smiling. Gilly traced the line of his face with one finger. It was Todd.

He was in other photos, too, in some as young as perhaps eight and others as old as sixteen. It was the younger faces that grabbed her attention. Something about him as a boy seemed so familiar to her, but she couldn't quite figure out why.

Gilly put the pictures away and used the other drawers to store the things Todd had bought for her. In the chest at the foot of the bed she found sheets, blankets, pillowcases. These were cleaner than those on the bed and fragrant with the biting scent of cedar. She stripped the bed and made it up again. Smoothing the sheets and plumping the pillows gave her hands something to do while her mind worked, but when the task was over her mind was as blank as it had been before.

In the kitchen, she opened cupboards and saw the supplies he'd bought in the hours she'd been asleep. Beneath the sink she found bottles and cartons of soap, sponges, bleach. They weren't new, but they'd work. She rolled up her sleeves and bent to the task.

The day passed that way, and Gilly lost herself in the work. At home, Gilly was lucky if she got to fold a basket of laundry before being pulled away to take care of some other chore. Floors went unmopped for weeks, toilets went unscrubbed, furniture went undusted. Gilly hated never finishing anything. She'd learned to live with it, but she hated it. She felt she could never sit, never rest, never take some time for herself. Not until she was done, and she was never done. Later in her life, with spotless floors and unrumpled bedspreads, she might look back to this time with wistful nostalgia. But she doubted it. She hated never finishing anything.

Most of her girlfriends complained about it incessantly, but Gilly liked cleaning. Not just the end results, but the effort. Making order out of chaos. For her, it was much the same feeling she'd heard long-distance runners or other athletes describe. When she was cleaning, really working hard, Gilly could put herself into "the zone."

Everything else faded away, leaving behind only the scent of bleach and lemon cleanser, the ache of muscles worked hard and a blank, serene mind. It wasn't a state she often reached. Always, there were too many distractions, too many interruptions. Too many demands on her time.

Now, today, the dirty cabin and time reeled out in front of her without an end to either of them. By concentrating on one small part at a time, the task didn't seem so daunting. Todd had cleaned the fridge before loading it with groceries, but the rest of the kitchen was a disaster. Gilly started with the counters, then the cupboard fronts, the stove. She cleaned the scarred table of as much grime as she could. She discovered the pantry, as fully stocked as the fridge and cupboards, and through it the door to the backyard. She scrubbed the floor on hands and knees and dumped buckets of black water off the back porch, forming a dirty puddle that quickly froze.

Early-falling dark and the grumbling of her stomach forced her to stop. Gilly surveyed her efforts. The kitchen would never be fresh and new, but it was now, at least, clean. Her back ached and her fingers cramped, stiff and blistered from the scrub brush, but satisfaction filled her. She'd accomplished something, even if it was irrelevant and useless to her situation.

She went to the windows. Snowflakes flirted through the sky, promising a storm. As she watched, the soft white flakes grew thicker. Maybe they weren't just flirting after all.

She thought of Arwen and Gandy. Who was with them? Did they miss her? And Seth, dear, sweet Seth who couldn't find his own pair of socks…what must he be going through?

She thought of the stack of bills waiting to be paid and the poor dog missing his vet appointment. Laundry, baskets of it overflowing, and dishes piled in the sink. The house would be falling apart without her.

When Gilly was pregnant with Arwen, her grandmother had given Gilly a sampler. Embroidered in threads of red and gold, it read simply: "There is a special place in Heaven for mothers." Gilly had thought she understood the sentiment, but it wasn't until after Arwen's birth, as her daughter grew from baby to child and Gandy came along, that Gilly really did understand. She'd embraced motherhood with everything inside her, determined to be the kind of mother she'd always wanted but hadn't had.

Good mothers cooked and cleaned and read stories to their children before bed. They sang songs. They played the Itsy Bitsy Spider until their fingers fell off, if that was the game that made their babies giggle. They changed diapers, filled sippy cups, sewed the frayed and torn edges of favorite blankies to keep them together just another few months. They gave up everything of themselves to give everything to their children.

Good mothers did not run away.

Gilly pressed her fingertips to the cold glass. She'd wanted to run away. How often had she thought about simply packing a bag, or better yet, nothing at all? Just leaving the house with nothing but herself.

Gilly understood having children meant sacrifice. It was the only thing about motherhood she'd been certain of before actually becoming a mother. Impromptu dinners out, going to the movies, privacy in the bathroom, had all become luxuries she didn't mind foregoing, most of the time. She didn't even mind the grubby clothes, which were far more comfortable than the pinching high heels and gut-busting panty hose she'd worn when she worked. Gilly cherished her children. Lord knew, they drove her to the edge of madness, but wasn't that what children did? Staying home to raise them had become the most challenging and rewarding task she'd ever undertaken. She'd conceived her children in love and borne them in blood, and her life without them wouldn't be worth living. It was just the constant never-endingness of it that some days made her want to scream until her throat burst.

She loved Seth, the solid man she'd married more than ten years before. Seth did his share, when he was home, of bathing and diapering and taking out the garbage. Yes, he needed reminding for even the simplest tasks and no, he never quite managed to complete any of them without asking her how to do it, but he tried.

She had a good life. Her children were healthy and bright, her husband attentive and generous. They lived in a lovely house, drove nice cars, went on vacation every year. She had as many blessings as a woman could want. If there were still days Gilly thought she might simply be unable to drag herself out of bed, it wasn't their fault.

They were her life. They consumed every part of her. She was a mother and a wife before she was a woman. Feminism might frown on it, and Gilly might strain against the shackles of responsibility, but when it came right down to it, she'd lost sight of how else to be.

The hours of cleaning had cleared her mind. Everyone would believe a knife to her head had made her toss her children out the car window, and nobody would question that fear for her life had kept her moving. Only Gilly would ever know the real and secret truth. She'd wanted to escape, but not from Todd. From her precious and fragile life. From what she'd made.

Gilly opened the pantry door and surveyed what she found. She ran her hands along the rows of canned spaghetti, the jars of peanut butter and jelly, the bags and cartons of cookies and snacks. He'd bought flour, sugar, coffee, pasta, rice. Cartons of cigarettes, which she moved away from the food in distaste. He'd stocked the cabin with enough food for an army...or for a siege.

Gilly took a box of spaghetti and a jar of sauce from the shelf and closed the pantry door behind her. He'd already told her he didn't plan to let her go and warned her of the risks of trying to leave on her own. Two choices, two paths, and she couldn't fully envision either of them. Yesterday she'd been ready to toss her kids out a window to get away from them, and Todd had appeared. Now she felt tossed like dandelion fluff on the wind.

Gilly slapped the box of pasta on the counter. She found a large pot and filled it with water, then a smaller one. She lit the burners on the stove with an ancient box of matches from the drawer and set the water boiling and the pasta sauce simmering. She stood over them both, not caring about the old adage about watched pots. The heat from the stove warmed her hands as she stared without really seeing.

There was a third choice, one she'd already imagined even though now her mind shuddered away from the thought. If she could not manage to convince Todd to voluntarily let her go, and if she couldn't somehow be smart and strong enough to escape him, there was one other option. And, of the three choices, it was the one Gilly was sure would work.

Some pasta sauce had splashed on the back of her hand, rich and red. She licked it, tasting garlic. The water in the pot bubbled, and she opened the box of spaghetti, judged a handful, then tossed in the whole box. Dinner would be ready in a few minutes, and Todd was likely to return soon.

If she couldn't change his mind or break for an escape, Gilly thought she might just have to kill him.

Todd walked in the door just as Gilly finished setting the table with a red-and-white-checkered cloth and a set of lovely, Depression-era dishes and silverware she'd found in the drawer. Though the silver was tarnished and several of the plates cracked or chipped, she could only imagine what pieces like this would sell for in an antiques shop. Hundreds, maybe thousands of dollars. He paused in the doorway to sniff the air. Again, he reminded her of a hungry, loveless dog hanging around the kitchen door.

"Smells good." He jingled the pocket of his sweatshirt, then took out her keys. He tossed them on the counter.

Gilly purposefully kept her eyes from them. "I hope you're hungry," she said flatly. "I made a lot."

Todd pulled out his chair with a scrape that sent chills up her spine, like fingernails on a chalkboard. "Fucking starving."

Gilly poured the spaghetti into the strainer she'd put

in the sink. Clouds of steam billowed into her face and she closed her eyes against it. She scooped some onto a plate and went to the table, taking the seat across from him.

Todd didn't serve himself, just stared at her expectantly. With a silent sigh she got up from her seat and took his plate to the sink, plopped a serving of spaghetti on top and splashed it with the sauce. She tossed a piece of garlic bread beside the spaghetti and handed it to him.

"Thanks." At least he did have some manners.

They ate in silence interrupted only by the sounds of chewing and slurping. Surreptitiously Gilly watched the movement of his mouth as he gobbled pasta. A few days' worth of beard stubbled his tawny cheeks, the dark hairs glinting reddish in the light from above.

"This is good." He wiped his mouth with the napkin she'd folded next to his plate. "Really good."

"Thank you." Cleaning had made her hungry. She'd polished off a large plateful herself and now sat back, her stomach almost too full.

Todd burped loud and long, the kind of noise that at home would have earned a laugh followed by a reprimand. Gilly did neither. She sipped some water, watching him.

"Where did you go?"

"Out."

She hadn't really expected him to tell her. She sipped more water and wiped her mouth. Todd eyed her, his mouth full. He chewed and swallowed.

"Why'd you do this?" Todd twirled another forkful of spaghetti but didn't eat it.

"To be nice," Gilly said. There was more to it than that.

Todd's eyes narrowed. He knew that. "Why?"

Only honesty would suffice. Gilly took a deep breath. "Because I'm hoping that if I'm nice to you, you'll let me go home."

Todd sat back in his chair, tipping it. "I can't. You know my name. You know where we are. You'd tell someone. They'd come."

Desperation slipped out in her voice. "I don't know where we are, remember? You could blindfold me. Take me someplace far away, dump me off."

Todd shook his head.

Her voice rose with tension. "I won't tell anyone your name. Or anything. I'll say I don't know anything, I swear to you. If you let me go, I'll…"

"Don't you get it? I can't ever let you go now. Not ever." His hands clutched the tabletop. His face twisted in loathing. "Don't you get it?"

"No! I don't! You don't want me here, so just…" Her voice broke, softened, slipped into a murmur. "Please, Todd. Please."

Again, he shook his head. His voice got lower, too. "You say you won't tell them anything, but even if you mean it, I know you will. You'll have to. They'll keep at you and keep at you. It's what they fucking *do,* Gilly."

"Who?"

"Them. The cops. Your therapist. Your fucking husband, I don't know. Someone will want to know where the fuck you were, and with who, and you can't tell me you won't break down and tell them. You'll spill it all, and I'll be totally fucked. And I'll tell you something," Todd said, voice lower still, his body stiff and tense, "I won't go back to jail."

Gilly wasn't surprised Todd had been to jail. He

must've seen the lack of shock in her expression, because he looked first ashamed, then defiant. He lifted his chin at her.

"I mean it. Not going back. Ever. I can't."

"You should've thought of that before," Gilly said under her breath but loud enough for him to hear her.

"You think I fucking didn't?"

Gilly shrugged. "I don't know what you thought. But you have to see that no matter what happens, you're going to get caught, Todd. Whether you let me go or I get away."

He studied her, dark eyes pulling her apart and leaving big gaps in the seams of her composure.

"No. I'll do…whatever I have to." The words were clipped and tight, his expression hard.

Gilly had thought the same. Whatever she had to, to survive. To get away from here and back to her family. If Todd was as desperate as she was—but she couldn't let herself think about that right now. Couldn't let herself be afraid.

Time spun out as they stared each other down. From the corner of her eye, Gilly spotted a glint of metal on the counter beside them. Though she tried not to let her eyes flicker, something in her gaze must have given her away. She saw it in his eyes, the sudden wariness that showed he knew what she was thinking.

Todd launched himself across the table as Gilly pushed back in her chair so hard it toppled to the floor. His fingers, not clenched now but stretched into grappling talons, scratched at her neck but didn't gain purchase.

Gilly would've hit the floor if the wall hadn't been so close behind her. Instead, she cracked the back of her head hard enough to see stars. She rolled along the short length of wall until she reached the opening to the living room. Her feet twisted on themselves and she almost fell, but her hand, grasping, found the edge of the counter, and she stayed upright. Her fingers clenched over the bundle of keys.

Todd moved fast, with swift, athletic grace, but Gilly had the thoughts of her children to fuel her. She turned, swiftly, as he grabbed at her. Keys bristled between her knuckles, and she sliced at him, hard. The metal slashed his cheek. He clapped a hand over the wound, which gushed bright blood.

He caught her just inside the living room and knocked her feet out from under her. Gilly hit the floor on her hands and knees, the keys still gripped tight in her fist. With a low growl, Todd grabbed her ankles and yanked her closer, scrabbling at the back of her shirt but not quite able to catch her.

Gilly rolled, kicking, as he loomed over her. Todd's eyes glittered, fierce, the blood on his face like war paint. He grabbed the front of her shirt, tearing it.

She kicked him in the nuts. Her foot didn't connect squarely, hitting part of his thigh, but it was enough. Todd went to his knees with a strangled groan.

Gilly got up and ran.

Adrenaline exhilarated her. She flew to the front door and leaped through it, leaving it hanging open. She'd misjudged the stairs and the icy ground beyond, and so went sprawling onto her hands and knees. Rocks tore her pants and her skin. She didn't drop the keys even though the sharp metal sliced her.

Gilly got up, palms bloodied, and ran for the truck.

She heard Todd shouting and cursing on the porch behind her. She didn't stop to look around.

The lightly falling snow had turned into thick, soft blankets of white, hiding the treacherous ice beneath. Gilly slid but kept herself from falling this time. She hit the driver's side full on, hard enough to send spikes of agony into her shoulder and dent the door. The keys scratched the paint like four claws as she grabbed the door handle to keep from falling. He'd locked it. Her numb fingers fumbled with the key-ring remote.

"Don't do this!" Todd cried from the porch. A sudden gust of wind tore his words to tatters.

Gilly ripped open the door and pulled herself into the driver's seat. Her palms stung as she gripped the wheel and plunged the keys into the ignition. She had to do this now, because she hadn't before. Because she'd been crazy before, crazy stupid. She'd let this man drive her away from her home, her husband, her children.

The Suburban roared into life. Gilly kept her foot steady on the accelerator. Her right knee, already bruised from when he'd hit her there before, had taken the worst of her fall and now throbbed with every motion. Blood slicked her palms and her hands slipped until she forced her frozen fingers to curl. She yanked the gearshift into Reverse and the truck revved backward, narrowly missing the tree that loomed in her rearview mirror.

Drive.

Her wet feet slipped on the gas pedal and light from the headlights swung wildly as she forced the truck through the snow. She hadn't realized it had gotten so deep. The vehicle slid a little, bouncing in the ruts when she jammed the gas pedal.

Her heart hammered. Everything in front of her was black, and the headlights weren't helping much. She tried to remember how long this road was, where it turned, how far to the gate, and couldn't. All she could do was drive.

On her left, the mountain. On the right of the narrow, ice-slick road, a steep incline. A line of trees reared up in front of her as the road bent. Gilly braked, forgetting in her panic everything she'd ever learned about driving. The truck went into a long, slow slide. It seemed impossible she'd actually hit the tree row, not in slow motion.

Her mind was in slow motion. Her reactions, too. But not the truck. It mowed down the trees with a vast and angry crashing that pounded Gilly's ears. The big vehicle tilted, throwing her against the door, and slammed back to the ground with a thud that jarred her to the bone. She had time to think she was going to be okay before she looked out the side window and saw the side of the mountain reaching for her.

The Suburban veered into the wall of rock. Metal screeched. Gilly, not wearing a seat belt, was flung forward into the steering wheel hard enough to knock the breath out of her. It didn't end there—the truck shuddered and groaned, sliding on ice and snow.

She was going over.

Gilly had no breath to scream. She did have time to pray, but nothing came but the sight of her children's faces. That was prayer enough.

The Suburban jolted off the road and over the edge, nearly vertical at first and then with a huge, thumping slam, it came to rest with the hood crumpled against a tree. The airbag didn't even go off, something she only noticed when she could see, very clearly, the bent and broken trees barely managing to keep the truck from sliding down the mountain. The horn bleated and died. The interior lights had come on and the pinging noise signifying an open door sounded although all the doors were closed.

Everything blurred. She tasted blood. Warmth coated her lap and dimly Gilly was embarrassed to think she might've wet herself. It wasn't urine but more blood gushing from a slice in the top of her thigh. She groaned, the sound of her voice too loud.

The door opened. Gilly screamed, then, thin and whistling but with as much force as she could muster. In the next minute Todd yanked her from the driver's seat, shoving her against the metal. Gilly swung and missed.

"Let me go!"

"You crazy dumb bitch! The fuck you think you're doing?" Todd shook her.

Beside them, the truck groaned. The trees snapped. The metal behind her back shifted and moved, and Todd yanked her a few steps toward him. Gilly fought him but couldn't get free.

Nothing seemed real. The pain in every part of her wasn't as bad as knowing she'd tried and failed to escape. She fought him with teeth and the talons of fingernails Arwen had painted pale blue only yesterday.

Todd dodged her swinging fists and her teeth. He slapped her face, first with his palm. Then, when she didn't stop flailing at him, with the back of his hand so hard her head rocked back. Gilly fell into the snowy brush and was instantly soaked. Red roses bloomed in front of her eyes.

"You dumb bitch," Todd said again, this time into

her ear. He'd lifted her though she was suddenly as limp as a rag doll.

He'd hit her. Nobody had hit her that way in a very long time. Blood dripped from her mouth, though everything was so shadowed she couldn't see it hit the snow.

Todd's fingers dug into her arms as he jerked her upright and shook her. Everything was dark and cold around them, and the sound of creaking branches was very loud. The lights from the truck abruptly dimmed.

"Wake up. I can't get your ass up this hill if you're deadweight."

Gilly blinked and struggled feebly. "Don't…hit me… again."

"I don't *want* to hit you, for fuck's sake." Todd sounded disgusted. "Just get your ass moving. What happens if that tree won't hold, huh? You want to get wiped out by that truck when it goes crashing down the rest of this hill? Look up there, how fucking far we have to get back up to the lane!"

Gilly didn't look. She couldn't, really. Turning her head made bright, sharp pain stab through her. Besides, it was too dark. The headlights were pointing the other way, down the steep slope, and as she watched they guttered and went out, followed an instant later by the ding-ding alert of the interior light cutting off.

"Ah, fuck," Todd muttered in the sudden silence. "Just stay still. Don't move."

As if she could've moved. Gilly, limp, went to her knees when Todd let her go. The snow was soft and thick but not deep enough to cradle her. Rocks and bits of broken branches stabbed at her.

"All right. Let's go. Get up. I can see," Todd said, and jerked her by the back of her collar.

Gilly couldn't. Everything was still black. She scrabbled along the slope with Todd yanking her hard enough to pull her off her feet a few times.

This was a nightmare. It had to be. Right? Pain and darkness and fear.

They got to the top of the slope and Todd paused, breathing hard. Now instead of rocks and broken trees, gravel bit into Gilly's skin as she went to her hands and knees. It was easier to get to her feet, though, when Todd yanked the back of her collar again.

Somehow they made it back to the clearing and the cabin, still ablaze with light that hurt her eyes after so many long minutes in darkness. Gilly was beyond fighting him by then. She barely made it up the front steps and into the living room. She definitely didn't make it up the steep, narrow stairs to the second floor. Todd, cursing and muttering, did that by yanking and pushing her.

With rough hands he forced her toward the bed she'd slept in. When he tried to take off her shirt, Gilly found the strength to fight him again. Todd shouted out another slew of curses.

"Stop fighting me!"

But she would not. If this was a nightmare, she was going to keep swinging and scratching, even though every movement made her cry in pain. Todd, finally, ripped her shirt completely down the front, pushed her onto the bed and yanked at her pants, too.

Gilly kicked out as hard as she could. Maybe Todd dodged it, maybe she missed. She couldn't tell. All she knew was he grabbed her by the upper arms, fingers digging deep into her flesh, to yank her to her feet.

"I'm trying to help you!" Todd shouted into her face, breath hot and spittle wet on her cheeks. Then, "Oh, shit. Don't you pass out on me, Gilly."

But Gilly did.

7

Gilly woke up blind. She lurched upright, clawing at her face. "My eyes!"

Her eyes were merely gummed shut, not blind. Her head ached in the dull, persistent manner that meant no amount of aspirin would stop it. The cold air stung a long gash on her cheek. She put trembling fingers to it and felt the wound's curve from the left side of her jaw all the way to the corner of her eye. The crash had taken its share of skin and blood from her face, which felt puffy and tender. Her chest ached from the impact with the steering wheel, but, though she sensed bruises, nothing appeared to be broken.

She wore a thick flannel nightgown that had rucked up about her thighs. She hated nightgowns for just that reason. She touched the soft fabric with her jagged, broken fingernails and shivered with distaste.

Gilly tested her limbs one at a time, cataloging aches and pains that ranged from mild to agonizing. Her neck hurt the worst. The pain when she looked to the left was excruciating enough to twist her stomach. The gash on her thigh proved to be shallow but ugly, sore to the touch and still oozing blood and clear fluid.

Still, she was alive. There was that.

A shuffle of feet from the stairs told her he was coming. She spoke before she saw him. "What time is it?"

"Does it matter?"

He'd paused at the top of the stairs but she could see him through the partition. Gilly rubbed at her temples but the throbbing didn't ease. "No. I guess it doesn't."

Todd took a few steps closer. "How are you?"

"Bad."

"You're a mess," he said flatly. "You know that?"

Gilly shrugged slightly. It was the greatest motion she could make without ripping herself open. It wasn't slight enough; she ached and more pain flared.

"The fuck were you thinking?"

She looked at him. "I want to go home."

"Yeah, well, I want a million dollars."

Gilly blinked at this attempt at…humor? Sarcasm? He'd said it with a straight face, so she couldn't be sure. "My head hurts. My neck, too. I think I strained something. And this cut on my leg needs stitches."

"No shit. You're lucky you didn't get hurt worse. That was some crash." Todd let out a low whistle. "Nice shiner."

Gilly got out of bed and went to the dirt-encrusted attic window. Her entire left side felt rubbed raw. She winced at every step but could walk.

Everything outside was white. Snow piled against the cabin in drifts that looked nearly waist high. One giant drift reached almost to the windowsill.

No. Oh, no.

"All of this in one night?" she cried, incredulous. She put her hands to the cold glass.

Todd moved to her side. She shrank from him, but he didn't seem to notice. He leaned forward to peer out the window.

"It snowed all night and all morning, too. It stopped about an hour ago. Sky's still gray. I don't think it's finished yet."

"The truck?"

He shrugged. "Totaled. Halfway down the mountain, unless that tree broke. Then that bitch is all the way at the bottom, and you can forget about ever getting it back."

She knew that already but let out a gusting sigh that became a small moan. "Oh, no."

"Hope you have good insurance."

Another joke Gilly didn't find amusing. She pressed her face to the glass, eyes closed, and let out another small, despairing sigh. "Does that even matter now?"

Todd laughed and moved away from her. "Probably not. You shouldn't have tried to run away. That was stupid."

Gilly looked at him. She searched his face for sign of a threat, but what would she do even if she saw it? Run? Fight? She'd failed miserably at both.

"You gave me no choice. I have to get home to my kids. My husband's probably worried sick."

Todd shrugged. "Neither one of us will be going anywhere until this snow melts. Not without the truck. We're pretty much fucked."

Gilly went back to the bed and sat. "I want to go home."

His face went hard, the soft, dark eyes bitter. He

threw her own words back at her. "Maybe you should've thought about that before."

Don't lose it...

But it was already lost.

"Fuck you! You think I don't know that? Fuck you, Todd!" Gilly shrieked, lurching to her feet with fists flailing.

If she'd aimed for his face she probably wouldn't have hit him, but one of her wild swings caught him just under the eye. Todd stumbled back, muttering curses. The wound she'd inflicted on him earlier broke open, oozing blood. Gilly stood her ground, fists clenched and teeth chattering, ready to batter him again.

He reached out, quick as a cat, and grabbed her shoulders. He shook her like one does a naughty child, or a pet, each shake emphasizing a word. "That's twice. Don't do it again."

"Or what?" she cried. "What could you possibly do that's worse than what you've already done?"

Todd stared at her with a flat black gaze for too long before answering, "I could do worse."

He let her go so suddenly she stumbled back, her aggression puffed out like a breath-blown match. They were at a standoff. Gilly rubbed the sore spots his fingers had left, just a few more to add to the plethora already aching all over her.

Without another word, Todd went down the stairs. She went to the window again and stared out at the vast expanse of blankness. Even the trees had been covered in heavy quilts of white, blurring their lines and making them nothing more than vague humps. She wasn't going anywhere until that melted. Perhaps as early as March or as late as April, but April was three months away.

Her throat was dry. She needed a drink. Gilly looked around the walls of the prison she'd inflicted upon herself. A wave of dizziness washed over her and she sat on the bed, then put her head on the pillow, hoping it would pass. She'd caught every flu bug Arwen brought home from kindergarten, from the nastiest stomach virus to the most persistent of colds. No amount of hand washing had seemed to help, and she was wary of overusing hand sanitizer, fearing the creation of a superbug more than risking the chance of catching yet another case of the sniffles. She'd been on antibiotics, on and off, for the past few weeks, to get rid of a bad sinus infection. Now she felt even worse, aching from head to toe and shivering with chills. She got up just long enough to slide back beneath the covers again and closed her eyes against the pain stabbing her behind the lids.

If there was any relief for her, it had the same source as her anxiety. She felt sick; she could lie down without fear of little hands plucking at her, little voices calling her name. The last time she'd taken herself to bed, unable to stand up without the world spinning, Gandy had decided to remove all the DVDs from their cases and, for some reason known only to his toddler brain, stick them in and out of the jumbo-size tub of margarine she used for making grilled cheese. That had been the day she called Seth, desperate for him to come home early from work, and he had.

There'd be no Seth to rescue her this time.

Desperation gnawed at her, a frenzied yearning to burst into action. She forced herself still, resting. Nothing to be gained by wild action; she'd learned that lesson the hard way. She thought of the snow outside, and she thought of Todd.

She supposed the real question was what did she think he would do to keep her, if he couldn't or wouldn't let her go? Did she think he would kill her if he had to? She remembered the desperation in his cry "I won't go back to jail!" And she thought that yes, he might. He might be slow of thought, and he might be kind at heart, but something had happened to him that made him what he was today. Gilly didn't think Todd had brought her here to kill her, but she did believe he would if he felt he had to.

But hadn't she determined that she'd do the same? If the chance arose, if she was left with nothing else. The thought of it now sent a shudder cascading up and down her spine, like cold fingers stroking the nape of her neck. She'd tried to change his mind, and she'd tried to escape. Both had failed. But what would happen if she killed him? The third option that had seemed so matter-of-fact and to-the-point didn't feel that way now.

Even if she managed to bring herself to kill him, she was still trapped in this cabin without a phone, without a map, without proper clothes. No vehicle, that was her own stupid fault. Even if he died, there was nothing for her to do until the snow melted. She snuggled deeper into the cave of warmth her body heat created beneath the blankets. It turned out she had a fourth option.

Waiting.

8

Three days gone. She'd never been away from her babies for that long. Not to visit a friend, not to go on a girls' weekend away, not even to a scrapbooking seminar.

In her college days and just after, before meeting Seth, Gilly had been a traveler. She'd stayed in youth hostels or taken summer jobs at tourist destinations in different states. She'd jaunted on spur-of-the-moment trips based on whatever cheap airfare she'd found. Once she'd bought a companion ticket on an ocean liner from an elderly woman whose friend had been unable to make it at the last minute. The woman's name was Esther and though Gilly had been nervous about sharing a cabin with a stranger, the two of them had hit it off superbly. They'd kept in touch for years, until Esther passed away. Gilly hadn't traveled like that in a long, long time and probably never would again.

Seth traveled sometimes for work. He came home with the news of a conference or business trip, how many days he'd be gone, what time his flights left and returned. He made his plans and took the trips without a second thought about who'd pick up Arwen from kindergarten or take Gandy to preschool. Who'd feed and walk the dog, sign for deliveries. Pay the bills or take care of the loads of laundry. Seth decided he was going, and he went.

A trip for Gilly would take weeks of planning and countless favors called in from friends to juggle her children's schedules and her time commitments. The effort it took for her to step out the door for a trip to the grocery store by herself would be magnified to such extent even a few days spent in a spa getting hot-stone massages and foot rubs from handsome, oiled men in loincloths wouldn't be worth the hassle.

This was not even close to a hot-stone massage. Paused at the bottom of the stairs, Gilly looked across the room at Todd sitting at the table, still sorting through his folder of papers. He had a cigarette in one hand and sucked in long, deep draws of smoke he held for an impossibly long time before letting it seep from his nostrils. His hair fell forward as he bent over the papers, but she could still see the wounds she'd inflicted on his face. The cuts were evidence she'd done what she could to get away, but small consolation compared to her aches and bruises.

She'd stayed upstairs for what felt like an hour but might've been two. Might've been fifteen minutes. She didn't have a watch, the cabin had no clocks, and the daylight outside was set permanently to twilight. More snow drifted down in spurts, dandruff brushed from a giant's shoulders.

Todd looked up when her foot creaked on the bottom step. He closed the folder and stood. "Hi."

Walking stiffly so as to jar her sore muscles as little as possible, Gilly limped into the living room. She kept a wary distance, but Todd acted as though he'd never raised a hand to her. He came around the couch but stopped when she took a step back.

"I got your stuff," he said.

"What stuff?" Gilly asked. She didn't think he was capable of being particularly subtle, but she *was* wary of some sort of trick she couldn't anticipate.

Todd hesitated, then gestured at the front door. "Your stuff. From the truck. I got what I could, anyway. It was fuckall tough. That little tree's not going to hold it much longer. But…I thought you might want stuff out of it before it hits the bottom of the mountain."

Gilly's aching knees buckled. The doorway saved her from falling as she gripped it with her sore hand. He'd brought her things.

She moved on stumbling feet, three, four, five steps, to crouch by the pile of miscellaneous junk Todd had brought back from the wreck. Most of it *was* junk. A scattering of plastic toys. A stray sock that had been missing for months and was now too small for either of the kids. A sippy cup, thick with the remnants of some red juice. Gandy's blankie, many times repaired and badly in need of a wash. He'd be missing it by now. Crying for it, unable to sleep.

Gilly grabbed it. Held it to her face. Breathed in the scent of her son. She made a wordless noise of grief into the fabric.

You're never going to see him again. Or Arwen, or

Seth. This is what you did, Gilly. This is what you de-serve.

"Gilly?"

Todd's hand came to rest on her shoulder, and she shook it off. Clutching the blankie to her chest, she glared up at him. "Don't. Just don't!"

Todd held up both hands, face grim. "Fine. Jesus. What a bitch."

He slouched away, boots heavy and clomping on the bare boards of the floor. Gilly crouched over her meager pile of belongings. The detritus of motherhood. Tiny, mismatched pieces of her heart.

She found her iPod, safe in the soft eyeglass case she used to transport it, the earbuds still wrapped around it. He'd also brought the black CD case bulging with discs she only listened to while driving. Bat Boy, scratched probably beyond repair.

Behind her, Gilly heard Todd pacing, but she didn't look. She held the CD close to her. She'd bought this disc with Seth at one of the last few shows this cast had performed at an off-Broadway theater, four days after the Twin Towers had fallen.

"We took the ferry," she said.

Todd's boots stopped thumping.

Gilly bent her head over the disc. Her fingers left misty marks on the silver back. "We parked in the lot and took the ferry across. It was full of people going to volunteer to help. There was a federal marshal on board. I could see his gun. I looked out across the water and saw the smoke."

Gilly closed her eyes, her memories clutched in bruised and aching hands.

"There were posters everywhere. Pictures of people

who were still missing, with numbers to call. When we got to the other side, there were parking lots blocked off by wire fencing, filled with pallets of water. I saw a bundle of axes, maybe twenty of them, leaning against the fence."

"The fuck are you talking about?" Todd asked, but softly. Gentle. It was the way someone might speak to someone standing on a ledge or a bridge.

Gilly opened her eyes. She gathered up what he'd brought to her, careful not to lose anything. "It was the worst thing I'd ever seen."

"You messing with me again?"

She stood and looked at him. "No. I'm not. I'm trying to tell you that I've seen bad things."

"Yeah?" Todd frowned. "Well, so have I."

"I thought at the time that was the worst experience I'd ever have. Seeing what had been left behind. The grief of people who'd lost someone they loved. The bravery of the ones who'd traveled from all over to help dig out the dead. I thought it was the very worst thing, and it was bad…" She looked up at him. "But I think this is worse."

Todd took a step back, mouth thinning. "Why don't you shut up now, Gilly."

"Yes," she said faintly and held her things close to her. "Yes. I think I will."

Todd scuffed a boot on the floor. It left a black mark on the boards she'd so painstakingly swept earlier. "I'm making dinner. Come have some."

Gilly shook her head. "No."

"You should eat something."

Her stomach, empty, was nonetheless too shriveled

for hunger. The thought of food made her feel sick. "Why?"

Todd's mouth opened and closed. He scowled, then tossed up his hands and turned on his heel to stalk to the kitchen. Gilly watched him go, then stood, juggling her belongings, and went upstairs.

She put everything he'd salvaged in the top drawer of the dresser she was nauseated to realize she thought of as "hers." Then she climbed into bed and burrowed under the blankets with the iPod.

Though it didn't look broken, the iPod wouldn't turn on. It gave a low, chugging *whir* when Gilly pressed the button. She slapped it into her palm as if she was tamping a pack of cigarettes, once, then harder. The screen lit, then shut off. She tamped it again. This time, the Apple logo showed up as the unit rebooted or did whatever it was doing.

She slipped the earbuds in and thumbed the controls. It was an old model, inherited from Seth after he'd upgraded, but that had never mattered. It had enough space on it to store some music and photos. She scrolled to the picture slideshow she'd loaded to show Seth's parents the last time they'd visited. In moments the bright and bouncy music, some instrumental piece that came with the photo software, came on. So did the photos.

Arwen in pink tights and a ballerina sweatshirt, curly dark hair pulled into pigtails, showing off a hole where her front tooth had been. Gandy dressed like Scooby Doo, holding an empty pumpkin pail, chocolate smeared on his face. Photo after photo of her children, each one precious and remote, unforgettable and unreachable.

And finally, Gilly wept.

9

Gilly woke again to the morning sun and frozen cheeks. She hunched the covers up around her face to warm it. From the other side of the barrier she heard the low, familiar rumble of male snoring.

It was early, judging by the slant of sunlight made brighter by its reflection off the snow. Her entire body still hurt, possibly worse than it had the day before. Her bruises had bruises. Joints popped and crackled as she stretched. Her stomach wasn't too happy, either. She hadn't eaten much of anything, but the thought of food made her swallow a gag.

Her head hurt. Gilly had been prone to headaches her entire life, most of them tension related, but this was a bad one. Pain cradled her skull and spiked her eyes from the combination of infected sinuses, lack of food and anxiety. She'd never been diagnosed with migraines, but now she blinked away what sure as hell looked like an aura.

Groaning seemed worthless, but she did it anyway.

No cease from the snoring on the room's other side. Gilly pressed her thumbs to the magic spots just above the bridge of her nose, willing the pain to go away. It didn't, but it did ease a little. Long experience told her that eating would help, even if she didn't feel like it. A hot shower would, too, but she was out of luck on that one.

She flung the covers off and swung her legs over the bed. Her head spun and her stomach rocked alarmingly. Clenching her jaw didn't help her headache, but she refused to puke. Absolutely refused. Raw bile burned in her throat, and she swallowed convulsively, over and over.

Breathe, Gilly. In. Out. Keep it together.

She must've groaned louder because suddenly Todd appeared, leaning on the partition. "You okay?"

She didn't dare speak, and so only nodded. She pressed her thumbs more firmly against her forehead. The throbbing subsided. Sheer willpower kept her stomach's contents inside it rather than all over the floor.

"You don't look good."

"I don't feel good."

He didn't say anything. Gilly looked up at him. Sleep had mussed his hair and still clouded his eyes. He wiped a hand across bristled cheeks. "You gonna puke?"

"No!" Her indignation chased the last of her sour stomach away.

"Just asking. You look kinda pale."

"I'm always this color."

He raised his eyebrows at her. "If you say so."

"I just need to eat something." Gilly pushed past him and hobbled down the stairs. In the kitchen, she toasted bread and poured cereal. The single half-gallon container of milk was almost empty. She swished it around thoughtfully before pouring it. There'd be no more for a long time after this was gone. She poured it anyway.

Todd had bought the kind of sugary cereals she never bought at home because she knew they'd rot her kids' teeth or give them cancer or send them into hyperactive spirals. Now Gilly dug into the bowl and crunched the sweetness. She gobbled it. She watched the colored cereal turn her milk the color of a tropical sunset.

Todd appeared at the bottom of the stairs. He wore a loose-fitting pair of sweatpants, slung low across his hips. When he lifted his arm to scrub at his face she saw the tan expanse of his belly, not taut and buff but soft and slightly curved. A long, angry scar dimpled the skin.

"It's starting to snow again," Todd remarked as he looked out one of the back windows. "Goddamn, look at that coming down. Fucking snowpocalypse out there."

Gilly filled her bowl again and kept crunching. Famine had replaced her earlier nausea. The sweet cereal made her teeth ache.

"There's no more milk," she said when he entered the kitchen, and waited to see what he would say.

"There's five gallons outside in the lean-to," Todd replied. "As long as it's cold like this, it'll stay frozen out there."

Gilly felt somehow defeated in her defiance. "You've thought of everything."

Todd got a bowl from the cupboard and sat across from her to fill it with Lucky Charms. He shrugged. "Didn't want to get caught needing something I didn't have."

Gilly pushed her bowl away, suddenly no longer so hungry. "You planned this."

His spoon stopped halfway to his mouth, then lowered. "I had a plan, yeah. And then it changed. I wasn't sure what the hell was going to happen, so I tried to make sure I was ready for whatever. Lucky for us, huh?"

He had that wary look in his eyes again. Gilly toyed with the floating rainbow chunks in the bright pink milk. She watched him lift the spoon to his mouth, watched him chew.

"It was a pretty piss poor plan." Todd shrugged, pretending it didn't matter. "I didn't plan on you."

"You took my truck! How could you not plan on me? Why not just steal a car if you wanted one so bad?"

"First, you obviously don't know how fucking hard it is to steal a car in the middle of a busy parking lot, duh. If I even knew how to hot-wire one which I fucking don't. And…I didn't know you had kids in the back, okay?" Todd pushed back from the table, and his spoon clattered to the floor. He stalked to the sink and hunched over it, his hands splayed on the green countertop. "I didn't see the kids. When you went to the money machine, I just saw you."

Gilly thought back to what seemed like so long ago. "I left them in the truck to run to the ATM for one second."

"I thought I'd just take the truck and tell you to drive someplace quieter, then make you get out," Todd continued. "The fuck were you thinking? Leaving your kids in the car. Don't you know you're not supposed to leave your kids alone in the car?"

"Don't you…don't you question my parenting skills!" Gilly cried. "You don't know anything about it!"

"I didn't know they were in there."

His voice shuddered and his face twisted. Gilly sat

motionless. It would have been easy for her to pity him, to soften her heart. But she did not.

"I'd never hurt a kid." His mouth pulled down in distress. "I might be a fuckup, but I'd never hurt a kid!"

She believed him, strangely enough. "That's a damn good thing, Todd. Because if you'd harmed one hair of my children's heads, I would've...I *would* have killed you."

Saying it aloud, she knew it was true. There'd have been no hesitation. If he'd hurt her kids, she'd have done it.

He turned to face her, his eyes wide. "Shut up."

She leaned forward, hands flat on the table, one on each side of her cereal bowl. Her voice was steadier than she expected. Full of truth. "I would have killed you."

He wet his lips, thinking. Then he scoffed. "No, you wouldn't have."

His easy dismissal irritated her. "Yes. I would."

He stared at her, frowning. "You have no idea how hard it would be to kill somebody. You're not hard like that, Gilly. I can tell."

Under any other circumstances, his comment would have been a compliment. Now she was as insulted as if he'd called her a vile name. Her eyes bored into his. "If you hurt my children, nothing in this world could have kept you safe from me."

Todd's gaze flickered. He put his hands on the table, too, and leaned to look into her eyes. "You're full of shit."

He was wrong about her—she did know how hard it was to kill. Her mother, at the end, had begged for Gilly to put a pillow over her face, to give her pills, to turn up the drip on the morphine until it sent her off to sleep for good. Her mother, sallow and scrawny by then, with nothing left of the beauty Gilly had always envied, had wept and pleaded. She'd called Gilly names and raged with breathless whispers, the loudest she could make. She'd demanded.

Gilly hadn't killed her mother, but she'd wanted to.

Gilly leaned forward, too. She could've kissed him, if she'd chosen. Or bitten him. "I'm a mother and I would do anything for my children. I *would* kill you. Believe it."

She had never meant anything more.

"Mothers don't love their children that much." Todd stood and shrugged. "It's something they made up for TV. You don't have a clue about killing."

"Do you?" she shot back, and was instantly afraid of the answer.

"Are you asking me if I ever killed someone?"

Did she want to know?

"Yes," Gilly said.

Todd gave her no answer other than a shake of his head.

Gilly swallowed hard, choking for a second on the breath she'd been holding. "Would you kill me?"

"Aw, hell! I already told you that's not why I brought you here, Jesus."

"I didn't ask if you wanted to kill me. I asked if you would." She didn't like this side of herself, the re- lentlessness, but she didn't stop herself. "If I run away again, and you catch me, will you kill me? Will you kill me anyway? Because someone will come, Todd. Someone will find out where I am, and come for me. You know they will."

He ran both hands through his hair, gripping his

head for a moment before replying through gritted teeth. "Shut the fuck up, okay?"

She moved closer, tiny compared to his height, but pushing him back with every step she took. "I want to hear you say it. I want to know. I deserve to know!"

"Why?" He backed away, shaking his shaggy head, the dark hair swinging like the mane of some wild stallion. "Why the fuck do you deserve a fucking thing from me?"

"Because you took me!" The words tore her throat. "At the gas station I thought you'd leave and it would be all over. You'd call the cops, they'd come, whatever. I figured that was it. I went in the store and bought my shit, the whole time thinking I was gonna come back out and find you gone. I thought for sure I was screwed, but you stayed in the truck. Why didn't you get out? Why the hell didn't you get out?"

"Why didn't you make me get out?"

"Fuck if I know. I figured…what the hell, if you didn't get out, you wouldn't tell the cops…I dunno. Christ, you scared the shit out of me, Gilly. That's all. I didn't know what the hell to do with you. You had the chance to get out and you didn't…." Todd's grin reminded her of the Big Bad Wolf. All teeth. "You're as crazy as I am."

Crazy meant medication, hospitals, long narrow corridors smelling of piss and human despair. Crazy was her mother, locked away in a room with only her mood swings for company. It was the grit of shattered glass underfoot and the smell of spilled perfume.

"No, I'm not." Her words weren't as convincing this time.

Todd snorted and turned back to the window with

the same easy knack he had of pushing away the tension, making it appear that it hadn't happened at all. "Man, it's really coming down. We might get another foot, at least."

Gilly stood and took her bowl to the sink. She had to push past him to get there, but he stepped aside and didn't crowd her. Side by side they stared out the window.

"So," she said. "What happens now?"

Todd shrugged again. "I don't know."

Gilly wanted to slap him. Instead, she rinsed her bowl and spoon and set them to dry in the drainer. He didn't move, only watched her.

"I won't stop trying, you know," she whispered. "To get away, I mean."

"I'll always stop you."

"No," Gilly said. "One day, you won't."

10

Short days passed into long nights. Gilly's body ached, but she forced herself to appreciate every ache and pain and hobble around the cabin to keep her stiff muscles limber. She didn't think there'd be another chance for escape, but if one came she didn't want to be too disabled to take it.

Todd didn't say much to her, and if he noticed Gilly keeping her distance from him, he didn't show it. Again, she was struck at how easy he was about all of this, how commonplace he made it. While every gust of wind scraping a tree branch on the house startled her into jumping, Todd barely glanced up. When she padded past him to the kitchen to forage for something to eat, he called out casually for her to grab him a beer.

She did, not sure why. The bottle, a longneck, chilled her palm as she brought it to him. She watched while he took a pocketknife, much smaller than the one he'd threatened her with, and used the bottle-opener part to open it. He tipped it to his lips, drinking it back with a long sigh.

"Want one?" he said. "There's a couple in the fridge, couple of six-packs on the back porch in cans. I should've bought more."

"No."

Todd lipped the bottle's rim and drank again. His throat worked. She was looking at him but her gaze fell on the knife on his belt. He watched her looking and tipped the bottle at her.

"Might be good for you," Todd said.

Gilly felt her mouth go tight and hard. "To get drunk?"

"Might loosen you up."

"I don't need to be loose," Gilly muttered, and turned her back on him.

In the kitchen she opened drawer after drawer. He'd taken away all the sharp knives. She went through the cupboards, too, aware he'd come to watch her. Todd leaned in the doorway, one ankle crossed over the other, beer in his hand.

"What are you looking for?"

She slammed a drawer, making the silverware inside jump. She shrugged. She didn't really know. Todd laughed, and Gilly glared at him over her shoulder.

"Have a beer," he said. "It'll make you feel better, really."

"I don't drink." She pulled down a glass and filled it with cold, clear water that must've come straight up from a hundred feet underground. It went down the back of her throat like a shot, delicious, and sent a spike of pain to the center of her forehead.

Todd took a long pull from the bottle and set it on the counter next to him. "How come?"

Gilly blinked slowly and rinsed her glass from the faint imprint of her lips. She dried it with a hand towel and put it back in the cupboard. She didn't answer.

"Whatever," Todd said, and went back into the living room, where he lit a cigarette and fiddled with the small radio he'd pulled from someplace when she wasn't watching.

At first it blatted static interspersed with gospel music. Finally, after several minutes fidgeting with the knob, Todd tuned in a station playing some contemporary music. The song ended and the disc jockey came on.

"...worst blizzard in twenty years..." The static broke the words into burps and fizzles, but the message was clear. More snow had fallen on the region than in twenty years, and more was predicted.

"Fuck me," Todd murmured. "More damned snow."

She'd already paced the length and width of this place while he was gone. There wasn't enough room to keep between them. She could find privacy in the bathroom, though not for long since he had to share it, or upstairs, where she'd lain for hours listening to random songs on her increasingly finicky iPod. Here in the living room, though, he was too close even when he was across the room.

Gilly went to the window. Crossing her arms over her chest, she rubbed her elbows even though she wasn't cold. He'd filled the woodstove with logs and it had heated the downstairs, at least. Heat was supposed to rise but maybe the vents were blocked or something, because upstairs stayed cold enough to show her breath.

She couldn't see much through the glass. The propane lanterns that illuminated the room didn't quite reach outside. She couldn't see the snow falling, but she could hear it. It sounded like a mother shushing a ceaselessly cranky child.

Shh. Shh. Shhh.

Todd clicked off the radio with an annoyed grunt. "Good thing I got the supplies when I did. Uncle Bill always said to shit when you had the paper."

Gilly didn't turn. "How eloquent."

She'd spoken thick with sarcasm, but Todd only laughed. "He had a way with words, all right. He liked 'em. Big ones, especially."

She flicked a glance toward him. "I wouldn't say *shit's* a particularly big word."

"Nah. I mean he liked other big words. Like *stygian* and *bumptious* and *callipygian.*" He laughed, shaking his head. "That means you have a nice ass."

"It doesn't!"

"Sure it does. You can look it up if you want. Uncle Bill kept a list of words he ran across that he didn't know. He'd look them up in the dictionary and write them down. He said a man who could use big words had something over the man who didn't." Todd paused. "Obviously I don't much take after my uncle. Of course, Uncle Bill always said it was good to know your own faults, too."

She wasn't sure if he were being self-deprecating or simply brutally honest. "He's right."

"He *was* right," Todd said. "Now he's just dead."

Gilly had nothing to say to that but "I'm sorry."

Todd snorted. "Why? You didn't even know him. No point in being sorry about something you didn't do."

"Is that something else your uncle Bill said?"

"As a matter of fact, he did."

Moments of silence passed with nothing but the sound of the snow outside and her own heart beating its slow tempo in her ears. Gilly stared out into the darkness, seeing nothing. Thinking of everything.

"I'm hungry," Todd said.

She wasn't, and didn't answer. Gilly shut her eyes and leaned her forehead against the glass. The cold soothed her bruises.

Shh. Shh. Shhh.

"How about some dinner?"

"No, thanks." Her stomach turned over again at the thought of food, her throat so tight she wouldn't be able to swallow anyway. And even if she did, it felt like all of it would come right back up.

"I meant," he said, "how about making *me* some dinner."

Oh, no, he did not just ask me that.

"No." Gilly twisted to face him for a moment, her face set in the look her husband called Wrath of the Gorgon. It was usually enough to send her family scattering, but not Todd. He just tilted his head to stare.

"No?" Todd said as though he hadn't heard her.

"No," Gilly repeated, and turned back to the window.

Shh.

Tears licked at the back of her eyelids, burning them. She swallowed another lump in her throat. Her fingers clutched tight into fists, her broken nails digging without mercy into her palms.

"What do you mean, no?"

She heard him get up from the table and braced herself for his touch. She already knew he had no trouble using his hands to get what he wanted. Well, he could force her into the kitchen if he wanted. Make a puppet of her, forcing her hands to cook, if that was important enough to him. Gilly thought about the promise she'd made to herself that she'd get out of this alive, but three months was a long time to serve as someone's slave. She'd be damned if she would. Gilly straightened her spine and kept her face against the glass.

"I'm not hungry. If you are, you can make yourself something to eat. I won't do it for you."

He let out a low, confused snuffle. She pictured him shrugging, frowning, though she hadn't turned around to see it. "Why not?"

One. Two. Three.

She wouldn't make it to ten. "Because I'm not your wife and I'm not your mother. I'm not here to take care of you."

"But…" She heard the struggle in his voice as he tried to understand. "But you made dinner for me before, the other day when I came back."

"I made dinner for *me,*" Gilly said. "And I made enough for you while I was at it. It's an entirely different thing. I was trying to be nice."

"Why don't you try to be nice now?"

His question was simple, and she had a simple answer.

She turned to look at him. "Because there's no point in it, now, is there?"

She waited for him to speak. Instead, he left the room and went to the kitchen. She smelled garlic and ground beef, good smells that should've made her hungry but only sent bitterness surging onto her tongue. She heard the clatter of dishes and silverware, the sound of the kitchen chair scraping on the linoleum. Later, a belch.

Gilly stayed looking out at the night, eyes not seeing the dark outside or the reflection of her face in the glass facing her. She looked beyond those things to the faces of her children and drew strength from them, and she listened to the soft sound of the snow covering the world outside.

Shh. Shh. Shhh.

11

She'd woken earlier than him again. Gilly listened to the soft sound of Todd's snoring from beyond the partition. Though an initial slow stretch proved her aches and pains had eased a little, her stomach rocked and her head pounded. Somehow this was worse than feeling as though she'd been beaten with a mallet.

Why bother getting up? You have no place to go. Nothing to do. Nobody needs you. Go back to sleep. When's the last time you stayed in bed so long?

Gilly couldn't convince herself to get up. She'd given up the luxury of sleeping in for babies, and it was one she missed the most. Admitting to herself she was enjoying not having to get out of bed felt wrong, but she forced herself to own it. She'd never been the sort to poke herself on purpose with pins, but something about this pain felt right.

She still didn't get up.

Lethargy weighted her limbs. Beneath the layers of quilts, warmth cocooned her. She shifted her legs and the soft flannel of the nightgown rubbed against the heavy fleece sweatpants she wore beneath it. Turning onto her side, face snuggled into the pillow, Gilly sighed and drifted.

When her leg cramped and her hip ached, she turned onto her back. When that position started to hurt, she rolled to her other side. She didn't sleep, not really, no matter how much she wanted to. She did dream, though. Random patterns of memory and thought, currents of imagination painting pictures in her brain.

Long, lazy nights spent making love. Burrowing deep under blankets against the light of morning, against the chill of winter air. Snuggling up tight against naked flesh, the sound of Seth's voice and low laughter warming her as much as the layers of quilts. Pressing against him. Loving him.

How long had it been since they'd spent a day like that together, staying in bed for hours? Enjoying each other's company beyond just sex? Would she ever have the chance again?

Her stomach gurgled, more in hunger than nausea this time. Gilly ran her tongue over her teeth and wrinkled her nose at the film there. She hadn't showered or bathed, *really* bathed in four days.

Until Todd built up the fire for the day, the cabin would stay cold. There was nothing else to do but brave it. She flung off the covers and jumped out of bed. Her head pounded harder at the motion, but she forced herself to continue.

With a quick glance over the partition at still-sleeping Todd, Gilly slipped the heavy flannel gown over her head and tucked it under her pillow, then tugged the covers over it. She grabbed the turtleneck shirt and sweater from the rocking chair next to the bed and pulled them both on. Later, she'd be reduced to short sleeves and sweating even, but for now she wanted both the protection of "real" clothes, not pajamas, and as many layers as she could.

Todd muttered in his sleep, rolling onto his belly and pulling the pillow over his head as she walked past him. The floor creaked and she paused, but he didn't wake. Downstairs, Gilly used the poker on the red coals until they flared and then put on a log. She warmed her hands for a few minutes at the stove and watched the huff of her breath shine silver and ephemeral before disappearing.

She hated being cold. Really hated, not just disliked. Growing up, the house had always been chilly and dark. Gilly had vowed she'd never live that way, shivering and piling on sweaters to stay warm. And yet here she was, covered in goose bumps with the tip of her nose an ice cube.

"Bleah," Gilly muttered.

The room warmed, slowly. Her stomach rumbled. She was no more eager to move from her spot near the stove than she'd been to get out of bed, but eventually she forced herself to get up and wander into the kitchen on toes still too miserably cold for her good humor.

She finished her breakfast, more sugary cereal, with no sign or sound of Todd from above. Strangely, the sweetness again settled her stomach. She craved coffee, which was also odd since even at home she usually preferred tea.

She washed her bowl and spoon and set them in the drainer to drip dry. So domestic, so normal. Gilly paused, hands still in the sink, fingers ringed with bubbles. She tried hard to find some outrage or anger or fear, but none came.

As a kid, the only constant in their house had been inconstancy. From one day to the next Gilly was never sure whether her dad would be home or traveling, if her mother would be a bright and smiling TV-perfect mom, baking cookies, or something rather less pleasant. Gilly could adapt to anything. Even, it appeared, this.

With her bowl and spoon washed, Gilly had nothing else to do. Todd had brought her sparkly tights and flannel pajamas, but he hadn't brought her anything to read. A search of the large armoire in the corner revealed a large selection of board games including Monopoly, Parcheesi and Trouble. Decks of cards, poker chips, a checkerboard with a plastic Baggie of checkers stacked on top. She found a hinged box full of spent shotgun shells and stared at it for a long time as though looking would give her some clue as to why anyone had saved them, but in the end she couldn't think of any reasons that made sense. On one of the shelves she discovered a stack of *Field & Stream* and *People* magazines from the 1980s.

Princess Diana stared out at her from one cover, Mel Gibson from another. She touched the slick paper and ran her fingers over his piercing blue eyes. *Sexiest Man Alive.* Would anyone think so now? Probably not after the adultery and anti-Semitic rants.

"Morning." Todd startled her out of her reverie. "You been up long?"

"A little while."

He yawned and stretched, showing the pale worm of his scar twisting across his belly. His face had scabbed. He was healing. They both were.

"Still snowing?" he asked, not waiting for a reply before looking out one of the back windows. He glanced over his shoulder at her. "It's ugly out."

Gilly shrugged. Did it matter? What would be a few more inches on top of what had already fallen?

Todd yawned again and scrubbed at his hair. "I thought we were supposed to have whatchamacallit. Global warming."

Gilly gathered a handful of magazines and closed the armoire door. "That's what they say."

"They." Todd laughed, shaking his head. "Who's they, anyway? Bunch of scientists sitting around yanking their cranks, figuring out stuff to scare everyone. That's what I think. You eat already?"

She nodded and Todd padded into the kitchen. He ate breakfast while Gilly read about celebrities and fads from thirty years ago. The room grew warmer as he added more wood to the stove. Gilly shed her sweater, at last warm if not exactly cozy.

Perhaps an hour passed while Gilly read. During that time, she was aware of Todd drifting around the room. She kept her eyes on the pages as he walked aimlessly from window to window. He checked the stove, adding logs and pushing them around with the poker until sparks flew. He went out onto the front porch, letting in a burst of air that ruffled the pages and raised goose bumps on her flesh.

At last, irritated, Gilly snapped. "Can't you find something to do?"

Todd flopped on the sofa across from her and sighed. "There *is* nothing to do."

He looked so much like Arwen when she said the same thing that Gilly bit her lip against a chuckle. Todd drummed out a beat on the arm of the couch, something rhythmic and annoying. Gilly ignored him, concentrating on the magazine, but Todd wouldn't be ignored. He shifted, muttered, wriggled, thumped. At last she set aside the issue in her hands; Princess Di slithered off the couch and onto the floor.

"Why don't you go have a beer," she said. "Or something."

He paused in the incessant motion and raised a brow. "I thought you didn't drink."

"I don't. Doesn't mean you can't."

He glanced toward the kitchen, then back at her with a raised eyebrow. "Why, you want me drunk?"

"Oh, God, Todd. Why on Earth would I *want* you drunk?"

"Maybe so I'll pass out."

He didn't say the rest, that she'd use the chance to escape, but Gilly knew what he meant. It was unreasonable to feel stung that he might be as wary of her as she was of him, but Gilly sniffed anyway. "Actually, no. I don't like being around drunk people. Does one beer make you drunk?"

"Not usually." He grinned and thumped his feet on top of the coffee table, shifting the pile of magazines she'd finished.

"Could you not do that? You're making a mess." She bent to pick up all the magazines and stacked them neatly, then looked up to see him staring at her curiously.

"Does it make a difference?" Todd said.

Gilly stood, stretching against the lingering bumps and bruises. "Yes. It does."

Todd put his feet down with a thud and a frown. "Sorry."

For once he'd been the one to say it, and Gilly looked him over. "It's just nicer if things are clean, that's all."

"Yeah, well, nothing stays..." Todd began and stopped. He scowled. "Yeah. I guess so."

Restless, Gilly stretched again. The passage of time struck her. She'd lost track of the days. "What's today?"

"Friday. I think. Right? Fuck if I know."

Friday. At home she'd be spending the day cleaning and cooking in preparation for Shabbat. By nightfall she'd be exhausted, but seeing the faces of the ones she loved in the light of the Sabbath candles always rejuvenated her. Gilly looked forward to Friday nights for just that reason.

She baked fresh challah, the Jewish Sabbath bread, every week. Her stomach muttered at the thought. She didn't remember seeing any yeast in the kitchen, but she might be able to find something. If her ancestors had survived fleeing Egypt with only unleavened bread to take with them, Gilly Soloman could make do.

The heat from the woodstove didn't quite reach the pantry. Her breath plumed out in great gusts as she searched the shelves. Todd's more recent purchases, many of them still in plastic grocery bags, cluttered the front of the shelves, but further back were items that had probably been there as long as the magazines.

Her fingers were growing numb. "Todd!"

He appeared in the doorway after a moment. "Yeah?"

Gilly waved her hand at the chaos. "Get this stuff all put away, will you? You can't just leave it like this."

"Why not?"

She gave him an exasperated sigh. "Because it's a mess, that's why. Who raised you, wolves?"

She'd meant the question as rhetorical, but by the way his expression slammed shut she knew she'd touched a sore spot. "Sorry."

He set his jaw but brushed past her. The pantry wasn't really big enough for the two of them. As he began taking cans and jars out of the bags, Gilly felt the heat radiating from him. He was his own furnace.

She stepped away, uncomfortable with the contact. "I'll go work in the kitchen. Shut the door so the heat doesn't come out."

He grunted in reply but kept unpacking. She gave him a look. Todd made an exasperated sputter.

"What? You think I'm that much of a douche bag that I don't even know enough to keep the freaking door shut?"

She didn't answer that, just went into the kitchen and closed the door behind her. Gilly opened cupboards, pulling out ingredients she'd need as she found them and organizing the ones she didn't. Uncle Bill must have used the cabin fairly frequently, for it was well stocked with staples like salt and spices, and lots of nonperishable goods. Todd had also made good choices in his grocery buying. Not just all sugar cereals, cigarettes and booze like she'd thought.

It chilled her, a little, how methodical he'd been about shopping. Making sure there was enough of everything. She should be grateful for it now, considering the circumstances, but he hadn't known they'd be snowed in when he'd bought it all, which only further hit home how long he'd intended to be here.

Todd emerged from the pantry blowing on his hands

and shivering. He shut the door behind him. The look he gave her was defiant but proud. "It's all done."

Gilly didn't shame him by checking, which is what she'd have done for one of the kids. But he wasn't a child, much less one of hers. "Thanks."

"What are you doing?"

"I'm going to make challah, if I can find the right ingredients," she said.

His puzzled look told her he had no clue what she was talking about.

"Bread," she explained. "For the Sabbath."

Thankfully he didn't ask her more, and so she didn't have to explain a whole lot. He did look skeptical, though. "Bread?"

"We'll see how it turns out," Gilly told him. "I don't suppose you bought any yeast?"

To her surprise, he had. Not the sort of thing she'd have expected to find in a bachelor's mountain hideaway, but he went back into the pantry and came out with several packets.

"Eggs," Gilly said, looking in the fridge. "Butter. Margarine will do, I guess."

She found both and set them on the table. Todd watched as she found a bowl and mixing spoons. Gilly laid out the ingredients carefully, working from inadequate memory and hoping for the best. They'd have to do without poppy seeds, but if everything else turned out okay she supposed that was all right.

"Do you want to crack the eggs?" She asked him what she always asked Arwen and Gandy. To her surprise, Todd said yes.

She gave him the eggs, and he first made a well in the flour before he cracked them into the bowl. Then he expertly separated the final egg yolk from its white and plopped the golden glop in with the rest.

"You've done this before," Gilly said.

He shrugged. "I've had a lot of jobs. Worked in a bakery for a while. At a diner. I guess I can cook okay."

Gilly kneaded the dough, then set it aside to let it rise. She remembered seeing something in the pantry, an item she'd thought a strange choice. "We...we could make some chocolate chip cookies. If you want."

He gave her a guarded expression. "Why?"

Why did she want chocolate chip cookies, or why was she being nice? Gilly wiped carefully at the sprinkles of flour on the table. "Because I feel like it."

The grin began on the left side of his mouth, where it twitched his lips until it reached the other side. "I make good cookies."

"So do I."

She hadn't intended a challenge, but there it was. Todd brushed the hair out of his eyes and looked at her thoughtfully. Gilly lifted her chin, staring back.

"Mine are better," Todd said.

"Why don't we find out?" Gilly asked.

Wasting the eggs and butter seemed foolish when both knew there could be no more until the snow thawed. Todd didn't mention it, so neither did Gilly. Both gathered what they needed with an unspoken agreement not to peek while the other worked.

Gilly's recipe had come straight off the back of the store-brand chocolate chips she bought in bulk from the warehouse club. It was only a little different from the one on the package Todd had bought. With the exception of walnuts, which she despised and Todd hadn't bought anyway, she'd made the same kind of cookies for years with fine results.

She measured and mixed from memory, handing off the measuring cups and spoons without a word. There weren't any rubber scrapers and the wooden spoons looked to be of questionable cleanliness, so she mixed the dough with a metal fork that clanked against the edge of the bowl in a steady rhythm. As with cleaning, the mixing and making put her mind on auto-pilot.

Todd took a half-used jar of ground ginger from the cupboard. She heard him humming under his breath as he mixed and scraped. Ginger?

"Wanna lick?"

She turned to see him holding out a fingerful of dough. Gilly shook her head. "No, thanks. I don't want to get salmonella."

Todd shrugged. "You don't know what you're missing."

Gilly had sneaked spoonfuls of cookie dough and risked food poisoning more times than she could count, but she wouldn't have taken the sweet, sticky dough off his finger if he'd held his knife to her head again. It might be a matter of stilted, silly pride, but it was her pride. "No, thanks."

"Okay." He put his finger in his mouth and licked the dough. He made a groaning noise of pleasure and dipped again into the bowl for another fingerful.

Gilly shivered as she watched him. Something about Todd was as raw as the cookie dough he sucked off his finger. What made it worse was that he did these things as innocently and unselfconsciously as a child. He finished with the second glob of dough and held out a third to her.

"Sure you don't want any?"

Her voice shook just a little, probably unnoticeable to him. Gilly concentrated on her own mixing bowl. "I said no."

They put the cookies on trays that had seen better times and slid them into the oven. The timer on the oven wasn't digital and took some figuring, but she managed to set it. Fifteen minutes was a very long time to sit and stare at each other. Todd thumped out a pattern on the table with his fingers, caught her looking and smiled sheepishly. He turned his hands palm up and shrugged.

"I'm a spaz. Sorry."

Gilly herself hadn't moved, though she'd felt as restless as his dancing hands had proved Todd to be. "My son is like you. Can't stop moving. It's like he runs on batteries that never wear down."

"Like that rabbit in the commercials," Todd offered.

She smiled before she could stop herself. "Yeah, like that."

"I used to drive my teachers crazy," Todd confided. He laughed and tapped out another rhythm on the tabletop, but consciously this time.

"I'm sure you did."

The timer dinged, then, saving her from having to make more conversation. Both sets of cookies came out golden-brown and smelling like heaven. Todd unceremoniously dumped his on a tea towel, cursing when he burned his fingers on the edge of the ancient blackened cookie sheet. Gilly used a spatula to pry hers from the sheet, then set them carefully on a pink ceramic plate.

"Milk," Todd said. "Gotta have milk."

"I'll get it."

She needed something fresh to breathe, some space.

Gilly left the kitchen and went through the pantry to the back door, then the rickety back porch and the lean-to. Ten half-gallons of milk in white plastic jugs were lined up on one of the shelves alongside some packages of bacon, sausages, lunch meat, some cheese. Everything wore a thin silver coating of frost.

After the stifling warmth of the kitchen, the air out here was cold enough to burn. Her earlobes and the tip of her nose had gone almost instantly numb, and she was losing sensation in her fingers.

Despite all that, the cold felt good. Cleansing. Gilly didn't want to admit that she'd enjoyed the past hour, that it had actually been…pleasant. She searched inside her for the hate but, just as she had earlier, came up empty. Like joy and terror, anger was too fierce an emotion to sustain for long.

Gilly grabbed a half gallon of milk and went back inside. Todd had put two of each type of cookies on two plates and set them on the table. He'd even set out glasses.

Gilly ran the milk under the water for a few minutes until it was at least no longer frozen solid. It filled the glasses in crystalline white chunks. Todd laughed.

As it turned out, his cookies were better.

Later, as night descended, she asked him for some candles. He gave her two, squat and half-burned and ugly. She lit them with the blessings that ushered in the Sabbath. Gilly waited for the calm that always filled her, but all that came was a sense of emptiness and sorrow.

12

Gilly marked the passage of time by the aching of her heart. Each day seemed like an eternity. How long had it been since she'd smelled Gandy's hair or helped Arwen tie her shoes? How long since Seth had kissed her on the way out the door, his mind already on his job and hers on how nice it would be when nap time came? Too long.

Gilly ducks into the pantry when the kids are mesmerized by relentlessly running cartoons. In the dark and quiet she breathes in deep. Scents of cinnamon and spices. Wooden floor cool under her toes. The door has a lock on it because Gandy will sneak sweets if she doesn't keep an eye on him. She locks it now and sits on the step stool she keeps there so she can reach the highest shelves.

She only wants a few minutes' quiet. Some time to herself. She's not hungry, not thirsty, but she is bone-achingly tired. She wants to take a nap but when she tried to lie down on the couch, Gandy had made her his

*personal trampoline. She can't go upstairs and leave
them alone down here while she sleeps. They'll destroy
the house.*

*She wants to simply sit and breathe but the patter
of small feet happens almost at once. They're tuned to
her, those precious angel-monsters. She might as well
put up a red alert when she goes to the bathroom, because they're instantly there. A phone conversation is
a certain beacon, bringing them clinging to her legs
as she tries to get in a word with friends. And, oh, she
dare not sit down at the computer to check her emails
before little voices beg for time on the online pet store
or whatever games the cartoon shows are promoting.*

*"Mama?" The knock comes. Shadows shift under
the door as two small humans pace back and forth.
"Mama? Mama? Mama!"*

*And for a few seconds she pretends she doesn't hear
them. Doesn't answer. For one long, eternal moment,
she hopes they will simply give up and go away.*

"What do you want for breakfast?" Todd's words
startled her out of her thoughts.

She left the window and slid into a seat at the kitchen
table. "Nothing."

He turned from the stove and looked at her critically.
"C'mon. You got to eat something."

"I'm not hungry." She wasn't. Her appetite had ebbed
and flowed, changing drastically over the past week.
She blamed stress. She went from the edge of starva-
tion to having her stomach want to leap from her throat
at the very thought of eating anything at all, much less
the skillet of eggs he was frying.

"You got to have a good breakfast if you want to get

through the day." His words sounded so scholarly, so fourth-grade teacherly, so damned smug.

She wanted to give him the finger.

"I'm serious," Todd said. "Breakfast is the most important meal of the day."

"Who told you that?" she asked cruelly. "Your dear sainted mother?"

The skillet clattered against the burner rings. Todd switched off the propane with a sharp and angry twist of his wrist. "No. Not from her."

The word dripped with a vehemence so thick Gilly could practically see it. She found herself apologizing to him again for remarks she'd made about his upbringing. "Sorry."

The set of his shoulders said the apology hadn't been accepted. Gilly told herself she didn't care. It was nothing to her if she hurt his feelings. Situation and circumstance should have given her the perfect reason to forget the sort of fake politeness she'd always hated and never been able to stop herself from offering.

Todd shook himself slightly, then set the eggs on the table. "Eat."

"I'm not hungry," Gilly repeated. "What are you going to do, force me?"

He cocked his head. "Uncle Bill always said if you had to force someone to do something it probably wasn't worth making them do it."

More words of wisdom from Uncle Bill. Gilly sat back in her chair and fixed him with a glare. "Oh, really?"

He stabbed a pile of yellow fluff with his fork. Before he brought it to his lips, he paused. Searched her gaze with his own in a manner so forthright it brought heat to stain Gilly's cheeks.

Todd pointed with his fork to the snow-laden window. A drift had formed outside, one large enough to nearly cover the glass. "Even if I *wanted* to let you go, I couldn't."

"But you don't *want* to." She teased out this truth between them as though he'd tried to deny it.

Todd set down the utensil with its uneaten clump of egg still clinging to it. His eyes glinted but his voice remained soft when he answered her. "I can't go back to jail, Gilly. I just can't. Don't you get it?"

"I get it."

Todd paused, gaze not shifting from hers. Serious. "And if I get caught for this, that's what would happen. They'd put me back in jail. I'd rather die."

Her fingers tapped a random pattern on the faded tabletop before she stopped them. Her voice went tight and hard, unsympathetic. "You should have thought about that before you kidnapped me."

His sigh was so full of disgust it made her flinch. "I didn't kidnap you."

Gilly shoved away from the table and went to the sink. Nothing outside but white. She gripped the edge of the counter, forced herself to lower her voice. "Don't act like you picked me up in a bar during fifty cent draft night."

She'd had moments like this before, days when every little thing worked at her like a grain of sand against an eyeball. One minute close to tears, the next ready to scream until her throat tore itself to bloody shreds. Seth knew to stay out of her way when she was like this, blaming it on her hormones or menstrual cycle with a man's bland acceptance that the mysteries of a woman's body could be blamed for everything. Her temper was hot but brief, and Gilly had learned to hold it in as best she could. She had to.

Her mother had screamed a lot, when she wasn't facing Gilly with cold silence that was somehow worse than the shrieking accusations. Her mother had alternated between rage and despair with such little effort Gilly hadn't known until adulthood there could be a difference in the emotions.

Counting to ten. Counting to twenty. Biting her tongue until it bled. Sometimes, most times, those tactics worked. It hurt, holding in all that anger, but she wasn't going to put her kids through what she'd gone through as a child. Some days that had meant hiding in the pantry, clinging to the very last shreds of her patience with everything she had, just to keep herself from flying apart.

She wasn't feeling very patient now. Not even counting to a hundred was going to work. Angry words wanted to fly from her lips, to strike him, to wound. She bit the inside of her cheek. Pain helped her focus. Fury wouldn't help her. Todd was right about the snow and their situation. He couldn't let her go, and she couldn't realistically, practically or logically escape. It was keep her temper or lose her mind.

"You should just kill me," she said through clenched jaws, knowing even as she said it she was poking him too hard.

Todd shook his head, facing away from her. He hunched over the table, stabbing at his plate with the tines of his fork. "Shut up."

But she couldn't. The words tumbled out, bitter and

nasty. Harsh. "You could've let me freeze to death out there. You wouldn't have to worry about me, then. You should've left me in the truck. Then I'd be dead and you'd have nothing to worry about."

"I said," Todd muttered tightly, "shut up."

She'd never pulled the legs off daddy longlegs, never tied a can to a puppy's tail. Gilly had never been the sort to tease and torture. But now she found a hard, perverse and distinct pleasure in watching Todd squirm.

"The only way you'll ever be safe is if I'm dead," she continued, gleeful, voice like a stick stabbing him in tender places. "So you should just do it. Get it over with. Save us both the hassle—"

"Shut up, Gilly."

She slapped the counter hard enough to make some dishes jump. "Do it or say you'll let me go!"

He stood and whirled on her, sending her stumbling back against the sink. The chair clattered to the floor. The cold metal pressed against her spine; her elbow cracked painfully on the counter's edge.

"I only wanted the truck. I told you that. I was going to dump you off by the side of the road, but then you had the kids in the back. I didn't want to hurt the kids. I just wanted to come up here and stay away from people, to get away! I didn't want to keep you, for fuck's sake! But now here you are, right? Right up in my fucking face. Yeah, I could've left you out there to freeze, but I didn't. But that doesn't make me a hero, right? Just makes me an asshole. I'm fucked no matter what. So why don't I just kill you, Gilly? Why don't I? Because I don't. Fucking. Want to."

She'd thrown her hands up in a warding-off gesture, but Todd didn't touch her. He raked one hand through his hair instead and backed off. It would've been easier if he'd hit her. She was waiting for it. She was pushing him to do it. She wanted him to hit her, she realized with sickness thick in her throat.

"Uncle Bill died. He left me this place, and the money. Five grand," Todd said in a low, hoarse voice. A broken voice. "Not a whole lot of money, but nice. I was doing okay without it. I was making it. Doing whatever I had to, to get by. Working shit jobs, never doing anything but work and sleep. Shitty apartment, piece-of-shit car, mac-and-cheese for dinner four times a week. And not the good kind," he added, this affront clear. "The four-for-a-dollar crap from the dollar store."

Gilly remembered the flavor of that kind, made with water instead of milk when her bank account had run low. She could taste it now, the flavor nostalgic and gritty on her tongue. It wasn't necessarily a bad memory.

"The money was going to make a difference, pay some bills, so that was good. I thought I might actually get ahead for once instead of always being behind. But it didn't get released right away. Some bunch of legal shit I had to sift through and I didn't know how. But I was doing okay."

He shot her a narrow-eyed look, emphasizing it. "I was doing *okay*. Then they fired me at the diner for being late. I was late because my car broke down. My buddy Joey DiSalvo was going to sell me a car, real cheap, but he needed a thousand bucks. It was everything I had. I mean everything. Rent, food, everything. But no car, no job. That son-of-a-bitch took my money and ran off...."

The words tumbled out of him in a rush, breathless,

but with the same precise manner she'd noted about him before. As though every word he spoke had been carefully thought out before he pronounced it.

Todd paced the worn linoleum. There wasn't really enough room for him to do that, not without bumping against her, but he didn't seem to notice or care. He stalked to the pantry door and slipped a crumpled pack of Marlboros from his shirt pocket. Without pause, he lit a cigarette from the stuttering flame from his lighter and drew the smoke deep into his lungs. It streamed forth from his nostrils as he paced. Her eyes watered at the acrid stench as he passed.

He talked and smoked, the cigarette tipping against his lip but never falling out of his mouth. "They fired me because I was late," he repeated. "One time. One fucking time. They wouldn't give me a second fucking chance, you know?"

"Because you'd been in jail." The sight of him fascinated her. She was no less angry than she'd been a few moments before, but Todd had a way of defusing her fury that Seth, despite their years together, had never mastered.

Todd slammed his fist against the cupboard, rattling the dishes inside. Gilly jumped. "Yeah. Because of that. You want to know what I did? I robbed a liquor store because I owed some guys some money. I thought it would be an easy gig, right? Bust in, get the cash, get the fuck out. The state doesn't need that money, why the fuck do we pay all those taxes, right? Old man doing inventory wasn't supposed to be there. But he was. Shit, Gilly, my fucking gun wasn't even real. I bought it at a garage sale. It was a fucking *lighter*."

"You robbed a store. Did you think that was someone else's fault, too, like it was my fault I have kids?"

Todd's lip curled, his dark eyes glinting. "You don't know shit about a damn thing."

"I've never robbed a liquor store, I know that." Gilly pointedly waved a hand in front of her face to disperse the smoke stinging her eyes and coughed, though she doubted Todd would care.

His gaze through the wafting smoke became assessing. "You don't know what it's like to be poor. That's what I know."

She thought of college, living on ramen noodles and dollar-store macaroni-and-cheese to make ends meet, but always knowing she could go home if she really needed to. And of how living in near poverty was often better than going home. "There are plenty of disadvantaged people who don't turn to crime."

He sneered again, taking another drag on the cigarette. This time instead of letting the smoke seep from his nostrils he held it in his mouth and let it drift out one side. "I wasn't *disadvantaged*."

"No?"

"I was royally screwed, that's what I was."

She raised her eyebrows at him. "What happened? Kids make fun of you at school because you didn't have the right clothes?"

"Sometimes." Todd's gaze went flat. "Sometimes for other things."

It was her turn for a curled lip. "Poor baby."

"You don't know anything about what my life was like. Don't even try. You can't even guess." Now his voice shook, just barely, and he swallowed hard before turning away.

She couldn't, actually. She had no experience with people who thought living on the other side of the law was fair compensation for the slights society had made against them. Her voice was hard and humorless, though not quite as poking as it had been before.

"Everybody thinks their lives are hard, Todd. It's human nature to think you're special. Especially when you're not."

She'd meant that to hurt him, but it seemed to miss the mark, because Todd didn't even flinch. He leaned toward her much as she had done to him earlier. Smoke laced the hot breath caressing her cheek. Gilly forced herself to stand still, to meet his eyes. To not turn away. She'd put herself in this place. She had to face it.

"*Your* life didn't seem too hard. Nice car. Wallet full of money." He reached out and flicked the pendant dangling from her neck. "Nice husband to buy you pretty jewelry. Nice kids. You had it *real* hard, Gilly. Poor fucking you. Poor little rich girl."

Guilt raged through her, because what he said was true. She couldn't deny it. She'd let him steal her from that good life, the good man and the children who were her reason for everything. Gilly slapped his hand away.

"Don't touch me."

Todd drew back. He threw the remains of the cigarette on the floor and ground it out with the toe of his boot. He rested for a minute, sagging against the counter, and slipped his hands into the pockets of his jeans. "It was the first time I'd ever robbed a place. But I got into a lot of trouble as a kid. He…the judge said…maybe some time behind bars would change my attitude."

"Did it?" The question was rude, but Gilly couldn't take it back.

"Hell if I know." Todd shot her a grin then, shocking in its unpredictability. "Guess not."

Gilly shook her head, unbalanced by his shift in attitude. "Stealing my truck wasn't too smart."

"You got stupid people and smart people," Todd said with another of his dangerously charming and artless shrugs. "I'm just not smart."

He was no genius, she knew that. Yet something about his reply told her that he'd been told he was stupid so many times that it had become the truth, rather than the other way around. He'd been told it, and he believed it. He had become it.

"Didn't you think they'd trace the truck?"

He snorted. "Trucks get stolen all the time. I had a buddy who was going to take care of it for me. Not DiSalvo, that piece of shit. Some other dude. Said he'd give me a good deal on a trade-in. I'd have been out of it and into something else before anyone even knew where to start looking for it. It would've been in a hundred pieces, sold for parts."

He sounded so confident and made it sound so plausible, she thought he might be right. Not that it mattered, now, with her Suburban probably in a hundred pieces at the bottom of a mountain ravine instead of a junkyard. "Forgive me if I don't feel bad for you."

Todd lit another cigarette and puffed the smoke at her. He cocked his head again, the puppyish tilt of it at odds with the harshness of the smoke curling from his nostrils. "C'mon, Gilly. I haven't been such a prick to you, have I?"

"You've been a real Prince Charming," Gilly muttered. She had a headache, and her stomach had begun its incessant churning again. She was frustrated and annoyed, but no longer in a raging fury. She only wanted to lie down and go back to sleep.

Todd reached out as casually as if he were plucking a flower and grabbed a handful of hair at the back of her head. Faster than a moment, he'd pressed her against him. Todd's fingers twisted in her hair, the pressure just on the edge of becoming pain.

"I could have hurt you. Could've pulled over the side of the road and gutted you like a deer." Todd nuzzled his cheek against her neck in the sensitive part just below her ear, though there was nothing sensual about the caress. Nothing sexy. Beneath the harsh smell of tobacco smoke, she caught the scent of soap and flannel. His lips brushed her ear when he whispered, "But I didn't, did I?"

"Don't." Unable to move away from him with his hand fixed in her hair, Gilly stiffened her spine against a shiver.

"Even though you act like that's what you want me to do." His fingers curled tighter, knuckles pressed to the back of her skull. Her scalp protested, skin smarting. "Is that really what you want?"

Gilly closed her eyes.

"Answer my question," he said without letting go. When she didn't answer, he tugged sharply until she looked at him. "Haven't I been good to you, Gilly?"

"No, you haven't," Gilly muttered, bracing herself for more pain that didn't come.

"I didn't want you here." He put his forehead on hers. His deep brown eyes bored into hers, hardly even blinking. "I even tried to let you escape. But you didn't go."

She twisted her head, fighting him. He was too big, too strong. She felt the strength of him in every movement. She could not wriggle free. He was violating her more surely than if he'd forced his tongue into her mouth or his hand between her legs.

"Why didn't you go when you had the chance, huh? Why not just run away to the hubby and the kiddies and the nice white house with the yard and the dog—"

"Fuck you!" The words tore out of her.

"Don't feel good, does it? Being judged? Seems to me like you should be thanking me, not treating me like I'm something gross you stepped in."

"You don't know me." Gilly ground the words from between clenched jaws.

"You know what I think? I think," Todd said slowly, deliberately, his gaze pinning her like a beetle to a board, "I'm the best thing that ever happened to you."

Gilly stopped struggling.

He let her go. Gilly stumbled back, whacking her elbow on the counter again. More pain. She forced back a gag.

"I want to be nice to you," Todd told her. He sat at the table with his back to her. He stubbed out his smoke, then began to eat his eggs. "But you make it really fucking hard."

Gilly left the kitchen and walked to the front door. The back of her head still smarted, but her cheek fairly burned from the caress he'd put on it. She scrubbed at the flesh with her hand, the long sleeve of the sweatshirt he'd bought her fleecy-soft against the skin.

She paused by the scarred wooden table, staring without really seeing the faded plastic flowers. Roses. They were roses, faded and plastic and not real. As she wished none of this was real.

Slowly, methodically, she pulled the sweatshirt over

her head. She folded it carefully, one arm over the other, then into a bulky square. She set it on the table.

Her hands went to the waist of her sweatpants. She'd had to tie the string in a double tight knot to prevent the large pants from falling off her hips. From the kitchen came the clatter of dishes in the sink. Gilly didn't pause. Her fingers worked the string, and all the while she stared at the flowers.

Roses needed lots of care. A lot of responsibility. Love wasn't enough, you had to trim them, water and fertilize them. Roses were precious and fragile things that took a lot of time and effort to grow and sometimes, no matter how much time you gave them, they still failed.

Gilly wore no shoes, only a thick pair of white athletic socks. She slid her sweatpants down over her thighs, her ankles, and over the socks, which came off with a small twist of each foot. Goose bumps rose on her skin, though with the woodstove going the room was quite warm. She was left in her panties and bra, her own that she'd been wearing the day he took her, and a cotton T-shirt that had Princess on the front in tacky rhinestone letters.

She folded the sweatpants and put them with the sweatshirt, then added the socks to the pile. She slipped the T-shirt over her head and stood nearly naked. Still staring at the flowers. Thinking about roses.

She heard the back door open as Todd went out through the pantry and to the lean-to for something. Gilly touched her breasts, her belly, the triangle of pink material between her legs. This was what was hers. She'd brought these things with her, and she didn't owe him anything for them.

The frigid air outside forced a gasp when she stepped out onto the front porch. Gilly didn't bother to shut the door behind her. She went down the rickety steps into the knee-deep snow outside.

It was cold. Very cold. She shuddered and kept walking, fixing the picture of roses in her mind. Her feet went numb so fast she could easily forget she wasn't wearing boots. Her hands reached out as though she were blind, though everything in front of her was as crisp and clear as if she were viewing it all through a magnifying glass.

She didn't know what she was doing, or why, just that his touch had made her feel unclean. Fire could burn it away; ice could sear her clean. She stumbled and went to one knee. The snow, when she threw out her hands to catch her fall, covered her arms all the way to the shoulders.

Hadn't he been good to her? Hadn't he been nice? He'd bought her clothes, he hadn't hurt her. She thought of the pale worm of a scar twisting across the softness of his belly, of cigarette smoke curling dragonlike from his nostrils, of the way his eyes glowed when he grinned. Gilly's stomach rose again at the feeling of his cheek on hers. Not because it had been repulsive, but because it had not.

He's right. You were glad to let him take you away. You wanted to be taken away, so you wouldn't have to run. Because then you could blame someone else for what you really wanted. He's right, you did this. This is all you, Gillian. All you.

She let out a small cry, unable to tell if it was of anger or despair. She forced herself to her feet. Chunks of ice littered the snow, and she'd cut her hand on one of them. A crimson rose, her blood, bloomed on the otherwise pristine surface of the drift. She swept it away with her hand, punching at it. Her fist broke through the thin crust of ice, smearing the blood into the soft snow beneath.

He'd taken her, but she'd allowed it. Nothing could ever change that. No amount of screaming, no number of accusations or lies. Todd hadn't done this to her, she'd done it to herself.

How many times did you wish for someone or something to take you away? How many times did you imagine how nice it would be to get sick, really sick, so you could be hospitalized and have someone else take care of you for a change?

The thoughts penetrated her mind over and over as she scrubbed herself with snow. Her skin turned pink, then red, and still Gilly forced her deadened hands to scoop more and rub it all over.

"The fuck are you doing?"

Todd grabbed her up out of the snow. His fingers must have dug into her skin, but she didn't feel them. He shook her so hard her teeth rattled. Gilly got to her feet and kicked out at him, feeling nothing as her bare toes crunched on his shin.

"Jesus Christ, Gilly!"

"Let me go!" The chattering of her teeth made the words a gobbledygook.

"You're out of your goddamned mind! You're crazy, you know that?"

She swung at him, but feebly, and he held her off as easily as if she hadn't even tried. "Don't touch me!"

"It's freezing out here, you dumb bitch. Get inside."

Todd yanked her arm, his fingers pinching down on numbed flesh.

Gilly resisted with a strength that surprised them both. She slipped from his grasp and went sprawling back into the snow. Todd grabbed her up again, shrugging out of his battered gray sweatshirt and wrapping it around her shoulders. Gilly had no more strength to fight.

"Let me go," she thought she whispered, but neither one of them heard.

When he saw she couldn't walk he scooped her up. In the movies he would've strode through the snow cradling her against his chest without faltering. But this was not the movies, it was real life, and Gilly was no anorexic starlet. Todd stumbled and went onto one knee, dropping her.

He ground out a curse and picked her up again. He staggered up the steps and tripped through the open doorway. Gilly spilled out of his arms and onto the living room floor next to the table.

"Goddamn it." Todd grabbed her under the arms and dragged her in front of the woodstove, her heels thumping on the floorboards as she hung limp in his grasp. He began chafing her hands. "The fuck was that all about?"

She couldn't explain, not even to herself. Sheer stupidity had made her go out there, and it made no sense. It had felt right, that was all. She yelped as the feeling began returning to her hands and feet, and swatted him away.

"Don't touch me!"

He backed off, hands in the air. He went to the table and grabbed up the pile of clothes she'd left there. He came back, knelt beside her, tried to wrap her in the clothes. She shoved him away and struggled into them by herself.

"Don't touch me," she repeated. "Ever again."

He backed off again and pulled out another smoke. She felt his eyes on her as he lit up. The curl of smoke rising from the tip of the cigarette wavered in the air. His hands were shaking.

"You scared the shit out of me," he said.

Now that she was warming up her teeth chattered incessantly. She'd been out there for perhaps only fifteen minutes, but that was long enough for the first angry red patches to appear on the backs of her hands and probably other places, too. She hitched closer to the stove. Shudders racked her body.

"I want to go home." It wasn't what she'd thought she was going to say.

"I know you do."

"I miss my kids," she whispered. "And Seth."

He sighed. "I know. But you can't."

A sob hitched from her chest, burning her throat. "I want to go *home,* Todd. Where it's warm. With my family. I want to tell them that I'm sorry...I shouldn't have let you keep me...."

She sank to the floor, pressing her face to the faded rug. It smelled of dust and age. She closed her eyes, aware of the rug's nubbly surface making grooves in her skin but too tired to care.

From somewhere very far away she heard him say her name, but then she didn't hear anything else.

13

His hands were on her again, but Gilly couldn't fight them. He held her too tightly. A mountain of blankets covered her, suffocating. She kicked at them, writhing, and whimpered in gratitude at the blessed blast of cool air that covered her.

"Water," she begged, and he pressed a glass to her lips.

It choked her and she gagged. Bile burned her throat and tongue. He was there with a basin, whispered soothing things to calm her as she retched. He pushed the hair back from her forehead and gave her a cool cloth for her forehead.

Gilly sank back on her pillow, exhausted. The headache that had been plaguing her for weeks had become agonizing again. Even blinking made her head throb worse than a thumb hit by a hammer.

She remembered her stupid run out into the snow, and looked at her hands. They were still red and chapped, but it didn't look like she'd lose any fingers. She wiggled her toes under the heavy weight of the blankets, relieved to feel them all.

Todd sat back, watching her, the expression in his dark eyes veiled. "You okay?"

She nodded, though fresh pain flared behind her eyes at the movement. Gilly pressed her thumbs just inside the curve of her eye socket. It didn't help.

"Advil," she managed to say. Then as an afterthought, "Please."

"I have aspirin." Todd left and returned a few minutes later with a gigantic bottle in one hand. "This okay?"

Aspirin would barely touch the horrendous throbbing, but Gilly took the two white pills he shook out and offered. "Two more."

Todd looked at the bottle and squinted. "It says…"

"I know what the dose is," Gilly said, careful not to raise her voice and send spears of agony ripping through her head. "It's not enough. It won't help me."

"I don't want you to OD on me," Todd said, but he shook out two more pills into her outstretched hand.

She struggled to sit up. Todd slipped a hand behind her elbow to help her, and she stiffened. "Don't."

He dropped her arm as though her words had burned him. "Jesus, sorry."

Gilly shifted herself upright, which helped relieve some of the pressure. She took the cup of water he offered and swallowed the aspirin, fighting back the urge to puke it all up again.

Already she felt herself drifting again. Her eyes became heavy lidded, her limbs leaden. Gilly let herself sink back into sleep.

"You want to go up to bed?"

She did, but didn't want him to take her. Gilly opened

her eyes. The room blurred. She forced herself to sit and waited until everything around her stopped spinning.

"I can do it," she said quietly when Todd made a move to help her.

She made it to the kitchen where she drank a full glass of cold water, then refilled it and took it with her upstairs. Her former aches and pains had intensified along with the throbbing agony in her head. She thought again of her old wish to be taken so ill she'd need nursing. She put the cup close at hand on the dresser, then slipped into bed.

Her cheeks flushed, hot with fever or, more likely, embarrassment at her run out into the snow. She'd been stupid, not even trying to get away. Not even sure what she was trying. Todd must think she was nuts, and… well, wasn't she?

Her chest felt tight, her throat ticklish. Gilly coughed experimentally and groaned at the throb in her temples. She didn't think she'd be able to sleep, but she did, and dreamed.

Not of her mother, or of Seth and the children. Not even of Todd. Gilly dreamed of fields of roses, vast acres of red blooms and green stems. Beautiful, vibrant roses protected by thorns. She grabbed and grabbed again until blood ran slick and hot from her fists, and it was the same as dreaming of all of them.

14

She woke again, this time to darkness. She'd thrown off the layers of blankets and now chills assaulted her. Gilly shuddered, twisting against the pillow and struggling to pull the covers back up. Just as she did, her cheeks flared with sudden, urgent heat.

She understood in the back of her mind that she was feverish but could do nothing about it. She seemed to float in the darkness, and without the bed beneath her to anchor her to the earth, Gilly wondered if she might have just floated all the way to heaven.

She groped for the cup of water. Her fingers tipped the cup, spilling it onto her pillow. She pressed her cheek against the welcome wetness, but all too soon even that brief chill was gone. The heat from her face was so great it dried the tiny spill in no time.

She thought about calling for Seth, knowing even as she did so that he wouldn't come. She couldn't exactly remember why and didn't want to try. Where were her pills, the extrastrength antibiotics and heavy-duty de-congestants that worked to make the pain in her head disappear?

She must be sicker now. Was she at home? Gilly had the sudden fear that her wish had come true. That she'd been hospitalized, taken from her children. Who was with them if she was here?

She cried their names, reaching into the blackness as though she might find their faces there beneath her fingertips. She found only frigid air and emptiness. Gilly plunged her hands back beneath the covers, hugging herself and burying her face in the pillow.

Someone had wrapped her in cotton. The thickness of it, the weight, surrounded her, pressed in on all sides. Someone had covered her eyes with gauze, so that even the blackness had taken on a fine white haze. Someone had gloved her hand, so that all she touched seemed far-away and unrecognizable.

Hands stroked her forehead. Fingers ran a delicate pattern down her cheek. Gilly turned her head, her hand trapped beneath the cotton and the gloves, unable to fight off the caresses she did not want.

"No," she mumbled. "The drugs…it's not safe…."

Antibiotics interfered with the effectiveness of birth control pills. She couldn't let Seth make love to her, not this cycle, not without some other protection. They hadn't used other protection in years.

"No," Gilly muttered as she gained the strength to push at the hands now slipping beneath her shoulders. "Don't touch me."

Not until after her next period, when the cycle would

be unaffected. But when would that be? Thinking was hard, the effort enormous and ineffective, because she couldn't remember anyway. Two weeks? One? A few days?

"Don't touch me!" She found the force of will to say, and the hands underneath her slipped away and left her alone.

She had to get to the children. Baby Gandy was crying for her. Gilly's breasts tingled with a surge that meant it was feeding time.

Then she realized it was not baby Gandy sobbing for her to nurse him, but Arwen crying out for her. "Mama!" Then it was the two of them, crying her name over and over, the sound of it agonizing to hear.

She had to go to them, had to get to her babies. Gilly struggled free of the covers anchoring her to the bed. Even the darkness would not prevent her from finding them.

Her hands paddled at the air, swimming through it, but gaining no purchase. Her legs were leaden. She couldn't move them. She managed to push herself out of bed.

She hit the floor with a thud that jarred her head so badly she cried out. The ceaseless cries of "mama" stopped abruptly, and a sob of despair threatened to rip from her throat. Something was wrong with her babies. She had to get to them, *had* to.

The wood floor scraped at her cheek. Gilly pushed against it with little result, too weak to sit up, much less stand. Her breath whistled in her lungs, forcing her to cough until bright sparks flashed in her vision.

She couldn't breathe. Gilly gasped for air, but it felt

like soup in her lungs, thick and suffocating. She struggled, choking and coughing, flopping on the floor.

Her mind cleared a little, and she remembered where she was. But she *had* heard someone saying "mama." She hadn't imagined it. Gilly pushed again at the floor, but couldn't really move.

The dark began to turn gray, but not because the sun was coming up. Fringes of red flickered in the gray. She was going to pass out.

She'd been sleeping a long time, she could sense that. Dozing in and out for hours. Maybe even days. But now true unconsciousness threatened, and Gilly fought it as though it were a physical being. The red fringes thickened and clung together, taking over the gray.

The darkness had been difficult, frightening but not terrifying. It was natural, part of the night. The gray and red were horrifying in their casual replacement of the simple darkness; the gray and the red were not outside of her, they were in her mind.

Her arms stiffened even as she twitched. Every meager breath she managed to take sounded like a freight train, rumbling. Gilly wheezed, unable to do anything more now than clutch at the pain in her head, squeezing her temples with frozen fingers.

She was losing the battle. She could not get up from the floor; she could not get to her children. She'd abandoned them. Even as unconsciousness threatened, her thoughts became clear.

The gray and the red had been replaced by blackness, black as ink, as tar, as eternity. Not the darkness of night, but of the void. Gilly fought it, too, but fared no better. She closed her eyes but the blackness followed her even there.

She would never see her children or Seth again. Whatever sickness she'd been fighting for the past few weeks had taken root and bloomed. Without medicine to battle it, and with the circumstances to aid it, it was going to overtake her.

She coughed again, feebly, unable to bring up the mess in her lungs stealing her ability to breathe. Gilly choked and choked, unable to stop.

Slow down. One breath at a time. Breathe in slow, breathe out slow.

It didn't help. Her breath was too thick. It lodged in her throat, refusing to get down into her lungs. The floor beneath her spun.

Was this it? The blackness filled her vision from side to side so there was nothing left. Gilly couldn't win.

Gilly dives to the bottom of the lake on a dare to retrieve a weighted ring. She makes it to the muddy bottom, finds the garish-colored piece of plastic, but the search has taken her too long. She hasn't gone more than a quarter of the way back to the surface before her lungs begin to burn. Halfway back her legs stop kicking hard enough to get her back to the surface in time.

She sees daylight, golden as it slants through green water, and beyond that the shimmery image of the wooden raft moored at the lake's center. She glimpses her friend's faces, watching, laughing, pointing. Gilly lets go of the weight, feels it knock against her ribs and snag the lilac nylon of her bathing suit. She reaches to the sky, grasps for the air, but cannot reach it.

What of all the boys she'll never kiss? The songs she'll never hear? She'll never finish school, marry, move from her parents' house. Regret and yearning give her enough strength to kick once, twice more, but it isn't enough. A flurry of bubbles, the last desperate few, escape her lips like butterflies dancing in the breeze.

Only one of her friends has seen her distress. David Phillips reaches one of his long arms down into the water and hauls Gilly out by her hair. She breaks the surface choking and gasping, breathing in deep. Shaking while everyone laughs. For the rest of the day, she endures the good-natured teasing of the group at losing the weight and thus the dare, but Gilly won't so much as dip a toe in the water for the rest of that summer.

She'd only nearly drowned then, but she was going to drown now. This time there would be no hand reaching down to pluck her to safety. This time, she had so much more to regret losing.

She heard her name and thought it part of the dream. The voice came again, louder this time. Hands grasped her own and pulled. Gilly didn't fight the touch this time, recognizing they were saving her from drowning. From dying.

A light shone in her eyes, and at first she thought it must be the hand of God. She blinked, and the golden glow revealed Todd's face instead. Gilly felt instant relief and disappointment at the same time.

"Don't die, Gilly." Todd's fingers bit into her wrists as he hauled her upright. "Don't die, please, don't die…."

He didn't put her back on the bed. He lifted her, and Gilly had time to think she must've lost weight, because he didn't stagger beneath her this time. Despite everything, she smiled. Would she be skinny, now?

He must have seen her smile and taken it for something else. "Jesus, Gilly. Don't you fucking die on me!"

"…easier for you…" she wheezed.

They were in the stairway now, her feet and head thumping on the narrow walls with every step.

"Shut up." He grunted with the effort of carrying her. So she wasn't skinny, after all.

"...what you want..."

"It's not what I want, goddamn it!" At Todd's shout pain flared again behind her eyes, but Gilly welcomed that pain as a good sign. She wasn't slipping away any more.

He plopped her down on the ugly plaid couch; her head banged on the arm. He left her to light the propane lantern on the table. Gilly managed to stay upright, though without the support of his arms she barely had the strength. All at once it seemed like someone had taken a huge vacuum cleaner and sucked the garbage right out of her lungs and nose. She could breathe again, albeit with a wheezing, grumbling snort, but she *could*.

If she could breathe, that also meant that she could cough. The first bout brought up a bunch of gunk that she spit into the palm of her hand, not caring how disgusting that was. Mothering had made her immune to bodily fluids. She'd had worse on her fingers. The second bout of coughing brought a fine spray of blood from her lips.

The green mucus disgusted her, but the blood scared her. With trembling hands she took the wad of paper towels Todd handed her and wiped her hand and mouth. She waited to see if more blood would come, perhaps a gout of it, but it didn't. It looked even worse on the paper towel, small blots of crimson against the white paper. She crumpled it in her fingers so she wouldn't have to see.

He hovered over her. "Are you going to be all right?"

"I need a doctor."

He shook his head. "I can't get you one."

"I need medicine."

He held up his hands helplessly. "I don't have any. Just aspirin."

Another cough swelled in the back of her throat, but she was afraid to let it out. She swallowed convulsively to get rid of the tickle. The feeling of thick snot draining down the back of her throat sickened her, but vomiting would be worse than the coughing.

Another round of chills racked her, clattering her teeth. More pain stabbed behind her eyes and in the hollows beneath them. In her cheeks, too, and her ears, which popped mercilessly with every swallow. Gilly rocked with the pain, body jerking. Todd paced the floor in front of her, each stride long enough to take him out of her area of view and then back into it again as he turned. With nearly every step his calf rubbed against the couch until not even the shaking and the pain in her head could stop her from yelling, even though her shout came out as no more than a hissing whisper.

"Stop that. You're shaking me."

He stopped and dropped to his knees beside her. "I don't know what to do."

She was sick, sicker than she'd ever been in her adult life, and yet she *still* had to be the one in charge. To take care of herself. Resentment burbled in her, but she didn't have the strength to do anything about it.

"Blankets" was all she managed to get out before another round of coughs ripped through her. "Hot tea…"

Todd put his hand gently on her arm, timidly, as though afraid she would order him to take it off. She didn't have the strength for it, and now it didn't seem like such a big deal. Like so much else that had happened over the past few days, what difference did it make any longer?

When he saw she wasn't going to yell, he bent forward to look at her. "You got to tell me what to do."

Wasn't that what she was doing? Gilly clenched her jaw to keep herself from biting her tongue. "Get me some blankets, some hot tea. Some more aspirin."

"Okay."

An idea struck her like a hammer between the eyes, so hard and strong she gasped and coughed. "The truck!"

"It's wrecked," Todd said. "I can't drive it anywhere. Shit, it might be totally gone, I told you that."

"Not drive," Gilly managed. "In the truck. Medicine. It's in the center console. You didn't bring it."

"I didn't know," he started, sounding defensive, but Gilly shushed him.

She'd stopped at the pharmacy just before going to the ATM. Her prescription, the decongestants and antibiotics, were in the truck. She gripped his arm, her fingers slipping and falling away without strength. "Just go. Try. I have pills in there. They'll help."

He left her, and was back in a moment with an afghan he tucked around her tightly. Todd tucked the edges around her, smoothing them. And after that, Todd didn't come back for a long time.

Gilly closed her eyes. Sleep took her again almost instantly, but it was fretful. She twisted on the couch, coughing relentlessly every time it seemed she'd drift off. Her neck and back cramped from the force of it, and shudders still swept over her.

Had she ever felt this bad? If she had, she couldn't

remember it. There'd never been time to be sick when she was a kid, not when she had to be awake and alert to take care of her mother, who was hardly ever well. Even in later years, when Gilly came down with everything the kids did and often twice as hard, she didn't get "sick days."

"He's not coming back," her mother said, clear as sunlight, unmistakable.

Gilly's eyes opened, and she screamed in a breathless whistle. She was alone. She fell back against the arm of the couch, unable even to weep.

She didn't know how much time passed before cold air caressed her. She heard the clomp of boots. The next whistle came not from her throat but the teakettle. Todd brought her a mug of tea and held it to her mouth. It burned her mouth and she winced, and the tea itself was bitter, but she sipped anyway. He slipped a couple of pills into her mouth and she washed them down.

"What else can I do?"

The warmth of the tea and blankets eased her chill; or perhaps the aspirin was helping with her fever, she didn't know. His fingers were chilly on her forehead, and that felt just fine. Gilly let her eyes close again.

"I need to sleep. Give the medicine time to work."

She sensed him leaving, but sleep wouldn't take her. The couch was old and lumpy, and her head rested at an awkward angle. The blankets that had given her such welcome warmth now lay on her like stones. Briars had bloomed in her throat, dry and scratching.

She coughed again and he was there, helping her to sit and holding out another wad of paper towels to catch what came out of her mouth. She ought to have been embarrassed, but couldn't seem to manage.

The soft fringes of his hair brushed her cheek as he slipped a pillow behind her head to ease the awkward position. Gilly turned her face away, accepting the comfort he offered but even in her delirium unwilling to accept the man who gave it. Todd tucked the blankets tighter around her and then sat on the couch facing hers.

"You shouldn't have run out in the snow," he said. "And the truck…I got the stuff out, but it's really gone, now. The tree broke when I closed the door. It's at the bottom of the mountain."

Hot tears leaked from beneath Gilly's closed eyelids and slipped down her cheeks. She didn't speak. Todd sighed. She heard the smack of his lighter and smelled the smoke.

It made her start to cough again. The few moments of clarity she'd had began to fade again. Gilly slipped back into the twilight world.

15

She thought several days passed, but she wasn't sure. Gilly left the couch only when Todd dragged her into the bathroom to use the toilet. He didn't leave her, even there. He brought her soup and tea and medicine, and he changed the cool cloths on her forehead when the fever dried them. The more he offered her, the more she took until she had given herself up to him entirely.

This was what she'd wanted, but not the way she wanted it. After having her children there'd been nurses in the hospital who'd brought her food and helped her to pee. One kind nurse had even lifted Gilly's breast with steady efficiency to help her learn to nurse Arwen, an intimacy that Todd hadn't had reason to employ. As for the rest of it, it wasn't much different than allowing him to drive away with her. Her reasons for letting him were the same. Lying on the couch, Gilly didn't have to think. She didn't have to remember that she was missing her children, that her husband must be sick with grief at losing her. Her illness gave her detachment a legitimacy she would not otherwise have allowed herself. She'd finally been granted her wish, an illness so deep she was unable to care for herself.

The days passed, one blurring into the other, while she slept and dreamed. There were times when she truly did not know where she was, or who Todd was, times when his comforting hand on her brow became Seth's, or even her mother's.

Gilly wept in the throes of these fever dreams, because her mother had died more than twelve years ago, before she and Seth had married, before Gilly had become a mother herself and could talk about the joys and sorrows of motherhood with her.

Gilly didn't want to die. In fact, she refused. Not like this, not from a stupid, simple bout of flu. Not in a cabin with a man she couldn't trust and wouldn't like. Not away from her family.

The power of her will had been a driving force in her since childhood and the secrets she'd had to keep about her mother's illnesses. It had seen her through high school, when good grades and snack cakes had substituted for slumber parties and prom dates. And in college, when success had frightened her more than failure.

It would save her now, too.

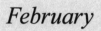

February

16

There came a day when her head no longer threatened to explode every time she moved, and her throat didn't constantly scratch with the urge to cough. She was far from well, but she recognized with vivid relief that she felt better. She no longer needed him, and as he put an arm beneath her to help her up, she spoke in a dull, flat voice.

"Please don't touch me."

Todd's fingers twitched briefly on her shoulder, and then he withdrew. "I was just…"

She spoke stiffly, not looking at him, her chin lifted to keep her voice from trembling. "I'm better now. You don't have to do that."

His breath hissed from between his lips, and he sat back. "Thanks, Todd."

"What?"

He hadn't smoked around her during the worst of her illness since it made her erupt into violent coughing, but now he pulled out a cigarette and lit it. "Thanks, Todd.

For helping me while I puked my guts out. Thanks, Todd, for taking me to the can so I didn't have to piss myself. I could've left you to choke on your own snot."

The spot on the inside of her cheek was still sore, but she bit it anyway. "But you didn't. So...thank you."

Todd grunted and cocked his head to peer at her. "Jee-sus. Women are all the same. Ungrateful bitches."

Gilly set her jaw. "I said thank you."

"Yeah, I could really tell you meant it. You know what your problem is, Gilly? You're too fucking prideful," Todd snapped, and stalked away. He went to the kitchen and slammed some cupboard doors but didn't take anything out. He went out through the pantry and the lean-to, slamming the door behind him.

Gilly sat rigidly on the couch, her hands clenched together in her lap. He'd called her ungrateful, and he was right. He *had* helped her during the worst illness she could ever remember having. Just as he hadn't left her in the snow to freeze, just as he hadn't stabbed her through the heart. She might've died without him. Not wanting that to be fact didn't make it any less true. Pride kept her from gratitude. Still, wasn't that all she had left?

17

After that, he left her alone. Gilly had spent so many days lying on the sofa she itched for a change. She managed to set herself up in one of the armchairs with the pile of blankets and a pillow for her head, but once seated she had no more strength to do anything else. She spent the day there, and the closest Todd came to her was when he bent to put more logs on the fire.

He ate in the kitchen, alone, without offering to bring her anything. When she hobbled to the kitchen table and had to put her head down to keep herself from fainting, he ignored her and left the room. That night she managed only a glass of water and a handful of stale saltine crackers.

Facing the steep stairs by herself was a more daunting task. She almost broke down then, but stopped herself from asking for his help. She felt his eyes on her as she put her foot on the first step, and it was only his gaze that allowed her to straighten her back and take the next step. Another step had her head reeling. She put both hands on the railing. One more step and she had to sit to catch her breath.

Gilly nearly cried, wanting only to slip into bed and sleep. She slapped at the tears, forcing them away, and then she took another step. By the time she reached the top of the stairs, she was on her hands and knees. Crawling, she crossed the attic room and made it only halfway before she collapsed in exhaustion.

Just a little bit farther. You can do it. You can get yourself into that bed, and then you can sleep again. But you can't sleep here.

She pushed herself on her arms with a low groan, her head spinning. She'd left the pills downstairs, and at the realization let out a low groan. Her forehead again touched the dirty wooden planks. Dust made her sneeze until harsh, barking coughs replaced it. The world grayed, but she forced herself to stay conscious.

She hadn't realized Todd had followed her until he spoke. "You okay?"

"Fine," she managed to say.

"You're dumber than I am." Todd crouched next to her and put a gentle hand between her shoulder blades. "C'mon. Let me help you."

She assumed he'd simply pull her upright, but Todd waited. Gilly looked at him through swollen eyes and the fringe of her hair, greasy and unkempt. She licked cracked lips. "Why?"

Why should I? Why would you want to? Gilly wasn't sure what she meant.

Todd sat back on his heels and cocked his head at her again as though looking at her from an angle would help him understand her better. "Wouldn't you do the same for me?"

Gilly managed a hoarse noise that sounded as dusty as the floor beneath her. Todd smiled a little. He pushed his hair out of his eyes with a quick flick of his fingers.

"Maybe not. Okay, so you'd let me choke to death on my own snot. I get it." He shrugged.

Gilly, still on hands and knees, blinked slowly. The truth pricked her. A thorn.

"I know you think I'm some sort of monster," Todd said after a moment when she didn't say anything.

He didn't look at her. He shifted his weight, his boots sliding on the wood. She could count the threads hanging from the hem of his jeans. The cracks in the leather of his boots.

"Well…maybe you're right," he continued. "Maybe I am. But I ain't going to let you just…die. You can't lay here on the floor like this. If you want to get into bed, I'll help you. But you got to tell me you want it."

Screw you.

The words formed in her brain but not on her tongue. She'd always hated being told what to do. Gilly blinked again, knowing to fight this was useless and ridiculous and petty. She felt his touch between her shoulder blades again.

She nodded.

He put his hands under her armpits and lifted. Not gently. The room spun as he hoisted her upright and walked her to the bed where he let her fall ungracefully. Todd stood back, watching as Gilly squirmed into the blankets.

"You need anything?"

She managed a croaking reply. "No."

He flicked his hair from his eyes again. "I'm going downstairs. If you need something, holler."

She closed her eyes. "Okay."

She listened to the sound of his boots, heavy on the floor, and the thud of him going down the stairs. The softness of the bed cradled her, and there was no denying it was better than the couch had been. Better than the floor, where she'd still be if Todd hadn't come to check on her.

She wanted to think of him as a monster, but she knew the real monster here wasn't Todd.

18

The next day was better. Her vision was clearer, her head not so heavy. She woke feeling refreshed, and though her legs still wobbled when she got out of bed, Gilly could walk.

In a cabin as small as this, she couldn't avoid him forever. It seemed trivial and childish not to speak to him when they were no more than a few inches apart at the breakfast table. Especially when he pushed the sugar across to her as she stirred her tea.

"Thank you." Gilly cleared her throat and tried again. "Thank you, Todd."

He grunted, shoveling oatmeal into his mouth. "Whatever."

She reached out hesitantly, hating herself for it but unable to stop herself from being decent. "I mean, thank you for…everything. You didn't have to."

He stared at her. "Lots of things I didn't have to do."

She nodded. "But you did."

"Ain't life funny that way?" Todd asked her, then

shot her one of his wolflike grins. He gave his next words an exaggerated Pennsylvania Dutch accent. "One great big fuckup, ain't?"

His comment almost made her laugh but, in the end, did not. "Yeah. It sure is."

Todd shrugged, looking down. His face had started healing. The wounds she'd inflicted might not leave any scars, but Gilly would never look at him without remembering how she'd made him bleed.

Nobody would blame her. Probably not even Todd. But as she watched him get up from the table and take her plate with him to the sink, Gilly blamed herself.

"Anyway," she said. "Thanks."

Todd shrugged, his back to her, and put on the kettle. He brought down two mugs, two tea bags. He opened the cupboards, searching until he found a package of chocolate sandwich cookies, the chocolate chip ones they'd made long gone. He opened the package, arranged the cookies on a flowered plate and slid it across the table in front of her.

"Here," he said gruffly.

"No, thanks. I'm not hungry." Her stomach still hovered on the edge of nausea even as her mouth squirted saliva at the sight of the junk food.

A faint smile tugged the corner of his lips. "Why aren't women ever hungry?"

"I'm really not," she said, but took a cookie anyway. White frosting edged her fingertip and she licked it off. The sweetness was almost too much, but after a second it settled her stomach.

"Right." Todd leaned his rear on the counter and crossed his arms over his chest. "How about just a salad? You want that instead?"

Gilly frowned. "No. Yuck."

He laughed at that and turned off the gas just as the kettle began to whistle. He refilled their mugs, then sat. Today he wore a white tank top beneath an unbuttoned, snap-front Western shirt. He'd rolled the sleeves up to his elbows.

For the first time, Gilly noticed the tattoo on the inside of his left arm, halfway between his wrist and his elbow. Black ink, stylized numbers. At first she assumed it was a piece of Japanese calligraphy of the sort that had become so trendy over the past few years, people getting inked with words they didn't know how to read. Or maybe it was tribal ink, another trend she'd never understood unless it was by someone with Native American heritage. Jews weren't supposed to get tattoos, anyway, but if she'd ever considered getting something permanently embedded in her skin, it would be something that made sense to her personally, not something everyone got just because it was popular.

She saw it more clearly when he stretched his arm to grab a couple of cookies from the plate. Not calligraphy and not tribal markings, though the numbers had been drawn in a highly stylized form that made them almost indecipherable.

1 of 6

It took her a few seconds to puzzle out what it meant, sort of like trying to read a custom license plate, or that funky cross-stitch piece that said Jesus when you looked at it one way and looked like nonsensical blocks the other. As with those things, once she'd figured it out there was no way to not see it, of course. Gilly snorted lightly, feeling stupid.

"One of six," she said aloud.

Todd jumped. His hand hit his mug, sending it to the floor where it shattered. Hot tea splattered. Gilly jumped, too, at the sound, and the sudden motion sent a wave of dizziness through her.

Todd stood. "Shit. Look at that."

He sounded too distressed for a simple accident— even though the mug had broken, the cupboard was stocked with at least a dozen more. It bore the name of a bank and she didn't see how it could possibly have any sentimental value. Todd kicked at a shard of porcelain, sending it skittering across the floor as he went to the sink for a dish cloth.

"Be careful," Gilly said automatically when he bent to wipe at the spill. "Use the broom, first."

He paused, head down, shoulders hunched. "I can clean up a broken mug."

"I'm not saying you can't. I just meant…"

"I know what you meant." He stood and tossed the towel into the sink while Gilly watched, helpless to understand.

Todd went through the pantry, out to the lean-to, and came back with an ancient, straggly straw broom. The handle had been painted with whimsical designs and looked utterly out of place here in this cabin that didn't look like it had seen a woman's touch in a long time, if ever. In his other hand he gripped a red metal dustpan that looked as old as the chairs on the front porch. He put it on the floor and held it with his boot as he swept up the mug. The straw broom left dirt marks on the floor she'd scrubbed not so long ago, and Gilly made an inadvertent noise of protest.

Todd looked up at her, brow furrowed. She opened

her mouth to complain about the mess he'd made of what had been a relatively clean floor, but stopped herself. He wasn't hers to scold.

He finished with the mug while she sipped at her tea and nibbled the cookie his scorn had forced her to take. Sitting while someone else cleaned was such a novelty she had to enjoy it, at least a little, even though she didn't want to. But when he left again to return the broom and dustpan, Gilly couldn't stay in her seat.

She took the dish towel, dampened it, and swiped at the smudges he'd left behind. She looked up at the sound of his boots and discovered him staring down at her. She got up to rinse out the towel, though the water from the tap was too cold to make it easy to clean it.

"Thanks," Todd said.

"You're welcome."

She wrung out the cloth and let it hang over the edge of the sink. "I can make you another cup, if you want. The water's probably still pretty hot."

"Nah." Todd hovered between her and the table. "I'm good."

He'd pulled his sleeves down, a fact Gilly noticed but didn't comment upon. They stared at each other until he straightened up. He was always taller than she thought he was, probably because he slouched a lot. Taller and with broader shoulders. He took up a lot of space but just now Gilly didn't feel threatened.

"Going out for a smoke," Todd said, though he'd never bothered to either warn her or ask permission in the past.

She watched him go out the front door. Then she got the broom again and made sure nothing remained on the floor to cut their feet. He'd returned by the time she was rehanging the broom, but if he minded her cleaning up after him, Todd didn't say.

19

She was down to the last few pills and probably didn't need them, but took them anyway. Medicine that was supposed to make other people wakeful always knocked her out, so she stayed in bed. Besides, beneath the blankets she was warm, and under their protection she didn't have to face Todd.

The more she slept, the easier sleep seemed to find her. Gilly, who hadn't gone one night through without interruption in more than five years, now spent more than half the day in bed, creeping downstairs only to use the toilet and sneak a few slices of stale bread while Todd was outside smoking or chopping wood for the stove. She was back upstairs before he came in, and when he came into the attic to stand over her, staring, Gilly closed her eyes and pretended to be dreaming. She'd always been a vivid dreamer, but now her dreams became more real to her than her life.

Sometimes she dreamed of things that had already happened. Her wedding to Seth, dancing in a high school musical, falling off her bike and cutting her leg badly enough to need stitches. Other things she dreamed of had never happened and likely never would—appearing on Broadway in the role of Annie Oakley, flying, attending Harvard.

She dreamed of her children, the sweet scent of their skin and the softness of their cheeks as she cuddled them. The days of nursing them as infants, when their tiny mouths puckered so sweetly against her breast and their fingers curled around hers. Those dreams left her aching and desperate to sleep again, both to escape and embrace the dreams.

And she dreamed of roses. Always roses, never tulips or daffodils or lilies, all flowers she actually had in her yard. Giant fields of roses and herself in the middle of them, watching them bloom and die over and over while she tried to grab them up and never succeeded. She didn't know what a dream dictionary would say about the symbolism of roses. She knew what they meant to her.

When night fell and Todd again climbed the stairs, this time to go into his own bed, Gilly waited until she heard the soft rumble of his snores before she went down again to use the toilet. She was back under the blankets in less than ten minutes.

As a child it had never made sense to her, why her mother complained of being so tired all the time when she barely got out of bed. How her mother could be still for so long without moving. Gilly understood her mother much better now.

Gilly drifted that way, until morning when a glance from her pillow showed nothing but white outside the window. Nothing had changed. Maybe nothing ever would.

Her lethargy grew deeper every day. She woke to eat and use the bathroom, but spent as little time as possible at either of those activities before returning to the sanctity of her bed. Beneath the covers, she was protected from the world.

20

"**Y**ou gonna sleep your whole life away?"

Gilly cracked open one bleary eye and peeled her face from the pillow. Apparently, at some point during the night, she'd drooled. She swiped her gummy tongue across equally sticky lips and teeth.

"…time…?" She mumbled.

"Time for you to get your lazy ass out of bed." Todd leaned against the dresser and sniffed loudly, then recoiled. "Clean yourself up. You reek."

Gilly shook her head and rolled over. "Go away."

"Get out of bed, Gilly."

"No!"

Gilly pulled the covers over her head, ignoring him. Todd muttered a string of curses under his breath and clomped away. Then he came back.

"I ain't going to ask you again," he told her. "Get out of bed."

Gilly untangled her hand from its citadel of blankets and waved her middle finger at him. "No, and fuck off."

"Goddamn it, Gilly," Todd said. "You are one impossible bitch! The fuck is wrong with you?"

"I want you to leave me alone," Gilly told him, and wriggled farther down beneath the blankets. "Just go away and leave me alone."

"So you can rot up here? No fucking way."

She pulled the pillow over her head, knowing it was immature and doing it anyway. "I'm tired. Let me sleep."

"You been sleeping for three days!"

"Leave me alone!" Shouting hurt her throat and made her cough, though even she couldn't pretend to still be sick.

"No way."

Todd grabbed the covers and tore them away from her, ripped the pillow from her hands and threw it on the floor. Gilly flailed at him, grabbing without effect at the sheets as he tugged them away, too. Red-hot rage filled her, and she screamed, a wordless roar of anger like shards of glass in her already wounded throat.

Without hesitation, Todd reached down and grabbed the front of her nightgown. The cloth tore as he pulled her from the bed. Gilly fought him, twisting in his grip. Her feet hit the floor and her ankle turned, sending tingling sparks of pain flaring up her leg. She bit out a curse, her words as harsh as his, and punched him in the stomach.

Todd barely flinched as he backhanded her across the cheek without letting go of the front of her gown. Gilly reeled, hand to her face. Bright blood dripped from the corner of her mouth and stained her fingers. The gown ripped completely from her neck to her waist, exposing the shirt and sweatpants she wore beneath, and she fell back onto the bed.

"You son of a bitch," she said, incredulous, showing him the crimson stain. "You hit me! Damn you, you hit me!"

"Get up."

He had struck her before and there'd been a time she'd actually wished for him to hit her, but that felt surreal compared to this. She rubbed the blood on her fingertips. "You're an asshole."

His eyes narrowed. "Get up or I'll crack you again."

Apparently, she didn't move fast enough for him. He reached down and grabbed her by the front of her shirt with both hands and hauled her upright. Gilly managed to smack him in the face.

Todd grunted, face turning from the force of her blow. When he looked back at her with glistening eyes, his mouth had gone pinched and thin. His nostrils flared.

"I told you not to do that."

"You hit me!" she cried, dangling in his grip, noticing even in her distraught state at how his nose wrinkled and he turned his face from the gust of her sour breath. "You! Hit me!"

Todd's eyes didn't widen. "And I'll fucking do it again if you don't get your shit together."

Gilly blinked, swallowing a retort. He was so much bigger he'd lifted her onto her tiptoes, and in socks she couldn't do any damage by stepping on his toes or kicking his shins, either. She couldn't even get another good strike at his face, if she was going to be so stupid.

"You going to be sensible?" he asked.

She didn't nod or shake her head, but Todd must've

seen something in her face because he let go of the front of her shirt. Gilly kept her feet, mostly because he took hold of her upper arm. His fingers could almost encircle her biceps, bunching her sleeve.

"C'mon," Todd said. "Downstairs."

She dug in her feet and tried to turn back toward the bed. "I'm tired. I want to stay in bed."

"No." He pulled her harder. "You can't stay up here all the time. You got to take care of yourself."

"You said you wouldn't," Gilly muttered.

Todd didn't let go of her arm. "Wouldn't what?"

"Make me do anything I didn't want to do."

He grunted. "For chrissake, Gilly, you stink. You haven't changed your clothes in a week. When's the last time you brushed your teeth? How can you stand it?"

She couldn't, actually, now that she was fully awake and aware of it. But she wouldn't let him know that. She tried to pull her arm away, but his grip was too tight.

"You're hurting my arm."

"I know."

"Just leave me alone," Gilly begged with a glance at the bed. "Why do you care?"

"You can't sleep all the time," Todd told her, punctuating his words with a shake. "If you're not sick, you can't stay in bed all day. You can't just fucking…fade away."

"I'm not fading away, I'm waiting!" Gilly shouted.

Todd dropped her arm and stepped away from her. He didn't need to ask her what she was waiting for. "You said you didn't need me to take care of you anymore. Then you got to take care of yourself."

"Why do you care?" Gilly repeated.

"You ain't no good to anybody up here," Todd said. "Not me, not yourself…not them, either."

"Don't. Don't you talk about them."

He sighed and rubbed at his eyes. "I'll make you a deal. You promise to come downstairs and act like a human being…"

"And what? You'll let me go?" Gilly sniffed, rubbing the spot on her arm where the bruise would appear.

He shook his head. "No, I'm not going to let you go, for fuck's sake, Gilly, that's getting pretty old. But you want to run out in the snow again? Be a dumbass? Be my guest. See what happens this time, see if I save your sorry ass one more time."

"What about when the snow melts, Todd? What then?"

His gaze wavered for a second before he shoved her away from him and stalked to the center of the room, head hung low. When he swung around to look at her, his dark eyes were large in his face, his mouth a pensive frown.

"Why can't you just like me?" he asked her. "I ain't done anything real bad to you, Gilly. Not real bad."

"I won't ever like you. Don't you see I can't?"

"Why not?" Todd held out his hands, giving her that kicked-dog look. "Why?"

"Because you're my enemy." Gilly pulled the torn pieces of her gown back together with one hand, the fabric a useless shield but one she couldn't put down. Her mouth stung when she spoke, but the blood had ceased dripping. "Because you are keeping me from the things I love."

He sighed as if the weight of the world had come to

rest on his broad shoulders. "We could get along better than we do."

"No!" She recoiled, grimacing.

"I didn't mean like that," he said quietly.

"I know you didn't. The answer's still no."

He looked angry again. "We're stuck here, Gilly. Ain't no way around it. We're fucking stuck out here in the middle of no place up to our assholes in snow. That's the way it is. Don't keep pushing me into being something you wish I was just so you can feel better about what *you* did."

It wasn't the statement of a stupid man but of an insightful one, and Gilly wondered at what the people in his life had done to him, and for how long, to convince him he was so dumb.

"I don't *want* to hurt you," Todd said. "I don't *want* to."

But he would. The words unsaid nevertheless hung between them, loud and clear.

She turned her face away. "When the snow melts, I'm going to try to get away. Are you going to tie me up?"

"I'm not that kinky," Todd said, "though a girl did ask me once to put on her panties."

This was serious and she hated he was making a joke of it. "The only thing keeping me here is the snow. You know that."

"Ah, fuck me. Yes. I know it." Todd scowled.

"So, what happens when the snow melts?" She asked the question more quietly this time, not pushing so hard. Truly curious. She wanted to know the answer.

"I knew an old hound dog once," Todd said after a pause. "He wasn't mine—I never had a dog. He belonged to this guy who lived down the street from one of the places they put me after...one of the places I lived as a kid."

Despite herself, Gilly lifted her face to meet his unwavering gaze. Todd's voice was solid, deep, precise even in its uneducated manner. He stood with his feet planted slightly apart, hands at his sides. Telling her.

"This dog was one mean son of a bitch. The guy kept him outside on a chain, and that dog would run so fast to bite your ass he'd choke himself right off his own feet. Every day, I'd walk by that dog on my way to school, every fucking day he'd try to get me. But he never did."

Todd laughed, low. "The guy that owned him could've just kicked that dog when he saw him, but he never did. That guy always made sure that dog had plenty of food and water, and he gave him chew toys and rawhide bones. And every night, when that guy came out to feed the dog, he'd pat him on the head and scratch him behind the ears. And the dog, that ass-biting dog, always growled.

"The guy loved that dog, even though the dog never loved him back, and never thanked him for all the nice things he did for it. Then one night, when the guy went out to feed the dog and pat him on the head, the little fucker didn't bother growling. This time, he took a big chunk right out of the guy's hand."

Her throat had gone dry during the telling of his tale. "What happened then?"

Todd smiled, an empty expression that bared his teeth and did not reach his eyes. "The guy went inside his house and got his shotgun, and he blew that little fucker's head right off."

There was no mistaking the meaning of his story, but Gilly wasn't afraid of it. "Which one of us is the dog?"

"I don't know, Gilly," Todd said. "I guess we'll just have to wait and see."

21

She got out of bed on her own the next morning. Washed and dressed. Sat across the table from him and ate her breakfast. She did not speak.

Todd didn't seem to mind. He ate as heartily as he ever did, and after breakfast lit up a cigarette as if it was dessert. Gilly waved away the smoke hanging in front of her face and coughed deliberately, but Todd either didn't notice or did not care.

"You giving me the silent treatment?" he asked her finally, when she got up to put her dishes away.

Gilly paused before answering. "I don't have anything to say to you."

"How about good morning?"

She repeated the words without enthusiasm. Todd got up from the table and touched her shoulder to turn her to face him. Gilly moved without resistance, her gaze on the ground.

"Gilly. Look at me."

She did so grudgingly.

"We got to go through this again?"

She shook her head and tried to turn her face away. "No."

He lifted her chin so she had to continue looking at him and asked her the question he'd asked her once before. "You afraid of me?"

"No."

"You're not a good liar," Todd said, and let her go. He followed her to the living room. "Will you just stop for a minute?"

She whirled to face him. "Can't you just let it go? What do you want from me?"

"Just thought we were going to try and be friends, that's all. Seems better than not being friends." Todd shrugged. The tip of his cigarette glowed red as he drew the smoke deep into his lungs.

"I never said I was going to be your friend." Lip curling on the word, Gilly crossed her arms in front of her.

"You just gonna keep being that growling dog, ain't you?" Todd grinned. "Okay. I'll just keep patting you on the head…."

"And maybe one day I'll bite you," Gilly retorted.

"Maybe one day you will," Todd conceded. "Or maybe, one day, you'll just stop that growling."

"I don't think so." She went to the front window, watching the snow outside. A rabbit hopped along the white drifts, leaving behind its footprints. Then it was gone.

"Ah, Gilly, why not?" He sounded so sincerely curious, she turned to face him.

"The idea is ridiculous."

"How come?"

He wanted to know, so she told him. "We have nothing in common. There's nothing about our lives that would ever have brought us together."

"Not true. We did get brought together."

"Not by my choice!"

Todd made a thoughtful face. "Not by mine, either, but it happened. What, you can only be friends with someone you met on purpose? The fuck kind of fun is that? You must not have many friends if that's how you go about it."

"You have a lot of friends?" she asked, sounding snide, expecting the answer to be negative.

Todd shrugged. "Depends on what you consider a friend. I know a lot of people. And most of them I didn't meet on purpose. But yeah, some of them are friends. Some are douche bags who run off with my money and turn me to a life of crime."

He was making another joke. She saw it in his eyes and the slight tilt of his lips, though his voice was dead serious. Gilly realized suddenly she envied Todd his sense of humor, even amongst all of this. His ability to somehow laugh at what was going on. She'd had a great sense of humor, once upon a time, but she hadn't been able to find the humor in lots of things for a long time. Certainly not this, now.

"We would never be friends under any circumstances, and this situation is certainly not conducive to friendship," she said stiffly.

"Huh. You like big words just like Uncle Bill." Todd shrugged. "This situation is all we got. How fortuitous for both of us to have made each other's acquaintance. See? I know some big words, too."

"It doesn't matter, Todd," Gilly said tiredly.

"Now who won't let it go?" Todd drew in another

deep lungful of smoke, watching her with narrowed eyes. Thinking. "You sure are stubborn."

Gilly lifted her chin. "I've been called worse."

"I bet." Todd shrugged. "Well, I guess it's up to me, then."

She eyed him suspiciously. "What's up to you?"

"Guess I got to prove to you I really am a nice guy." Todd smiled. "Prove we can be friends. You and me, besties. It'll be great. Maybe we can even braid each other's hair."

His eyes glinted with humor even in the face of Gilly's answering glower. In fact, he laughed out loud, right into her face. Gilly crossed her arms.

"Keep dreaming," she said.

"Ah, c'mon. Not even if I make you a friendship bracelet?" Todd fluttered his eyelashes at her.

He looked so utterly harmless and innocent Gilly almost laughed out loud, but she cut it off, tight. Locked it up. "No. Forget it. Not happening."

"You could at least think about it."

"No. I can't." She watched the light of his humor fade. "Really, Todd. You should understand that."

He nodded, just barely, after a long minute of looking at her. "Yeah. Sure, sure. I get it."

Why now did she feel that she was the one in the wrong again? She held her apology, a pearl on her tongue created from the sand of their argument. "We'll never be friends, Todd."

"We'll see," Todd said. "Maybe we'll be something else."

22

Danica is Gilly's best friend until their junior year of high school, when Danica's braces come off and she replaces her glasses with contact lenses. A perm, a tan, a few pounds lost and an inch in height had transformed her over the summer from a band geek into a hottie, and the boys have noticed. That would be fine, but Danica notices, too.

They've shared most everything over the years. Secrets, dreams. They'd practiced kissing their pillows during sleepovers at Danica's house, and she's the only person Gilly's ever told about her crush on their gym teacher, Mr. Grover, in seventh grade. Danica has a lot of brothers and sisters, but Gilly has none. Danica's her sister. Her best friend.

At first, Danica's new popularity with the opposite sex is sort of a boon to Gilly, who's had her share of giggling crushes and notes passed to her in study halls but never really had a boy like her. Not like her, like her, not the way she liked him. Now, walking the halls

*of school before the bell rang for homeroom, Gilly fol-
lows Danica and the boys follow them both. Surely one
or two of them will look Gilly's way when they see her
friend is busy with the others.*

And sure enough, one does.

*Not the one Gilly likes. That's Bennett Longenecker,
who looks like he just stepped out of one of those teen
movies. Perfect hair, perfect skin, perfect teeth, perfect
smile. He likes Danica, of course, but he's nice enough
to Gilly because he also has a perfect personality. Gilly
swoons inside whenever he looks her way, which is just
often enough to keep her pleasantly tingly all throughout the school day and sometimes even into the evening.*

*The boy who likes her has the unfortunate name
of Reginald Gampey. He was named for his ___d and
his grandfather, and he goes by Reg...but it do__n't
help. With a name like Reginald Gampey he's ___stin_d
for thick glasses, an overbite and bad ac___. Being __
brainiac might've made up for it but h___cks even the
smarts to be considered one of the ___'s's top students.*

And, he likes Gilly.

*He manages to become a part of the little crowd of
those who hang out before and after school. Danica
and her admirers, Bennett, who seems to soak up all
the adoration directed his way without really absorb-
ing it. Gilly. Another girl, Marie. And Reg.*

*Things are bad at home again. They'd been okay for
a while, but over the summer when Danica was growing
breasts, Gilly'd been dealing with her mother's increasingly difficult behavior. Mom didn't want Gilly going
to the pool or out with friends, to the movies, out late
at night. She wanted to know where Gilly was all the*

time, to keep her from "trouble." The only trouble Gilly had was hiding the fact that her home life was so shitty.

Danica knows something's up—she's been Gilly's best friend since grade school, after all. But things have changed. Looking back now, Gilly thinks there would've been distance between them without the boys and the new look. But back then Gilly doesn't notice or doesn't want to see how Danica's eyes slide past her, or how Danica doesn't laugh at Gilly's old jokes, or how she mostly just ignores her whenever she can and makes up excuses about how she's too busy to hang out.

The night of the Homecoming dance that fall, the plan is to go as a group date. A lot of the kids from school are doing it rather than springing for limos and corsages. It probably was Danica's idea anyway, so she doesn't have to choose which one, single boy can take her. Reg had asked Gilly but with the group date thing in place she has a reason to say no.

Gilly's having a great time. She slow-dances with Bennet once and a couple other boys. Even Reg, though the way he gazes so longingly into her eyes unnerves her. The DJ plays all the best songs and afterward, the plan is to go out to the local diner to eat and stay out a whole hour after curfew.

"I don't think you should come," Danica says. "Don't you have to get home to your...mom?"

"My dad's with her."

Danica shrugs, so much said in that artless response. "I think you should find someone else to hang out with, Gilly."

"Tonight?" Gilly asks, stunned.

Danica looks at her. Another shrug. "Just...all the time. I think you should find a new best friend."

Then she goes off with the rest of their friends, leaving Gilly to stand with Reg, who offers to drive her home. She lets him, too. Lets him feel her up in the front seat, parked in front of her parents' house. Lets him French-kiss her.

She lets Reg think she likes him, until Monday at school when she tells him the same thing Danica had said to her. "I think you should find another girlfriend."

Gilly never asked Danica what had prompted the change in their long friendship. She never had the courage. She played it off, pretended it didn't matter, but for the rest of that year she watches Danica laugh and joke with everyone else but her. It's a rejection worse than any from a boy could ever have been.

Gilly chooses her friends very carefully after that.

23

"Fuck my life!" Todd hissed and stuck his fingers in his mouth as he knelt by the stove to poke at the logs. "Burned myself."

Gilly looked up from the magazine crossword puzzle she was working on. "Do you have to drop the f-bomb with everything you say?"

Todd looked up from the fire and dusted off his hands on the thighs of his already dirty jeans. He'd been wearing the same pair for the past few days. Gilly had a few unworn shirts from the stash he'd bought her and had done some laundry in the bathtub, but Todd was apparently far less concerned with recycling his clothes. His forehead furrowed.

"Huh?"

"You curse all the time."

"I do?"

"Yes," Gilly said patiently. "Almost every sentence you're saying *fuck* or *shit* or something like that."

Todd shrugged. "So?"

"Well...can't you think of a better way to express yourself?" Gilly prompted. "You know, Todd, words don't have to be big to be effective."

"No." He held out his forefinger and thumb a scant inch apart. "Sometimes they're really tiny and they work great. Like, for instance, *fuck*."

She cocked an eyebrow at him. Todd stood. He put his hands on his hips, looking down at her.

"You've said it," he told her. "I heard you."

"Well, yes, I've said it, but I don't say it all the time."

"Maybe you should say it more." He grinned. "Fuck! Say it. It feels really good. Besides, the more you say it, the less scary it is. Go on."

"I'm not scared of saying it. I just choose to express myself with different word choices." God, she sounded prissy even to herself.

"Ooh." Todd fluttered his fingers over his heart. "Fancy."

She bit the inside of her cheek, but not in anger. "The more you say it, the less effective it actually becomes. You should try it. Using something else."

"What do you want me to stay instead?"

"Fudge?"

Todd laughed aloud. "Oh, right. That's so cool. 'Hey baby, wanna fudge?' Wow, I bet I'd get laid so much my dick would fall off."

"Gross!"

"Slow your roll, Gilly, jeez. You act like you never heard a dude talk about his dick before. And don't tell me you haven't, because we all do it."

Seth had, indeed, talked about his "junk" on more than one occasion, but Gilly wasn't going to talk about that with Todd. "Use whatever words you want. I'm just saying that society will look at you less askance if you clean up your mouth."

As soon as she said it, Todd's grin faded. "Yeah. Because society really gives a fuck about my mouth."

"You never know," Gilly said, "what makes an impression."

Todd pointed at his chest. "See this? See me, standing right here in front of you?"

"You're hard to miss since you are standing right there," she said.

"Yeah, well, let me tell you something. I could put on a suit and tie and slick my hair back and shave, and I'm still always going to be a guy society looks upon like an ass can'ts, whatever the fuck that is."

"*Askance*. It's like…" She demonstrated with her expression.

"Scared?"

"No. Not… More like this." She tried again, raising her brows and parting her lips.

He laughed. "Yeah. Scared. Like I might mug you."

"Well…" She looked him up and down but didn't finish the thought.

Todd's smile faded. He stalked to the window and looked out, silent for a few minutes. "It's snowing again."

"Again?"

He pointed out the window. "Yeah."

Beyond the glass, she could see nothing but white. Gilly turned her attention back to the puzzle and shrugged. She needed an eleven-letter word for a noun meaning "anything abominable; anything greatly disliked or abhorred" and "mother-in-law" didn't fit. She knew because she'd tried. She tapped the pencil, worn to a soft-nosed nub, against her chin. "Nothing we can do about it."

Todd paced a little bit in front of the stove, stopping every now and then to peer out the window again. He discovered a ball in some drawer, along with a suction-cupped basketball hoop. He took shot after shot, making most of them but occasionally needing to dive after the ball as it bounced wildly along the floor or rolled under the couch where she was sitting.

Gilly forced herself to concentrate on the crossword puzzle, though Todd's constant motion agitated her. The third time she had to lift her feet so he could get beneath them, she fixed him with a glare Todd didn't seem to notice. Cheek pressed to the worn carpet, one long arm snaking under the couch to grab the ball, his ass in the air, he didn't look so threatening. In fact, she thought suddenly, catching sight of the knife in the sheath on his belt, his face was at just the right place to kick.

"Gotcha." Todd got up, ball in hand, and the moment, such as it was, passed.

She filled in another few words and sighed. Now would've been a good time for the use of the word she'd told Todd to find a substitute for. Todd, tossing the ball back and forth from hand to hand, looked down at the paper.

"Abomination," he said.

"What?"

"Abomination." There was a pause as he waited, mouth quirked, for her to reply, but he spoke before she did. "Even has more than four letters."

Gilly filled in the letters carefully. "Abomination."

It was sort of the same thing as mother-in-law.

She hated crossword puzzles, normally. She wasn't

good at figuring out definitions from vague clues and vocabulary had never been her strongest talent. She knew what words meant when she read them, but thinking of them when she needed to use them often left her grasping. Still, it was better than sitting staring at the wall, which is what she'd have been reduced to, otherwise.

Or, she thought, biting the familiar spot to keep from growling, she could pace up and down like a caged animal and totally annoy everyone else in the room. Todd had lost interest in the makeshift basketball game and now wandered from window to window, looking out and muttering. That was bad enough, but when he plopped onto the couch beside her and put his feet on the coffee table, then started jiggling them so the entire couch shook, Gilly'd had enough.

"Todd!"

He jumped, looking guilty, and thumped his feet to the floor. "Sorry."

Gilly closed the magazine with a sigh. "Can't you sit still? It's like you're being electrocuted."

Todd frowned and shrugged. "I'm fucking bored as fuck. What do you want me to do?"

She sighed again. "Take a nap. Sew that hole in your shirt. Better yet, wash the shirt, it's disgusting."

Todd looked down at the front of it and ran his fingertips over the mother-of-pearl snap buttons. "I like this shirt."

"Obviously, since you've worn it for the past three days."

"Aw, Gilly," Todd said with a grin. "You noticed."

She sighed. "Just…do something that doesn't involve you annoying me!"

"Is there anything that wouldn't annoy you?" Todd got up from the couch. He shifted on his feet, looking for all the world like a cat ready to pounce on a mouse. Everything about him reminded her of some feral creature. He went to the window again. "I'm so fudging bored!"

Gilly fixed him with an impatient stare. "What do you want me to do about it?"

"You like Monopoly?"

Actually, she loved the game, but hadn't played for years. A house with small children was no place for a game with a myriad of tiny pieces. Todd went to the large armoire in the corner and pulled out the familiar box.

"We could play," he said.

"I'm busy."

The idea was tempting. She was more than a bit bored herself, but Gilly forced her attention back to the magazine. She couldn't allow herself to relax with him or she'd be lost, and yet each passing moment in his company made it harder and harder to hold him at a distance. Not when he asked her to do innocent things like play Monopoly.

"Your head hurting again?"

She shook her head. Her fingers fluttered on the magazine's slick pages. Todd sat down across from her and pulled the magazine from her hands.

"Hey!"

"Play with me, Gilly."

"No."

He sighed. "Shit."

Gilly snatched back the crumpled pages and turned her face from him. "Leave me alone, Todd."

"Just one game. C'mon. I'll let you pick whatever piece you want. Top hat, race car, thimble, whatever. Hell, you can even roll first."

"I said no!" The words spit from her mouth like bullets from a gun.

He recoiled, his mouth twisting. A spark that didn't look like anger glimmered in his eyes, but Gilly didn't flinch. She lifted her chin, daring him to protest.

"Christ, you're a bitch," he said.

Gilly put the magazine on the coffee table between them and stood up, hands on her hips. "Why do men always say that when they don't get what they want?"

Her head spun a little at the speed of her retreat, but she managed to walk away with some semblance of dignity. That he was right didn't bother her. He'd called her a growling dog, too. If being a bitch meant she could survive this ordeal, then she'd be one.

Todd's voice stopped her at the foot of the stairs. "Is that what your husband calls you?"

She stiffened. "Seth has never called me a bitch."

"Not to your face," Todd muttered.

Gilly bit back a retort. There'd been days when she knew her frustration spilled out in sharp words, her tongue a keener weapon than any knife. She knew she'd send her husband from her with his pride smarting, his love for her the only reason he'd kept his own replies civil. She knew it when it happened and had felt helpless to stop it, and she knew it now.

She did with Todd what she'd so often felt incapable of doing with Seth—she held her tongue. Gilly went up the stairs and changed into her nightclothes: thick socks, heavy sweatpants, the flannel nightgown she hated but wore because it kept her warm. She got into bed and pulled the covers up to her chin. Daylight still filtered through the window, but through the densely falling snow the light was diffuse enough to ignore. She closed her eyes and waited for him to come and demand she get out of bed, but he didn't.

Much later, when night had fallen, she woke to the sound of Todd's boots on the stairs. For once, she'd slept without dreaming. Within minutes the light he'd brought with him went out and they lay in the dark again. Together but separated by more than just the low half-wall. After a time, she heard his soft, slow breathing, and knew he slept.

She desperately had to pee. Gilly blinked against the dark. Since she'd gone to bed so early, she hadn't brought a light. She pressed her thighs together, but the dull, cramping ache in her bladder meant there was no way she'd be able to make it until morning.

She swung her legs out of bed and shivered instantly. Without constant stoking, the woodstove quickly stopped heating the cabin. The shivering didn't help her need to pee, and she took a few deep breaths to convince her body she was going to make it to the bathroom without embarrassing herself.

Darkness would make the trip hazardous, and Gilly had a vision of herself tripping over something. Falling and wetting herself at the same time. Once upon a time she'd been able to go without bathroom breaks for hours, but not since having babies. She'd almost embarrassed herself enough times to know better than to tempt fate. Only the dimmest glimmer of light shone in through the windows on either end of the room, not enough to see by. She'd have to make it by memory.

Think about it. Picture the room in your mind. You

*can find your way to the stairs, no problem. Just take
one step at a time.*

Gilly walked with her hands held out like a sleep-
walker. Instead of lifting her feet high, she slid them
along the floor, shuffling to prevent herself from tripping. Her thighs bumped the edge of the dresser and
her hands felt empty space in front of her. She shuffled
forward.

Her eyes had adjusted to the darkness, not enough
to see anything clearly but enough to let her know ap-
proximately where she was going. From the opening in
the partition, there was a clear space between the rows
of beds all the way to the steep stairwell. If she could
make it all the way there without falling down them,
she'd do all right.

Once at the stairs, Gilly gripped the railing hard.
Step by step. Downstairs a soft red glow from the
stove's vents gave her some meager light, but she used
the wall to guide her to the bathroom where she sat
with an audible sigh.

On the way back through the living room, she
paused. Her house was never this quiet. There was always the ambient hum of appliances, the sound of occasional traffic and the dog, who could never be content
to simply sleep but had to yip and pant and scrabble
in constant doggie dreams. This cabin was silent, not
even any wind outside blowing snow against the walls.

Yet this felt familiar, being awake while everyone
else slept. She had spent many nights wandering the
house in the dark, unable to sleep. Sometimes because
she was simply waiting to be woken, sometimes because
of an overwhelming need to check on everything one
last time. Sometimes because no matter how exhausted

she was, she couldn't go to bed until toys that would simply be dumped again in the morning had been put away, or that last load of laundry tossed in the washer. The dishes soaking in the sink scrubbed and dried and put away so she didn't have to face them in the morning.

Gilly always felt like the only member of her household who cared if any of those tasks were completed. It didn't stop her, though. Those were things she could control, make happen. Now she tipped her face to the ceiling. This nighttime wandering felt familiar, but she couldn't let herself forget that it wasn't.

She climbed the steps, the journey up in darkness somehow easier than it had been going down. Todd's breathing grew louder as she got closer. She picked out his form in the darkness, a huddled lump in the middle bed on the right-hand side. The moon had risen and by chance or luck a pale shaft of moonlight managing to trickle through the window highlighted the curved metal headboard. Gilly glimpsed a tuft of dark hair on the white pillow.

He shifted as she drew near and flung one long arm above his head. Now the soft light seemed to almost caress the curve of his jaw, the line of his lips. He muttered something, softly, and Gilly froze.

She drew closer to the bed, watching the way his mouth pursed with his breath. In sleep, with the covers shielding most of his body from her, he looked far less threatening. He didn't look like a man, really. More like an overgrown boy.

"Mama." He spoke with a child's voice, timid, small and broken of heart.

What was this? The man who'd held her at knifepoint and threatened to kill her was asking for his mother? It might have been comical if not for the utter desolation in his voice, if not for the way the word caused her nipples to peak and her heart to ache with remembrance of baby voices crying out her name in the night just that way.

Three short steps on whispering feet took her to the side of his bed, and she took them without thinking twice. Automatic, the way she did at home when the murmur of a child caught her ear. Todd spoke the word again, this time with a sigh. Tears glittered like fallen diamonds on his cheeks as he shifted again in the bed.

Gilly reached out a hand to brush the hair from his forehead, to wipe away the tears shining on his face. She stopped herself just before she touched his skin, before she could condemn herself to pity and kindheartedness. Todd took in a hitching breath and whispered one last time, "Mama." Then he began to snore softly, and Gilly finished her journey in the dark without hearing him speak again.

24

Todd was quiet in the morning, shadows beneath his dark eyes. He toyed with his lighter, snapping it again and again as it sparked, until the sharp, gassy smell of the fluid tickled a sneeze from Gilly's nose. He didn't offer a "God bless you."

"The funniest thing I ever seen was a fat lady in a bikini trying to do the limbo," Todd said suddenly.

At the sheer incongruity of his statement, Gilly turned from the sink where she was washing her breakfast plate. "Where did you see that?"

"At the beach. I only went one time." Todd leaned back in his chair, rocking. "Laughed so hard I pissed my pants and…the people I was with got mad and took me home."

She watched him tilt the chair, waiting for him to tumble backward. By luck or skill he kept the chair hovering in place while he balanced. He was graceful that way. Comfortable and competent with his body in a way he wasn't with his intellect.

Todd looked at her. "What's the funniest thing you ever seen?"

Gilly shrugged. It didn't seem that conversation should be so easy, no matter how much he made it so. "I don't know."

Todd sighed dramatically. "You're never any fun."

His comment stung. "*Young Frankenstein*. That's a funny movie."

Todd rolled his eyes. "Not a movie. What's the funniest thing you ever seen in your real life? Bet it ain't as funny as a fat lady in a bikini trying to do the limbo."

He was challenging her again, and Gilly rose to the bait. "When I was just out of college, I bought a new mattress from this factory outlet store. When I went to pick it up, the guy from the store helped me put it in the back of this van I'd borrowed. He tried carrying it on his back, but he got stuck, and then the mattress fell on him and only his legs were sticking out...."

Todd raised both eyebrows. Gilly frowned. "What? It was funny. I guess you had to be there."

"I made you smile." Todd thumped his chair down onto all four legs. "See?"

Gilly pushed her mouth back into the frown, but it was too late. "I wasn't smiling at you."

"You got a nice smile." Todd winked.

Oh, how she wanted and needed him to be loathsome to her! Gilly thought of the way his hand had felt when he hit her mouth, drawing blood. The memory was still vivid enough to make her put a hand to her lips. It was also enough to wipe the smile from her face.

"I wasn't smiling." Her denial was transparent, but Gilly didn't care.

"Are you this much fun at home, too?" Todd pulled

a crumpled pack of cigarettes from his T-shirt pocket and scowled to find it empty. He tossed it onto the kitchen table and stood. His gaze swept her up and down. "Maybe they don't miss you as much as you think they do."

He stomped into the pantry while Gilly, stunned, stared after him. In the months before he'd taken her, Gilly had felt more often like screaming than laughing. She thought hard, tears springing to her eyes, about the last time she had laughed with her children. Really laughed. It had been a long time. There had been too many days when her palms hurt from clenching her fists too hard to keep from striking out, too many nights when the last words she uttered were not "I love you," but "for God's sake, go to sleep!"

People always vowed to change, if given a second chance. Gilly was no different, no better. She sat rigid, her back as straight as a poker, and vowed that if she was allowed to return to them, she would cherish her family as something more precious than diamonds. Later, when most of her time with Todd had begun to fade into a series of hazy memories, this moment at the kitchen table would forever stand out as clear as crystal. She wouldn't spend the rest of her life without yelling at her kids or arguing with her husband; such a thing would be impossible and impractical. But when those moments came, the times of anger and grief, it was the moment at Todd's kitchen table she always recalled, and that was usually enough to make her put out her hands and forgive.

"I know you want to hate me," Todd said from the doorway, a fresh pack of cigarettes in one fist. "I know you want to, real bad. But admit it. You just can't."

"You're wrong." Her voice stuttered, giving away her emotions.

"You just ain't that hard." Todd dismissed her protest like it meant nothing. "And if you do hate me, it isn't because of what I done, really. It's because of what you done. So you're mad at yourself."

His observation was the truth, but Gilly wasn't about to admit it to him. "Don't try to psychoanalyze me. You're not smart enough to get inside my head."

He smoothed a hand through his hair. "Shit, Gilly, you seem like a sad, uptight bitch to me. Why the hell would I want to get inside your head?"

She exploded. "Just shut up!"

"Ooh." Todd raised his hands in mock fear. "That's a smart comeback. Wish I could think of something that smart."

Gilly left the table and stalked to the living room, but there was no place to escape him. She paced the wooden planks, wishing suddenly she smoked so she could have the comfort of a cigarette to occupy herself.

She was hard enough to hate, she thought spitefully, watching him as he set out a game of solitaire on the dining table. And she had every reason to hate him. But she also had every reason to hate herself.

Thinking of the evil he'd committed against her, holding her at knifepoint, slapping her face, should have been enough to keep the fires of her hatred burning. Gilly, however, feared that Todd was right about her. She wasn't hard enough to keep hating, not in the face of kindness and good humor. Not even when she should.

Relationships were like machines. Gears fit together, turning to make the machine work. Boss, roommate, parent, child, spouse. The cogs moved, the gears turned or stuck and needed to be oiled. Todd was none of these to her and yet there was no denying they had a relationship, and that it was as much a machine as any other. If they couldn't find some way to make it work, it would break down. A day before, Gilly would've said without question she didn't want to make it work. Now she wasn't sure she could stop herself.

"I don't like to tell anyone," Gilly said, "but I like to watch videos of people falling down."

Todd sat back in the chair, cigarette dangling. "Yeah?"

"Yeah." She nodded.

"Well…" Todd paused as though considering this. "That *is* funny, sometimes. When someone falls. Even if they get hurt, you know, it's funny to see it happen."

"It's wrong to laugh at someone who's hurt, but I can't help it."

Both of Todd's eyebrows lifted. "That's messed up."

"I know," Gilly said, but with a sense of relief, as if she'd confessed to some sort of crime. "It's awful. I'm a terrible person."

"Nah. Or if you are, you're not the only one," Todd pointed out. He shuffled the cards back and forth so fast they became a blur and then again in an intricate pattern. Seeing her look, he paused. "I worked in a casino for a while, too…before."

She wasn't surprised. She took the chair across from him. "So deal something out."

She hated the wary way he looked at her, as though waiting for her to change her mind. Todd shuffled the cards, then caught them all in one hand to take his cigarette from his lips with the other. He tapped the cards into a tidy pile on the table.

"What do you want to play?"

"I don't care. I'm not good at anything," Gilly said.

"I bet you're great at fifty-two pickup."

She made a face. "Yeah, I'm also not that stupid."

"No," Todd said quietly. "I know you're not."

They passed the day that way, hours of cards. He taught her games she'd never known and even a trick or two. By the end of the day, they were not friends but no longer enemies.

25

"What's in that file you keep peeking at?" Gilly turned from where she'd been poking the woodstove to catch Todd sifting through his papers again.

"Nothing." He wasn't in a friendly mood today, which perversely had made Gilly bright and chipper.

"Something you need to throw in the fire?" she asked suspiciously, because he seemed to keep dancing around that decision. "We could use something in there."

"No!"

Gilly blew out a gust of air. "Sorry."

Todd stuffed the papers back in the file and put them on top of the armoire, a gesture she could in no way misinterpret since the only way she could have reached up there was to stand on a chair. Gilly poked the logs one last time and watched them crumble into glowing ruby embers. She sat back on her heels, holding her hands out to the warmth.

"Want to play some cards again?" she asked, to make

him turn away from the window where he stared out into the darkness.

"No."

"Best out of three…?" she began, her tone lightly teasing, in a better mood than she'd been in the weeks since he'd brought her here.

"Just shut the fuck up, okay?" Todd snapped.

Gilly wilted like a flower without water, then set her jaw. "Fine."

Todd was agitated, rocking on the balls of his feet, lighting cigarettes from the ends of others. He shrugged into his ratty sweatshirt and pulled a large plaid hunting jacket over top. "I'm going out."

"Out where?" Gilly got to her feet, alarmed. "It's freezing out there."

"I've got to get out of here!" His eyes looked through her without seeing her. He took one last drag on his smoke before dropping it to the floor and stubbing it out with the toe of his boot.

Gilly recognized the edge of panic in his voice, but could not imagine what had caused it. "Todd…"

He slapped himself in the face. Gilly stopped, stunned. A runner of blood appeared at the corner of Todd's mouth, and he didn't even bother to wipe it away. He slapped the other side. His bent his head, his dark hair hanging to obscure his face.

"What's wrong with you?" This new behavior frightened Gilly more than any other had. She stepped toward him, not thinking, and grabbed his arm.

Todd flung off her touch and fled out the door. He disappeared into the night, leaving only footprints in the snow to show where he had gone. Gilly stood in the doorway, mindless of the frigid night air against her skin for a full few minutes as she searched the darkness for him. He was gone.

Gilly shivered and went inside, closing the door behind her. The sight of Todd's blood had left her with a chill that even sitting by the fire could not chase away. What had made him do that?

Something in that ragged file of papers had upset him. She had to know what it was. Without a second thought, Gilly grabbed one of the dining table chairs and dragged it over to the huge armoire in the corner.

Someone, a long time ago, had lovingly carved the armoire to fit the cabin's corner space. The massive piece rose nearly to the ceiling, its heavy doors shielding four deep drawers and eight roomy shelves. Todd, easily taller than six-two, had no problem tucking the file away on top of the armoire, but Gilly at almost a foot shorter wasn't nearly tall enough to reach. Even with the chair, and standing on her tiptoes, she couldn't quite grab the file. She strained, fingers scrabbling, but all that happened was the chair wobbled and she nearly fell.

The door banged open, and cold air swirled in. Startled and guilty, Gilly jumped from the chair. Todd slammed the door behind him and shrugged out of his coat. He stamped the snow from his boots.

There was no hiding what she'd been doing. Gilly waited for his reaction. Todd stared at her for a long time, so long that the silence became uncomfortable and Gilly had to break it.

"You came back."

His slanting grin lacked its usual luster. "You think I wouldn't?"

"I didn't know." Gilly took the chair back to the table

and hung his snow-covered coat over the back of it. "Are you okay?"

"Nope," Todd said with a trace of his former cheeriness. "But I'm used to it."

"I can make some tea," Gilly said, surprising herself with the offer.

She must have surprised him, as well, because he cocked his head to stare at her thoughtfully. "Thanks."

She nodded, uncertain exactly what had passed between them but knowing something had begun to change. As she headed for the kitchen to boil water, he called after her.

"Don't look in that file," Todd said. "There's some pretty awful shit in there. Especially for someone like you."

Someone like her? But Gilly was afraid to ask, and so he didn't tell.

26

"*I've been waiting for a girl like you...*" Seth sings this loudly and off-key. He's had too much to drink. He's not charming when he's drunk. He might be charming all the rest of the time, but not when he's drunk. Or maybe it's her, maybe it's just that she doesn't like it.

A girl like you, Seth sings again, lifting his glass toward her.

Karaoke sounded like a good idea when she agreed to go along with a bunch of other people from the office and some of their friends, and some random strangers who'd ended up coming along. Gilly doesn't like to sing, not in public, anyway, and has been more than content to sit and watch.

Seth is a friend of her boss's wife. Gilly met him at a barbecue a few months ago, and he's shown up fairly often at group dates like these. He's always been nice. They have something in common, both of them Jews in a widely Christian area. He's handsome and funny, *when he's not drinking and making an ass of himself singing in falsetto.*

Tonight she was supposed to have a date with Joe, but he stood her up. Well, he called to cancel. That wasn't any better. He thinks Gilly loves him, but she doesn't.

Later, though, she's glad Joe passed on the night. Gilly realizes Seth's not drunk. Sure, he's had a couple of beers, but it's not alcohol that gets him up there to sing and dance and make a fool of himself. He just doesn't care if people think he's a goofball.

She likes that about him, Gilly realizes, the third or maybe it's the fourth time they go out like that. She likes Seth. She offers him her number without thinking too much about it. Not a big deal, really. He'll call or he won't.

But Seth holds the number in his hand as though she's given him something precious. "I didn't think..."

Gilly's been laughing, having fun with friends. This didn't seem like something important until just now, but watching Seth look at her she understands it's all become very significant, indeed. "You didn't think what?"

"I didn't think a girl like you would go out with a guy like me. That's all."

"What," she says, laughing, "is a girl like me?"

Seth's answer is a kiss, soft and lingering.

He never does give her an answer other than that.

27

Whatever had been bothering him the night before had left him. Gilly watched him carefully, trying not to let him know she was doing it. Todd might call himself dumb, but he noticed her scrutiny.

"I'm okay today," he told her. "I'm not going to freak out on you or anything like that."

"Whatever," Gilly said as though she didn't really care. "Want to play some checkers?"

"Sure." Todd got out the board and checkers from the armoire and put them on the coffee table in front of the woodstove.

They played three games, and Todd won every one. After the third victory, he lit a fresh cigarette and gave Gilly a sideways, thoughtful glance. She pretended not to notice as she set the board up again.

"How come you were letting me win?"

Gilly feigned ignorance. "I wasn't letting you win."

He snorted. "Yeah, you were."

Gilly forced herself to look offended, though he *had* caught her out. "Why would I do that?"

For once, Todd let the cigarette burn without smoking it. "You tell me."

Gilly sighed. "I didn't want you to get upset again."

"And you thought if I lost a stupid game of checkers, I'd get whacked-out again?" Todd's eyebrows disappeared behind his bangs and shook his head. "I'm a piece of work, I know, but I ain't that bad."

Now she was on the defensive. "I just thought…"

"You do that for your kids? Let them win so they don't get upset?"

"Sometimes." Gilly fiddled with the checkers.

"You think that helps them?"

"I don't think it hurts them," Gilly said.

Todd rolled his neck on his shoulders, cracking it, and stretched out his impossibly long legs. "The world is shit, Gilly, and the sooner they learn that, the better off they'll be."

Gilly thought of her sweet babies, her innocent darlings. "I don't agree."

He fixed her with a look. "It's true."

"If the world is such shit, like you say, then I want to protect them as long as I can. Keep them safe." Gilly waved her hand over the checkerboard. "My kids are little, still. There's plenty of time for them to learn the world isn't always a happy place."

He snorted. "They'll grow up thinking everything's got to go their way."

"They will not." She frowned at his casual dismissal of her parenting choices. "They'll grow up with self-confidence and security."

"You going to let them win off you all the time?"

Gilly shook her head. "Of course not."

"How old?" Todd crumpled his package of cigarettes, but didn't light another one. "Your kids, I mean."

"Five and two." Gilly closed her eyes briefly at the thought of them, and the sight of their faces in her mind had her smiling instead of crying.

"I was five when my mother…" He stopped himself. "When she died."

Instant pity flooded Gilly. "I'm sorry."

He shrugged it off, though clearly the memory wasn't dismissed. "Not your fault. What are their names?"

He was deliberately changing the topic, but Gilly let him. "Arwen and Gandy."

Todd pulled a funny face. "Arwen and Gandy? What kind of names are those?"

Gilly had been asked that question so many times it could no longer offend. "They're names from Tolkein. Gandy's real name is Gandalf."

"What's Toll-keen?"

"J.R.R. Tolkein," Gilly explained. "He wrote *The Hobbit, The Lord of the Rings.* Seth, my husband, he's really into the Middle Earth series."

She thought he might laugh, but he only nodded. "Oh, yeah. I seen that movie."

"They were books first."

"Figures someone like you would name their kids after someone from a book."

"Someone like me?" Gilly furrowed her brow at him. "You keep saying that. What does that mean?"

"You know." Todd began stacking the small wooden disks with swift and efficient movements, making a tower. "Smart. High-class. Rich."

Gilly shook her head, though his assessment of her was complimentary. "Oh, God. No, Todd."

He looked at her from beneath the fringe of bangs and grabbed her hand. He turned it over so that her engagement ring glittered. "Looks pretty high-class to me. And you must've been smart to catch a man who could buy a rock like that."

"This ring was my grandmother's." Gilly took her hand away and rolled the diamond with the back of her finger. "She brought it with her when her family fled Europe to escape the Nazis."

Todd tapped the pile he'd made, and the checkers scattered across the board. "You mean like Anne Frank? See, that's a book, too. I had to read it in school."

"That's not just a book. It was real," Gilly said. "And Anne Frank did not escape."

Suddenly, uncomfortably, she was forcibly reminded of her situation. She could see in Todd's eyes that he, too, had not missed the parallel. He cleared his throat.

"That was different," he said.

"Yeah." She refused to look at him. On her finger, the diamond winked. "Anne Frank was hidden away to save her life. It was completely different than this."

"Gilly…" His voice trailed off.

She shrugged, mimicking him. Gilly picked up the checkers and replaced them, snapping the small wooden pieces onto the board with firm gestures. "Let's play again."

This time, she won.

28

She didn't try to lose any more games. Sometimes she won and sometimes she lost, but victory or defeat were fair results. At least Uncle Bill had stocked the cabin with plenty of board games and decks of cards. They wouldn't lack for that form of entertainment.

"What did you plan to do here all by yourself?" Gilly asked as they set up the board for another game, this time Monopoly.

Todd picked out the little silver shoe he claimed gave him good luck and set it on Go. "Nothing."

"What do you mean nothing? How can you do nothing? What does that even mean?" Gilly dealt the money and laid out the property cards.

Todd gave her fierce look. "I came up here to be by myself…and do nothing."

Gilly persisted, her curiosity piqued. "There's no TV, no DVDs, no internet…."

"Didn't have any of that anyway."

She grimaced. "How could you live without internet?"

Some days, the internet was her sole adult entertainment. The television ran constantly on the kiddie channels during the day and at night she was often too tired to watch any more than an hour of whatever reality TV show Seth had chosen before falling asleep. On the worst days she had a few minutes here and there to check her email, maybe chat online with a friend. On the best days she wasted hours surfing sites, looking at photos with funny captions, watching videos of people falling down.

"I didn't have a computer. Besides, online's for porn and shopping," Todd said succinctly. "I can buy a skin mag cheaper, and I don't shop."

Gilly gaped. "I don't look at porn!"

Todd rolled his eyes.

"I don't!"

"Everyone looks at porn." He shrugged. "Anyone who says they've never looked at porn is full of shit."

Gilly's mouth worked on a reply that came out stuttering with affront. "I don't look at porn."

"Never once?" Todd leaned back in his chair, tipping it again. He looked her up and down, and under his scrutiny Gilly's cheeks heated, even though she was telling the truth. "Not even one time?"

"No!" She shook her head. "First of all, my kids are with me almost all the time. I can't have them looking at something like that. It's my job as their mother to make sure they don't see anything like that. My daughter uses the computer to play games. I have parental controls to block all that stuff."

"Yeah? What about your husband? I bet he looks at porn."

"Seth has his own laptop," Gilly said stiffly. "I don't think he looks at porn."

"Even if he doesn't talk about it, he's got a dick, right? Then he looks at porn. I guarantee it." Todd closed his fist on air and jerked it. "Nothing to be scared of."

Gilly rolled the dice and moved her piece, the top hat, five spaces to land on her own property. "I'm not scared of it. If he looks at porn, I don't know about it, okay? And that's the way I'd like to keep it."

She couldn't keep her lip from curling with distaste at the idea of her husband masturbating to video clips of huge-breasted, spread-eagled women in trashy shoes. Todd laughed and took his turn, also landing on one of her properties. Gilly collected his money without hesitation or remorse.

"So, you shop, then."

Gilly straightened a row of houses on the property closest to her, thinking about buying a hotel the next time around. "Hmm?"

"You don't watch porn. You must shop."

She laughed. "You think I have so much money I can shop all day?"

"Don't you?"

To him, she realized, it must seem like it. The engagement ring. The truck, now totaled. The money from the ATM. He didn't know they ate rice and beans so often because it was worth it to her to sacrifice fancy, gourmet meals to spend a week at the beach in a house nicer than the one they lived in full-time. Todd didn't know how some months the choice between dinner and a movie lost to a pair of shoes for Arwen, or about the number of payments Gilly still had to make on her mother's medical bills that had gone uncovered by insurance. He didn't know about the money she squirreled away every month against a time when something might unexpectedly break or get lost, how she hoarded paper towels and toilet paper and ramen noodles against the impending apocalypse.

"You know it's not money that makes a person rich, Todd."

"Oh, fuck, here we go with the Chinese fortune cookie shit."

"F—" she began and stopped herself.

Todd laughed. "Go ahead and say it. You know you want to. Fuck you, fuck me. Fuck everyone."

She flipped him off, not giving him the satisfaction of saying it aloud. "I don't have enough money to spend all day shopping online. Okay?"

"So, you don't shop. You don't watch porn. What do you do? Connex?" Todd made air quotes around the term and rolled his eyes again.

"Sometimes."

"Lame." He snorted.

Gilly bristled. "What do you know about it, if you don't have one?"

"I don't," Todd said off handedly, "have anyone to Connex with."

"What about all your alleged friends?"

"They don't do lame shit like that. They're too busy committing felonies," he said with a straight face.

She thought he might be kidding but this time couldn't really be sure. "Nice."

He laughed. "Connex sucks."

"How can you say it sucks if you've never done it?" Gilly had nearly five hundred "friends" on Connex and knew maybe about a third of them personally.

"I don't want to do it. Have a bunch of friends—" again with the air quotes "—reading about when I take a dump and how many times a day I jerk off?"

"You're so crude," she said, though truthfully that was pretty close to what a lot of the people on her list did status updates about.

He made a jerking-off motion with curled fingers. "Dear Connex, today I shot my load four times. I wanted to try for five, but I ran out of lube."

"Todd."

He laughed again. "Yeah, really. People don't give a shit about that stuff. What's the point?"

"To connect with people who share similar interests. It's why they called it Connex." Gilly had no idea why she was defending a website she thought was sort of stupid, too.

"I don't have similar interests to anyone."

"I'm not surprised."

Todd blinked. Then grinned. "You're such a bitch."

Gilly wasn't insulted this time; he'd sounded almost fond. "It's called social networking for a reason. To be social. I stay home with my kids all day long. If I didn't do something online, talk to people, I'd go…"

"Crazy?" he prompted after half a minute when she stalled.

"Yes. I'd go crazy." Gilly fussed with her houses again.

She thought of the sound of muffled sobs behind a bedroom door and the cloying scent of spilled perfume. The sting of splintered glass in her feet. This, like the mysteries of her bank account, wasn't something Todd knew or would ever know.

"Who do you talk to?"

"Oh...family. People I went to school with or used to work with. I belong to a few groups for things I like."

"Like what?"

Gilly looked at him. "Authors. Television shows. Rock bands. Whatever."

Todd snorted and rattled the dice in his palm but didn't throw them. "Huh. That sounds like a fuckton of boring."

"Hey," Gilly said, annoyed. "You asked, didn't you? I'm not going to tell you things if you're going to make fun of me once you know."

Too late, she'd admitted she'd tell him things. Todd grinned as Gilly scowled. He handed her the dice.

"Besides," she added. "It's not just the people and the groups. There are games to play. And other things to do."

"Like what?"

"Oh. Take surveys. Are you going to roll those dice or what?"

He rolled, took his turn. "Surveys for what?"

She didn't want to admit her shameful secret, that she whored herself for "seeds" in her favorite Connex game, Farmburg. "Anything."

Todd nodded and helped himself to two hundred bucks for passing Go. "Yeah, right. For cash. I had a friend who got a bunch of stuff doing that. Crap, mostly. But some money."

"I don't do it for money." Though she had heard stories about people who'd won big.

"The fuck would you do an online survey for, if not money?" Todd looked up at her, brow furrowed.

Gilly sighed. No reason not to tell him. Stranded in a mountain cabin with a stranger who'd abducted her at knifepoint, after tossing her kids out a vehicle window, she really shouldn't be worried about telling him she had an addiction to a silly online game. "For seeds."

"Huh?" Todd brushed hair from his eyes and tipped his chair back, going to his pocket for a cigarette he stuck in his mouth but didn't light. "What kind of seeds?"

"For a game," she said, and took the dice, rolling. She landed on Boardwalk, as-yet-unowned, and crowed. "Yes! I'm buying it."

Todd passed her the card. "So you do surveys for… seeds."

Gilly settled her card amongst the others and looked up at him. "Yeah. You need seeds to plant, to get crops. To expand your farm and level up."

Todd raised an eyebrow.

"It's fun," Gilly said.

"Sooo…" Todd drew out the word, long and slow. "How many surveys do you do?"

"I don't have a lot of time, you know," Gilly began defensively, and stopped at another of Todd's raised-eyebrow looks. "Maybe three or four."

"A day?"

"Yes."

Or five. Once a memorable ten while Gandy napped and Arwen had a playdate. Her wrist had begun to ache from scrolling through the choices and the seeds had been spent in fifteen minutes. She'd had to filter out junk mail for the next six weeks.

"I'll be damned." All four legs of Todd's chair hit the floor. "Surveys are your porn."

"Shut up!" Gilly gasped, horrified. "Gross."

Todd grinned, unapologetic, and pointed at her. "They are."

"You're disgusting!"

"Well, yeah, maybe," Todd said. "But that don't make me wrong."

Gilly lifted her chin and gave him a cool glare. "It's your turn."

They rolled the dice, moved their pieces around the board, collected the paper cash when they passed Go. There was a suspicious absence of Go To Jail cards in this set, but Gilly didn't question it. She played for keeps, though, trying to strategize while Todd gambled his way around the board picking up properties at random without seeming to care about the cost or location.

"I'll trade you the Electric Company for Indiana and Illinois." Gilly already owned Kentucky and was itching to get hotels on those spots.

"Nope."

"C'mon, Todd. When I land on it, I'll have to pay you four times the number I roll on the dice."

Todd snorted, the unlit cigarette still dangling from his lower lip. "Nope."

"Electric Company and Water Works. Ten times the roll of the dice when you own both."

"No fucking way, Gilly. I'm dumb but I'm not that dumb." He made another of those jerking-off gestures. "You'll put hotels on those bitches and I'll land on them every fucking time."

"You won't," she scoffed, though she had to give him grudging admiration for outplaying her. He'd been merrily buying up properties, keeping her from owning more than two per set, therefore making it impossible for her to complete them. "It's statistically impossible for you to land on it every time."

"Yeah, well, you can forget it." His hair fell over his eye.

"Fine," she said. "But I'm buying Park Place and putting hotels up, and you can kiss my ass."

"Ooh, scary."

She was angrier than she should've been about a game and understood it wasn't that at all. Her cheek hurt when she bit it and hurt worse when she rubbed the sore spot with her tongue over and over to keep from saying something she didn't mean. But to her surprise, the mantra of *Count to ten, Gilly,* didn't start. She didn't need it. She snorted a little under her breath and looked up to Todd's curious glance.

"It's just a game," she said.

He studied her. "Well…yeah."

She shrugged. "I mean, it's *just* a game."

She looked around the room, then got up to go to the window. More snow. She snorted louder this time and pressed her forehead to the glass, relishing the chill.

Just a game. Slow your roll, Gilly. Chill out.

"Are we gonna finish the game, or what?"

She looked over her shoulder. "I guess so. Nothing else to do, right?"

Todd gave her a strange look and half got to his feet. "Gilly, you're not gonna freak out on me again, are you? Run out in the snow?"

She shook her head, took her seat. "No. I'm okay. Let's play."

They did for another few rolls of the dice, before Todd said, "What's he like?"

"Who? My husband?"

"Yeah."

She shrugged, concentrating on the board to keep emotion from overtaking her. "He's a good man. He's a good dad, fantastic with the kids. I love him very much."

"You're lucky, then. Really fucking lucky."

"Yes," Gilly said. They played in silence for a minute before the words rose to her lips, unbidden and undeniable. She'd never said this aloud before, not even to her girlfriends sitting around a coffee table, bitching about their husbands. "He doesn't listen to me."

The dice, tipped from Todd's hand, rolled across the board and came to rest. Snake eyes. He didn't move his piece right away; she felt his eyes on her and didn't want to meet them, but did.

"I mean, I think he hears me. He just doesn't listen."

Todd moved his racing car to an open property but didn't look to see the cost or offer to buy it. He didn't even glance toward the thin piles of paper money he'd carefully laid out in front of him. He gathered the dice again, rolling them in his palm. They clattered like bones against the board and he moved again, this time to one of his own properties.

"He's a good man," Gilly repeated in a low voice.

"What doesn't he listen to you about?"

Gilly picked up the dice, warm from Todd's palm. Her fingers curled over the plastic. "Never mind. Forget it."

It was wrong to talk about her husband like that

with Todd. It was a betrayal. Gilly rolled the dice. They played the game.

She lost.

29

At home, just as it was never totally quiet, the house was never fully dark. Too many night-lights and appliances with clocks. Navigating her house in the night meant hopscotching from shadow to faint green glow. Gilly was the one who rose in the night and paced the floors, listening. Never Seth.

He never listened for the sound of the subtle shift in a child's breath that predicted a cough or a cry, or the dreaded, always-at-three-in-the-morning puke. He never listened for the dog's claws clicking toward the garbage can on the hardwood floor of the kitchen, or the neighbor's revving engine that meant their teenage son had finally returned. Seth went to bed and slept, sprawling and snoring. He probably didn't even know about the nights Gilly spent awake, checking the locks and the stove burners, or leaning over her children's beds just to make sure they still breathed.

He didn't listen to any of those things, and Seth didn't listen to her. Saying it to Todd had been like some bitter confession she could still taste hours later as she lay in the dark and stared up at a ceiling she couldn't see. Gilly swallowed hard now, her ears popping with the effort. She burrowed deeper into the blankets and curled on her side in a bed that would've been too small to share with her husband and was infinitely too vast when she was in it alone.

She loved her husband. He was a good man. A wonderful father, a loving husband. If he didn't listen to her, maybe it was because she didn't make herself heard. Or he couldn't understand that when she told him something it was real and true, not empty words said for the sake of conversation.

If Seth thought she was joking when Gilly told him she was going to lose her mind if he didn't replace the garbage bag after emptying the trash, or put a new roll of toilet paper on the holder when he'd used the last scrap, whose fault was that? His for not taking her seriously, or hers for not impressing upon him how utterly serious she was? Or hers, for allowing such minor, small things to eat away at her? It didn't matter now. Their marriage was a machine, the gears and cogs turning or sticking. What more could she ask for? What more could she expect?

"How'd you meet him?" Todd's voice parted the darkness.

Gilly lifted her head, turning her face toward him but not her body. "My husband?"

"Yeah. How'd you meet him?"

She settled back into the blankets, shrugging them higher on her shoulders. "A friend introduced us."

"At a party?"

"Yes." She paused, curiosity winning. "How'd you know?"

She heard him shifting in his sheets and imagined a shrug. "Lots of people get introduced at parties."

"It was a barbecue at his boss's house. His boss's wife was my friend." Gilly paused again, the dark room a perfect screen for the movie of her memories.

Seth had been wearing a pink polo shirt and khaki shorts, a beer in the hand he hadn't held out for her to shake. His hair had been too long for her taste, his smile nice enough, but Gilly hadn't been looking at him "like that."

"Did you like him right away?"

Gilly blinked away the vision of the first time she'd seen the man she'd marry. "No. God, no."

Todd laughed a little louder. "Huh?"

"I was with someone else. I thought he was okay, but I wasn't interested in him that way."

"So how you'd end up together?"

Was this wrong, to talk about this with Todd? She hadn't thought about it for years. The kids weren't old enough to ask about it, and the story had never seemed romantic enough to retell. "We went out a bunch of times with friends."

"And then you hooked up with him?"

Gilly smiled, bittersweet, at the memory. "Not that first time. I was still seeing the other guy, the one I'd gone to the barbecue with. I thought I liked him, but... he turned out to be sort of a jerk."

"What did he do to you?" Todd's voice broke on a yawn and triggered one from her.

"Oh, the usual stuff."

"Knocked you around? Stole shit from you? Ran around on you?"

"No! Is that what you think the usual stuff is?" Gilly shifted in her blankets, indignant.

"Sure. If you don't like a dude, yeah, I mean, that's some bad stuff, right?" He paused. "I mean…you don't think that's okay, do you?"

"Of course it's not. *You* don't think that's okay, do you?"

"No. Of course not. A man who hits a woman isn't much of a man," Todd said in a low voice.

They both ignored the fact they'd hit each other, and more than once.

"He didn't hit me. He probably did run around on me, yes. Mostly he didn't call when he said he would, stood me up. That sort of thing." Gilly frowned as she remembered. "I didn't even like him that much, that guy. He thought I was in love with him, though, which made it even worse."

"Huh?"

Gilly sighed. "If he'd treated me badly knowing I didn't really love him, that would've been one thing. But if he thought I was in love with him and he still did that stuff…that's worse. That it didn't matter how I felt about him. I went out with Seth, finally, because that other guy had promised to call and didn't."

"And you knew he was the guy for you."

She smiled a little at the certainty in Todd's voice. "Oh…I don't know about that. I didn't know right away, that's for sure."

"You didn't?"

"No. I don't think anyone can ever know right away."

More shifting and rustling from his side of the room. "You don't believe in love at first sight and all that shit?"

"No. Do you?"

"Fuck no." Todd's laugh grated, rusty and sharp. "Love's just another word for sucker."

"Oh, Todd." Gilly bit back a laugh. "That's not true. Haven't you ever…haven't you had…?"

She trailed to a stop. They weren't giggling girlfriends at a sleepover. She burrowed deeper into the blankets.

Todd stayed silent long enough Gilly thought he'd gone to sleep. "What? Like a girlfriend?"

"Someone," Gilly amended at the way he'd sneered the word.

Todd made a low, derisive noise. "Girls like men with money."

"That's not the only thing women like about men." The urge to defend her gender was automatic and not necessarily sincere.

"Well, let me put it like this. They don't like guys without money as much as they like guys with cash," Todd said. "It don't matter if you're nice to 'em. Hell. Some of 'em like it better when you're mean, so long as you've got bank."

The question tripped off her tongue before she could stop it. "So, no girlfriend, ever?"

"I had girlfriends." Todd sounded angry at first, then, quieter. "I had one, once.…"

She waited.

"Her name was Kendra. I met her at work."

"At the diner?"

"No." He sounded gruff. "This was a long time ago,

before the diner. I was working for a landscaping company. Planting trees, hauling brush, that sort of shit."

"Did she work for the landscaping company?"

More silence. She thought he'd fallen asleep. "No. She was…the daughter of a customer."

He didn't really have to say more than that. Gilly could guess the outcome. She made a sympathetic noise, anyway, not necessarily to encourage him but not trying to put him off, either.

"I broke up with her," Todd said.

"Oh." It was so not the scenario she'd imagined— irate customer waving off "the help" to protect his daughter's virtue.

"Yeah, I know," Todd said in a voice dripping with sarcasm, showing he guessed what she'd been thinking. "Who'd have guessed it would be me who bailed, huh?"

"I didn't say anything."

"You didn't have to."

Another few minutes of silence until Gilly said, tentatively, "What happened?"

"She wanted to get married."

"Oh." It wasn't the first time she'd heard about a relationship ending because the woman had wanted more of a commitment than the man. "And you didn't want to."

"Fuck no!" Todd sounded as thoroughly disgusted as if she'd suggested he eat feces.

There didn't seem much to say after that. Gilly closed her eyes and noticed no difference in the darkness behind her lids than when she'd been staring. During the past few years, there'd been many nights Gilly had greeted her husband at the door with her car keys already in one hand, her purse in the other, so desperate to get out of the house by herself she manufactured errands to run. There'd been far fewer times lately that she'd greeted him the way she had in the early days of their marriage, with a kiss and a hug and questions about his day.

Those days seemed faraway now. All of them. The good and the bad, both. The cliché would've been that if she had the chance to greet him at the door again, she'd choose the kiss rather than escape, but listening to the soft sound of Todd's snoring slipping through the chill and black, Gilly wasn't quite able to convince herself it was true.

30

Gilly hadn't watched the television show *Lost* in a long time, not since the end of the second season when the show had totally, well…lost her. Yet there was a moment during the show's first season she would never forget—the part when Hurley's CD player finally gave up and died. She couldn't remember what the character had said to commemorate the occasion, but the words that came out of her mouth were definitely not allowed on network television.

She tugged the headphones from her ears and thumbed the iPod's controls. Nothing. Totally dead. Worse, she'd been listening to a song she didn't even like. She'd wasted the last few minutes of music time on garbage.

Todd had gone outside to bring in some wood for the stove. Now he came in and dumped the logs into the bin. Snorting and stamping, he slapped his bare hands against his thighs and blew into his curled fingers. He looked up at the sound of her curse and raised both eyebrows.

"It's dead," Gilly said in a tone more appropriate to the loss of a pet than an inanimate piece of electronic equipment. She held up the iPod.

Todd toed off his boots and left them to drip snow onto the floor by the door. He shivered, still rubbing his hands together and shook his hair, coated with a light mist of flakes from the seemingly constant snowfall. "That sucks, huh?"

"Yes. It does." Gilly got up, put the iPod on the table.

She hadn't wept in weeks, but she wanted to cry now. Instead she scrubbed furiously at her eyes until they stung and her breath caught in her throat. "It's just an iPod," she said.

She felt him watching her but Todd said nothing, just disappeared into the kitchen. She heard him rummaging around in the drawers. He was back before she had time to even turn around.

"Here." Todd held out a handful of batteries. "There's an old CD player in the cupboard. It should work."

She didn't move toward him to take what he offered. After half a minute Todd sighed, shoulders slumping, and rolled his eyes. He went to the cupboard himself, pulled out the boom box. He brought it to the table and set it beside the iPod, then flipped the CD player on its side to pry open the back and fill the empty slot with the batteries.

"I took them from the flashlight," he said. "If you don't fucking listen to something, I'm going to be pissed off."

The threat sounded empty. Gilly was too touched by the gesture to do more than stare, anyway. Todd sighed again, heavier this time, and stomped upstairs. She heard the scrape of a drawer, then his feet on the stairs. He brought her the CD case he'd rescued from the truck.

"Here." Todd opened it. "Pick something."

Gilly unzipped the case and flipped through the plastic pages. The sight of the silver discs, such a vivid link to her life, made her throat burn. She gave herself a mental shake and forced the feeling away. "Like what?"

Todd took the case from her and looked through the choices. His forehead wrinkled in consternation. "What the hell is this stuff?"

Gilly bit a smile, knowing instantly the reason for his question. Her taste in music was eclectic, to say the least, her iPod filled with everything from classical to reggae. She rarely listened to CDs anymore except in the truck, and the discs she'd chosen to keep in there had all been chosen for their "singability." She had to be able to belt out the lyrics, sing with abandon, and generally make the kind of fool of herself that she could only do in the privacy of her vehicle with no one to hear but the kids.

"Hedwig and the Angry Inch? The Rocky Horror Picture Show? Phantom of the Opera?" He faked a gag. "Don't you have anything good?"

"Hey. All of those CDs are good."

Todd flipped some more pages. *"One Hundred and One Silly Kids Songs? The Wiggles? Jesus, Gilly."*

She smiled. "You might like it."

Todd rolled his eyes and pulled out another disc. *"Simon and Garfunkel. Jason Manns,* who the hell is he? Oh, hell, no. Spare me that folk shit. Okay, this is better. *The Doors.* Greatest hits. Sweet."

"That's my husband's..." Gilly stopped herself. She didn't want to talk about Seth with Todd any more than she already had. "But we can listen to it."

Todd punched the button on the small CD player and inserted the disc. In a few seconds, the first opening strains of "The End" came out of the speakers. He grabbed the bowl of popcorn he'd made earlier and sat down on the couch, long legs stretched out on the coffee table, head back on the cushions.

"This is good."

The music made Gilly restless. At the window, she peered out into the rapidly falling night. More snowflakes, light now but promising to get heavier, drifted down. She hadn't been outside in nearly a month. Todd's footprints still broke the span of white, but with the new snow coming down it wouldn't be long until they disappeared, too.

Jim Morrison's achingly clear voice spouted poetic lyrics that reminded her of college parties, lights dim in the basement of some fraternity house, warm beer and cigarette smoke. The song made her think of Seth, too, who'd owned the CD before they'd met. He'd taken her to see the film *The Doors,* Val Kilmer playing a perfect Morrison, at some college art department film series on their fourth date. He'd bought her popcorn and nonpareils, and later had licked the salt and chocolate from her fingers before leaning over in the dark movie theater to kiss her. Gilly touched the frosted window and watched her fingertips make small, clear ovals in the rime.

She missed him. Missed his strength, his quiet humor. She missed the way he put up with her sniping and complaining, and the way he laughed with her at silly old movies. She missed the scent of him, fresh soap and water, and the way he never failed to squeeze her when she passed him.

She had no tears, not now, not when they would serve no purpose. Watching the snow outside, it seemed impossible it would ever melt. That she would ever be able to get away from this place. It seemed as though she might be here forever, listening to a dead man sing and watching darkness swallow the world.

"What do you think he means, anyway?" Todd's voice broke her concentration, and Gilly jumped a little.

Her fingers skidded in the frost, leaving slashed marks like wounds on the glass. "Who?"

"Morrison." Todd crunched some popcorn. "The killer picks a face from the ancient gallery and all that shit. What's that mean, do you think?"

Gilly tore her gaze from the window to contemplate the man on the couch. "I suppose you could take it to mean that…well…" She struggled to put her thoughts into words. *Her* thoughts, not anything she'd read that someone else had postulated. "That there's a killer in all of us. Or that we can choose our actions. I think he means we can choose the face we wear."

"Gilly." Todd gave her a look. "The fuck's that mean? Choose your face. You get the face you're born with."

"Not your real face." She made a circle with her finger, outlining her features. "Not your eyes and nose and mouth, not like that. The face you put on for people. For the rest of the world. I think he meant you choose that face."

Todd cocked his head. "Huh. You think that's true?"

She nodded. "Yes. I do."

Her answer seemed to satisfy him, because he nodded thoughtfully. But then Todd said, "That's a bunch of crap."

Gilly sniffed. "Why'd you ask if you didn't want to know?"

"I asked what you thought. Doesn't mean I have to agree. What about the rest of it?" Todd reversed the CD for a few seconds until the passage started again. "The blue bus and all that stuff?"

Gilly pondered, aware that for whatever reason, he expected her to have an answer. "Life is a journey?"

She waited for his scoffing.

Todd glanced at her. "Hell, it sure ain't one I want to take on a bus. You ever take a trip on a bus, Gilly?"

She had, several times, to visit a college boyfriend. "Sure." The memory made her smile. "Bus stations are scary."

"You got that right." Todd cocked his head to listen to the music. "Morrison was one fucked-up dude."

"Some people think he was a great poet for his time," Gilly said, uncertain why his casual assessment of the long-dead rock star should affect her at all, much less cause her to rise to his defense. Hell, she didn't even like Morrison all that much, despite his sexy ways and liquid lyrics.

Todd turned up the volume. "The dude wanted to kill his father."

"And fuck his mother," Gilly said matter-of-factly, and was completely unprepared for Todd's reaction.

His face went pale, and his mouth gaped. He turned his attention from the small CD player and stared at her with stunned disgust. He even went so far as to take a step back.

"What?"

Gilly took her own step back from the force of his glare. "That's what he says at the end there...well, at least, that's what people think he meant to say...."

"People are sick!" Todd shuddered. "For crissakes, Gilly, that's sick."

Gilly chewed on her response before saying anything. This was not the first time the topic of motherhood had set him off. And he had mentioned that his mother died. Gilly wasn't sure what to say.

Todd shuddered again and ran a hand over his hair. "You think he really wanted to do that?"

"I don't know," she admitted. "Maybe it's an urban legend or a rumor, but that's what I always thought he meant. It would fit with the whole Oedipus thing, with wanting to kill his father...."

She stopped at Todd's blank look.

"I told you before, I ain't smart."

She hadn't meant to throw his lack of education in his face. "Oedipus is an old story about a man who accidentally kills his father and marries his mother."

"How in the hell do you accidentally kill your father to marry your mom?"

On the CD, "The End" became "Touch Me." She wished he'd asked about that song. It would've been way easier to interpret.

Gilly sighed, not sure she remembered all the details and not up to the task of teaching the Greek classics. "It's complicated."

"Yeah, I bet."

"It's Greek," she said, like that made a difference.

Todd rolled his eyes. "They have good salad and shitty stories."

It took her a minute before she realized he was making another one of his jokes. A giggle almost squeezed out of her throat, but she pinched it off. She might not be able to hate him, but Gilly wasn't ready to laugh with him.

"It wouldn't kill you to laugh," Todd said, as if reading her mind.

But Gilly thought it might do just that. She got up and turned off The Doors and slipped in *Hedwig and the Angry Inch.* "Enough Morrison."

Todd listened to the first few words of the song that came on, and looked as shocked as he had when she told him what Jim Morrison wanted to do to his mother.

"What the…?" He was too stunned even to utter his favorite curse word.

Gilly had chosen the track on purpose to shock him. She felt another giggle coming on, a nasty one this time, but she satisfied herself with an evil grin. "His sex-change operation got botched. It's pretty self-explanatory."

Though she'd removed the CDs from their plastic jewel cases to put them in the travel case, she'd also put in the inner sleeves. Todd pulled out the one for Hedwig and stared in utter amazement at the photo of the man in a bright yellow wig and tons of glam makeup screaming into a microphone.

"Is that a dude?"

"Yes," Gilly said. "I guess you've never seen the movie."

Todd gave her a look. "This is from a movie? Figures."

"It was a good movie," Gilly replied somewhat wistfully. It had been a long time since she'd watched a movie.

Todd waved the travel case. "Why do you listen to this shit. You got a thing for guys in makeup, or what?"

"I guess I have a thing for the underdog." The self-assessment surprised her. Bat Boy. Hedwig. Even poor, misunderstood tragic antihero Frank-N-Furter. All underdogs who met bad ends when the world they lived in rejected them for being who they were.

"If you like the underdog," Todd said, "then you should practically be in love with me."

Without looking at him, Gilly took the CD out and put it back in the travel case. She slid another into the player and hit Play. She thought he'd grumble, but she didn't care. When the music began, she went to the window and pressed her face against the glass to look out at the snow. It was the same view. The same snow. Constant, not changing. As was all of this.

Todd, quiet, took a place beside her at the window. Gilly straightened up, her forehead cold from where it had rested on the glass. They stared out into the darkness, but all Gilly could see was their reflection, blurry. Her and Todd.

"This song," he said, after it had played nearly all the way through.

She looked at him, not in the mirror made by the light inside shining to the outside, but at his face. His real face. "What about it?"

"This one's right," Todd said. "The part where he says I told the truth, didn't come here to fool you. That's a good song."

It ended. Todd left her side and messed around with the CD player's buttons. It was a song Gilly loved, though not the lyric he'd quoted. She thought of the part that made the most sense to her—love was not a victory march.

"C'mon," she told him as the song began again. "I'll make us something to eat."

31

Board games and their dozens of tiny pieces were scattered all over the place. Gilly looked around the room and frowned. "This place is a pigsty."

Todd looked up from the couch, where he'd been silently contemplating the ceiling for the past fifteen minutes. "So clean it up."

Her fingers itched to do just that, but she refused to be a slave to this house. "*You* clean it up."

"I'm relaxing."

"Relaxing implies rest," Gilly said sourly. "Like you've been actually working."

Todd scratched his head with his middle finger, and Gilly fumed. She envied him the ability to sit and stare at nothing for an hour at a time. She crossed her arms and glared.

"Is it nice?" she asked another fifteen minutes later when Todd hadn't moved and she'd been unable to stop herself from putting away the Monopoly game.

Todd looked at her, then. "Is what nice?"

She gestured at the ceiling. "Being entertained by the ceiling? Is that an advantage to being a meathead?"

"I guess it is." Todd smirked.

A strand of hair had come loose from her ponytail, and she grimaced as she tucked it back. She'd bathed every day since he'd forced her out of bed, quick rinses bent over the tub, using tepid water. Nothing thorough or luxurious.

"I want a bath."

Todd flapped a languid hand toward the bathroom. "Go ahead. Who's stopping you?"

In the bathroom, door closed, Gilly flipped him off but felt no better for the gesture. If anything, she felt petty and stupid again, which only made her grouchier. A hot bath would fix her temper. Hot baths could fix a lot of things.

She turned on the taps, which sputtered and spit and groaned but let loose a flood of water that rang against the bottom of the iron tub like Jamaican kettledrums. She grimaced as she stripped out of her clothes and felt the prickly stubble of her armpits and legs. Greasy hair, unshaven legs, no wonder she felt gross and grumpy.

The water had filled the tub only halfway when she thought to run a hand under the stream. It would've been generous to call it lukewarm. Gilly wilted and dipped her fingers into the water in the tub's bottom. That was hot enough, but not deep enough.

She turned off the faucet and yanked on her clothes, then opened the door. "Todd. The hot water's not working."

He looked over his shoulder at her. "Oh. Yeah."

"What do you mean, 'oh, yeah'?" She put her hands on her hips.

He gave her a shrug that had become familiar. "Water heater's probably fucked. And shit, Gilly, it's not like we have a fuckton of propane. Maybe we're running out. In which case we really are fucked."

She swallowed a bitter retort at that. "Really?"

Another shrug.

"Todd!" she cried, exasperated, and left the bathroom to face him. "Are you serious? Why didn't you say anything?"

She hated the grin and the wicked glint in his eyes that told her he enjoyed teasing her. She hated the fact he knew he was getting under her skin even more. She tried forcing her expression to smooth with little success.

"You said you wanted a bath. What was I going to do? Tell you no?"

"I don't want it," she said with tense jaw and narrowed eyes, "if it means we're going to run out of propane. I've suffered with sponge baths up to now. I could get by with it."

Todd got up, stretching to his full height and looked down at her. "This is a hunting cabin. Dudes mostly don't go for long bubble baths. We always had enough hot water for a couple of showers. The water heater's small and it's old. It probably needs time to refill, that's all."

She wanted to punch his arm. Or someplace more tender. "And if it's the propane tank?"

He shrugged a third time. "Then we go without lights and have to use the hand pump outside for water, if that bitch hasn't frozen solid. Heat'll be fine so long as we have wood for the stove."

"You don't sound too worried about it!"

Todd looked at her this time. "Would it matter if I was? Nothing I can do about it. You can't, either."

"How do you check?"

He jerked a thumb at the window. "Tank's out back. There's a gauge." He paused. "Last time I checked, there was plenty, should get us through until spring anyway. Uncle Bill always made sure to top off the tank before winter."

Her mouth tightened. "The last time you…so you know how much we have? We're not close to running out?"

"Nah. I don't think so." Todd grinned, eyes glinting again.

"You're an asshole," Gilly muttered, arms linked tight across her chest.

"Aw, hey."

"Hey, nothing! I was…worried," she admitted, hating it.

"I'm sorry," Todd said.

He sounded as if he meant it, but Gilly wasn't going to take his apology. "You could've told me that before I tried filling the tub."

Todd's brows went up as the corners of his mouth turned down. "How was I supposed to know the hot water'd run out before you could fill the tub? The fuck you think I am, psychic?"

"Well, I know you're not as funny as you think you are!"

Todd's frown tightened. He slouched back to the couch, feet on the table. "Fuck you. Go take a bath. Freeze your tits off. The fuck I care?"

She was not going to freeze, and she *would* have a hot bath. Gilly went to the kitchen and filled the largest pots she could find with water. Also the kettle. While the water boiled, she sorted through the last few fresh items in the refrigerator. She took an apple and some cheese and went to the pantry for a box of wheat crackers.

By the time she'd finished peeling and slicing the apple and cubing the cheese, the water was boiling. Grabbing a set of oven mitts, she carried the pots to the cast iron bathtub and poured them in. She refilled the containers and set them to boil again.

Todd watched her with undisguised interest. "You going to fill up the whole tub that way?"

Gilly put her snack on a plate and sat at the kitchen table to wait for the water. "Yes."

He snorted. "It'll get cold before you're done."

She didn't think so. The tub would hold in most of the heat, and she hoped that by the time the tub had enough water in it for soaking, the boiling water would have become cool enough to bathe in but not too cold. And if it wasn't, it would be simple enough to add some cold water to it.

When she dumped the second set of pots, the tub water was still steaming. However, she needed more water, and faster. Gilly dug around in the bottom cupboards while the next batch of water heated. She found several large, deep stockpots. They were incredibly heavy when she finally got them filled, and she didn't try to put them on the stove. She put them on the woodstove.

"You're wasting good propane," Todd told her.

Gilly shrugged, an echo of him, not worried now that he'd told her there was enough propane to last until spring. "I need a bath. I *want* a bath."

She ate the rest of her food and took another set of

pots to the bathroom. The water in the tub had cooled considerably, but was still luxuriously warm. The pots on the woodstove began to boil next.

Gilly lugged gallon after gallon of boiling water to the tub. She burned her wrists and hands when the water slopped over the sides, and she hurt her back lifting the heavy pots. But she did it.

When she finally shed her clothes and sank up to her chin in the water, she was sure she'd caused herself permanent injury. Every part of her body throbbed and ached even worse than after she'd wrecked the truck. To finally feel clean, though…well, she thought the pain was worth it.

Water had always soothed her. She preferred showers to baths, usually. She loved the way the hot water made steam and pounded down all around her, blocking out the noise of a whining child or the phone or any other of a dozen disturbances. This wasn't as nice as a shower, but it was wonderful all the same.

Floating. Gilly was floating. She'd drifted off to sleep, letting her body slip almost completely beneath the water. Only her face stuck out, just far enough for her to breathe. She didn't dream, wasn't far enough down for that. Gilly simply floated.

Sweet summer corn.

She didn't know why that came into her mind, but now it was all she could think about. Corn on the cob slathered with butter and salt, fresh from the farm stand. The last time she'd eaten corn, she'd bought it from the side of the road. A young Mennonite girl, hair in long braids, her feet bare, had taken the money and counted sufficient change in her head faster than Gilly could've done with a calculator. She'd taken it home and boiled it to eat with burgers on the grill, sliced tomatoes from the garden and home-sliced French fries she'd seasoned with sea salt and fresh-ground pepper.

Gilly's mouth watered as she drifted in the bath, eyes closed. Thinking of summer. Heat. Her stomach rumbled.

Gilly's mother had loved sweet corn. Even in the worst times, when she insisted all she could drink was cola—heavily laced with rum, but nobody was supposed to know it—her mother could be tempted to eat sweet corn. At the end it was all she would eat. Her mother had loved it so much Gilly sometimes felt she should hate it just to be ornery, be different, or because remembering how much her mother had loved it was too painful.

But Gilly didn't hate it. She wanted some, right now, even though it was out of season and she wasn't at home. She was…someplace else, far away, craving something she couldn't have.

The water cooled, and her body protested. Gilly left the haze of sleep to which she'd so gratefully succumbed, and opened her eyes. And screamed.

Todd stood over her. How long had he been watching? Gilly scrambled upright, sloshing water over the side of the tub, wetting the legs of his jeans. Her hands were inadequate for the task, but she tried futilely anyway to cover herself.

He stepped back, expression unreadable. "I thought you drowned. I thought you were dead."

"Go away!" Gilly cried, hunching forward to protect her body from his emotionless eyes.

"Get out of the tub now, Gilly." Todd left the bathroom.

There would be no more peace for her here. Gilly

shivered from more than the chilly air as she got out of the water and dried herself. Her fingers had gone pruney, but her stomach rumbled. She could still taste the memory of sweet corn, but it had gone sour on her tongue.

32

"No more eggs for breakfast. These are the last." Gilly cracked the last two into the challah dough.

Todd stubbed out his cigarette into the puddle of tea in his saucer until Gilly, with a sigh, pushed an ashtray from the cupboard across the table at him. "It's okay. I like your bread."

"Thanks." The word slipped off her tongue far more easily than it would have even a few days before.

She finished kneading the dough and left it on the counter to rise, then went to the sink and cleaned her hands with a scant palmful of soap, mindful of the emptying bottle. Outside, the winter sun glared brilliantly off the still-immense piles of snow. No sign of any melting, and the temperatures hadn't dropped so none seemed likely anytime soon.

Gilly let out a long, hard sigh.

Todd got up to put his dishes in the sink. He leaned against the counter and stretched, cracking his neck. "I need a new pillow."

The ghost of a grin painted Gilly's mouth. "Let me run out and get you one."

Todd didn't laugh. He rolled his head on his neck with a grimace and a bit of a groan. "It always kinks up on me like this after a while. It's from a car wreck I was in. Feels like someone stabbed me with an ice pick."

Gilly raised her eyebrows at him and held up her hands, wiggling the fingers. "Don't look at me."

"Wow. Ha-ha-ha. You know you ain't as funny as you think you are?" Todd rubbed the junction of his shoulder and neck with his fingertips.

Gilly brushed past him and went to the living room, restless. She'd read all the magazines and finished the crossword puzzles. She picked up one of the magazines anyway and sat down with it.

"Will you rub it for me?"

"What? No!" Gilly shrank away from Todd, who'd suddenly appeared before her.

"Please?" He grimaced again. "It really hurts bad."

He sank to the floor in front of her and sat cross-legged. He let his head hang down, and the thick dark hair parted, exposing his neck. A downy line of dark fuzz dusted his skin there.

Gilly stared at him but didn't touch him. "I can't do that. I'm…I'm not any good at massage."

He shot her a grin over his shoulder. "I seen you kneading that bread. Just do the same on my neck. C'mon. Right there."

He waited, and Gilly faltered. She did not want to touch him. And yet, she was tired of being the growling dog. Her defenses were slipping in the face of Todd's constant forgiving spirit.

Gilly put her hands on Todd's shoulders and felt the knots there. "You're really tense."

"No shit."

She spread out her fingers, resting them lightly on the bare skin of his neck. His hair brushed her knuckles. His arms pressed against the inside of her calves.

Todd let out a low, guttural groan as she began the massage. She faltered a moment at the sound but then continued, working the muscles the way she kneaded her dough. He hung his head, allowing her to access the sides of his neck and shoulders.

"That feels good."

Todd relaxed and went boneless under her fingers, but Gilly remained tense. This didn't feel right. At last she had to pull away. Gilly got up from the chair and surreptitiously wiped her hands on the seat of her jeans as she went to the kitchen.

Todd followed. "Why'd you stop?"

"I have to check the bread dough." A blatant lie. Gilly lifted the damp cloth to peek at the rising dough, which didn't need her attention. Her face felt flushed with the untruth, her palms sweaty.

Todd was behind her. She was aware of him, how he towered over her, how the aura of his strength surrounded her. He was so much bigger, taller and broader, that she was made tiny. Gilly turned to leave, to make her escape. His hand on her arm stopped her.

"What's wrong?" Todd asked.

"Nothing."

She shrugged the lie and pushed past him into the living room. It wasn't enough. She needed more distance. Gilly went upstairs and sat on her bed.

"What's the matter with you?" Todd had followed her but stopped at the top of the stairs.

"I have a headache." The third lie slipped out. She lay down, facing away from him, on top of the covers.

"That's what you're supposed to tell your husband, not me."

She didn't look at him, just made a disgruntled sound.

Todd sighed. He wasn't wearing boots and his tread was lighter than usual across the bare floor. "Sorry. I know that wasn't funny. Hey, Gilly, c'mon. Look at me."

She refused. "I'm tired. Let me take a nap."

His weight dented the bed. She still didn't turn. Gilly closed her eyes, willing him to go away. His hand weighted her shoulder, but his touch was gentle. Inquiring, not demanding.

"What did I do?" he asked, in a low voice unlike his normal tone. "Talk to me. Please?"

"You didn't do anything." Gilly rolled into a tight ball, knees to her chest. "I told you, I'm just tired. I have a headache. That's all. Let me sleep."

He sighed and did not remove his hand. "You're acting like I done something real bad to you. Something scary. And I didn't even touch you."

Gilly sat, twisting her body away from him and scooting across the double bed as far as she could to get out of his reach. "No, I touched you."

Todd rolled his head on his neck again. No popping or cracking of the joints this time. No grimace of pain. "Yeah, thanks. It was great."

She shivered. "You don't understand."

His gaze flickered. He tried to joke. "I got cooties, huh?"

She didn't even smile. "I don't want to touch you. Anymore. Ever."

"It's okay to hit me, but not to help me," Todd said, with a touch to his cheek where the faint line of the earlier injuries she'd inflicted still remained. "Making me bleed is okay, though, huh? That's just fine?"

She looked down at her betraying hands. "You couldn't possibly understand."

Todd's mouth thinned. "Christ, Gilly. I didn't ask you to give me a hand job."

"Stop it!" She clapped her hands over her ears. "Stop!"

She could still hear his voice, low, and angry. "Still got to be that growling dog, huh?"

She took her hands away from her ears. "Can you blame me?"

He was not, she realized with some alarm, angry. Todd was upset. His mouth trembled, and did she see a glint of tears in his eyes? He hung his head, making it impossible for her to be sure.

"You act like touching me was going to burn your hands or something." Todd splayed his fingers on his thighs, then gripped the denim of his jeans as though he was trying to stop from clenching his fists. "Like I'm dirty."

Touching him with compassion had made her *feel* dirty. Gilly didn't deny it. She watched him with wide eyes, waiting to see what he would do.

"Is that what you think?" He looked at her with naked honesty in his face. "I'm dirty to you?"

Gilly remained silent. Todd sighed again. He set his jaw, waiting for her to talk to him.

"You ain't going to say anything?"

She shook her head slowly. Todd got up from the

bed and left the room. A few moments later, she heard a tremendous crash that nearly startled her into falling off the bed. More crashes followed, interspersed with cursing.

Gilly crept beneath her covers, shaking, and tried to warm herself. She could close her eyes, but even putting the pillow over her head wasn't enough to drown out the noise. She bit her lip to keep from crying out at every bang and crash.

The silence that followed was worse than the crashing. She waited, aching from breathlessness, to hear the sound of his footsteps on the stairs. She fell asleep waiting for it.

A cry woke her from another dream of roses. Gilly shot straight up in bed, heart pounding so hard she saw bright flashes of light in front of her eyes. The room had fallen into blackness while she slept.

She pressed her hands to her mouth, shaking, listening for the cry to come again. In the first few moments of wakefulness she'd again thought she was home, listening for one of her children. Maybe she would always think that. Now she remembered where she was, knew it couldn't be Arwen or Gandy, but still strained to hear the cry.

It came again from downstairs, lower this time, a sound so filled with grief and agony it brought sympathetic tears to Gilly's eyes. She swung her legs over the bed, waiting to hear it again. It did, the low, destitute cry of a child who's given up on his mother ever coming to comfort him.

It was Todd.

She did not have to go to him. It would've been easy enough to close her ears to his anguish, to roll over in bed and force herself back into sleep. His suffering did not have to become her own. She owed him nothing. Yet she got out of bed and sought him, because listening to his pain without offering solace went against every instinct she had. Gilly couldn't close her heart.

She made her way down the dark stairs. He'd lit candles, not a propane lantern, and the flickering light turned his skin to gold. Todd sat in front of the fire, his familiar pile of crumpled and stained papers in front of him. He held the red folder, creased and also stained, and bulging with what looked like newspaper clippings. The scraps of yellowing newsprint fell from the folder to his lap, covering his knees. Todd rocked from side to side, muttering.

"Todd?"

He whipped around to face her. His eyes were red rimmed and awful looking, like pools of blood surrounding the darkness of his pupils. His cheeks, grown pale from so many days without the sun, had bloomed with two red roses. His mouth worked, and his hands opened helplessly. The rest of the folder fell to the floor. He pressed the heels of his hands to his eyes, fingers tipped with raw, chewed nails.

"Oh, Todd." She said his name softer the second time. Gentler.

He held out the papers to her, a sheaf of clippings falling to the floor like dirty snowflakes. He didn't speak. Gilly forgot all that had passed between them and went to him, knelt beside him. She took the papers.

Squinting in the candlelight, she read the first article. A black-and-white photograph filled most of the page. Five children encircled a woman whose mouth twisted in an insincere smile. She held the sixth, smallest child, a small boy with smooth dark hair and wearing bibbed overalls, in her lap. The headline above the photo didn't match the picture of familial bliss.

One of Six Survives

Gilly was slammed back in time to elementary school. The story had been huge back then with its gruesome details and tragic ending. The worst kind of legend, based on truth but grown from repeated whispers in the hallway, the bathroom, the playground. Everyone knew what had happened. They said if you went up to the church where she'd done it, you could see their ghosts.

"Oh, my God," Gilly breathed. "You're that boy?"

She sifted through the rest of the pile, catching bits of the story here and there. Though she'd been too young to follow the story in the papers or on the news, what she'd heard in school had been pretty accurate.

Boy survives mother's wrath. Five children slain. Mother dies by own hand.

"She said we were going to see Jesus," Todd said in a voice filled with rust and razor blades. "I thought she meant church. She took us there sometimes, when she thought we were being bad, and she'd make us sit in those little benches and pray. The little church back there in the woods. The one her family built way back a couple hundred years ago."

Gilly knew the place. It had always had a reputation of being haunted, even before Todd's mother had killed her children there. A set of famed murderers, the last criminals to be hanged in Pennsylvania, had been buried in the cemetery. It had been a place to go at midnight on Halloween, a place to scare yourself stupid.

"She put us in the Fuego, even though there wasn't

enough seat belts for us all. She always made us wear
our seat belts. But not that night. Katie and Mary sat in
the front with her. Stevie, Joey, Freddy and me were in
the back. Stevie was my oldest brother." Todd pointed
to the tallest boy in the photo.

"My Grandma Essie sometimes called Mama Fertile Myrtle, because she had us six kids in ten years.
Daddy left around the time I was born, just run off with
the truck-stop waitress from Ono, but we all lived with
Grandma and Uncle Bill."

He took a deep, shuddering breath that didn't seem to
calm him. Gilly's legs had gone to rubber, and she was
thankful she was already kneeling instead of standing.
The details of the story had rushed back to her as soon
as he began speaking. It had been told in horrified yet
fascinated whispers, passed from mouth to ear like a
game of telephone. Particulars had been exaggerated,
some lost, but the sadness of it hadn't been diluted.
Even as a kid Gilly had wanted to cry when she heard it.

"She told us to be real quiet, and we'd get to see a star
shower." Todd looked into the fire, the flames reflected
in his eyes. "'Hush up,' she said. 'You'll see Jesus in the
stars.' Katie started to cry because she had to go to the
bathroom, and Mama kept telling her to hush up, hush
up now. It was cold out there in the dark, and spooky,
too. Stevie held my hand because he knew I was afraid.
He was always good like that, I remember. He'd push
me on the swings when nobody else would. He let me
lay down next to him under the old blanket that still
smelled like puke from when Freddy threw up on it,
and we looked out the big glass hatchback up to the sky.
But I didn't see stars.

"I looked, though. I looked hard. I looked hard. Mama left the car running, and she got out once and did something to the tailpipe, but I didn't know what she was doing. She was laughing and talking to herself, like something was really funny. Then she started crying, too. After a while, we started to get sleepy, and Mama said 'It's not enough.' Then she took out the knife.''

Todd stopped. His hands drifted up to bury themselves in his hair, like squeezing his head would press out the rotten memories. He let out a low moan, and though it came from a man's throat, it was a little boy's cry.

"There was so much blood," he said. "And the smell of it, like lightning, like biting on a penny, I couldn't breathe. She took Katie first, and Mary didn't even cry when Mama did her, too. Joey tried to get away but she grabbed him by the shirt and hauled him up front, and she did him, too. Right across the throat, like killing chickens.

"Freddy screamed, and when she was fighting with him, Stevie started kicking at the glass. Stevie was my oldest brother, but he was still just a kid, and that glass wouldn't break. Freddy fell on the backseat like he was broke, just like the doll Katie got one year for Christmas that fell down the stairs. Mama was reaching for us, and all the time she was singing. 'Go to sleep, little baby,' she sang, that song she used to sing when we was wakeful and wouldn't go down at night for her.

"She caught Stevie by the hair, but he was near as big as her, and he pulled away. She couldn't get into the backseat too easy, not with Freddy in the way, gurgling and kicking. Stevie grabbed the jack from alongside us and he whacked that glass window with everything he had. The glass fell in on us. It got in my hair, all sticky and gummy, and all over my clothes.

"Mama yanked Freddy out of the way and went for Stevie. She looked like she'd dipped herself in black paint, and all's I could see was her eyes and her teeth as she grinned. She grabbed Stevie by the back of his shirt, but he pushed me through the hatchback like I wasn't nothing more than air. 'Run, Todd!' he hollered. Then he couldn't say anything else. I fell over the bumper and landed on my head, and that was the only time I saw any stars that night. I was froze to the ground, couldn't run. I heard her scream, and then it was quiet. I stayed there all night, until the cops came."

"Oh..." No endearment seemed right, no matter how much he needed one. "Oh, Todd."

She put her hand on him, and it landed upon a piece of lined notebook paper. Todd looked at her, then down to the paper. He took it from her and opened it, smoothed it out, handed it back.

"She left a note," he said.

Gilly didn't want to see what sort of words a woman who killed her children might have thought important enough to leave behind, but she took the paper. She smoothed it as Todd had done. In the dim candlelight she'd have been happy not to be able to read it, but she could.

Nothing stays clean. Three words only, written in a rounded, careful hand in dark ink gone faded with time. *Nothing stays clean.*

Gilly imagined that would be true for a mother with six children each only a year or so apart. She thought of her own two children and the swath of destruction they left in their path. No, nothing ever did stay clean.

Gilly didn't forget what Todd had done. She didn't forget her vow to escape him in any way she could. She simply put those things aside. She dropped the folder without care, not bothering to notice if the pages in it scattered on the floor. She opened her arms to him in invitation, and without hesitation.

"Come here, Todd," Gilly said, and enfolded him in her arms to weep there until his sobs faded away, and at last, he slept.

33

The next morning, Gilly helped Todd clean up the mess he'd made. Together they swept up broken glass and the shattered remains of one of the dining table chairs. Gilly piled all the papers, the newspaper clippings and the note, inside the battered red file and handed it to him.

"Burn it," Todd told her.

She did without hesitation. Then she went to the kitchen sink to wash her hands, because touching those papers had left her feeling as though she'd laid her hands down in the fly-blown corpse of something only recently dead. Todd waited until she had washed, rinsed, then dried her hands.

"I never told anybody that stuff before." His gaze was earnest, not shifty. "Lots of people knew, but I never told nobody that story. Not the cops, not the Social Services zombies, not the people in the hospital or even my uncle Bill. You're the first person I ever told that story to."

Would she rather have lived her entire life without

hearing that? Definitely yes. But she had heard it, and hearing it, could never forget it. Gilly put the towel back on the hanger.

"Did telling it make you feel better?"

The shaggy head moved from side to side, then hesitantly, up and down. "I don't know for sure. I guess so."

"Sometimes, getting something like that off your chest can make a world of difference." Gilly meant what she said but it still sounded wrong. Sort of patronizing, which wasn't what she felt at all. It was daytime television psychobabble. There was no way talking about what had happened could ever make it better.

"You ever have something bad like that happen to you?" Todd's left hand went habitually to his pocket for the package of cigarettes.

Gilly thought of her mother's "vacations," which were better in many ways than the silent dinners or the bouts of screaming that became weeping. At least, when her mother was in the psychiatric hospital or in rehab, life moved in an orderly fashion. With her mother home, nothing was standard, nothing was reliable. Everything was chaos. Time and prescription drugs had cleared her mother's mind and helped her stop drinking. Before she died of cirrhosis at age fifty-six, Gilly's mother had actually become a woman she felt she could be proud to call "mom."

"No," Gilly said. "Nothing so bad as that."

"Uncle Bill used to say all families had their dirty little secrets." Smoke filtered from Todd's mouth while he spoke. "Ours was just dirtier than most."

"God gives us what we can handle." Again, Gilly wished she could say something more meaningful. Something real that would actually help him, not something regurgitated and lame. "It doesn't seem fair, but that's how it is."

"Pfft. I stopped believing in God when I was five years old. Not sure I can start now."

What kind of God would allow a mother to slaughter her children? Would allow a child to witness it? The same God who would allow a man to take a mother from her children, and a mother to let him take her.

"I guess that doesn't matter, as long as God believes in you." Even as she said them the words tasted false. Sanctimonious. She didn't blame him for rolling his eyes.

Todd's laugh was an ugly sound. "Bullshit. God doesn't believe in fuckall. Do *you* believe that, Gilly? Really?"

"I don't know, Todd." It was the truth. Gilly'd spent her share of years wondering about the existence of a higher power. She'd decided believing in God was easier than not, but the real truth was, she spent very little time praying. Religion had become a set of holidays and habits, not of faith.

"You don't even believe in Jesus."

That was true, too. Gilly shrugged. "Yeah, so? You think Jesus is the only way to believe in God?"

"It's the only way I know about."

"Well," Gilly said gently, because she wasn't trying to lecture or condemn him, "it's not."

Todd shook his head and scrubbed at his face with the back of his hand. He wouldn't look at her just now. Gilly found herself wanting to take his chin in her hand the way she did with Gandy when he'd made a mess and knew he was in trouble.

"She used to tell us Jesus suffered the little children.

Whatever the fuck that meant. I don't think it meant what she thought it meant, anyway. But we…they… suffered. Didn't they?"

Gilly thought the one who'd suffered most had been Todd, the one left behind. The pain the other children had felt had, at least, been blessedly brief. He'd had to live with the pain for his entire life, and there didn't seem any way Gilly could see for something like that to ever fade.

"They were scared," Todd said. "That was the last thing they had in them. Fear."

He did look at her then, brown eyes bright with tears that didn't seem to shame him. Gilly thought of how she'd cradled him the night before, but comfort that seemed all right to give in the dark wasn't the same now the sun had come up. Things had changed between them, but not as much as that.

She could be sincere, though. "I'm sorry, Todd."

His lip curled at her sympathy, and he backed away. "Forget it. It was a long time ago."

He hadn't forgotten it, and how could he, ever? Gilly hadn't forgotten it and she hadn't lived it. She'd never forget it now, either.

Todd turned his back. Walking away. He was giving up on her, and though Gilly didn't necessarily want the responsibility of trying to help him, she found herself speaking anyway.

"When I was about nine years old, my dad started traveling for business. Before that he'd worked normal hours, nine to five or so. He was always home for dinner. But his job changed…actually, he lost his job. He was fired." Gilly drew in a sharp breath. "That's the first time I've ever told anyone that."

Todd cocked his head and drew out a cigarette he held between his thumb and forefinger but didn't light. He didn't say anything. He offered her the comfort of a listening ear the way she'd done the night before, without trying to diminish any part of what she was saying.

"Anyway. He started traveling. Days at a time. Three, four. Or he'd get up early in the morning and be gone until after I went to bed. I didn't know it at the time, but he probably didn't have to work so hard…it was easier for him, I think. Than being at home."

Todd put the cigarette in his mouth and lit it, nodding. His eyes squinted shut against the smoke. He took care to blow it away from her face.

"I was an only child. My mom had been pregnant a couple times before and after me, but hadn't carried to term. It was something with her uterus, it was tipped or something." Gilly had spent the bulk of both her pregnancies worried she'd miscarry the way her mother had, even though there were no indications it was likely.

"So it was just you and your mom?"

"Yes."

"What happened when your dad started traveling?"

Gilly needed something to do with her hands while she told this story and found it in the task of making tea. They'd both drunk a lot of tea over the past few weeks. She filled the kettle and settled it on the burner before turning back to him.

"Well, my mom didn't like it when he was gone. She relied on my dad for a lot. Everything, really. She didn't work. I mean, she had worked, but when I was born she decided to stay home. She hadn't had a baby for other people to raise, she always said." Gilly's voice hitched on that, remembering long hours with her mother reading stories or playing dolls.

From the cupboard she took a mug and added sugar. Holding the mug kept her focus on something other than the story. She felt the weight of Todd's gaze and didn't want to face him, but did.

"It's why I stayed home with my kids."

"Because of your mom?"

"Yes. Because I hadn't had them for other people to raise." Tears burned the back of her eyes and she blinked to keep them from overflowing. This wasn't the time for weeping. This was the time for telling.

Todd smiled faintly. "I had a foster mom once. She stayed home, too. She was nice. She's the one who taught me how to bake cookies."

It was good to hear someone had been kind to him. The kettle whistled and she poured hot water over the tea bag, then took the mug to the table to sit. He followed.

"When my dad was gone, my mom was always more... nervous."

Nervous.

It was what her mother had always called it.

"She drank a lot when she was nervous," Gilly continued in a voice as flat and emotionless as she could make it. It was the only way to get through this. "She was too nervous to cook or clean the house. Mostly she stayed in bed all day."

"I bet that sucked."

That was succinct. Gilly smiled a little. "Yeah. It did. I got myself up in the morning to go to school, and when I got home, she'd still be in bed, all the curtains closed. She kept the bottle in her nightstand. What a fucking cliché."

She surprised herself, but said it again. "A cliché. A fucking stereotype. It was like she'd put herself in some Tennessee Williams play. Pathetic!"

The mug warmed her hands, even though she had no desire to drink the tea. It sloshed, burning her fingers. Gilly didn't let go of the mug; if she did, she might make a fist. If she made a fist, she might use it to punch something. A wall, the door, herself.

She could tell Todd didn't know Tennessee Williams, but it didn't matter. He understood what she meant. He nodded. Gilly kept talking.

"One day, I was late coming home from school. I'd gone to a friend's house to play. I didn't tell my mom, or even call. I knew she wouldn't get out of bed to answer the phone, and we didn't have an answering machine. God. That was so long ago."

"I've never had one," Todd offered with a laugh. "Hell. I never even got a cell phone."

Both of them contemplated the turning of time and technology for a moment.

"I knew she'd worry about me," Gilly said softly. "I think I wanted her to."

"What happened?"

"I got home. She was in her room. I could smell something bad, really strong. I went in, and…" Gilly swallowed hard against the memory and had to close her eyes for a minute to clear her brain. To make it just a memory, not something she was reliving. It was hard.

Todd breathed out. Gilly breathed in. She opened her eyes.

"She'd smashed all her perfume bottles. And the

bottle of booze. She'd broken the mirror on her vanity table, too. There was glass everywhere. I ran into the room in bare feet—Mom always insisted on taking off our shoes in the house, even when she wasn't keeping up with the cleaning. Anyway, I ran in, right onto the glass. It cut my feet pretty bad." Gilly gripped the mug. "She wasn't cut at all."

"Of course she wasn't." Todd sneered. "She'd have been careful, right?"

Gilly looked up at him, no longer surprised at his insight. "Yes. She was careful not to hurt herself. She was crying, though. Blaming my dad for being gone, me for being late. Saying over and over again how nobody loved her. Not enough. I went to her on bleeding feet and tried to tell her I loved her, but it wasn't enough. Nothing was. Not when she was…nervous."

"Shit. No wonder you don't drink."

He had a way of summing it up her husband had never managed. It felt disloyal to think that, but it was true. Seth couldn't comprehend what it had been like for her, growing up. Seth's parents believed they meant well and were interminably pushy and self-centered, but nevertheless "normal." If any family could ever be considered nondysfunctional, which Gilly doubted.

"I needed four stitches in my foot. I called the ambulance myself. She wanted to drive me. I wouldn't let her. I knew she'd been drinking."

Todd leaned the chair, balancing, his hands laced behind his head. "You were a smart little kid."

"Yeah. Well. You see why I laugh when you say someone 'like' me."

His chair came down. "But you don't laugh."

Gilly could now sip from the mug, the story finished and tea cool. "Hmm?"

"You don't laugh," Todd pointed out. "Not ever. I've never heard you laugh."

Gilly met his eyes. "I have nothing to laugh about right now."

Todd's eyes narrowed, his mouth pursed, but he gave her a curt nod. "Oh. Right. Stupid me."

If only whatever this was between them could be balanced as easily as he balanced his chair, she thought as he pushed away from the table and left the kitchen. She didn't go after him. Gilly sat and drank her tea, even though it had gone cold, instead.

34

They'd given up on the radio. Even with batteries stolen from the CD player it picked up nothing more than static. Todd finally snapped it off and blew a ring of smoke into the air.

"Must be the snow," he commented with a wave to the window. Outside, more snow fell as dusk began coating the trees. "Messing up the signal."

Gilly nodded. She walked from one end of the room to the other, pacing. Going stir-crazy. Weeks of regular snow had kept them indoors, and her last foray outside had made her leery about going out even for a few minutes. A line from a television production of *Pride and Prejudice* suddenly came to her.

"Won't you join me in a turn about the room? It's so refreshing."

Todd looked at her as if she'd lost her marbles. A wild gust of laughter threatened to burst out of her mouth, but Gilly bit it off like a piece of licorice, chewed and swallowed her mirth though it stuck in her throat. She waved a hand at him.

"It's from a book."

"You and books," Todd said.

"You should read one sometime," Gilly told him loftily.

Todd snorted. "I've read books. Stroke books."

Gilly wrinkled her nose. "Todd. Gross."

He laughed, loud and long, and pointed at her. "Gotcha. No, seriously, I've read books."

She didn't read as much as she used to. Not enough time. She missed it, though. "Yeah? Like what?"

Todd shrugged. "I like horror. And science fiction."

"Me, too." Gilly perched on the edge of the chair. "Like what?"

Todd gave her another look. "You want me to tell you about what books I read?"

"Yes. Maybe I've read them, too. We could talk about them."

"The fuck you think this is, *The Oprah Show?*" Todd laughed again and shook his head. "Right."

"Never mind. Don't tell me." Gilly sighed and started pacing again.

To the window. To the door. To the kitchen, where she filled a glass with water and drank only half before dumping it down the drain.

Todd gave her another look but settled back onto the couch. Again, she envied him the ability to sit for long periods of time doing nothing. Now, however, she did not cruelly assume the skill came from his lack of intelligence. Now she imagined the trait had grown within him out of necessity.

"I liked this book called *Swan Song,*" Todd offered. "You ever read that one?"

"No." Gilly turned from the sink and looked at him from under the hanging cabinets dividing the living room from the kitchen, then came around to lean in the doorway. "What's it about?"

"Nuclear war. Bunch of bombs go off and then the people have to survive nuclear winter. It scared the shit out of me as a kid," Todd said with a grin. "I read it about four times. Took me for-fucking-ever, though. It's really long."

"I wish I had a book now," Gilly said.

Todd looked around, frowning. "Yeah. Sorry. Uncle Bill wasn't much of a reader, and I didn't think about it when…well. You know."

She did know and didn't really want to go over all that ground again. She left the doorway to look out the front windows. Snow and more snow. She sighed.

Her stomach growled, but the thought of actually eating made her want to gag. A twinge of headache ran behind her eyes, telling her to sit down and close them or suffer the consequences. Gilly made a place for herself on one of the couches, plumped the sagging cushions, rescued a crocheted afghan from one of the drawers in the armoire. She laid her head back, letting her body sink into the barely comfortable couch.

"What's your favorite book?" Todd asked.

"I have so many, I'm not sure I could pick one."

"If you had to," Todd said.

She turned her head to look at him on the couch's other end. "Oh. Maybe the collected works of Ray Bradbury. Something like that. I could read all those stories over and over again."

"Ray Bradbury!" Todd's eyes lit. "Electric Grand-mother."

"You know it?"

"Yeah, sure. I used to wish for one." Todd was silent for a moment, and when he spoke again his tone wasn't sad or wistful, just resigned. "Of course I never had one, I mean, even if they were real I'd never have been able to get one. But I always thought it would be great to have."

"Yeah," Gilly said.

They fell into companionable silence.

Did she sleep, or only dream? In the silence, and with only the flickering red-gold light from the woodstove to illuminate the room, Gilly didn't know for sure. This was different from earlier, when she'd sought the realm of sleep to escape reality. Now she embraced the reality of being here, the snow outside, the man slouched at the other end of the couch. Cigarette smoke tickled her nose, and the glowing ember of the tip of Todd's Marlboro winked at her.

Only a few weeks ago she'd never have sat this way with him. Things were different now. After what he'd told her, how could they not? Gilly rescued stray kittens, donated her time and money to the local soup kitchen, was always the first to weep at the tragedies she saw on the evening news. She couldn't have hardened her heart against Todd any more than she could've refused to go to her children when they wept for her in the night.

She knew the date only because she could see it on the dial of her watch. February, the coldest and dankest month. The one with Valentine's Day right in the middle, a made-up holiday people needed just to get through—and someone had made it shorter, too, knowing that February just couldn't be borne for thirty days. It was only February.

But March would come soon, and with it, warmer days. Days when the snow would melt and she could… she could…

Gilly opened her eyes to the yellow glow of the propane lantern and the sight of Todd banking the fire for the night. She would not think of March now, not when she could do nothing to hasten its arrival.

"Ready for bed?" Todd asked her.

She rose lazily from her self-made nest and nodded, surprised to find herself tired after the hours of inactivity. "Yes."

He climbed the stairs in front of her, leading the way with the light so she would not trip. He gave her the lantern to put on her dresser, then turned away without being asked to give her privacy while she dressed for bed.

"Good night," she called across the partition as she turned out the light. It was the first time she'd ever said the words to him.

Later, his moans woke her from dreamless sleep. Gilly blinked in the darkness, confused for a moment before remembering where she was. She heard the shuffling of sheets, the whisper of bare feet on the wooden floor.

She didn't need the light to know he was there. Todd hesitated in the opening of the partition. Gilly had been woken countless times by just such an apparition, albeit one usually much smaller, but with the same intent.

She flipped back the covers and slid over, whispering: "It's all right. You can come in."

Anxiety filled her for one moment, for despite all

he'd shared with her, Todd was not a child. He slid in beside her, his own heat radiating like an oven even though he'd been standing in the frigid air.

"I have bad dreams, sometimes," he whispered.

"It's okay." Gilly pushed him onto his side so she could curl against his back. She pressed her cheek to the softness of his T-shirt, took the warmth he provided and prepared to offer comfort of her own. "So do I."

35

Todd laid the yellow three on top of the blue three, and crowed, "Uno!"

Gilly sighed dramatically. "I don't have any threes... or any yellows..."

He hooted and rapped the table with his hands, managing to do a victory dance while still seated. Gilly pretended to reach for the draw pile, but then drew back.

"Oh, wait," she said. "I do have this wild card...the one that says Draw Four."

She put the multicolored card on the pile and smirked. "Uno. The color is red."

Todd narrowed his eyes at her. "You suck."

Gilly rolled her eyes. "And you're a poor loser."

"No, I ain't." Todd grinned, and Gilly had to look away so as not to let herself be taken breathless with how the smile swept his face into beauty. "I can still win."

He proved it by picking up four cards and slapping down a red skip card, followed by a yellow skip card.

Gilly, who could no longer use her remaining red card, had to draw from the pile.

"Me and Uncle Bill had some pretty good Uno tournaments," Todd said as he gathered up the scattered cards to reshuffle. "Don't feel bad."

"I don't."

He shot her a glance. "What would you be doing if you was home, now?"

The question startled her. "What?"

Todd dealt another hand of cards. "What would you be doing?"

Gilly crossed her hands on the table and stared down at them. "I wouldn't be playing Uno."

He waited for her to speak. She heard the soft rise and fall of his breathing and became intensely aware of his gaze upon her. Hot, like a flame held too close to her skin.

"It's ten-thirty on a Sunday morning," Gilly said. "I would probably be at the synagogue, watching the door during Hebrew School."

His puzzled look showed her he didn't understand.

"The synagogue is always locked," Gilly explained. "During Hebrew School hours, a parent volunteers to sit in the office to push the button to open the door for anyone who needs to get in."

"Why's it locked? I thought churches were always open."

"Unfortunately, some people don't have the same open minds as others about religion," Gilly said lightly, and raised her head to see Todd looking confused. "There were some threats to the synagogue. The congregation decided it was better to lock the doors for safety."

"That's fucked-up."

"Yeah, well, it's a fucked-up world."

Todd rearranged his cards. "And after that? What would you do then?"

She thought, her throat tightening but glad to talk of it. "I'd take Arwen, and we'd go to the grocery store for some things. Come home. Fix lunch. Clean the house. Do laundry. Maybe we'd go to the movies, if there was something good for the kids. Maybe we'd go out to dinner, or order a pizza. Sunday's family day."

Todd put down his cards, got up from the table and went to the window. From the tense line of his shoulders, Gilly could tell something had upset him. She carefully gathered the cards and put them back into their box.

"It sounds real nice," Todd said finally.

"It is."

He turned to her. "Your kids are lucky. You're a good mom."

A good mother wouldn't be here. Gilly rested her head in her hands for a moment, plagued by a sudden onset of weariness that made her want to cry. The moment passed, leaving behind only a vague nausea that unsettled her stomach.

She hadn't disagreed aloud, but now Todd argued with her silence. "You are. You give your kids stuff… love and stuff."

She didn't say, *Of course.* For Todd, there could be no *Of course* about it. What was natural and expected from a mother hadn't existed for him.

She motioned for him to sit back at the table. She took his hand, held his arm out flat against the wood.

She pushed his sleeve up, gently, and touched the inked pattern. She knew what it meant now.

"One of six," she murmured.

This time, Todd didn't jump away from her. Below her fingertips, his pulse jumped. Gilly touched the tattoo again before withdrawing.

"I used to be one of six," Todd said, voice hoarse, eyes bright. "But then I was the only one."

"What happened to you, after?" Gilly asked quietly.

He hunched his broad shoulders. "They took me to the hospital. But there was nothing wrong with me. The blood...it wasn't mine. They made me sleep there."

"Alone?"

"There was a big room, with a bunch of kids...." He stopped. "But they were all there because they were sick. Some of them were crying because it hurt them. I didn't cry."

Gilly bit the inside of her cheek, the spot tender with old scars from many bites. "What about your Grandma? Uncle Bill?"

Todd shuddered, then seemed to catch himself. "They called my Grandma to tell her what happened. Grandma...had a bad heart, Gilly."

The story grew worse. Gilly put her hand over his. "Oh, Todd."

His sigh was like the bitter wind outside. "I didn't know she died until they came to take me away. They took me to a foster home. It smelled like cat piss and baby puke. They didn't let me take my nonnie..." He looked embarrassed. "My blanket. You know, like babies have? But I was five. They didn't let me have it."

Her heart broke a little more at the picture of Todd as a child. "And then what?"

She didn't prompt him out of her own need to listen to the story. They were past that, anyway. Todd needed to tell her these things. She would never have thought she'd want to understand him. But that was before.

"They sent me to another place, after a while. They brought me some of my stuff, but they didn't know they gave me some of Freddy's stuff, too. His shirts. One shirt he had, it had the Dallas Cowboys on it. I always wanted it, but he'd never let me wear it. They brought me that shirt, and I put it on, and it still smelled like Freddy. I wouldn't let the foster mom wash it. She got real mad at me. Finally, when I was at school, she took it and threw it away. Because it stank so bad, she said. She didn't know it was all I had of my brother."

Her throat closed. She remembered cleaning Arwen's room of its collection of broken toys, discarded playthings, clothes that had become too small. Junk her daughter had loved and wept to discover gone.

"How many homes?" Gilly asked.

Todd ran a hand through his hair and looked at her sideways. "A lot. I started being bad. I don't know why, except being bad made me feel better. I didn't *want* to be bad. I just was."

Just as he didn't want to keep her. He just was. Gilly didn't point that out, though she was pretty sure he was thinking it, too.

"The Social zombies started making me go to a shrink. I had four different homes in two years before they put me in the group home. I lived there until I was twelve."

Gilly waited for the rest of the story. She sat patiently, without moving. Watching him. The weak February sun cast lines on his cheeks, highlighting the dark scruff with hints of gold.

"I almost burned it down." Todd waited for her response, which Gilly purposefully masked. "They sent me to the hospital for that."

"For attempted arson?"

He shook his head. "For attempted suicide. I poured gasoline on myself and tried to light a match." He laughed. "Damn wind kept blowing the fucking thing out. They said it was a suicide attempt. I don't know. It probably was."

"How many times did you try?" Gilly asked, horrified yet fascinated.

"On purpose?" He thought a moment. "Three on purpose. Fire. Pills, twice. How many times just by doing stupid shit, hoping it would be the last time I had the chance? A lot more."

Todd stood and lifted his shirt over his head. It was the first time she'd seen him completely bare, and her heart thudded in her throat at the intimacy of the sight. His chest was smooth, dark nipples surrounded by a smattering of sleek black hairs. Muscles corded in his biceps and shoulders as he moved, though his stomach was soft. The white scar rippled across his belly; Gilly flinched at the sight though she'd seen it before. A smaller, deeper scar dimpled the flesh next to his navel.

Todd pointed to both of them. "I crashed my car doing eighty around a curve when I was seventeen. This is where they took out my spleen. This is where they stuck a tube in me to drain out all the bad shit."

Gilly made a sad noise.

"But I always fucked it up," Todd said with forced

lightness. "Couldn't even kill myself right. Stupid fucking loser. Always fucked it up, let someone find me…."

"Maybe…maybe you didn't really want to die," Gilly said. "Maybe…"

"Don't give me that cry for help shit, Gilly." Todd shook his head and pulled his shirt back on. "I wanted to die. I'm just too fucking stupid to pull it off."

"What changed your mind? What made you decide living would be better?"

He looked at her with his sideways glance. "What makes you think I did?"

"You're here," she pointed out. "Not in the ground."

Todd lifted the edge of his shirt. His hand went to his waist, and he unsnapped the leather holster. He pulled out the knife. The blade glinted in the sunlight as he turned it from side to side so she could see every inch of the long blade.

"Once you asked me what I came up here planning to do." Todd let the blade rest lightly on the skin of his forearm. When he took it away, a thin line of blood remained.

"You told me 'nothing.'"

"I lied," Todd told her. "Did you ever feel so bad you wanted to die?"

She had not. Even during the worst times in her youth, she'd clung to the idea of life with desperation. If she lived, she knew she would grow up and eventually get away from the horror of living with her mother. If she died then, she'd die with grief in her heart.

But it wasn't hard for her to understand the pain that must've driven Todd to thoughts of suicide. Gilly, who could perhaps imagine better than some people how a mother's betrayal affected a child, could only begin to imagine how deeply Todd's mother's death had messed him up. She'd never wanted to die, but she knew too well the craving for oblivion.

"I ain't never been good at anything," Todd said. "Not in school. Not even shop. I can't make things. I ain't good with my hands. Can't hold a job for shit. Can't even rob a damn liquor store without getting caught."

His litany urged her to murmur "It can't be that bad," even as she knew it must be.

"Girls don't like me," Todd continued. "No chick wants to hang out with a dumbass like me with no job, no money, a jail record. Least, not any girl I'd like to hang with. Not nice girls…not like you."

Gilly put the cards back in the box, guessing their game was over. She didn't remind him of the girl he'd said wanted to marry him. In her palm, the box of cards felt slick and cool. Heavier than it looked.

"You know that's not true, Todd."

"You're not nice?"

She looked up at him, their eyes meeting with neither flinching away. Gilly shook her head a little. The inside of her cheek felt torn and raw; she chewed it anyway in lieu of an answer.

Todd studied her. He reached in his pocket, stroking the crinkly wrapping of his pack of cigarettes, but didn't pull one out. "You're good, Gilly. I'm not."

"Oh, Todd."

How many times had she said this, now? How many more would his name come from her lips that way? Gilly's chair rocked, but she didn't get up. She clenched the cards tight, tighter. "You have this idea about me, but you don't really know me at all."

He reached across the table and flicked the ends

of her hair, unsecured in its usual ponytail. Then her sleeve, her shirt the one she'd been wearing the day he got into the passenger seat beside her. "Look at you."

"It has nothing to do with what I look like."

"I know that." Todd's quiet dignity was a splinter in her skin, stinging. "Anyway. I figured, if I kept going on the way I was, I was going to get sent back to jail. Guys like me just don't turn their lives around, Gilly. I'm not smart enough to do it, and I can't work hard enough, either." He paused, looking out the window. "A guy like me...I figure I was gypped out of a lot of good stuff, and it really pisses me off."

His expression darkened, and his hands clenched on the table. "Seems like I been in some sort of jail all my life, Gilly. And I swore I'd never go back. They...they do stuff to you in jail."

He didn't elaborate with words, only with a shudder and a grimace of disgust. "Worse even than some of the homes I was in. They hurt you in jail. I figured...fuck. I figured there'd been a lot of shit in my life I didn't get to choose. I thought it was time I got to decide what happened to me."

"That's why you didn't care about the truck. About being found. You didn't intend to be caught."

She thought he might get angry. Todd touched the knife on the table between them. His fingers tightened on the handle, and he tilted the blade again to catch a ray of weak February sunshine. It was the kind of knife a hunter used to gut a deer. It was the knife he'd pointed at her throat on that evening what seemed a lifetime ago. Now he moved it back and forth and made something pretty with it, sunshine in stripes on the table.

"You know how easy this knife cuts?" he said quietly. "It's real sharp. I made sure of that. It won't snag on anything. It'll just cut. Human skin's not even an inch deep, you know that? But most people who cut themselves to die, they do their wrists. The blood clots."

He drew the flat of the knife crossways over his wrist, then up from the heel of his hand to his elbow. "You're supposed to go down the lane, not across the street. You ever hear that?"

"No."

"It works better that way. But you know what works even better than that?" He looked at her.

She looked back. "Todd, don't."

He put the flat of the blade to his throat, then turned it so the edge pressed lightly. His skin dented. "Cutting the carotid artery would fuck you up pretty good. It's how I'd do it. I thought it all out. One quick slice, and it would be all over. No coming back from that, really. You'd have to be one lucky prick to get through that."

He looked at the knife. "I've never been lucky."

Gilly had nothing more to say than that. Any words she'd find would be empty. Useless.

Todd put the knife back in its sheath on his belt and pulled his shirt down over it. He put his head in his hands for a moment. When he looked back at her, his face was bleak. "I figured I deserved it, you know? Just once. To decide what happened to me."

She couldn't disagree with that, but she tried. "It doesn't have to be…"

"No. Look at you, sitting there. Tell me I'll get out of this, Gilly. Tell me you'd be able to convince any-one I didn't take you on purpose. Hell, see if that even matters if it was by accident. I still did it. I still took the truck, I still took you. Tell me anything you could say would make a difference." He tilted his head, studying her. "Tell me you'd say anything, anyway. Tell the police you ran away with me, right? You'd never."

"I have no idea what I'll say," she told him honestly. "But I could tell them it was a mistake. It *was* a mistake, Todd."

"There isn't any room in my life for more mistakes."

She believed him when he said he couldn't survive another stay in jail. "Why didn't you do it?"

"You," Todd said simply. "I didn't do it because of you."

"I couldn't have stopped you." And wouldn't have, not when he'd first taken her. Now? Now Gilly wasn't sure what she would do should he take the knife from the table and slash at himself with it.

She'd bind his wounds, she thought suddenly. She would do what she could to save him, if she could. She wouldn't let him die in front of her any more than he'd allowed *her* to perish in what had been as much a suicide attempt as he'd planned.

Todd shook his head. "At first, you had me so rattled I didn't know what to do. Then, you were so sick…I couldn't just let you die up here. Couldn't have that one more mess on my head, you know?"

She nodded. "Yes."

Todd tugged on his shirt hem, covering up the scars no mother's love had ever soothed. He went to the window and looked out at the blinding whiteness of the snow. "I'm not so sure I want to die anymore, Gilly."

Gilly didn't ask him what had changed his mind. She didn't want to hear his answer, didn't want to accept responsibility for his decision not to take his life. But she thought maybe she already had.

"Tea?" she asked instead, because that was safe.

Todd didn't turn from the window. "Yeah. Sure."

Gilly boiled the water, and they sat at the table and drank cup after cup until it was gone. Their silence was not hostile. It was the quiet of two people who didn't need to speak to know what the other was thinking.

36

Todd refused to listen to any more of what he termed "that freaky music." So they stuck to The Doors, some Simon and Garfunkel, and an old Guns N' Roses CD Gilly'd forgotten she had.

Gilly found a thousand-piece jigsaw puzzle in one of the armoire drawers, and she set it up on the dining room table. She didn't like jigsaw puzzles any better than crosswords, as a rule, having neither the patience nor the time to devote to their creation. But here she had nothing but time, even if her patience hadn't grown. The puzzle was a hard one, an intricate mess of swirling colors without rhyme or reason. Gilly hated it, loathed it, despised, abominated and abhorred it…but every piece set into its proper place gave her an immense satisfaction that had quickly become addictive.

She glanced up from the puzzle to see Todd in a corner of the room, whaling away on an air guitar to "Welcome to the Jungle." His dark hair fell across his face as he strummed the imaginary instrument.

"Wyld Stallynz," she murmured to herself, but he heard her.

With no embarrassment, he turned to her. "What?"

"You remind me of that movie with Bill and Ted," Gilly said.

He could always surprise her. With a cock of his head and a smile, a mere hand gesture, Todd transformed himself into the character from the movie.

"Bogus! Party on, dude!"

"You've seen the movie, I take it," Gilly said dryly.

Todd struck a pose with his invisible guitar. "Yeah. Never thought I looked like Ted, though. That dude is good-looking."

"You're—" Gilly clipped the words and looked down to her puzzle, her cheeks heating.

She didn't want him to get the wrong idea, not when their co-existence was so precarious. She picked up a piece, set it against one, fitted it beside another. When she finally looked at him, his face was stormy.

"Don't make fun of me," he said. "I know I'm an ugly cuss."

With another man she might've thought he was fishing for a compliment or trying to make her uncomfortable. Gilly bit her lip and sighed, cursing her own inconstant tongue. She set the puzzle pieces down.

"Did someone tell you that?"

He shrugged in a way that showed her the answer was yes. Gilly tapped her fingers on the table. The people in Todd's life hadn't been very kind.

"You're not ugly." Gilly touched the puzzle lightly. "I don't know who told you that, but they were wrong."

"Monkey boy," he muttered, and the way he said it showed it had not been a term of endearment. "Big hands, big feet. Always tripping over myself. Always making a mess of things. I wasn't little and blond and cute like Ricky Buckwalter, who stole money from the housemother's purse and bought weed."

"Todd, you aren't ugly." Gilly put firmness into her voice, the voice of authority.

He gave her his sideways glance and the ghost of a smirk. "Right, I'm a regular fucking Keanu Reeves."

Todd didn't have that actor's smoothness, his ethereal beauty. The resemblance was slight, a similarity in the eyes and the hair, in the curve of his jaw. His grin had the same goofy light as Ted Logan in *Bill and Ted's Excellent Adventure,* but Todd was not that man. He was Todd himself. Unique.

Gilly shook her head. "Bogus."

"Shit." Todd frowned. "If I looked that good I'd have been swimming in pu—girls. Ah, well. Girls...shit. All's they want is to get married, have babies...and I know I won't ever do that."

"Why not?" Gilly ran her fingers over the puzzle pieces, hoping for some intuition that would lead her to the one that would fit next. It was hard work, this puzzle. Took a lot of thought. It was why she liked it even though she hated it at the same time.

"Like I'd make somebody a good father," Todd said scornfully. "Right."

Gilly, puzzle piece in hand, looked at him thoughtfully. "Maybe you would be a good father, because you would have learned all the things not to do. You'd do the opposite."

"Bad seed."

"What?"

Todd pointed at himself. "I got bad seed. You think I

ought to go out and spread that around? Think of what I come from, Gilly. You think any kid deserves a dad like me?"

"There are plenty of people who come from worse who don't give a damn how many kids they spawn. Lots of people don't deserve to be parents, but they go ahead and have kids anyway."

"I guess I did at least one good thing with my life, then," Todd said with a grin. "I always used a rubber and I never knocked anybody up."

"Well, amen to that," Gilly said, and fit another piece into the puzzle. She let out a hoot of pleasure. "Yeah!"

"You've got a pretty smile," Todd told her in a wistful tone that froze Gilly's hand over the scattered pieces on the table.

"Go put in another CD," she told him without looking up. "I'm tired of Guns N' Roses."

He did as she asked, and didn't mention her smile again.

37

"I'm bored!" Todd groaned and flopped onto the couch. He flung his arm over his head. "Damn, Gilly! I'm so fucking bored I could get a hard-on watching paint dry."

She grimaced. "Ew."

Todd sighed and squirmed to look at her. "Why do you always say 'ew' like that?"

"Because you're crude when you talk about sex."

He gave a snort of laughter. "Sorry. You want me to talk about surveys?"

She ignored his wiggling eyebrows, though the thought of surveys being her porn seemed funnier now, in retrospect. "Find something to do."

"Like what?"

"It's not my job to entertain you," Gilly said calmly.

She'd said that often, at home, up to her ears in laundry and dinner and the scrubbing of toilets. What excuse did she have here? She left the horrendous puzzle and peered out the front window.

The sun was bright. It looked warm, though she knew the temperature outside remained bitter. Still, with layers of clothes…

"Can't we go outside?" she said.

Todd sat up. "It's colder than a vanilla ice cream cone up a polar bear's ass out there!"

Gilly rolled her eyes. "So? We've been cooped up in here for too long." She wrinkled her nose. "It stinks in here. We should go outside, get some fresh air."

"Are you nuts?" He got up from the couch and crossed to the window. "What do you want to do out there?"

"I don't know," Gilly said. "We could build a snowman."

Todd barked out a laugh. "Yeah, right."

"Okay, a snow woman," Gilly said. "We can give her great big boobs if you want. Like Pam Anderson."

Todd's laugh was more genuine this time. "I never built a snow woman. Or a snowman."

"What?" Gilly looked at him in surprise. "Never?"

Todd shifted uncomfortably. "There was never anyone… I never…"

She put her hand on his arm. "It's okay. I get it."

She suddenly felt very bad for him. Worse even than before. As if sensing her pity, Todd scowled.

Suddenly desperate to go outside, Gilly quickly changed the subject. "I guess it's about time, right? C'mon. Let's do it."

She could see his growing excitement with the idea. He was as transparent as Arwen and Gandy. His grin faded for a minute, as he looked down at her feet.

"You don't have boots."

She'd forgotten. It had been weeks since she'd entertained the idea of running away. Gilly faced him squarely. "Did you throw my boots away?"

Todd hesitated. He looked from her feet to the window, then raised his gaze to hers. "No. I just took them away so you couldn't—"

She cut him off, wanting for the moment to forget his reasons. "But you have them."

He nodded, slowly. "But, Gilly…"

She reached out and took his hand. "Todd. I won't run away. Not now. How far would I get, even with boots? The snow is three feet deep out there, deeper in the drifts. I don't even know where I am."

She wasn't convincing him. His warm fingers twitched against her palm. He bit at his lower lip, worrying it. When he looked her again, she could tell he was going to say no.

"I got to know…"

"What, Todd?"

He sighed. "I want to know you won't run away…"

"I won't. I told you that."

He made a face of frustration. "No. Not because of the snow, or any of that. Just…because."

Gilly dropped his hand and took a step back. "You want me to say I won't run away because I don't want to?"

Slinking dog faced growling dog.

"Yeah."

"No." Gilly's voice was ice. "I can't say that. You know I can't."

He reached for her hand, but she pulled it away. "How come?"

"I would be lying."

His face turned hard. "Then stay inside."

All at once the need to go outside burned inside her brighter than any desire she'd had for months. Any desire she could ever remember, as a matter of fact. Gilly drew herself up, not nearly as tall as Todd but making herself bigger. "You'd spite yourself to hurt me?"

"If that's what you want to call it," Todd told her.

"We're both bored," Gilly said in a low voice. "We both want this. We both *need* this."

"Yeah? Maybe I need a lot of things. Going outside to play in the snow ain't one of them."

She turned from him to hide the tears of angry frustration. "Fine. Be a stupid asshole."

"Don't call me that!" His hand gripped her shoulder, turning her.

She yanked herself from his grasp. "Don't you raise your hand to me!"

His eyes were flat, black, obsidian. The eyes of a snake. She had time to marvel again at how quickly he could change, but then he'd grabbed her. Pulled her close.

"Tell me," he ordered.

"No!"

"Why not?"

She wasn't proud of her temper. She could blame tight quarters and circumstance for it, but in the end would know it was simple bitterness with no excuse. It was just her. The way she was built. It didn't matter what triggered it, Gilly had the choice to hold her tongue and didn't.

She sneered and dug where it would hurt the most. "You really *are* stupid if you can't even figure that out."

"You're still thinking about it? Getting away? Fucking up my life?"

"You fucked up your life, not me!" Gilly twisted fruitlessly in his grip. "Don't you blame me! Blame yourself!"

"You'd have them send me back to jail in one second, wouldn't you?" His breath was hot on her face. "One fucking second."

"I thought," Gilly said harshly, "you were going to kill yourself before that could happen. And why not? Maybe that would be the best thing for you!"

He pushed her away from him so hard she stumbled backward. "The fuck are you trying to do? You want to make me so mad I—"

"Don't you threaten me!" Gilly cried. She'd twisted her ankle and it throbbed, but she refused to even wince. "Don't you dare!"

"Quit riding me! Get off my back!" Todd advanced on her.

He was like a great wolf, snarling. Gilly stood her ground. Toe to toe, he towered over her, but Gilly didn't move.

If anything, she forced herself to stand taller. Look him in the eyes. "You want me to lie to you? I give you honesty, and you want lies?"

"Why not?" Todd said. "It's all I've had my whole damn life."

He pushed past her and disappeared into the pantry. A moment later he returned, her boots in his hand. He threw them at her feet.

"Go outside," he said. "Make a fucking snowman."

She did not go out into the snow, and they didn't speak to each other the rest of the day. The boots lay where Todd had thrown them on the floor. Gilly didn't touch them.

Stubborn, he'd called her. He was right. He hadn't returned her boots to her out of kindness but disdain.

Besides, even with her boots, her fashionable but useless boots, she couldn't expect to make it out of here. Not for a while. Not if she was smart.

Oh, the thought crossed her mind. Of layering her clothes, packing food and drink. Of somehow rendering Todd incapable of stopping her and hiking out of here…

Of dying in the woods, in the snow. Of never making it home. She was stubborn, but she was also afraid. Once she started, there'd be no going back…and what if she failed?

38

The first contraction ripples over her belly like finger-tips, tickling. Not painful, not yet. That will come later. Later, Gilly will sweat and scream and moan and lie glassy-eyed with agony in a big bed with smooth sheets. But just now she puts her hands to the watermelon her stomach has become and she smiles.

It's going to happen, finally. Nine months of waiting, six months of trying before that. The baby's coming.

A little boy? A little girl? She and Seth have both agreed it won't matter, though in her deep and secret heart Gilly has prayed for a daughter. It's important to her, to have a daughter. To be a mother to a daughter. A son would be fine; she will love a son. But she really wants a daughter.

She quit her job last month in preparation for the baby coming, already planning to stay home and raise her child because, after all, she wasn't bearing this baby for someone else to raise. She's spent the past month getting the nursery ready, even if Jewish tradi-

tion says you're not supposed to do anything until the baby's born. Bad luck or some such thing, but Gilly doesn't believe in luck.

Little socks, little shoes, tiny little caps and blankets in yellows and soft greens. Things suitable for either boy or girl. Seth doesn't know that Gilly found a perfect little dress outfit complete with matching cap and ruffled diaper cover on a trip to the baby outlet, or that she bought it and tucked it away here beneath the stacks of burp cloths and Onesies.

It was only a few dollars, less than ten. On sale. But perfect, just the thing she'd buy to dress her daughter in. If she has one. And as another contraction tightens across her stomach and echoes deep inside her, Gilly puts her hands on the dresser she'll use as a changing table, and she prays once more to whoever will listen that the baby on its way is a girl.

Seth is at work. She won't call him just yet. The pain isn't bad and she's had Braxton Hicks several times already. Gilly folds tiny clothes instead. She tests out the rocker and imagines how it will be when she sits there at three in the morning with her baby in her arms.

She plans to nurse and now she cups her breasts, thinking how heavy they are. What will it be like to feed a child from them? It's sort of a disgusting idea, actually, but it seems the right one. Just as she's not having this baby for someone else to raise, knowing that her body naturally will make something to sustain her child seems the right choice to make.

Oh, she knows it won't be easy. She'll have to be the one getting up at all hours since Seth won't be able to feed the baby. But it'll be all right. It's going to be marvelous.

By evening she's sick to her stomach and has been on the toilet all day long. Everything in her guts wants to come out. The midwife assures her this is normal, her body's way of getting ready to give birth, but to Gilly it feels like a bad case of food poisoning.

When Seth gets home unexpectedly late, she's already packed and ready to go. She snaps at him when he takes too long changing his clothes and making a sandwich. When he fumbles with the suitcase they're taking to the birth center. When he pulls out of the driveway without putting on his seat belt.

This is a time when they're supposed to feel closer to each other than ever, but everything he does is a splinter of glass in all her tender places. The way he laughs with the midwives, joking about the drive. How he lingers in the hall instead of bringing her suitcase to her so she can get into the soft nightgown she's going to wear. Gilly presses her lips together and makes fists of her hands, wanting to tell him to move his fucking ass, but instead she breathes in deep. Out slowly. In and out, concentrating on the pain, willing herself to get through it.

Nothing she has read or watched or listened to prepared her for this. Natural birth? What a fucking joke. What is natural about being torn apart from the inside out? What is natural about stinking fluid gushing out of her as she squats once more on the toilet, groaning and pale faced, her hands gripping the metal railings.

Birth is slippery and smelly, coated in blood. Labor takes forever. The contractions consume her—this pain doesn't sting like a wound, not an ache like a break or strain. This pain is white-hot, lava, it rips through her with dreadful regularity every minute and gives her no time even to breathe in between.

"Do you want something for the pain?" the nurse asks.

Stubborn, Gilly shakes her head. "No."

"You can go ahead and push," says the midwife sometime later, Gilly's not sure how long, from between Gilly's legs. The midwife's just used her fingers to decide if it's time. The intrusion was worse than the pain.

Push? Gilly pushes. Nothing happens.

"From your bottom," the midwife says unhelpfully. "Push from your bottom."

Gilly has no fucking idea what that even means. Exhausted, she strains. Nothing. The baby isn't coming. Not moving. The contractions keep coming and she bites down on the inside of her cheek to keep from screaming...but no baby.

There is the hush of whispered conversation that's not quiet enough for her not to overhear. Hey, morons, Gilly wants to say. I can hear you. They talk of a C-section, of calling in the on-call obstetrician for a consult.

She is going to have this baby no matter what. Not by cutting it out of her. She is going to push this child out of her body and make this pain stop. Gilly's never been more determined to do anything in her life.

But no matter how hard she tries to push from her bottom, whatever the fuck that means, what does that even mean? No matter how hard she pushes, or strains, how hard she grips the bed railings, no matter how many times Seth squeezes her hand and offers terrifically unhelpful encouragement, this baby will not come.

"I can't do it," Gilly says.

She's failed.

"You can do it," Seth tells her, patting her face.

She almost bites his hand. She wants to. Bite his fucking fingers off and spit them in his face for touching her now.

"I can't do it," she says again. She thinks she's shouting but really, it's only a whisper.

"Breathe," Seth offers.

She wants to kick him in the face for that.

The nurse beside her says to him, *"The next time she pushes, you hold her knee back."*

Seth looks confused. It's not fucking brain surgery, Gilly wants to tell him. She gets it. Hold her knees back so she can open up her birth canal and push this baby the fuck out of her vagina. But Seth doesn't get it, even when the nurse shows him.

The next contraction comes. The nurse puts both hands flat on Gilly's belly and pushes down. The midwife makes a tutting noise but doesn't stop her.

"Push now," the nurse says. *"The baby will come."*

And...it does. Gilly can feel the baby moving down and out of her. Something rips inside her. She wants to scream and bites it back, still stubborn. Her hand clutches Seth's so hard it goes numb and he winces. She doesn't care.

She pushes. The nurse presses down. The baby is coming, finally, and the midwife eases the child into the world as she's done with hundreds already.

But this baby is not like those. This is Gilly's baby. The midwife coos and there's a scuffle of activity as they clean the baby. Seth goes around to the foot of the bed and makes strange, excited noises. He might be saying something, but all Gilly can hear is the sound of an ocean roar.

"She's passing out," someone says.

There comes the insensitive and insulting sting of a needle. A rush of clarity. The pain eases, and she thinks she was crazy for not taking this sooner. Why would it have been a failure to take even this small comfort?

Then they put the baby, wrapped in a blanket, on her chest. Nobody's told her if it's the daughter she wanted or a son she'll love just as much. She stares with tear-blurred eyes at a tiny, ugly face, blotchy red and still coated in places with white, waxy goo.

"Who is it?" she asks. Not what. But who.

Her husband puts his hand on the baby's head, the other on Gilly's shoulder. "It's a girl. It's Arwen."

And Gilly trembles in the aftermath of birth, barely twitching as the midwife between her legs stitches her intimate places. Gilly stares in wonder at this small creature she created and carried and has now ejected from her body. She touches tiny eyebrows with the tip of her finger and waits to feel...something. Anything. She waits for the rush of emotion that has so often hit her over the past few months and feels only the weight of responsibility and reality. Fear.

Love doesn't come until later.

39

Todd greeted her over breakfast with a sunny smile that might have fooled someone…but not her. Gilly watched his guarded eyes.

Breakfast didn't sit well with her. She got up from the table to pace off the nausea, but when the cold sweat broke out on her forehead and spine, she knew it was no use. She vomited quietly in the bathroom, heaving until she had nothing left to bring up and then heaving some more. The world spun, and she clung to the worn linoleum floor as if that would keep her from flying off.

Gray faced and shaking, she splashed cold water on her face. After a few moments, she began to feel better. She rinsed her mouth and brushed her teeth with the purple sparkly toothbrush.

"You okay?" he asked when she came out.

Her voice was an old woman's, hoarse and raw and quavery. "Yeah."

She went to the table and sat down, staring at the half-finished puzzle with no desire to try to fit any of the pieces. The swirling, vibrant colors made her head ache. Gilly closed her eyes against the sight, feeling suddenly weary.

She felt the thump of something heavy hit the table. She opened her eyes to see her boots. She looked up.

"I'm sorry, Gilly."

She nodded, reached out and touched the leather. She'd bought these boots because she wanted something nice, something fashionable. Any single thing to make her feel less frumpy and matronly. More like…a woman. Now the effort seemed ridiculous, that a pair of shoes could make her feel anything. That she'd put so much value into something she wore rather than anything she did.

"Me, too," she said.

"I always had a temper. Guess I should've learned my lesson by now, huh?" Todd laughed without humor.

"I know about temper. It's okay." She meant the words the same as she'd meant the apology, but Todd looked at her as though she'd lied. "I lose mine, too."

His smile looked a little more natural. "No shit."

"I just can't hold it in sometimes." Gilly got up from the table. Sitting was making her feel worse, not better. She needed to walk. She didn't think she had to puke again…not quite.

Todd watched her as she went to the row of windows at the front of the house. She looked out each one. She turned to face the room. He hadn't spoken.

She didn't want to tell him about the days she went into her closet and stuffed her face into the racks of hanging clothes, screaming until her throat ripped and left her hoarse and sore. She didn't want to even think about those days. Gilly didn't want to tell Todd about the taste of blood she'd grown so used to, or the constant sore spot on the inside of her cheek from biting it.

"I don't want to be angry so much. I just am," Gilly said quietly. "Too much. It's too much, Todd."

"I make you angry?"

She threw out her hands and turned in a slow circle. "This place makes me angry. This situation. Everything about it makes me mad, Todd. You're part of it... I'm a part of it."

She looked at him. "I know I did this to myself, and I'm angriest about that. I wouldn't be here if I hadn't been so stupid. If I'd just gotten out of the truck at the gas station..."

She bit down on the words; chewed them into blood-tasting paste. Swallowed and waited for them to choke her. They went down smoother than she'd thought through a throat closed tight with emotion.

"Everything would've been different if you had," Todd said. "I know you're upset. But I'm not. Not really."

Of course he wouldn't be. Gilly took a deep breath, and another. One more. She counted slowly to ten while Todd watched her, and at the end of it, she held out her hand. He looked at it without taking it.

"I'll try not to lose my temper," Gilly said firmly, reaching to grab his hand and shake it. "If you do the same."

Todd's hand engulfed hers, as warm as the rest of him. He gave her a quizzical look. "Ooohkay."

"It will be better for us both. Easier to get along, if we both try. Deal?"

Todd squeezed her fingers and let them drop. He

looked wary, then broke into a grin. "You are one weird woman."

"Deal?" she repeated.

"Sure," Todd said. "It's a deal."

40

Gilly watched the gray sky, thinking that if she saw one more snowflake come down she would lose her mind. So far the clouds had kept their contents inside. She pressed her fingers to the window, feeling the cold.

"I'd like to go for a walk," she blurted.

Todd's calm response showed no indication of surprise. "You're crazy."

"I know." Gilly looked back outside, twisting her neck to catch a glimpse of blue sky that simply wasn't there. "But I need to get outside, Todd. I have to. I'm going to explode if I don't, and trust me, you don't want to see that."

He didn't argue with her, just flapped a hand in her direction. He was whittling a piece of firewood. She didn't think he actually meant to make something from it, at least nothing she could tell.

"Fine. Go ahead."

Gilly went upstairs and layered herself with as many clothes as she could. She slipped her feet into thick

socks, then put on the boots he'd given as a peace offering, and tied them. They pinched, tight on her feet.
After so many weeks without shoes at all, her feet hurt
from the constriction of the leather. The thick socks
only made it worse.

She wouldn't be out long, she told herself. Not in
this weather. Not with these clothes. But she had to get
out of the cabin. Feel the fresh air on her face, breathe
it deep into her lungs. She was stagnating.

Todd hadn't moved from his chair when she came
downstairs. He sat in his usual position, head thrown
back, face slack. He wasn't sleeping.

"I'm going," Gilly said.

"Be careful."

She paused to consider him, carefully. "Thanks. I
will."

Stepping outside was a kick in the ass and a kiss
on the cheek all at the same time. Bitter wind slapped
at her face. She had no scarf, so struggled to pull her
sweatshirt's neckline up over her mouth and nose. Her
eyes instantly stung with tears that froze and burned.
She'd never smelled anything so sweet.

Gilly hopped off the porch and into the knee-high
snow. She would walk in this? She *was* insane. She
struggled forward. The heavy snow weighed her down,
but she pushed forward.

She didn't want to go back inside. Not with the fresh
air whisking away the stink of all that had happened
these past few weeks. Outside, she could almost forget
where she was and what was happening. Close her eyes,
picture herself on a ski slope somewhere…

That was no use. Skiing created warmth. Standing in

the drifted snow there was only coldness. Gilly forced her foot forward, then the other. She'd taken two steps.

She glanced over her shoulder but could see nothing inside the cabin windows. She put her attention back to her feet, lifting one and then the other. Two more steps.

"Just once around the house," she told herself through gritted teeth. "Once around. Then back inside."

The cabin was so small, it didn't seem like such a daunting task. Gilly, who could carry two bags of groceries and a tired toddler, should be able to forge a path around the house. Just once.

"Yeah, right," she muttered and clapped her hands together sharply, though the sound was muffled. "Right. Let's go."

As with most things, the first step was the hardest. She forced her feet forward again anyway. The snow clung in great white clots to her sweatpants and the bootlaces. She'd added a good pound to each of her legs just from the clumping snow, which was heavy and wet.

Heart attack snow. Make sure you take a break when you're shoveling. You don't want to end up in the E.R.

Gilly blinked for a moment, distracted by her father's voice. He hardly ever popped into her mind like this, not like her mother, who Gilly seemed doomed to never escape. It had been a while since she'd talked to him. She'd spoken to him in September, for Rosh Hashanah. Maybe for the last time.

She pushed the thought from her mind and shifted her weight forward, yanking her foot free of the heavy snow and putting it down. One step. Then another.

She could do this. She *had* to do it. She was well aware her mind had twisted again, that her compulsion was anything but healthy. But, shit, she thought, tilting her head to the sky and drinking in the frigid, fresh air like wine, didn't it feel good?

She let out a whoop of joy, then tossed a double handful of snow into the air. It fell down around her with solid thumps, creating pockets in the drifts. No tiny, dainty flakes here. This snow was serious. She looked up to the gray sky again, daring it to open up. Gilly stuck out her tongue and did as much of a dance as she could while up to her knees in snow that felt like wet sand.

Ten arduous steps took her to the edge of the house. Already her thighs burned, her calves ached. Her feet, which before had felt pinched and aching in the boots, had gone numb. Her hands, wrapped in layers of thick socks in lieu of the gloves Todd had not provided, were okay as long as she clenched and unclenched the fingers to keep them warm. Her face above the sweatshirt was numb, too.

Outside she was frozen, but inside Gilly felt warm. She'd spent too many days idle, too many hours lying on the couch. Her body ached with the efforts she forced upon it, but she felt exhilarated, too. She was moving! Doing something, not just being done to. Powerful, not powerless. Active, not passive. This was more than exercise. It was freedom.

She trudged ahead until she could touch the corner of the house. Now she faced the side with the lean-to and pantry. Green and black shingles, many rotted or missing, covered the walls of the small addition to the cabin. Three rickety steps led up to it.

She'd tossed buckets of black water off those steps. They'd made dirty ice underneath the white snow. She would have to walk carefully. She didn't want to break an ankle. She lifted her feet one at a time, shook them free of their load of snow and dropped them. On this side of the house, the snow wasn't as deep. Perhaps the wind had blown more of it to other parts of the yard. There was a bit of path, too, from Todd's trips to the woodpile. She was crossing it, not moving along it, but her legs were grateful for the respite.

The door to the lean-to opened as she stood there. Todd, wearing no coat, no hat, just the same familiar hooded sweatshirt, was already lighting up a cigarette. He snapped his lighter closed and tucked it in his front jeans pocket, then jerked his chin toward her.

"Hey."

"Hey." She sounded breathy, winded.

"How's it going?"

Gilly stretched, not wanting to lose her momentum or get chilled. "Good. Fine. Great, as a matter of fact."

"You coming back in?"

"Not yet." She stepped off the path of beaten-down snow into the depths of a small drift and sank up to her shins. "Still walking."

"It's cold as fuck out here, Gilly."

She glanced over her shoulder at him. She was already nearing the house's second corner. She had a rhythm starting, and she grinned. It seemed to take him aback, because he flinched.

"Crazy bitch," Todd muttered. He went inside and closed the door firmly. The scent of smoke lingered for only half a second before the wind whisked it away.

Gilly looked at the sky and, laughing, did her best Todd imitation. "Fucking insane."

She pushed on. Five more steps. She experimented, taking small half steps interspersed with lunging strides. She stopped to rest after just a few steps. Her breath whistled in her throat, her mouth parched, and she scooped a handful of snow to melt on her tongue.

Gilly had never understood those people who risked their lives to climb mountains or explore wastelands. One of Seth's favorite shows was that one about the man who put himself out into the wilderness and survived by eating insects and drinking urine. Gilly didn't even like to read about that sort of thing, much less watch it on television. So what on earth was possessing her to live it now?

Without looking at her watch she could only guess at the amount of time she'd been out here already, but it hadn't been too long. Perhaps half an hour. Thirty minutes to move a few hundred feet!

Sweat streamed down her back and froze on her forehead. She sucked in gusts of air, burning her lungs and enjoying it. Determination fueled her. It would be so easy to give up. Gilly forced herself to move forward two more steps, the weight of the snow even heavier on her legs now that she'd taken a few minutes to rest.

If she gave up now, it would be a failure she could never forgive herself for. Somehow, for some stupid reason, making her way around this cabin had fixed itself in her mind as something important. Sacrifice for redemption…for penance? An idea completely at odds with what she believed, totally against her faith.

However, knowing what she was doing was crazy didn't make Gilly change her mind. She set her jaw, biting at the thick fabric of her sweatshirt to keep it from slipping down off her face. She lifted her legs, the muscles burning, and set them down. Two more steps.

By the time she made it around the cabin's second

corner, her mood had changed from exhilaration to doubt. She reached out to touch the side of the cabin. Like a talisman, touching the rough shingles gave her strength.

Evening, by her reckoning, was a few hours away, but the sky had grown dark enough to make it seem as though night were beginning to fall. She had to finish this journey before that happened. She might be crazy, but she wasn't insane enough to stay out here after dark.

Gilly had only seen the back of the cabin through the windows. Once out here, the humped and hilly landscape of snow seemed as foreign to her as an alien planet. She made it to a dilapidated picnic table, heaped high with snow, with a minimum of huffing and puffing and steadied herself on its snow-covered top.

Gilly glanced to the windows, half expecting to see Todd's broad silhouette checking on her again, but all she saw was the glow of the lights he must've recently lit. She paused long enough to sit on the table's bench seat and wiggle her toes inside the boots. She could still feel her feet pushing against the leather, though all other sensation had numbed. The foolishness of this undertaking struck her as she thought of blackened and amputated toes.

Don't think of it. You'll be okay. Just keep moving.

She whacked the snow off her bottom and looked at the cabin. Through the windows she saw Todd moving. It looked warm in there, and though she wasn't cold yet—not really, aside from her toes—she was tired and hungry and worn-out.

"Move your ass," she said aloud. "C'mon, Gilly. You came out here and wanted to do this. Don't be a baby."

Time ceased ticking as she stumbled through the

mounds of whiteness. One foot in front of the other, lifting and plunging. The sound of her breath came loud in her ears, like a freight train. Like the roar of a lion. It gave her strength, that sound, and when she opened her mouth and let out a scream of triumph as she touched the cabin's third corner, she didn't care how crazy or bestial she sounded. Her shriek echoed off the trees, startling a rabbit from its hiding place beneath the thick undergrowth. The sound of it, though it had come from her own throat and of her own volition, frightened Gilly, too.

She was almost there. The world tilted in front of her eyes, but Gilly managed to bring it back into focus. No fainting out here, not even if it meant she could lie down in the deep, soft snow. Sleep had never been so appealing, but to sleep here meant certain death. She must keep moving.

Had she ever done anything this physically hard? Gilly thought again of childbirth, the never-endingness of it, the fact that once begun she could not have stopped it if she tried. There are moments in life that once started cannot be stopped; she would have to see this through to completion as surely as she'd given birth to her children. There was no going back. Only forward.

She gathered her strength again, feeling it ebb with every moment she remained still. Her body screamed a protest when she forced her foot forward. Gilly stumbled, the first time since she'd stepped off the porch earlier this afternoon, and hit the snow.

It engulfed her, enveloped her, wrapped her in clouds of stinging softness. Whiteness filled her eyes, her nose, her throat while she coughed and gagged. She was drowning in it.

Gilly got her feet beneath her and pushed with her hands, lifting herself out of the drift with an effort she could only classify as superhuman. She shivered, then quaked with reaction and cold.

"C'mon," she muttered, slapping her hands together. "Stupid, Gilly! Stupid to do this!"

But even as her body stung and ached, and the bitter wind tore at her flesh, Gilly didn't feel stupid. She was almost done. She would do this, and in doing it become stronger.

She forged ahead, battling her weakness with grunts and curses. She touched the fourth corner of the cabin, viewed the front porch, and found no strength for screams this time. Instead she gathered her breath and forced herself to drag herself through the snow.

"To the steps," she breathed. "Then I'm done."

And she made it to the steps, though without recall of how she did it. Every painful step of the trip around the house was clear like ice in her brain, but not the final steps. She simply found herself inside the front door, shedding her clothes, and realized she'd done it.

Her hands wouldn't loosen her clothes. Gilly staggered to the dining room table, knocking puzzle pieces to the floor. She didn't have the strength to do more.

The room felt blessedly, unbearably hot. She raised her face to the warmth, letting it seep into her as she tried to shed her sodden, frozen clothes.

"Get out of that stuff," Todd told her.

Gilly looked up, feeling the goofy grin paint itself on her face. "I did it. All the way around the house!"

"You're a real jerkoff, Gilly, do you know that?"

She should've felt worse for her adventure. Should've been cringing and whimpering as the heat leached into

her frozen bones. Instead, Gilly felt joyous. Exuberant.
She almost, but not quite, laughed.

The almost-laugh sobered her. "I need to warm up."

"I heated some water for you."

"What?" His statement was so unexpected, she
blurted the question though she had heard him perfectly.

"It should still be hot," Todd told her. He held up one
hand to show her a splash of red across it. "Burned myself just for you, so you better fucking enjoy it."

Enjoy it? Gilly almost bent down and kissed Todd's
feet for the kindness. "Thank you, thank you, oh, God.
Thank you!"

She didn't need his help to make it to the bathroom,
and once inside, even managed to slide out of her layers of clothes. Naked, she worked her fingers and toes
and was relieved to see they looked all right.

Sliding into the hot water made her cry out, moan,
whimper. In seconds her body adjusted to the temperature, and it became paradise. He'd filled the tub nearly
to overflowing, a task that must've taken him nearly the
same amount of time for her to make it around the cabin.

Gilly sank into the water, letting it heal her. No one
would probably ever understand why she'd done it. She
wasn't sure she understood, herself. But she had, and it
was something she would never forget. Gilly grinned
and sank beneath the water.

By all rights, when she got out she should have been
stiff and sore. That would come later, maybe, when her
muscles tightened as she slept. Now, though, she felt
just fine. Relaxed. Even…content. Not with her situation, which she could be resigned to but not content
with. Content with herself. It was a feeling she hadn't
had in a long, long time.

"Todd?"

His answer came garbled and muffled. "Yeah?"

"Can you bring me something to wear?"

She heard him pound up the stairs and then down. The door creaked. His hand appeared with a pile of dry clothes. The door closed again.

Gilly dressed, combed her hair, brushed her teeth. She peered at her windburned cheeks in the mirror and noted the sparkle in her eyes. She bared her teeth at the image and then ignored it.

She walked out into a candlelit haven. The smell of something delicious wafted from the kitchen, and her stomach grumbled. She was starving.

"What's for…?" Gilly stopped, stunned.

Todd had set the table. Though the candles were utilitarian and white, they highlighted pretty china plates and silverware on a delicate flowered cloth. He turned from the stove as she came into the kitchen.

"I hope you're hungry," he said.

She nodded, not trusting herself to speak. Todd motioned for her to sit, and she did, sliding into the chair that had become hers by habit. She touched the silverware, the plates, the tablecloth.

Todd had brushed his hair. It swept off his face to curl softly behind his ears and to his shoulders. The permanent scruff of his beard had been shaved. He wore a black turtleneck shirt and jeans, and his feet were bare.

Gilly saw all these things because she could not look away from him. Todd's smile was brief before it disappeared. The cautious look in his eyes was belied by his confident stance.

"Happy Valentine's Day, Gilly."

Her heart met her stomach as one sank and the other

leaped to her throat. She bent her head to stare at the plate, no longer able to look at him.

Oh, no. Oh, God.

"It's only macaroni and cheese," Todd said, "but it's the good kind. Shells. It's the best of what's left. I thought you might like it."

He'd also made canned potatoes, soft and white, and added slivers of some kind of potted meat the origin of which she knew better than to question. He'd added a plate of saltines painted with grape jelly. Her stomach, which had been growling only moments before, twisted at the sight of the haphazard dinner. She picked up her fork anyway.

"You were out there a real long time," Todd said. "I thought I might have to go out for you."

"No," Gilly said faintly, raising a forkful of cheesy pasta to her lips. "I was okay."

"I don't have any candy, but I made a white cake for dessert. Box mix. Didn't have eggs, but I think it turned out okay."

"Good." She chewed carefully, still unable to look at him.

"Gilly."

She raised her gaze to his. In the candlelight, his eyes were the color of warm caramel. The black turtleneck emphasized the darkness of his hair and the paleness of his skin. He could've passed for a gothic novel's vampire lover, save he had no fangs.

"I never did this for anyone before. It's probably shit compared to what you're used to."

"I…we…don't celebrate Valentine's Day," Gilly said. His brow furrowed. She explained further. "The holiday started as a way to honor Saint Valentine…many Jews don't recognize Christian saints."

Todd slid into his chair and rested his hands on the table. "So you never got cards or chocolates or stuff like that?"

Gilly shook her head. "Not usually, no."

He grinned. "Then it's a first for you, too."

"Todd…"

"Please, Gilly," Todd said softly. "Just this once, for tonight. Can you let me be nice to you?"

Something inside her broke, agonizing in its painlessness. Gilly sighed, brushing her forehead with the fingertips of one hand. She was helpless to deny him, despite the strength she had gained only hours before.

"All right. Sure."

The smile lit up his face, creasing his cheeks and sending sparks to flare in the chocolate-colored eyes. He forked a bite of macaroni and cheese but seemed unable to eat it. Todd wriggled in his seat like a puppy thrilled with praise from its master.

It was only a meal. She would think no further than that. Just this once, for a reason she could not explain and would not ponder, she would let him be nice to her.

He charmed her over the sorry meal. Todd had already proved himself to be insightful. When he wasn't self-conscious about being stupid, he actually turned out to be knowledgeable on a lot of subjects, and Gilly told him so.

"Nah. It's just a bunch of stupid shit nobody cares about. Just trivia." He mixed potatoes and macaroni and cheese without eating it.

"No, it's not," she insisted. "It's not just trivia, Todd.

Being smart isn't always about what big words you can spout out or how fast you can do math, you know."

He shrugged. "I guess I've just...lived more, or something. Done a lot of stuff. Hey, that's one good thing about never hanging on to a job, I guess. I learned how to do a lot of stuff. But I'm still stupid."

He had indeed lived a lot more than she ever had. She didn't envy him the experience. "Doing stupid things doesn't mean you're stupid, Todd."

"No?" His brows arched beneath the fringe of his dark hair. "What does it mean?"

"Well. It means you're...not...it just means...you need to think before you act." She nodded firmly, the voice of authority.

The food disappeared as they talked. At the end of the meal, Todd presented the cake with a flourish, though it was flat and crumbly without the eggs for the batter. It tasted strongly of cinnamon and honey, two flavors Gilly didn't like. She ate it anyway, and praised him for the effort.

Todd gave her his curious puppy look. "You're being nice."

"Do you want me to stop?"

"No." He shook his head. "Ain't so hard, is it?"

That it wasn't difficult would've frightened her had Gilly allowed it. Instead, she put it from her mind, too. A thought for a later time.

They'd never assigned each other chores, each usually taking care of their own meal prep and cleanup, but tonight Todd cleared and washed the dishes, insisting she sit.

"Happy Valentine's Day," he insisted at her protest

that he'd done enough by preparing the meal. "Take a load off."

Gilly had never really minded missing out on the national day of romance. Seth had been fond of reminding her that every day in their marriage was a celebration of their love. Gilly didn't always agree, particularly on the days when the children's hijinks had shortened her temper and Seth breezed in late from work asking "What's for dinner?" Still, she didn't miss the overpriced chocolates and bouquets of flowers that were heavy on guilt and lacking in sentiment. Her husband told her he loved her every day, and didn't need the words on a greeting card to do it.

Because she didn't share Valentine's Day with Seth, sharing it with Todd somehow didn't seem like betrayal. At least not so far, with his innocuous offering of food and service. Gilly sat on the couch, watching the play of candlelight on the ceiling.

She shivered and wanted the chill to come from the room's lowering temperature and not from her sudden anxious anticipation. She got up to put some more logs on the fire, and took the last three from the battered wicker basket next to the stove. They were almost out of wood.

"We need more wood," Gilly called.

Todd appeared beside her, startling her. "The pile out back's all, gone," he said, using the typical Pennsylvania Dutch phrasing that usually made her cringe. "I didn't have time to cut more today."

Gilly hadn't realized their supply was so low. She felt stupid for not noticing. "Oh."

Todd poked at the logs she'd put on. Red sparks

hissed in the fire. The logs popped and complained at their fiery fate.

"I'll cut some more tomorrow."

He'd leaned across her to reach the poker. Now they faced each other from no more than a few inches apart. The red and orange flames reflected in his eyes, and Gilly knew she didn't imagine the questions she saw there.

Self-consciously, she got to her feet and moved away. She wasn't certain exactly where she meant to go when there was no place to escape. His voice, low and uncertain, froze her solid.

"Gilly..."

She murmured a reply. "Hmm?"

He sighed. She closed her eyes and her teeth found the inside of her cheek. She prayed he wouldn't find the courage to ask her the question she'd seen glimmering in his eyes. He cleared his throat, and she tensed. Waiting.

"Gilly, would you dance with me?"

It wasn't the question she'd expected, though not much better. Gilly turned to face him, her face a careful, neutral mask. "What?"

He got to his feet, all arms and legs, gangly. "Dance? I'm not any good. But would you...?"

"Dance with you?" Gilly murmured. She allowed his touch on her fingers, her thoughts elsewhere. Her breath caught in her throat before coughing out. "Oh, Todd."

"Please?"

What harm could it do? She knew even as she nodded her reply that she was dooming herself. And him. No good could come from this. But...could harm? What could giving him this one thing hurt?

"Great!"

For once the radio didn't let them down. Todd tuned in a station playing classic golden oldies. "Smoke Gets In Your Eyes" made way for "Unchained Melody."

They moved to a clear spot on the floor. He didn't know where to put his hands, and Gilly showed him. They were large and encircled her waist in a way that made her feel he could squeeze her in half with little effort. The top of her head just barely reached his shoulder. Gilly was not a small woman, but once again he'd made her tiny.

"I told you I'm not good," Todd said.

"You're doing fine," Gilly whispered, her throat dry.

His innate grace took the place of his inexperience. The songs playing on the radio flowed one into the other with no more than a few seconds of break between them. Todd and Gilly danced, their movements slow but unhesitating.

He pulled her slowly, hesitantly closer. His hands didn't stray from her hips. The puff of his breath ruffled her hair.

She knew this had been a mistake. This didn't mean the same things to her as it must to him. This was Reg Gampey all over again. This was giving someone something he wanted because she felt so bad about something else she didn't know how to say no.

But then she'd been a kid. She was a woman now. She shouldn't let pity move her into doing something she knew would end badly.

The slow songs kept playing. Todd and Gilly kept dancing. She rested her hands on his shoulders and just barely kept her face from touching even the soft flannel of his shirt.

She was reminded of middle-school dances where the girls and boys were too scared to even touch. But this wasn't quite like that. In middle school Gilly had known the mechanics of what sex was but hadn't had a clue about what it could be. Even later, in high school, when dancing close often led to making out in shadowy corners, there'd still been an innocence to sharing a dance that was missing here.

At last the music stopped. An announcer spoke. The moment broke.

Gilly tried to pull away, but Todd's hands stayed her. Her head dropped. She saw the floor, his bare feet, the ragged hem of his jeans.

"Gilly?"

"No, Todd."

For an instant she sensed anger. His fingers clutched at her waist, then relaxed. He tried again.

"Gilly…"

"No." Her voice came more firmly this time. Definite. She moved out of his embrace, clutching her elbows and turning from him.

"Look at me?"

Because it was a plea and not a demand, she obliged. She could hardly bear the look of longing on his face. Gilly swallowed, hard, and shook her head again.

"Don't ask, and I won't have to tell you no again."

"Why?" The question was simple, and the answer should've been simpler, but was not.

"My mother used to tell me, 'be happy with what you have,'" Gilly said at last. "Be happy with what you have, Todd."

He looked around the cabin, at her, and then down

at himself. "What I have? That looks like a whole lot of nothing."

She moved, still trembling, to the stairs before changing her mind. She didn't want to lead him up there, where the line of beds would be all too tempting. She went instead to the dining room table and one of her puzzles but couldn't find rest there, either. Finally, she turned and faced him squarely.

"I can't change things," she told him. "And I wouldn't if I could. I have too much to lose and nothing to gain."

His face broke, his head dropped. His knees buckled for an instant before he caught himself and made his way to a chair. Todd buried his face in his hands, his sigh soft but as loud and mournful as the howling of wolves. He pressed the heels of his hands to his eyes.

"Is it wrong to want just one thing? One good thing?" He spoke so low she could've pretended not to hear him.

But she did hear him, every word.

"No. But I'm not it."

"You could be. If you wanted to."

"But I don't want to, Todd." She hated the words the second they came out, even though she meant them.

"See? I am stupid."

He hadn't moved from the chair. She was still by the table. A vast distance separated them, too far for her to touch him, but she put out her hand anyway.

"You're not—"

He cut her off with a low noise from deep inside him. Gilly stopped, uncertain. Todd looked up at her.

"Go away," he told her, and she went.

41

The gears had jammed, the machine ground to a halt. Todd replied when she spoke to him, but only in the gruffest, briefest words. Gilly didn't really blame him. There wasn't much more to say. She should've been grateful for it and could only be sad.

They fixed lunch at the same time but not together, bound by mutually growling stomachs if nothing more. Long weeks of confinement meant they'd worked out a routine in the kitchen. A step here, a dodge there. Today she zigged when he zagged, and Gilly found herself with both hands pressed to his chest to keep them from colliding.

He pushed her away, gently but firmly. "Don't touch me."

Now she understood how it must've felt for him when she'd said those same words. "Todd."

"Don't." He jerked his hands away, lifting them out of her reach as though she'd tried to take one, then moved around her to grab his plate. He turned his back on her to take a seat at the kitchen table.

Gilly had fixed herself the last handful of wheat crackers and some squares of defrosted lunch meat that was a little too pink to be turkey. Was it only weeks ago she'd refused a plate of eggs mixed with bacon? She'd have eaten it, now. They were far from starving but they'd had an unspoken agreement to cut back on their meals. Their stomachs, like the pantry and fridge, were emptier every day.

At the table across from him, Gilly attempted to start a conversation that Todd shut down with one-word answers. They ate in uncompanionable silence. Her food tasted bad because of it.

"Don't blame me for what I can't change," she blurted finally, unable to help herself.

He lifted his eyebrows at her and leaned back in the kitchen chair, tipping it. The smoke from his cigarette wreathed his features, made them softer, even as his scowl became harsher. He said nothing.

"I can't," Gilly whispered, and got up from the table. She left her plate.

Behind her she heard the thump of all four chair legs hitting the floor, but she didn't turn. The scent of his cigarette smoke tickled her nose, but she refused to cough. She went to the bathroom and ran the cold water, splashed her face again and again until her eyes burned and her face turned red.

When she came into the living room, he'd gone upstairs. She heard the sound of his footsteps on the creaking wooden floor. She tilted her head toward the ceiling, but he didn't seem to be coming back down. This time, Todd was the one who'd escaped upstairs.

"I can't change things, damn it!" she cried to the ceiling, her fists clenched in impotent anger. Even as she said it, she could taste the lie on her tongue. Could not and would not were two separate things altogether.

Gilly pressed the heels of her palms to her eyes, willing away the urge to cry. She owed him no tears. If she wept it should be for Seth, for Arwen, for Gandy. Perhaps even for herself. But not Todd. Not over this.

All at once, she couldn't breathe. Her throat burned with the effort, and Gilly sank onto the sofa. She pushed her hands against her chest, feeling and hearing the thunder of her heart.

"I'm sorry," she whispered. He couldn't hear her, but that didn't matter. She knew she'd said it.

42

"Coming to bed?" This is Seth's code for wanting to make love.

Gilly looks at the pile of bills as-yet-unpaid. From the laundry room, the dryer buzzes with a load of sheets and towels, with one last load in the washer ready to be transferred. It's only a little after nine o'clock, and she could easily stay up until eleven without suffering too much in the morning. Two whole hours with a house sleeping around her—how much she could finish in that solitude!

"I have to finish a few things first."

He comes up behind her to kiss her neck. Gilly stiffens. The inside of her cheek burns and stings as she bites, though at least she doesn't taste blood. Not yet.

"Come to bed," her husband says as his hands come around to cup her breasts even though she's told him time and again that nursing made them too sensitive for her to enjoy being grabbed that way. "I'm horny."

She isn't.

Her mind races, calculating if she can satisfy him with a quick hand-job at the desk so he'll go away and leave her alone. He's already taking her hand and rubbing his crotch with it. Seth thinks this will make her want to have sex with him, when all it really does is make her want to grab as hard as she can and yank.

It wasn't always this way. Gilly remembers a time when she was the one chasing her husband for sex, he the one complaining about being tired. That was before children, though, back in the days when she had nobody to take care of but herself. When she could stay up until midnight and still get seven hours of uninterrupted sleep. Back when her belly had been smooth and curved, not loose and doughy and road-mapped with scars.

She has friends whose husbands don't like to screw the way they used to—something about their wives gaining weight or being matronly, something about being unable to look at them as lovers any longer. She should be thankful her marriage is still strong, that her husband watched two children come out of her vagina and still finds her not only just attractive but sexy enough to chase around the house.

He shouldn't have to chase her.

At the very least, she shouldn't mind when he catches her.

But she does, and Gilly sighs as Seth whispers in her ear again, adding a stroke of tongue to her earlobe that makes her shudder with nothing resembling passion.

"Come to bed," Seth says.

Gilly does, because appeasing him has become one more thing on a long list of chores she needs to complete before the night is through. She goes through the motions and the noises, wanting to please him because she does love him, after all, this man who quickly turns to snoring beside her in their bed. He doesn't notice when she gets up to go back downstairs and finish the chores she'd left undone so she could take the time to satisfy him.

"Don't forget to take your pills," Todd says from the bathroom when Gilly at last finishes the last load of laundry, closes the checkbook and heads for a hot, steamy shower. She wants to stay in the water for a long time, letting it beat on her neck and shoulders, blocking out the world. She stops, instead, to listen to him say, "They're on the counter. You're sick, remember? The antibiotics."

As the steam begins to fill the room, Gilly thinks she ought to scream. There's a stranger in her house. He's staring at her like he knows her. Not a stranger, after all.

Gilly doesn't scream.

But she did wake up, heart pounding and stomach sick. She rushed to the bathroom to hover over the toilet, hoping she wouldn't vomit and yet somehow relieved when she couldn't hold it back. She was in there for a long time and when she came out, unlike all the others, Todd didn't ask her if she was okay.

43

Gilly wasn't used to being the bad guy, and she definitely didn't like it. Three days had passed since Todd had asked her to dance. Early on in all of this, she'd have thought it better if they didn't speak, but they'd gone beyond that now. Todd turned his back on her when she entered a room and ignored her when she spoke. He'd even taken to sleeping downstairs on the couch so they didn't have to share the room upstairs. It was killing her.

She'd spent the morning tidying just to keep herself busy, but at last she turned to him. "Are you ever going to talk to me again?"

Todd said nothing.

"Please?" Gilly said, exhausted. She sank into a chair across from him. "C'mon, Todd. Please. Don't do this."

Todd got up when she sat down, but before he could escape Gilly had snagged his sleeve. He set his jaw and deliberately pulled it from her grip. He didn't look at her.

"I'm going to get some wood." He might've been talking to himself for all the attention he gave her.

"Do you need some help?"

He fixed her with a look so contemptuous and bitter she recoiled from it the way she would've if she'd stumbled on a snake in a woodpile. Without answering, he shrugged into an extra sweatshirt and pulled his hood up over the fall of silky dark hair. Then he stomped outside.

It always seemed to come back to sex, with men. Whether they wanted it and didn't get it, or got it but not enough of it, it led to more arguments and hard feelings than anything else Gilly could think of. In the beginning she'd been afraid Todd meant to rape her— and that would've been about power, not sex. Now it was simply about longing, and somehow that made it so much more frightening.

She couldn't repair the hurt she'd caused him. Any apologies she made would ring false, and Gilly wasn't sure she could convince him of the difference between being sorry she couldn't give him what he wanted and sorrow that her decision had caused him pain.

She cradled her head in her hands for a minute, willing her headache to subside. The rolling of her stomach had woken her early this morning. She'd been sick again. She didn't want to contemplate what that might mean.

She watched Todd from the window as he trudged through the thigh-deep snow. She gained some small measure of satisfaction from seeing that he didn't have a much easier time wading through the snow than she had. He disappeared into the woods.

He'd only taken a small hand ax. Guilt nudged her

when she glanced at the empty wicker basket next to the woodstove. She hadn't ever thought about where the wood came from, or wondered what would happen when the stockpile outside the lean-to disappeared. Then again, neither of them had expected so much snow, or to be here this long.

She busied herself with her puzzle, nearly completed now, but could find no pleasure in it. She heard the thump of wood against the back of the house, and jumped. Todd didn't come back inside.

More time passed. Gilly finished the puzzle, but her triumph was empty. She sat at the table and stared at the brightly colored picture she'd made. Then she took it all apart.

She heard another load of wood thump against the house. She looked at her watch. An hour had passed. Plenty of time for him to have cut enough wood to last a few days. She went again to the window, and was just in time to see Todd vanish again into the woods.

Gilly went to the back door and gaped at the size of the pile. How had he managed to cut and carry all of that in so short a time, and alone? Her gaze followed the trampled path in the snow to where it led to the trees.

Heart attack snow.

What if Todd had gone out there alone and fallen ill? Hurt himself? What if the ax had slipped and he was lying in a pool of his own frozen blood? What if he was exhausted and hypothermic?

What would she do out here, alone, without him?

Gilly boiled water, found a mug, dunked a tea bag. She added extra sugar. While it steeped she wrestled herself into several layers of clothing and forced her feet into her boots. As an afterthought, she found the large deep stockpot, filled it and put it on top of the woodstove.

She carried the mug carefully through the path Todd had made and into the woods. She found him seated on a fallen tree, the ax resting at his side. His breath plumed out in front of him. His hair had frozen, stiff with sweat, into random spikes.

"Here." She handed him the mug.

He took it with cold-reddened hands. "Thanks."

"You've been out here a long time."

"We needed wood."

She glanced at the pile at his feet. "I think we have enough."

"I needed to work." He cupped the mug with his hands and tested the still steaming liquid with the tip of his tongue.

"It's cold out here," Gilly said. "Why don't you take a break?"

"Why don't you get the fuck out of my face?" he replied evenly, and handed her back the mug. "Don't you get it, Gilly? I *need* to work."

His gaze swept her from head to toe, burning her even through the many layers. She nodded quickly, her cheeks heating, and took the cup. She hurried back through the snow and into the cabin.

Inside, she tore her top layer of clothes off and flung them to the floor. She splashed frigid water on her hot face. Dripping and gasping, Gilly pushed back from the sink and dried herself with the hem of her shirt.

She let herself rest at the table. She put her head in her hands. Stifled a groan.

The thud of logs against the pile outside again startled her into standing. In another moment, the back door opened. Todd stomped in, scattering clods of snow onto the linoleum. He blew into his hands. His teeth started to chatter.

"You need to get those wet clothes off...I didn't have time to fill the tub like you did for me...but I heated some water...." She was babbling, and realized it. Gilly closed her mouth abruptly. "Come sit over on the couch."

He did. Gilly found a smaller pan and set it on the floor in front of him. She added enough cold water to make the temperature bearable and got up. "Take off your boots."

Todd bent, but she could clearly see that his fingers were too numb to work the laces. Gilly knelt and did it for him. He groaned as she pulled off the battered hiking boots, and then the socks beneath. His toes were ice cubes.

"I'll make some more tea."

He caught her hand as she turned and tugged her close to him. "Now you're being nice to me again. I don't get it."

At first, Gilly couldn't form her answer into words. She held his icy feet between her hands to warm them a bit before she slipped them into the hot water. He hissed and clenched his fists, but didn't protest.

"Todd," Gilly said finally with a sigh. "Being nice doesn't have to mean..."

She stopped, mouth working as she tried to put her thoughts into speech. "I can take care *of* you without caring *for* you."

She raised her gaze to his face and instantly wished she hadn't. Beneath the ruddy color from the cold, he'd gone pale. His mouth set in a thin line.

"I guess you can," he said.

"I have a home," Gilly said. "I have a family. And I will get back to them someday. Whether you want to believe it or not. I believe it. I have to."

He nodded twice, sharply. "You still want to get away from me."

"How can you ask me that?" Gilly reached for a towel, lifted his feet from the water, dried them. "Todd, can you expect anything else from me?"

He leaned forward, grasped her upper arms. His eyes searched hers. "Yeah. I think I can."

Gilly shook her head. "No. You can't. It's too much to expect. Even for you."

"What's that mean? Even for me? Even for a dumbass like me, you mean?"

"That's not what I meant, and you should know that," Gilly said. "I meant that no matter what I know…"

His fingers tightened. She restrained a wince. "You pity me."

"I empathize with you, Todd. There's a difference."

His grip softened, but not by much. His gaze did, too. "I ain't asking for so much. Am I, really?"

"It's too much."

He shook her a little, and the role of power had shifted. Now kneeling at his feet felt subservient instead of caretaking. Gilly started to get to her feet, but Todd's grasp stopped her.

"What *can* you give?"

She looked at him, then waved her hand at his feet. "This. It's all I have for you, Todd."

He gave a low, growling laugh. "You want to be my fucking mother?"

"Interesting choice of words," Gilly murmured.

"You shut…you shut your mouth." He pushed away from her, got up, took long, limping strides to the edge of the room before turning back to her. "Is that what you think of me?"

Gilly shook her head, her knees hurting on the bare floor. She got up. "No, of course not."

He drew a cigarette from the crumpled pack and threw the empty paper to the floor. The smoke seeped from his nostrils in slow, twin tendrils, Fog. He picked a bit of tobacco off his tongue with one finger, turned and spit onto the floor. When he looked at her, Gilly wanted to turn away from the bluntness in his eyes.

"What, then?" he shouted. "The fuck am I to you, then, Gilly? Because I know I'm something to you."

Todd's voice dipped low and soft. Hopeful. "I am, right?"

She couldn't answer and he seemed to take her silence as assent.

"I never met anyone like you, Gilly." Todd's smile was lopsided. "You…you're clean. When I'm around you, I feel clean, too."

"Then let me stay that way," Gilly said. "Please."

Todd shook his head and bent his head to stare up at her through the sheaf of his dark hair. "I don't think I can."

"You have to."

He shook his head. "I ain't that good a person, Gilly."

A drop of cold sweat trickled down her spine, but she refused to shiver. "You can be. If you try."

Todd drew deep on his cigarette, watching her. Thinking. When she saw he wasn't going to say anything else, Gilly took the basin into the kitchen and emptied it. They did not continue the conversation.

44

What did he mean to her? The answer wasn't "nothing." Gilly knew it, even if she wasn't going to tell him. She thought about what it might be through the night as she fought sleep so she wouldn't have to face her dreams. She'd sought refuge in them before, but now they only made everything hurt worse.

For the first time ever, Gilly waited for the sound of her mother's voice to ring in her head, and it didn't come. She could hear her mother's words, but it wasn't like she was there, speaking them, and they were only memory, time-faded and inexact.

Roses, she thought, prompting with no response. What had her mother said about roses? What had she said about…love?

No. Not that. It was impossible.

Love had many shapes, but this was not and could not be one of them. She couldn't love Todd. It was wrong. It was a perversion of the very word. Whatever she felt for him—and she could admit it was something, yes, she could do that, it was most emphatically not love.

She felt as responsible for him as she did for her children, yet she didn't feel maternal toward him. She believed he knew her as well as her husband did, but she didn't feel romantic toward him, either. Everything about Todd was chaos and conflict.

She heard his step on the stairs, the shuffle of his feet along the floor to his bed. The creak of the springs. She waited for the soft sigh of his snore, which she'd missed while he was avoiding her by sleeping on the couch. Instead, she heard him murmur her name.

"Yes, Todd."

His reply came with the shuffle of feet on the floor-boards and a shadow standing, hesitating, in the space between the partition. There was no moon, or it hadn't yet risen, and all she could see was the black, hunched shape of his shoulders. She heard his breathing.

She tensed.

He came closer and sat, close enough to touch her if he wanted but not touching her. He was always so warm, tonight no exception. She could feel him even through the blankets.

"I told you about Kendra," Todd said.

"Yes. Your girlfriend. She wanted to get married and you didn't." Gilly shifted in the covers, turning onto her side to face him though she couldn't see anything more than the shape of him.

"Yeah. See, the thing about Kendra, was that she wasn't like the other girls I'd ever been with. I mean, I never really had a lot of girlfriends. Just some girls I got with every once in a while when I could. But when

I met her, it was different. She was nice. She lived in a nice house. She had a job."

"What did she do?"

"She taught kindergarten." Todd laughed harshly. "Can you believe that, Gilly? Me with a fucking kindy teacher. She spent all day with little kids. And she went out with me at night. I bet if those parents had known what she was up to, they wouldn't have been so happy."

Gilly was a parent. If she'd found out her daughter's teacher was dating a convict, she'd have had trouble with it, no doubt. "It was her social life, not any of their business."

"Yeah, well. You know how people are."

"Yeah. I do."

Todd shifted and the bed dipped a little as he half turned toward her. "She had the prettiest laugh. And she laughed a lot when she was with me. I laughed, too. When I was with Kendra, I felt…"

Gilly waited.

"Luminescent," Todd said finally. "You know that word?"

"Yes. I do."

"It's a good one."

She smiled in the dark. "A very good one."

"One of Uncle Bill's favorites," Todd said offhandedly. "But that's how I felt when I was with Kendra."

"So what happened?"

"She wanted to get married. And I just couldn't do it. She said it would all work out and everything would be okay, but I couldn't do it."

Gilly put out her hand. Her fingertips grazed his back. She kept them there, barely touching.

"She didn't really know me," Todd said. "She loved me, though. But I didn't lose her. I pushed her away."

Gilly put her hand flat on his back, but it fell away when Todd stood. She missed his heat right away and shivered. He moved, and the floorboards creaked.

"I shouldn't have asked you for more," Todd said. Then he went back to his bed.

45

Todd slid a hand through his hair in irritation. "Damn it."

Gilly looked up from the list she was writing. "What?"

"My hair." Todd blew upward, causing the strands to lift off his forehead. "It's too long."

She looked at him critically. It hung past the edges of his shoulders and obscured the crows' wings of his eyebrows. "It sure is."

He snorted. "I hate dirty hair."

She put a hand up to her own hair, pulled back into a ponytail for the same reason. Neither of them had been much concerned about washing their hair. It was hard enough taking a bath.

He tugged at a handful. "It's driving me crazy."

"I could cut it for you." She meant the offer casually, not thinking he would take it.

Todd's eyes lit. "Yeah?"

Gilly shrugged. "Sure. I can't promise you how

pretty it will turn out, but I can do it. I cut my kids'
hair all the time."

"Cool!" Todd went to the kitchen and began rummaging around in one of the drawers. He came back
with his trophy held high: a large pair of scissors.
"Here."

She took the dull and ancient tool and looked at it
skeptically. "I don't know about this."

"Just try. I can't stand it."

"Okay, so long as you're not planning on entering
any beauty pageants." She motioned to him. "Sit down."

He sat so she could stand behind him, and his head
still came up to her chin. Gilly snapped the scissors
open and shut a few times and touched Todd's hair. It
was dirty, but still smooth. She ran it through her fingers, catching the snags.

"Ouch!"

"Sorry." She tried again, with the same response.
"It's too tangled."

"Cut the knots out."

"No," Gilly said sternly. "You'd look horrible. I have
to comb it first. And I think I should wash it."

He protested, but only feebly. Gilly led him to the
bathroom and bent him over the bathtub. He yelped
as the lukewarm water hit his scalp, but didn't fight
to get away.

Gilly worked quickly, mindful of how quickly the
hot water ran out. She soaped Todd's head and rinsed
it, then used a palmful of conditioner. It was the last
in the bottle.

She finished, and he wrapped his head in a towel.
They returned to the living room, moving the chair
closer to the fire. She combed his hair until it lay smooth

and shining against his scalp and hung straight to the middle of his back.

"It seems a shame to cut it. You have such nice hair, Todd."

"Sissy hair," he said. "I have girl's hair."

"No," Gilly admonished. "Just because it's long doesn't make it girl's hair."

"It's too pretty," Todd said in a mocking tone. "Faggot hair."

Gilly shook her head, thinking of one of her best friends from college. Mark would've said the very same thing, only with envy in his tone. Mark's partner wore his hair long and straight, like Todd's, but Mark kept his short in a buzz cut to disguise a receding hairline.

Todd twisted to look at her. "You think that's funny?"

His vehemence took her aback. "No."

"My uncle Bill was a fag," Todd said, his face stony. "And he was the best man who ever was. If you got a problem with that you'd better keep it to yourself."

"Todd." Gilly cut him off. She laid her hand on his shoulder. "I don't."

He wet his lips. "Some people do."

"I'm not some people."

He nodded. "Yeah. Right."

She pushed his head until he looked forward again, and brandished the scissors. "If you want me to cut it, I'll cut it."

"Do it."

In a few minutes, the deed was done. Todd's hair lay in loose curls all over the towel draped across his shoulders and the floor. He ran a finger through the short, cropped strands.

"Feels nice," he commented.

The short hairstyle emphasized the line of his cheekbones and curve of his jaw. He'd grown thinner, Gilly noted. His scalp showed white in places, and a few tiny silver hairs glittered in places she hadn't noticed before.

"All done." Before she could stop herself, Gilly reached out and stroked his cheek. Then, not wanting to make a scene, she pretended she was merely brushing some stray hairs from his face.

He pressed his face against her hand and closed his eyes for a minute. Gilly took her hand away. She busied herself with tidying up.

When he wasn't looking, she gathered a hank of his hair and twisted it together before slipping it into her pocket. She couldn't have said what compulsion had made her do it; she didn't want to dwell on it. Later, she took it out and put it in her dresser drawer. She didn't look at it again, but she always knew it was there.

46

"What are you doing?"

Gilly looked down at the piece of paper now mostly filled with lines of her sloping handwriting. "Writing a list."

Todd bent to look over her shoulder. "A list of what?"

Gilly moved her hand to show him. "Things I want to do. Or that I've never done."

"Shit, it would take a lot more than one piece of paper for me to do that."

Gilly looked at what she'd written. "This is just a start."

"What do you got on it?"

For a moment, she didn't want to tell him. Her list, like her laugh, was private. A piece of herself. But then, unlike her laughter, Gilly shared what she'd written.

"'Take my kids to the beach,'" she read. "They've never seen the ocean. I'd like to see Gandy get out of diapers. See Arwen start first grade."

"Are they all about your kids?" Todd's voice was carefully neutral.

Gilly looked over the list and read some more aloud. "'Learn to play the piano. Go scuba diving. Research my family tree.'"

She continued. "'Buy Seth the golf clubs he's been wanting. Finish painting Arwen's bedroom.'"

"You have a lot of stuff on your list."

She ran her fingers over the ink. "Yes. I do."

He didn't offer her false comfort. Gilly knew he wouldn't say she'd do those things someday. He didn't believe she ever would. All at once, the thought she'd never hold her children in her arms again made her start to cry.

The sobs tore from her throat with a force and vehemence that left her gasping. A hot fist clutched her heart, squeezed it, made her moan. She no longer had the strength to grasp the paper, and it floated from her fingers. Gilly buried her face in her hands, breathless with sobs, agonized in her grief.

"Hey," Todd said, and then again. "Hey. Shh. Shh, Gilly, it's okay."

She felt his arm curl around her shoulders, and he drew her close to him. The flannel of his shirt was soft against her cheek. The scent of tobacco permeated him, underlying the scent of fresh air he always seemed to carry with him.

Gilly pushed away from him but was too weakened by grief to move far. His arms held her, loosely but firmly, in his comforting grasp.

"I love them!" she sobbed, spitting the words against his chest. "Ah, God, I miss them!"

He rocked her, slowly, as she had once rocked him. He smoothed her hair. She felt the touch of his lips on her forehead. Gilly sagged into Todd's embrace, not welcoming it but helpless to fight it.

"I miss them," she whispered raggedly, her throat raw from tears. Her fingers clutched a handful of flannel shirt. "My family."

"Don't cry, Gilly."

The tears were tapering off into sniffles. He let her pull away from him. Her eyes ached, swollen and hot.

"I want to see my children again."

He shook his head slowly, back and forth, once. "If you go back, they'll make you tell them what happened. They'll make you tell them where I am. *Who* I am. They'll send me back to jail. And I won't go."

The truth of his statement was undeniable, but Gilly didn't care. She railed at him, flailing her arms. "You son of a bitch! Didn't you hear me? I want to see my children! Don't you understand? I miss my kids!"

"I understand," Todd growled, catching her hand in midstrike and holding it. His voice softened. "I know, Gilly. What do you want me to do about it?"

"Tell me you'll let me go home."

Todd shook his head. "Can't."

"Just tell me," she said. "Even if you don't mean it!"

He shook his head again.

"Then do what you came up here to do," she said through gritted teeth and yanked her hand from his grasp.

His eyes flickered. "I can't. I could've before. But now I can't."

"You," she said with deliberate cruelty, "are afraid."

He frowned. "Shut up!"

"You're chickenshit!" Gilly cried. "You're a pussy!"

"Shut up, Gilly, or so help me…"

"Or what?" she asked and held out her hands. "What? You'll hit me? You'll kill me?"

"Shut up," he said for a third time, his voice low. He turned from her. "Just shut your mouth."

"If I knew that I would never see my kids or Seth again, I would kill myself," Gilly said with a faint contemptuous sneer. "And I wouldn't be afraid, either."

"Oh, no?" Todd's hand went to the leather sheath on his belt. He unbuckled the huge knife and drew it out. "Then do it. Here you go. Take it."

She didn't.

He put the knife away. "I didn't think so. Not so easy, is it, when it comes right down to it?"

Her smile felt hot and wild, plastered to her face. "I believe I will get back to my family, Todd."

He bowed his head. "I can't let you do that. You know that."

"You won't have a choice," Gilly said.

March

47

For the first morning in a long time, Gilly's stomach didn't hurt. She got out of bed without the rumble and roil of nausea, and that alone was enough to put a smile on her face. The bright morning sunshine, too, lifted her spirits. Its yellow glow meant warmth. Soon, the days would get longer, the sun hotter. Soon, she thought, as she opened the pantry to look for food, the snow would melt entirely.

Todd had risen before her. He said nothing as she prepared pancakes from a boxed powder mixed with water. Even the smell of the food didn't make him stir from his seat. An ashtray overflowed beside him.

"Ugh." Gilly wrinkled her nose as she sat down across from him with her plate of pancakes. "Todd, do you have to do that at the table?"

Silently he got up and went through the pantry. She heard the back door open and close. When he returned, the ashtray was empty.

"Want some pancakes?" she asked around a full mouth.

He shook his head. Brooding. Gilly took a deep breath, not sure what she was going to say, but ready to say it anyway. He cut her off with a short hand gesture.

"Hush."

She chewed, though now the golden cakes stuck in her throat. She washed them down with a glass of cold, clear water, then stabbed another. She was starving.

"My life has always been shit," Todd said. "Can you blame me for wanting to turn it around, now?"

"Of course not. But you broke the law, Todd. You can't expect it to be without consequences." She sipped water, paused, searched his face. "I'm sorry, but that's the way it is."

He grimaced. "Do you really think I deserve to go back to jail? Is that what you want?"

Did she want that? "I don't know."

"Why didn't you get out of the truck when I gave you the chance?" he asked. "None of this would've happened if you'd just got out of the damn truck."

"One of life's greatest mysteries," Gilly told him. "I don't know that, either. It was wrong."

"So now we're both fucked."

She got up and put her empty plate in the sink. "Maybe."

"Those were my last smokes," he told her. "All gone. No more."

"Smoking is a bad habit," Gilly said.

"Bad seems to be the only kind I have," Todd replied. "Let's play a game."

48

More days passed that way, with board games and puzzles, but Todd didn't seem to have the patience to pay attention to any one thing for long. Gilly couldn't blame him. Aside from her kamikaze jaunt around the house and his trips outside to cut wood, neither of them had left the tiny cabin for more than a few minutes.

He shuffled the cards again but only halfheartedly dealt out the hand. Gilly didn't take them. She got up from her chair and stared out the window.

"Looks like a nice day," she commented.

He sighed and reached up to run a hand through his now short hair. "Yeah."

"Come outside with me."

He rolled his eyes. "Didn't we talk about that before?"

Gilly looked back out the window. "The sun is shining. It looks a little warmer outside. It's better than staying in here all day."

"Okay."

Gilly grinned. "You mean it?"

"Yeah, yeah, I mean it. I'll help you build your damn snowman." He stood and stretched, seeming impossibly tall.

"Snow woman," Gilly corrected. "With huge boobs."

Todd laughed and shook his head. "Jeez. Okay."

"C'mon," Gilly said, and reached over to take his hand. "It'll be fun."

But a few hours later, with snow in her face and up her shirt, Gilly didn't think it was so fun. Todd, however, was having a blast. Now he laughed in her face while he held a huge handful of sopping snow ready to throw at her.

"You're bigger than I am!" Gilly cried, wriggling. "Not fair!"

"If you can't play with the big boys," Todd said with an evil grin, "don't start the game."

Perhaps throwing that first snowball hadn't been such a smart idea. Gilly was willing to admit that. Taunting him hadn't been so smart, either.

"Get off me," she gritted out, feeling another inch of snow creep beneath her layers of clothes. They'd stomped it down in a lot of places, but most of it was still up to her knees.

He did, then held out a hand to help her up. "You started it."

His dripping face was evidence of that. Gilly slapped at the snow on her clothes, then lifted her face to the sunshine. Thank God it was warmer today than it had been last week. It hadn't made a lot of difference in the depth of the snow…not yet. But it would.

She waved her hand at the huge snow woman they'd

built. "Aren't you ashamed to act this way in front of your girlfriend?"

Todd trudged over and slapped a couple of handfuls onto the already gigantic chest. "She can't be my girlfriend unless her hooters are bigger."

Gilly shook herself so the snow slipped out from under her clothes. "If they get any bigger she won't be able to walk."

"She's made out of snow," Todd said. "She can't walk anyway."

For a moment she wasn't sure he knew she'd been joking, but the devilish twinkle in his eyes proved otherwise. "You're a smart-ass."

He bowed, low, with a sweeping gesture of his hand. "Yeah. I know."

Gilly felt a burble of laughter welling up in her throat, but quenched it. "I'm cold. Let's go back in."

The noise reached them both at the same time; she knew it by the way Todd stood suddenly, head cocked, face turned toward the woods. A low, buzzing rumble. It had been so long since Gilly had heard anything like it she couldn't, at first, figure out what it was.

Todd had no trouble. "Snowmobile."

Her guts clenched, the snow-packed earth beneath her feet tripping her so she stumbled. Todd grabbed her arm to hold her up. His fingers pinched hard even through the layers. He wasn't looking at her, but Gilly had no doubt he was completely, totally aware of her.

The buzzing came closer.

"Get inside." Todd yanked Gilly so hard she stumbled again, her feet tangling. He didn't even give her the chance to get up before he was dragging her.

Snow got up inside her shirt, cold and stinging, and Gilly swung at him. "Todd, stop it!"

He waited, but only the barest moment before grabbing her with his other hand, too, and hoisting her over his shoulder. Dangling this way, her hair in her face and the blood rushing to her head, Gilly couldn't even scream. She clutched the back of his sweatshirt as Todd stumbled. She closed her eyes and prayed they wouldn't fall.

He banged open the door to the lean-to and put her down. Gilly wobbled, the world spinning. Her flailing hands knocked a couple of cans from the decimated pantry shelves and a moment later, Todd had done the same but on purpose.

"Shit," he muttered. "Shit, shit, shit."

"Todd—"

Without even looking at her, he pushed her back against the wall opposite the shelves hard enough to knock the breath from her. He reached a long arm into the shadows of the shelves behind the supplies and pulled. The shelf moved aside, exposing a narrow closet.

"No!" Gilly cried.

Todd looked at her. "Get in there."

"No, Todd!"

He grabbed her arm and pulled her close, gaze boring into hers. "It's where Uncle Bill hung meat to cure. It's been empty a long time. It won't even smell bad. Get in there and be quiet."

The revving rumble of the snowmobile's engine was much, much louder. Gilly shivered. Time had turned to syrup again. She shook her head.

The motor cut off. Gilly tensed; Todd went stiff. Gilly strained to hear the crunch of boots on snow.

"If you don't get in there, if you make a sound, I will kill whoever's out there. And then I'll kill you," Todd said flatly. "And then I'll do myself, too."

He pushed her into the closet and slid the door closed. It wasn't dark or warm. Stripes of light shafted in through the gaps between the wallboards, the only solid surface being the back of the door through which he'd pushed her. Large hooks hung from the ceiling and lined the boards, stained from long-ago kills. He was right, it didn't smell bad, no matter how many corpses had hung here. In fact, the only scent tickling her nose was the faintest whiff of gasoline from outside and the lingering undercurrent of wood smoke. The stove vented into this space, or around it, or something, maybe to aid in curing the meat. She didn't know. She didn't care. Gilly pressed her fingers to the wall and looked through a crack.

It was a ranger.

Todd opened the back door and went out into the snow. The ranger was admiring the snow woman, and he turned with a grin as Todd walked up. Gilly pressed her forehead to the boards, trying to see.

"Hey," Todd said.

"Hi, sir. How's it going?"

"Good. Fine." Todd didn't even glance toward the cabin. "What can I do for you?"

"Just doing a routine check. We're making a run on all the places out here that back up to the state game lands. Making sure everyone's got what they need."

"I do," Todd said.

She'd never heard him sound like that—cool but friendly. Todd had ceased to be a stranger to her, but his voice was utterly alien just then. The ranger didn't notice, and why would he? Todd wasn't acting suspicious. The ranger had no idea she was there, and wouldn't, unless she screamed.

Even from here she could see the leather sheath on Todd's belt. She knew too well the length of the blade inside. With his hands on his hips it would take him a second to whip out the knife. Did the ranger have a weapon? Even if he had a gun, would he be able to draw it before Todd stabbed him?

Gilly stayed quiet.

"That's quite a snowman. Snow lady." The ranger laughed and looked around at the cabin.

What would he see? Gilly clutched at the wood, not caring about what blood might have darkened it in the past. The snow, trampled. Smoke coming from the chimney. No vehicle.

No vehicle.

Notice. How did Todd get here without a car? Please, notice.

"How about this snow, huh?" The ranger kicked at some of it. "Worst we've had in as long as I can remember. Lots of folks buried back here. Got a fellow a few miles up on Timberline Road, he's got a plow. I could send him over if you need it."

"Ah…no, thanks. I'm okay. Snow can't last forever, right? And I stocked up good before the storms started."

The ranger took another look around the yard and swung his gaze back to Todd. "You all alone out here, sir?"

"Ah…no. My wife's with me." In profile, Todd's grin was just as transforming as it was full-on—the ranger seemed calmed by it, anyway. "Sort of a…honeymoon."

The ranger laughed and tipped a finger to his hat. "Gotcha. Don't want to be disturbed, huh?"

"You got it."

"But you've got a working phone? Someone to call in case of an emergency? I see you don't have a vehicle here, sir."

"Had to park it at the end of the lane," Todd said easily, evenly, breezily. "Though it's not there, now, my wife's brother's borrowing it for a couple weeks until we get back. He'll come pick us up on a snowmobile if he has to. Like the one you have. What is that, a Bearcat five-seventy?"

The ranger looked over his shoulder. "Yep."

"Sweet." Todd walked over to it farther from the house. He shot a glance over his shoulder, seeming to look right into her eyes, then turned to openly admire the snowmobile.

The men talked about vehicle specs while Gilly shivered. This wasn't the way it had been at the gas station, when she'd lost her senses. Now she wanted to scream out, to batter the door open with her fists.

He said he'd kill the ranger. Then you. Then himself. Even if he doesn't...what will happen if you scream and the ranger doesn't hear you? What if he does and he manages to keep Todd from attacking him? What if Todd doesn't kill him, and the ranger gets away? What would happen then, Gilly?

Gilly turned her back to the crack she'd been peeking through and slid down the wall to bury her face in her hands. Shuddering with cold and anxiety, she wept. Her tears froze on her lashes.

You know what would happen.

You have to take care of what you love, Gillian. Even if it makes you bleed.

After another few minutes, she heard the snowmobile's buzz moving away. A minute after that, Todd opened the door and pulled her out. His eyes were wide and staring, a little crazy. When he pulled her against him, hugging her tight, Gilly was too surprised to stop him. They breathed together, in and out. His hand stroked down her back. She pulled away.

"Thank you, Gilly. Thank you."

"C'mon," Gilly said tensely. "Let's have some tea. I think there are some cookies left, too."

"Maybe you should lay off the cookies," Todd joked as they went into the kitchen. "I about busted myself lifting you."

Gilly, nerves already strung tight, gaped at this sad attempt at humor. Her hands flew to the mound of her stomach. Even beneath the layers of clothes she could feel a small, round bulge. Her face had grown thin, her arms and legs, too, but her belly had not. Her face heated. "That's an awful thing to say!"

She stormed into the bathroom and stripped off her clothes, tossing them into a pile on the floor. The small mirror above the sink could not reflect her entire body, so she had to rely on her own eyes and the movement of her hands as she felt her stomach.

She cupped her breasts in her hands, felt their weight and the way they ached. She slid her palms over the rounded curve of her belly. Still small. But there.

Gilly pawed through the depleted supplies Todd had bought for her so many weeks ago. Shampoo. Soap. Toothbrush. Toothpaste. No tampons, no sanitary napkins. And she hadn't noticed, had she? Hadn't paid attention to something missing that she hadn't needed to use? And she hadn't needed those monthly reminders of her fertility, because...

I'm pregnant. Oh, my God. No.

"Gilly? You okay?" Todd rapped on the door and tried the handle, but Gilly grabbed it tight before he could open it.

"I'll be out in a minute."

She was not okay. Not at all. Gilly bit the familiar sore spot inside her cheek to stifle a moan. She sank to the floor, mindless of the cold air that had her skin humped into prickly gooseflesh. She knelt in the pile of sopping wet clothes and pressed her hands to her face.

Not this. Not now, when Arwen starting first grade and Gandy graduating from diapers meant she would begin to have some of her life back.

A baby? Breastfeeding, diaper explosions, sleepless nights? Soft, sweet heads that smelled of baby soap. Tiny fingers and toes. The first toothless grin.

She was not a woman who "oohed" and "aahed" over babies in the grocery store or on the street. Both her pregnancies had been fraught with illness, complications and hard, relentless labor. The beauty of her children more than made up for the pain, but she'd vowed after Gandy's forty-eight-hour labor and birth that she'd never go through it again.

"Damn, damn," she swore softly. Goose bumps as hard as rocks pebbled her skin. She had nothing dry or warm to put on. "Todd...?"

He'd already anticipated her. The door edged open, and his hand appeared. He gave her underwear, socks, T-shirt, sweatshirt, sweatpants. Layers of warmth that would do nothing to chase away the chill. She took them with thanks, dried herself, slipped them on.

"You okay?" he asked when she finally ventured forth from the bathroom. He looked at her face and guessed the answer before she could reply. "You puke again? Are you sick?"

Gilly sat on the ugly plaid chair. "I'm pregnant."

The stunned look on his face would've been comical if she'd been in a better mood. For several long moments, Todd appeared unable to speak. Finally he ran a hand over his face, then up through the cropped remains of his hair.

"The fuck?" he asked.

"What the fuck, indeed," Gilly replied. She plucked at the front of her sweatshirt, peeling away bits of the logo with her fingernails.

"Jesus, Gilly. Pregnant? But...we...I mean..."

Todd struggled for the words, and Gilly decided to help him. "Not you. Seth. My husband. I was sick and needed antibiotics...they interfere with birth control pills."

Todd's hand reached naturally for his pocket, but found nothing except an empty cigarette package. He tossed it to the floor, then got up. He paced in front of her, finally turning to face her.

"What are you going to do?"

"Do?" Gilly asked. "There's not much to do, is there?"

"Whoa." Todd's voice turned gruff. "A baby. Damn, that's a big pile of shit, huh?"

The casual echo of her own earlier thoughts seemed heartlessly cruel. Gilly burst into tears. She felt foolish even as she wept, even as Todd handed her a hankie to wipe her face. Now the tears made sense, though, her hormones racing.

In seconds her tears had disappeared, replaced by weary hilarity. "A baby!" she said, not quite able to bring herself to laughter. "Oh. My. God."

Todd sat down on the couch nearest her and reached for her hand. "Gilly."

He said her name as though there should be more, but nothing else came.

"Oh, my God," Gilly replied, wiping at her face.

"I'll take care of you."

She lowered the cloth from her eyes to stare at him. "Surely you must see this changes everything."

He shook his head. "It doesn't have to. Stay here with me. Let me take care of you."

"What?" Gilly forced herself up from the chair. She couldn't make sense of what he'd just said. "What exactly do you want?"

"Have your baby with me," Todd said, a note of growing desperation in his voice. "Just…just say you'll stay here with me. We can raise it together."

"Are you out of your fucking mind?" Gilly shrieked. She backed away from him, toward the stairs. The horror of his suggestion raced through her. "Are you crazy?"

"Don't you call me that!" Todd was across to her in two strides. His fingers closed around her upper arms, holding her. "Just don't!"

Gilly didn't fight him. She didn't strike back. The child swimming in her belly made that impossible. She had more than herself to care for now. Protective instinct surged forth, overwhelming her. She'd *thought* she'd do anything to get back to her children, but now, to protect the life growing inside her, she *knew* she would. Whatever it took.

Lie. Cheat. Steal.

Kill.

"I'm sorry," she whispered and let him pull her closer again.

"I just wanted to tell you something." He didn't wait for her to reply before continuing. "I want you to know...I didn't mean it. About the ranger, or you. I would never...I'd never hurt you, Gilly. Not ever."

"I know you wouldn't."

"Do you?"

"Of course, Todd." Cheek pressed to the soft flannel of his shirt, she nodded. "I know you."

"And you'll stay with me, right?"

"All right," Gilly said in a voice as cold as the icicles hanging from the roof outside. "Okay, Todd. I'll stay with you."

She did know him, she thought as he let her go with one last squeeze. Todd was a rose. He'd be beautiful if tended properly, but would always have thorns.

49

"I'm pregnant, not disabled," Gilly told Todd, who'd just insisted on bringing her lunch to the couch. "Really, it's better for me to be active."

"You sure?" His worried expression was so sincere, it scraped at Gilly's heart.

She touched his cheek. "I'm sure."

He set the tray he'd prepared on the table. "Don't you got to have good food, though? Milk and eggs and shit? Vitamins?"

"Well, yes. I should." Gilly eyed the plate of boxed macaroni and cheese made with water instead of butter and milk. He'd sprinkled some peanuts on top. "But we don't have those things."

"Won't it hurt the baby?"

She'd had no doctor's appointments, no checkups. She'd been battered and stressed. She'd suffered trauma. But she couldn't allow herself to dwell on those things. Not when she had no way of changing them.

"I'll be fine. Women have been having babies for thousands of years."

"And lots of them died," Todd said.

Gilly's hands fisted at the bluntness of his words. "Todd!"

He shrugged, then sat down beside her. "I don't know anything about pregnant ladies. I just don't want anything bad to happen to you."

"I'll be fine," she said tightly, though images of blood-soaked sheets filled her mind. Her womb twinged in memory, and a sharp pain stabbed between her legs. Cold sweat trickled down her spine.

Todd put his arm around her. "Do you think it will be a boy or a girl?"

"I don't know." She shook herself mentally, though the image had been so vivid she could practically smell the copper tang of blood.

"If it's a boy," Todd said slowly. "Do you think we could name him Bill?"

The very thought of naming her child after Todd's dead uncle turned her stomach. Gilly smiled. "Of course."

His answering smile was like the sun parting rain clouds. "Cool!"

He got up and took the tray to the kitchen. Gilly poked a fork at the urine-colored pasta, but didn't eat it. She touched the small bulge of her tummy, knowing it was too early to feel anything but imagining the flutter of movement anyway. She had to care for this child. She ate the macaroni, every last bite of it.

Later, when the afternoon had passed into evening, Todd brought out a pair of white candles and set them on the counter. "I thought you might want these."

Gilly looked at him in surprise. She'd allowed the past few Sabbath evenings to pass without lighting candles to commemorate them. She'd been unable to perform the rituals that usually so calmed her. Lighting the candles had made her ache for her family too much.

"Thank you." Gilly took the pack of matches and lit one, touching it to the first wick and then the other. She closed her eyes and waved her hands toward her face, then said the blessing aloud.

"Why do you do that thing with your hands?" Todd asked when she'd finished.

For a moment she didn't know what he meant. The habit of candle-lighting was so ingrained she didn't have to really think about any one part of it. Then she understood.

"You mean this?" She repeated the gesture.

"Yeah."

"When I do that," Gilly said with a sigh that came from her toes, "I'm gathering up all the bits of wonder I've found since last Shabbat and offering them up to Adonai. To God. All the blessings and things to be thankful for."

"What did you send up this week?" Todd asked her as innocently as any child.

Gilly touched her stomach. "This." She thought, then touched his shoulder. "And you, I guess."

She hadn't thought she would say such a thing until it popped out of her mouth. The awful and hilarious thing was, she meant it. Hate and love were two pages back to back in the same story. What she felt for him now was no different than what she'd felt in the beginning, and yet it was vastly, immensely dissimilar. As was everything inside her. Nothing could ever be the same.

Todd looked pleased. "Yeah?"

"Yeah," Gilly said. "Sure, Todd."

Even she couldn't be certain if she was lying.

50

Drip. Drip. Drip. The icicles on the porch grew longer every day. First the sun melted them enough to allow the water to drip from the ends, and when night came they froze. Now they looked like great, jagged teeth in the mouth of an enormous beast.

Was it better to be on the inside looking out, already consumed by the giant? Or to be outside, looking at the teeth ready to snap down on tender flesh? Gilly leaned her forehead against the window, pondering.

"Want to play a game?" Todd asked.

"No." Gilly's hands caressed her belly absently. Her thoughts were on the baby. Boy or girl, this time?

"There's another puzzle in the cabinet. I'll help you put it together. It's got trains on it."

"No, thanks."

Todd let out a frustrated sigh. "C'mon, Gilly. Let's do something!"

She blinked, focusing on him. "I don't feel like doing anything."

He groaned. "Damn it!"

In the light of her hormonal glow, his childishness was endearing rather than annoying. Gilly smiled and rolled her eyes. "What game would you like to play?"

Todd crossed to the large armoire and opened the doors. "Monopoly. Life. Checkers. Battleship…ah, shit, half the pieces are missing out of that one. Shit. We've played all these a million times."

It certainly felt as though they had. "What's up on that shelf, up there?"

Gilly pointed. Despite his height, Todd stood too close to the shelves to see to the back of the ones above his head. From her vantage point across the room, though, Gilly saw some boxes tucked back in the shadows. Perhaps more games, or another puzzle. Something fresh to them, anyway, and something to relieve the tedium.

Todd reached up and stuck his hand back along the shelf. He still wasn't quite tall enough to grab it. "Grab me a chair, will you?"

Her attention now was piqued. Gilly took him one of the tottery dining chairs and held the back of it while he stood on top. Todd peered back into the shelf and grabbed one of the boxes, handed it down to her and stepped from the chair.

"What is it?" Todd asked.

Gilly brushed at the thick coating of dust. The wooden box was fairly large, big enough to need two hands to hold it properly. She sniffed. Cedar. Gilly smiled. Seth always said no tourist trap would be complete without a display of cedar boxes and moccasins.

"I'm not sure." Gilly cracked open the lid, which squealed on its hinges. "Pictures?"

"Let me see." Todd took the box from her and flipped through the sheaf of yellowed photographs and pieces of paper. He stopped, the color draining from his face. "Oh."

"What is it?"

He held up one. "My mother."

Gilly took his elbow and led him to one of the couches. "Here. Sit down. Let's look at them."

Todd shoved the box away from him. Paper scattered across the battered coffee table. "No! I don't want to look at her!"

Gilly gathered them up gently and tucked them back into the box. "They're only pictures, Todd. They can't hurt you."

He shook his head, fingers going to the cigarettes that weren't there and then running through the length of hair that was no longer long. His feet jittered on the nasty shag carpet. Gilly put a hand on his arm to soothe him, and he quieted suddenly.

"We can look at them together. It'll be okay." Gilly pulled out the one on top and held it so he could stare down at it if he chose.

At first he shook his head, but then he nodded his assent. He took the photo from her. "That's my mom."

The young woman in the picture looked vastly different from the haggard zombie in the newspaper clippings. Her smile was genuine here, her eyes bright.

"She's pretty," Gilly said.

"Yeah." Todd touched the smiling face.

"You look like her."

He looked surprised. "You think so?"

Gilly studied the dark-eyed woman whose hair fell in sheaves to her waist. "Yes. I do."

He put the picture aside and picked up the next. "Uncle Bill with Mom."

The siblings faced the camera, smiling, heads together and arms around each other's waists. They wore bathing suits, the colors of their vintage style still noxiously vivid even though time had faded their intensity. Todd's mother's belly peeked out from the opening of her bikini, perhaps in pregnancy?

Todd confirmed the thought. "My brother Stevie, probably."

He sifted through more of the pictures. He lifted one and let out a sigh that was half moan. "There we all are."

The picture, taken a few years earlier than the one featured in the paper, clearly showed the decline of Todd's mother. Her face had gone from smiling and pretty to glassy-eyed and rigid. Her arms encircled a blue wrapped bundle. Her hair, once dark and shining, had been cropped short and lay flat against her head. Tiny red sores clustered in one corner of her mouth.

"The baby…that's me." Todd showed her another photo, of only the children grouped around the blue bundle. He touched the faces of each of his brothers and sisters, naming them. "Stevie. Freddie. Mary. Joey. Katie."

One hand went to his face to cover his eyes. His shoulders heaved. He wept.

Gilly, uncertain, put a hand on his arm. Todd bent and buried his face in her neck. His face was hot on the skin of her throat. His tears splashed her, burning.

She held him tightly, not knowing what to say and so comforting him as best she could with her silence. She put one hand to the back of his head, stroking the shorn strands. His hands clutched her.

"We were just kids!" he sobbed against her, his words nearly unintelligible.

"It wasn't your fault."

He still wept. "We were only little kids! Why? What did we do that was so bad that she wanted to kill us?"

"It wasn't you," Gilly repeated more firmly. "Todd, your mother was mentally unstable. She was in pain. She couldn't decide what was right and wrong, or she would have never—"

"I should've died there, too," he whispered. "Along with Stevie and the others. I wasn't no better than them! I ain't never been better!"

"Todd!" She shook him until he sat up. "Listen to me!"

She used her "Mommy means business" voice, the one guaranteed to stop a rampaging toddler in his tracks seconds before grocery store disaster. It worked on Todd, too. He knuckled his eyes, but stopped protesting.

"There is nothing you could have done to stop your mother," Gilly said. "She was sick. You were only five years old. You and your brothers and sisters didn't do anything to make her do what she did. You didn't deserve it. She was wrong."

"She didn't love us...." He sighed, scrubbing at his face. "Why didn't my mom love me?"

Without thinking, Gilly put her hand on her stomach. "She must have loved you, Todd. There's no way she couldn't have. But what she did…as sick as it was…she probably did it out of that love. She must have thought you would be better off…"

Her explanation trailed off, insufficient.

"That ain't love," Todd said fiercely. "You love your

kids. You told me you'd do anything to stop them from getting hurt. You'd never do what she did!"

"No. I wouldn't."

He lifted another photograph, another of his mother while still young and pretty. "Look at her there, Gilly. See how she looked before she had us?"

"Mothers love their babies—"

"*Some* mothers love their babies," Todd interrupted. "Some don't know how to."

"Maybe that's true," she conceded. "But that's not your fault. Stop blaming yourself. You were only a kid! You're still…"

He would always be a child where this was concerned. Always a wounded, damaged boy who'd been left for dead by the person who was supposed to love him more than anything in the world. Gilly swallowed hard.

"It's not your fault," she repeated. "None of it."

"This must've been Uncle Bill's box," Todd said. "He never showed it to me."

"Maybe he thought it would upset you too much."

Todd stared off into the distance. "Nobody ever talked about them, you know? Nobody ever said their names. It was like they didn't just die, they never even were born. I didn't have anything even to remember them by. If I'd had this box maybe things would've been at least a little different. If I'd had this instead of a file full of newspaper clippings and a note."

He shrugged, hand going absently to his pocket and falling away again when it found no cigarette package there. "Maybe it would've been a little easier."

She doubted it. "Maybe."

He took out a faded piece of ruled notebook paper. "Uncle Bill wrote this. I recognize the writing."

It was a poem, and not a very good one. What it lacked in creative imagery it made up for in emotion. Todd read the first few lines aloud.

"'She's pretty like the red rose, with skin as soft as butterfly wings. Hair as dark as the night that has to shield our love.'"

He frowned, turning the paper over. "I didn't know Uncle Bill wrote poems."

And to women, no less, Gilly thought, remembering that Todd had claimed his uncle to be homosexual. "People usually manage to surprise us."

He read to the bottom of the page. "For Sharon. That's my mother."

"Are you sure Uncle Bill wrote this?"

Todd put the paper back into the box. "Hell if I know. But this is his box and it sure looks like his writing. Why would he have somebody else's poem in it?"

He opened a creased envelope, looked over the lined paper, and handed it to Gilly without a word. Todd got up from the couch, spilling the box's contents. Gilly read the letter, written in a looping, uneducated hand, the same from the note he'd shown her weeks before.

Bill,
The test shows positive. Im knocked up again &
this time we know for shore who the dad is, huh?
We said it wuldn't happen again but God knows
more than us and so we are caught again. Stevie
is ok but what if this one ain't right?

The letter continued, mostly into ramblings about God and Jesus and whether or not the child she carried would be normal or deformed. Gilly's hands shook as she set the paper down, and her stomach twisted in a way that had nothing to do with morning sickness. If she'd read the letter correctly, Bill Lutz and Sharon Blauch had created two children, Stevie and Todd. Sharon didn't name the father of her other four children, but Gilly assumed from the woman's disjointed words that they hadn't been Bill.

"I...I thought you said he was gay," she finally said, wishing after she spoke to take the words away.

Todd hadn't gone far, just to the window. Now he turned to look at her. "He was."

"But..." She stopped, unable to say anything more.

"He fucked men and he knocked up his sister," Todd said. "And I guess he was my father. Shit."

He pulled up his sleeve and looked at the tattoo. "I thought I was one of six. I guess I was just one of two, huh? One of fucking two."

His voice broke on that, and Gilly's heart broke a little listening to it. He crossed to her and gathered the pile of pictures and letters. He took the one of himself as an infant, surrounded by his smiling siblings, and put it in the pocket that used to hold his smokes. He stuffed the rest into the box and returned it to the armoire, where he slid it back onto the highest shelf.

"Some things," Todd said, "just aren't right to know."

51

Gilly eyed the empty basket by the woodstove and debated getting some more logs from the pile outside the back door. The longer it took her to decide, the less she felt like heaving herself up from the couch and going outside. And really, she comforted herself, it was downright balmy in here. With the warmth outside now, they didn't even need a fire at all.

Todd set a plate of crackers and aerosol cheese in front of her. "Here."

She grimaced.

He looked serious. "All we got for snacks. Better eat it. Besides, Gilly, it's cheese. Good for you and the baby."

He hadn't asked again to call the child after his uncle. Gilly picked up the plate and looked at it critically. "Todd, this stuff has more sodium and chemicals in it than anything else. I don't think it even came from a cow."

He snatched one of the crackers and tucked into his

mouth, chewing solemnly. "Yeah, but this and a handful of Slim Jims is like eating a piece of heaven."

Gilly snorted. "There's no accounting for taste."

Her stomach rumbled, and she ate a cracker. She was taking her mother's advice and being happy with what she had. Which wasn't much.

"When the snow melts, I'll hike out to the main road and hitch a ride to town. Get us a truck. Buy some stuff."

The utter improbability of what he proposed made Gilly stuff another cracker in her mouth to keep from laughing out loud. His face showed he was serious. He meant that she should stay with him. Have her baby here in this cabin. Raise it together like some perverted Little House in the Big Woods family.

"I know you don't think it's going to work," Todd said in a low voice.

"Oh, Todd." Gilly took a deep breath. "Don't talk about it. There's nothing we can do about it right now, anyway."

"I'm a fucking moron, ain't I?" His self-deprecating question had the lilt of humor in it, but Todd wasn't smiling. "A foron. A stupid foron."

"I don't think so."

"You don't want to stay with me," Todd said matter-of-factly. "No matter what you said before."

Gilly faced him, the taste of slick processed cheese bitter on her tongue. "So, what are you going to do about it?"

"Nothing." Todd met her eyes. "I told you before I couldn't ever let you go. But I know you think about getting away. I know you're going to try."

Had she really thought she could continue to lie to

him? That she could convince him of her willingness to stay and raise her child with him? She'd underestimated him.

"Yes. When the snow melts." Gilly touched his hand. "I have to."

"Even if you promised not to tell them anything, they'd come here, wouldn't they? They'd find me. Even if I ran, I guess they would. I'd have no chance, huh?"

"I don't think so. And I couldn't promise you I wouldn't say anything. I'd have to, you know. Tell them something."

"I'd go to jail. Or I'd cut myself and bleed to death up here, all alone. Not much of a choice." He poked at one of the crackers, then swallowed it.

Gilly rested her hands on her belly. "No. I'd say it's not."

"A good person would give up, let you go. I wish I was a good person." He said suddenly, "But I just ain't!"

"People can change."

Todd shook his head. "Tell me again that you'll stay here with me."

"I'll stay here with you," Gilly said.

He stretched out beside her and put his head in her lap. "Wouldn't it be nice if that were true?"

She threaded her fingers through his hair. "Sure it would."

He closed his eyes and nestled close to her. Gilly stroked his hair, watching the sun paint lines on the planes of his face. When he slept, she watched the rise and fall of his chest. How hard would he hang on to life, she thought, when she tried to take it away?

52

Todd was balancing a straw on the end of his nose. Arms out at shoulder height, fingers spread, he bobbed and weaved, trying to keep the straw from falling. The sight was completely ridiculous, especially since he went about the feat with so much determination.

"I seen this on TV once," he said as the straw hit the floor again. "You're supposed to watch the end. Then you can balance it."

He watched the end all right, but since the straw was so short, watching it crossed his eyes. Gilly bit her lip against a giggle. Todd caught the gesture from the corner of his eye and let the straw fall off without retrieving it.

"Aren't you ever going to laugh? Not ever?"

Gilly shook her head. "I don't think so."

"Not ever again?"

Not here, with him. Gilly just shook her head again, unwilling to answer. Todd scowled and left the kitchen.

A few minutes later, she heard him call her name.

She looked across to the living room to see what her college roommate had fondly called a "moon." Gilly clapped her hands over her eyes in mortification.

"Todd!"

"Make you laugh?"

"No!" she cried, and covered her eyes.

"Shit."

She peeked through her fingers to see him tucking in his shirt. "That was really uncalled-for."

"I just wanted to see if I could make you laugh." Todd sauntered closer. "Figured the sight of my hairy a—"

"Todd! For goodness' sakes!" Gilly felt a burble of hilarity in her chest, but it didn't come out. She smiled, but kept her laughter to herself as she had vowed to do.

"Whatever." He shrugged, then waggled his eyebrows. "It sure made your cheeks go all pink."

Gilly rolled her eyes. "I guess it did."

Todd leaned against the half wall, ducking his head to peer under the hanging cabinets at her. "Tell me something."

"About what?" she asked, thinking he had something specific in mind.

He waved his hand at her. "I don't know. Just something. Anything."

"Are we going to tell stories, is that it?"

Todd didn't smile back. "I figure you know a hell of a lot about me. Thought maybe I ought to get to know you."

"There isn't much to tell." Gilly thought. That wasn't really true, was it? She had lots of stories, none quite so tragic and horrendous as Todd's, but tales of her life that showed why she had become the woman she was.

"What about your family?" Todd tapped the counter restlessly, and she could tell he was missing his smokes.

"I told you about my family."

"Not all of it."

Gilly came around the counter and motioned with her head for him to follow her to the couch. "You sure you want to know?"

"What the hell else is there to do?"

Todd flopped onto the couch and spread out his arms and legs, then patted the seat beside him. Gilly looked at the couch across from him but sat where he'd indicated. His thigh touched hers, but there was no point in moving away. Not now. They'd come too far for her to play at coyness, or to pretend she didn't recognize their closeness.

She looked outside, where snow still covered every surface though the sun had risen high in the sky. "My family. Okay. Well, my mother was an alcoholic with paranoid and depressive tendencies. She spent a lot of time in the hospital when I was in my early teens. By the time she got on the proper medication and stopped drinking, I was in college. She died before my children were born."

"Do you miss her?"

Unexpected tears stung her eyes. "Sometimes. Yes. I miss her."

Todd made a low noise. "Even though she was all messed up?"

Gilly's memories could in no way compete with Todd's for heartbreak, but her childhood and adolescence had been far from the sweetness and light of a television sitcom. "Yes. Even though she was all messed up."

He bit at his nails, a habit he'd taken up since running out of cigarettes. "Why do you think that is?"

"Because she was my mother," Gilly said in surprise, as though the answer should be obvious. Well, it should be. But she understood his question, and why he asked it. "Because…no matter how much bad she gave me, I loved her."

"Because she was your mom."

"Yes."

Todd sighed heavily, leaning his head back on the couch. A moment later he slouched down to rest it on Gilly's shoulder. He'd washed his hair that morning, cursing and shouting at the cold water, but now the cropped strands smelled faintly of citrus. It tickled her cheek.

"What made you decide to have kids?" Todd reached over and took her hand. He turned it palm up and traced the lines there. "Did you think you'd be a better mother than yours?"

"Oh, no," Gilly said. "I wasn't sure I'd be a good mother at all. I didn't think I knew how." She trailed off, picturing her children. "I'm still not sure I know how."

"But you love your kids."

"Of course. You know I do."

"And you're going to have another one," Todd said, resting his hand on her belly.

Gilly snorted. "Not on purpose, believe me."

"But you'll love it, right?" He peered up at her, the slinking dog look returning after long absence. "Even though you didn't want it?"

Gilly placed her hand over his. "Yes. I will love this child. And I will protect it."

"I never wanted kids." The weight of his hand was

not unwelcome on her stomach. "I knew I'd fuck them up. Big-time."

"Understandable that you would feel that way." Gilly leaned her head back and closed her eyes.

"Do you think I could be a good father?"

She cracked open one eye to look down at him, but his attention was focused on her stomach. "It's not something anyone can know until it happens."

"Funny thing is," he said, "I think I might like to try. I think I could be okay at it."

"You do?"

"Yeah." Now he looked at her, a light of excitement in his eyes. His hand rubbed slow, hypnotizing circles on her stomach. "How long until it comes?"

Gilly thought. "Six or seven months."

"My birthday is in November," Todd told her. "Maybe it'll come on my birthday."

"You never know." The slow rhythm of his hand was putting her to sleep. The conversation had become dreamlike. Unreal. She knew what he was asking but could not answer him.

"Stay with me," he whispered, and she was awake as instantly as if someone had popped a balloon in her ear. "Let me show you. Help me be good, Gilly."

"Only you can make that choice, Todd."

"I think I could love a baby. A kid."

"They're hard not to love," Gilly said.

They fell silent together, and she thought of mothers who didn't love their children, and those who loved them in the wrong way. Perhaps Todd was thinking of that, too. But since he didn't speak, Gilly didn't know.

53

The sound of rushing water had been constant over the past few days. Bright sunshine every day. Warmth. The snow was melting, finally. Not quite there yet. And then…

Gilly gasped when she saw green. Grass, showing through one of the bare patches from where they'd rolled the snowman. She pressed her face to the glass, unable to believe it. Only one small patch, and only in the places they'd already mostly cleared. But there.

"Spring," she murmured, then said a blessing. "*Baruch Ha-Shem*. Thank you, God."

It was time to get prepared.

Her hands went to her belly automatically as she thought. She would still need appropriate clothes. Food. Water. She didn't know how long it would take to hike the road, if she even could, but…she would do it, now. She had to.

She heard Todd's heavy tread upstairs, and turned from the window as he came down. "Todd…"

But she couldn't tell him that the snow was melting, not with so much joy in her voice. She wouldn't be able to hide it. She couldn't be deliberately cruel to him. Not anymore.

He looked at her curiously. "Yeah?"

"Nothing," Gilly replied with a smile that felt as though it stretched across her entire face.

She wanted to run outside, to throw herself down in the tiny emerald patch, to rub her face and hands all over it. Her hands shook with the desire, so intense she had to shove her hands in her pockets to stop their trembling. She forced herself to look away from it. To pretend it wasn't there.

"It's hot in here," Todd said. "I won't even have to light the stove today."

Gilly nodded and walked on stiff legs to the dining table. She'd begun another puzzle, this one of a thousand different kinds of lollipops. Her fingers patted the scattered pieces, but she did not place any. She would not, if God was willing, finish this puzzle.

It was almost time for her to go home.

54

"I'm so hungry I could eat a bowl of cigarette butts with a hair in it." Gilly groaned and grabbed her stomach. "Hurry up with those potatoes!"

"Calm down." Todd brandished his knife. "They've got a million eyes in them, all over the place."

"You're going to cut off your fingers. Use a paring knife."

Todd concentrated on gouging out another eye, then tossed the edible potato into the pot with the others. "This is the sharpest knife we got."

"Just be careful, that's all. I don't want to have to stitch you up." Gilly went to the window over the sink. It seemed that for almost three months, all she'd done was look, from one window or the other, out at the white wasteland of imprisonment.

No more. Water ran from the gutters with a sound like a running brook. Large patches had rotted in the snow, revealing the brown and green of earth underneath. At the edge of the woods, the first shoots of crocuses poked their purple and yellow heads up to reach the sun.

She couldn't sit still. Gilly paced constantly, like a tiger in a cage. Each day she'd woken to brilliant sunshine was one she was closer to release.

"That's the last of the oil," Todd said, setting a pot of it on the stove.

She'd been craving French fries since yesterday. Today, Todd had pulled out the last crinkly sack of potatoes that had weathered the winter. Some of them had been salvageable.

In contrast to Gilly's edginess and constant monitoring of spring's progress, Todd was actively ignoring the season's change. He had to notice, had to see, but Gilly didn't mention the decreasing blanket of snow outside and neither did he.

His nightmares had returned, and his cries often woke her from her own dreams. The fields of roses had stopped blooming. Now she dreamed of rows and rows of barren, thorn-ridden stems. Each time she soothed him and herself back to sleep with wordless lullabies. It was easy to do, in the dark, with his tears wetting her shoulder. Easy to pretend he was just another child to care for.

In the light of day, it was different. She watched him without looking at him. Saw how his face had grown thinner and haggard over the past few days, while her own in the mirror glowed with vibrant, unvoiced joy. If she was kinder to him then, it was because she was helpless to be anything else.

Their time together was running short. She knew it, and he had to know it, too. Every hour that passed took her farther away from him, though she hadn't gone anywhere at all.

"Stay with me," he asked her in the night, and her lie hung between them like the strands of a caterpillar's silk. "Stay with me," he whispered with increasing desperation, but only in the dark. In the light, Todd no longer asked.

Gilly turned from the window, powerless to stop the smile stretching her lips. Sunshine filled her soul, her heart, even her womb, where the life inside gave her the strength she would need to do what she must. When he saw her face, Todd flinched, but recovered.

"Almost done," he said, and waved the huge knife at her and the potato. "French fries, coming right up."

"Yummy!" Gilly cried. Seeing the early spring flowers had made her positively giddy.

The potato slipped from Todd's fingers and landed on the floor. He reached for it, smacking his head on the table with a resounding thud and a muffled curse. The accident did what his silly jokes and awkward wordplay had not.

Gilly laughed.

The delight that filled her from the soft spring breeze now burst from her throat in a loud guffaw. The noise was loud. It startled both of them. And it didn't stop.

Gilly laughed until her sides ached and tears streamed down her face. Todd, who could have been offended by her making such fun of his misfortune, merely gazed at her gape-mouthed. He reached up to rub the lump on his forehead, and hit himself in the eye with the potato.

Gilly laughed harder. Todd met her with a smile, then a chortle. He joined her hilarity. They laughed together, and it was all right. She gave him the last secret part of herself she'd been holding back, and it didn't matter.

Todd put the knife on the table to hold his sides in laughter. Gilly's eyes fell on it, the blade so huge and glinting. Her laughter stopped. She met Todd's gaze.

In that last moment, his smile faded. His eyes closed briefly and when they opened, she saw he knew what she meant to do. There was no future for Todd if Gilly left this place. There could be no future for her if she stayed.

She had nothing more for him than this, a cruelty that was in fact a simple mercy.

The knife was heavy in her hand, but her aim was true. She slashed once. Todd went to his knees in front of her as if he was praying, hands to his throat. Crimson jetted between his fingers.

The knife fell, turning over and over, and clattered to the floor beside her, but Gilly didn't pay attention. She went to her knees, too, arms reaching to catch him as he slumped.

Not long ago she'd asked herself how hard he'd hold on to life when she took it away. She had her answer now. Todd didn't struggle or fight. His back arched as his life ran out over his hands and hers. As she cradled him against her, fingers stroking in his hair.

She sang to him, the same lullabies from their long nights together, all mixed up yet somehow making sense. A long stream of words and melody, broken now and again by the relentless hitch of her breath as she fought sobs. She didn't make it through one verse.

There was more blood than she'd expected, gouts of it, splattering the floor and legs of the table. It painted everything, the color too bright. Unreal. Too real.

And too short. She'd had months to convince herself she'd do this to survive. It took only seconds to make it happen. She'd thought she would do this for herself, but in the end she did it for him.

Todd's lips moved, though he had no voice. He clutched at her. He drew her close, and she let him. She kissed his forehead and looked into his eyes as he mouthed two words she didn't have to hear to understand.

"You're welcome," Gilly said.

And then Todd died.

55

"See, Arwen. Roses don't like to get their feet wet. Just a little bit of water." Gilly handed her daughter the watering can and looked up at the warm spring sunshine.

"I like red roses," Gandy said matter-of-factly.

No more baby words for him. He spoke in full sentences now and no longer needed a blankie. Arwen had shot up two inches and a dress size. Sometimes Gilly looked at the two of them and couldn't believe how much they'd changed.

Baby Tyler in the sling across her chest let out a small, muffled wail and Gilly reached to unbutton the flap of her nursing shirt so he could reach her breast. The tingle of her milk letting down had started at the first whimper and her youngest son latched on, sucking hard while she cupped the back of his tiny head. Gilly, sitting on a blanket in the sunshine with her children beside her, surveyed the yard where last year only dandelions had grown.

She'd planted roses.

Red roses, all of them, different varieties and shades but every one of them red. She'd worked hard in the garden, digging and turning the soil, making raised beds in the places where it was too boggy and moist for roses to thrive. She'd spent hours on her efforts and would see no results until they bloomed, but that was all right. She could wait.

"Mama?"

"Yes, baby." She smoothed Arwen's hair back from her forehead.

"I missed you."

Gilly shifted Tyler so she could pull Arwen into her lap. She didn't have to ask when. Arwen had had more trouble with what had happened last year than Gandy. She still woke from nightmares, sometimes. Gilly cradled her daughter close, even when the baby let out a "meep" of protest before getting back to the business of nursing.

"I know you did, baby. But Mama's here now."

"And you won't go away again, right?"

"No."

Gandy, who'd taken the watering can to fill it from the spigot, was having trouble with it now. His sturdy legs weren't as chubby as they'd been last year. He'd stretched up. He set the can down and furrowed his brow to give it a hard stare before picking it up again. Water sloshed as he struggled, but he finally got it back to the bush they'd last planted.

"Good job, Gandy." Gilly waved at her son. "Come here. Mama needs a squeeze."

All three of them crowded onto her lap and Gilly held

them as close as she could. She breathed them. These, her children, whom she loved so dearly.

"That man won't ever come back, will he?" Arwen insisted.

"No."

"Because he's dead," Gandy offered.

There would always be pieces of the story Gilly wouldn't tell anyone, ever, about those three months. Nobody had ever questioned what she'd said about how Todd had held her against her will, or that he'd died by his own hand. She thought he'd forgive her that.

She hadn't given her children all the details, though she knew some day they might ask. "Yes. His name was Todd. And he died."

Gandy struggled to his feet, eager to be off and away. Arwen snuggled closer for a moment, plucking at the sling and petting the top of her baby brother's head. Gilly's thighs cramped but she held her daughter tight.

"Do you miss him, Mama?" Arwen asked, looking into Gilly's face. "Do you ever miss that man?"

Gilly stroked her hand down Arwen's hair. She looked out across the roses, bare now but promising beauty. She watched her son running and felt her infant taking nourishment from her body. She looked into her daughter's eyes.

The crunch of tires on the driveway made them both look up. A familiar gray Volvo was pulling into the garage, Arwen already tumbling off Gilly's lap in her eagerness.

"It's Daddy! I'm going to give him what I made in school!" Arwen cried, and ran, her brother following.

Gilly got to her feet and watched her husband gather their children into his arms for hugs and kisses. He lifted Gandy upside down, sending the boy into fits of giggles, then bent to take the linked necklace of paper rings Arwen had made in first grade. Seth lifted his hand to her, waving, his grin familiar and beloved and just for her.

"Yes," Gilly murmured with only the roses as witness. "Sometimes, I do."

And then she went to her husband, whom she greeted with kisses, and together with their children they went inside. This was her family. Precious and fragile and beloved.

This was the life she'd made, and she'd never again lose sight of what it meant.

* * * * *

ACKNOWLEDGMENTS

As always, I could write without music, but I'm ever so grateful I don't have to. Much appreciation goes to the following artists, whose songs made up the playlist for this book. Please support their music through legal sources.

"Give It Away"—Quincy Coleman
"Take Me Home"—Lisbeth Scott and Nathan Barr
"Everything"—Lifehouse
"This Woman's Work"—Kate Bush
"You've Been Loved"—Joseph Arthur
"Iris"—Goo Goo Dolls
"Look After You"—The Fray
"The End"—The Doors
"One Last Breath"—Creed
"A Home for You"—Kaitlin Hopkins, Deven May
"Over My Head"—Christopher Dallman

And a special thanks to Jason Manns, whose version of "Hallelujah" wasn't there when I started this book but was there all through the end.

DIANE CHAMBERLAIN

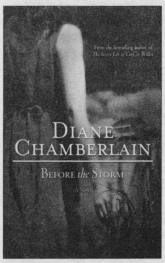

Laurel Lockwood lost her son once through neglect. She's spent the rest of her life determined to make up for her mistakes, and she's succeeded in becoming a committed, protective parent. Still, she loosens her grip just enough to let Andy attend a local church social—a decision that terrifies her when the church is consumed by fire. But Andy survives...and remarkably, saves other children from the flames.

But when the suspicion of arson is cast upon Andy, Laurel must ask herself how well she really knows her son...and how far she'll go to keep her promise to protect him forever.

Available wherever books are sold.

REQUEST YOUR
FREE BOOKS!

2 FREE NOVELS
FROM THE ROMANCE COLLECTION
PLUS 2 FREE GIFTS!

YES! Please send me 2 FREE novels from the Romance Collection and my 2 FREE gifts (gifts are worth about $10). After receiving them, if I don't wish to receive any more books, I can return the shipping statement marked "cancel." If I don't cancel, I will receive 4 brand-new novels every month and be billed just $5.99 per book in the U.S. or $6.49 per book in Canada. That's a savings of at least 25% off the cover price. It's quite a bargain! Shipping and handling is just 50¢ per book in the U.S. and 75¢ per book in Canada.* I understand that accepting the 2 free books and gifts places me under no obligation to buy anything. I can always return a shipment and cancel at any time. Even if I never buy another book, the two free books and gifts are mine to keep forever.

194/394 MDN FVU7

Name   (PLEASE PRINT)

Address   Apt. #

City   State/Prov.   Zip/Postal Code

Signature (if under 18, a parent or guardian must sign)

Mail to the **Harlequin® Reader Service:**
IN U.S.A.: P.O. Box 1867, Buffalo, NY 14240-1867
IN CANADA: P.O. Box 609, Fort Erie, Ontario L2A 5X3

Want to try two free books from another line?
Call 1-800-873-8635 or visit www.ReaderService.com.

* Terms and prices subject to change without notice. Prices do not include applicable taxes. Sales tax applicable in N.Y. Canadian residents will be charged applicable taxes. Offer not valid in Quebec. This offer is limited to one order per household. Not valid for current subscribers to the Romance Collection or the Romance/Suspense Collection. All orders subject to credit approval. Credit or debit balances in a customer's account(s) may be offset by any other outstanding balance owed by or to the customer. Please allow 4 to 6 weeks for delivery. Offer available while quantities last.

Your Privacy—The Harlequin® Reader Service is committed to protecting your privacy. Our Privacy Policy is available online at www.ReaderService.com or upon request from the Harlequin Reader Service.

We make a portion of our mailing list available to reputable third parties that offer products we believe may interest you. If you prefer that we not exchange your name with third parties, or if you wish to clarify or modify your communication preferences, please visit us at www.ReaderService.com/consumerschoice or write to us at Harlequin Reader Service Preference Service, P.O. Box 9062, Buffalo, NY 14269. Include your complete name and address.

Sophie Littlefield

IN THE DARK DAYS *of* WAR, A MOTHER MAKES THE ULTIMATE SACRIFICE

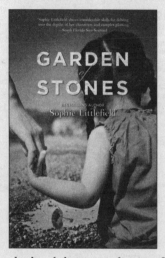

Lucy Takeda is just fourteen years old, living in Los Angeles, when the bombs rain down on Pearl Harbor. Within weeks, she and her mother, Miyako, are ripped from their home—along with thousands of other innocent Japanese Americans—and taken to the Manzanar prison camp.

Buffeted by blistering heat and choking dust, Lucy and Miyako must endure the harsh living conditions of the camp. Corruption and abuse creep into every corner of Manzanar, eventually ensnaring beautiful, vulnerable Miyako. Ruined and unwilling to surrender her daughter to the same fate, Miyako commits a final act of desperation that will stay with Lucy forever…and spur her to sins of her own.

Available wherever books are sold.

DEBORAH CLOYED

Leda desperately seeks the "real world" when she flees her life of privilege to travel to Kenya. What she doesn't expect is to fall for Ita, the charismatic and thoughtful man who gave up his dreams to offer children a haven in the midst of turmoil.

Their love is threatened by Ita's troubled childhood friend Chege, a gang leader with whom he shares a complex history. As political unrest reaches a boiling point and the slum erupts in violence, Leda is attacked…and forced to put her trust in Chege. Their worlds upturned, they must now face the reality that sometimes the most treacherous threat is not the world outside, but the demons within.

Available wherever books are sold.